Stephen Arnold Douglas, Henry M. (Henry Martyn) Flint

Life of Stephen A. Douglas

United States Senator from Illinois

Stephen Arnold Douglas, Henry M. (Henry Martyn) Flint

Life of Stephen A. Douglas
United States Senator from Illinois

ISBN/EAN: 9783337054212

Printed in Europe, USA, Canada, Australia, Japan

Cover: Foto ©Raphael Reischuk / pixelio.de

More available books at **www.hansebooks.com**

LIFE

OF

STEPHEN A. DOUGLAS,

UNITED STATES SENATOR FROM ILLINOIS.

WITH

His most Important Speeches and Reports.

BY H. M. FLINT.

NEW YORK:

DERBY & JACKSON, PUBLISHERS.

1860.

W. H. TINSON, Stereotyper.

GEO. RUSSELL & Co., Printers

THE proofs of this work having been submitted to several of Mr. Douglas' most judicious friends, it is believed by them to be a true and faithful exposition of the leading incidents of his career, and is by them cordially recommended as authentic and reliable.

CONTENTS.

---•••---

CHAPTER V.

CHAPTER VI.

CHAPTER VII.

CHAPTER VIII.

CHAPTER IX.

CHAPTER X.

CHAPTER XI.

CHAPTER XII.

CHAPTER XIII.

LIFE AND SPEECHES

OF

STEPHEN A. DOUGLAS.

———•••———

INTRODUCTORY CHAPTER.

THE object of the author of this book is to present to the people of the United States a truthful delineation of the character and qualities of the greatest American statesman now living.

The public life of Mr. Douglas naturally divides itself into five periods. The first, from his entrance into Congress in 1843, to the close of the war against Mexico, in 1848. Second, from the close of the Mexican War to the passage of the Compromise measures of 1850. Third, from the passage of the Compromise of 1850, to the passage of the Nebraska Bill in 1854. Fourth, from the passage of the Nebraska Bill, to the third election of Mr. Douglas to the Senate, in the fall of 1858. Fifth, from the commencement of his third Senatorial term, in March, 1859, to the meeting of the Charleston Convention in April, 1860.

During the first period, Mr. Douglas appears among the most active and influential friends of the re-annexation of

1*

Texas to the United States, and causes to be run through Texas the Missouri Compromise line of 36° 30′; and when the war with Mexico breaks out, he is found among the ablest supporters of the administration, and one of the foremost of our statesmen in upholding the honor of our flag and in prosecuting the war with a vigor and prudence that led to an honorable and satisfactory peace. In this period, too, Mr. Douglas is seen endeavoring to carry out in good faith the principles of the Missouri Compromise, by extending the line of 36° 30′ westward through our acquisitions from Mexico to the Pacific Ocean; in which attempt he was frustrated by northern Freesoilers.

GREAT MEASURES OF MR. DOUGLAS.

The second period was one of the most important in the whole life of Mr. Douglas. He is seen at this time, shaping and molding for the territories of the United States, those institutions of government upon which his fame as a statesman rests, and upon which depend the happiness of millions of American citizens, and the prosperity of a dozen new States. In treating of this period of the life of Mr. Douglas, I have shown that he is the real author of the Compromise measures of 1850, so generally attributed to Henry Clay. In this period, too, we see Mr. Douglas coming home to his constituents, and in the presence of an infuriated mob, proclaiming the propriety and expediency of those measures with such matchless eloquence, that the voices of faction and fanaticism were hushed, and the citizens of Chicago passed resolutions declaring their adherence to those very measures which they had the day before denounced.

Toward the close of the third period, we see Mr. Douglas bringing forward the details of his great plan for the government of the territories, in the shape of the Kansas and

Nebraska bills; explaining and elucidating the principles upon which they are based, and urging their adoption by Congress. And when these measures were passed, we see him coming home to a constituency that refused to hear him vindicate their justice and propriety.

During the fourth period, we see the evils that resulted in Kansas, from attempts to evade or disregard the principles of the Nebraska Bill. We see the President of the United States exerting the whole strength of his administration in attempting to force a constitution repugnant to their wishes on the people of Kansas; and Mr. Douglas energetically and with all his might resisting the tyrannical proceeding, and vindicating the right of the people of the territories in all time to come, to form and regulate their domestic institutions in their own way. When the British also, in 1858, attacked no less than thirty-three of our vessels in the space of four weeks, and when the Senate were about to pass the customary resolutions, declaring that such acts were very annoying to the United States, and ought not to be committed, we see Mr. Douglas urging upon Congress the instant adoption of such energetic measures on our part as should compel Great Britain not only to cease such outrages in future, but also to make reparation for those she had committed.

"THE RETURN FROM ELBA."

During this period also, we see the great campaign in the autumn of 1858, the election of a senator from Illinois for the next six years, the gallant stand made by Mr. Douglas, and the unscrupulous efforts made by federal officials and Abolitionists to crush him. Like Napoleon on his return from Elba, Mr. Douglas, on his return to Illinois, inspired his numerous friends with unbounded enthusiasm. We see the momentous struggle between Mr. Douglas and the

Democratic party on the one side, and the allied forces of the Republicans, Abolitionists, and office-holders on the other. We see the battles and skirmishes of the campaign; in every engagement, we see the utter discomfiture of the unholy alliance, and the triumph of the right—and always, in the forefront of the battle, we hear the clarion voice of the great leader of the democracy. Finally, we see his victory over all his enemies, and witness his triumphant return to the Senate, bearing high aloft the glorious banner of the Democracy, unstained and untarnished.

During the last period, we see the hostility of the Executive manifested in the removal of Mr. Douglas from the chairmanship of the Committee on Territories; the war of the pamphlets; the Senate proceedings following the horrible plot of John Brown; and the ridiculous attempt on the part of a few senators to make a platform for the Charleston Convention entirely incompatible with the known principles of Mr. Douglas. We see the uprising of the people all over the nation in favor of Mr. Douglas for the Presidency, the proceedings of the several State conventions, and their unanimity in designating Mr. Douglas as their choice above all other men. Finally, we see the meeting of the Charleston Convention; and we may reasonably hope to see the nomination of Judge Douglas for the Presidency, and his triumphant election.

PERSONAL APPEARANCE.

The Rev. Wm. H. Milburn, the blind preacher, in his interesting book, "Ten Years of Preacher Life," gives the following graphic sketch of his impressions of Mr. Douglas :

"The first time I saw Mr. Douglas was in June, 1838, standing on the gallery of the Market House, which some of my readers may recollect as situate in the middle of the square of Jacksonville. He and Colonel John J. Hardin were engaged in canvassing Morgan County for Congress. He

was upon the threshold of that great world in which he has since played
so prominent a part, and was engaged in making one of his earliest stump
speeches. I stood and listened to him, surrounded by a motley crowd of
backwood farmers and hunters, dressed in homospun or deerskin, my
boyish breast glowing with exultant joy, as he, only ten years my senior,
battled so bravely for the doctrines of his party with the veteran and accomplished Hardin. True, I had been educated in political sentiments
opposite to his own, but there was something captivating in his manly
straightforwardness and uncompromising statement of his political principles. He even then showed signs of that dexterity in debate, and vehe-
ment, impressive declamation, of which he has since become such a master.
He gave the crowd the color of his own mood as he interpreted their
thoughts and directed their sensibilities. [His first-hand knowledge of the
people, and his power to speak to them in their own language, employing
arguments suited to their comprehension, sometimes clinching a series of
reasons by a frontier metaphor which refused to be forgotten, and his determined courage, which never shrank from any form of difficulty or danger, made him one of the most effective stump-orators I have ever heard.]
  "Less than four years before, he had walked into the town of Winchester, sixteen miles southwest of Jacksonville, an entire stranger, with
thirty-seven and a half cents in his pocket, his all of earthly fortune. His
first employment was as clerk of a ' Vandu,' as the natives call a sheriff's
sale. He then seized the birch of the pedagogue, and sought by its aid
and by patient drilling, to initiate a handful of half-wild boys into the sub-
lime mysteries of Lindley Murray. His evenings were divided between
reading newspapers, studying Blackstone, and talking politics. He, before
long, by virtue of his indomitable energy, acquired enough of legal lore to
pass an examination, and ' to stick up his shingle,' as they call putting up
a lawyer's sign. And now began a series of official employments, by
which he has mounted within five and twenty years, from the obscurity of
a village pedagogue on the borders of civilization, to his present illustrious
and commanding position. In the twelve or thirteen years that had
elapsed from the time of his entering the State, a friendless, penniless
youth, he has served his fellow-citizens in almost every official capacity,
and entered the highest position within their power to confer.
  "No man, since the days of Andrew Jackson, has gained a stronger hold
upon the confidence and attachment of his adherents, or exercised a more
dominating authority over the masses of his party than Judge Douglas.
Whether upon the stump, in the caucus, or the Senate, his power and success in debate are prodigious. His instincts stand him in the stead of
imagination, and amount to genius.   •

"Notwithstanding the busy and boisterous political life which he has led with all its engrossing cares and occupations, Mr. Douglas has, neverthe less, by his invincible perseverance, managed to redeem much time for self-improvement. He has been a wide and studious reader of history and its kindred branches. Contact with affairs has enlarged his understanding and strengthened his judgment. Thus, with his unerring sagacity, his matured and decisive character, with a courage which sometimes appears to be audacity, but which is in reality tempered by prudence, a will that never submits to an obstacle, however vast, and a knowledge of the people, together with a power to lead them, incomparable in this generation, he may be accepted as a practical statesman of the highest order.

The correspondent of the New York "Times" describes Mr. Douglas as follows: "The Little Giant, as he has been well styled, is seen to advantage on the floor of the Senate. He is not above the middle height; but the easy and natural dignity of his manner stamps him at once as one born to command. His massive head rivets undivided attention. It is a head of the antique, with something of the infinite in its expression of power: a head difficult to describe, but better worth description than any other in the country. Mr. Douglas has a brain of unusual size, covered with heavy masses of dark brown hair, now beginning to be sprinkled with silver. His forehead is high, open, and splendidly developed, based on dark, thick eyebrows of great width. His eyes, large and deeply set, are of the darkest and most brilliant blue. The mouth is cleanly cut, finely arched, but with something of bitter and sad experience in its general expression. The chin is square and vigorous, and is full of eddying dimples— the muscles and nerves showing great mobility, and every thought having some external reflexion in the sensitive and expressive features. Add now a rich, dark complexion, clear and healthy; smoothly shaven cheeks; and handsome throat; small, white ears; eyes which shoot out electric fires; small white hands; small feet; a full chest and broad shoulders;

and with these points duly blended together, we have a picture of the Little Giant.

As a speaker, Mr. Douglas seems to disdain ornament,
and marches right on against the body of his subject with
irresistible power and directness. His rhetorical assault has
nothing of the cavalry slash in its impressiveness, rather
resembling a charge of heavy infantry with fixed bayonet,
and calling forcibly to mind the attack of those ' six thousand
English veterans " immortalized by Thomas Davis :

> " ' Steady they step adown the slope,
> Steady they climb the hill ;
> Steady they load—steady they fire—
> Marching right onward still.'

His voice is a rich and musical baritone, swelling into occa-
sional clarion-blasts toward the close of each important
period. He is heard with breathless attention, except when
now and again the galleries feel tempted to applaud—these
demonstrations appearing to give particular uneasiness to the
Administration, Secession, and Republican senators."

Mr. Douglas has been twice married. He has two little
sons, the children of his first wife, who was a southern
lady. In 1857, he married Miss Adele Cutts, daughter of
James Madison Cutts, Esq., second Controller of the Treasury, a beautiful and accomplished woman, and well known
in Washington for the amiability of her disposition, and the
goodness of her heart. He has had one child, a daughter,
since his second marriage.

CHAPTER II.

Parentage, Birth, and early Life of Stephen A. Douglas—He Studies Law
—Goes to the West—Teaches School—Admitted to Practise Law—His
Success as a Lawyer, and the Causes of it—Becomes Attorney General
of Illinois—Elected to the State Legislature—Electioneers for Martin
Van Buren for President, in 1840—Makes 207 Speeches in that Year,
and carries Illinois for the Democracy—Becomes a Judge of the
Supreme Court—Is Elected to Congress in 1843.

STEPHEN A. DOUGLAS was born in the town of Brandon,
Vermont, on the 23d day of April, 1813. His father was a
native of the State of New York, and a physician of high
repute. His grandfather was a Pennsylvanian by birth, and
a soldier in the Revolutionary War. He was one of those
soldiers of Washington who passed that terrible winter at
Valley Forge, and was present at the surrender of Lord Corn-
wallis. His great-grandfather was also an American by birth,
but his ancestors came originally to this country from Scotland. Dr. Douglas died when his little son Stephen was only
three months old. From the age of ten to that of fifteen
years, Stephen was sent to the common schools of the neighborhood. During the last two years of this term, he was
noted for remarkable aptitude for his studies, and was extremely diligent and attentive. His quick perception, excellent memory, and determination to excel in his studies, were
subjects of remark by his teachers, even at that early period.
His disposition was amiable and kind, of which fact there
are numerous instances related by those who were his school

fellows. His temper, however, was naturally quick and vivacious.

At the age of fifteen, he expressed to his mother his earnest desire to prepare for college ; but it was decided at a family council that the expense of a collegiate education would make that idea impossible. " Well, then," said Stephen, " I will earn my own living ;" and he immediately engaged himself as an apprentice to the trade of cabinet-making, which was then an excellent and lucrative business. He worked at this trade for eighteen months, and then abandoned it altogether, as it proved entirely too severe for his constitution. His master has since jocularly remarked, that during the time Stephen was with him, he displayed his greatest ingenuity in the construction of *bureaus, cabinets, and secretaries.* At the age of seventeen, he entered the academy at Brandon, and pursued his studies there for more than a year. His mind was extremely active at this time, and he made rapid advancement in those branches of learning to which he directed his attention. When the family removed to Canandaigua, New York, he attended the academy there as a student. Having decided to make the law his profession, he entered the office of Mr. Hubbell, and studied law till 1833.

EARLY LIFE.

In the spring of that year he went to the West, in search of an eligible place in which to establish himself as a lawyer. He went to a number of cities and towns in the West, among them Cincinnati, Louisville, St. Louis, and Jacksonville, Illinois. At Winchester, a little town sixteen miles from Jacksonville, he found there was no school, and immediately opened one. He obtained forty pupils without any difficulty, whom he taught for three months, at $3 00 per quarter. He devoted his evenings, during this time, to the prosecution of his law studies. In March, 1834, he was admitted to practise law, by the judges of the Supreme Court of the State. He at once opened a law office, and became remarkably successful as a legal practitioner.

Within a year after his admission, and while not yet twenty-two years of age, he was elected by the legislature of Illinois, attorney-general of the State. In 1836, he was elected to the legislature by the Democrats of Morgan County, and resigned the office of attorney-general. At the time he took his seat in the legislature, he was the youngest member of that body. In 1837, he was appointed by President Van Buren register of the land-office at Springfield, Illinois. In November of the same year, he received the Democratic nomination for Congress, although he was then under twenty-five years of age, and consequently ineligible. He attained the requisite age, however, before the day of election, which was in August, 1838. At this election upward of 36,000 votes were cast, of which Mr. Douglas received a majority. About twenty votes were rejected by the canvassers, because in them the name of Mr. Douglas was spelled incorrectly. The quibble was a most unworthy one, and would not stand at this day. As it was, the Whig candidate was declared to be elected by a majority of only five votes; and the election was everywhere regarded as a triumph of Mr. Douglas.

MR. DOUGLAS AS A LAWYER.

Retiring now from political life, Mr. Douglas devoted himself with assiduity to the practice of his profession. He was an able and successful lawyer, and his business increased rapidly. There are many persons now living, who were clients and neighbors of Mr. Douglas at this time, and who remember well his demeanor as an advocate. He was noted, among other things, for the careful preparation of his cases, and for his tact and skill in the examination of witnesses, He never went into court with a case until he thoroughly understood it in all its bearings. His addresses to the jury were generally plain and clear statements of the matters of fact, the arguments logical and conclusive, and his manner earnest and impressive. He rarely failed to enlist the feelings and sympathies of a jury.

In the year 1840, Mr. Douglas entered with ardor into the celebrated "Hard Cider and Log Cabin" campaign, and threw the whole weight of his influence in favor of Martin Van Buren, the democratic candidate for President, and against the "Tippecanoe and Tyler too" candidates of the Whig party. During seven months of that year, he traversed the State of Illinois in all directions, and addressed 207 meetings of the people. General Harrison was elected President, but Illinois was carried for the Democratic candidates, and Mr. Douglas was mainly instrumental in bringing about this result.

MR. DOUGLAS ELECTED TO CONGRESS.

In December, 1840, Mr. Douglas was appointed secretary of state of Illinois. In February, 1841, he was elected by the legislature a judge of the Supreme Court of the State. This was only seven years after he had received, from the judges of that court, his license to practise law. He remained upon the bench of the Supreme Court for three years. In 1843 he was elected to Congress by 400 majority; and in 1844 by a majority of 1,900 votes. He was elected a representative a third time in 1846, by a majority of 3,000 votes.

CHAPTER III.

On taking his seat in Congress, Mr. Douglas did not at once rush into the debates of the House. He was perfectly informed concerning the interests of his constituents, over which he exercised a watchful care. But for the first session or two of Congress, he spoke rarely, and briefly; familiarizing himself, by study and observation, with the rules of debate, and the usages of parliamentary bodies. When he did rise to address the House, it was on some practical question; and his remarks were always forcible, and to the point.

IMPROVEMENT OF WESTERN RIVERS.

His first speech in Congress was upon the improvement of western lakes and harbors, delivered December 19, 1843. He had moved that so much of the President's message as referred to that subject, be referred to a select committee. He insisted upon a select committee, "because the question involved important interests requiring an accurate knowledge of the condition of the country, its navigable streams, and the obstructions to be removed. A thorough examination of subjects so various, extensive, and intricate, and requiring so much patient labor and toil, could not be expected from those who reside at a great distance. He desired a full, elaborate, and detailed report from those whose local positions would stimulate them. Let this be granted, and the friends of the measure would be content to leave its policy and propriety to the judgment of the House." While Mr. Douglas has never ceased to take a lively interest in river and harbor improvements and the protection of inland navigation, experience soon convinced him that the practice of appropriating from the federal treasury for such purposes had utterly failed to accomplish its object, and that a system of tonnage duties which he matured, and on several occasions has introduced into the Senate, should be substituted for Congressional appropriations. Since the system of tonnage duties has been elaborated in Congress, and is becoming understood by the public, the most enlightened friends of the navigating interests are becoming satisfied that the substitute proposed by Mr. Douglas would prove not only more economical, but more effective and beneficial in the accomplishment of their views.

In connection with this subject, it should be added, that Mr. Douglas was mainly instrumental in securing the passage of the law by which the maritime and admiralty jurisdiction of the federal courts was extended over the northern lakes.

SPEECH IN FAVOR OF REMITTING GEN. JACKSON'S FINE.

On the 7th of January, 1844, he delivered an eloquent speech on the bill to refund to Gen. Jackson, the fine unjustly imposed on him by Judge Hall, of New Orleans. From this speech we make the following extracts :

"I maintain," said Mr. Douglas, "that in the exercise of the power of proclaiming martial law, Gen. Jackson did not violate the Constitution, nor assume to himself any authority not fully authorized and legalized by his position, his duty, and the necessity of the case. Gen. Jackson was the agent of the government, legally and constitutionally authorized to defend the city of New Orleans. It was his duty to do this at all hazards. It was then conceded, and is now conceded, that nothing but martial law would enable him to perform that duty. His power was commensurate with his duty, and he was authorized to use the means essential to its performance. This principle has been recognized and acted upon by all civilized nations, and is familiar to all who are conversant with military history. It does not imply the right to suspend the laws and civil tribunals at pleasure. The right grows out of the necessity. The principle is, that the commanding general may go as far, and no further than is absolutely necessary to the defence of the place committed to his protection. There are exigencies in the history of nations, when necessity becomes the paramount law, to which all other considerations must yield. If it becomes necessary to blow up a fort, it is right to do it. If it is necessary to sink a ship, it is right to sink it. If it is necessary to burn a city, it is right to burn it."

*   *   *   *   *   *   *   *   *

Mr. Douglas then gave a graphic description of the state of affairs at New Orleans in December, 1814, and January, 1815; concluding thus: "The enemy, composed of disciplined troops, four times as numerous as our own force, were in the immediate vicinity of the city, ready for the attack at any moment; the city, filled with traitors, anxious to surrender; spies transmitting information to the enemy's camp. The governor of the State, the judges, the public authorities, and all the chief citizens, earnestly entreated Gen. Jackson to declare martial law, as the only means of maintaining the safety of the city. Gen. Jackson promptly issued the order, and enforced it by the weight of his authority. The city was saved. The country was defended by a succession of the most brilliant military achievements that ever adorned the annals of any country or any age. Martial law was continued no longer than the danger existed. Judge Hall himself had advised, urged, and solicited Gen. Jackson to declare it."

* * * * * * * * *

"The last of the high crimes and misdemeanors imputed to Gen. Jackson at New Orleans, is that of arresting Judge Hall, and sending him beyond the limits of the city, with instructions not to return till peace was restored. The justification of this act is found in the necessity which required the declaration of martial law, and its continuance and enforcement until the enemy should have left, or the treaty of peace be ratified. Judge Hall, who was by birth an Englishman, had confederated with Louallier's band of conspirators. Their movements were dangerous. Gen. Jackson took the responsibility, and sent the judge beyond the lines of his camp. Was this a contempt of court?"

* * * * * * * * *

"I envy not the feelings of the man who can calmly reason about the force of precedents in the fury of the war-cry, when 'booty and beauty' is the watchword. Talk not to me of 'forms, and rules of court' when the enemy's cannon are pointed at the door! The man who could philosophize at such times, would fiddle while the Capitol was burning. There was but one form necessary on that occasion, and that was, to point cannon and destroy the enemy."

* * * * * * * * * ,

"I grant that the bill is unprecedented : but I desire, on this day, to make a precedent that shall command the admiration of the world. Besides, sir, the government has repeatedly recognized and sanctioned the doctrine, that in cases of necessity, the commander is fully justified in super seding the civil law; and that Congress will make remuneration, when the commander acted with the view of promoting the public interests. The people demand this measure, and they will never be satisfied till their wishes shall have been respected, and their will obeyed."

JACKSON'S OPINION OF THIS SPEECH.

The bill was passed, and the fine refunded. A year afterward, Mr. Douglas, in company with several other members of Congress, paid their respects to the venerable hero and patriot, at the Hermitage. When Mr. Douglas was introduced, the old general grasped him warmly by the hand, and requested him to step with him into a private room. There, in the presence of two other gentlemen now living, and from one of whom we have received this relation, the venerable soldier, in a voice trembling with emotion, thus addressed the young statesman : "Mr. Douglas, I read, with feelings of lively gratitude, your speech in Congress last winter, in favor of remitting the fine imposed on me by Judge Hall. I knew when I proclaimed and enforced martial law, that I was doing right. But never, until I had read your speech, could I have expressed the reasons which actuated my conduct. I knew that I was not violating the Constitution of my country. When my life is written, I wish that speech of yours to be inserted in it, as my reasons for proclaiming and enforcing martial law in New Orleans."

and requiring so much patient labor and toil, could not be expected from those who reside at a great distance. He desired a full, elaborate, and detailed report from those whose local positions would stimulate them. Let this be granted, and the friends of the measure would be content to leave its policy and propriety to the judgment of the House." While Mr. Douglas has never ceased to take a lively interest in river and harbor improvements and the protection of inland navigation, experience soon convinced him that the practice of appropriating from the federal treasury for such purposes had utterly failed to accomplish its object, and that a system of tonnage duties which he matured, and on several occasions has introduced into the Senate, should be substituted for Congressional appropriations. Since the system of tonnage duties has been elaborated in Congress, and is becoming understood by the public, the most enlightened friends of the navigating interests are becoming satisfied that the substitute proposed by Mr. Douglas would prove not only more economical, but more effective and beneficial in the accomplishment of their views.

In connection with this subject, it should be added, that Mr. Douglas was mainly instrumental in securing the passage of the law by which the maritime and admiralty jurisdiction of the federal courts was extended over the northern lakes.

SPEECH IN FAVOR OF REMITTING GEN. JACKSON'S FINE.

On the 7th of January, 1844, he delivered an eloquent speech on the bill to refund to Gen. Jackson, the fine unjustly imposed on him by Judge Hall, of New Orleans. From this speech we make the following extracts :

"I maintain," said Mr. Douglas, "that in the exercise of the power of proclaiming martial law, Gen. Jackson did not violate the Constitution, nor assume to himself any authority not fully authorized and legalized by his position, his duty, and the necessity of the case. Gen. Jackson was the agent of the government, legally and constitutionally authorized to defend the city of New Orleans. It was his duty to do this at all hazards. It was then conceded, and is now conceded, that nothing but martial law would enable him to perform that duty. His power was commensurate with his duty, and he was authorized to use the means essential to its performance. This principle has been recognized and acted upon by all civilized nations, and is familiar to all who are conversant with military history. It does not imply the right to suspend the laws and civil tribunals at pleasure. The right grows out of the necessity. The principle is, that the commanding general may go as far, and no further than is absolutely necessary to the defence of the place committed to his protection. There are exigencies in the history of nations, when necessity becomes the paramount law, to which all other considerations must yield. If it becomes necessary to blow up a fort, it is right to do it. If it is necessary to sink a ship, it is right to sink it. If it is necessary to burn a city, it is right to burn it."

*   *   *   *   *   *   *   *   *

Mr. Douglas then gave a graphic description of the state of affairs at New Orleans in December, 1814, and January, 1815; concluding thus: "The enemy, composed of disciplined troops, four times as numerous as our own force, were in the immediate vicinity of the city, ready for the attack at any moment; the city, filled· with traitors, anxious to surrender; spies transmitting information to the enemy's camp. The governor of the State, the judges, the public authorities, and all the chief citizens, earnestly entreated Gen. Jackson to declare martial law, as the only means of maintaining the safety of the city. Gen. Jackson promptly issued the order, and enforced it by the weight of his authority. The city was saved. The country was defended by a succession of the most brilliant military achievements that ever adorned the annals of any country or any age. Martial law was continued no longer than the danger existed. Judge Hall himself had advised, urged, and solicited Gen. Jackson to declare it."

* * * * * * * * *

" The last of the high crimes and misdemeanors imputed to Gen. Jackson at New Orleans, is that of arresting Judge Hall, and sending him beyond the limits of the city, with instructions not to return till peace was restored. The justification of this act is found in the necessity which required the declaration of martial law, and its continuance and enforcement until the enemy should have left, or the treaty of peace be ratified. Judge Hall, who was by birth an Englishman, had confederated with Louallier's band of conspirators. Their movements were dangerous. Gen. Jackson took the responsibility, and sent the judge beyond the lines of his camp. Was this a contempt of court?"

* * * * * * * * *

" I envy not the feelings of the man who can calmly reason about the force of precedents in the fury of the war-cry, when ' booty and beauty' is the watchword. Talk not to me of ' forms, and rules of court' when the enemy's cannon are pointed at the door! The man who could philosophize at such times, would fiddle while the Capitol was burning. There was but one form necessary on that occasion, and that was, to point cannon and destroy the enemy."

* * * * * * * * *

" I grant that the bill is unprecedented: but I desire, on this day, to make a precedent that shall command the admiration of the world. Besides, sir, the government has repeatedly recognized and sanctioned the doctrine, that in cases of necessity, the commander is fully justified in super seding the civil law; and that Congress will make remuneration, when the commander acted with the view of promoting the public interests. The people demand this measure, and they will never be satisfied till their wishes shall have been respected, and their will obeyed."

JACKSON'S OPINION OF THIS SPEECH.

The bill was passed, and the fine refunded. A year afterward, Mr. Douglas, in company with several other members of Congress, paid their respects to the venerable hero and patriot, at the Hermitage. When Mr. Douglas was introduced, the old general grasped him warmly by the hand, and requested him to step with him into a private room. There, in the presence of two other gentlemen now living, and from one of whom we have received this relation, the venerable soldier, in a voice trembling with emotion, thus addressed the young statesman: " Mr. Douglas, I read, with feelings of lively gratitude, your speech in Congress last winter, in favor of remitting the fine imposed on me by Judge Hall. I knew when I proclaimed and enforced martial law, that I was doing right. But never, until I had read your speech, could I have expressed the reasons which actuated my conduct. I knew that I was not violating the Constitution of my country. When my life is written, I wish that speech of yours to be inserted in it, as my reasons for proclaiming and enforcing martial law in New Orleans."

CHAPTER IV.

RE-ANNEXATION OF TEXAS.

Speech in Favor of the Re-Annexation of Texas—Mr. Douglas reports Joint Resolutions, declaring Texas to be one of the United States—Texas Annexed.

MR. DOUGLAS was among the earliest advocates of the annexation of Texas; on which subject he made an able speech on the 6th of January, 1845. In this speech he showed that the Texas question was not at that time a new one : that it did not originate with Mr. Tyler : that one of first acts of the administration of Gen. Jackson had been to re-open negotiations with Mexico for the annexation of Texas: that Mr. Van Buren, then secretary of state, had addressed a long dispatch to Mr. Poinsett, our minister to Mexico, instructing him to endeavor to secure Texas, and directing him to give $5,000,000 for it: that the attempt had been renewed by President Jackson in 1833, and again in 1835. He showed by the authority of John Quincy Adams, in his official letters, especially the one dated March 12, 1818, that the western boundary of Louisiana extended to the Rio del Norte : that the settlements made between the rivers Sabine and Rio del Norte, by La Salle, in 1685, under the authority of Louis XIV., king of France, together with those on the Mississippi and the Illinois, formed the basis of the original French colony of Louisiana, which was ceded to the United States in 1803 ; and quoted the language of Mr. Adams, "that the claim of the United

States to the boundary of the Rio Bravo del Norte was as clear as their right to the island of New Orleans."

He then went on to show that as the Rio del Norte was the western boundary of Louisiana, and Texas was included in the cession of 1803, all the inhabitants of that country were, by the terms of the treaty, naturalized, and became citizens of the United States; and all who migrated there between 1803 and 1819 went there under the shield of the Constitution and laws of the United States, and with the guaranty that they would be forever protected by them; and quoted from the treaty of cession as follows: "The inhabitants of the ceded territory shall be incorporated into the Union of the United States, and admitted as soon as possible, according to the principles of the Constitution, to the enjoyments of all the rights of the United States."

"To the fulfillment of these stipulations," said Mr. Douglas, "the sacred faith and honor of this nation were solemnly pledged. Yet, in violation of one of them, Texas was ceded to Spain by the treaty of 1819. The American Republic was severed by that treaty, a part of its territory joined to a foreign kingdom, and American citizens were transformed into the subjects of a foreign despotism. Texas did not assent to the separation; she protested against it promptly and solemnly. The protest and declaration of independence of Texas, in June, 1819, says, 'The recent treaty between Spain and the United States has dissipated an illusion, and has aroused the citizens of Texas. They see themselves abandoned to the dominion of Spain; but, spurning the fetters of colonial vassalage, they resolve, under the blessing of God, to be free and independent.'

"Most nobly have they maintained that righteous resolve; first, against the despotism of Spain, and then the tyranny of Mexico, until, on the plains of San Jacinto, victory established their independence and made them free."

Mr. Douglas proceeded to enumerate the advantages that would attend the annexation of Texas, and then went on to show that it must be done in accordance with the principles of the Constitution ; proving the doctrine to have been sanc tioned and settled, that foreign territory may be annexed, organized into territories and States, and admitted into the Union on an equal footing with the original States. In concluding his remarks upon this point, Mr. Douglas said, "The conclusion is irresistible that Congress, possessing the power to admit a State, has the right to pass a law of annexation. I do not say that territory cannot be acquired in any other way than by act of Congress. We may acquire it by conquest, or by treaty, or by discovery. We claim the Oregon Territory by virtue of the right of discovery and occupation. But if we wish to acquire Texas without making war or relying upon discovery, we must fall back upon the power to admit new States, and acquire the territory by act of Congress, as one of the necessary and indispensable means of executing that enumerated power. Our federal system is admirably adapted to the whole continent; and while I would not violate the laws of nations, nor treaty stipulations, nor in any manner tarnish the national honor, I would exert all legal and honorable means to drive Great Britain, and the last vestiges of royal authority, from the continent of North America, and extend the limits of the Republic from ocean to ocean. I would make this an ocean-bound republic, and have no more disputes about boundaries or red lines upon maps."

The treaty for the annexation of Texas having failed in the Senate, Mr. Douglas, among others, introduced joint resolutions in the House of Representatives for the annexation of Texas to the United States ; and at the next session, being chairman of the Committee on Territories, reported the bill by which Texas was declared one of the States of the Union, on an equal footing with the original States. In this joint resolution there was inserted, at the instance of Mr. Douglas, a provision extending the Missouri Compromise line westward through Texas to the Rio del Norte, its western boundary. The reasons which induced Mr. Douglas to bring forward that provision are explained by him in his speech on the Nebraska Territory, delivered January 30, 1854, and which will be found in a subsequent chapter of this work.

The joint resolution as passed is as follows:

JOINT RESOLUTION FOR ANNEXING TEXAS TO THE UNITED STATES.

"*Resolved,* by the Senate and House of Representatives of the United States in Congress Assembled, That Congress doth consent that the territory properly included within, and rightfully belonging to, the Republic of Texas, may be erected into a new State, to be called *the State of Texas,* with a Republican form of government, to be adopted by the people of said Republic, by deputies in convention assembled, with the consent of the existing government, in order that the same may be admitted as one of the States of this Union.

"SEC. 2. *And be it further resolved,* That the foregoing consent of Congress is given upon the following conditions, and with the following guaranties, to wit:

"*First,* Said State to be formed, subject to the adjustment by this government of all questions of boundary that may arise with other governments; and of the constitution thereof, with the proper evidence of its adoption by the people of said Republic of Texas, shall be transmitted to the President of the United States, to be laid before Congress for its final action, on or before the first day of January, one thousand eight hundred and forty-six.

"*Second,* Said State, when admitted into the Union, after ceding to the United States all public edifices, fortifications, barracks, ports, and harbors, navy and navy-yards, docks, magazines, arms, armaments, and all other property and means pertaining to the public defence, belonging to the said Republic of Texas, shall retain all the public funds, debts, taxes, and dues of every kind which may belong to, or be due or owing said

Republic; and shall also retain all the vacant or unappropriated lands lying within its limits, to be applied to the payment of the debts and liabilities of said Republic of Texas; and the residue of said lands, after discharging said debts and liabilities, to become a charge upon the United States.

" *Third*, New States of convenient size, not exceeding four in number, in addition to the said State of Texas, and having sufficient population, may hereafter, by the consent of said State, be formed out of the territory thereof, which shall be entitled to admission under the provision of the Federal Constitution; and such States as may be formed out of that portion of said territory lying south of thirty-six degrees thirty minutes, north latitude, commonly known as the Missouri Compromise line, shall be admitted into the Union with or without Slavery, as the people of each State asking admission may desire. And in such State or States as shall be formed out of said territory north of said Missouri Compromise line, Slavery or involuntary servitude (except for crime) shall be prohibited.

[WALKER'S AMENDMENT—ADDED.]

" *And be it further resolved*, That if the President of the United States shall, in his judgment and discretion, deem it most advisable, instead of proceeding to submit the foregoing resolution to the Republic of Texas, as an overture on the part of the United States, for admission, to negotiate with that Republic; then,

" *Be it resolved*, That a State to be formed out of the present Republic of Texas, with suitable extent and boundaries, and with two representatives in Congress, until the next apportionment of representation, shall be admitted into the Union by virtue of this act, on an equal footing with the existing States, as soon as the terms and conditions of such admission, and the cession of the remaining Texan territory to the United States, shall be agreed upon by the Governments of Texas and the Un'ted States.

" *And be it further enacted*, That the sum of one hundred tho-sand dollars be, and the same is hereby, appropriated to defray the expenses of missions and negotiations, to agree upon the terms of said admission and cession, either by treaty to be submitted to the Senate, or by articles to be submitted to the two Houses of Congress, as the President may direct.

" Approved, *March* 2, 1845."

2*

CHAPTER V.

WAR WITH MEXICO.

Speech in Vindication of the Administration—Mr. Douglas elected to Congress a third time.

Mr. Douglas vigorously supported the administration of President Polk, in the measures it adopted for the prosecution of the war against Mexico; and on the 13th of May, 1846, made a long and able speech in favor of the bill making appropriations for the support of the army. The object of this speech was to vindicate our government, and to demonstrate that it had not been in the wrong, in the origin and progress of the war. It will be remembered that the war was denounced by the Whig party as unholy and damnable, and the government of the United States was vilified and traduced without measure, for taking the only course that could be taken, in order to preserve the national honor. Henry Clay, the great leader of the Whigs, did not, indeed, join in this shameful cry. His eldest son, Henry Clay, jr., fought gallantly in the war, and fell at Buena Vista : and the old patriot was not one of those who gave aid and comfort to the enemy. But Thomas Corwin, and others like him, declared in Congress that while the President could command the army, they thanked heaven that *they* could command the purse, and that he should have no funds to prosecute this war; and called upon the Mexicans to welcome the soldiers of the American army, with "bloody hands and hospitable graves!"

In reply to this, Mr. Douglas presented a mass of evidence from official documents, showing that for years past we had had ample cause for war against Mexico, and quoting the declaration of President Jackson's last special message, that the wanton character of the outrages upon the persons and property of our citizens, upon the officers and flag of the United States, independent of recent insults to this government and people, would justify in the eyes of nations, immediate war.

' MEXICAN OUTRAGES.

"Aside from the insults to our flag," said Mr. Douglas, "the indignity to the nation, and the injury to our commerce, not less than ten millions of dollars are due to our citizens, for these outrages which Mexico has committed within the last fifteen years. The Committee on Foreign Relations of the U. S. Senate, said in their report in 1837, that they might ' with justice recommend an immediate resort to war or reprisals;' and the House Committee, at the same session, reported that ' the merchant vessels of the United States have been fired into, and our citizens put to death.' It should be borne in mind that all these insults and injuries were committed before the annexation of Texas—before the proposition of annexation was ever seriously entertained by this government. For offences much less aggravated, France made her demand for reparation, and proclaimed her ultimatum from the deck of a man-of-war off Vera Cruz. Redress being denied, the French fleet opened their batteries on the Castle of San Juan de Ulloa, compelled the fortress to surrender, and the Mexican government to accede to their demands, and to pay $200,000 in addition, to defray the expenses of enforcing the payment of the claim. Our wrongs are ten fold greater than those of France, in number and enormity; yet her complaints have been heard in tones of thunder from the mouths of her cánnon.

"When the question of annexation was recently agitated, Mexico gave notice to this government that she would regard the consummation of the measure as a declaration of war. She made the passage of the resolution of annexation the pretext for dissolving the diplomatic relations between the two countries."

HOUSTON'S TREATY WITH SANTA ANNA.

Mr. Douglas then briefly related the facts relative to Mr. Slidell's appointment as minister to Mexico, the contemptuous reception that he met with there, and his final rejection by the government of Paredes; and also gave a brief sketch of the early military operations on both sides. By references to the documentary archives of the government, he proved that the Rio Grande was the western boundary of Texas, and cited the fact that immediately after the battle of San Jacinto, Santa Anna proposed to General Sam Houston, commander of the Texan army, to make a treaty of peace by which Mexico would recognize the independence of Texas with the Rio del Norte as the boundary, and that such a treaty was made, in which the independence of Texas was acknowledged by the government *de facto* of Mexico, and the Rio del Norte recognized as the boundary. He showed that according to the well-established principles of international law, the acts of the government *de facto* are binding on that nation in respect to foreign states: and concluded by a defence of the course pursued by President Polk, in ordering General Taylor to occupy with his forces territory that was as much ours as Florida or Massachusetts.

Mr. Douglas was prominent among those who, in the Oregon controversy with Great Britain, maintained that our

title to the whole of Oregon was clear and unquestionable.
He declared in the House of Representatives, that he would
never, now or hereafter, yield up one inch of Oregon, either
to Great Britain or to any other foreign government. He
advocated the policy of giving notice to Great Britain to terminate the joint occupation; of establishing a territorial
government over Oregon, protected by a sufficient military
force ; and of putting the country at once into a state of preparation, so that if war should result from the assertion of our
just rights, we might drive Great Britain and the last vestige
of royal authority from the continent of North America.

CHAPTER VI.

THE WAR WITH MEXICO : 1847–1848.

Mr. Douglas Elected to the United States Senate—He opposes the Wilmot Proviso—Speech on the Ten Regiment Bill—Bill for the Establishment of the Territory of Nebraska—Pass to Gen. Santa Anna—Exertions of Mr. Douglas in procuring Grants of Land to the Illinois Central Railroad —He endeavors to extend the Missouri Compromise Line to the Pacific Ocean—The Design defeated by Northern Votes—Bill for the Admission of California—Indian Titles in the Northwest—Protection to Emigrants.

THE WILMOT PROVISO.

MR. DOUGLAS had been reëlected to Congress in 1846 ; but before Congress met, the legislature of the State of Illinois elected him a senator for six years from the 4th of March. 1847.

So far as the question of slavery was involved in the organization of territories and the admission of new States, Mr. Douglas early took the position that Congress ought not to interfere on either side ; but that the people of each Territory and State should be allowed to form and regulate their domestic institutions in their own way.   In accordance with this principle, he opposed the Wilmot Proviso whenever it was brought up.

SPEECH ON THE TEN REGIMENT BILL.

On the 30th of January, 1848, Mr. Douglas made a speech in the Senate on the Ten Regiment Bill, which provided for the raising, for a limited time, of an additional military force. In this speech, Mr. Douglas alluded to the fact that the war with Mexico had been in progress nearly two years. The campaign of 1846 had resulted in the most brilliant victories that ever adorned the annals of any nation. The States of California, New Mexico, Chihuahua, New Leon, and Tamaulipas, besides many towns and cities in other Mexican States, had been one after another reduced to our possession. After a defence of President Polk from the charge of changing his grounds in regard to the causes of the war and the objects of prosecuting it, he showed that the war was not one of conquest, but of self-defence forced on us by Mexico; and that the declaration of the President, that the first blood of the war was "American blood shed upon American soil," was the simple truth. "That in order to compel Mexico to do us justice, it was necessary to follow her armies into her territory, to take possession of State after State, and hold them until she would yield to our reasonable demands. Indemnity for the past, and security for the future, was the motive of the war." When Mr. Douglas rose to make this speech, his desk was piled with original Mexican documents, all official, from which he proved that the Rio Grande always was the western boundary of Texas. After first defeating the Mexicans, the Texans on the 2d of November, 1836, adopted a declaration of independence, and on 17th published their constitution. In both of these documents, the Rio Grande was stated as the boundary. After the memorable victory of San Jacinto, on the 21st of April following, a treaty was made and ratified May 12th, between Santa Anna on the part of the Mexican government, and Gen. Houston on the part of Texas, which prescribed the boundary of Texas, the Rio Grande being the western line.

Mr. Douglas then proceeded to show that the war had been commenced by the act of Mexico, and cited the official instructions from President Paredes to the Mexican general commanding on the right bank of the Rio Grande, in which he says, April, 18, 1846, "It is indispensable that hostilities be commenced, yourself taking the initiative against the enemy." In closing this speech, Mr. Douglas paid a glowing tribute to the volunteers who had so gallantly rushed to the standard of their country, and especially to the 7,000 volunteers from Illinois.

PASS TO SANTA ANNA.

Gen. Santa Anna had been an exile from his country when the Mexican War began; and, desiring to return to Mexico, he was permitted to pass through our squadron. This was done in pursuance of orders from the War Department to the commander of our fleet in the Gulf of Mexico. The Government was violently assailed for having permitted this; Mr. Clayton of Delaware having charged the President, by giving this pass to Santa Anna, with being guilty of a blunder worse than a crime. On the 17th of March, Mr. Douglas, in a brief, but comprehensive speech, defended the policy of the administration in this matter, and showed that the admission of Santa Anna, so far from being a blunder, was a wise and politic measure. The results of the war proved that he was right, and that Mr. Clayton was mistaken.

ILLINOIS CENTRAL RAILROAD.

The bill granting to the State of Illinois the right of way through the lands of the United States, which had been originally introduced into the Senate by Mr. Douglas, April 10, 1848, was passed on the 31st of May: the measure owing its success mainly to his exertions. The object of the bill was to construct a railroad connecting Chicago and the

great lakes of the North, with the Mississippi River at
Cairo. The road was built, and it has proved to be of incalculable benefit, not only to the State of Illinois, but to the
whole country.

In the debate on the bill, Mr. Douglas explained that the
proposed road was to be the entire length of the State from
north to south, not far from 400 miles. The bill proposed
to grant the land in alternate sections, increasing the price
of the other sections to double the minimum price. It was fol
lowing the same system that had been adopted in reference tt
improvements of a similar character in Ohio, Indiana, Alabama,
Iowa, and Wisconsin, by which principle each alternate
section of land was ceded, and the price of the alternate
sections not ceded was doubled, so that the same price is received for the whole. These lands had been in the market
about twenty-three years; but they would not sell at the usual
price of $1 25 per acre, because they were distant from any
navigable stream. A railroad would make the lands salable
at double the usual price. The road was begun by the
State of Illinois in 1836, and about a million of dollars were
expended upon it by the State. With the exception of the
county at the northern end of the road, more than one-half
of the whole of the lands along the line were then vacant;
in most of the counties, it was so. Around the towns the
land was all taken up and cultivated, but there were large
prairies where the land was in all its original wildness.

ITS BENEFIT TO ILLINOIS.

It must be remembered that this was twelve years ago.
Illinois twelve years ago was very different from the Illinois
of to-day. There was then not a single mile of railroad in
the State; and the greater part of the line of the proposed
railroad passed for miles and miles without coming in sight

of a house, or any other indication of civilized life. What a contrast now! The proposed road built, known even in Europe as one of the most prosperous in America; other railroads crossing it in all directions; the reserved alternate sections of land nearly all sold, at prices ranging from two dollars and a half to seven and a quarter per acre, thus yielding to the government a much larger sum for one half than was before asked for the whole; the whole of the soil of Illinois, acknowledged to be the richest in the world, redeemed from its primitive wildness, blooming and blossoming like a garden, and teeming with abundant harvests; a market brought to every farmer's door; and this prosperity owing its origin and material progress to the exertions or Mr. Douglas in securing the passage of this bill.

It is but an act of simple justice to those illustrious states men to add, that John C. Calhoun, Henry Clay, Danie Webster, Thomas H. Benton, and Lewis Cass, seconded the efforts of Mr. Douglas by able and eloquent speeches in favor of this great measure.

MISSOURI COMPROMISE REPUDIATED.

In August, 1848, Mr. Douglas offered an amendment to the Oregon Bill, extending the Missouri Compromise line to the Pacific Ocean, in the same sense and with the same understanding with which it was originally adopted in 1820, and extended through Texas in 1845. The amendment was adopted in the Senate, but was rejected in the House of Representatives by northern votes.

It is important to mark well this fact. The first time that the principles of the Missouri Compromise were even abandoned, the first time they were ever rejected by Congress, was by the defeat of that provision in the House of Representatives, in 1848. That defeat was effected by northern votes with Freesoil proclivities. It was that defeat which reopened the slavery agitation in all its fury, and caused the tremendous struggle of 1850. It was that defeat which created the necessity for making a new compromise in 1850. Who caused that defeat? Who was faithless to the principles of the compromise of 1820? It was the very men who in 1854, insisted that the Missouri Compromise was a solemn compact that ought never to be violated. The very men who, in 1854, arraigned Mr. Douglas for a departure from the Missouri Compromise, were the men who successfully violated it, repudiated it, and caused it to be superseded.

CALIFORNIA, INDIAN TITLES, ETC.

By the time the next session of Congress assembled, California had been settled by an enterprising people, whose numbers entitled them to admission into the Union as a State. A bill " for the admission of California as a State into the Union," was introduced by Mr. Douglas on the 29th of January, 1849 ; but was not acted on till long afterward.

On the 18th of December, 1849, Mr. Douglas was reëlected chairman of the Senate Committee on Territories, by 33 out of 40 votes; a position to which he was constantly thereafter reëlected, until December, 1858.

The tribes of Indians which had, until a few years before, occupied the lands in Minnesota, Oregon, California, and New Mexico, had never been fully divested of their title to the same ; and their constant presence there, and their depredations on the settlers, were very annoying ; so much so that the settlement of those new Territories was much impeded. In order to remove the cause of all the trouble at once, Mr. Douglas, on the 7th of January, 1850, offered a resolution providing for the complete extinguishment of the Indian title in the Territories above named. The resolution was debated at some length, but it was adopted ; and the measures proposed have been faithfully carried out. Ample provision was made for treating the Indians with fairness and justice : and while their rights have been respected, and their comforts secured, the vast regions which they occupied have been secured for all time to come for the abodes of civilized men ; and for the spread of those great fundamental principles on which our national prosperity rests.

At the time that Mr. Douglas introduced his resolution, however, the emigrants to those Territories, and especially to those of Oregon and California, were annoyed and attacked to such an extent, by roving bands of Indians, that it was considered positively unsafe for emigrants to go any further west than the Missouri River. It was clearly the duty of the Government to afford protection to its citizens on its own soil ; and accordingly, on the 31st of January, Mr. Douglas offered a resolution, instructing the committee on military affairs to inquire into the expediency of providing, on the usual emigrant line from the Missouri River to the South Pass of the Rocky Mountains, a sufficient movable military force to protect all emigrants to Oregon and California.

To the legislation growing out of this resolution, many hundreds of families now living in comfort and even in affluence in the smiling villages of Oregon, California, and Minnesota, are indebted, not only for their safety, but their very lives. The instances of emigrant trains saved from the attack and spoliation of the savages, by our gallant troops on the frontier, from 1851 to 1857, are numerous and well authenticated. The settlers in those new countries owe a debt of gratitude to Mr. Douglas which they will not soon forget.

CHAPTER VII.

COMPROMISE OF 1850.

Mr. Douglas supports the Compromise Measures of Henry Clay—Great Speech on the 13th and 14th of March—Speech in favor of the Omnibus Bill, June 3—The Nicholson Letter of General Cass—Mr. Douglas returns to Chicago—He is Denounced by the Local Authorities—He beards the Lions in their Den—Speech to the Citizens of Chicago—Its Effect.

WHEN the Compromise measures of Mr. Clay were brought forward in 1850, Mr. Douglas supported them with zeal and vigor. On the 13th and 14th of March, he delivered a speech on the general territorial questions, which has scarcely been surpassed by any of his subsequent efforts. It was by far the ablest speech that had ever been delivered in the Senate by any western man. It was in this speech that Judge Douglas first enunciated the doctrine of which he has ever since been the most distinguished advocate, that it is the true Democratic principle in reference to the Territories, that each one shall be left to regulate its own local and domestic affairs in its own way.

In the beginning of this great speech, Senator Douglas showed that all the acts of the Tyler administration in reference to the annexation of Texas (including the proposed treaty with Mexico for that object, and the correspondence between our secretary of state on the one part, and Mr. King, minister to France and Mr. Murphy, chargé d'affaires in the republic of Texas, on the other part), had been indignantly and contemptuously rejected by the Senate ; and that this had been done in order to repudiate and rebuke the administration of Mr Tyler, and in order that the Democratic party might come to the support of the annexation of Texas as they did come, and consummated the annexation upon broad, national grounds, elevated far above and totally disconnected from the question of slavery.

ORDINANCE OF 1787 HAD NO EFFECT ON SLAVERY.

A distinguished southern senator having said that the South had been deprived of its due share of the territories, Mr. Douglas responded, " What share *had* the South in the territories? or the North? I answer, none at all. The territories belong to the United States as one people, and are to be disposed of for the common benefit of all, according to the principles of the Constitution. No geographical section of the Union is entitled to any share of the territories. What becomes of the complaint of the senator, that the Ordinance of 1787 excluded the South entirely from that vast fertile region between the Ohio and the Mississippi? That ordinance was a dead letter. It did not make the country to which it applied, free from slavery. The States formed out of the territory northwest of the Ohio, did not become free by virtue of the Ordinance, nor in consequence of it. Those States became free by virtue of their own will, recorded in the fundamental laws of their own making. That is the source of their freedom. In all republican states, laws and ordinances are mere nullities, unless sustained by the hearts and intellects of the people for whom they are made, and by whom they are to be executed.

SLAVES IN ILLINOIS.

"The Ordinance of 1787 did the South no harm, and the North no good. Illinois, for instance, was a slave territory. Even in 1840, there were 331 slaves in Illinois. How came these slaves in Illinois? They were taken there under the Ordinance, and in defiance of it. The people of Illinois, while it was a territory, were mostly emigrants from the slaveholding States. But when their convention assembled at Kaskaskia in 1818, to form the constitution of the State of Illinois, although it was composed of slaveholders, yet they had become satisfied, from experience, that the climate and productions of Illinois were unfavorable to slave labor. They accordingly made provision for a gradual system of emancipation, by which the State should become eventually free. These facts show that the Ordinance had no practical effect upon slavery. Slavery existed under the Ordinance ; and since the Ordinance has been suspended by the State governments, slavery has gradually disappeared under the operation of laws adopted and executed by the people themselves. A law passed by the national legislature to operate locally upon a people not represented, will always remain a dead letter, if it be in opposition to the wishes and interests of those who are to be affected by it.

" In regard to the effects of the Missouri Compromise on the question of slavery, I do not think that it had any practical effect on that question, one way or another : it neither curtailed nor extended slavery one inch."

A GLANCE AT THE FUTURE.

" We recognize the right of the South, in common with our right, to emigrate to the Territories with their property, and there hold and enjoy it in subordination to the laws in force there. The senator from South Carolina desires such an amendment to the Constitution as shall stipulate that in all time to come, there shall be as many slaveholding States in the Union as there are States without slaves. The adoption and execution of such a provision would be an impossibility. We have a vast territory which is filling up with an industrious and enterprising population, large enough to form seventeen new States, one-half of which we may expect to see represented in this body during our day. Of these, four will be formed out of Oregon, five out of our late acquisition from Mexico, including the present State of California, and two out of Minnesota. Each of these will be free Territories and free States, whether Congress shall prohibit slavery in them or not. Where are you to find the slave territory with which to balance these seventeen free Territories? In Texas? If Texas should be divided into five States, at least three of them will in all probability be free."

*   *   *   *   *   *

ADMISSION OF CALIFORNIA.

Mr. Douglas then proceeded to advocate, at great length, the immediate admission of the State of California under her constitution; and concluded his speech by declaring that "this nation owes to the venerable senator from Kentucky (Mr. Clay) a debt of gratitude for his services to the Union on this occasion. The purity of his motives cannot be doubted. He has set the ball in motion which is to restore peace and harmony to the Union."

THE OMNIBUS BILL.

On the 3d of June, 1850, Mr. Douglas spoke in favor of the Omnibus Bill, and in the course of his remarks said: "In respect to African slavery, the position that I have ever taken has been, that this, and all other questions relating to the domestic affairs and domestic policy of the Territories, ought to be left to the decision of the people themselves. I would therefore have much preferred that the bill should have remained as it was reported from the Committee on Territories, with no provision on the subject of slavery; and I do hope that that clause in the bill will be stricken out. It ought not to be there, because it is a violation of principle I do not see how we who have argued in favor of the right of the people to legislate for themselves on this question, can support such a provision without abandoning all the arguments which we urged in the Presidential campaign of 1848, and the principles set forth by the senator from Michigan in the Nicholson letter.

"And, sir, is an institution to be fixed upon a people in opposition to their unanimous opinion? I, for one, think that such ought not to be the case. I desire no provision whatever in respect to slavery in the Territories. I wish to leave the people of the Territories free to enact such laws as they please. But on this one point, I am not left to follow my own judgment, nor my own desire. I am to express the will of my constituents. My vote will be in accordance with their instructions."

We give, in a subsequent part of this work, the Nicholson letter referred to by Mr. Douglas, and commend it to the perusal of our readers. It will amply repay the time thus spent.

On the 6th of June, and also on the 26th, Mr. Douglas addressed the Senate in support of the Compromise measures.

ABOLITIONISM IN CHICAGO.

The Compromise measures of 1850 having been adopted by Congress, and that body having adjourned, Mr. Douglas proceeded to Chicago, where he had recently purchased property, with a view of making that city his permanent residence. It is a well known fact that Chicago has always been the hot-bed of abolitionism, and a prominent station on the Underground Railroad. There are many men there who have never bowed the knee to the Baal of fanaticism and treason, but the majority of the people have always been abolitionists. These restless beings had been violently opposed to the Compromise measures, and they raised a storm of execration and abuse against Mr. Douglas, because he had been prominent in procuring their adoption. The excitement was fierce and terrific. A venal press, and pulpits disgraced by crazy fanatics, joined in the work of misrepresentation, abuse, and denunciation. The city council met, and passed resolutions denouncing the Compromise and Fugitive Slave Law as violations of the law of God and the Constitution of the United States ; enjoined the city police to disregard the law, and called upon the citizens not to obey it. On the next evening a meeting was held, composed of twenty-five hundred citizens, and in that meeting, in the midst of terrific applause, it was determined to defy " death, the dungeon, and the grave," in resistance to the execution of the law. Mr. Douglas was then in Chicago : he knew that this meeting was to take place; and he knew, from the character of the men who composed it, what the nature of the resolutions would be. He walked into the meeting, and from the stand gave notice that on the next evening he would appear there and defend every measure of the Compromise, and especially the Fugitive Slave Law, from every objection : and he called upon the entire people of the city to come and hear him. The announcement was made in the midst of profound silence, but was immediately followed by a storm of groans and hisses. Mr. Douglas, however, calmly stood his ground till the noise subsided, and then, addressing those who had hissed and groaned, told them that he was right and they were wrong, and that if they would come and hear him he would prove it to them.

MR. DOUGLAS SPEAKS IN CHICAGO.

On the next evening, in the presence of 4,000 people, with the city council and abolitionists in front of the stand, which was surrounded in the rear by a large body of armed negroes, including many fugitive slaves, Mr. Douglas made a speech in which he vindicated the Compromise measures and the Fugitive Slave Law, and proved that the latter was both necessary and constitutional; and he answered every objection that had been urged against them. The objections relating to the right of trial by jury, to the writ of habeas corpus, to records from other States, to the fees of the commissioners, to the pains and penalties, to the "higher law"—every objec tion which the ingenuity and fanaticism of abolitionism could invent, was brought up by different persons in the meeting, and fully and conclusively answered by Mr. Douglas. What was the effect of that speech upon that meeting, comprising three-fourths of all the legal voters of the city of Chicago? The people composing that meeting, a majority of whom had, the night previously, pledged themselves to open and violent resistance to the law, after the conclusion of the speech of Mr. Douglas, unanimously adopted a series of resolutions in favor of sustaining and carrying into effect every provision of the Constitution and laws in respect to the surrender of fugitive slaves. The resolutions were written, and submitted to the meeting by Mr. Douglas, and cover the entire ground. The city council having nullified the law and denounced Mr. Douglas as a traitor, the Hon. Buckner S. Morris offered the following resolution, which was also adopted : "*Resolved*, That we, the people of Chicago, repudiate the resolutions recently passed by the Common Council of Chicago upon the subject of the Fugitive Slave Law."

EFFECT OF THE SPEECH.

On the following evening, the city council met again, and repealed their nullifying resolutions by a vote of twelve to one.

This speech of Mr. Douglas was the first one ever made in a free State in defence of the Fugitive Slave Law, and that Chicago meeting was the first public assemblage in any free State that determined to support and sustain it. In the very nest of rebellion and treason, the rebels and traitors received their first check: the fanatical spirit was rebuked, and the supremacy of the Constitution and laws asserted and maintained. Such is the power of eloquence and the force of truth, even in modern times.

In the Appendix to this work, will be found the two documents referred to by Senator Douglas in his speech of the 13th and 14th of March, 1850; namely, the official dispatch of John C. Calhoun, secretary of state under John Tyler, to the Hon. Wm. R. King, our ambassador to Paris: and the Nicholson letter of Gen. Cass. The former is valuable as a part of the history of the Tyler administration, and as showing their views on the subject of the annexation of Texas. It is a rare document, and as curious as any State paper in the history of the country.

CHAPTER VIII.

1851–1854.

Speech in favor of making Gen. Winfield Scott a Lieutenant-General—Speech on the Fugitive Slave Law—Speech on the Foreign Policy of the United States—Retrospective View of the Course of Mr. Douglas in Congress up to this Time (1852)—Mr. Douglas the real Author of the Compromise Measures of 1850—Bill for the Organization of the Territories of Kansas and Nebraska—Mr. Douglas opposes the Oregon Treaty with England—Opposes the Peace Treaty with Mexico—Speech on the Clayton and Bulwer Treaty—Report on the Organization of Nebraska and Kansas—The Nebraska Bill—Debate on it—The bill passed.

On the 12th of February, 1851, Mr. Douglas spoke in favor of conferring the rank of Lieutenant-General on General Winfield Scott. In the course of his remarks, he said, " I would have preferred, however, to have seen this proposition put in a shape which would have been more consistent with the organization of the army, with reference to what may occur in the future. I think that the highest grade in the army of the United States should be always vacant in time of peace, to be filled when war should occur, by a commission to expire at the end of the war. I think that when a war occurs, the President of the United States should be at liberty to look through the whole line of the army, and through the whole line of the citizen soldiery, to select a commander-in-chief to conduct that war. I would, therefore, like to see the office of lieutenant-general created, to be

filled when a war arises, and to become vacant at its termination."

On the 22d, in the debate on the execution of the Fugitive
Slave Law, shortly after the riot at Boston, Mr. Douglas said:
" The laws of Illinois have always discouraged negroes from
coming there.   In regard to runaway slaves coming into the
State, we have a law imposing penalties at the discretion of
the court, upon any citizen of Illinois who would harbor a
runaway slave.   It has been my fortune, in the course of my
brief judicial experience, to impose severe penalties upon
citizens of Illinois for a violation of that law : it remains upon
the statute book at this day.   The senator from Ohio looks
upon this matter of the rescue of a fugitive at Boston, as a
trivial transaction.   I do not.   It is well known that there is
a systematic organization in many of the free States of this
Union, for the purpose of evading the obligations of the Constitution, and to prevent the enforcement of the laws of the
United States in relation to fugitive slaves.   It has, at its
head, men of daring and of desperate purpose; and the opposition to the Fugitive Slave Law is a combined and concerted
action.   It is in the nature of a conspiracy against the government.   I say, therefore, that these conspirators, be they in
Boston or in Illinois, are responsible for all that any of their
number may do in resistance to this law.   Sir, I hold white
men now in my sight responsible for the violation of the law
at Boston.   It was done under their advice, under their
teaching, under the influence of their speeches.   The negroes
in the free States have been armed by the abolitionists during
the last six months, for the express purpose of violating the
Fugitive Slave Law.   I have stood in a meeting of 2,000 men,
and heard white men tell the negroes to kill the first white

man who attempted to execute this law. I have seen the weapons that have been prepared by white abolitionists, to enable the negroes to resist. I trust the penalty will fall upon the white abolitionists."

On the 26th of August, 1852, Mr. Sumner, of Massachusetts, made a most violent speech against the Fugitive Slave Law, and in favor of its repeal.

Mr. Douglas said in reply: "The arguments against the Fugitive Slave Law, are arguments against the Constitution of our country. Gentlemen should pass over the law, and make their assaults directly upon the Constitution of the United States, in obedience to which the law was passed. Let them proclaim to the world that they feel bound to make violent resistance to the Constitution which our fathers have transmitted to us. The Constitution provides that no man shall be a senator unless he takes an oath to support the Constitution. And when he takes that oath, I do not understand that he has a right to have a mental reservation, or entertain any mental equivocation that he excepts that clause which relates to the surrender of fugitives. I know not how a man reconciles it to his conscience to take that oath to support the Constitution, when he believes that Constitution is in violation of the law of God. A man who thus believes, and yet takes the oath, commits perjury before God for the sake of the temporary honors of a seat on this floor."

KOSSUTH.

On the 11th December, 1851, when the resolution giving a national welcome to Louis Kossuth, of Hungary, was pending before the Senate, Mr. Douglas said: "I regret that this resolution has been introduced, not because I do not cordially sympathize in the proposed reception, but because it cannot pass unanimously. Its discussion and a divided vote deprive it of its chief merit. I do not deem it material whether the reception of Gov. Kossuth will give offence to the crowned heads of Europe, provided it does not violate the laws of nations, and give just *cause* of offence. The question with me is, whether the passage of this resolution gives just cause of offence according to the laws of nations. I would take no step which would violate the law of nations, or give just cause of offence to any power on earth. Nor do I think that a cordial welcome to Gov. Kossuth can be properly construed into such cause of offence. Shall it be said that democratic America is not to be permitted to grant a hearty welcome to an exile who has become the representative of liberal principles throughout the world, lest despotic Austria and Russia shall be offended? I think that the bearing of this country should be such as to demonstrate to all mankind that America sympathizes with the popular movement against despotism. The principle laid down by Gov. Kossuth as the basis of his action, that each state has a right to dispose of her own destiny, and regulate her internal affairs in her own way, is an axiom in the laws of nations which every state ought to recognize and respect. The armed intervention of Russia to deprive Hungary of her constitutional rights, was such a violation of the laws of nations as authorized England or the United States to interfere and prevent the consummation of the deed. To say in advance that the United States will not interfere in vindication of the laws of nations, is to give our consent that Russia may interfere to destroy the liberties of an independent nation. I will make no such declaration. On the other hand, I will not advise the declaration in advance that we *will* interfere. Something has been said about our alliance with England. I desire no alliance with England."

RETROSPECTIVE VIEW.

Let us now take a brief retrospective view of the Congressional life of Mr. Douglas, up to this time. The first important vote he ever gave in the House of Representatives was in favor of excluding abolition petitions, and his vote stands so recorded. His action, ever since he has been a member of the Senate, has been governed by the same principle. Whenever the slavery agitation has been forced upon Congress, he has met it fairly, directly and fearlessly, and endeavored to apply the proper remedy. When the stormy agitation arose in connection with the annexation of Texas, he originated and first brought forward the Missouri Compromise as applicable to that territory, and had the gratification to see it incorporated in the bill which annexed Texas to the United States. He did not deem this a matter of much moment as applicable to Texas alone; but he did conceive it to be of vast importance in view of the probable acquisition of New Mexico and California. His preference for the Missouri Compromise was predicated on the assumption that the whole people of the United States would be more easily reconciled to that measure than to any other mode of adjustment; and this assumption rested upon the fact that the Missouri Compromise had been the means of an amicable settlement of a fearful controversy in 1821, which had been acquiesced in cheerfully by the people for more than a quarter of a century, and which all parties and sections of the Union respected and cherished as a fair, just and honorable adjustment.

COURSE OF MR. DOUGLAS IN CONGRESS.

Mr. Douglas could see no reason for the application of the Missouri line to all the territory owned by the United States
3*

in 1821, that would not apply with equal force to its extension to the Rio Grande, and also to the Pacific, as soon as we should acquire the country. In accordance with these views, he brought forward the Missouri Compromise at the session of 1845 as applicable to Texas, and had the satisfaction to see it adopted. Subsequently, after the war with Mexico had commenced, and when, in August, 1846, Mr. Wilmot first introduced his proviso, Mr. Douglas proposed to extend the Missouri Compromise to the Pacific, as a substitute for the Wilmot Proviso. The Wilmot Proviso not only designed to prohibit slavery in the territories while they remained territories, but proposed to insert a stipulation in the treaty with Mexico, pledging the faith of the nation that slavery should never exist in the country acquired, either while it remained a territory, or after it should have been admitted into the Union as States. Mr. Douglas denounced this proviso as being unwise, improper, and unconstitutional: he never voted for it, and more than once declared that he never would vote for it. When California and New Mexico had been acquired without any condition or stipulation in respect to slavery, the Wilmot Proviso was disposed of for ever.

At the time that the question began to be discussed, what kind of territorial governments should be established for those countries, a severe domestic affliction called Mr. Douglas from Washington, and detained him several weeks. On his return to the Senate he supported the Clayton bill, which passed the Senate, but was defeated in the House of Representatives. Mr. Douglas then brought forward his original proposition, to extend the Missouri Compromise to the Pacific, in the same sense and with the same understanding with which it was originally adopted. This proposition passed the Senate by a large majority, but was rejected, as we have seen, by the House of Representatives. Mr. Douglas then conceived the idea of a bill to admit California as a State, leaving the people to form a constitution, and to settle the question of slavery afterward to suit themselves. This bill was introduced by Mr. Douglas with the sanction of President Polk. It recognized the right of the people of California to determine all questions relating to their domestic concerns in their own way; but the Senate refused to pass the bill. All this took place before the Compromise measures of Mr. Clay were brought forward. During the period of five years that Mr. Douglas had been laboring for the adoption of the Missouri Compromise, his votes on the Oregon question, and upon all questions touching slavery, were given with reference to a settlement on that basis, and were consistent with it.

MR. DOUGLAS THE AUTHOR OF THE COMPROMISE OF 1850.

When Congress met, in December, 1849, Mr. Douglas was again placed by the Senate at the head of the Committee on Territories, and it became his duty to prepare and submit some plan for the settlement of those momentous questions, the agitation of which had convulsed the whole nation. Early in December, within the first two or three weeks of the session, he wrote and laid before the Committee on Territories, for their examination, two bills: one for the admission of California into the Union, and the other containing three distinct measures; first, for the establishment of a territorial government for Utah; second, for the establishment of a territorial government for New Mexico; and third, for the settlement of the Texas boundary. These bills remained before the Committee on Territories from the month of December, 1849, to the 25th of March, 1850. On that day Mr. Douglas reported the bills, and they were, on his motion, ordered to be printed. These printed bills having laid on the tables of all the senators for four weeks, the Senate appointed a committee of thirteen, Henry Clay, of Kentucky, chairman. That committee took the two printed bills of Mr. Douglas, pasted them together, and reported them to the Senate as one bill, which was thenceforth known as the Omnibus Bill. Mr. Douglas made this statement to the Senate on the 23d of December, 1851, while the original Omnibus Bill was yet upon the clerk's table. The Committee of Thirteen had drawn a black line through the words, " *Mr. Douglas, from the Committee on Territories,*" and in place of them, interlined these other words, " *Mr. Clay, from the Committee of Thirteen,* reported the following bill."

The report of the committee will be found in a subsequent part of this work.

Mr. Douglas supported the Omnibus Bill as a joint measure; but the Senate refused to pass the measures together. Each one, however, was passed separately; and each one was supported by Mr. Douglas. Well might Mr. Polk remark in the House of Representatives, in April, 1852, after speaking of the eminent services of Mr. Douglas: " History will cherish the record of such fearless and faithful service, and administer the proper rebuke to those who from malice or envy may seek to detract from his fair fame."

We give the material features of these bills as they were passed, as a part of the history of the times, in the Appendix.

THE RIGHT OF INSTRUCTION.

On the 23d of December, 1851, Mr. Douglas made a speech in the Senate, on the resolutions declaring the Compromise measures of 1850 to be a definitive and final settlement of all the questions growing out of the subject of domestic slavery, in the course of which he took a brief review of the votes he had given since the introduction of the Compromise measures, and showed that he had supported them all.. In this speech he said:

MR. PRESIDENT: I claim no merit for having originated and proposed the measures contained in the Omnibus Bill. There was no remarkable feature about them. They were merely ordinary measures of legislation, well adapted to the circumstances, and their merit consisted in the fact that separately they could and did pass both Houses of Congress. Being responsible for these bills, as they came from the hands of the Committee on Territories, I wish to call attention to the fact that they contained no prohibition of slavery—no provision upon the subject. And now I come to the point which explains my object in stating my votes. The legislature of Illinois had passed a resolution instructing me to vote for a bill for the government of the territory acquired from Mexico, which should contain an express prohibition of slavery in that territory while it remained as territories, leaving the people to do as they pleased when they became a State. The instruction was designed in order to compel me to resign my seat and give place to a Freesoiler. The legislature knew my inflexible opposition to the principles asserted in the instructions, and wished me to give place to a Freesoiler, who would come here and carry out abolition doctrines. Notwithstanding these instructions, I wrote the bills and reported them from the Committee on Territories without the prohibition, in order that the record might show what my opinions were; but, lest the trick against me might fail, a Freesoil senator offered an amendment in the language of my instructions. I knew that the amendment could not prevail, even if the vote of Illinois was recorded in its favor. But if I resigned my place to an abolitionist, it was almost certain that the bills would fail on their passage. I came to the conclusion that duty required me to retain my seat. I was prepared to fight and defy abolitionism in all its forms, but I was not willing to repudiate the settled doctrine of my State, in regard to the right of instruction. Before the vote was taken, I defined my position. I denounced the doctrine of the amendment, declared my unalterable opposition to it, and gave notice that any vote which might be recorded in my name seemingly in its favor, would be the vote of those who gave the instructions, and not my own. Under this protest, I recorded a vote for this and two other amendments embracing the same principle, and then renewed my protest against them, and gave notice that I should not hold myself responsible for them. Immediately on my return home, and in a speech to my constituents, I renewed my protest against these votes, and repeated the notice to that infuriated meeting, that they were their votes, and not mine. In that speech at Chicago, I said of the territorial bills : ' These measures are predicated on the great fundamental principle that every people ought to possess the right of forming and regulating their own internal concerns and domestic institutions in their own way. If those who emigrate to the territories have the requisite intelligence and honesty to enact laws for the government of white men, I know of no reason why they should not be deemed competent to legislate for the negro. If they are sufficiently enlightened to make laws for the protection of life, liberty, and property, of morals and education, to determine the relation of husband and wife, of parent and child, I am not aware that it requires any higher degree of civilization to regulate the affairs of master and servant. My votes and acts have been in accordance with these views in all cases, except in the instances in which I voted under your instructions. Those were your votes. and not mine. I entered my protest against them at the time, before and after they were recorded, and shall never hold myself responsible for them.' I made a good many speeches of the same tenor, the last of which was at the capital of Illinois. A few weeks afterward the legislature of Illinois assembled, and one of their first acts was to repeal the resolution of instructions to which I have referred, and to pass resolutions approving of the course of my colleague, General Shields, and myself, on the Compromise measures. From that day Illinois has stood firm and unwavering in support of the Compromise measures, and of all the compromises of the Constitution.

Mr. President, if I have said anything that savors of egotism, the Senate will pardon me. If I had omitted all that was personal to myself, my defence would have been incomplete. I am willing to be held responsible for all my acts, but I wish to be judged by my acts, and not by malicious misrepresentations. I may have committed errors; but when I am convinced of them, I will acknowledge them like a man, and promptly correct them. The Democratic party is as good a Union party as I want, and I want to preserve its principles and its organization, and to triumph upon its old issues. I desire no new tests, no interpolations upon the old creed."

In December 1853, Mr. Douglas reported the bill to organize the Territories of Kansas and Nebraska, which formed the issues upon which the Democratic and Republican parties became arrayed against each other. He opposed the treaty with England in relation to the Oregon boundary, contending that England had no rights on that coast. He opposed the Trist peace treaty with Mexico upon the ground that the boun· daries were unnatural and inconvenient, and that the provisions in relation to the Indians could never be executed. The United States government has since paid Mexico ten millions of dollars to change the boundaries; and to relinquish the stipulations in regard to the Indians. He opposed the Clayton and Bulwer treaty, because it pledged the United States in all time to come, never to annex Central America. He declared that he did not desire to annex Central America at that time, but maintained that the isthmus routes must be kept open as highways to the American possessions on the Pacific; that the time would come when the United States would be compelled to occupy Central America, and that he would never pledge the faith of the republic not to do in the future what its interests and safety might require. He also declared himself in favor of the acquisition of Cuba, whenever that island can be obtained consistently with the laws of nations and the honor of the United States. We give this speech entire in a subsequent part of this work.

On the 4th of January 1854, Senator Douglas made the following Report relative to the organization of the Territories of Nebraska and Kansas:

The Committee on Territories, to whom was referred a bill for an act to establish the Territories of Nebraska, have given the same that serious and deliberate consideration which its great importance demands, and beg leave to report it back to the Senate, with various amendments, in the form of a substitute for the bill:

The principal amendments which your committee deem it their duty to commend to .the favorable action of the Senate, in a special report, are those in which the principles established by the Compromise measures of 1850, so far as they are applicable to territorial organizations, are proposed to be affirmed and carried into practical operation within the limits of the new Territory.

The wisdom of those measures is attested, not less by their salutary and beneficial effects, in allaying sectional agitation and restoring peace and harmony to an irritated and distracted people, than by the cordial and almost universal approbation with which they have been received and sanctioned by the whole country. In the judgment of your Committee, those measures were intended to have a far more comprehensive and enduring effect than the mere adjustment of difficulties arising out of the recent acquisition of Mexican territory. They were designed to establish certain great principles, which would not only furnish adequate remedies for existing evils, but, in all time to come, avoid the perils of similar agitation, by withdrawing the question of Slavery from the halls of Congress and the political arena, committing it to the arbitration of those who were immediately interested in, and alone responsible for, its consequences. With a view of conforming their action to what they regard as the settled policy of the government, sanctioned by the approving voice of the American people, your Committee have deemed it their duty to incorporate and perpetuate, in their Territorial Bill, the principles and spirit of those measures. If any other consideration were necessary to render the propriety of this course imperative upon the Committee, they may be found in the fact that the Nebraska country occupies the same relative position to the slavery question, as did New Mexico and Utah, when those Territories were organized.

It was a disputed point, whether slavery was prohibited by law in the country acquired from Mexico. On the one hand, it was contended, as a legal proposition, that slavery, having been prohibited by the enactment of Mexico, according to the laws of nations, we received the country with all its local laws and domestic institutions attached to the soil, so far as they did not conflict with the Constitution of the United States; and that a law either protecting or prohibiting slavery, was not repugnant to that instrument, as was evidenced by the fact that one-half of the States of the Union tolerated, while the other half prohibited, the institution of slavery. On the other hand, it was insisted that, by virtue of the Constitution of the United States, every citizen had a right to remove to any Territory of the Union, and carry his property with him under the protection of law, whether that property consisted of persons or things. The difficulties arising from this diversity of opinion, were greatly aggravated by the fact that there were many persons on both sides of the legal controversy, who were unwilling to abide the decision of the courts on the legal matters in dispute; thus, among those who claimed that the Mexican laws were still in force, and, consequently, that slavery was already prohibited in those Territories by valid enactment, there were many who insisted upon Congress making the matter certain, by enacting another prohibition. In like manner, some of those who argued that Mexican law had ceased to have any binding force, and that the Constitution tolerated and protected slave property in those Territories, were unwilling to trust the decision of the courts upon the point, and insisted that Congress should, by direct enactment, remove all legal obstacles to the introduction of slaves into those Territories.

Such being the character of the controversy in respect to the territory acquired from Mexico, a similar question has arisen in regard to the right to hold slaves in the Territory of Nebraska, when the Indian laws shall be withdrawn, and the country thrown open to emigration and settlement. By the 8th section of "an act to authorize the people of Missouri Territory to form a constitution and State government, and for the admission of such State into the Union on an equal footing with the original States, and to prohibit slavery in certain Territories," approved March 6th, 1820, it was provided; "That in all that territory ceded by France to the United States under the name of Louisiana, which lies north of 36 degrees 30 minutes north latitude, not included within the limits of the State contemplated by this act, slavery and involuntary servitude, otherwise than in the punishment of crimes whereof the parties shall have been duly convicted, shall be, and are hereby, prohibited: *Provided always*, That any person escaping into the same, from whom labor or service is lawfully claimed in any State or Territory of the United States, such fugitive may be lawfully reclaimed, and conveyed to the persons claiming his or her labor or services as aforesaid."

Under this section, as in the case of the Mexican law in New Mexico and Utah, it is a disputed point whether slavery is prohibited in the Nebraska country by *valid* enactment. The decision of this question involves the constitutional power of Congress to pass laws prescribing and regulating the domestic institutions of the various Territories of the Union. In the opinion of those eminent statesmen who hold that Congress is invested with no rightful authority to legislate upon the subject of slavery in the Territories, the 8th section of the act preparatory to the admission of Missouri is null and void; while the prevailing sentiment in large portions of the Union sustains the doctrine that the Constitution of the United States secures to every citizen an inalienable right to move into any of the Territories with his property, of whatever kind and description, and to hold and enjoy the same under the sanction of law. Your Committee do not feel themselves called upon to enter upon the discussion of these controverted questions. They involve the same grave issues which produced the agitation, the sectional strife, and the fearful struggle of 1850. As

Congress deemed it wise and prudent to refrain from deciding the matters in controversy then, either by affirming or repealing the Mexican laws, or by an act declaratory of the true intent of the Constitution, and the extent of the protection afforded by it to slave property in the Territories, so your Committee are not prepared to recommend a departure from the course parsued on that memorable occasion, either by affirming or repealing the 8th section of the Missouri act, or by any act declaratory of the meaning of the Constitution in respect to the legal points in dispute.

Your Committee deem it fortunate for the peace of the country, and the security of the Union, that the controversy then resulted in the adoption of the Compromise measures, which the two great political parties, with singular unanimity, have affirmed as a cardinal article of their faith, and proclaimed to the world as a final settlement of the controversy and an end to the agitation. A due respect, therefore, for the avowed opinions of senators, as well as a proper sense of patriotic duty, enjoins upon your Committee the propriety and necessity of a strict adherence to the principles, and even a literal adoption of the enactments of that adjustment, in all their territorial bills, so far as the same are not locally inapplicable. Those enactments embrace, among other things less material to the matters under consideration, the following provisions:

When admitted as a State, the said Territory, or any portion of the same, shall be received into the Union, with or without Slavery, as their constitution may prescribe at the time of their admission;

That the legislative power and authority of said Territory shall be vested in the Governor and a Legislative Assembly;

That the legislative power of said Territory shall extend to all rightful subjects of legislation, consistent with the Constitution of the United States, and the provisions of this act; but no law shall be passed interfering with the primary disposal of the soil; no tax shall be imposed upon the property of the United States; nor shall the lands or other property of non-residents be taxed higher than the lands or other property of residents.

Writs of error and appeals from the final decisions of said Supreme Court shall be allowed, and may be taken to the Supreme Court of the United States in the same manner and under the same regulations as from the Circuit Courts of the United States, where the value of the property or amount in controversy, to be ascertained by the oath or affirmation of either party, or other competent witness, shall exceed one thousand dollars; except only that, in all cases involving title to slaves, the said writs of error or appeals shall be allowed and decided by the said Supreme Court, without regard to the value of the matter, property, or title in controversy; and except, also that a writ of error or appeal shall also be allowed to the Supreme Court of the United States from the decision of the said Supreme Court by this act, or of any judge thereof, or of the district courts created by this act, or of any judge thereof, upon any writ of *habeas corpus* involving the question of personal freedom ; and each of the said district courts shall have and exercise the same jurisdiction, in all cases arising under the Constitution and laws of the United States, as is vested in the circuit and district courts of the United States ; and the said supreme and district courts of the said territory, and the respective judges thereof, shall and may grant writs of *habeas corpus*, in all cases in which the same are granted by the judges of the United States in the District of Columbia.

To which may be added the following proposition affirmed by the act of 1850, and known as the Fugitive Slave Law.

That the provisions of the " act respecting fugitives from justice, and persons escaping from the service of their masters," approved February 12, 1793, and the provisions of the act to amend and supplementary to the aforesaid act, approved September 18, 1850, shall extend to, and be in force in, all the organized Territories, as well as in the various States of the Union. AND IN CONCLUSION

From these provisions it is apparent that the Compromise measures of 1850 affirm, and rest upon, the following propositions :

First : That all questions pertaining to Slavery in the Territories, and the new States to be formed therefrom, are to be left to the decision of the people residing therein, by their appropriate representatives, to be chosen by them for that purpose.

Second : That " all cases involving title to slaves," and " questions of personal freedom," are to be referred to the adjudication of the local tribunals, with the right of appeal to the Supreme Court of the United States.

Third : That the provisions of the Constitution of the United States, in respect to fugitives from service, is to be carried into faithful execution in all " the original Territories," the same as in the States.

The substitute for the bill which your Committee have prepared, and which is commended to the favorable action of the Senate, proposes to carry these propositions and principles into practical operation, in the precise language of the Compromise measures of 1850.

The bill thus reported was considered in Committee of the Whole, and then made the special order for the following Monday. The debate was continued Jan. 31st, Feb. 3d, 5th, and 6th.

On the 23d of January, Mr. Douglas, from the Committee on Territories, reported a substitute for the original bill, in nearly the same terms, in which, after defining the limits of the territory, it was proposed to constitute it a Territory, to be afterward admitted as a State, with or without slavery, as their constitution may prescribe at the time of their admission.   It was declared to be the true intent and meaning of the act to carry into practical operation the principles of the Compromise measures of 1850, to wit, That all questions pertaining to slavery in the Territories, and in the new States to be formed therefrom, are to be left to the decision of the people residing therein ; and that the provisions of the Constitution and laws of the United States, in respect to fugitives from service, are to be carried into faithful execution in all the organized Territories.   To the words " the Constitution and all laws of the United States not locally inapplicable, shall have the same force and effect within the said Territory as elsewhere in the United States," the substitute proposed to add these words : " Except the 8th section of the Act for the admission of Missouri into the Union, approved March 6, 1820, which was superseded by the Compromise measures of 1850, and is declared inoperative.'

DEBATE ON THE NEBRASKA BILL.

On the 30th of January, Mr. Douglas made his first speech in favor of the Nebraska Bill.   We give the speech in a subsequent part of this work.

On the 15th of February, Mr. Douglas moved to strike out of his substitute the assertion that the Missouri restriction " was superseded by the Compromise measures of 1850," and insert instead the following :

" Which, being inconsistent with the principle of non-intervention by Congress with Slavery in the States and Territories, as recognized by the legislation of 1850 (commonly called the Compromise measures), is hereby declared inoperative and void; it being the true intent and meaning of this act not to legislate slavery into any Territory or State, nor to exclude it therefrom, but to leave the people thereof perfectly free to form and regulate their domestic institutions in their own way, subject only to the Constitution of the United States,"

which prevailed—yeas 35, nays 10—as follows :

YEAS—*for Douglas' Amendment* : Messrs. Adams, Atchison, Bayard, Bell, Benjamin, Brodhead, Brown, Butler, Cass, Clayton, Dawson, Dixon, Dodge of Iowa, Douglas, Evans, Fitzpatrick, Geyer, Gwin, Hunter, Johnson, Jones of Iowa, Jones of Tenn, Mason, Morton, Norris, Pierce, Pettit, Pratt, Sebastian, Slidell, Stuart, Thompson of Ky. Toombs, Weller, Williams—35.

NAYS—*against the Amendment* : Messrs. Allen, Chase, Dodge of Wisc., Everett, Fish, Foote, Houston, Seward, Sumner, Wade—10.

The vote on this amendment is significant, and we invite to it the attention of the reader. Here we have the emphatic declaration of every Democratic senator, especially of every Democratic senator from the slave States, in favor of the great peace measure of non-intervention with slavery in the States and Territories, avowing "the true intent and meaning of this act to be, not to legislate slavery into any *Territory* or *State,* nor to exclude it therefrom, but to leave the *people thereof* free to form and regulate their domestic institutions in their own way, subject only to the Constitution of the United States." How this doctrine, deemed sound, then, contrasts with the late shibboleth of the Senate caucus, that *if the people of a Territory want slavery, Congress shall not interfere, but if they do not want it, Congress is to legislate it on them.*

Mr. Badger of N. C. moved to add to the aforesaid section :

" *Provided,* That nothing herein contained shall be construed to revive or put in force any law or regulation which may have existed prior to the to the act of 6th of March, 1820, either protecting, establishing, prohibiting, or abolishing Slavery."

Carried—yeas 35, nays 6.

It had been charged by Edmund Burke, of New Hampshire, and other Abolition enemies of the measure at the north, that the repeal of the restriction would revive slavery in Kansas and Nebraska, by putting in force the old French laws. The object of Mr. Badger was to set this slander at rest. Every Southern Democrat voted for the proviso.

The question on the engrossment of the bill was now reached, and it was carried—yeas 29, nays 12—as follows :

YEAS—*To engross the bill for its third reading:* MESSRS. Adams, Atchison, Badger, Benjamin, Brodhead, Brown, Butler, Clay, Dawson, Dixon, Dodge of Iowa, Douglas, Evans, Fitzpatrick, Gwin, Hunter, Johnson, Jones of Iowa, Jones of Tenn., Mason, Morton, Norris, Pettit, Pratt, Sebastian, Shields, Slidell, Stuart, Williams—29.

NAYS—*against the engrossment:* Messrs. Chase, Dodge of Wisc., Fessenden, Fish, Foot, Hamlin, James, Seward, Smith, Sumner, Wade, Walker—12.

On the night of the 3d of March, 1854, Mr. Douglas closed the debate in a speech of great eloquence and ability. The attention of the reader is particularly directed to those passages in which Mr. Douglas speaks of the necessity for the organization of these Territories; and to his elucidation of what had generally been called the Missouri Compromise, in which he proves that Missouri was not admitted into the Union under the Missouri restriction, the Act of 1820, but under Mr. Clay's compromise, or joint resolution, of March 2, 1821 ; and also to the broad nationality of the views of the whole speech. We give it entire in a subsequent part of the work.

The vote was then taken, and the bill passed—yeas 37, nays 14. So the bill was passed, and its title declared to be "An Act to organize the Territories of Nebraska and Kansas." The bill being approved by the President, became a law. We give it entire, in a subsequent part of this work.

CHAPTER IX.

MR. DOUGLAS AT CHICAGO, 1854.

IT is difficult to give a full idea of the excitement that prevailed at Chicago, at the time of the passage of the Nebraska bill. It far surpassed the excitement in 1850, relative to the Compromise measures. The ranks of the Abolitionists, always full there, had been largely recruited during the last three years: and among the new converts were many professed ministers of the Gospel. These men eagerly seized on any pretext that would give them a little notoriety, and as the public mind, that is to say, the Abolition sentiment in Chicago, was already worked up to a high pitch, they conceived the idea of treating Senator Douglas as a delinquent schoolboy. Accordingly, they addressed to him, and published in the Chicago daily papers at the same time, a most scurrilous and abusive letter, in which they impiously arrogated to themselves the authority to speak " in the name of Almighty God," and soundly berated Mr. Douglas for his course in the Senate. With admirable temper, Mr. Douglas wrote them a letter, which will be found in a subsequent part of this work.

In the autumn of 1854, Mr. Douglas returned to Chicago. The city was convulsed with excitement. The Nebraska Bill, and its author, were denounced in the most bitter and violent manner. Neither were understood. The opposition organs, the " Tribune," the " Journal," and the " Press," had for months teemed with articles written in the most savage style, in which the Nebraska Bill and its provisions had been studiously misrepresented and misquoted, and Mr. Douglas vilified and abused as the author of countless woes to generations yet unborn. It is no compliment to the intelligence of the readers and supporters of these papers to state what is, nevertheless, the fact, that these statements were swallowed with eager credulity, and that Mr. Douglas was regarded by the Abolitionists as a monster in human form.

In a few days after his arrival in Chicago, Mr. Douglas caused the announcement to be made that he would address the citizens in vindication of the Nebraska Bill. A meeting was accordingly appointed, to take place at North Market Hall. At the hour of meeting, the vast space in front of the Hall was filled with men, the crowd numbering nearly ten thousand persons. Probably one-third of the number were really desirous to hear the senator's speech; but by far the greater part of the crowd were violent and radical Abolitionists, who were determined that he should not speak.

HIS SPEECH THERE.

Mr. Douglas appeared before the meeting, on an open balcony, and commenced his address. He alluded to the excitement that prevailed, but asked a patient hearing, and promised his audite : to be as brief as he could be, consistently with a full exposition of the subject. He spoke of the sacred rights of the people of the Territories to form and regulate their domestic institutions in their own way; the great principle that lay at the foundation of the Nebraska Bill. At this part of his remarks, several prominent Abolitionists commenced to groan and hiss. Others followed the example. The noise and tumult increased.

The senator stopped speaking, and stood calmly, with his

4

arms folded upon his breast, and his eye surveying the angry and excited multitude. He waited patiently till the noise subsided, and then, stretching forth his hand, he proceeded. He described the Territories of Kansas and Nebraska, and alluded to the fact that for the last ten years, he had endeavored, at every session of Congress, to have them organized. Here the groans and hisses were redoubled in violence, and came from all parts of the meeting. The most opprobrious epithets were applied to Mr. Douglas, and the most insulting language used to him by rowdies in the crowd. In vain several gentlemen endeavored to restore order. The Abolitionists were determined that Mr. Douglas should not be heard; and they succeeded. For nearly four hours after this did Mr. Douglas essay to make himself heard; and each time did the yells and hootings of the infuriated multitude drown his voice. At last, it being Saturday night, he deliberately pulled out his watch under the gaslight, and observing that it was after twelve o'clock, he said in a stentorian voice, which was heard above the din of the crowd: "Abolitionists of Chicago! it is now Sunday morning. I will go to church, while you go to the devil in your own way."

A SCENE FOR A PAINTER.

In her whole history, Chicago has never witnessed so disgraceful a scene as this. There was a parallel occurrence in the life of Rienzi, the last of the Roman Tribunes, thus described by the great English novelist:

"On they came, no longer in measured order, as stream after stream—from lane, from alley, from palace, and from hovel—the raging sea received new additions. On they came—their passions excited by their numbers—women and men, children and malignant age—in all the awful array of aroused, released, unresisted physical strength and brutal wrath: 'Death to the traitor—death to the tyrant—death to him who has taxed the peo ple!' 'Mora 'l traditore che ha fatta la gabella!—Mora!' Such was the cry of the people—such the crime of the senator! They broke over the low palisades of the capitol—they filled with one sudden rush the vast space—a moment before so desolate—now swarming with human beings athirst for blood!

"Suddenly came a dead silence, and on the balcony above stood Rienzi —his face was bared, and the morning sun shone over that lordly brow, and the hair grown grey before its time, in service of that maddening multitude. Pale and erect he stood—neither fear, nor anger, nor menace— but deep grief and high resolve upon his features! A momentary shame —a momentary awe, seized the crowd.

"He pointed to the gonfalon, wrought with the republican motto and arms of Rome, and thus he began :

"'I too am a Roman and a citizen; hear me!'

"'Hear him not; hear him not! his false tongue can charm away our senses!' cried a voice louder than his own; and Rienzi recognized Cecco del Vecchio.

"'Hear him not; down with the tyrant!' cried a more shrill and youthful tone; and by the side of the artisan stood Angelo Villani.

"'Hear him not; death to the death-giver!' cried a voice close at hand, and from the grating of the neighboring prison glared near upon him, as the eye of a tiger, the vengeful gaze of the brother of Montreal.

"Then from earth to Heaven rose the roar—'Down with the tyrant— down with him who taxed the people!'

"A shower of stones rattled on the mail of the senator—still he stirred not. No changing muscle betokened fear. His persuasion of his own wonderful powers of eloquence, if he could but be heard, inspired him yet with hope. He stood collected in his own indignant but determined thoughts; but the knowledge of that very eloquence was now his deadliest foe. The leaders of the multitude trembled lest he *should* be heard; '*and doubtless*,' says the contemporaneous biographer, '*had he but spoken he would have changed them all*.' "

Thus it was at the meeting at the North Market Hall. The leaders of the multitude trembled lest Douglas should be heard; they remembered the effect of his eloquence in 1850, and they knew that if he was permitted to speak now, he could and would convince the citizens of Chicago, for the second time, that he was right and they were wrong.

SPEECH AT THE TREMONT HOUSE.

After the close of the canvass of that year, in which Mr. Douglas had addressed the people in every portion of Illinois, he returned to Chicago, and on the 19th of November, two hundred and fifty gentlemen of that city, personal and political friends of Senator Douglas, tendered him the compliment of a public dinner at the Tremont House. After the repast, and in response to a toast in compliment to the "distinguished guest, the originator and successful advocate of the Illinois Central Railroad, and the champion of State Rights and Constitutional Liberty," Mr. Douglas made the speech which we give in a subsequent part of this work.

In this speech, Mr. Douglas takes up and critically examines the Nebraska Bill, and proves the soundness of the principles on which it is founded : he fastens upon the House of Representatives in 1848 the responsibility for all the subsequent slavery agitation, by their rejection of the Missouri Compromise line, after it had passed the Senate : he proves that the Abolitionists and Freesoilers, by supporting Van Buren, pledged themselves to blot out the Missouri Compromise line : he calls to the recollection of his hearers the fact, that he was abused and vilified in the year 1848, and called "Stephen A. Douglas the solitary exception," meaning that he was the only northern member of Congress who was in favor of adhering to the Missouri Compromise line ; and the other fact, that the same Abolitionists and Freesoilers *now* pretend to support a measure which they *then* declared infamous. He graphically describes the manner in which the Compromise measures of 1850 were formed ; and then, passing again to the Nebraska Bill, he shows that its great principle was to guarantee to the people of all the new Territories the right (which the Constitution of the United States had already secured, but which the Missouri Compromise had taken away) of determining the question of slavery for themselves. He proves, by the unequivocal testimony of the oldest and wisest patriots of the country, that the Abolitionists have proved to be the very worst enemies of the slaves, have riveted stronger their chains, taken away some of the privileges which they had before enjoyed, and actually put a stop to their owners emancipating them.

THE "REPUBLICAN" PARTY ANALYZED.

The last part of the speech is a complete and searching exposition of the platform and principles of the new "Republican party" which had just been formed. He proves it to be purely an abolition party, the principles of which were entirely sectional, arraying the North against the South, and which, of course, could never be a national party. We give this speech entire in a subsequent part of this work.

CHAPTER X.

TERRITORIAL POLICY OF MR. DOUGLAS, 1856.

Report of Mr. Douglas on the Territorial Policy of the Government—
Speech in Reply to Trumbull, and in Support of the Bill authorizing the
People of Kansas to form a Constitution and State Government—Speech
in Reply to Mr. Collamer—The Bill passed by the Senate—Report of
Mr. Douglas on the House Bill.

AFFAIRS IN KANSAS.

The 34th Congress met on the first Monday in December,
1855, but the House of Representatives was unable to
organize or to choose a Speaker for nine weeks. On the
31st of December, President Pierce transmitted his Annual Message to Congress, in which he only slightly alluded
to the recent troubles in Kansas. On the 24th of January,
however, he sent a special message to Congress in regard to
the affairs in Kansas, which will be found in a subsequent
part of this work.

On the 12th of March, 1856, Mr. Douglas made his great
report on the affairs of Kansas Territory. In this report, he
elucidates the constitutional principles under which new
States may be admitted, and Territories organized. He exposes the designs of the Massachusetts Emigrant Aid Society; traces from their inception the treasonable acts of that
secret military organization, the "Kansas Legion;" and

proves that all the troubles in Kansas originated in attempts to violate or circumvent the principles and provisions of the Nebraska Bill. This report will be found in a subsequent part of this work.

Mr. Jacob Collamer, of Vermont, who constituted the minority of the committee, made a minority report on the same day.

TRUMBULL'S SPEECH.

Two days afterward, on the 14th of March, Mr. Lyman Trumbull, who had taken his seat a few days before, as a senator from Illinois, in the place of General Shields, addressed the Senate in opposition to the views expressed in the report of Mr. Douglas. Mr. Douglas was absent from the Senate chamber at the time, but notwithstanding his knowledge of this fact, Mr. Trumbull was offensively personal. It might have been supposed that in making his first speech in the Senate, Mr. Trumbull would have had some regard to common decency and propriety. But in point of fact, he was so violent and coarse in his invective as to disgust the whole body of senators. As soon as the rules of the Senate would permit, he was stopped by Mr. Weller of California, who called for the special order of the day, which was the bill to increase the efficiency of the army. But as this was his first speech, he had the effrontery to insist upon continuing his rigmarole of abuse, and did go on till nearly 4 o'clock. Shortly before that time, Mr. Douglas entered the Senate chamber, and when Mr. Trumbull had exhausted the vials of his wrath, and sat down, Mr. Douglas said :

Mr. President, I was very much surprised when it was communicated to me this afternoon that my colleague was making a speech on the Kansas question, in which he was arraigning my own conduct and the statements and principles set forth in the report which I had the honor to submit to the Senate two days since from the Committee on Territories.

The feeble state of my own health, which is well known to the Senate, rendered it imprudent for me to be in the Senate chamber to-day, and I stayed away for that reason. I never dreamed that any man in this body would so far forget the courtesies of life, and the well known usages of the Senate, as to make an assault in my absence in violation of the distinct understanding of the body when the subject was postponed.

My colleague says that he did not know that I was not here. Now, I am informed that my friend from Texas (Mr. Rusk), when the morning hour expired, suggested, among other reasons for a postponement, that I was absent. The senator from Texas told my colleague that I was absent, and, therefore, according to the courtesies of the Senate, his speech should have been postponed. In the face of a fact known to every man present, my colleague now dares to say that he did not know I was absent.

Sir, I believe in fair and free discussion. Whatever speeches I may have to make in reference to my colleague or his political position, or in reference to other senators, will be made to their faces. I do not wish to avoid the responsibility of a reply to the points that shall be made. I will not attempt to reply to my colleague upon hearsay, having been absent, from the causes which I have stated during the delivery of the greater portion of his speech. I desire, however, to ask him, with a view to fix the time for the discussion of the subject, at what period of time I may reasonably look for his printed speech? I desire to reply to its statements, and I ask the question with a view to have the subject postponed until the time which he may name.

MR. TRUMBULL.—I think my remarks will be published on Monday.

MR. DOUGLAS.—If I can rely on seeing the speech published in the "Globe" on Monday, I will reply to it on Tuesday; and I shall ask the Senate to accord to me that courtesy. I propose to reply on the next day after its publication.

MR. SEWARD and MR. TRUMBULL.—Take your own time.

MR. DOUGLAS.—Sir, I understand this game of taking my own time. Last year, when the Nebraska Bill was under consideration, the senator from Massachusetts (Mr. Sumner) asked of me the courtesy to have it postponed for a week, until he could examine the question. I afterward discovered that, previous to that time, he had written an exposition of the bill—a libel upon me—and sent it off under his own frank; and the postponement thus obtained by my courtesy was in order to take a week to circulate the libel. I do not choose to take my own time in that way again. I wish to meet these misrepresentations at the threshold. If I am right, give me an opportunity to show it. If my colleague is right, I desire to give him the fullest and fairest opportunity to show it.

●

TRUMBULL REBUKED.

I desire now to say a word upon another point. I understand that my colleague has told the Senate, as being a matter very material to this issue, that he comes here as a Democrat, having always been a Democrat. Sir, that fact will be news to the Democracy of Illinois. I undertake to assert there is not a Democrat in Illinois who will not say that such a statement is a libel upon the Democracy of that State. When he was elected, he received every Abolition vote in the Legislature of Illinois. He received every Know Nothing vote in the Legislature of Illinois. So far as I am advised and believe, he received no vote except from persons allied to Abolitionism or Know Nothingism. He came here as the Know-Nothing-Abolition candidate, in opposition to the united Democracy of his State, and to the Democratic candidate. How can a man who was elected as an Abolition-Know Nothing, come here and claim to be a Democrat, in good standing with the Democracy of Illinois? Sir, the Illinois Democracy have no sympathies or alliances with Abolitionism in any of its forms. They have no connection with Know Nothingism in any of its forms. If a man has ever been a Democrat, and becomes either an Abolitionist or Know Nothing, or a Free Soiler, he ceases that instant to be a Democrat in Illinois.

Sir, why was the statement of my colleague being a Democrat made, unless to convey the idea that the Illinois Democracy would harbor and associate with a Know Nothing or an Abolitionist? Sir, we do no such thing in Illinois. There is a high wall and a deep ditch between the national Democracy of that State, including the old national Whigs, on the one side, and all Know Nothing and Abolition organizations on the other. I can say to senators that Know Nothingism and Abolitionism in Illinois are one and the same thing. Every Know Nothing lodge there adopted the Abolition creed, and every Abolition society supported the Know Nothing candidates. It may be different in the South; but in the Northwest, and especially in Illinois, a Know Nothing or an Abolitionist means a Republican. My colleague is the head and front of Republicanism in Illinois in opposition to Democracy. You might as well call the distinguished senator from New York (Mr. Seward), or the member from Massachusetts (Mr. Sumner), or any other leader of the Republican forces, a Democrat, as to call my colleague a Democrat. Why has that assertion been brought into this debate? Did it prove that my report was wrong? Did it prove that it was courteous to make an assault on that report in my absence?

On the 17th of March, Mr. Douglas reported from the Committee on Territories, "A bill to authorize the People

4*

of the Territory of Kansas to form a Constitution and State government, preparatory to their admission into the Union when they have the requisite population."

On the 20th of March, Mr. Douglas addressed the Senate in support of this bill, and in reply to the tirade of Mr. Trumbull. In this speech, he vindicates his report; shows that the report of Mr. Collamer keeps out of sight the material facts of the case; and proves that it was the design of the reckless leaders of the Freesoil party, to produce a conflict with the Territorial government. He defends the Missourians from the charge of invading and conquering Kansas, and proves that the whole responsibility of all the disturbances in Kansas, rests upon the Massachusetts Emigrant Aid Society. When he reached the concluding paragraph of his remarks, he turned to where Trumbull uneasily sat, and fixing upon him his eagle eye, pronounced in a clear and sonorous voice, and in emphatic tones, those words referring to the certainty of the fact that even in the United States, the traitor's doom would fall upon the traitor's head. Trumbull turned pale, and his head sank upon his breast. He *felt* that he was convicted.

The speech will be found in a subsequent part of this work.

REPUBLICAN HYPOCRISY EXPOSED.

Mr. Collamer made a speech upon the same subject, on the 3d of April, and on the 4th, Mr. Douglas responded. Mr. Collamer had labored hard to show that the free State men in Kansas were not such bad fellows after all. But in this speech Mr. Douglas shows by incontestable evidence, their blood-thirsty nature, their determination to *conquer* all who did not believe with them, and to resist the constituted authorities to a bloody issue, and their preparations of arms and munitions of war, with which to resist. He raises the specious veil of "peaceful emigration," which concealed the movements of the free State party in Kansas, and exposes the secret springs by which they were really actuated, showing that they were guilty of rebellion and treason. This speech is a full and complete exposition of the real history of Kansas, up to that time. The reader will not fail to observe, toward the conclusion of the speech, how completely Mr. Douglas exposes the hypocrisy of the Black Republican party; and how conclusively he shows the hollowness and insincerity, as well as the inconsistency and heartlessness, of their professions of regard for the negro. Strong in the consciousness of the rectitude of the principles of the Democratic party, he delineates, with withering scorn, the inconsistent and jarring elements that make up the creed of the Republican faith, and dares the leaders of that party to the fight. Like some experienced general, at the head of a numerous and well disciplined army, an army which loves, idolizes, and trusts in their leader—knowing his own strength and confident of victory because he knows that his cause is just, he throws down the gage of battle, and challenges the onset of the opposing squadrons. The leaders of the Republican party quailed before him in the Senate; as that party itself afterward quailed under the irresistible charge of the Democracy. The speech will be found in a subsequent part of this work.

On the 30th of June, Mr. Douglas reported to the Senate on several bills submitted for the pacification of Kansas, as also most decidedly against Mr. Seward's proposition to admit Kansas as a State under the bogus "Topeka" constitution.

Mr. Seward then moved to strike out the whole of Mr. Douglas' bill, and insert instead, one admitting Kansas under the Topeka constitution. This motion was defeated—ayes 11, nays 36.

The bill was now reported as amended, and the amendment made in Committee of the Whole concurred in. The bill was then (8 A.M. on the 3d, the Senate having been in session all night), ordered to be engrossed and read a third time; and, on the question of its final passage the vote stood —yeas 33, nays 12—as follows:

YEAS—Messrs. Allen, Bayard, Bell of Tennessee, Benjamin, Biggs, Bigler, Bright, Brodhead, Brown, Cass, Clay, Crittenden, Douglas, Evans, Fitzpatrick, Geyer, Hunter, Iverson, Johnson, Jones of Iowa, Mallory, Pratt, Pugh, Reid, Sebastian, Slidell, Stuart, Thompson of Kentucky, Toombs, Toucey, Weller, Wright, and Yulee—33.
NAYS—Messrs. Bell, of New Hampshire, Collamer, Dodge, Durkee, Fessenden, Foot, Foster, Hale, Seward, Trumbull, Wade, and Wilson—12.

So the bill passed the Senate. We give it, in the shape in which it was sent to the House, in a subsequent part of this work.

On the 8th of July, Mr. Douglas reported back from the Committee on Territories the House bill to admit Kansas as a State, with an amendment striking out all after the enacting clause, and inserting instead the Senate bill (No 356) just referred to.

Mr. Trumbull, of Illinois, moved that all the Territorial laws of Kansas be repealed and the Territorial officers dismissed: rejected—yeas 12, nays 32.

Mr. Collamer of Vermont, proposed an amendment, prohibiting slavery in all that portion of the Louisiana purchase north of 36° 30' not including the Territory of Kansas. rejected—yeas 12, nays 30.

The amendment reported by Mr. Douglas (*i. e.* the Senate bill as passed) was then agreed to—yeas 32, nays 13—and the bill in this shape passed the Senate.   But the House of Representatives, where the majority was composed of a *fusion* of Republicans, Abolitionists, Know Nothings, Freesoilers, Freethinkers, Free-lovers, and Freemonters, refused to act upon it, or to concur in it, and the session terminated without the concurrence of the House.

CHAPTER XI.

RETROSPECTIVE.

A Retrospect—Origin and Causes of Disagreement with the President—
Not Provoked by Mr. Douglas—Mr. Buchanan owes his Nomination at
Cincinnati to Mr. Douglas—Telegraphic Dispatches—His Efforts to Elect
Mr. Buchanan in 1856—Speech at Springfield in 1857, defending the
Administration—President's Instructions to Governor Walker—Constitution to be Submitted—Executive Dictation—Differences of Opinion
tolerated on all Subjects except Lecompton—Mr. Douglas' Propositions
for Adjustment—Resolutions of Illinois Democracy—Controversy terminated by the English Bill—War Renewed by the Administration—Coalition between the Federal Officeholders and the Abolitionists—Mr. Douglas' last Speech in the Senate preparatory to Illinois Canvass.

IN order that the reader may appreciate the nature and importance of the issues involved in the memorable senatorial
canvass in Illinois in 1858, it is but proper we should state
distinctly the origin and causes of the unfortunate disagreement between Mr. Douglas and the administration of Mr.
Buchanan.

It will be remembered that Mr. Buchanan owed his nomination at Cincinnati to the direct and personal interposition
of Mr. Douglas. But for the telegraphic dispatches which
he sent to his friends urging the withdrawal of his own name
and the unanimous nomination of Mr. Buchanan, that gentleman could never have received the nomination by a two-
thirds vote, according to the rules of the convention and the
usages of the party.

These dispatches are important, serving to show the magnanimity of Mr. Douglas, and his anxiety to promote the union and harmony of the Democratic party.

The names of James Buchanan, Franklin Pierce, Lewis Cass, and Stephen A. Douglas, were put in nomination by their respective friends. There were 296 votes in the Convention. On the first ballot Buchanan received 135½, Pierce 122½, Douglas 33, and Cass 5. Judge Douglas' votes were from the following States: Ohio, 4; Kentucky, 3; Illinois, 11; Missouri, 9; Iowa, 4; Wisconsin, 2. There were very few changes in the ballotings until after the fourteenth, when Pierce was withdrawn. The two succeeding ballots were about the same. The sixteenth was as follows: Buchanan, 168; Douglas, 122; Cass, 6. When this ballot was announced, Col. Richardson, of Illinois, arose, and after making a short explanatory speech, said that he had just received a dispatch from Judge Douglas, which he sent to the chair to be read, after which, he said he would withdraw that gentleman's name from before the Convention. This dispatch is so characteristic of Senator Douglas, that we cannot refrain from reproducing it here. Its self-sacrificing spirit, its conciliatory tone, and its pure Democracy, commend it to the attention of the country at the present state of political affairs. It breathes the spirit of devotion to the Democratic party which has ever characterized the public life of its great author. It applies to the Presidential Convention system the great principle for which his whole life has been devoted —the principle that the majority should rule. Let it be remembered, that in the Cincinnati Convention he would not allow his name to be used one moment after any other statesman had received a *majority of the votes!* But here is Judge Douglas' letter, and we ask for it the careful perusal of every Democrat in the nation:

WASHINGTON, *June 4*, 1856.

DEAR SIR: From the telegraphic reports in the newspapers, I fear that an embittered state of feeling is being engendered in the Convention, which may endanger the harmony and success of our party. I wish you and all my friends to bear in mind that I have a thousand fold more anxiety for the triumph of our principles than for my own personal elevation.

If the withdrawal of my name will contribute to the harmony of our party, or the success of our cause, I hope you will not hesitate to take the step. Especially is it my desire that the action of the Convention will embody and express the wishes, feelings, and principles of the Democracy of the republic; and hence, if Mr. Pierce, or Mr. Buchanan, or any other statesman, who is faithful to the great issues involved in the contest, *shall receive a majority of the Convention, I earnestly hope that all my friends will unite in insuring him two-thirds, and then in making his nomination unanimous.* Let no personal considerations disturb the harmony or endanger the triumph of our principles.

S. A. DOUGLAS.

To HON. W. A. RICHARDSON, Cincinnati, O.

The reading of this dispatch was interrupted by frequent and tremendous applause. The other dispatches are as follows:

June 5, 1856, 9 A.M.

DEAR SIR: I have just read so much of the platform as relates to the Nebraska Bill and slavery question. The adoption of that noble resolution by a unanimous vote of all the States, accomplishes all the objects I had in view in permitting my name to be used before the convention. If agreeable to my friends, I would prefer exerting all my energies to elect a tried statesman on that platform to being the nominee myself. At all events do not let my name be used in such manner as to disturb the harmony of the party or endanger the success of the work so nobly begun.   S. A. DOUGLAS.

HON. W. A. RICHARDSON, of Illinois,
    Burnet House, Cincinnati, Ohio.

WASHINGTON, *June* 5*th*—9¼ A.M.

Mr. Buchanan having received a majority of the convention, is, in my opinion, entitled to the nomination. I hope my friends will give effect to the voice of the majority of the party.

S. A. DOUGLAS.

HON. W. A. RICHARDSON.

(See "Washington Union," June 7th, 1856.)

Many of Mr. Douglas' warmest friends complained of him bitterly for having thus withheld his own name and secured the nomination of his rival, at the critical moment, when it became evident the latter could not possibly have been nominated without the positive and efficient aid of the former; and this withdrawal in favor of Mr. Buchanan, is, at this time, used in some quarters as a point of objection to Mr. Douglas' nomination at Charleston. But the whole political course of Mr. Douglas, for a quarter of a century, has been in harmony with the sentiment enunciated and enforced in those despatches, that he felt "a thousand fold more interest in the success of the principles of the Democratic party than in his own individual promotion."

Immediately after the adjournment of the convention, Mr. Douglas entered the canvass with that energy and vigor for which he is so remarkable, and it is but fair to add that to his herculean efforts, in Illinois, Indiana, Pennsylvania, and other States in the campaign of 1856, is Mr. Buchanan indebted for his election, more than to any other man living or dead.

When the election was secured, and the inauguration had taken place, Mr. Douglas had no personal favors to ask of the President for either himself or friends, and hence had no grievances to complain of or disappointments to resent. Before he left Washington for his home, it is well known that he was personally consulted by the President, and approved of the policy of his administration in regard to Kansas affairs, to be promulgated by Governor Walker in his message and address to the people of that Territory, viz., that the constitution which was about to be formed at Lecompton should be submitted to and ratified by the people, at a fair election to be held for that purpose, before the State could be admitted into the Union.

Subsequently, when Governor Walker was on his way to Kansas, he called on Judge Douglas at Chicago by direction of the President, as he himself says, and read to him the inaugural address which he was to publish on his arrival in the Territory, in which the governor stated that he was authorized by the President and his cabinet to give the assurance that he and they would oppose the admission of Kansas into the Union as a State under any constitution which was not first submitted to and ratified by the people.

After copying his instructions from the President in favor of the submission of the constitution to the people, Governor Walker added: "I repeat, then, as my clear conviction, that unless the convention submit the constitution to the vote of all the actual resident settlers of Kansas, and the election be fairly and justly conducted, the constitution will be and ought to be rejected by Congress."

In this interview, Judge Douglas assured Governor Walker, as he had previously assured the President, that he might rely on his cordial and hearty coöperation in carrying out the policy that Kansas should not be forced into the Union with any constitution which had not been previously submitted to and ratified by the people at a fair election regularly held for that purpose.

A short time afterward, June 12th, 1857, Mr. Douglas made his celebrated Springfield speech, in which he warmly defended the administration of Mr. Buchanan, commended his territorial policy, and predicted for him a successful and brilliant administration. We have the best reasons for the assertion that his friendly relations with, and kind feelings toward Mr. Buchanan continued uninterrupted and undiminished until after their well-known interview in Washington city, about the first of December of that year, upon the question of admitting Kansas into the Union under the Lecompton constitution, *without* submitting the constitution to the people for ratification or rejection. Mr. Douglas insisted that he was bound in honor, good faith, and due regard for the fundamental principles of all free government, to resist the measure at every hazard and under all circumstances.   Here we find the origin and sole cause of the disagreement between the President and Mr. Douglas, so far as the friends of the latter have ever been able to discover. The difficulty was not of Mr. Douglas' own seeking or procurement. He only claimed that so far as he was concerned it was his right and duty to carry out in good faith the policy to which he, Governor Walker, the President, and every member of his cabinet, stood publicly and irrevocably pledged. The President claimed that it was his right and duty, in a message to Congress, to recommend the admission of Kansas under the Lecompton constitution. Mr. Douglas did not question either the right or the duty of the President, provided "he thought the Lecompton constitution was the act and deed of the people of Kansas, and a fair embodiment of their will." While conceding to the President entire freedom of action according to his sense of duty, Mr. Douglas claimed the same privilege for himself, as a senator representing a sovereign State.

The President, however, would tolerate no difference of opinion among friends on this question. Upon the tariff—upon specific and ad valorem duties—upon the Pacific Railroad—upon the Homestead Bill—upon the Neutrality Laws—and, indeed, on any and every other question, Democratic senators and representatives, and cabinet officers, were at liberty to think and act as they pleased, without impairing their personal or political relations with the President. But on the Kansas question, having determined to abandon the principles and reverse the policy to which he had pledged the administration and the party, he regarded Mr. Douglas' refusal to follow him in his change of principles and policy as a serious reflection upon his own conduct. All freedom of judgment and action was denied. Implicit obedience to the behests of the President was demanded. The senator was required to obey the mandate of the Executive, instead of to represent the will of his constituency. The representa-

tives of the States and of the people were required to surrender their convictions, their judgments and their consciences
to the Executive, and to receive instructions from him instead
of them.

These were the terms and the only conditions upon which
Mr. Douglas could preserve friendly relations with the President. He met the issue with characteristic alacrity and
boldness. He denounced the Lecompton constitution in
firm but respectful terms, not because it provided for a slave
State, but because it was not the act and deed of the people
of Kansas, and did not reflect their will.

Foreseeing the rent the agitation of this unfortunate
question was likely to make in the Democratic party, and the
irreparable damage to which it would be likely to lead, Mr.
Douglas was anxious to heal the breach and settle the difficulty on any fair and just terms, that were consistent with
fidelity to his own constituency, and to those principles of
popular rights and self-government to which he was so
solemnly pledged, and upon which he believed the peace and
harmony of the country depended. He submitted various
propositions in a spirit of conciliation and fraternal feeling
for the pacification of the difficulty.

He proposed to refer the Lecompton constitution back to
the people of Kansas, for their adoption or rejection, at a
fair election, to be held in pursuance of law for that purpose,
and if ratified by a majority of the legal votes cast at such
election, Kansas was to be declared a State of the Union
without further legislation.

He proposed to pass an act of Congress authorizing the
Territorial legislature to call a new convention and form a
constitution, and submit the same to the people for adoption
at the polls, and if ratified at such election, Kansas should
be received into the Union, with or without slavery, as such
constitution should prescribe, as provided in the case of Min-

nesota, to which the President had referred as affording an example to be followed in all future cases of admission of new States.

He offered to accept what is known as the "Crittenden-Montgomery Amendment," as a satisfactory solution of the question, in harmony with the fundamental principles of self-government.

And finally, he proposed a general law, which would not only settle the existing difficulty, but prevent all future controversies on the subject, providing that "neither Kansas nor any other Territory shall be admitted into the Union as a State, until it shall have been ascertained, by a legal census, to contain population requisite for a member of Congress, according to the existing ratio of representation for the time being; and that the example of the Minnesota case shall be a rule of action in the future, as recommended in the President's message."

This proposition was offered substantially at a later period of the session in the House, by General Quitman, of Mississippi, who intended to have called it up in the event of the failure of the English bill. It would have been happy for the Democratic party and the country had it been accepted. Besides thoroughly uniting the party, it would have laid the foundation of a sound and healthy principle governing the admission of new States, and have saved the present Congress from acting on the Kansas Wyandot constitution.

These several propositions and all others for conciliation and harmony, were unceremoniously rejected by the partisans of the President, and the unconditional submission of the rebels demanded under the penalty of having all their friends removed from office and made victims of Executive vengeance. The system of proscription and persecution which followed is too fresh in the public mind to require recapitulation.

The wisdom and forecast evinced by Mr. Douglas in opposing the admission of Kansas under the Lecompton constitution, has been amply vindicated by succeeding events. The immense vote by which it was rejected when submitted under the temptations of the English bill—the subsequent confession of actors in the fraudulent voting—the discovery of the bogus election returns—the statements of Governor Denver, and other well-authenticated facts and circumstances attest the correctness of Mr. Douglas' position; while the declaration of Senator Hammond, who voted for the measure, that "the constitution ought to have been kicked out of Congress," and the high repute in which Governor Wise and other leading southern statesmen who opposed the project enjoy in the respect and confidence of the Southern people, clearly indicate that their "sober second thought" does justice to the statesmanlike view which Mr. Douglas took of this unfortunate issue.

RESOLUTIONS OF ILLINOIS DEMOCRATIC CONVENTION.

Notwithstanding the ferocity with which the warfare was continued against Mr. Douglas and his friends during the Lecompton controversy, all fair-minded men took it for granted that hostilities would cease with the settlement of the question out of which the contest arose. Mr. Douglas and the Illinois Democracy seem to have entertained this reasonable expectation, as appears from the proceedings of the Illinois Democratic State Convention, which assembled at Springfield, on the 21st of April, 1858, for the nomination of candidates for State officers. While the resolutions were explicit and firm in the assertion of the principles on which they had rejected the Lecompton constitution, they were conciliating in spirit and respectful in language. They contain no assault on the President, no attack upon the adminis-

tration, and indulge in no complaint at the unprovoked, and
vindictive warfare which had been waged against them.
They maintain a dignified and manly silence, a generous
forbearance on all these points, with a view to the preservation of the organization, the usages, and the integrity of the
Democratic party upon its time-honored principles, as enunciated in the Cincinnati Platform. The resolutions adopted
by the Convention were introduced into the Senate by Mr.
Douglas on the 25th of April, "AS FURNISHING THE PLAT-
FORM ON WHICH THE ILLINOIS DEMOCRACY STAND, AND BY
WHICH I MEAN TO ABIDE."

They were as follows: .

Colonel McClernand, from the committee to prepare solutions for the
consideration of the convention, made the following report; which was
read, and, on motion, each resolution was separately read and unanimously
adopted:

1. *Resolved*, That the Democratic party of the State of Illinois, through
their delegates in general convention assembled, do re-assert and declare
the principles avowed by them as when, on former occasions, they have
presented their candidates for popular suffrage.

2. *Resolved*, That they are unalterably attached to, and will maintain
inviolate, the principles declared by the national convention at Cincinnati
in June, 1856.

3. *Resolved*, That they avow, with renewed energy, their devotion to
the Federal Union of the United States, their earnest desire to avert sectional strife, their determination to maintain the sovereignty of the States,
and to protect every State, and the people thereof, in all their constitutional rights.

4. *Resolved*, That the platform of principles established by the national
democratic convention at Cincinnati is the only authoritative exposition of
Democratic doctrine, and they deny the right of any power on earth,
except a like body, to change or interpolate that platform, or to prescribe
new or different tests; that they will neither do it themselves nor permit it
to be done by others, but will recognize all men as democrats who stand
by and uphold Democratic principles.

5. *Resolved*, That in the organization of States the people have a right
to decide, at the polls, upon the character of their fundamental law, and

that the experience of the past year has conclusively demonstrated the wisdom and propriety of the principle, that the fundamental law under which the Territory seeks admission into the Union should be submitted to the people of such Territory, for their ratification or rejection, at a fair election to be held for that purpose; and that, before such Territory is admitted as a State, such fundamental law should receive a majority of the legal votes cast at such election; and they deny the right, and condemn the attempt, of any convention, called for the purpose of framing a constitution, to impose the instrument formed by them upon the people against their known will.

6. *Resolved*, That a fair application of these principles requires that the Lecompton constitution should be submitted to a direct vote of the actual inhabitants of Kansas, so that they may vote for or against that instrument, before Kansas shall be declared one of the States of this Union; and until it shall be ratified by the people of Kansas, at a fair election held for that purpose, the Illinois Democracy are unalterably opposed to the admission of Kansas under that constitution.

7. *Resolved*, That we heartily approve and sustain the manly, firm, patriotic, and democratic position of S. A. Douglas, Isaac N. Morris, Thomas L. Harris, Aaron Shaw, Robert Smith, and Samuel S. Marshall, the Democratic delegation of Illinois in Congress, upon the question of the admission of Kansas under the Lecompton constitution; and that, by their firm and uncompromising devotion to Democratic principles, and to the cause of justice, right, truth, and the people, they have deserved our admiration, increased, if possible, our confidence in their integrity and patriotism, and merited our warm approbation, our sincere and hearty thanks, and shall receive our earnest support.

8. *Resolved*, That in all things wherein the national administration sustain and carry out the principles of the Democratic party as expressed in the Cincinnati platform, and affirmed in these resolutions, it is entitled to, and will receive, our hearty support.

By the adoption of the English bill a few days afterward, the Lecompton controversy was at an end so far as Congress was concerned. By that act the question was banished from the halls of Congress and remanded to the people of Kansas to be determined at an election to be held on the first Monday in August, 1858.

In a speech in the Senate after the passage of the English

bill, Mr. Douglas referred to the Lecompton controversy as at an end—a dead issue which should no longer distract and divide the Democratic party, in these words :

But when the bill became a law, the whole question was remanded to Kansas, to be decided at an election, which has been fixed for the first Monday in August. Whichever way the people of Kansas may decide the question at that election will be final and conclusive. If they reject the proposition submitted by Congress, the Lecompton constitution is dead, and there is an end of the controversy. If, on the contrary, they accept the 'proposition,' Kansas, from that moment, becomes a State of the Union, and thus the controversy terminates. Whether they shall accept or reject the proposition is a question for the people of Kansas to decide for themselves, and with which neither Congress nor the people of the several States, nor any person, official or otherwise, outside of that Territory, has any right to interfere. Hence, the Lecompton controversy is at an end ; for all men, of all parties, must be content with and abide by whatever decision the people of Kansas may make.

NO POINT OF DIFFERENCE NOW BETWEEN DEMOCRATS.

And again, in the same speech, Mr. Douglas said :

Under these circumstances the question naturally arises, what con- troverted principle is there left for Democrats to differ and divide about ?

In the first place, we all agree, not only Democrats, but men of all par- ties, that whatever decision the people of Kansas may make at the election, on the first Monday in August must be final and conclusive.

Now, if we can agree, as I have always avowed my willingness to do, to sustain President Buchanan's recommendation, that in all future cases the constitution shall be submitted to the people, as was required in the Minnesota case, all matters of dispute and controversy will be at an end, and our Territorial policy will be firmly placed on a wise and just basis.

Whatever justification or excuse may be urged for the war- fare upon Mr. Douglas and his friends during the Lecompton controversy, no patriotic reason can be assigned after the passage of the English bill and the adoption of the magnanimous and conciliating resolutions of the Illinois State convention, for forming a coalition in that State with the Abolitionists to defeat the regular Democratic nominee for State officers, members of the legislature, congressmen, and a United States senator, and filling their places with abolitionists. No other reason can be assigned for keeping up the warfare after the question had been finally settled than an insatiable desire for revenge. No administration can be justified in dividing and destroying the party by which it was elevated to power upon the plea of resentment for real or imaginary grievances growing out of a past political issue. The coalition between the Republicans and the federal officeholders in Illinois, for the purpose of electing Mr. Lincoln to the Senate in the place of Mr. Douglas, by violating all the usages and bolting the regular nomination of the Democratic party, must form a dark page in the history of Mr. Buchanan's administration. Having been voted down and defeated by overwhelming majorities in the regular organization in every county in the State for the election of delegates to the State convention, the federal officeholders called a new convention at Springfield on the 9th of June, 1858, and formed a separate ticket to be supported by the bolters, for the avowed purpose of defeating the regularly nominated ticket of the party, and securing the ascendency of Black Republicanism in Illinois by means of the division thus produced in the Democratic ranks.

On the 15th of June, 1858, Mr. Douglas made a speech in the Senate, in which he exposed the combination between the federal officeholders and the Abolitionists in Illinois, and called the attention of the Democratic party in Congress, and of the whole country, to this unholy and unnatural alliance; and after showing that the federal officials professed to have the authority of the President and his cabinet for the course they were pursuing, said:

A refusal to disavow the authority, after a full knowledge of the facts shall have been brought home to the administration, should, of course, be regarded and treated as an approval and indorsement of the act as having been done by authority. . . . .

I intend to denounce this treason to the Democratic party; this system of bolting regular Democratic nominations—this coalition of officeholders with the enemies of Democracy. I intend to denounce it in every part of Illinois, and I mean to hold all men responsible for it, who, by their action, become justly responsible. I now point out the fact that a conspiracy against the unity and integrity of the Democratic party exists, and is being executed by a portion of the federal officeholders in Illinois, who profess to be acting under the sanction of the administration, but who, in my opinion, are acting under the direction of a small squad of selfish and unscrupulous politicians here, who care less for the present than for the next administration. I am as confident that the Democracy of the whole Union will visit the conspirators with condemnation when the facts are fully understood, as I am now assured that the movement itself is disapproved and condemned by a large majority of the Democrats in both houses of Congress. All good Democrats, all fair-minded men of every party, will unite in denouncing such an unscrupulous alliance between the leaders of the Republican party and that portion of the officeholders who receive orders from the Danite chief. What is the issue now pending in Illinois? What is the inducement to the great struggle for which the Republican leaders and their allies are now preparing? The motive cannot be disguised, nor, indeed, is there much effort to conceal it. The object of this combination is to strike down and crush out the Democratic delegation in the two houses of Congress, and the Democratic party in Illinois, which has unanimously indorsed their course in State convention, for having acted fully up to their conscientious convictions in carrying out in good faith the great principle of self-government, in its application to Kansas. This is the extent of our offending. For this offence we are to be pursued and hunted down by an unscrupulous coalition. The Republican leaders, with all the machinery of their party organization in motion, are fighting us with more fierceness, and, I may add, with more ferocity, than they ever did on any former occasion. They go into the battle with more energy and confidence, relying for success solely upon the aid which may be rendered them by the bolting officeholders in dividing the Democratic party.

It is natural that the Republican leaders should feel great anxiety to humble and defeat the Democracy of Illinois. They are restive under the reflection that Illinois is the only northern State which never struck her flag to the enemies of the Democracy at a Presidential election. While every

other northern State has, at some time, under some momentary panic or
fanatical excitement, struck her flag and surrendered to the enemy, Illinois
never! Pennsylvania has, on more than one occasion, abandoned the
Democratic party, and secured the election of an opposition President.
New York has done the same thing frequently; Ohio often; Indiana several times; and so with each State in turn, leaving Illinois standing bravely
alone, a solitary exception among her northern sisters. Now, it is proposed, in view of these facts, to humble that gallant State, and make her
trail her glorious old flag in the dust, and strike her ever-victorious colors
to an allied army, composed of the Republican organization and the bolting
officeholders under a Democratic administration!

CONSTITUTION FOR MINNESOTA.*

The 3d Session of the 34th Congress assembled in December, 1856. One of the most important acts of this session
was the passage of a bill to authorize the people of the Territory of Minnesota to form a constitution and State government, preparatory to their admission into the Union on an
equal footing with the original States. In the debate on this
bill, on the 21st of February, 1857, Mr. Douglas said.

The organic act creating the Territory of Minnesota many years
since provided that:

"Every free white male inhabitant above the age of twenty-one years, who
shall have been a resident of the said Territory at the time of the passage of
this act, shall be entitled to vote at the first election, and shall be eligible to
any office in the said Territory; but the qualifications of voters and of holding
office at all subsequent elections shall be such as shall be subscribed by the
Legislative Assembly: *Provided,* That the right of suffrage and of holding
office shall be exercised only by citizens of the United States and those who
have declared on oath their intention to become such, and shall have taken an
oath to support the Constitution of the United States and the provisions of
this act."

That was the organic law of the Territory. Under that law the
Territorial legislature have prescribed the qualifications of voters.
The present bill provides that the legal voters of Minnesota may
assemble and elect delegates to a convention to form a constitution
and State government for admission into the Union, leaving the
qualifications of voters in the Territory for this purpose precisely
what they have been ever since the Territory was organized, and as
they are now fixed by law. I see no reason why we should change

* Chronologically, the conclusion of this chapter belongs elsewhere. It
will be arranged in a subsequent edition.

the existing law of Minnesota on that point for this one election, when there is no pretence that any evil consequences have grown out of the exercise of the elective franchise under the present law. If my friend from North Carolina could show me that any injurious consequences had grown out of the law of Minnesota fixing the qualifications of voters, there would be an argument in favor of the change; but there is no objection on that score; no consideration of that kind has been urged. The amendment, therefore, is only to carry out a theory of the senator, and not to remedy any practical existing evil in the Territory.

My friend from North Carolina is entirely mistaken in the supposition that it has been the uniform practice in laws enabling Territories to become States, to restrict the right of voting to citizens of the United States. I have sent for the laws, and will present them if it be necessary, in the course of the discussion, to show that he is entirely mistaken in that respect. The rule is rather the reverse, if there be any rule on the subject. The fact is, that there has been a variety of laws on that point. In some Territories where there was no contest about it, the right was confined to citizens of the United States; in others, all the inhabitants possessing certain qualifications were allowed to vote. In all the Northwestern Territory, in Ohio, Indiana, Illinois, Michigan, and Wisconsin, aliens, under certain conditions, were permitted to vote, not only while those States were Territories, but when they became States; and this provision was not peculiar to the Northwestern States, as has been supposed.

My friend from Alabama is mistaken in saying that it has not been done at the South. I remember well that I served some years ago on the Committee of Elections in the House of Representatives when there was a contested seat between Mr. John W. Jones and Mr. John M. Botts; and it turned out that Mr. Jones had received some eighty-nine votes, I think, of foreigners unnaturalized according to the laws of the United States, but who were legal voters according to the laws of Virginia. There certainly was a class of persons in Virginia, who, under her laws, were allowed to vote, although they were not naturalized citizens of the United States, and they did vote in that election between Jones and Botts under the law of Virginia, authorizing them to become voters, although they were not citizens of the United States according to the laws of the United States. It was under some special law. The impression is on my mind' firmly, because I was on the committee that investigated this question.

Virginia prescribes who shall be citizens of Virginia, and in some cases has not confined the right of voting to citizens of the United States. That is just what Michigan did when she came into the Union with a constitution providing that all citizens of the United States should be permitted to vote, and also, all other persons who were inhabitants of the State at the time of the adoption of the constitution. By that constitution, Michigan made those other inhabitants who had not been naturalized, but possessed certain specified qualifications, citizens of the State of Michigan, although they were not citizens of the United States. That is precisely what we did in Illinois under the old constitution. We allowed an unnaturalized foreigner who possessed certain qualifications to vote in that State, although he had not become a citizen of the United States; in other words, we made him a citizen of the State of Illinois, and authorized him to vote at our elections, notwithstanding the fact that he had not complied with the law of Congress in regard to citizenship. That is all Virginia has done, and I believe it is only in limited cases.

But, sir, I did not wish to open a debate on this subject. I referred to the Virginia case only for illustration. The simple question here is, shall we authorize the present legal voters of Minnesota to vote for the election of delegates to form a State constitution? I hope the amendment will not be adopted.

I appeal to the Senate not to go into a political discussion upon aliens and Know Nothingism, and other questions, on these measures, for the reason that we are near the end of the session. This day was set apart for Territorial business, and there is as much as we can dispose of if we confine ourselves to the bills themselves, without these long discussions. I appeal, therefore, to the Senate to allow us to have a vote. This question is well understood by every senator present. It has been thoroughly discussed. I have not the slightest idea that any gentleman can have his opinions changed, or his stock of knowledge added to or diminished materially by a discussion. The only effect of this discussion will be to occupy the entire day, and compel us to have a night session, or else oblige us to lose all these Territorial bills for to-day. Of course, if I cannot get a vote to-day, I shall feel compelled to press these measures every day until I can get a vote. I refrain from replying even to that part of the argument which touched my own State, and where I think it did her injustice, in order to get a vote.

As I do not wish to reply to my friend, I desire now to call his attention to an error into which he has fallen. He overlooks one clause in the Indiana and Illinois laws to which he has referred. I will read the Illinois law:

" That all white male citizens of the United States who shall have attained to the age of twenty-one years, and have resided in said Territory six months previous to the day of election, and all persons having in other respects the legal qualifications to vote for a representative in the General Assembly of said Territory, be, and they are hereby, authorized to vote "—

—at the election to form a State constitution. That includes inhabitants unnaturalized, who, by the Territorial laws, and the Ordinance of 1787, were authorized to vote. If the senator will turn to the Indiana law, he will find a similar clause there:

" That all male citizens of the United States who shall have attained the age of twenty-one years, and resided in said Territory at least one year previous to the election, and shall have paid a country tax," . . . . "and all persons having, in other respects, the legal qualifications to vote for representatives in the General Assembly of said Territory, be, and they are hereby, authorized to choose representatives."

The organic law of Indiana Territory was the Ordinance of 1787; or organic law of Illinois Territory was the Ordinance of 1787; and so with all the northwestern Territories. The Ordinance of 1787, which constituted the organic law of those Territories, expressly provided that citizens of the different States residing there and having a certain amount of property, should vote; and it expressly authorized unnaturalized persons to vote, as well as naturalized citizens, provided they owned property. If my friend will look into the matter, he will find that there is no question that, under the organic law of those Territories, unnaturalized foreigners could and did vote while they were Territories; and then the acts authorizing those Territories to form constitutions and State governments, provided that all citizens of the United States could vote, and also, all such other persons as were qualified to vote in the Territories by existing laws, showing clearly that there was an express recognition of the rights of unnaturalized foreigners to vote who were authorized to vote under the Territorial laws. That brings those cases exactly within the limits of the bill now under consideration.

OPPOSITION TO MINNESOTA.

The bill met with considerable opposition in both houses of Congress. In the Senate, Mr. Thompson, of Kentucky, made a most remarkable speech against it, which is entirely too rich to be lost, but which our limits preclude our giving here. This was on the 24th of February; and in reply to it, Mr. Douglas made a speech which we give in a subsequent part of the work.

On the 12th of June, 1857, Mr. Douglas being at Springfield, Illinois, addressed the Grand Jury of the United States Court, at their request, upon the affairs of Kansas and Utah, and the recently decided Dred Scott case. The reader will observe that at the time Mr. Douglas made this speech, he had no doubt but that President Buchanan would remove Brigham Young and all his followers from office, would cause a searching investigation to be made into all the crimes that have been perpetrated in Utah, and would execute the laws, by military force if necessary. No temporizing policy, no half-way measures, says Mr. Douglas, will answer. " He would first repeal the organic act, absolutely and unconditionally, blotting out of existence the Territorial government, and bringing Utah under the sole and exclusive jurisdiction of the United States government."

No man can fail to see that the mode of grappling with the Utah question which Mr. Douglas suggests, is the only way in which the great problem of " What is to be done with Utah ?" can be solved. It must be settled in the way he indicates, sooner or later. We give this speech in a subsequent part of the work.

CHAPTER XII.

THE LECOMPTON CONSTITUTION—BRITISH AGGRESSION—1858.

New Aspect of Affairs at the Federal Capitol—Mr. Douglas calls on the President for Information in regard to Affairs in Kansas—Great Speech of Mr. Douglas against the Lecompton Constitution—Speech in Favor of the Crittenden-Montgomery Amendment—Speech on the English Bill—Speech in favor of conferring on the President Power to punish British Outrages.

THE LECOMPTON CONSTITUTION.

THE first session of the 35th Congress met in December, 1857. On the 8th, President Buchanan sent to Congress his first annual message. On the 9th, Mr. Douglas addressed the Senate on that part of the message referring to affairs in Kansas.

This speech is a calm and clear examination of the question —whether or not Kansas could be received into the Union, with the Lecompton constitution.

MR. PRESIDENT: When yesterday the President's message was read at the clerk's desk, I heard it but imperfectly, and I was of the impression that the President of the United States had approved and indorsed the action of the Lecompton convention in Kansas. Under that impression, I felt it my duty to state that, while I concurred in the general views of the message, yet, so far as it approved or indorsed the action of that convention, I entirely dissented from it, and would avail myself of an early opportunity to state my reasons for my dissent. Upon a more careful and critical examination of the message, I am rejoiced to find that the Presi-

5*

dent of the United States has not recommended that Congress shall pass a law to receive Kansas into the Union under the constitution formed at Lecompton. It is true that the tone of the message indicates a willingness on the part of the President to sign a bill, if we shall see proper to pass one, receiving Kansas into the Union under that constitution. But, sir, it is a fact of great significance, and worthy of consideration, that the President has refrained from any indorsement of the convention, and from any recommendation as to the course Congress should pursue with regard to the constitution there formed.

The message of the President has made an argument—an unanswerable argument, in my opinion—against that constitution, which shows clearly, whether intended to arrive at the result or not, that, consistently with his views and his principles, he cannot accept that constitution. He has expressed his deep mortification and disappointment that the constitution itself has not been submitted to the people of Kansas for their acceptance or rejection. He informs us that he has unqualifiedly expressed his opinions on that subject in his instructions to Governor Walker, assuming, as a matter of course, that the constitution was to be submitted to the people before it could have any vitality or validity. He goes further, and tells us that the example set by Congress in the Minnesota case, by inserting a clause in the enabling act requiring the constitution to be submitted to the people, ought to become a uniform rule, not to be departed from hereafter in any case. On these various propositions I agree entirely with the President of the United States, and I am prepared now to sustain that uniform rule which he asks us to pursue, in all other cases, by taking the Minnesota provision as our, example.

I rejoice, on a careful perusal of the message, to find so much less to dissent from than I was under the impression there was, from the hasty reading and imperfect hearing of the message in the first instance. In effect, he refers that document to the Congress of the United States—as the Constitution of the United States refers it—for us to decide upon it under our responsibility. It is proper that he should have thus referred it to us as a matter for Congressional action, and not as an administration or executive measure, for the reason that the Constitution of the United States says that " *Congress* may admit new States into the Union." Hence we find the Kansas question before us now, not as an administration measure, not as an Executive measure, but as a measure coming before us for our free action, without any recommendation or interference, directly or indirectly, by the administration now in possession of the Federal Government. Sir, I propose to examine this question calmly and fairly, to see whether or not we can properly receive Kansas into the Union with the constitution formed at Lecompton.

The President, after expressing his regret, and mortification, and disappointment, that the constitution had not been submitted to the people in pursuance of his instructions to Governor Walker, and in pursuance of Governor Walker's assurance to the people, says, however, that by the Kansas-Nebraska Act the slavery question only was required to be referred to the people, and the remainder of the constitution was not thus required to be submitted. He acknowledges that, as a general rule, on general principles, the whole constitution should be submitted ; but according to his understanding of the organic act of Kansas, there was an imperative obligation to submit the slavery question for their approval or disapproval, but no obligation to submit the entire constitution. In other words, he regards the organic act, the Nebraska Bill, as having made an exception of the slavery clause, and pı vided for the disposition of that question in a mode different from that in which other domestic or local, as contradistinguished from federal questions, should be decided. Sir, permit me to say, with profound respect for the President of the United States, that I conceive that on this point he has committed a fundamental error, an error which lies at the foundation of his whole argument on this matter. I can well understand how that distinguished statesman came to fall into this error. He was not in the country at the time the Nebraska Bill was passed; he was not a party to the controversy and the discussion that took place during its passage. He was then representing the honor and the dignity of the country with great wisdom and distinction at a foreign court. Thus deeply engrossed, his whole energies were absorbed in conducting great diplomatic questions that diverted his attention from the mere territorial questions and discussions then going on in the Senate and the House of Representatives, and before the people at home. Under these circumstances, he may well have fallen into an error, radical and fundamental as it is, in regard to the object of the Nebraska Bill and the principle asserted in it.

Now, sir, what was the principle enunciated by the authors and supporters of that bill when it was brought forward ? Did we not come before the country and say that we repealed the Missouri restriction for the purpose of substituting and carrying out as a general rule the great principle of self-government, which left the people of each State and each Territory free to form and regulate their domestic institutions in their own way, subject only to the Constitution of the United States? In support of that proposition, it was argued here, and I have argued it wherever I have spoken in various States of the Union, at home and abroad, everywhere I have endeavored to prove that there was no reason why an exception should be made in regard to the slavery question. I have appealed to the people if we did not all agree, men of all parties, that all other local and domestic questions should be submitted to the people. I said to them, " We agree that the people shall decide for themselves what kind of a judiciary system they will have ; we agree that the people shall decide what kind of a school system they will establish ; we agree that the people shall determine for themselves what kind of a banking system they will have, or whether they will have any banks at all ; we agree that the people may decide for themselves what shall be the elective franchise in their respective States ; they shall decide for themselves what shall be the rule of taxation and the principles upon which their finance shall be regulated ; we agree that they may decide for themselves the relations between husband and wife, parent and child, guardian and ward ; and why should we not then allow them to decide for themselves the relations between master and servant? Why make an exception of the slavery question by taking it out of that great rule of self-government which applies to all the other relations of life ?" The very first proposition in the Nebraska Bill was to show that the Missouri restriction, prohibiting the people from deciding the slavery question for themselves, constituted an exception to a general rule, in violation of the principle of self-government, and hence that that exception should be repealed, and the slavery question, like all other questions, submitted to the people to be decided for themselves.

Sir, that was the principle on which the Nebraska Bill was defended by its friends. Instead of making the slavery question an exception, it removed an odious exception which before existed. Its whole object was to abolish that odious exception, and make the rule general, universal, in its application to all matters which were local and domestic, and not national or federal. For this reason was the language employed which the President has quoted; that the eighth section of the Missouri Act, commonly called the Missouri Compromise, was repealed because it was repugnant to the principle of non-intervention established by the Compromise measures of 1850, " it being the true intent and meaning of this act not to legislate slavery into any Territory or State, nor to exclude it therefrom, but to leave the people thereof perfectly free to form and regulate their domestic institutions in their own way, subject only to the Constitution of the

United States." We repealed the Missouri restriction because that was confined to slavery. That was the only exception there was to the general principle of self-government. That exception was taken away for the avowed and express purpose of making the rule of self-government general and universal, so that the people should form and regulate all their domestic institutions in their own way.

Sir, what would this boasted principle of popular sovereignty have been worth, if it applied only to the negro, and did not extend to the white man? Do you think we could have aroused the sympathies and the patriotism of this broad Republic, and have carried the Presidential election last year in the face of a tremendous opposition, on the principle of extending the rights of self-government to the negro question, but denying it as to all the relations affecting white men? No, sir. We aroused the patriotism of the country, and carried the election in defence of that great principle, which allowed all white men to form and regulate their domestic institutions to suit themselves—institutions applicable to white men as well as to black men—institutions applicable to freemen as well as to slaves—institutions concerning all the relations of life, and not the mere paltry exception of the slavery question. Sir, I have spent too much strength and breath, and health, too, to establish this great principle in the popular heart, now to see it fritted away by bringing it down to an exception that applies to the negro, and does not extend to the benefit of the white man. As I said before, I can well imagine how the distinguished and eminent patriot and statesman now at the head of the government, fell into the error—for error it is, radical, fundamental—and, if persevered in, subversive of that platform upon which he was elevated to the Presidency of the United States.

Then, if the President be right in saying that, by the Nebraska Bill, the slavery question must be submitted to the people, it follows inevitably that every other clause of the Constitution must also be submitted to the people. The Nebraska Bill said that the people should be left " perfectly free to form and regulate their domestic institutions in their own way "—not the slavery question, not the Maine liquor law question, not the banking question, not the school question, not the railroad question, but " their domestic institutions," meaning each and all the questions which are local, not national—State, not federal. I arrive at the conclusion that the principles enunciated so boldly, and enforced with so much ability by the President of the United States, require us, out of respect to him and the platform on which he was elected, to send this whole question back to the people of Kansas. and enable them to say whether or not the constitution which has been framed, each and every clause of it, meets their approbation.

The President, in his message, has made an unanswerable argument in favor of the principle which requires this question to be sent back. It is stated in the message, with more clearness and force than any language which I can command; but I can draw your attention to it and refer you to the argument in the message, hoping that you will take it as a part of my speech—as expressing my idea more forcibly than I am able to express it. The President says that a question of great interest, like the slavery question, cannot be fairly decided by a convention of delegates, for the reason that the delegates are elected in districts, and in some districts the delegate is elected by a small majority; in others by an overwhelming majority, so that it often happens that a majority of the delegates are one way, while a majority of the people are the other way; and therefore it would be unfair and inconsistent with the great principle of popular sovereignty, to allow a body of delegates, not representing the popular voice, to establish domestic institutions for the mass of the people. This is the President's argument to show that you cannot have a fair and honest decision without submitting it to the popular vote. The same argument is conclusive with regard to every other question as well as with regard to slavery.

But, Mr. President, it is intimated in the message that although it was an unfortunate circumstance, much to be regretted, that the Lecompton convention did not submit the constitution to the people, yet perhaps it may be treated as regular, because the convention was called by a Territorial legislature which had been repeatedly recognized by the Congress of the United States as a legal body. I beg senators not to fall into an error as to the President's meaning on this point. He does not say, he does not mean, that this convention had ever been recognized by the Congress of the United States as legal or valid. On the contrary, he knows, as we here know, that during the last Congress I reported a bill from the Committee on Territories to authorize the people of Kansas to assemble and form a constitution for themselves. Subsequently, the senator from Georgia (Mr. Toombs) brought forward a substitute for my bill, which, after having been modified by him and myself in consultation, was passed by the Senate. It is known in the country as "the Toombs Bill." It authorizes the people of Kansas Territory to assemble in convention and form a constitution preparatory to their admission into the Union as a State. That bill, it is well known, was defeated in the House of Reprosentatives. It matters not, for the purpose of this argument, what was the reason of its defeat. Whether the reason was a political one; whether it had reference to the then existing contest for the Presidency; whether it was to keep open the slavery question ; whether it was a conviction that the bill would not be fairly carried out; whether it was because there were not people enough in Kansas to justify the formation of a State—no matter what the reason was, the House of Representatives refused to pass that bill, and thus denied to the people of Kansas the right to form a constitution and State government at this time. So far from the Congress of the United States having sanctioned or legalized the convention which assembled at Lecompton, it expressly withheld its assent. The assent has not been given, either in express terms or by implication ; and being withheld, this Kansas constitution has just such validity and just such authority as the Territorial legislature of Kansas could impart to it without the assent, and in opposition to the known will of Congress.

Now, sir, let me ask what is the extent of the authority of a Territorial legislature as to calling a constitutional convention without the assent of Congress? Fortunately this is not a new question; it does not now arise for the first time. When the Topeka constitution was presented to the Senate nearly two years ago, it was referred to the Committee on Territories with a variety of measures relating to Kansas. The committee made a full report upon the whole subject. That report reviewed all the irregular cases which had occurred in our history in the admission of new States. The committee acted on the supposition that whenever Congress had passed an enabling act authorizing the people of a Territory to form a State constitution, the convention was regular, and possessed all the authority which Congress had delegated to it ; but whenever Congress had failed or refused to pass an enabling act, the proceeding was irregular and void, unless vitality was imparted to it by a subsequent act of Congress adopting and confirming it. The friends of the Topeka constitution insisted that although their proceedings were irregular, they were not so irregular but that Congress could cure the error by admitting Congress with that constitution. They cited a variety of cases, amongst others the Arkansas case. In my report, sanctioned by every member of the Committee on Territories, except the senator from Vermont (Mr. Collamer), I reviewed the Arkansas case as well as the others, and affirmed the doctrine established by General Jackson's administration and enunciated in the opinion of Mr. Attorney General Butler, a part of which opinion was copied into the report and published to the country at the time.

Now, sir, in order to ascertain what we understood on the 12th of March, 1856—little more than a year and a half ago—to be the true doctrine on this point, let me call your attention to the opinion of Mr. Butler in the Arkansas case. The governor of the Territory of Arkansas sent a printed address to President Jackson, in which he stated that he had been urged to call together the legislature of the Territory of Arkansas, for the purpose of allowing them to call a convention to form a constitution, preparatory to their admission into the Union as a State. The governor stated that, in his opinion, the legislature had no power to call such a convention without the assent of Congress first had and obtained; but he asked instructions on that point. The President referred the case to the secretary of state, and he asked for the advice of the attorney general, whose opinion was given, and adopted, as the plan of action, and communicated to the governor of Arkansas for his instruction. I will read some extracts from that opinion:

"Consequently, it is not in the power of the General Assembly of Arkansas to pass any law for the purpose of electing members to form a constitution and State government, or to do any other act, directly or indirectly, to create such new government. Every such law, even though it were approved by the governor of the Territory, would be null and void. If passed by them, notwithstanding his veto, by a vote of two-thirds of each branch, it would still be equally void.

"If I am right in the foregoing opinion, it will then follow that the course of the governor, in declining to call together the Territorial legislature for the purpose in question, was such as his legal duties required; and that the views he has expressed in his public address, and also in his official communication to yourself, so far as they indicate an intention not to sanction or concur in any legislative or other proceedings toward the formation of a State government until Congress shall have authorized it, are also correct."

That is what I have understood to be the settled doctrine as to the authority of a Territorial legislature to call a convention without the consent of Congress first had and obtained. The reasoning is very clear and palpable. A Territorial legislature possesses whatever power its organic act gives it, and no more. The organic act of Arkansas provided that the legislative power should be vested in the Territorial legislature, the same as the organic act of Kansas provides that the legislative power and authority shall be vested in the legislature. But what is the extent of that legislative power? It is to legislate for that Territory under the organic act, and in obedience to it. It does not include any power to subvert the organic act under which it was brought into existence. It has the power to protect it, the power to execute it, the power to carry it into effect; but it has no power to subvert, none to destroy ; and hence that power can only be obtained by applying to Congress, the same authority which created the Territory itself. But while the attorney general decided, with the approbation of the administration of General Jackson, that the Territorial legislature had no power to call a convention, and that its action was void if it did, he went further :

"No law has yet been passed by Congress which either expressly or impliedly gives to the people of Arkansas the authority to form a State government."

Nor has there been any in regard to Kansas. The two cases are alike thus far. They are alike in all particulars so far as the question involving the legality and the validity of the Lecompton convention is concerned. The opinion goes on to say :

" For the reasons above stated, I am, therefore, of opinion that the inhabitants of that Territory have not at present, and that they cannot acquire otherwise than by an act of Congress, the right to form such a government."

General Jackson's administration took the ground that the people of Arkansas, by the authority of the Territorial legislature, had not the power to hold a convention to form a constitution, and could not acquire it from any source whatever except from Congress. While, therefore, the legislative act of Arkansas was held to be void, so far as it assumed authority to authorize the calling of a convention to form a constitution, yet they did not hold, in those days, that the people could not assemble and frame a constitution in the form of a petition. I will read the rest of the opinion, in order that the Senate may understand precisely what was the doctrine on this subject at that day, and what the committee on Territories understood to be the doctrine on this subject in March, 1856, when we put forth the Kansas report as embodying what we Nebraska men understood to be our doctrine at time. Here it is. This was copied into that report:

" But I am not prepared to say that all proceedings on this subject, on the part of the citizens of Arkansas, will be illegal. They undoubtedly possess the ordinary privileges and immunities of citizens of the United States. Among these is the right to assemble and to petition the government for the redress of grievances. In the exercise of this right, the inhabitants of Arkansas may peaceably meet together in primary assemblies, or in conventions chosen by such assemblies, for the purpose of petitioning Congress to abrogate the Territorial government, and to admit them into the Union as an independent State. The particular form which they may give in their petition cannot be material, so long as they confine themselves to the mere right of petitioning, and conduct all their proceedings in a peaceable manner. And as the power of Congress over the whole subject is plenary and unlimited, THEY MAY ACCEPT ANY CONSTITUTION, HOWEVER FRAMED, WHICH IN THEIR JUDGMENT MEETS THE SENSE OF THE PEOPLE TO BE AFFECTED BY IT. If, therefore, the citizens of Arkansas think proper to accompany their petition with a written constitution, framed and agreed on by their primary assemblies, or by a convention of delegates chosen by such assemblies, I perceive no legal objection to their power to do so, nor any measures which may be taken to collect the sense of the people in respect to it; provided always, that such measures be commenced and prosecuted in a peaceable manner, in strict subordination to the existing Territorial government, AND IN ENTIRE SUBSERVIENCY TO THE POWER OF CONGRESS TO ADOPT, REJECT, OR DISREGARD THEM, AT THEIR PLEASURE."

While the legislature of Arkansas had no power to create a convention to frame a constitution, as a legal constitutional body, yet if the people chose to assemble under such an act of the legislature for the purpose of petitioning for redress of grievances, the assemblage was not illegal; it was not an unlawful assemblage; it was not such an assemblage as the military power could be used to disperse, for they had a right under the Constitution thus to assemble and petition. But if they assumed to themselves the right or the power to make a government, that assumption was an act of rebellion which General Jackson said it was his duty to put down with the military force of the country.

If you apply these principles to the Kansas convention, you find that it had no power to do any act as a convention forming a government; you find that the act calling it was null and void from the beginning; you find that the legislature could confer no power whatever on the convention. That convention was simply an assemblage of peaceable citizens, under the Constitution of the United States, petitioning for the redress of grievances, and, thus assembled, had the right to put their petition in the form of a constitution if they chose; but still it was only a petition—having the force of a petition—which Congress could accept or reject, or dispose of as it saw proper. That is what I understand to be just the extent of the power and authority of this convention assembled at Lecompton. It was not an unlawful assemblage like that held at Topeka; for the Topeka constitution was made in opposition to the Territorial law, and, as I thought, intended to subvert the government without the consent of Congress, but, as contended by their friends, not so intended. If their object was to subvert it without the consent of Congress, it was an act of rebellion, which ought to have been put down by force. If it was a peaceable assemblage, simply to petition and abide the decision of Congress on the petition, it was not an unlawful assemblage. I hold, however, that it was an unlawful assemblage. I hold that this Lecompton convention was not an unlawful assemblage; but, on the other hand, I hold that they had no legal power and authority to establish a government. They had a right to petition for a redress of grievances. They had a right in that petition to ask for the change of government from a Territorial to a State government. They had a right to ask Congress to adopt the instrument which they sent to us as their constitution; and Congress, if it thought that paper embodied the will of the people of the Territory, fairly expressed, might, in its discretion, accept it as a constitution, and admit them into the Union as a State; or if Congress thought it did not embody the will of the people of Kansas, it might reject it; or if Congress thought it was doubtful whether it did embody the will of the people or not, then it should send it back and submit it to the people to have that doubt removed, in order that the popular voice, whatever it might be, should prevail in the constitution under which that people were to live.

So far as the act of the Territorial legislature of Kansas calling this convention was concerned, I have always been under the impression that it was fair and just in its provisions. I have always thought the people should have gone together *en masse* and voted for delegates, so that the voice expressed by the convention should have been the unquestioned and united voice of the people of Kansas. I have always thought that those who staid away from that election stood in their own light, and should have gone and voted, and should have furnished their names to be put on the registered list, so as to be voters. I have always held that it was their own fault that they did not thus go and vote; but yet, if they chose, they had a right to stay away. They had a right to say that that convention, although not an unlawful assemblage, is not a legal convention to make a government, and hence we are under no obligation to go and express any opinion about it. They had a right to say, if they chose, "We will stay away until we see the constitution they shall frame, the petition they shall send to Congress; and when they submit it to us for ratification we will vote for it, if we like it, or vote it down if we do not like it." If say they had a right to do either, though I thought, and think yet, as good citizens, they ought to have gone and voted; but that was their business and not mine.

Having thus shown that the Convention at Lecompton had no power, no authority, to form and establish a government, but had power to draft a petition, and that petition, if it embodied the will of the people of Kansas, ought to be taken as such an exposition of their will, yet if it did not embody their will, ought to be rejected—having shown these facts, let me proceed and inquire what was the understanding of the people of Kansas, when the delegates were elected? I understand, from the history of the transaction, that the people who voted for delegates to the Lecompton convention, and those who refused to vote—both parties—understood the Territorial Act to mean that they were to be elected only to frame a constitution, and submit it to the people for their ratification or rejection. I say that both parties in that Territory, at the time of the election of delegates, so understood the object of the convention. Those who voted for delegates did so with the understanding that they had no power to make a government, but only to frame one for submission; and those who staid away did so with the same understanding.

Now for the evidence. The President of the United States tells us, in his message, that he had unequivocally expressed his opinions, in the form of instructions to Governor Walker, assuming that the constitution was to be submitted to the people for ratification. When we look into Governor Walker's letter of acceptance of the office of governor, we find that he stated expressly that he accepted it with the understanding that the President and his whole cabinet concurred with him, that the constitution, when formed, was to be submitted to the people for ratification. Then look into the instructions given by the President of the United States, through General Cass, the secretary of state, to Governor Walker, and you there find that the governor is instructed to use the military power to protect the polls when the constitution shall be submitted to the people of Kansas for their free acceptance or rejection. Trace the history a little further, and you will find that Governor Walker went to Kansas and proclaimed, in his inaugural, and in his speeches at Topeka and elsewhere, that it was the distinct understanding, not only of himself, but of those higher in power than himself—meaning the President and his cabinet—that the constitution was to be submitted to the people for their free acceptance or rejection, and that he would use all the power at his command to defeat its acceptance by Congress, if it were not thus submitted to the vote of the people

Mr. President, I am not going to stop and inquire how far the Nebraska Bill, which said the people should be left perfectly free to form their constitution for themselves, authorized the President, or the cabinet, or Governor Walker, or any other Territorial officer, to interfere and tell the Convention of Kansas whether they should not submit the question to the people. I am not going to stop to inquire how far they were authorized to do that, it being my opinion that the spirit of the Nebraska Bill required it to be done. It is sufficient for my purpose that the administration of the Federal Government unanimously—that the administration of the Territorial government, in all its parts, unanimously understood the Territorial law under which the convention was assembled to mean that the constitution to be formed by that convention should be submitted to the people for ratification or rejection; and, if not confirmed by a majority of the people, should be null and void, without coming to Congress for approval.

Not only did the national government and the Territorial government so understand the law at the time, but, as I have already stated, the people of the Territory so understood it. As a further evidence on that point, a large number, if not a majority, of the delegates were instructed in the nominating conventions to submit the constitution to the people for ratification. I know that the delegates from Douglas County, eight in number, Mr. Calhoun, president of the convention, being among them, were not only instructed thus to submit the question, but they signed and published, while candidates, a written pledge that they would submit it to the people for ratification. I know that men, high in authority, and in the confidence of the Territorial and national government, canvassed every part of Kansas during the election of delegates, and each one of them pledged himself to the people that no snap judgment was to be taken; that the constitution was to be submitted to the people for acceptance or rejection; that it would be void unless that was done; that the administration would spurn and scorn it as a violation of the principles on which it came into power, and that a Democratic Congress would hurl it from their presence as an insult to Democrats who stood pledged to see the people left free to form their domestic institutions for themselves.

Not only that, sir, but up to the time when the convention assembled, on the 1st of September, so far as I can learn, it was understood everywhere that the constitution was to be submitted for ratification or rejection. They met, however, on the 1st of September, and adjourned until after the October election. I think it was wise and prudent that they should thus have adjourned. They did not wish to bring any question into that election which would divide the Democratic party, and weaken our chances of success in the election. I was rejoiced when I saw that they did adjourn, so as not to show their hand on any question that would divide and distract the party until after the election. During that recess, while the convention was adjourned, Governor Ransom, the Democratic candidate for Congress, running against the present delegate from that Territory, was canvassing every part of Kansas in favor of the doctrine of submitting the constitution to the people, declaring that the Democratic party were in favor of such submission, and that it was a slander of the Black Republicans to intimate the charge that the Democratic party did not intend to carry out that pledge in good faith. Thus, up to the time of the meeting of the convention, in October last, the pretence was kept up, the profession was openly made, and believed by me, and I thought believed by them, that the convention intended to submit a constitution to the people, and not to attempt to put government in operation without such submission. The election being over, the Democratic party being defeated by an overwhelming vote, the Opposition having triumphed, and got possession of both branches of the legislature, and having elected their Territorial delegate, the convention assembled, and then proceeded to complete their work.

Now let us stop to inquire how they redeemed the pledge to submit the constitution to the people. They first go on and make a constitution. Then they make a schedule, in which they provide that the constitution, on the 21st December—the present month—shall be submitted to all the *bonâ fide* inhabitants of the Territory on that day, for their free acceptance or rejection, in the following manner, to wit : thus acknowledging that they were bound to submit it to the will of the people, conceding that they had no right to put it into operation without submitting it to the people, providing in the instrument that it should take effect from and after the date of its ratification, and not before ; showing that the constitution derives its vitality, in their estimation, not from the authority of the convention, but from that vote of the people to which it was to be submitted for their acceptance or rejection. How is it to be submitted ? It shall be submitted in this form : " Constitution with slavery, or constitution with no slavery." All men must vote for the constitution, whether they like it or not, in order to be permitted to vote for or against slavery. Thus a constitution made by a convention that had authority to assemble and petition for a redress of grievances, but not to establish a government—a constitution made under a pledge of honor that it should be submitted to the people before it took effect ; a constitution which provides, on its face, that it shall have no validity except what it derives from such submission —is submitted to the people at an election where all men are at liberty to come forward freely without hinderance and vote for it, but no man is permitted to record a vote against it.

That would be as fair an election as some of the enemies of Napoleon attributed to him when he was elected First Consul. He is said to have called out his troops, and had them reviewed by his officers with a speech, patriotic and fair in its professions, in which he said to them : " Now, my soldiers, you are to go to the election and vote freely just as you please. If you vote for Napoleon all is well ; vote against him, and you are to be instantly shot." That was a fair election. (Laughter.) This election is to be equally fair. All men in favor of the constitution may vote for it—all men against it shall not vote at all. Why not let them vote against it ? I presume you have asked many a man this question. I have asked a very large number of the gentlemen who framed the constitution, quite a number of delegates, and a still larger number of persons who are their friends, and I have received the same answer from every one of them. I never received any other answer, and I presume we never shall get any other answer. What is that? They say if they allowed a negative vote the constitution would have been voted down by an overwhelming majority, and hence the fellows shall not be allowed to vote at all. (Laughter.)

Mr. President, that may be true. It is no part of my purpose to deny the proposition that that constitution would have been voted down if submitted to the people. I believe it would have been voted down by a majority of four to one. I am informed by men well posted there—Democrats—that it would be voted down by ten to one; some say by twenty to one.

But is it a good reason why you should declare it in force, without being submitted to the people, merely because it would have been voted down by five to one if you had submitted it? What does that fact prove? Does it not show undeniably that an overwhelming majority of people of Kansas are unalterably opposed to that constitution? Will you force it on them against their will, simply because they would have voted it down if you had consulted them? If you will, are you going to force it upon them under the plea of leaving them perfectly free to form and regulate their domestic institutions in their own way? Is that the mode in which I am called upon to carry out the principle of self-government and popular sovereignty in the Territories—to force a constitution on the people against their will, in opposition to their protest, with a knowledge of the fact, and then to assign, as a reason for my tyranny, that they would be so obstinate and so perverse as to vote down the constitution if I had given them an opportunity to be consulted about it?

Sir, I deny your right or mine to inquire of these people what their objections to that constitution are. They have a right to judge for themselves whether they like or dislike it. It is no answer to tell me that the constitution is a good one and unobjectionable. It is not satisfactory to me to have the President say in his message that that constitution is an admirable one, like all the constitutions of the new States that have been recently formed. Whether good or bad, whether obnoxious or not, is none of my business and none of yours. It is their business, and not ours. I care not what they have in their constitution, so that it suits them and does not violate the Constitution of the United States and the fundamental principles of liberty upon which our constitutions rest. I am not going to argue the question whether the banking system established in that constitution is wise or unwise. It says there shall be no monopolies, but there shall be one bank of issue in the State, with two branches. All I have to say on that point is, if they want a banking system let them have it; if they do not want it, let them prohibit it. If they want a bank with two branches, be it so; if they want twenty, it is none of my business, and it matters not to me whether one of them shall be on the north side and the other on the south side of Kaw River, or where they shall be.

While I have no right to expect to be consulted on that point, I do hold that the people of Kansas have the right to be consulted and to decide it, and you have no rightful authority to deprive them of that privilege. It is no justification, in my mind, to say, that the provisions for the eligibility for the offices of governor and lieutenant-governor requires twenty years' citizenship in the United States. If men think that no person should vote or hold office until he has been here twenty years, they have a right to think so; and if a majority of the people of Kansas think that no man of foreign birth should vote or hold office unless he has lived there twenty years, it is their right to say so, and I have no right to interfere with them; it is their business, not mine; but if I lived there I should not be willing to have that provision in the constitution without being heard upon the subject, and allowed to record my protest against it.

I have nothing to say about their system of taxation, in which they have gone back and resorted to the old exploded system that we tried in Illinois, but abandoned, because we did not like it. If they wish to try it, and get tired of it, and abandon it, be it so; but if I were a citizen of Kansas, I would profit by the experience of Illinois on that subject, and defeat it if I could. Yet I have no objection to their having it if they want it; it is their business, not mine.

So it is in regard to the free negroes. They provide that no free negro shall be permitted *to live* in Kansas. I suppose they have a right to say so if they choose; but if I lived there, I should want to vote on that question. We, in Illinois, provide that no more shall come there. We say to the other States, "take care of your own free negroes and we will take care of ours." But we do not say that the negroes now there shall not be permitted to live in Illinois; and I think the people of Kansas ought to have the right to say whether they will allow them to live there, and if they are not going to do so, how they are to dispose of them.

So you may go on with all the different clauses of the constitution. They may be all right; they may be all wrong. That is a question on which my opinion is worth nothing. The opinion of the wise and patriotic chief magistrate of the United States is not worth anything as against that of the people of Kansas, for they have a right to judge for themselves; and neither Presidents, nor Senates, nor Houses of Representatives, nor any other power outside of Kansas, has a right to judge for them. Hence, it is no justification, in my mind, for the violation of a great principle of self-government, to say that the constitution you are forcing on them is not particularly obnoxious, or is excellent in its provisions.

Perhaps, sir, the same thing might be said of the celebrated Topeka constitution. I do not recollect its peculiar provisions. I know one thing, we Democrats, we Nebraska men, would not even look into it, to see what its provisions were. Why? Because we said it was made by a political party, and not by the people; that it was made in defiance of the authority of Congress; that if it was as pure as the Bible, as holy as the ten commandments, yet we would not touch it until it was submitted to and ratified by the people of Kansas, in pursuance of the forms of law. Perhaps that Topeka constitution, but for the mode of making it, would have been unexceptionable. I do not know; I do not care. You have no right to force an unexceptionable constitution on a people. It does not mitigate the evil, it does not diminish the insult, it does not ameliorate the wrong, that you are forcing a good thing on them. I am not willing to be forced to do that which I would do if I were left free to judge and act for myself. Hence, I assert that there is no justification to be made for this flagrant violation of popular rights in Kansas, on the plea that the constitution which they have made is not particularly obnoxious.

But, sir, the President of the United States is really and sincerely of the opinion that the slavery clause has been fairly and impartially submitted to the free acceptance or rejection of the people of Kansas, and that, inasmuch as that was the exciting and paramount question, if they get the right to vote as they please on that subject they ought to be satisfied; and possibly it might be better if we would accept it, and put an end to the question. Let me ask, sir, is the slavery clause fairly submitted, so that the people can vote for or against it? Suppose I were a citizen of Kansas, and should go up to the polls and say, "I desire to vote to make Kansas a slave State, here is my ballot." They reply to me, "Mr. Douglas, just vote for that constitution first, if you please." "Oh, no!" I answer, "I cannot vote for that constitution conscientiously. I am opposed to the clause by which you locate certain railroads in such a way as to sacrifice my county and my part of the State. I am opposed to that banking system. I am opposed to this Know Nothing or American clause in the constitution about the qualification for office. I cannot vote for it." Then they answer, "You shall not vote on making it a slave State." I then say, "I want to make it a free State." They reply, "vote for that constitution first, and then you can vote to make it a free State; otherwise you cannot." Thus they disqualify every free State man who will not first vote for the constitution. They disqualify every slave State man who will not first vote for the constitution. No matter whether or not the voters state that they cannot conscientiously vote for those provisions, they reply, "You cannot vote for or against slavery here. Take the constitution as we have made it, take the elective franchise as we have established it, take the banking system as we have dictated it, take the railroad lines as we have located them, take the judiciary system as we have formed it, take it all as we have fixed it to suit ourselves, and ask no questions, but vote for it, or you shall not vote either for a slave or free State." In other words, the legal effect of the schedule is this : all those who are in favor of this constitution may vote for or against slavery, as they please; but all those who are against this constitution are disfranchised, and shall not vote at all. That is the mode in which the slavery proposition is submitted. Every man opposed to the constitution is disfranchised on the slavery cause. How many are they? They tell you there is a majority, for they say the constitution will be voted down instantly, by an overwhelming majority, if you allow a negative vote. This shows that a majority are against it. They disqualify and disfranchise every man who is against it, thus referring the slavery clause to a minority of the people of Kansas, and leaving that minority free to vote for or against the slavery clause, as they choose.

Let me ask you if that is a fair mode of submitting the slavery clause? Does that mode of submitting that particular clause leave the people perfectly free to vote for or against slavery as they choose? Am I free to vote as I choose on the slavery question, if you tell me that I shall not vote on it until I vote for the Maine liquor law? Am I free to vote on the slavery question, if you tell me that I shall not vote either way until I vote for a bank? Is it freedom of election to make your right to vote upon one question depend upon the mode in which you are going to vote on some other question which has no connection with it? Is that freedom of election? Is that the great fundamental principle of self-government, for which we combined and struggled, in this body and throughout the country, to establish as the rule of action in all time to come?

The President of the United States has made some remarks in his message which it strikes me it would be very appropriate to read in this connection. He says:

" The friends and supporters of the Nebraska and Kansas Act, when struggling on a recent occasion to sustain its wise provisions before the great tribunal of the American people, never differed about its true meaning on this subject. Everywhere throughout the Union they publicly pledged their faith and honor that they would cheerfully submit the question of slavery to the decision of the *bona fide* people of Kansas, without any restriction or qualification whatever. All were cordially united upon the great doctrine of popular sovereignty, which is the vital principle of our free institutions."

Mark this:

"Had it then been insinuated, from any quarter, that it would have been a sufficient compliance with the requisitions of the organic law for the members of a convention, thereafter to be elected, to withhold a question of slavery from the people, and to substitute their own will for that of a legally ascertained majority of their constituents, this would have been instantly rejected."

Yes, sir, and I will add further, had it been then intimated from any quarter, and believed by the American people, that we would have submitted the slavery clause in such a manner as to compel a man to vote for that which his conscience did not approve, in order to vote on the slavery clause, not only would the idea have been rejected, but the Democratic candidate for the Presidency would have been rejected; and every man who backed him would have been rejected too.

The President tells us in his message that the whole party pledged our faith and our honor that the slavery question should be submitted to the people, without any restriction or qualification whatever. Does this schedule submit it without qualification? It qualifies it by saying, "you may vote on slavery if you will vote for the constitution; but you shall not do so without doing that." That is a very important qualification—a qualification that controls a man's vote, and his action, and his conscience, if he is an honest man—a qualification confessedly in violation of our platform. We are told by the President that our faith and our honor are pledged, that the slavery clause should be submitted without qualification of any kind whatever; and now I am to be called upon to forfeit my faith and my honor in order to enable a small minority of the people of Kansas to defraud the majority of that people out of their elective franchise? Sir, my honor is pledged; and before it shall be tarnished, I will take whatever consequences personal to myself may come; but never ask me to do an act which the President, in his message, has said is a forfeiture of faith, a violation of honor, and that merely for the expediency of saving the party. I will go as far as any of you to save the party. I have as much heart in the great cause that binds us together as a party as any man living. I will sacrifice anything short of principle and honor for the peace of the party; but if the party will not stand by its principles, its faith, its pledges, I will stand there, and abide whatever consequences may result from the position.

Let me ask you, why force this constitution down the throats of the people of Kansas in opposition to their wishes, and in violation of our pledges. What great object is to be attained? *Cui bono?* What are you to gain by it? Will you sustain the party by violating its principles?

Do you propose to keep the party united by forcing a division? Stand by the doctrine that leaves the people perfectly free to form and regulate their institutions for themselves in their own way, and your party will be united and irresistible in power. Abandon that great principle, and the party is not worth saving, and cannot be saved, after it shall be violated. I trust we are not to be rushed upon this question. Why shall it be done? Who is to be benefited? Is the South to be the gainer? Is the North to be the gainer? Neither the North nor the South has the right to gain a sectional advantage by trickery or fraud.

But I am beseeched to wait until I hear from the election on the 21st of December. I am told that perhaps that will put it all right, and will save the whole difficulty. How can it? Perhaps there may be a large vote. There may be a large vote returned. (Laughter.) But I deny that it is possible to have a fair vote on the slavery clause; and I say that it is not possible to have any vote on the constitution. Why wait for the mockery of an election when it is provided, unalterably, that the people cannot vote—when the majority are disfranchised?

But I am told on all sides, "Oh, just wait; the pro-slavery clause will be voted down." That does not obviate any of my objections; it does not diminish any of them. You have no more right to force a free State constitution on Kansas than a slave State constitution. If Kansas wants a slave State constitution she has a right to it; if she wants a free State constitution she has a right to it. It is none of my business which way the slavery clause is decided. I care not whether it is voted down or voted up. Do you suppose, after the pledges of my honor that I would go for that principle and leave the people to vote as they choose, that I would now degrade myself by voting one way if the slavery clause be voted down, and another way if it is voted up? I care not how that vote may stand. I take it for granted that it will be voted out. I think I have seen enough in the last three days to make it certain that it will be returned out, no matter how the vote may stand. (Laughter.)

Sir, I am opposed to that concern because it looks to me like a system of trickery and jugglery to defeat the fair expression of the will of the people. There is no necessity for crowding this measure, so unfair, so unjust as it is in all its aspects, upon us. Why can we not now do what we proposed to do in the last Congress? We then voted through the Senate an enabling act, called "the Toombs Bill," believed to be just and fair in all its provisions, pronounced to be almost perfect by the senator from New Hampshire (Mr. Hale), only he did not like the man, then President of the United States, who would have to make the appointments. Why can we not take that bill, and, out of compliment to the President, add to it a clause taken from the Minnesota Act, which he thinks should be a general rule, requiring the constitution to be submitted to the people, and pass that? That unites the party. You all voted, with me, for that bill, at the last Congress. Why not stand by the same bill now? Ignore Lecompton, ignore Topeka, treat both those party movements as irregular and void; pass a fair bill—the one that we framed ourselves when we were acting as a unit; have a fair election, and you will have peace in the Democratic party, and peace throughout the country, in ninety days. The people want a fair vote. They will never be satisfied without it. They never should be satisfied without a fair vote on their constitution.

If the Toombs Bill does not suit my friends, take the Minnesota Bill of the last session—the one so much commended by the President in his message as a model. Let us pass that as an enabling act, and allow the people of all parties to come together and have a fair vote, and I will go for it. Frame any other bill that secures a fair, honest vote to men of all parties, and carries out the pledge that the people shall be left free to decide on their domestic institutions for themselves, and I will go with you with pleasure, and with all the energy I may possess. But if this constitution is to be forced down our throats, in violation of the fundamental principle of free government, under a mode of submission that is a mockery and insult, I will resist it to the last. I have no fear of any party associations being severed. I should regret any social or political estrangement, even temporarily; but if it must be, if I cannot act with you and preserve my faith and my honor, I will stand on the great principle of popular sovereignty, which declares the right of all people to be left perfectly free to form and regulate their domestic institutions in their own way. I will follow that principle wherever its logical consequences may take me, and I will endeavor to defend it against assault from any and all quarters. No mortal man shall be responsible for my action but myself. By my action I will compromit no man.

[At the conclusion of the honorable gentleman's speech, loud applause and clapping of hands resounded through the crowded galleries.]

MR. BUCHANAN'S MESSAGE.

Mr. Douglas had previously (Dec. 10) given notice of his intention to introduce a bill to enable the people of Kansas territory to hold a convention to form a constitution and State government, preparatory to their admission into the

Union on an equal footing with the original States. On the 18·h, he had introduced the bill (S. No. 15), which was read twice. and referred to the Committee on Territories.

Or the 2d of February, 1858, President Buchanan trans-mitted to Congress a copy of the proposed constitution of Kansas, framed by the convention at Lecompton ; accompanied by a message from himself, from which we make the following remarkable extracts :

The Kansas convention, thus lawfully constituted, proceeded to frame a constitution ; and having completed their work, finally ad-journed on the 7th day of November last. They did not think pro-per to submit the whole of this constitution to a popular vote ; but they did submit the question whether Kansas should be a free or a slave State to the people. No person thought of any other question. For my own part, when I instructed Governor Walker in general terms in favor of submitting the constitution to the people, I had no object in view except the all-absorbing question of slavery.

I then believed, and still believe, that under the organic act the Kansas convention were bound to submit this all-important question of slavery to the people. It was never, however, my opinion that, independently of this act, they would have been bound to submit any portion of the constitution to a popular vote in order to give it va-lidity.

It has been solemnly adjudged, by the highest judicial tribunal known to our laws, that slavery exists in Kansas by virtue of the Constitution of the United States. Kansas is therefore, at this mo-ment, as much a slave State as Georgia or South Carolina. Without this, the equality of the Sovereign States composing the Union, would be violated, and the use and enjoyment of a Territory acquired by the common treasure of all the States, would be closed against the people and the property of nearly half the members of the Confeder-acy. Slavery can, therefore, never be prohibited in Kansas, except by means of a constitutional provision, and in no other manner can this be obtained so promptly, if a majority of the people desire it, as by admitting it into the Union under its present constitution.

On the other hand, should Congress reject the constitution, under the idea of affording the disaffected in Kansas a third opportunity of prohibiting slavery in the State, which they might have done twice before if in the majority, no man can foretell the consequences. If Congress, for the sake of these men who refused to vote for dele-gates to the convention, when they might have excluded slavery from the constitution, and who afterward refused to vote on the 21st December last, when they might, as they claim, have stricken slavery from the constitution, should now reject the State, because slavery remains on the constitution, it is manifest that the agitation upon this dangerous subject will be renewed in a more alarming form than it has ever yet assumed.

DOUGLAS INTERROGATES THE PRESIDENT.

Two days after the reception of this extraordinary message by Congress, Senator Douglas called on the President for more definite information regarding the facts to which the message alluded, as follows :

MR. DOUGLAS—I desire to offer a resolution, calling for information which will hasten our action on the Kansas question. I will read it for information; but if it gives rise to debate, of course it will go over :

Resolved—That the President be requested to furnish all the information within his possession or control on the following points :

1. The return and votes for and against a convention at an election held in the Territory of Kansas, in October, 1856.

2. The census and registration of votes in the Territory of Kansas, under the provisions of the act of the said legislature, passed in February, 1857, providing for the election of delegates and assembling a convention to frame a constitution.

3. The returns of an election held in said Territory on the 21st of December, 1857, under the schedule of the Lecompton constitution, upon the question of "constitution with slavery" or "constitution without slavery."

4. The returns of an election held in the Territory of Kansas on the 4th day of January, 1858, under the authority of a law passed by the legislature of said Territory, submitting the constitution formed by the Lecompton convention to a vote of the people for ratification or rejection.

5. The returns of the election held in said Territory on the 4th day of January, 1858, under the schedule of the Lecompton constitution, for Governor and other State officers, and for members of the legislature, specifying the names of each officer to whom a certificate of election has been accorded, and the number of votes cast and counted for each candidate, and distinguishing between the votes returned within the time and in the mode provided in said schedule, and those returned subsequently and in other modes, and stating whether at either of said elections any returns of votes were rejected in consequence of not having been returned in time, or to the right officer, or in proper form, or for any other cause, stating specifically for what cause.

6. All correspondence between any of the Executive departments and Secretary or Governor Denver relating to Kansas affairs, and which has not been communicated to the Senate.

Resolved—That in the event all the information desired in the foregoing resolution is not now in the possession of the President, or of any of the Executive departments, he be respectfully requested to give the proper orders and take the necessary steps to procure the same for the use of the Senate.

MR. SLIDELL objected, and the resolutions, under the rules, were laid over.

MINORITY REPORT ON KANSAS AFFAIRS.

The majority of the Committee on Territories being in favor of the admission of Kansas under the Lecompton constitution, submitted through Mr. Green a report to that effect. On the same day, February 18, 1858, Mr. Douglas submitted a Minority Report, which will be found in a subsequent part of this work.

This report is a most vigorous argument, showing that there was no evidence that the Lecompton constitution was the act of the people of Kansas, or that it embodied their will; that the right of admission accrued to a Territory only when they had sufficient population; that the President and his cabinet had solemnly assured the people of Kansas that the constitution should be submitted to them for their free acceptance or rejection; that the 60 delegates composing the Lecompton convention were chosen by 19 of the 38 counties of the Territory, while the other 18 counties were entirely disfranchised; he tears away the thin veil that covered the designs of the members of the Lecompton convention, and shows that while knowing that an immense majority of the people of Kansas were opposed to the introduction of slavery they yet determined that they *would* form a constitution sanctioning slavery, and submit it in such a form as to render it impossible for them to reject it; that the election held in Kansas on the 21st of December, 1857, was not valid and binding on the people of the Territory, for the reason that it was not held in pursuance of any law; that the election of January 4, 1858, was lawful and valid, having been fairly conducted under a valid law of the Territorial legislature; and that there was a majority of 10,000 votes against the Lecompton constitution.

DEBATE ON LECOMPTON.

During the month of March, 1858, the proposition to admit Kansas under the Lecompton constitution was warmly debated in the Senate. On the 22d, Mr. Douglas made a speech which was one of the ablest efforts of his life, and will be read with interest and admiration, as long as a vestige of the political history of the Union exists. In this speech, after a rapid and brief review of his course in Congress, he shows that it was the chief merit of the Compromise measures of 1850, that they provided a rule of action which should apply everywhere, north and south of 36° 30′, not only to the territories we then had, but to all we might afterward acquire; and thus prevent all strife and agitation in future. He shows that the Lecompton constitution is not the act and deed of the people of Kansas, and does not embody their will. In concluding, he alludes to the approaching termination of his senatorial term, and to the efforts that the Executive would make to prevent his reëlection. In tones that rang through the Senate chamber clear and sonorous as the blast of a trumpet, he gave utterance to these noble sentiments:

"I do not recognize the right of the President to tell me my duty in the Senate chamber. When the time comes that a Senator is to account to the Executive, and not to his State, what becomes of the sovereignty of the States? Is it intended to brand every Democrat as a traitor who is opposed to the Lecompton constitution? Come what may, I intend to vote, speak, and act, according to my own sense of duty. I have no vindication to make of my course. Let it speak for itself. Neither the frowns of power nor the influence of patronage will change my action, or drive me from my principles. I stand immovably upon the principles of State Sovereignty, upon which the campaign was fought and the election won. I will stand by the Constitution of the United States, with all its compromises, and perform all my obligations under it. If I shall be driven into private life, it is a fate that has no terrors for me. I prefer private life, preserving my own self-respect, to abject and servile submission to executive will. If the alternative be private life, or servile obedience to executive will, I am prepared to retire. Official position has no charms for me, when deprived of freedom of thought and action."

We give this great speech entire in a subsequent part of this work. It was delivered in the evening, the Senate chamber being brilliantly illuminated, and the galleries crowded, many ladies being admitted to seats on the floor of the Senate.

On the next day, however, March 23, the bill admitting Kansas into the Union under the Lecompton constitution, passed the Senate by a vote of 33 to 25. Previous to taking this vote, Mr. Crittenden, of Kentucky, moved a substitute for the bill, to the effect that the Constitution be submitted to the people of Kansas at once; and if approved, the State to be admitted by the President's proclamation. If rejected, the people to call a convention and frame a constitution to be submitted to the popular vote. Special provisions made against frauds at elections. The substitute was lost—yeas 24, nays 34.

On the first of April, the bill as passed was taken up in the House of Representatives, and Mr. Montgomery, of Pennsylvania, offered, as a substitue, the same one proposed by Mr. Crittenden. This was adopted in the House, ayes 120, nays, 112.

THE ENGLISH BILL.

The Senate refused to concur in this substitute, and a committee of conference was appointed by each House, who reported what has since been known as the English bill, which passed both Houses of Congress, and became a law. But in the debate in the Senate on the Crittenden-Montgomery amendment, Mr. Douglas spoke in its favor and against the English bill, and in the course of his remarks said :

"I had hoped that the principle of self-government in the Territories, the great principle of popular sovereignty which we all profess to cherish, on which all our institutions are founded, would have been carried out in good faith in Kansas. I believe, sir, that if the amendment inserted by the House of Representatives be concurred in by the Senate to-day, and become the law of the land, the great principle of popular sovereignty, on which all our institutions rest, will receive a complete triumph, and there will be peace and quiet and fraternal feeling all over this country.

" We are told that this vexed question ought to be settled ; that the country is exhausted with strife and controversy ; and that peace should be restored by the admission of Kansas. Sir, why not admit it ? You can admit it in one hour, and restore peace to the country, if you will concur with with the House of Representatives in what is called the Crittenden amendment. This amendment provides that Kansas is admitted into the Union on the fundamental condition precedent that the constitution be submitted to the people for ratification, and if assented to by them, it becomes their constitution ; if not assented to, they are to proceed to make one to suit themselves, and the President is to declare the result, and Kansas is to be in the Union without further legislation. Concur with the House of Representatives, and your action is final ; Kansas is in the Union, with the right to make her constitution to suit herself ; and there is an end to the whole controversy."

The English bill, as passed, will be found in a subsequent part of this work.

On the 29th of April, Mr. Douglas again addressed the Senate on the same general subject, with more particular reference to the English bill, for the admission of Kansas, which had passed the House of Representatives. In this speech, he says :

Mr. President : I have carefully examined the bill reported by the committee of conference as a substitute for the House amendment to the Senate bill for the admission of Kansas, with an anxious desire to find in it such provisions as would enable me to give it my support. I had hoped that, after the disagreement of the two houses upon this question, some plan, some form of bill, could have been agreed upon, which would harmonize and quiet the country, and reunite those who agree in principle and in political action on this great question, so as to take it out of Congress. I am not able, in the bill which is now under consideration, to find that the principle for which I have contended is fairly carried out. The position, and the sole position, upon which I have stood in this whole controversy, has been that the people of Kansas, and of each other Territory, in forming a constitution for admission into the Union as a State, should be left perfectly free to form and mold their domestic institutions and organic act in their own way, without coercion on the one side, or any improper or undue influence on the other.

The question now arises, is there such a submission of the Lecompton constitution as brings it fairly within that principle ? In terms, the constitution is not submitted at all; but yet we are told that it amounts to a submission, because there is a land grant attached to it, and they are permitted to vote for the land grant, or against the land grant; and, if they accept the land grant, then they are required to take the constitution with it; and, if they reject the land grant, it shall be held and deemed a decision against coming into the Union under the Lecompton constitution. Hence it has been argued in one portion of the Union that this is a submission of the constitution, and in another portion that it is not. We are to be told that submission is popular sovereignty in one section, and submission in another section is not popular sovereignty.

Sir, I had hoped that when we came finally to adjust this question, we should have been able to employ language so clear, so unequivocal, that there would have been no room for doubt as to what was meant, and what the line of policy was to be in the future. Are these people left free to take or reject the Lecompton constitution ? If they accept the land grant they are compelled to take it. If they reject the land grant, they are out of the Union. Sir, I have no special objection to the land grant as it is. I think it is a fair one, and if they had put this further addition, that if they refused to come in under the Lecompton constitution with the land grant, they might proceed to form a new constitution, and that they should then have the same amount of lands, there would have been no bounty held out for coming in under the Lecompton constitution; but when the law gives them the six million acres in the event they take this constitution, and does not indicate what they are to have in the event they reject it, and wait until they can form another, I submit the question whether there is not an inducement, a bounty held out to influence these people to vote for this Lecompton constitution?

It may be said that when they attain the ninety-three thousand population, or if they wait until after 1860, if they acquired the population required by the then ratio—which may be one hundred and ten thousand or one hundred and twenty thousand—and form a constitution under it, we shall give then the same amount of land that is now given by this grant. That may be so, and may not be so. I believe it will be so; and yet in the House bill, for which this is a substitute, the provision was that they should have this same amount of land, whether they came in under the Lecompton constitution or whether they formed a new constitution. There was no doubt, no uncertainty left in regard to what were to be their rights under the land grant, whether they took the one constitution or the other. Hence that proposition was a fair submission, without any penalties on the one side, or any bounty or special favor or privilege on the other to influence their action. In this view of the case, I am not able to arrive at the conclusion that this is a fair submission either of the question of the constitution itself, or of admission into the Union under the constitution and the proposition submitted by this bill.

There is a further contingency. In the event that they reject this constitution, they are to stay out of the Union until they shall attain the requisite population for a member of Congress, according to the then ratio of representation in the other House. I have no objection to making it a general rule that Territories shall be kept out until they have the requisite population. I have proposed it over and over again. I am willing to agree to it and make it applicable to Kansas if you will make it a general rule. But, sir, it is one thing to adopt that rule as a general rule and adhere to it in all cases, and and it is a very different, and a very distinct thing, to provide that if they will take this constitution, which the people have shown that they abhor, they may come in with forty thousand people, but if they do not, they shall stay out until they get ninety thousand; thus discriminating between the different character of institutions that may be formed. I submit the question whether it is not congressional intervention, when you provide that a Territory may come in with one kind of constitution with forty thousand, and with a different kind of constitution, not until she gets ninety thousand, or one hundred and twenty thousand? It is intervention with inducements to control the result. It is intervention with a bounty on the one side and a penalty on the other. I ask, are we prepared to construe the great principle of popular sovereignty in such a manner as will recognize the right of Congress to intervene and control the decision that the people may make on this question?

I do not think that this bill brings the question within that principle which I have held dear, and in defence of which I have stood here for the last five months, battling against the large majority of my political friends, and in defence of which I intend to stand as long as I have any association or connection with the politics of the country.

Mr. President, I say now, as I am about to take leave of this subject, that I never can consent to violate that great principle of State equality, of State sovereignty, of popular sovereignty, by any discrimination, either in the one direction or in the other. My position is taken. I know not what its consequences will be per

sonally to me. I will not inquire what those consequences may be.
If I cannot remain in public life, holding firmly, immovably, to the
great principle of self-government and state equality, I shall go into
private life, where I can preserve the respect of my own conscience
under the conviction that I have done my duty and followed the
principle wherever its logical consequences carried me.

SUBSEQUENT AFFAIRS OF KANSAS.

On the next day, however, April 30, the Senate passed the
English bill. So far as the action of Congress was concerned,
Kansas was admitted: that is, provided the people there
chose to come in under the English bill.

But they did not so choose. In order to give complete-
ness to this view of affairs in Kansas, we will state, though in
doing so we greatly anticipate the order of time, that when
the election took place, under the provisions of the English
bill, the people of Kansas indignantly rejected the propositions of the bill, and at the election held on the 3d of August,
1858, trampled the odious Lecompton constitution under
their feet, by a majority of 10,000 votes. Soon after the
election, Gov. Denver resigned, and Samuel Medary of Ohio
was appointed governor. The Territorial legislature met in
January, 1859, repealed many of the laws of the previous
session, passed a new apportionment act; and an act referring
to the people the question of a new constitutional convention,
the election to be held March 21. The people decided for a
constitutional convention by a majority of 3,881. The convention met at Wyandot, on the 5th of July, 1859, and
adopted a constitution by a small majority, the minority protesting against its adoption.

MR. DOUGLAS ON BRITISH AGGRESSION.

On the 29th of May, 1858, Mr. Douglas addressed the Senate,
on the general subject of the recent British aggression on

our ships, in a speech which made a most powerful impression, not only on the Senate, but on the whole country. He ridiculed the idea of simply passing resolutions on the subject; and urged the importance, nay, the necessity, of at once adopting such energetic measures as should convince England that the time had come at last when this nation would no longer submit to her aggressions. He urged that the President of the United States should be clothed with power to punish instantly and effectually, all outrages on our flag, as soon as committed: " confer the power, and hold him responsible for its abuse." He showed that the President of the United States was utterly powerless abroad, and that unless some such measures as he proposed should be adopted, the outrages of Great Britain would be continued. He then proceeded to prove, from his own observation, that the coast of America was not defenceless; that indeed, the coast of the United States is in a better condition of defence than that of Great Britain ; that New York was at this day better defended than London or Liverpool: and that it is easier for a hostile fleet to enter the harbor of either of those cities than the harbor of New York.

" While I am opposed to war," said Mr. Douglas, " while I have no idea of any breach of the peace with England, yet, I confess to you, sir, if war should come by her act, and not ours ; by her invasion of our rights, and our vindication of the same; I would administer to every citizen and every child Hannibal's oath of eternal hostility as long as the English flag waved, or their government claimed a foot of land upon the American continent, or the adjacent islands. Sir, I would make it a war that would settle our disputes forever, not only of the right of search upon the seas, but the right to tread with a hostile foot upon the soil of the American continent or its appendages."

The reader will find the whole of this eloquent and patriotic speech, in a subsequent part of this work. It electrified the whole nation. Men breathed freer and easier when they read it: and no one with a spark of American feeling in his breast failed to respond to the noble sentiments of the gallant senator from Illinois.

CHAPTER XIII.

Mr. Douglas returns to Chicago—Brilliant Reception—Makes his Speech opening the Campaign—Lays down Principles on which he conducted it.

SOON after Congress adjourned, in June, 1858, Mr. Douglas returned to Illinois to engage in his canvass for reëlection to the Senate, and to vindicate the line of policy which he had felt it his duty to pursue. He arrived at Chicago on the 9th of July, and was welcomed by such a reception as no public man has ever received in this country. The newspapers of that city, of all shades of political opinions, concur in representing it as one of the most magnificent orations on record. Many columns of their sheets were filled with descriptions of the arrangements for the reception, the vast concourse of people—estimated at 30,000—the processions, illumination of houses, fireworks, banners, cannon, etc., etc., which greeted Mr. Douglas' return to his home.

The great event of this imposing pageant, however, was the speech of Mr. Douglas, in reply to the address of welcome. After an appropriate and feeling acknowledgment of the honor done him in this grand testimonial, he proceeded to a discussion of the principles involved in the great controversy in which he was engaged. As this was the opening speech of the canvass, and clearly defines the principles on which it was afterward conducted through a series of more than one hundred joint and separate debates, we shall make such copious extracts as may enable the reader to understand the points in issue in that memorable campaign.

PRINCIPLES OF SELF-GOVERNMENT, AS APPLICABLE TO THE
LECOMPTON CONSTITUTION.

If there is any one principle dearer and more sacred than all others in
free governments, it is that which asserts the exclusive right of a free people to form and adopt their own fundamental law, and to manage and
regulate their own internal affairs and domestic institutions. (Applause.)
When I found an effort being made, during the recent session of Congress, to force a constitution upon the people of Kansas against their will,
and to force that State into the Union with a constitution which her people
had rejected by more than 10,000 majority, I felt bound, as a man of
honor and a representative of Illinois, bound by every consideration of
duty, of fidelity, and of patriotism, to resist to the utmost of my power the
consummation of what I deemed fraud. (Cheers.) With others I did
resist it, and resisted it successfully until the attempt was abandoned.
(Great applause.) We forced them to refer that constitution back to the
people of Kansas, to be accepted or rejected, as they shall decide at an
election, which is fixed for the first Monday of August next. It is true
that the mode of reference and the form of the submission was not such as
I could sanction with my vote, for the reason that it discriminated between
free States and slave States; providing that if Kansas consented to come
in under the Lecompton constitution it should be received with a population of 35,000; but if she demanded another constitution, more consistent
with the sentiments of her people and their feelings, that it should not be
received into the Union until she had 93,420 inhabitants. (Cries of "hear,
hear," and cheers.) I did not consider that mode of submission fair, for
the reason that any election is a mockery which is not free—that any election is a fraud upon the rights of the people which holds out inducements
for affirmative votes, and threatens penalties for negative votes. (Hear,
hear.) But whilst I was not satisfied with the mode of submission, whilst
I resisted it to the last, demanding a fair, a just, a free mode of submission,
still, when the law passed placing it within the power of the people of
Kansas at that election to reject the Lecompton constitution, and then
make another in harmony with their principles and their opinions (Bravo,
and applause), I did not believe that either the penalties on the one hand,
or the inducements on the other, would prevail on that people to accept a
constitution to which they are irreconcilably opposed. (Cries of "glorious," and renewed applause.) All I can say is, that if their votes can be
controlled by such considerations, all the sympathy which has been

expended upon them has been misplaced, and all the efforts that have been made in defence of their right to self-government have been made in an unworthy cause. (Cheers.)

NO RIGHT TO FORCE EVEN A GOOD THING ON AN UNWILLING PEOPLE.

I will be entirely frank with you. My object was to secure the right of the people of each State and of each Territory, North or South, to decide the question for themselves, to have slavery or not, just as they choose; and my opposition to the Lecompton constitution *was not predicated upon the ground that it was a pro-slavery Constitution* (cheers), nor would my action have been different had it been a free-soil Constitution. My speech against it was made on the 9th of December, while the vote on the slavery clause in that Constitution was not taken until the 21st of the same month, nearly two weeks after. I made my speech solely on the ground that it was a violation of the fundamental principles of free government; on the ground that it was not the act and deed of the people of Kansas; that it did not embody their will; that they were averse to it; and hence I denied the right of Congress to force it upon them, either as a free State or a slave State. (Bravo.) I deny the right of Congress to force a slaveholding State upon an unwilling people. (Cheers.) I deny their right to force a free State upon an unwilling people. (Cheers.) I deny their right to force a good thing upon a people who are unwilling to receive it. (Cries of "Good, good," and cheers.) The great principle is the right of every community to judge and decide for itself whether a thing is right or wrong, whether it would be good or evil for them to adopt it; and the right of free action, the right of free thought, the right of free judgment upon the question is dearer to every true American than any other under a free government. My objection to the Lecompton contrivance was that it undertook to put a constitution on the people of Kansas against their will, in opposition to their wishes, and thus violated the great principle upon which all our institutions rest. It is no answer to this argument to say that slavery is an evil, and hence should not be tolerated. You must allow the people to decide for themselves whether it is a good or an evil. You allow them to decide for themselves whether they desire a Maine liquor law or not; you allow them to decide for themselves what kind of common schools they will have; what system of banking they will adopt, or whether they will adopt any at all; you allow them to decide for themselves the relations between husband and wife,

parent and child, and guardian and ward; in fact, you allow them to decide for themselves all other questions, and why not upon this question? (Cheers.) Whenever you put a limitation upon the right of any
people to decide what laws they want, you have destroyed the fundamental principle of self-government. (Cheers).

ORIGIN OF THE IRREPRESSIBLE CONFLICT.

The Republican convention which nominated Mr. Lincoln
for United States senator in opposition to Mr. Douglas, was
held in the city of Springfield, on the 15th of June, 1858.
Immediately after Mr. Lincoln's unanimous nomination was
announced, he read to the convention a carefully elaborated
speech accepting the nomination which he had prepared in
anticipation of that event, and which was published for circulation by order of the convention, as an authoritative exposition of the principles of the Republican party. Mr.
Douglas referring to this speech, said :

Mr. Lincoln made a speech before that Republican convention which
unanimously nominated him for the Senate—a speech evidently well prepared and carefully written—in which he states the basis upon which he
proposes to carry on the campaign during this summer. In it he lays down
two distinct propositions which I shall notice, and upon which I shall take
a direct and bold issue with him. (Cries of "Good, good," and great
applause).

His first and main proposition I will give in his own language, Scripture quotation and all (laughter). I give his exact language :

"In my opinion it [the slavery agitation] will not cease until a crisis shall
have been reached and passed. 'A house divided against itself cannot stand.'
I believe this government cannot endure permanently half slave and half free.
I do not expect the house to fall, but I do expect it will cease to be divided. It
will become all one thing or all the other. Either the opponents of slavery will
arrest the further spread of it, and place it where the public mind shall rest in
the belief that it is in the course of ultimate extinction, or its advocates will
push forward till it shall become alike lawful in all the States—old as well as
new, North as well as South."

In other words, Mr. Lincoln asserts as a fundamental principle of this
government, that there must be uniformity in the local laws and domestic
institutions of each and all the States of the Union; and he therefore in-

vites all the non-slaveholding States to band together, organize as one body, and make war upon slavery in Kentucky, upon slavery in Virginia, upon slavery in the Carolinas, upon slavery in all the slaveholding States in this Union, and to persevere in that war until it shall be exterminated. He then notified the slaveholding States to stand together as a unit and make an aggressive war upon the free States of this Union with a view of establishing slavery in them all; of forcing it upon Illinois, of forcing it upon New York, upon New England, and upon every other free State, and that they shall keep up the warfare until it has been formally established in them all. In other words, Mr. Lincoln advocates boldly and clearly a war of sections, a war of the North against the South, of the free States against the slave States—a war of extermination—to be continued relentlessly, until the one or the other shall be subdued and all the States shall either become free or become slave.

Now, my friends, I must say to you frankly, that I take bold, unqualified issue with him upon that principle. I assert that it is neither desirable nor possible that there should be uniformity in the local institutions and domestic regulations of the different States of this Union. The framers of our government never contemplated uniformity in its internal concerns. The fathers of the Revolution, and the sages who made the Constitution, well understood that the laws and domestic institutions which would suit the granite hills of New Hampshire, would be totally unfit for the rice plantations of South Carolina (cheers); they well understood that the laws which would suit the agricultural districts of Pennsylvania and New York, would be totally unfit for the large mining regions of the Pacific, or the lumber regions of Maine. (Bravo.) They well understood that the great varieties of soil, of production, and of interests, in a republic as large as this, required different local and domestic regulations in each locality, adapted to the wants and interests of each separate State (cries of "bravo" and "good,") and for that reason it was provided in the federal Constitution that the thirteen original States should remain sovereign and supreme within their own limits in regard to all that was local, and internal, and domestic, while the Federal Government should have certain specified powers which were general and national, and could be exercised only by the federal authority. (Cheers).

IF UNIFORMITY WERE EITHER DESIRABLE OR POSSIBLE, HOW IS IT TO BE ACCOMPLISHED?

How could this uniformity be accomplished if it were desirable and possible? There is but one mode in which it could be obtained, and that must be by abolishing the State legislatures, blotting out State sovereignty, merging the rights and sovereignty of the States in one consolidated empire, and vesting Congress with the plenary power to make all the police regulations, domestic and local laws, uniform throughout the limits of the Republic. When you shall have done this you will have uniformity. Then the States will all be slave or all be free; then negroes will be free everywhere or nowhere; then you will have a Maine liquor law in every State or none; then you will have uniformity in all things local and domestic by the authority of the Federal Government. But, when you attain that uniformity you will have converted these thirty-two sovereign, independent States into one consolidated empire, with the uniformity of disposition reigning triumphant throughout the length and breadth of the land. ("Hear," "hear," "bravo," and great applause.)

From this view of the case, my friends, I am driven irresistibly to the conclusion that diversity, dissimilarity, variety in all our local and domestic institutions, is the great safeguard of our liberties; and that the framers of our institutions were wise, sagacious, and patriotic when they made this government a confederation of sovereign States with a legislature for each, and conferred upon each legislature the power to make all local and domestic institutions to suit the people it represented, without interference from any other State or from the general Congress of the Union. If we expect to maintain our liberties we must preserve the rights and sovereignty of the States, we must maintain and carry out that great principle of self-government incorporated in the Compromise measures of 1850; indorsed by the Illinois legislature in 1851; emphatically embodied and carried out in the Kansas-Nebraska Bill, and vindicated this year by the refusal to bring Kansas into the Union with a constitution distasteful to her people. (Cheers.)

NO CRUSADE AGAINST THE SUPREME COURT—THE DRED SCOTT DECISION THE LAW OF THE LAND AND MUST BE OBEYED.

The other proposition discussed by Mr. Lincoln in his speech consists in a crusade against the Supreme Court of the United States on account of the Dred Scott decision. On this question, also, I desire to say to you unequivocally, that I take direct and distinct issue with him. I have no warfare to make on the Supreme Court of the United States (Bravo), either on account of that or any other decision which they have pronounced from that bench. ("Good, good," and enthusiastic applause.) The Constitution of the United States has provided that the powers of government (and the constitution of each State has the same provision) shall be divided into three departments, executive, legislative and judicial. The right and the province of expounding the Constitution, and construing the law, is vested in the judiciary, established by the Constitution. As a lawyer, I feel at liberty to appear before the court and controvert any principle of law while the question is pending before the tribunal ; but when the decision is made, my private opinion, your opinion, all other opinions must yield to the majesty of that authoritative adjudication. (Cries of " it is right," " good, good," and cheers.) I wish you to bear in mind that this involves a great principle, upon which our rights, and our liberty and our property all depend. What security have you for your property, for your reputation, and for your personal rights, if the courts are not upheld, and their decisions respected when once firmly rendered by the highest tribunal known to the Constitution ? (Cheers.) I do not choose, therefore, to go into any argument with Mr. Lincoln in reviewing the various decisions which the Supreme Court has made, either upon the Dred Scott case, or any other. I have no idea of appealing from the decision of the Supreme Court upon a constitutional question to a tumultuous town-meeting. (Cheers.) I am aware that once an eminent lawyer of this city, now no more, said that the State of Illinois had the most perfect judicial system in the world, subject to but one exception, which could be cured by a slight amendment, and that amendment was to so change the law as to allow an appeal from the decisions of the Supreme Court of Illinois, on all constitutional questions, to two justices of the peace. (Great laughter and applause.) My friend, Mr. Lincoln, who sits behind me, reminds me that that proposition was made when I was judge of the Supreme Court. Be that as it may, I do not think that fact adds any greater weight or authority to the suggestion. (Renewed laughter and applause.) It matters not with me who was on the bench, whether Mr. Lincoln or myself, whether a Lockwood or a Smith, a Taney or a Marshall ; the decision of the highest tribunal known to the Constitution of the country must be final until it has been reversed by an equally high authority. (Cries of "bravo" and applause.) Hence, I am opposed to this doctrine of Mr. Lincoln, by which he proposes to take an appeal from the decision of the Supreme Court of the United States upon these high constitutional questions to a Republican caucus. (A voice—"Call it Freesoil," and cheers.) Yes, or to any other caucus or town-meeting, whether it be Republican, American, or Democratic. (Cheers.) I respect the decisions of that august tribunal; I shall always bow in deference to them. I am a law-abiding man. I will sustain the Constitution of my country as our fathers have made it. I will yield obedience to the laws, whether I like them or not, as I find them on the statute book. I will sustain the judicial tribunals and constituted authorities in all matters within the pale of their jurisdiction, as defined by the Constitution. (Applause.)

OURS A WHITE MAN'S GOVERNMENT—NEGROES NOT CITIZENS.

But I am equally free to say that the reason assigned by Mr. Lincoln for resisting the decision of the Supreme Court in the Dred Scott case does not in itself meet my approbation. He objects to it because that decision declared that a negro descended from African parents who were brought here and sold as slaves, is not, and cannot be, a citizen of the United States. He says it is wrong, because it deprives the negro of the benefits of that clause of the Constitution which says that citizens of one State shall enjoy all the privileges and immunities of citizens of the several States; in other words, he thinks it wrong because it deprives the negro of the privileges, immunities, and rights of citizenship, which pertain, according to that decision, only to the white man. [I am free to say to you that in my opinion this government of ours is founded on the white basis. (Great applause.) It was made by the white man, for the benefit of the white man, to be administered by white men, in such a manner as they should determine. (Cheers.) It is also true that a negro, or any other man of an inferior race to a white man, should be permitted to enjoy, and humanity requires that he should have all the rights, privileges and immunities which he is capable of exercising consistent with the safety of society. I would give him every right and every privilege which his capacity would enable him to enjoy, consistent with the good of the society in which he lived. ("Bravo.") But you may ask me what are these rights and these privileges. My answer is that each State must decide for itself the nature and extent of these rights. ("Hear, hear," and applause.) . Illinois has 'ecided for herself. We have decided that the negro shall not be a slave, and we have at the same time decided that he shall not vote, or serve on juries, or enjoy political privileges. I am content with that system of policy which we have adopted for ourselves. (Cheers.) I deny the right of any other State to complain of our policy in that respect, or to interfere with it, or to attempt to change it. On the other hand, the State of Maine

STEPHEN A. DOUGLAS.   145

has decided, as she had a right to under the Dred Scott decision, that in that State a negro may vote on an equality with the white man. The sovereign power of Maine had the right to prescribe that rule for herself. Illinois has no right to complain of Maine for conferring the right upon negro suffrage, nor has Maine any right to interfere with, or complain of, Illinois because she has denied negro suffrage. ("That's so," and cheers.) The State of New York has decided by her constitution that a negro may vote, provided that he owns $250 worth of property, but not otherwise. The rich negro can vote, but the poor one cannot. (Laughter.) Although that distinction does not commend itself to my judgment, yet I assert that the sovereign power of New York had a right to prescribe that form of the elective franchise. Kentucky, Virginia, and other States have provided that negroes, or a certain class of them in those States, shall be slaves, having neither civil nor political rights. Without indorsing or condemning the wisdom of that decision, I assert that Virginia has the same power, by virtue of her sovereignty, to protect slavery within her limits as Illinois has to banish it forever from our borders. ("Hear, hear," and applause.) I assert the right of each State to decide for itself on all these questions, and I do not subscribe to the doctrine of my friend, Mr. Lincoln, that uniformity is either desirable or possible. I do not acknowledge that the States must all be free or must all be slave.

I do not acknowledge that the negro must have civil and political rights everywhere or nowhere. I do not acknowledge that the Chinese must have the same rights in California that we would confer upon him here. I do not acknowledge that the Coolie imported into this country must necessarily be put upon an equality with the white race. I do not acknowledge any of these doctrines of uniformity in the local and domestic regulations in the different States. ("Bravo," and cheers.)

Thus you see, my fellow-citizens, that the issues between Mr. Lincoln and myself, as respective candidates for the U. S. Senate, as made up, are direct, unequivocal, and irreconcilable. He goes for uniformity in our domestic institutions, for a war of sections, until one or the other shall be subdued. I go for the great principle of the Kansas-Nebraska Bill, the right of the people to decide for themselves. (Senator Douglas was here interrupted by the wildest applause; cheer after cheer rent the air; the band struck up "Yankee Doodle;" rockets and pieces of fireworks blazed forth; and the enthusiasm was so intense and universal that it was some time before order could be restored and Mr. Douglas resume. The scene at this period was glorious beyond description.)

STANDS BY THE DEMOCRATIC ORGANIZATION AND THE CINCIN-
NATI PLATFORM.

My friends, you see that the issues are distinctly drawn. I stand by the
same platform that I have so often proclaimed to you and to the people of
Illinois heretofore. (Cries of "That's true," and applause.) I stand by the
Democratic organization, yield obedience to its usages, and support its
regular nominations. (Intense enthusiasm.) I indorse and approve the
Cincinnati platform (renewed applause), and I adhere to and intend to
carry out as part of that platform the great principle of self-government,
which recognizes the right of the people in each State and Territory to
decide for themselves their domestic institutions. ("Good, good," and
cheers.)

In conclusion, he denounces the "unholy alliance:"

Fellow-citizens, you now have before you the outlines of the propositions
which I intend to discuss before the people of Illinois during the pending
campaign. I have spoken without preparation, and in a very desultory
manner, and may have omitted some points which I desired to discuss,
and may have been less explicit on others than I could have wished. I
have made up my mind to appeal to the people against the combination
which has been made against me. (Enthusiastic applause.) The Republican leaders have formed an alliance, an unholy, unnatural alliance, with a
portion of the federal officeholders. I intend to fight that allied army
wherever I meet them. (Cheers.) I know they deny the alliance while
avowing the common purpose; but yet these men who are trying to divide
the Democratic party for the purpose of electing a Republican senator in
my place, are just as much the agents, the tools, the supporters of Mr.
Lincoln as if they were avowed Republicans, and expect their reward for
their services when the Republicans come into power. (Cries of "That is
true," and cheers.) I shall deal with these allied forces just as the Russians dealt with the allies at Sebastopol. The Russians when they fired a
broadside at the common enemy did not stop to inquire whether it hit a
Frenchman, an Englishman or a Turk, nor will I stop (laughter and great
applause), nor shall I stop to inquire whether my blows hit the Republican
leaders or their allies, who are holding the federal offices and yet acting in
concert with the Republicans to defeat the Democratic party and its nominees. (Cheers, and cries of "Bravo.") I do not include all of the federal
officeholders in this remark. Such of them as are Democrats and show

their Democracy by remaining inside of the Democratic organization and supporting its nominees, I recognize as Democrats, but those who, having been defeated inside of the organization, go outside and attempt to divide and destroy the party in concert with the Republican leaders, have ceased to be Democrats, and belong to the allied army whose avowed object is to elect the Republican ticket by dividing and destroying the Democratic party. (Cheers.)

Immediately after his reception at Chicago, Mr. Douglas entered actively on his canvass over the entire State, making more than one hundred speeches in less than four months, and enduring an unparalleled amount of physical exertion and fatigue. History fails to cite any public man who ever received such continued ovations at the hands of his people as greeted Mr. Douglas all through his Illinois campaign. We make room for a letter which appeared in one of the Chicago papers of the day, descriptive of his journey from that city to Bloomington, to fill his first appointment, with the remark that the same demonstrations of popular enthusiasm and manifestations of popular admiration and love met Mr. Douglas everywhere through his canvass. The picture of the correspondent does but bare justice to the facts as they existed.

SENATOR DOUGLAS AMONG THE PEOPLE—PASSAGE FROM CHICAGO TO SPRINGFIELD—GREAT ENTHUSIASM ALONG THE LINE OF THE ST. LOUIS AND ALTON RAILROAD—GLORIOUS DEMONSTRATIONS OF THE POPULAR FEELING.

BLOOMINGTON, *July* 16, 1858.

If there was ever any doubt that Senator Douglas possessed the popular heart of the people of Illinois, that doubt has been dispelled to-day. His passage from Chicago to this place has been a perfect ovation. There was not a station or cottage that the train passed from which there was not a greeting and a "God speed" sent forth; and the evidences of popular feeling evinced in his favor are conclusive that the result in November will be one of the most glorious triumphs of the Democracy ever achieved in this State.

Senator Douglas, as you are aware, left Chicago in the 9 o'clock train this morning, on the St. Louis, Alton and Chicago Railroad, to meet an appointment which he made at Springfield for to-morrow. The train which bore him was tastefully decorated with flags, the engine being almost hid beneath them, and banners were also displayed on the cars with the inscription "Stephen A. Douglas, the Champion of Popular Sovereignty." As the train passed along, the crowds who had assembled to give a parting cheer to the "Little Giant" performed their labor of love energetically and well. The train was soon out of Chicago and flying along the track; and now Mr. Douglas, having a few moments to devote to those "on board," shook hands and exchanged compliments with a number of impatient passengers who crowded around him, anxious to evince their respect and high admiration of the man.

As the train swept through Bridgeport, the employees of the road stationed there had assembled together, and greeted Senator Douglas with three hearty cheers.

A little incident occurred as we passed Bridgeport which is perhaps worthy of notice. One of the flags with which the train was decorated caught on the branches of a tree, and a gentleman seeing it, exclaimed, "See, Judge Douglas, there is one of your flags waving from that tree." "Yes," replied the Judge, "and before this campaign is over, my flags will be seen waving from every tree in the State."

At every station on the road—at Brighton Course, Summit, Athens and Lockport—the people were out waiting an opportunity to testify their respect to their patriot senator; and not a little interest was added to these demonstrations by the number of pretty girls and blooming matrons who took part in them, and testified by the waving of handkerchiefs and smiles of approval that there was one besides their lovers and husbands who had a place in their hearts.

As the train approached Joliet, the shrill whistle of the engine to "break up" was answered by the roar of artillery from the town; and when we reached the station, about 11 o'clock, we found some four or five hundred people awaiting us. The thunders of the guns were answered by the cheers of welcome by the crowd, who pressed around the cars anxious to get a glimpse of Senator Douglas. There being a delay at this place of twenty minutes for dinner, the senator spent it in shaking hands with and receiving the congratulations of those who had assembled to see him. The beaming countenances of the sturdy yeomanry, whose faces were lighted up with joy at meeting the man whom they delighted to honor, showed that the heart felt what the mouth uttered. One fine looking specimen of human nature, whose strong, sturdy frame, and sunburnt healthy cheek, bore testimony to his having spent the best part of his days in the open air, exclaimed, after shaking hands with the senator, "By G—d, that did me good!"

At Joliet, a platform car, decorated with thirteen flags, and bearing a twelve-pounder and gun-carriage, was hitched on to the train, and after we left that town, as we approached each station, "Popular Sovereignty," as the gun was called, gave lively notice that we were on hand. At Elwood, a crowd was awaiting us, and as the train passed through, cheer after cheer went up, whilst two or three individuals expressed their enthusiasm by the discharge of their revolvers.

As the train approached Wilmington, "Popular Sovereignty's" note was echoed by a piece of artillery in the town, and as we reached the station, we found the citizens, accompanied by a fine brass band, awaiting Senator Douglas. The cars had hardly stopped, when a gentleman, whose head was silvered o'er with age, jumped on the train, and seizing Senator Douglas by the hand, cried, "Welcome, Judge Douglas, welcome to Wilmington," and then three hearty cheers, such as only the farmers of the Prairie State can give, rose in the air, and the people crowded around to shake Mr. Douglas by the hand. The train was delayed here several minutes, in order to afford the people an opportunity of seeing their senator.

At all the other stations—Stewart's Grove, Gardner, Dwight, Odell, Cayuga, Pontiac, Rook Creek, Peoria Junction, Lexington, and Towanda, the people were out awaiting the train, and greeted Senator Douglas with loud hurrahs. At each of these stations large numbers got on board for Bloomington. As we approached Bloomington, "Popular Sovereignty" gave notice that we were about, and his roar was answered by another of welcome from the town. About 5,000 people had assembled here to meet Senator Douglas, and the whole town and surrounding country were present on horseback, in vehicles, and on foot, to welcome his arrival. The train was overrun with people who clambered on top of the cars, and tumbled in on all sides, and the enthusiasm manifested was similar to that shown on his arrival at Chicago on Friday last. The thunders of the guns, the music of the band, and the shouts of the multitude filled the air. The scene can better be imagined than described. The crowd closed in around the cars in an impenetrable mass, and, taking possession of Senator Douglas, they carried him over to the platform, where he received their personal welcomes. After some time spent in this manner, the senator was placed in an open carriage, provided by the Committee of Arrangements, and the escort, composed of the Bloomington Rifles, a cavalcade of horsemen, and citizens on foot, headed by the Bloomington brass band, took up its march for the London House where rooms had been engaged by the committee for their guest. Flags were displayed from the house, and strips of muslin ran along the balconies, bearing the inscription, "S. A. Douglas, the champion of Popular Sovereignty." Arriving at the house, the procession was dismissed, and after giving three times three cheers for Senator Douglas, gradually dispersed, to re-assemble at 7½ o'clock, P.M., in the court-house square, for the purpose of listening to his address.

At 7 o'clock, the roar of the cannon, and the firing of rockets, the ring of the court-house bell, and the music of the band attached to the Bloomington Guards, who attended the meeting in uniform, gave notice to the people to assemble; and in half an hour the large square surrounding the court-house was crowded with people, whilst Washington, Jefferson, and Madison streets were in the same condition; and the windows and doors of the houses fronting the square were thronged with ladies and gentlemen. There were about 10,000 persons in attendance, and the committee of arrangements expected a much larger number, who were prevented from coming in from the country by the heavy rain which fell in this neighborhood all last night and to-day. The court-house was illuminated, and a stage was erected on the west side for the meeting.

At about 8 o'clock, Allen Withers, Esq., chairman of the Committee of Arrangements, called the meeting to order. Dr. E. R. Roe, in a very eloquent speech, welcomed Senator Douglas, and assured him, on behalf of the people of McLean County, that his course, during the last session of Congress, was fully approved by them, and that they were ready to show that approval, in a substantial manner, at the polls in November next.

SPEECH AT BLOOMINGTON.

In the course of his speech at Bloomington, Mr. Douglas referred to the Compromise measures of 1850, and the instructions of the Illinois legislature of 1851 to carry out the same principle of self-government in the organization of new Territories, as follows:

Illinois stands proudly forward as a State which early took her position in favor of the principle of popular sovereignty, as applied to the Territories of the United States. When the Compromise measures of 1850 passed, predicated upon that principle, you recollect the excitement which prevailed throughout the northern portion of this State. I vindicated those measures then, and defended myself for having voted for them, upon the ground that they embodied the principle that every people ought to have the privilege of forming and regulating their own institutions to suit themselves—that each State had that right, and I saw no reason why it should not be extended to the Territories. When the people of Illinois had an opportunity of passing judgment upon those measures, they indorsed them by a vote of their representatives in the legislature—sixty-one in the affirmative, and only four in the negative—in which they asserted that the principle embodied in the measures was the birthright of freemen, the gift of Heaven, a principle vindicated by our Revolutionary fathers, and that no limitation should ever be placed upon it, either in the organization of a Territorial government, or the admission of a State into the Union. That resolution still stands unrepealed on the journals of the legislature of Illinois. In obedience to it, and in exact conformity with the principle, I brought in the Kansas-Nebraska Bill, requiring that the people should be left perfectly free in the formation of their institutions, and in the organization of their government. I now submit to you whether I have not in good faith redeemed that pledge, that the people of Kansas should be left perfectly free to form and regulate their institutions to suit themselves. ("You have," and cheers.) And yet, while no man can rise in any crowd and deny that I have been faithful to my principles, and redeemed my pledge, we find those who are struggling to crush and defeat me, for the very reason that I have been faithful in carrying out those measures. ("They can't do it," and great cheers.) We find the Republican leaders forming an alliance with professed Lecompton men to defeat every Democratic nominee, and elect Republicans in their places, and aiding and defending them in order to help them break down Anti-Lecompton men whom they acknowledge did right in their opposition to Lecompton ("They can't do it.") The only hope that Mr. Lincoln has of defeating me, for the Senate rests in the fact that I was faithful to my principles, and that he may be able, in consequence of that fact, to form a coalition with Lecompton men who wish to defeat me for that fidelity. ("They will never do it. Never in the State of Illinois"—and cheers.)

He again refers to the coalition between the federal officeholders and the abolitionists, to break down the Democratic party

This is one element of strength upon which he relies to accomplish his object. He hopes he can secure the few men claiming to be friends of the Lecompton constitution, and for that reason you will find he does not say a word against the Lecompton constitution or its supporters. He is as silent as the grave upon that subject. Behold Mr. Lincoln courting Lecompton votes, in order that he may go to the Senate as the representative of Republican principles! (Laughter.) You know that the alliance exists. I think you will find that it will ooze out before the contest is over. (" That's my opinion," and cheers.)

Every Republican paper takes ground with my Lecompton enemies, encouraging them, stimulating them in their opposition to me, and styling my friends bolters from the Democratic party, and their Lecompton allies the true Democratic party of the country. If they think that they can mislead and deceive the people of Illinois, or the Democracy of Illinois, by that sort of an unnatural and unholy alliance, I think they show very little sagacity, or give the people very little credit for intelligence. (" That's so," and cheers.) It must be a contest of principle. Either the radical abolition principles of Mr. Lincoln must be maintained, or the strong, constitutional, national Democratic principles with which I am identified, must be carried out.

There can be but two great political parties in this country. The contest this year and in 1860, must necessarily be between the Democracy and the Republicans, if we can judge from present indications. My whole life has been identified with the Democratic party. (Cheers.) I have devoted all my energies to advocating its principles, and sustaining its organization. In this State the party was never better united and more harmonious than at this time. (Cheers.) The State Convention which assembled on the 2d of April, and nominated Fondey and French, was regularly called by the State Central Committee, appointed by the previous State Convention for that purpose. The meetings in each county in the State for the appointment of delegates to the convention, were regularly called by the county committees, and the proceedings in every county in the State, as well as in the State Convention, were regular in all respects. No convention was ever more harmonious in its action, or showed a more tolerant and just spirit toward brother Democrats. The leaders of the party there assembled declared their unalterable attachment to the time-honored principles and organization of the Democratic party, and to the Cincinnati platform. They declared that that platform was the only authoritative exposition of Democratic principles, and that it must so stand until changed by another National Convention ; that in the meantime they would make no new tests, and submit to none ; that they would proscribe no Democrat, nor permit the proscription of Democrats because of their opinions upon Lecomptonism, or upon any other issue which has arisen ; but would recognize all men as Democrats who remained inside of the organization, preserved the usages of the party, and supported its nominees. (Great applause.) These bolting Democrats who now claim to be the peculiar friends of the national administration, and have formed an alliance with Mr. Lincoln and the Republicans, for the purpose of defeating the Democratic party, have ceased to claim fellowship with the Democratic organization, have entirely separated themselves from it, and are endeavoring to build up a faction in the State, not with the hope or expectation of electing any one man who professes to be a Democrat, to office in any county in the State, but merely to secure the defeat of the Democratic nominees, and the election of Republicans in their places. What excuse can any honest Democrat have for abandoning the Democratic organization, and joining with the Republicans ("None!") to defeat our nominees, in view of the platform established by the State Convention? They cannot pretend that they were proscribed because of their opinions upon Lecompton or any other question, for the Convention expressly declared that they recognize all as good Democrats who remained inside of the organization, and abided by the nominations. If the question is settled, or is to be considered as finally disposed of by the vote on the 3d of August, what possible excuse can any good Democrat make for keeping up a division for the purpose of prostrating his party, after that election is over, and the controversy has terminated.

DRED SCOTT DECISION—NEGRO EQUALITY.

But I must now bestow a few words upon Mr. Lincoln's main objection to the Dred Scott decision. He is not going to submit to it. Not that he is going to make war upon it with force of arms. But he is going to appeal and reverse it in some way; he cannot tell us how. I reckon not by a writ of error, because I do not know where he would prosecute that, except before an Abolition Society. ("That's it," and applause.) And when he appeals, he does not exactly tell us to whom he will appeal, except it be to the Republican party, and I have yet to learn that the Republican party, under the Constitution, has judicial powers; but he is going to appeal from it and reverse it either by an act of Congress, or by turning out the judges, or in some other way. And why? Because he says that that decision deprives the negro of the benefit of that clause of the Constitution of the United States which entitles the citizens of each State to all the privileges and immunities of citizens of the several States. Well, it is very true that the decision does have that effect. By deciding that a negro is not a citizen, of course it denies to him the rights and privileges awarded to citizens of the United States. It is this that Mr. Lincoln will not submit to. Why? For the palpable reason that he wishes to confer upon the negro all the rights.

privileges, and immunities of citizens of the several States. I will not quarrel with Mr. Lincoln for his views on that subject. I have no doubt that he is conscientious in them. I have not the slightest idea but that he conscientiously believes that a negro ought to enjoy and exercise all the rights and privileges given to white men ; but I do not agree with him, and hence I cannot concur with him. I believe that this government of ours was formed on the white basis. (Prolonged cheering.) I believe that it was established by white men—(applause)—by men of European birth and descended of European races, for the benefit of white men and their posterity in all time to come. ("Hear, hear.") I do not believe that it was the design or intention of the signers of the Declaration of Independence or the framers of the Constitution to include negroes or other inferior races with white men as citizens. (Cheers.) Our fathers had at that day seen the evil consequences of conferring civil and political rights upon the negro in the Spanish and French colonies on the American continent, and the adjacent islands. In Mexico, in Central America, in South America, and in the West India Islands, where the negro, and men of all colors and all races are put on an equality by law, the effect of political amalgamation can be seen. Ask any of those gallant young men in your own county, who who went to Mexico to fight the battles of their country, in what friend Lincoln considers an unjust and unholy war, and hear what they will tell you in regard to the amalgamation of races in that country. Amalgamation there, first political, then social, has led to demoralization and degradation until it has reduced the people below the point of capacity for self-government. Our fathers knew what the effect of it would be, and from the time they planted foot on the American continent, not only those who landed at Jamestown, but at Plymouth Rock and all other points on the coast, they pursued the policy of confining civil and political rights to the white race, and excluding the negro in all cases. Still Mr. Lincoln conscientiously believes that it is his duty to advocate negro citizenship. He wants to give the negro the privileges of citizenship. He quotes Scripture again, and says: "As your Father in Heaven is perfect, be ye also perfect," and he applies that Scriptural quotation to all classes, not that he expects us all to be as perfect as our Master, but as nearly perfect as possible. In other words, he is willing to give the negro an equality under the law, in order that he may approach as near perfection or an equality with the white man as possible. To this same end he quotes the Declaration of Independence in these words: "We hold these truths to be self-evident that all men were created equal, and endowed by their Creator with certain inalienable rights, among which are life, liberty, and the pursuit of happiness," and goes on to argue that the negro was included, or intended to be included, in that declaration by the signers of the paper. He says that by the Declaration of Independence, therefore, all kinds of men, negroes included, were created equal, and endowed by their Creator with certain inalienable rights, and further, that the right of the negro to be on an equality with the white man is a Divine right conferred by the Almighty, and rendered inalienable according to the Declaration of Independence. Hence no human law or constitution can deprive the negro of that equality with the white man to which he is entitled by Divine law. ("Higher law.") Yes, higher law. Now, I do not question Mr. Lincoln's sincerity on this point. He believes that the negro by the Divine law is created the equal of the white man, and that no human law can deprive him of that equality thus secured ; and he contends that the negro ought, therefore, to have all the rights and privileges of citizenship on an equality with the white man. In order to accomplish this, the first thing that would have to be done in this State would be to blot out of our State Constitution that clause which prohibits negroes from coming into this State and making it an African colony, and permit them to come and spread over these charming prairies until in midday they shall look black as night. When our friend Lincoln gets all his colored brethren around him here, he will then raise them to perfection as fast as possible, and place them on an equality with the white man, first removing all legal restrictions, because they are our equals by Divine law and there should be no such restrictions. He wants them to vote. I am opposed to it. If they had a vote I reckon they would all vote for him in preference to me, entertaining the views I do. (Laughter.) But that matters not. The position he has taken on this question not only presents him as claiming for them the right to vote, but their right, under the Divine law and the Declaration of Independence, to be elected to office, to become members of the legislature, to go to Congress, and to become governors, or United States senators (laughter and cheers), or judges of the Supreme Court; and I suppose that when they control that court that they will probably reverse the Dred Scott decision. (Laughter.) He is going to bring negroes here, and give them the right of citizenship, the right of voting, the right of holding office and sitting on juries, and what else ? Why, he would permit them to marry, would he not? and if he gives them that right, I suppose he will let them marry whom they please, provided they marry their equals. (Laughter.) If the Divine law declares that the white man is the equal of the negro woman; that they are on a perfect equality; I suppose he admits the right of the negro woman to marry the white man. (Renewed laughter.) In other words, his doctrine that the negro by Divine law is placed on a perfect equality with the white man, and that that equality is recognized by the

Declaration of Independence, leads him necessarily to establishing negro equality under the law; but whether even then they would be so in fact, would depend upon the degree of virtue and intelligence they possessed, and certain other qualities that are matters of taste rather than of law. (Laughter.) I do not understand Mr. Lincoln as saying that he expects to make them our equals socially, or by intelligence, nor, in fact, as citizens, but that he wishes to make them equal under the law, and then say to them "as your Master in Heaven is perfect, be ye also perfect." Well, I confess to you, my fellow-citizens, that I am utterly opposed to that system of abolition philosophy. ("So am I," and cheers.)

MIND YOUR OWN BUSINESS AND LET YOUR NEIGHBORS ALONE—CLAY AND WEBSTER.

In Kentucky they will not give a negro any political rights or any civil rights. I shall not argue the question whether Kentucky in so doing has decided right or wrong, wisely or unwisely. It is a question for Kentucky to decide for herself. I believe that the Kentuckians have consciences as well as ourselves; they have as keen a perception of their religious, moral and social duties as we have, and I am willing that they shall decide this slavery question for themselves, and be accountable to their God for their action. It is not for me to arraign them for what they do. I will not judge them lest I shall be judged. Let Kentucky mind her own business, and take care of her negroes, and we attend to our own affairs, and take care of our negroes, and we will be the best of friends; but if Kentucky attempts to interfere with us, or we with her, there will be strife, there will be discord, there will be relentless hatred, there will be everything but fraternal feeling and brotherly love. It is not necessary that you should enter Kentucky and interfere in that State, to use the language of Mr. Lincoln. It is just as offensive to interfere from this State, or send your missiles over there. I care not whether an enemy, if he is going to assault us, shall actually come into our State or come along the line and throw his bomb-shells over to explode in our midst. Suppose England should plant a battery on the Canadian side of the Niagara River, opposite Buffalo, and throw bomb-shells over, which would explode in Main street, in that city, and destroy the buildings, and that when we protested, she should say, in the language of Mr. Lincoln, that she never dreamed of coming into the United States to interfere with us, and that she was just throwing her bombs over the line from her own side, which she had a right to do, would that explanation satisfy us? ("No;" "Strike him again.") So it is with Mr. Lincoln. He is not going into Kentucky out he will plant his batteries on this side of the Ohio, where he is safe and secure for a retreat, and will then throw his bomb-shells—his abolition documents—over the river, and will carry on a political warfare and get up strife between the North and South until he elects a sectional President, reduces the South to the condition of dependent colonies, raises the negro to an equality, and forces the South to submit to the doctrine that a house divided against itself cannot stand, that the Union divided into half slave States and half free cannot endure, that they must all be slave or they must all be free, and that as we in the North are in the majority we will not permit them to be all slave, and, therefore, they in the South must consent to the States all being free. (Laughter.) Now, fellow-citizens, I submit whether these doctrines are consistent with the peace and harmony of this Union. ("No, no.") I submit to you, whether they are consistent with our duty as citizens of a common confederacy; whether they are consistent with the principles which ought to govern brethren of the same family. I recognize all the people of these States, North and South, East and West, old or new, Atlantic and Pacific, as our brethren, flesh of one flesh, and I will do no act unto them that I would not be willing they should do unto us. I would apply the same Christian rule to the States of this Union that·we are taught to apply to individuals, "do unto others as you would have others do unto you," and this would secure peace. Why should this slavery agitation be kept up? Does it benefit the white man or the slave? Who does it benefit except the Republican politicians, who use it as their hobby to ride into office. (Cheers.) Why, I repeat, should it be continued? Why cannot we be content to administer this government as it was made—a confederacy of sovereign and independent States. Let us recognize the sovereignty and independence of each State, refrain from interfering with the domestic institutions and regulations of other States, permit the Territories and new States to decide their institutions for themselves as we did when we were in their condition; blot out these lines of North and South and resort back to those lines of State boundaries which the Constitution has marked out and engraved upon the face of the country; have no other dividing lines but these and we will be one united, harmonious people, with fraternal feelings and no discord or dissension. (Cheers.)

These are my views and these are the principles to which I have devoted all my energies since 1850, when I acted side by side with the immortal Clay and the godlike Webster in that memorable struggle in which Whigs and Democrats united upon a common platform of patriotism and the Constitution, throwing aside partisan feelings in order to restore peace and harmony to a distracted country. And when I stood beside the death bed of Mr. Clay and heard him refer with feelings and emotions of the deepest solicitude to the welfare of the country, and saw that he looked upon the principle embodied in the great Compromise measures of 1850, the principle of the Nebraska Bill, the doctrine of leaving each State and Territory free to decide its institutions for itself, as the only means by which the peace of the country could be preserved, and the Union perpetuated, I pledged him, on that death-bed of his, that so long as I lived my energies should be devoted to the vindication of that principle, and of his fame as connected with it. ("Hear, hear," and great enthusiasm.) I gave the same pledge to the great expounder of the Constitution, he who has been called the "godlike Webster." I looked up to Clay and him as a son would to a father, and I call upon the people of Illinois, and the people of the whole Union to bear testimony that never since the sod has been laid upon the graves of those eminent statesmen have I failed on any occasion to vindicate the principle with which the last great, crowning acts of their lives were identified, or to vindicate their names whenever they have been assailed; and now my life and energy are devoted to this great work as the means of preserving this Union. (Cheers.) This Union can only be preserved by maintaining the fraternal feeling between the North and the South, the East and the West. If that good feeling can be preserved the Union will be as perpetual as the fame of its great founders. It can be maintained by preserving the sovereignty of the States, the right of each State and each Territory to settle its domestic concerns for itself, and the duty of each to refrain from interfering with the other in any of its local or domestic institutions. Let that be done and the Union will be perpetual; let that be done, and this republic, which began with thirteen States, and which now numbers thirty-two, which when it began only extended from the Atlantic to the Mississippi but now reaches to the Pacific, may yet expand North and South until it covers the whole continent and becomes one vast ocean-bound confederacy. (Great cheering.) Then, my friends, the path of duty, of honor, of patriotism is plain. There are a few simple principles to be preserved. Bear in mind the dividing line between State rights and federal authority; let us maintain the great principles of popular sovereignty, of State rights, and of the Federal Union as the Constitution has made it, and this republic will endure forever.

UNITY OF THE DEMOCRATIC PARTY.

In the course of Mr. Douglas' speech at Edwardsville, on the 6th of August, an old Democrat sprang to his feet and exclaimed, "These are the principles of all us Douglas Democrats!" To which Mr. Douglas replied:

My friend—you will pardon me for telling you that there is no such term in the Democratic vocabulary as Douglas Democrats. Let there be no divisions in our ranks—no such distinction as Douglas Democrats, or Buchanan Democrats, or any other peculiar kind of Democrats. Let us retain the old name of Democrat, and under that name recognize all men as good Democrats who stand firmly by the principles and organization of the party, and support its regular nominations. Let us have no divisions in our ranks on account of past differences, but treating bygones as bygones let the party be a unit in the accomplishment of the great mission which it has to perform.

This sentiment was received with rapturous applause.

SPEECH AT WINCHESTER—TOUCHING INCIDENTS.

At Winchester, where he settled when he first emigrated to Illinois, in 1833, he responded to the address of welcome, thus:

To say that I am profoundly impressed with the keenest gratitude for the kind and cordial welcome you have given me, in the eloquent and too partial remarks which have been addressed to me, is but a feeble expression of the emotions of my heart. There is no spot in this vast globe which fills me with such emotions as when I come to this place, and recognize the faces of my old and good friends who now surround me and bid me welcome. Twenty-five years ago I entered this town on foot, with my coat upon my arm, without an acquaintance in a thousand miles, and without knowing where I could get money to pay a week's board. Here I made the first six dollars I ever earned in my life, and obtained the first regular occupation that I ever pursued. For the first time in my life I then felt that the responsibilities of manhood were upon me, although I was under age, for I had none to advise with, and knew no one upon whom I had a right to call for assistance or for friendship. Here I found the then settlers of the country my friends—my first start in life was taken here, not only as a private citizen, but my first election to public office by the people was conferred upon me by those whom I am now addressing, and by their fathers. A quarter of a century has passed, and that pouniless boy stands before you, with his heart full and gushing with the sentiments which such associations and recollections necessarily inspire.

In the midst of that portion of his speech, in which he was vindicating the doctrine of popular sovereignty, applicable to the Territories, one of his early friends exclaimed, in a loud voice, "Stephen, you shall be the next President;" to which Mr. Douglas instantly replied:

My friend, I appreciate the kindness of heart which makes you put forth that prediction, but will assure you that it is more important to this country, to your children and to mine, that the great principles which we are now discussing shall be carried out in good faith by the party, than it is that I or any other man shall be President of the United States. (Three cheers.) I am also free to say to you that whenever the question arises with me whether I shall be elevated to the Presidency or any other high position, by the sacrifice of my principles, I will stand by my principles and allow the position to take care of itself. (Three cheers.) I have always admired that great sentiment put forth by the illustrious Clay, that he would rather be right than be President. ("Good.") I say to you that I have more pride in my history connected with the vindication of this great principle of popular sovereignty than I would have in a thousand Presidencies. (Three cheers.)

Mr. Douglas, again advocating that "by-gones be by-gones," when Kansas rejected the English bill, said, in a speech at Pittsfield:

By the rejection of the Lecompton constitution the controversy which it caused is terminated forever, and there will be no cause for reviving it, and it never will be revived unless it is brought up in an improper and mischievous manner, for improper and mischievous purposes. I say that the controversy can never rise again if we act properly, and for this reason: the President of the United States, in his annual message, declared that he regretted that the Lecompton constitution had not been submitted to the people. I joined him in that regret, and thus far we agreed. He further declared in that message, that it was a just and sound principle to require the submission of every constitution to the people who were to live under it, and to this I also subscribed. He then declared that, in his opinion, the example set in the Minnesota case, wherein Congress required the submission of the constitution to the people, should be followed here-after forever as a rule of action; in which opinion I heartily concurred. So far we agreed perfectly, and were together. Well, then, what did we differ about? He said that while it was a sound principle that the consti-tution should be submitted to the people, and while he hoped that here-after Congress would always require it to be done, yet that there were such circumstances connected with Kansas as rendered it politic and expedient to admit her unconditionally under the Lecompton constitution. I differed with him on that one point, and it was the whole matter at issue between him and me, his friends and mine. That point is now decided. The peo-ple of Kansas have set it at rest forever, and I trust that he is satisfied with their decision as well as myself. That being the case, why should we not come together in the future and stand firmly by his recommendation—that hereafter Congress shall, as in the Minnesota case, require the consti-tution of all new States to be submitted to the people in all cases? If we only do stand by that principle in the future, another Lecompton contro-versy can never arise—the friends of self-government will then all be united, and there will be no more discord or dissensions in our ranks. Why not rally on that plank as the common plank in the platform of our party, upon which not only all Democrats, but all national men, all friends of popular sovereignty, can stand together, shoulder to shoulder.

THE FREEPORT SPEECH.

In the joint debate at Freeport, Mr. Lincoln propounded to Mr. Douglas a series of questions, and among them was the following, to which he desired an explicit reply:

"Can the people of a Territory of the United States in any lawful way, against the wishes of any citizen of the United States, exclude slavery from its limits prior to the formation of a State constitution?"

To this question Mr. Douglas gave an affirmative reply, in accordance with the opinions which he had so often ex-pressed, in 1850, during the pendency of the Compromise measures, and in 1854, in support of the Kansas-Nebraska Bill, and in harmony with the known opinions of the most eminent men of the Democratic party, and especially of

General Cass, in his Nicholson letter, and of Mr. Buchanan, in his letter accepting the Cincinnati nomination.

It being a joint debate, in which his time was limited, and having a large number of other questions to answer, Mr. Douglas contented himself with a direct and unequivocal answer, without entering into any argument in support of the propositions. His reply, as published in the unrevised report of the debate, is as follows:

The next question propounded to me by Mr. Lincoln is, can the people of a Territory in any lawful way against the wishes of any citizen of the United States, exclude slavery from their limits prior to the formation of a State constitution? I answer emphatically, as Mr. Lincoln has heard me answer a hundred times from every stump in Illinois, that in my opinion the people of a Territory can, by lawful means, exclude slavery from their limits prior to the formation of a State constitution. (Enthusiastic applause.) Mr. Lincoln knew that I had answered that question over and over again. He heard me argue the Nebraska Bill on that principle all over the State in 1854, in 1855 and in 1856, and he has no excuse for pretending to be in doubt as to my position on that question. It matters not what way the Supreme Court may hereafter decide as to the abstract question whether slavery may or may not go into a Territory under the constitution; the people have the lawful means to introduce it or exclude it as they please, for the reason that slavery cannot exist a day or an hour anywhere, unless it is supported by local police regulations. (Right, right.) Those police regulations can only be established by the local legislature, and if the people are opposed to slavery they will elect representatives to that body who will by unfriendly legislation effectually prevent the introduction of it into their midst. If, on the contrary, they are for it, their legislation will favor its extension. Hence, no matter what the decision of the Supreme Court may be on that abstract question, still the right of the people to make a slave Territory or a free Territory is perfect and complete under the Nebraska Bill. I hope Mr. Lincoln deems my answer satisfactory on that point.

MR. DOUGLAS AT ALTON—REBUKES EXECUTIVE DICTATION.

And now this warfare is made on me because I would not surrender my convictions of duty, because I would not abandon my constituency, and receive the orders of the Executive authorities how I should vote in the

Senate of the United States. ("Never do it," three cheers, etc.) I hold that an attempt to control the Senate on the part of the Executive is subversive of the principles of our Constitution. ("That's right.") The Executive department is independent of the Senate, and the Senate is independent of the President. In matters of legislation the President has a veto on the action of the Senate, and in appointments and treaties the Senate has a veto on the President. He has no more right to tell me how I shall vote on his appointments, than I have to tell him whether he shall veto or approve a bill that the Senate has passed. Whenever you recognize the right of the Executive to say to a senator, "Do this, or I will take off the heads of your friends," you convert this government from a republic into a despotism. (Hear, hear, and cheers.) Whenever you recognize the right of a President to say to a member of Congress, "Vote as I tell you, or I will bring a power to bear against you at home which will crush you," you destroy the independence of the representative, and convert him into a tool of Executive power. ("That's so," and applause.) I resisted this invasion of the constitutional rights of a senator, and I intend to resist it as long as I have a voice to speak, or a vote to give. Yet, Mr. Buchanan cannot provoke me to abandon one iota of Democratic principles out of revenge or hostility to his course. ("Good, good, and three cheers for Douglas.") I stand by the platform of the Democratic party, and by its organization, and support its nominees. If there are any who choose to bolt, the fact only shows that they are not as good Democrats as I am. ("That's so," "good," and applause.)

UNION OF NATIONAL MEN FOR SAKE OF THE UNION.

My friends, there never was a time when it was as important for the Democratic party, for all national men, to rally and stand together as it is to-day. We find all sectional men giving up past differences and combining on the one question of slavery; and when we find sectional men thus uniting, we should unite to resist them and their treasonable designs. Such was the case in 1850, when Clay left the quiet and peace of his home and again entered upon public life to quell agitation and restore peace to a distracted Union. Then we Democrats, with Cass at our head, welcomed Henry Clay, whom the whole nation regarded as having been preserved by God for the times. He became our leader in that great fight, and we rallied around him the same as the Whigs rallied around old Hickory in 1832, to put down nullification. (Cheers.) Thus you see that whilst Whigs and Democrats fought fearlessly in old times about banks, the tariff distribution, the specie circular, and the sub-treasury, all united as a band of brothers when the peace, harmony, or integrity of the Union was imperilled. (Tremendous applause.) It was so in 1850, when abolitionism had even so far divided this country, North and South, as to endanger the peace of the Union; Whigs and Democrats united in establishing the Compromise measures of that year, and restoring tranquillity and good feeling. These measures passed on the joint action of the two parties. They rested on the great principle that the people of each State and each Territory should be left perfectly free to form and regulate their domestic institutions to suit themselves. You Whigs and we Democrats justified them on that principle. In 1854, when it became necessary to organize the Territories of Kansas and Nebraska, I brought forward a bill for the purpose on the same principle. In the Kansas-Nebraska Bill you find it declared to be the true intent and meaning of the act not to legislate slavery into any State or Territory, nor to exclude it therefrom; but to leave the people thereof perfectly free to form and regulate their domestic institutions in their own way. ("That's so," and cheers.) I stand on that same platform in 1858 that I did in 1850, in 1854 and 1856.

The Washington "Union," pretending to be the organ of the administration, in the number of the 5th of this month, devotes three columns and a half to establish these propositions: First, that Douglas, in his Freeport speech, held the same doctrine that he did in his Nebraska Bill in 1854; second, that in 1854 Douglas justified the Nebraska Bill, upon the ground that it was based upon the same principle as Clay's Compromise measures of 1850. The "Union" thus proved that Douglas was the same in 1858 that he was in 1856, in 1854 and in 1850, consequently argued that he was never a Democrat. (Great laughter.) Is it not funny that I was never a Democrat? (Renewed laughter.) There is no pretence that I have changed a hair's breadth. The "Union" proves, by my speeches, that I explained the Compromise measures of 1850 just as I do now, and that I explained the Kansas and Nebraska Bill in 1854 just as I did in my Freeport speech, and yet says that I am not a Democrat, and cannot be trusted, because I have not changed during the whole of that time. It has occurred to me that in 1854 the author of the Kansas and Nebraska Bill was considered a pretty good Democrat. (Cheers.) It has occurred to me that in 1856, when I was exerting every nerve and every energy for James Buchanan, standing on the same platform then that I do now, that I was a pretty good Democrat. (Renewed applause.) They now tell me that I am not a

Democrat, because I assert that the people of a Territory, as well as those of a State, have the right to decide for themselves whether slavery can or cannot exist in such Territory. Let me read what James Buchanan said on that point when he accepted the Democratic nomination for the Presidency in 1856. In his letter of acceptance, he used the following language:

"The recent legislation of Congress respecting domestic slavery, derived, as it has been, from the original and pure fountain of legitimate political power, the will of the majority, promise ere long to allay the dangerous excitement. This legislation 's founded upon principles as ancient as free government itself, and in accordance with them, has simply declared that the people of a Territory, like those of a State, shall decide for themselves whether slavery shall or shall not exist within their limits."

Dr. Hope will there find my answer to the question he propounded to me before I commenced speaking. (Vociferous shouts of applause.) Of course no man will consider it an answer who is outside of the Democratic organization, bolts Democratic nominations, and indirectly aids to put Abolitionists into power over Democrats. But whether Dr. Hope considers it an answer or not, every fair-minded man will see that James Buchanan has answered the question, and has asserted that the people of a Territory, like those of a State, shall decide for themselves whether slavery shall or shall not exist within their limits. I answer specifically, if you want a further answer, and say, that while under the decision of the Supreme Court, as recorded in the opinion of Chief Justice Taney, slaves are property like all other property, and can be carried into a Territory of the United States the same as any other description of property; yet, when you get them there, they are subject to the local law of the Territory just like all other property. You will find in a recent speech, delivered by that able and eloquent statesman, Hon. Jefferson Davis, at Portland, Maine, that he took the same view of this subject that I did in my Freeport speech. He there said:

"If the inhabitants of any Territory should refuse to enact such laws and police regulations as would give security to their property or to his, it would be rendered more or less valueless, in proportion to the difficulties of holding it without such protection. In the case of property in the labor of man, or what is usually called slave property, the insecurity would be so great that the owner could not ordinarily retain it. Therefore, though the right would remain, the remedy being withheld, it would follow that the owner would be practically debarred, by the circumstances of the case, from taking slave property into a Territory where the sense of the inhabitants was opposed to its introduction. So much for the oft-repeated fallacy of forcing slavery upon any community."

You will also find that the distinguished speaker of the present House of Representatives, Hon. James L. Orr, construed the Kansas and Ne-

braska Bill in this same way in 1856, and also that that great intellect of
the South, Alex. H. Stevens, put the same construction upon it in Congress that I did in my Freeport speech. The whole South are rallying to
the support of the doctrine that, if the people of a Territory want slavery,
they have a right to have it ; and if they do not want it, that no power on
earth can force it upon them. I hold that there is no principle on earth
more sacred to all the friends of freedom than that which says that no institution, no law, no constitution, should be forced on an unwilling people
contrary to their wishes; and I assert that the Kansas and Nebraska Bill
contains that principle. It is the great principle contained in that bill. It
is the principle on which James Buchanan was made President. Without
that principle he never would have been made President of the United
States. I will never violate or abandon that doctrine if I have to stand
alone. (Hurrah for Douglas.) I have resisted the blandishments and
threats of power on the one side, and seduction on the other, and have
stood immovably for that principle, fighting for it when assailed by
northern mobs, or threatened by southern hostility. ("That's the truth,"
and cheers.) I have defended it against the North and the South, and I
will defend it against whoever assails it, and I will follow it wherever its
logical conclusions lead me. ("So will we all," "hurrah for Douglas.") I
say to you that there is but one hope, one safety for this country, and that
is to stand immovably by that principle which declares the right of each
State and each Territory to decide these questions for themselves. (Hear
him, hear him.) This government was founded on that principle, and
must be administered in the same sense in which it was founded.

The Democracy of Illinois determined at the opening of
their campaign, in view of their relations toward the administration, to invite no speakers from abroad to participate in
the labor of their canvass. In the event of any gentlemen
volunteering their services, they would be most gratefully
accepted. A few exceptions, however, were made to this
rule, at the suggestion of friends in other States. Private
letters had been received by numerous gentlemen in the
State, to the effect that Vice-President Breckinridge warmly
sympathized with the Illinois Democracy in their fierce struggle with their confederated enemy, and that his feelings were
painfully exercised by the imminent dangers that environed

the prospects of Mr. Douglas' reëlection to the Senate. Indeed, it was suggested that the Vice-President had expressed a desire to lend the weight of his great talents and exertions in the good cause; and, if invited, would cheerfully engage in the canvass, as he had done before when himself a candidate in the contest of 1856. Accordingly, invitations were sent to Mr. Breckinridge, and Governor Wise of Virginia, who, it was understood, warmly sympathized with Judge Douglas in his struggle, as he had done through his whole anti-Lecompton course in Congress; to which invitations these gentlemen sent characteristic replies, which we think of sufficient importance to here insert.

LETTER OF MR. BRECKINRIDGE.

VERSAILLES, Ky., Oct. 4, 1858.

DEAR SIR: I received this morning your letters of the 28th and 29th ult., written as chairman of the Democratic State Committee of Illinois, also one of Mr. V. Hickox, who informs me that he is a member of the same committee. My absence from home will account for the delay of this answer.

In these letters it is said that I am reported to have expressed a desire that Mr. Douglas shall defeat Mr. Lincoln in their contest for a seat in the Senate of the United States, and a willingness to visit Illinois and make public speeches in aid of such result; and if these reports are true, I am invited to deliver addresses at certain points in the State.

The rumor of my readiness to visit Illinois and address the people in the present canvass is without foundation. I do not propose to leave Kentucky for the purpose of mingling in the political discussions in other States. The two or three speeches which I delivered recently in this State rested on peculiar grounds, which I need not now discuss.

The rumor to which you refer is true. I have often, in conversation, expressed the wish that Mr. Douglas may succeed over his Republican competitor. But it is due to candor to say, that this preference is not founded on his course at the late session of Congress, and would not exist if I supposed it would be construed as an indorsement of the attitude which he then chose to assume toward his party, or of all the positions he has taken in the present canvass. It is not necessary to enlarge on these things.

I will only add, that my preference rests mainly on these considerations: that the Kansas question is practically ended—that Mr. Douglas, in recent speeches, has explicitly declared his adherence to the regular Democratic party organization—that he seems to be the candidate of the Illinois Democracy, and the most formidable opponent in that State of the Republican party, and that on more than one occasion during his public life he has defended the union of the States and the rights of the States with fidelity, courage, and great ability.

I have not desired to say anything upon this or any other subject about which a difference may be supposed to exist in our political family, but I did not feel at liberty to decline an answer to the courteous letter of your committee.

With cordial wishes for the harmony of the Illinois Democracy, and the hope that your great and growing State, which has never yet given a sectional vote, may continue true to our constitutional Union,

I am, very respectfully, your obedient servant,

JOHN C. BRECKINRIDGE.

HON. JOHN MOORE, Chairman of the Committee.

LETTER OF GOVERNOR WISE.

RICHMOND, VA., 1858.

To HON. JOHN MOORE, Chairman of the Democratic
State Committee of Illinois:

DEAR SIR: I cannot express to you the emotions of my bosom, excited by your appeal to me for aid in the warm contest which your noble Democracy is waging with abolitionism. Every impulse prompts me to rush to your side. Your position is a grand one, and in some respects unexampled. In the face of doubt and distrust attempted to be thrown upon your Democracy, and its gallant leader, by the pretext of pretenders that you were giving aid and comfort to the arch enemy of our country, peace and safety, and our party integrity, I see you standing alone—isolated by a tyrannical proscription, which would, alike foolishly and wickedly, lop off one of the most vigorous limbs of national Democracy, the limb of glorious Illinois! I see you, in spite of this imputation, firmly fronting the foe, and battling to maintain conservative nationality—against embittered and implacable sectionalism—constitutional rights, operating *propriâ vigore*, and every way against all unequal and unjust federal or territorial legislation;

The right of the people to govern themselves against all force or fraud;

The right of the sovereign people to look at the "returns," and behind the "returns," of all their representative bodies, agents, trustees, or servants;

The responsibility of all governors, representatives, trustees, agents, and servants, to their principals, the people, who are "the governed," and the source of all political power;

Utter opposition to the detestable doctrine of the absolutism of conventions to prescribe and proclaim fundamental forms of government at their will, without submission to the sovereign people—a doctrine fit only for slaves, and claimed only by legitimists and despots of the old world;

Powers of any sort not expressly delegated to any man, or body of men, are expressly "reserved to the people;"

No *absolute* or dictatorial authority in representative bodies. The representative principle as claiming submission and obedience to the will of the constituents;

The sovereignty of the organized people supreme above all mere representative bodies, conventions, or legislatures, to decide, vote upon, and determine what shall be their supreme law;

Justice and equality between States and their citizens, and between voters to elect their agents and representatives, and to ratify or reject any proposed system of government;

Submission to the constitution and laws of the federal Union, and strict observance of all the rights of the States and their citizens, but resistance to the dictation or bribes of Congress, or any other power, to yield the inalienable right of self-government;

Protection in the Territories, and everywhere, to all rights of persons and of property, in accordance with the rights of the States, and with the constitution and laws of the Union;

Equity and uniformity in the mode of admitting new States into the Union, making the same rules and ratios to apply to all alike;

The rejection of all compromises, conditions or terms which would discriminate between forms of republican constitutions, admitting one, with one number of population, and requiring three times that number for another form equally republican;

The great law of settlement of the public domain of the United States, free, equal, and just, never to be "temporized" or "localized" by temporary or partial expedients, but to be adjusted by permanent, uniform and universal rules of right and justice.

Maintaining these and the like principles, I deem it to be the aim of the struggle of the devoted Democracy in this signal contest. And so understanding them, I glory in their declaration and defence. I would sacrifice much and go far to uphold your arms in this battle. I would most gladly visit your people, address them, and invoke them to stand fast by the standard of their faith and freedom, and never to let go the truths for which they contend, for they are vital and cardinal, and essential, and can never be yielded without yielding liberty itself.

But, sir, I am like a tied man, bound to my duties here; and, if my office would allow me to leave it, I could not depart from the bedside of illness in my family, which would probably recall me before I could reach Illinois; and my own state of health admonishes me that I ought not to undertake a campaign as arduous as that you propose. I know what the labors of the stump are, and am not yet done suffering bodily from my efforts for Democracy in 1855. For these reasons, I cannot obey your call; but, permit me to add: Fight on! fight on! fight on!—never yield but in death or victory! And, oh! that I was unbound and could do more than look on, throbbing with every pulse of your glorious struggle—with its every blow and breath—cheered with its hopes, and chafed by its doubts—You have my prayers, and I am,

Yours truly,
HENRY A. WISE.

The Democracy of Illinois were not satisfied with the spirit and tone of Mr. Breckinridge's letter, nor did they acknowledge the justice of the Vice-President's insinuation, that their position was no better than Black Republicanism, contained in the following paragraph:

I have often, in conversation, expressed the wish that Mr. Douglas may succeed over his competitor; but it is due to candor to say, that this preference is not founded on his course at the last session of Congress, *and would not exist* if I supposed it would be construed as an indorsement of the attitude which he then chose to assume toward his party, or of all the positions he has taken in the present canvass.

The speeches of Mr. Breckinridge, in favor of the Nebraska Bill, while that measure was pending in Congress, and in 1856, when a candidate for the Vice-Presidency, in each of which he advocated the doctrine of popular sovereignty, in terms quite as explicit as those employed by Mr. Douglas in his Freeport speech, were too fresh in the minds of Illinoisans to permit this implied rebuke from a gentleman whom they had so recently aided in electing to the second office in the gift of the people to pass without hard thoughts. Nor did the Illinois Democrats exactly relish the ambiguous and equivocal language in which the Vice-President gave his reasons for preferring Mr. Douglas to Mr. Lincoln.

The tone and temper of the noble letter of Governor Wise, replete with fervid interest in the struggle, is in striking contrast with that of Mr. Breckinridge, and the two letters appearing about the same time, produced a profound impression on the minds and feelings of the Illinois Democracy.

MR. DIXON'S LETTER.

Pending the campaign, the Hon. Archibald Dixon, late United States senator from Kentucky, addressed a letter to the Hon. Henry S. Foote, under date of September 30, 1858, in which the public career of Mr. Douglas was referred to, his position on the Lecompton constitution sustained, and his course on the Nebraska Bill vindicated. Mr. Dixon is an Old Line Whig, and will be remembered as having first moved the repeal of the Missouri restriction in the Senate, an amendment which was modified and accepted by Mr. Douglas, and subsequently incorporated into the Nebraska-Kansas Bill.

The following extract will show in what estimation Mr. Douglas is held by one of the retired statesmen of the country, no longer influenced by partisan feeling and personal rivalry :

Of Judge Douglas, personally, I have a few words to utter which I could not withhold, without greatly wronging my own conscience. When I entered the United States Senate a few years since, I found him a decided favorite with the political party then dominant both in the Senate and the country. My mind had been greatly prejudiced against him, and I felt no disposition whatever to sympathize, or to coöperate with him. It soon became apparent to me, as to others, that he was, upon the whole, far the ablest Democratic member of the body. In the progress of time my respect for him, both as a gentleman and a statesman, greatly increased. I found him sociable, affable, and in the highest degree entertaining and instructive in social intercourse. His power, as a debater, seemed to me unequalled in the Senate. He was industrious, energetic, bold, and skillful in the management of the concerns of his party. He was the acknowledged leader of the Democratic party in the Senate, and, to confess the truth, seemed to me to bear the honors which encircled him with sufficient meekness. Such was the palmy state of his reputation and popularity on the day that he reported to the Senate his celebrated Kansas and Nebraska Bill.

On examining that bill, it struck me that it was deficient in one material respect; it did not in terms repeal the restrictive provision in regard to slavery embodied in the Missouri Compromise. This, to me, was a deficiency that I thought it imperiously necessary to supply. I accordingly offered an amendment to that effect. My amendment seemed to take the Senate by surprise, and no one appeared more startled than Judge Douglas himself. He immediately came to my seat and courteously remonstrated against my amendment, suggesting that the bill which he had introduced was almost in the words of the Territorial acts for the organization of Utah and New Mexico; that they being a part of the Compromise measures of 1850, he had hoped that I, a known and zealous friend of the wise and patriotic adjustment which had then taken place, would not be inclined to do anything to call that adjustment in question or weaken it before the country.

I replied that it was precisely because I had been, and was, a firm and zealous friend of the Compromise of 1850, that I felt bound to persist in the movement which I had originated; that I was well satisfied that the Missouri restriction, if not expressly repealed, would continue to operate in the Territory to which it had been applied, thus negativing the great and salutary principle of *non-intervention*, which constituted the most prominent and essential feature of the plan of settlement of 1850. We talked for some time amicably, and separated. Some days afterward Judge Douglas came to my lodgings, while I was confined by physical indisposition, and urged me to get up and take a ride with him in his carriage. I accepted his invitation and rode out with him. During our short excursion we talked on the subject of my proposed amendment, and Judge Douglas, to my high gratification, proposed to me that I should allow him to take charge of the amendment and ingraft it on his Territorial Bill. I acceded to the proposition at once, whereupon a most interesting inter-change occurred between us.

On this occasion, Judge Douglas spoke to me, in substance, thus : " I have become perfectly satisfied that it is my duty, as a fair-minded national statesman, to coöperate with you as proposed in securing the repeal of the Missouri Compromise restriction. It is due to the South ; it is due to the Constitution, heretofore palpably infracted ; it is due to that character for *consistency*, which I have heretofore labored to maintain. The repeal, if we can effect it, will produce much stir and commotion in the free States of the Union for a season. I shall be assailed by demagogues and fana-tics there, without stint or moderation. Every opprobrious epithet will be applied to me. I shall be probably hung in effigy in many places. It is more than probable that I may become permanently odious among those whose friendship and esteem I have heretofore possessed. This proceed-ing may end my political career. But, acting under the sense of the duty which animates me, I am prepared to make the sacrifice. I will do it."

He spoke in the most earnest and touching manner, and I confess that I was deeply affected. I said to him in reply : "Sir, I once recognized you as a demagogue, a mere party manager, selfish and intriguing. I now find you a warm-hearted and sterling patriot. Go forward in the pathway of duty as you propose, and though all the world desert you, *I never will*."

The subsequent course of this extraordinary personage is now before the country. His great speeches on this subject, in the Senate and else-where, have since been made. As a true national statesman—as an inflexible and untiring advocate and defender of the Constitution of his country—as an enlightened, fair-minded, and high-souled patriot, he has fearlessly battled for principle ; he has with singular consistency pursued the course which he promised to pursue when we talked together in Wash-ington, neither turning to the right nor to the left. Though sometimes reviled and ridiculed by those most benefited by his labors, he has never been heard to complain. Persecuted by the leading men of the party he had so long served and sustained, he has demeaned himself, on all occa-sions, with moderation and dignity ; though he has been ever earnest in the performance of duty, energetic in combating and overcoming the ob-stacles which have so strangely beset his pathway, and always ready to meet and to overthrow such adversaries as have ventured to encounter him. *He has been faithful to his pledge ;* he has been true to the South and to the Union, and I intend to be faithful to my own pledge. I am sincerely grateful for his public services. I feel the highest admiration for all his noble qualities and high achievements, and I regard his reputation as part of the moral treasures of the nation itself.

And now, in conclusion, permit me to say that the southern people cannot enter into unholy alliance for the destruction of Judge Douglas, if they are true to themselves, for he has made more sacrifices to sustain southern institutions than any man now living. Southern men may, and doubtless have, met the enemies of the South in the councils of the nation, and sustained, by their votes and their speeches, her inalienable rights under the Constitution of our common country; northern men may have voted that those rights should not be wrested from us; but it has remained for Judge Douglas alone, northern man as he is, to throw himself "into the deadly imminent breach," and like the steadfast and everlasting rock of the ocean, to withstand the fierce tide of fanaticism, and drive back those angry billows which threatened to ingulf his country's happiness.

I have the honor to be, very respectfully and cordially, your friend and fellow-citizen,   ARCH. DIXON.

Our limits will not allow us to refer further to the incidents of the Illinois campaign. The canvass on both sides was conducted with unparalleled spirit and energy until the day of the election. The result is well known. The Republicans were completely routed, and a Democratic legislature chosen. Mr. Douglas' majority on joint ballot was eight, three in the Senate and five in the House. Most of the federal office-holders voted the Republican ticket, and the reason assigned for this act of treachery to the party was, that the entire Catholic vote had remained faithful to the party with which they had usually acted.

The "Chicago Herald," the organ of the Administration, on the day after the election, explained the reasons why the Administration ticket in that city received only 215 votes, when there were 600 persons in Government employ, as follows:

The fact having become known on the eve of the election, that *the entire Catholic vote of this city*, notwithstanding professions to the contrary, *would be thrown for Douglas*, the National Democrats became exasperated at such *wholesale treachery*, and despite all the efforts that could be made to prevent it, they voted *en masse* for *the Republican candidates*, as the most effectual way of defeating Douglas.

When full returns of the result had been received from all parts of the State, the Democracy celebrated their triumph with great eclat and rejoicing. Thousands of citizens from all quarters of the West flocked to Chicago to take part in the celebration.

When the immense procession reached the front of the Tremont House, they gave nine hearty cheers for Senator Douglas, and loudly called for a speech. Mr. Douglas made his appearance on the same balcony from which he had opened the canvas four months previous, and addressed the vast assemblage as follows :

My Friends and Fellow-Citizens : I return you my heartfelt thanks for this magnificent demonstration. The Democracy of Illinois have achieved a noble victory over the combined forces of Abolitionism and its allies. (Cheers.) You have a right to be proud of this glorious triumph. It is the triumph of the Constitution over faction ; it is the triumph of the glorious principles of the Union over fanaticism and sectionalism (applause) ; it is the triumph of the principle of self-government over Congressional interference and Executive dictation. (Immense applause.)

Four months ago, I opened the canvass in a speech from this balcony to countless thousands of my fellow-citizens ; I now appear before you to receive the congratulations of as many more thousands rejoicing over our great success. While it is right and proper that you should rejoice at the success of sound constitutional principles which insure peace and harmony to the republic, it is our duty to enjoy our victory with moderation. With the result of this election let all the asperities, the excitements and angry passions which have been aroused during the contest be buried forever. It is neither just nor magnanimous to rejoice over a vanquished foe. (Cheers.) Let us teach our political opponents that although we have triumphed, the victory is for their good as well as ours. (Great applause.) When we put sound, just and constitutional principles into practical operation in this government, the Republicans enjoy the blessings thus conferred as well as the Democrats. (Good, good, and cheers.) It is right, therefore, that all should rejoice in our triumph, but it is our duty to be kind, generous and magnanimous toward those whom we have differed with in opinion. (Cheers.) Let us remember, that while we are divided into political parties and separated from each other by antagonistic principles, yet as citizens of a common republic we all revere the glories of our past history, and trust that our posterity will share a common destiny in all time to come. (Applause.) This Union, through the Constitution, has conferred upon our country the greatest legacy that Divine Providence has ever vouchsafed to a free people. (Hear, hear.) Let that Constitution be administered as our fathers made it; let that bond of union which binds these States together continue forever, each State retaining its sovereign rights, disposing of its own internal affairs, and regulating its own domestic institutions to suit itself. (Cheers.) Let that great principle of popular sovereignty, which underlies our republican institutions, be carried out in good faith in the States and Territories alike. (Cheers.) Let Illinois regulate her own affairs, model her institutions according to her own wishes, and mind her own business, permitting every other State to do the same thing (cheers), and there will then be concord and fraternal feeling among the different States of the Union. (Renewed cheering.)

We must discard forever that fatal heresy which teaches that this Union, divided into free and slave States, as our fathers made it, cannot endure—that false philosophy which says that these States must all become free, or all become slave—that they must become all one thing, or all the other, should be discarded forever (applause); and the great principle of popular sovereignty, of State rights and State sovereignty should prevail, declaring the right of the people of each State and each Territory to manage their own affairs in their own way, subject only to the Constitution. (Three cheers.) When that principle shall be recognized and proclaimed by the whole American people, North and South, there will then be peace, and harmony, and fraternity among all the States of this confederacy (good, and applause); but so long as that monstrous political heresy shall prevail, that the North must combine against the South to abolish slavery everywhere, and that the South must combine against the North to establish it everywhere—that there must be an "irrepressible conflict" between the North and the South for the ascendency, so long there will be discord, strife and hatred between the different sections of the Union. ("That's it," and applause.) That great issue was directly and distinctly submitted to the people of Illinois at the recent election, and thank God, the principles of the Constitution and the Union have triumphed. (Immense applause.) Illinois now stands as she has ever stood, faithful to the Constitution and the Union; Illinois now stands as she has ever stood, immovable, upon Democratic principles, maintaining the Democratic organization. (Six cheers.) Every other free State in this Union at some time has wheeled out of line, except gallant Illinois. (Tremendous applause.) From the day that Illinois entered this confederacy, up to this hour, she has cast her vote for Democratic candidates for the Presidency and Vice-Presidency at every succeeding election. (Renewed applause.) And yet you have been told that the only State that has never failed to stand by the Democratic organization, and vote for the Democratic candidates for President, is now to be read out of that party by the politicians of those States which have all gone Abolition. When this dark cloud of fanaticism, which has spread over the New England States, rolled over New York, completely overwhelmed Pennsylvania, Indiana, Ohio, and reached in its course the Wabash River, it was there met by the invincible Democracy of Illinois, who turned back the tide and kept the flag of the Constitution and the Union floating over their beloved State. (Cheers.)

The victory you are now celebrating is one never to be forgotten, for it is the triumph of Union, constitutional men over fanaticism, sectionalism, and disunion. Illinois now occupies the proud position of having fought the good fight; Illinois is now greeted all over the Union—north and south, east and west—as the only northern State that was not overwhelmed in the recent elections. (Cheers.) To what cause do the Democracy of Illinois owe this triumph? It is due to fidelity to principle. (Applause.) In Illinois the true principle of popular sovereignty has been sustained; in Illinois the Cincinnati platform has been strictly adhered to ; In Illinois the Democratic organization has been maintained. (Six cheers, and long continued enthusiasm.) In Illinois there have been no new tests interpolated into the Democratic platform (applause) ; in Illinois Democrats have never been persecuted because of differences of opinion, provided they remained inside of the Democratic party and abided the usages of its organization. (Cheers.) In Illinois, a liberal, tolerant, just and generous policy has prevailed, and in Illinois a glorious triumph has rewarded that policy. (Applause.)

Now, my friends, the result in this State contrasted with the disasters in others, furnishes a lesson. Let the bitterness that has been excited, let the angry passions that have been aroused, be buried with the contest out of which they arose. (Good, and cheers.) Let us meet our fellow-citizens who differed with us in politics the same as if there had been no angry

8*

feeling engendered. It is our duty now to consolidate the party, to begin to combine our forces for the future, in order that we may present a full, united, invincible front to Abolitionism and all of its allied forces. (Cheers.) If wise and patriotic counsels now prevail, the great battle of Popular Sovereignty has been fought and the victory won forever. (Cheers.) If we expect to maintain our liberties as our fathers transmitted them to us, we must be vigilant and watchful, preserving our organization, and ever ready to present a united and irresistible front to the common enemy wherever he makes his appearance. (Cheers.)

My friends, I will now renew to you my grateful and profound acknowledgments for the magnificent demonstrations which you have made, to-night.

CHAPTER XIV.

Mr. Douglas leaves Chicago for New Orleans—Received at St. Louis and Memphis—Brilliant Reception at New Orleans—Speech at Odd Fellows Hall—Departs for New York—Received by Corporate Authorities—Voted Independence Hall in Philadelphia—Speaks at Baltimore — Receives news of his Reëlection as Senator on point of starting for Washington.

Soon after the close of the Illinois campaign, in November, 1858, Mr. Douglas, with his family, left Chicago for the purpose of making a brief visit to New Orleans, to attend to some pressing private matters which his public duties had constrained him too long to neglect. He gave no notice of his intention to make the trip, desiring to perform the journey as speedily and quietly as possible. Remaining in St. Louis a day, for a boat to convey him down the river, the news of his presence soon spread through the city, and that night he was honored with a serenade by a large concourse of citizens, who assembled around the hotel and insisted on a speech. Mr. Douglas acknowledged the compliment in a few appropriate remarks, and expressed his gratification that the people of Missouri, who were so deeply interested in the institution of slavery, so justly appreciated the nature and importance of the contest through which he had recently passed in Illinois.

Proceeding down the river without giving any public notice of his destination, Mr. Douglas was surprised when, nearly a hundred miles above Memphis, he was notified that the Democracy of that city had learned by telegraph of his intended visit to New Orleans, and had appointed a committee of one hundred persons and chartered a steamer to proceed up the river and meet him, for the purpose of inducing him to stop a day at Memphis and accept of the hospitalities of that city. Not feeling at liberty to decline so flattering an invitation, Mr. Douglas placed himself in the hands of the committee, and on the following day addressed a large meeting of the citizens of Memphis on the political topics of the day. In this speech Mr. Douglas confined himself mainly to a discussion of the points presented in the Illinois campaign, prefacing it with the declaration, that no political creed was sound which could not be proclaimed equally as well in one State of the Union as in the other. On a comparison of the published report of this speech, as it appeared in the newspapers of the day, we find that he asserted the same views on the Territorial question in Memphis as he had done in Illinois.

The cordial and enthusiastic approbation with which his audience received his speech, must have satisfied Mr. Douglas that Democracy was the same in Tennessee as in Illinois.

At New Orleans, Mr. Douglas' reception was truly grand and magnificent. Approaching the Crescent at 9 o'clock at night, he was received by the city authorities, the military and the citizens, amidst the firing of cannon and in the glare of a brilliant illumination. He was escorted to the St. Charles Hotel, where he was lodged as the guest of the city, and addressed by the mayor on behalf of the municipal authorities, and by Hon. Pierre Soulé on behalf of the citizens, in eloquent speeches of congratulation on his brilliant victory in Illinois over the enemies of the Constitution and the Union, to each of which he made an appropriate response.

On the 6th December, he addressed the people of New

Orleans at Odd Fellows Hall, on the political topics of the day, at the request of a large number of citizens, embracing all shades of political opinions. We deem this speech of sufficient importance to the reader to justify us in giving one or two extracts:

MR. PRESIDENT AND CITIZENS OF NEW ORLEANS: It was with much hesitation and no small degree of reluctance that I was induced to give my consent to address you on this occasion. I have just passed through a fierce conflict in my own State, which required me to perform more speaking than was either agreeable to my wishes or consistent with my strength. When I determined to visit New Orleans, it was only on private business of an imperative character; and it was my desire to arrive and depart as quietly as possible, and without in any way connecting myself with politics. I approached your city, as I supposed, unheralded and unknown, and I was amazed at the magnificent reception extended to me on the Levee by so vast a concourse of people, embracing the municipal authorities, the citizens in their individual capacity, my own political friends, and men of all political parties. This was a compliment which filled my heart with gratitude, and did not leave me at liberty to decline the first request you might make of me in return. I have, therefore, yielded to your solicitations, to make a few remarks on the political topics which now agitate the public mind throughout the length and breadth of our glorious Republic, and I have done so the more readily as I desire to know whether the principles which are admitted to be sound and orthodox in the free States can pass current in the slave States.

So long as we live under a common Constitution, binding on the people of all the States, any political creed which cannot be proclaimed in Louisiana as boldly as in Illinois, must be unsound and unsafe. I shall not attempt to enter upon any new views, or propound any original ideas, with the view of testing the truth of this proposition, but shall simply discuss these questions now at issue in the country, in the same manner that I am in the habit of doing before an Illinois audience. The tendency of events during the past fifteen years has been to force the organization of political parties on a geographical basis, to array the North against the South, embittering the one against the other, under the misapprehension that there is some irreconcilable antagonism in their interests which prevents harmony between them. For the last twenty-five years I have been in public life; fifteen years have been spent in the Congress of the United States, and the whole of my life has been devoted to the discovery and elucidation of some common ground on which northern and southern men might stand on terms of equality and justice. If you will take pains to examine the history of this sectional strife which has grown up in our midst, you will find that the whole contest has arisen from an attempt on the part of the Federal Government to assume, or usurp, the exercise of powers not conferred by the federal Constitution.

* * * * * * * * *

NON-INTERVENTION THE ONLY POLICY THAT CAN SAVE THE UNION.

The Democracy of Illinois, in the first place, accepts the decision of the Supreme Court of the United States in the case of Dred Scott, as an authoritative interpretation of the Constitution. In accordance with that decision, we hold that slaves are property, and hence on an equality with all other kinds of property, and that the owner of a slave has the same right to move into a Territory and carry his slave property with him, as the owner of any other property has to go there and carry his property. All citizens of the United States, no matter whether they come from the North or the South, from a free State or a slave State, can enter a Territory with their property on an equal footing. And, I apprehend, when you arrive there with your property, of whatever description, it is subject to the local laws of the Territory. How can your slave property be protected without local law, any more than any other kind of property? The Constitution gives you the right to go into a Territory and carry your slaves with you, the same as any other species of property; but it does not punish any man for stealing your slaves any more than stealing any other kind of property. Congress has never yet passed a law providing a criminal code or furnishing protection to any kind of property. It has simply organized the Territory and established a legislature, that legislature being vested with legislative power over all rightful subjects of legislation, subject only to the Constitution of the United States. Hence, whatever jurisdiction the legislature possesses over other property, it has over slave property—no more, no less. Let me ask you, as southern men, whether you can hold slaves anywhere unless protected by the local law? Would not the inaction of the local legislature, its refusal to provide a slave code, or to punish offences against that species of property, exclude slavery just as effectually as a constitutional prohibition? Would it not have that effect in Louisiana and in every other State ? No one will deny it. Then, let me ask you, if the people of a Territory refuse to pass a slave code, how are you going to make them do it? When you give them power to legislate on all rightful subjects of legislation, it becomes a question for them to decide and not for you.

If the local legislature imposes a tax on horses, or any other kind of property, you may think it a hardship, but how are you going to help it? Just so it is with regard to traffic in liquors. If you are dealing in liquors you have the same right to take your liquors into the Territory that anybody else has to take any other species of property. You may pass through and take your liquors *in transitu*, and you will be protected in your right of property under the Constitution of the United States; but if you open the packages they become subject to the local law ; and should the Maine law happen to prevail in the Territory, you had better travel with your liquors. Hence, if the local legislature has the same power over slave property as over every other species of property, what right have you to complain of that equality? But if you do complain, where is your remedy ? And let me say to you that if you oppose this just doctrine, if you attempt to exempt slaves from the same rules that apply to every other kind of property, you will abandon your strongest ground of defence against the assaults of the Black Republicans and Abolitionists. If the people of a Territory are in favor of slavery they will make laws to protect it ; if opposed to slavery they will not make those laws, and you cannot compel them to do it. But I will tell you when they will have it, and when slavery will find protection in a Territory. It is when the Territory lies in those latitudes and climates which adapt it to the profitable production of rice and sugar and cotton, and where slave labor will be remunerative. Thus, slavery will exist wherever soil, climate, and productions demand it, and it will exist nowhere else. Now, if climate, and soil, and self-interest will regulate this question, why should we quarrel about it ? When you arrive at a certain distance to the north of the line there cannot be any doubt of the result : and so when you go to a certain distance south, the result will be equally certain the other way. But in the great central regions, where there may be some doubt as to the effect of natural causes, who ought to decide the question except the people residing there, who have all their interest there ; who have gone there to live with their wives and children ? Any party which attempts, by a system of coercion, to force any institutions into regions not adapted to them, violates the great principles on which our government is founded.

You now have my views on the subject of slavery in the Territories.

Practically, they amount simply to this: If the people want slavery they will have it; if they do not want it they will not have it, and you cannot force it upon them. If these principles be recognized and adhered to, we can live in peace and harmony together; but just as surely as you attempt to force the people to have slavery, against their will, in regions to which it is not adapted, fanaticism will take control of the Federal Government.

FOREIGN POLICY—EXPANSION THE LAW OF OUR EXISTENCE.

A few words more and I am done. I will only say to you, in conclusion, that if we recognize and observe this principle of State rights and self-government for the people of the Territories, there will be peace forever between the North and South, and America will fulfill the glorious destiny which the Almighty has marked out for her. She will remain an example for all nations, expanding as her people increase and her interests demand more territory. I am not in favor of the acquisition of territory by fraud, violence, or improper means of any kind; on the contrary, I would never permit the Federal Government to be an instrument in the hands of foreign powers to carry out their purposes upon the American continent. Let us adopt a policy consistent with our destiny, and then bide our time.

[Mr. Douglas was apparently about to bring his remarks to a close at this point, when, in response to calls of "Cuba! Cuba!" from the audience, he proceeded thus:]

It is our destiny to have Cuba, and it is folly to debate the question. It naturally belongs to the American continent. It guards the mouth of the Mississippi River, which is the heart of the American continent, and the body of the American nation.

Its acquisition is a matter of time only. Our government should adopt the policy of receiving Cuba as soon as a fair and just opportunity shall be presented. Whether that opportunity occur next year or the year after, whenever the occasion arises and the opportunity presents itself, it should be embraced.

The same is true of Central America and Mexico. It will not do to say we have territory enough. When the Constitution was formed, there was enough, yet in a few years afterward, we needed more. We acquired Louisiana and Florida, Texas and California, just as the increase in our population and our interest demanded. When, in 1850, the Clayton-Bulwer treaty was sent to the Senate for ratification, I fought it to the end. They then asked what I wanted with Central America. I told them I did not want it then, but the time would come when we must have it. They then asked what my objection to the treaty was. I told them I objected to that among other clauses of it, which said that neither Great Britain nor the United States should ever buy, annex, colonize, or acquire any portion of Central America. I said I would never consent to a treaty with any foreign power, pledging ourselves not to do in the future whatever interest or necessity might compel us to do. I was then told by veteran senators, as my distinguished friend well knows (looking toward Mr. Soulé), that Central America was so far off that we should never want it. I told them then, "Yes; a good way off—half way to California, and on the direct road to it." I said it was our right and duty to open all the highways between the Atlantic and the Gulf States and our possessions on the Pacific, and that I would enter into no treaty with Great Britain or any other government concerning the affairs of the American continent. And here, without a breach of confidence, I may be permitted to state a conversation which took place at that time between myself and the British minister, Sir Henry Lytton Bulwer, on that point. He took occasion to remonstrate with me that my position with regard to the treaty was unjust and untenable ; that the treaty was fair because it was reciprocal, and it was reciprocal because it pledged that neither Great Britain nor the United States should ever purchase, colonize, or acquire any territory in Central America. I told him that it would be fair if they would add one word to the treaty—so that it would read that neither Great Britain nor the United States should ever occupy or hold dominion over Central America or Asia. But he said : "You have no interest in Asia ;" "No," answered I, "and you have none in Central America."

"But," said he, "you can never establish any rights in Asia." "No," said I, "and we don't mean that you shall ever establish any in America." I told him it would be just as respectful for us to ask that pledge in reference to Asia, as it was for Great Britain to ask it from us in reference to Central America.

If experience shall continue to prove, what the past may be considered to have demonstrated, that those little Central American powers cannot maintain self-government, the interests of Christendom require that some power should preserve order for them. Hence, I maintain that we should adopt and observe a line of policy in unison with our own interests and our destiny. I do not wish to force things. We live in a rapid age. Events crowd upon each other with marvellous rapidity. I do not want territory any faster than we can occupy, Americanize, and civilize i:. 1 am no filibuster. I am opposed to unlawful expeditions; but on the other hand, I am opposed to this country acting as a miserable constabulary for France and England.

I am in favor of expansion as fast as consistent with our interest and the increase and development of our population and resources. But I am not in favor of that policy unless the great principle of non-intervention and the right of the people to decide the question of slavery, and all other domestic questions, for themselves shall be maintained. If that principle prevail, we have a future before us more glorious than that of any other people that ever existed. Our republic will endure for thousands of years. Progress will be the law of its destiny; it will gain new strength with every State brought into the confederacy. Then there will be peace and harmony between the free States and the slave States. The more degrees of latitude and longitude embraced beneath our Constitution, the better. The greater the variety of productions, the better; for then we shall have the principles of free trade apply to the important staples of the world, making us the greatest planting as well as the greatest manufacturing, the greatest commercial, as well as the greatest agricultural power on the globe.

These are my views in regard to our foreign relations. They are questions I had not intended to discuss; and I should not have done so if some gentleman in the crowd had not called my attention to them. My votes in Congress have always been in harmony with the line of policy I have here marked out. It matters not whether you acquire more territory, or how much or how little you wish to acquire. Expansion is the law of our existence; when we cease to grow, we commence to decline. Hence our course is onward, on the principle established by our fathers, under Divine inspiration, as I believe, in the formation of the government.

And now permit me to return my grateful acknowledgments for the kindness with which you have listened to me, and to retire.

Mr. Douglas determined, at New Orleans, to take the steamer for New York, in order to secure relaxation from his recent labor. On the island of Cuba, where he stopped a few days *en route*, he was treated with marked attention by the authorities and people.

Arriving at New York, he found that elaborate preparations had been made in that city by the authorities for his reception. Both branches of the Council, by a unanimous vote, had extended to him the freedom of the city, and had invited him to become its guest.

PREAMBLE AND RESOLUTIONS OF THE BOARDS OF ALDERMEN AND COUNCILMEN OF THE CITY OF NEW YORK.

Whereas, Information has been received that the Hon. Stephen A. Douglas, United States senator from Illinois, will arrive in this city in a few days, *en route* for Washington, and

Whereas, It is eminently due this esteemed patriot and distinguished senator, that the city of New York, through its constituted authorities, should extend to him a cordial welcome on his arrival, in order to express our admiration of the man, and of the principles which he has so long and so ably advocated ;

Therefore, be it *resolved*, That a committee be appointed to extend to the Hon. Stephen A. Douglas the hospitalities of the city, and to become the guest of the corporation during his stay in New York.

And be it further *resolved*, That the flags be displayed on the City Hall during the day set apart for the reception of our distinguished guest.

Accordingly, Mr. Douglas was met at the wharf, on his arrival at New York, by the joint committee of the two boards of Common Council, and escorted to the Everett House. During his sojourn in the city, he was treated with such demonstrations of respect and regard as few public men have ever received.

No sooner had the news of Mr. Douglas' arrival in New York reached Philadelphia, than a committee of eminent citizens was appointed to repair to New York and tender him a public reception in Independence Hall, in pursuance of the resolutions of the Councils of Philadelphia, unanimously tendering its use for that purpose.

Although anxious to repair at once to Washington, and avoid all further demonstrations—for his journey so far had

been one continuous ovation—Mr. Douglas could not well decline an invitation which had rarely, if ever, been extended
to any American who had held a less position than President
of the United States.

The reader will hardly fail to admire the speeches which
were delivered on this interesting occasion.

Wm. E. Lehman, Esq., on behalf of the citizens' committee,
introduced Senator Douglas to the Mayor and Council. He
said:

MAYOR HENRY: It was my agreeable duty to be one of the committee
appointed to go to New York, and wait upon the distinguished senator of
Illinois, and extend to him a cordial invitation to visit our city. In the
performance of that duty, I not only represented his personal and political
friends, but, in a measure, the corporate authorities of the city. I informed
Senator Douglas that the councils of the city, without distinction of party,
had unanimously tendered him the use of Independence Hall to receive his
friends, and that it was your intention, as chief magistrate of this munici-
pality, to welcome him. I deem it proper to state that the senator, in his
reply, consented to waive all his private arrangements, and to forego engagements of a pressing public nature, to accept this grateful tribute of
respect. It is with great pleasure that I now introduce to you the illustrious senator.

Mayor Henry then addressed Senator Douglas in the following:

MR. SENATOR: The councils of Philadelphia have tendered you, in passing through this city, the use of the Hall of Independence for the
reception of your friends, and in their name I welcome you upon this
occasion.

This spot is the common heritage of American freemen. Within these
walls, memorable for the most illustrious deed in our country's history,
hallowed more than once by the ashes of the mighty dead, cherished as
the depository of the mementoes of patriots and heroes, all other sentiments merge in that of unalloyed devotion to the Union, its prosperity
and its perpetuity.

I greet you, sir, as a member of those national councils on whom devolves the guardianship of our nation's interest and destiny; as one whose eminent position in those councils has elicited the admiration and respect of so many of your fellow-citizens.

Permit me, individually, to express my wishes for your personal welfare, and the assurance that the hospitality of Philadelphia will be well cared for by your surrounding friends.

SENATOR DOUGLAS' SPEECH.

Senator Douglas, in response, said: MR. MAYOR—It has fallen to my lot, as a public man, and as a politician, to receive many testimonials from political and partisan friends, which, under the circumstances, were most grateful to my feelings; but the tender of the use of this hall voluntarily, and as I am informed, by the unanimous sentiment of the corporate authorities of the city of Philadelphia—this hall, within whose sacred precincts no thought, no sentiment, can enter any citizen's breast inconsistent with the peace of the republic and the perpetuity of the Union—is a compliment that overwhelms me with gratitude. In this hall we find the pictures, and we feel the influence of the spirit, of those sages and patriots to whom we owe our independence and our constitutional form of government. Here that sentiment which now animates all the free governments of the earth first found its authoritative exposition and proclamation. There stands the bell which "proclaimed liberty throughout the land, unto all the inhabitants thereof;" and it seems as if the inscription it bears was directed by the hand of Divine Providence, for it was placed upon it far in advance of the period when any human brain could foresee that it was to be used to proclaim the independence of America over the arbitrary decrees of a British parliament. The great principle proclaimed by the fathers of the republic in this hall, was the right of the people of all the States, of all the provinces and dependencies, and of every community, to regulate its own domestic concerns and internal affairs in its own way. Pennsylvania has always been true to that cardinal principle of representative government. Pennsylvania, with her Franklin, and those congenial spirits who gave impulse to the Revolution, foresaw that the time might come when, after having maintained her independence against the British parliament, another imperial parliament might be established on her own continent, equally destructive to the liberties of the people and the rights of the citizens, and hence Pennsylvania, in her instructions to her delegates who represented her in this hall, when she anticipated the Declaration of Independence, empowered them to give her assent to that declaration, on the fundamental condition that Pennsylvania retained unto herself forever the right to manage her local and domestic concerns and police regulations in her own way, independent of any other power on the face of the globe.

Sir: If we remain true to these great principles of constitutional liberty proclaimed by our fathers in this hall, and consummated by the Constitution of the United States within the precincts of Philadelphia, this Union may last forever as our forefathers made it, each State retaining just such local and domestic institutions as it shall choose. If my devotion to these constitutional, conservative principles of liberty have attracted to me the attention of the constituted authorities of this vast city, it is ample reward for all of the toils that have accompanied my public life. I appreciate it a thousand times more than any partisan triumph which a transient politician may acquire in the road through life, for such a triumph must necessarily be ephemeral in its character.

Mr. Mayor, discarding all partisan spirit, as you have done, I accept this honor with a grateful heart. I have not the vanity that would receive it as a mark of mere personal respect. I am glad to know that I have the esteem individually of yourself, and of those you represent; but it is far more grateful to me, as a public man, to know that your sympathy is aroused by public services calculated to sustain and perpetuate those principles of civil and religious liberty which our fathers have translated to us. May we be successful in handing down to our children, and through our children to our latest posterity, those immortal principles which were first proclaimed in this hall, the witnesses of which stand now, like guardian angels, looking down upon our every act, and inspiring our prayers to Heaven that this Union, this Constitution, these States, as they exist, and have existed, may last forever, not only for the protection of our own people, but as a guide to the friends of freedom throughout the world.

Returning my grateful acknowledgments, I can only say that when I leave here I shall carry with me a recollection of this day which will never be effaced while life lasts, and over the memory of which, I trust, my children will feel more proud than of any act that has heretofore marked my public life.

This great mark of respect to Mr. Douglas was to be the more appreciated, coming as it did from authorities the majority of whom were his political opponents, and was concurred in by the citizens, embracing every shade of political opinions.

The arrangements for Mr. Douglas' reception in Philadelphia by his political friends were imposing beyond description. Cannon, fire-works, music welcomed his arrival, while a vast concourse of citizens escorted him to his hotel, through thronged streets rendered brilliant by the illumination of the houses.

At Havre De Grace, Mr. Douglas was met by a deputation of citizens from Baltimore; the chairman of which delivered an eloquent address of congratulation upon the glorious triumph which he had recently achieved in Illinois over the enemies of the Constitution and the Union, and insisted that he should accept the hospitalities of his political friends in the Monumental City.

Yielding to their request, Mr. Douglas addressed that night a large assemblage of citizens on Monument Square, and the following day had a public reception.

After a brief recapitulation of the issues determined by the people of Illinois, at the late election, Mr. Douglas, in conclusion, said:

"My friends, I have given you an epitome of the principles which I discussed in Illinois in the late contest with the abolitionists and their allies. I appealed to the people of Illinois by their love for the American Union, to preserve sacred the fraternal feeling between the old and the new, the free and slave States; I pointed them to Bunker's Hill, to Bennington, to Saratoga and to Monmouth; I pointed them to King's Mountain, Guilford Court House, and to Yorktown; I showed them that in the Revolution, northern and southern men stood shoulder to shoulder in a common cause, fought under the same banner, poured out their blood in common streams, and shared common graves to secure the liberty which we now enjoy. Why cannot northern and southern men live under this Constitution in the same spirit in which our fathers framed it. I believe that if these principles are firmly adhered to and faithfully carried out, this glorious Union can exist forever, divided into free and slave States, as our fathers made it, each State retaining the right to have just such laws and institutions as it may choose, and to modify and change them as it may see proper. I renew to you my grateful acknowledgments for the kind and respectful manner in which you have listened to me, and beg to bid you good night.

The last and crowning feature of this triumphal tour was the receipt of a telegraphic dispatch by Mr. Douglas, at Baltimore, just as he was entering the cars for Washington, announcing his reëlection to the Senate of the United States by the legislature of Illinois, by a majority of eight votes, having received the vote of every Democratic member in each House.

CHAPTER XV.

Mr. Douglas again in Washington—Experiences a Change of Atmosphere—
Scene shifts—Removed from Post of Chairman of Territorial Commit-
tee—His Services as Chairman—Pretext of Removal—Freeport Speech—
Letter to California in reply to Dr. Gwin.

WHEN Mr. Douglas reached Washington, where Executive
power and patronage stifles popular sentiment, he found himself suddenly plunged into a very different atmosphere from
that which he had been breathing in the past few weeks.
Failing in their efforts to defeat his reëlection to the Senate
by a disreputable coalition with the abolitionists of Illinois,
his enemies contrived a new scheme to humble and degrade
the unsubdued rebel. For thirteen years previous, he had
been chairman of the Committee on Territories, two years in
the House and eleven in the Senate. In that capacity, he
had reported and successfully carried through Congress bills
for the admission of the following States: Texas, Iowa, Wisconsin, California, Oregon, and Minnesota.

During the same period, he had reported and successfully
carried through Congress bills to organize the following Territories: Oregon, Minnesota, New Mexico, Utah, Washington, Kansas, and Nebraska. In that time, he had met and
mastered every intricate question which had arisen connected
with the organization of the Territories and the admission of
new States. Confessedly, he was more familiar with all subjects pertaining to Territorial legislation, than any other living man. His peculiar qualifications and acquaintance with

9

the subject, induced the Senate, on the day of his first entrance into that body, to put him at the head of the Territorial Committee. He had been unanimously nominated in the Democratic caucus, and reëlected chairman of that committee each succeeding year. With a full knowledge on the part of every senator of his views and opinions on Territorial policy, what excuse can be given for the removal of a man from a position which he had so long filled with such distinguished ability, and for which he was so eminently qualified? With or without excuse, however, the deed was consummated in a secret caucus, and in Mr. Douglas' absence. The public indignation at his removal was almost universal. Indeed, so heavily has it fallen on those engaged in it, but three or four senators have ever had the boldness to confess themselves parties to the act, and ever these have assigned a reason as a pretext for the deed, which is an insult to the intelligence of the American people, and but a poor compliment to their own understanding; because they affect to call in question Mr. Douglas' political orthodoxy for the expression of an opinion in his Illinois campaign, which he had advanced and elaborated in his speeches on the Compromise measures of 1850, and upon the passage of the Kansas-Nebraska Bill, and indeed upon every discussion of the slavery question in which he had participated for the ten years previous to his removal.

Notwithstanding Mr. Douglas, in all his joint debates with Mr. Lincoln, in Illinois, had taken direct issue with him on all his abolition propositions—assuming bold ground against negro citizenship—reasserting his old position, that uniformity in the institutions of the various States was neither possible nor desirable—treating negro-slavery as purely a question of climate, production, and political economy, to be regulated by their inexorable laws—sustaining the Fugitive Slave Law, and avowing his willingness, if not strong enough, to vote to make it stronger—maintaining the binding force of all supreme judicial decisions—vindicating the equality of all the States, and proclaiming the right of all their citizens to emigrate into the common Territories on the basis of an entire equality under the local law, with their property of all descriptions, whether horses, clocks, negroes or what not—denouncing the doctrines of the "irrepressible conflict," when advanced by Lincoln four months prior to Seward's Rochester speech—sustaining the regular organization of the Democratic party, and maintaining the Democratic creed as enunciated in the Cincinnati platform;—notwithstanding all these facts, they seize on an answer of Mr. Douglas to a question propounded by Mr. Lincoln at Freeport, garble it from its context and present it to the country as the reason for his removal from the chairmanship of the Committee on Territories.

It went for nothing that Col. Jefferson Davis had uttered, a few weeks before, at Portland, similar views touching the power of the people of the Territories, which Mr. Douglas quoted and indorsed in a joint debate with Mr. Lincoln at Alton, as containing his own views—nothing that Stephens, Orr, Cobb, and a host of Democratic lights, great and small, were committed to the same proposition—nothing that Mr. Douglas was simply repeating as the Washington "Union" at that time in an elaborate article charged and proved (alleging that he was consistently unsound), what he had uttered frequently in the debates on the Compromise measures of 1850—nothing that Col. Richardson, when the Democratic candidate for Speaker, in 1855, had expressed similar opinions, and received, afterward, every Democratic vote in the House—it booted nothing that Mr. Douglas was on record one hundred times advocating the same doctrine while these very men (his present accusers) were his advocates for the Presidency. These things all stood for nothing.

MR. DOUGLAS' CALIFORNIA LETTER.

It is a remarkable fact, that while Mr. Douglas was removed from the Committee on Territories in December, 1858, no senator ever publicly assigned Mr. Douglas' Freeport speech as a cause for it, until in July, 1859, Dr. Gwin gave this reason in a speech in California. Mr. Douglas promptly replied to Dr. Gwin's speech, in a letter addressed to the editor of the San Francisco "National," from which we extract so much as relates to this subject:

The country is now informed for the first time that I was removed from the post of chairman of the Committee on Territories because of the senti- ments contained in my "Freeport speech." To use the language of Mr. Gwin, "The doctrines he had avowed in his Freeport speech had been condemned in the Senate by his removal from the chairmanship of the Territorial Committee of that body." The country will bear in mind this testimony, that I was not removed because of any personal unkindness or hostility ; nor in consequence of my course on the Lecompton question, or in respect to the administration ; but that it was intended as a condem- nation of the doctrines avowed in my "Freeport speech." The only posi- tion taken in my "Freeport speech," which I have ever seen criticised or controverted, may be stated in a single sentence, and was in reply to an interrogatory propounded by my competitor for the Senate : "That "the Territorial legislature could lawfully exclude slavery, either by non-action or unfriendly legislation." This opinion was not expressed by me at Free- port for the first time. I have expressed the same opinion often in the Senate, freely and frequently, in the presence of those senators who, as Mr. Gwin testifies, removed me "from the chairmanship of the Committee on Territories," ten years after they knew that I held the opinion, and would never surrender it.

I could fill many columns of the "National" with extracts of speeches made by me during the discussion of the Compromise measures in 1850, and in defence of the principles embodied in those measures in 1851 and 1852, in the discussion of the Kansas-Nebraska Bill in 1854, and of the Kansas difficulties and the Topeka revolutionary movements in 1856, in all of which I expressed the same opinion and defended the same position which was assumed in the "Freeport speeech." I will not, however, burden your columns or weary your readers with extracts of all these speeches, but will refer you to each volume of the "Congressional Globe" for the last ten years, where you will find them fully reported. If you cannot conveniently procure the the "Congressional Globe," I refer you to an editorial article in the Washington "Union" of October 5, 1858, which, it was reported, received the sanction of the President of the United States previously to its publication, a few weeks after my "Freeport speech" had been delivered. The "Union" made copious extracts of my speeches in 1850 and 1854, to prove that at each of those periods I held the same opinions which I expressed at Freeport in 1858, and, consequently, declared that I never was a good Democrat, much less sound on the slavery question, when I advocated the Compromise measures of 1850, and the Kansas-Nebraska Bill in 1854.

In the article referred to, the Washington Union said:

"We propose to show that Judge Douglas' action in 1850 and 1854 was taken with especial reference to the announcement of doctrine and programme which was made at Freeport. The declaration at Freeport was, that in his opinion the people can, by lawful means, exclude slavery from a Territory before it comes in as a State;' and he declared that his competitor had 'heard him argue the Nebraska Bill on that principle all over Illinois in 1854, 1855, and 1856, and had no excuse to pretend to have any doubt on that subject.'"

The Union summed up the evidence furnished by my speeches in the Senate in 1850 and 1854, that the "Freport speech" was consistent with my former course, with this emphatic declaration.

"Thus we have shown that precisely the position assumed by Judge Douglas at Freeport had been maintained by him in 1850, in the debates and votes on the Utah and New Mexican Bills, and in 1854 on the Kansas-Nebraska Bill; and have shown that it was owing to his opposition that clauses depriving Territorial legislatures of the power of excluding slavery from their jurisdictions were not expressly inserted in those measures."

The evidence thus presented by the Washington "Union"—the evidence of an open enemy—is so full and conclusive, that I have uniformly advocated for ten years past the same principles which I avowed at Freeport, that I cannot refrain from asking you to spread the entire article before your readers, as an appendix, if you choose, to this letter.

The question whether the people of the Territories should be permitted to decide the slavery question for themselves, the same as all other rightful subjects of legislation, was thoroughly discussed and definitively settled in the adoption of the Compromise measures of 1850. The Territorial bills, as originally reported on by the Committee on Territories, extended the authority of the Territorial legislature to all rightful subjects of legislation consistent with the Constitution, *without excepting African slavery.* Modified by the Committee of Thirteen, they conferred power on the Territorial legislature over all rightful subjects of legislation, *except African slavery.* This distinct question, involving the power of the Territorial legislature over the subject of African slavery, was debated in the Senate from the 8th of May until the 31st of July, 1850, when the limitation was stricken out by a vote of yeas 33, nays 19; and the Territorial legislature authorized to legislate on all rightful subjects, *without excepting Afrisan slavery.* In this form and upon this principle, the Compromise measures of 1850 were enacted.

When I returned to my home in Chicago, at the end of the session of Congress, after the adoption of the measures of adjustment, the excitement was intense. The City Council had passed a resolution nullifying the Fugitive Slave Act, and releasing the police from all obligations to obey the law or assist in its execution. Amidst this furious excitement, and surrounded by revolutionary movements, I addressed the assembled populace. My speech, in which I defended each and all of the Compromise measures of 1850, was published at the time, and spread broadcast throughout the country. I herewith send you a copy of that speech, in which you will find that I said—

" These measures are predicated on the great fundamental principle that every people ought to possess the right of forming and regulating their own internal concerns and domestic institutions in their own way. It was supposed that those of our fellow-citizens who emigrated to the shores of the Pacific and to our other territories, were as capable of self-government as their neighbors and kindred whom they left behind them ; and there was no reason for believing that they have lost any of their intelligence or patriotism by the wayside, while crossing the Isthmus or the Plains. It was also believed that after their arrival in the country, when they had become familiar with its topography, climate, productions, and resources, and had connected their destiny with it, they were fully as competent to judge for themselves what kind of laws and institutions were best adapted to their condition and interests, as we were, who never saw the country, and knew very little about it. To question their competency to do this was to deny their capacity for self-government. If they have the requisite intelligence and honesty to be intrusted with the enactment of laws for the government of white men, I know of no reason why they should not be deemed competent to legislate for the negro. If they are sufficiently enlightened to make laws for the protection of life, liberty, and property —of morals and education—to determine the relation of husband and wife, of parent and child—I am not aware that it requires any higher degree of civilization to regulate the affairs of master and servant. These things are all confided by the Constitution to each State to decide for itself, and I know of no reason why the same principle should not be extended to the Territories."

This speech was laid on the desk of every member of the Senate, at the opening of the second session of the 31st Congress, in December, 1850, when, with a full knowledge of my opinions on the Territorial question, I was unanimously nominated in the Democratic caucus, and reëlected by the Senate chairman of the Committee on Territories. From that time to this I have spoken the same sentiments, and vindicated the same positions in debate in the Senate, and have been reëlected chairman of the Committee on Territories at each session of Congress, until last December, by the unanimous voice of the Democratic party in caucus and in the Senate, with my opinions on this Territorial question well known to, and well understood by every senator. Yet Mr. Gwin testifies that I was condemned and deposed by the Senate for the utterance of opinions in 1858, which were put on record year after year so plainly and so unequivocally as to leave neither the Senate nor the country in doubt. Thus does Mr. Gwin, in his eagerness to be my public accuser, speak his own condemnation, for he voted for me session after session, with my opinions, the same that I spoke at Freeport, staring him in the face.

On the 4th of January, 1854, I reported the Nebraska Bill, and, as chairman of the Committee on Territories, accompanied it with a special report, in which I. stated distinctly " that all questions pertaining to slavery in the Territories, and in the new States to be formed therefrom, are to be left to the decision of the people residing therein, by their appropriate representatives to be chosen by them for that purpose." And that the bill proposed " to carry these propositions and principles into practical operation in the precise language of the Compromise measures of 1850." The Kansas-Nebraska Act, as it stands on the statute book, does define the power of the Territorial legislature " in the precise language of the Compromise measures of 1850." It gives the legislature power over all rightful subjects of legislation not inconsistent with the Constitution, without excepting African slavery. During the discussion of the measure it was suggested that it was necessary to repeal the 8th section of the act of the 6th of March, 1850, called the Missouri Compromise, in order to permit the people to control the slavery question while they remained in a Territorial condition, and before they became a State of the Union. That was the object and only purpose for which the Missouri Compromise was repealed.

On the night of the 3d of March, 1854, in my closing speech on the Kansas-Nebraska Bill, a few hours before it passed the Senate, I said : " It is only for the purpose of carrying out this great fundamental principle of self-government that the bill renders the 8th section of the Missouri Act inoperative and void." The article of the Washington " Union " of October

5, 1858, to which I have referred, quotes this and other passages of my speech on that occasion, to prove that the author of the Nebraska Bill framed it with express reference to conferring on the Territorial legislature power to control. the slavery question. And further, that I boldly avowed the purpose at the time in the presence of all the friends of the bill, and urged its passage upon that ground. I have never understood that Mr. Gwin, or any other senator who heard that speech and voted for the bill the same night, expressed any dissent or disapprobation of the doctrines it announced. That was the time for dissent and disapprobation ; that was the time to condemn, if there were cause to condemn, and not four or five years later. The record furnishes no such evidence of dissent or disapprobation ; nor does the history of those times show that the Democratic party, in the North or in the South, or in any portion of the country, repudiated the fundamental principle upon which the Kansas-Nebraska Act is founded, and proscribed its advocates and defenders.

If Mr. Gwin did not understand the Kansas-Nebraska Bill when it was under consideration, according to its plain meaning as explained and defended by its authors and supporters, it is not the fault of those who did understand it precisely as I interpreted it at Freeport, and as the country understood it in the Presidential canvass of 1856. Mr. Buchanan, and leading members of his cabinet, at all events, understood the Kansas-Nebraska Act in the same sense in which it was understood and defended at the time of its passage. Mr. Buchanan, in his letter accepting the Cincinnati nomination, affirmed that " this legislation is founded upon principles as ancient as free government itself, and, in accordance with them, has simply declared that the people of a Territory, like those of a State, shall decide for themselves whether slavery shall or shall not exist within their limits." General Cass, now secretary of state, has always maintained, from the day he penned the " Nicholson Letter " to this, that the people of the Territories have a right to decide the slavery question for themselves whenever they please. In 1856, on the 2d day of July, referring to the Kansas-Nebraska Act, he said: " I believe the original act gave the Territorial legislature of Kansas full power to exclude or allow slavery." Mr. Toucey, the secretary of the navy, interpreted that act in the same way, and, on the same occasion in the Senate, said:

" The original act recognizes in the Territorial legislature all the power which they can have, subject to the Constitution, and subject to the organic law of the Territory."

Mr. Cobb, the secretary of the treasury, in a speech at West Chester, Pennsylvania, on the 19th of September, 1856, advocating Mr. Buchanan's election to the Presidency, said :

"The government of the United States should not force the institution of slavery upon the people either of the Territories or of the States, against the will of the people, though my voice could bring about that result. I stand upon the principle—the people of my State decide it for themselves, you for yourselves, the people of Kansas for themselves. That is the Constitution, and I stand by the Constitution." And again, in the same speech, he said : " Whether they " (the people of a Territory) " decide it by prohibiting it, according to the one doctrine, or by refusing to pass laws to protect it, as contended for by the other party, is immaterial. The majority of the people, by the action of the Territorial legislature, will decide the question; and all must abide the decision when made."

Here we find the doctrines of the Freeport speech, including "non-action" and "unfriendly legislation" as a lawful and proper mode for the exclusion of slavery from a Territory clearly defined by Mr. Cobb, and the election of Mr. Buchanan advocated on those identical doctrines. Mr. Cobb made similar speeches during the Presidential canvass in other sections of Pennsylvania, in Maine, Indiana, and most of the northern States, and was appointed secretary of the treasury by Mr. Buchanan as a mark of gratitude for the efficient services which had been thus rendered. Will any senator who voted to remove me from the chairmanship of the Territorial Committee for expressing opinions for which Mr. Cobb, Mr. Toucey, and General Cass were rewarded, pretend that he did not know that they or either of them had ever uttered such opinions when their nominations were before the Senate ? I am sure that no senator will make so humiliating a confession. Why, then, were those distinguished gentlemen appointed by the President and confirmed by the Senate as cabinet ministers if they were not good Democrats—sound on the slavery question, and faithful exponents of the principles and creed of the party ? Is it not a significant fact that the President and the most distinguished and honored of his cabinet should have been solemnly and irrevocably pledged to this monstrous heresy of "popular sovereignty," for asserting which the Senate, by Mr. Gwin's frank avowal, condemned me to the extent of their power?

It must be borne in mind, however, that the President and members of the cabinet are not the only persons high in authority who are committed to the principle of self-government in the Territories. The Hon. John C. Breckinridge, the Vice-President of the United States, was a member of the House of Representatives when the Kansas-Nebraska Bill passed, and in a speech delivered March 23, 1854, said:

"Among the many misrepresentations sent to the country by some of the enemies of this bill, perhaps none is more flagrant than the charge that it proposes to legislate slavery into Kansas and Nebraska. Sir, if the bill contained such a feature it would not receive my vote. The right to establish involves the correlative right to prohibit, and denying both I would vote for neither. . . . . .

"The effect of the repeal, (of the Missouri Compromise,) therefore, is neither to establish nor to exclude, but to leave the future condition of the Territories dependent wholly upon the action of the inhabitants, subject only to such limitations as the federal Constitution may impose. . . . . It will be observed that the right of the people to regulate in their own way all their domestic institutions is left wholly untouched, except that whatever is done must be done in accordance with the Constitution—the supreme law for us all."

Again, at Lexington, Kentucky, on the 9th of June, 1856, in response to the congratulations of his neighbors on his nomination for the Vice-Presidency, Mr. Breckinridge said:

"The whole power of the Democratic organization is pledged to the following propositions: That Congress shall not interpose upon this subject (slavery) in the States, in the Territories, or in the District of Columbia; that the people of each Territory shall determine the question for themselves, and be admitted into the Union upon a footing of perfect equality with the original States, without discrimination on account of the allowance or prohibition of slavery."

Touching the power of the Territorial legislature over the subject of slavery, the Hon. James L. Orr, late speaker of the House of Representatives, on the 11th of December, 1856, said:

"Now, the legislative authority of a Territory is invested with a discretion to vote for or against the laws. We think they ought to pass laws in every Territory, when the Territory is open to settlement and slaveholders go there, to protect slave property. But if they decline to pass such law, what is the remedy? None, sir, if the majority of the people are opposed to the institution; and if they do not desire it ingrafted upon their Territory, all they have to do is simply to decline to pass laws in the Territorial legislature for its protection, and then it is as well excluded as if the power was invested in the Territorial legislature to prohibit it."

Mr. Stephens, of Georgia, in a speech in the House of Representatives on the 17th of February, 1854, said:

"The whole question of slavery was to be left to the people of the Territories, whether north or south of 86° 30', or any other line. . . . . . .

"It was based upon the truly republican and national policy of taking this disturbing element out of Congress and leaving the whole question of slavery in the Territories to the people there to settle it for themselves. And it is in vindication of that new principle—then established for the first time in the history of our government—in the year 1850, the middle of the nineteenth century, that we, the friends of the Nebraska Bill, whether from the North or South, now call upon this house and the country to carry out in good faith, and give effect to the spirit and intent of those important measures of Territorial legislation."

Again, on the 17th of January, 1856, he said:

" I am willing that the Territorial legislature may act upon the subject when and how they may think proper."

Mr. Benjamin, of Louisiana, in a speech in the Senate on the 25th of May, 1854, on the Nebraska Bill, said:

" We find, then, that this principle of the independence and self-government of the people in the distant Territories of the confederacy harmonizes all these conflicting opinions, and enables us to banish from the halls of Congress another fertile source of content and excitement."

On February 15, 1854, Mr. Badger, of North Carolina, said of the Kansas-Nebraska Bill:

" It submits the whole authority to the Territory to determine for itself. That in my judgment, is the place where it ought to be put. If the people of the Territories choose to exclude slavery, so far from considering it as a wrong done to me or to my constituents, I shall not complain of it. It is their business."

Again, on March 2, 1854, one day before the passage of the bill through the Senate, Mr. Badger said:

" But with regard to that question we have agreed—some of us because we thought it the only right mode, and some because we think it a right mode, and under existing circumstances the preferable mode—to confer this power upon the people of the Territories."

On the same day Mr. Butler, of South Carolina, said:

" Now, I believe that under the provisions of this bill, and of the Utah and New Mexico bills, there will be a perfect carte blanche given to the Territorial legislature to legislate as they may think proper. . . . . . . I am willing to trust them. I have been willing to trust them in Utah and New Mexico, where the Mexican law prevailed, and I am willing to trust them in Nebraska and Kansas, where the French law, according to the idea of the gentleman, may possibly be revived."

In the House of Representatives, June 25, 1856, Mr. Samuel A. Smith, Tennessee, said:

" For twenty years this question had agitated Congress and the country without a single beneficial result. They resolved that it should be transferred from these halls, that all unconstitutional restrictions should be removed, and that the people should determine for themselves the character of their local and domestic institutions under which they were to live, with precisely the same rights, but no greater than those which were enjoyed by the old thirteen States."

And further;

" In 1854, the same question was presented, when the necessity arose for the organization of the Territories of Kansas and Nebraska, and the identical principle was applied for its solution."

In the Senate, on the 25th of February, 1854, Mr. Dodge, of Iowa (now Democratic candidate for governor of that State), said:

"And, sir, honesty and consistency with our course in 1850 demand that those of us who supported the Compromise measures should zealously support this bill, because it is a return to the sound principle of leaving to the people of the Territories the right of determining for themselves their domestic institutions."

And in the House of Representatives, December 28, 1855, Mr. George W. Jones, of Tennessee, said:

"Then, sir, you may call it by what name you please—non-intervention, squatter sovereignty, or popular sovereignty. It is, sir, the power of the people to govern themselves, and they, and they alone, should exercise it, in my opinion, as well while in a Territorial condition as in the position of a State."

And again, in the same speech, he said:

" I believe that the great principle—the right of the people in the Territories, as well as in the States, to form and regulate their own domestic institutions in their own way— is clearly and unequivocally embodied in the Kansas-Nebraska Act, and if it is not, it should have been. Believing that it was the living, vital principle of the act, I voted for it. These are my views, honestly entertained, and will be defended."

I could fill you columns with extracts of speeches of senators and representatives from the North and the South who voted for the Kansas-Nebraska Bill and supported Mr. Buchanan for the Presidency on that distinct issue; thus showing conclusively that it was the general understanding at the time that the people of the Territories, while they remained in a Territorial condition, were left perfectly free, under the Kansas-Nebraska Act, to form and regulate all their domestic institutions, slavery not excepted, in their own way, subject only to the Constitution of the United States. This is the doctrine of which Mr. Gwin spoke when he said:

"To contend for the power—and a sovereign power it is—of a Territorial legislature to exclude by non-action or hostile legislation is pregnant with the mischiefs of never-ending agitation, of civil discord, and bloody wars.

          *   *   *   *   *   *   *   *   *   *   *

"It is an absurd, monstrous, and dangerous theory, which demands denunciation from every patriot in the land; and a profound sense of my duty to you would not permit me to do less than to offer this brief statement of my views upon a question so vital to the welfare of our common country."

Why did not the same " profound sense of duty " to the people of California require Mr. Gwin to denounce this " absurd, monstrous, and dan gerous theory when pronounced and enforced by General Cass, in support of the Compromise measures of 1850, and thence repeated by that eminent statesman at each session of Congress until 1857, when Mr. Gwin voted for his confirmation as secretary of state? Why did not Mr. Gwin obey the same sense of duty by denouncing James Buchanan as the Democratic candidate for the Presidency, when he declared, in 1856, that "the people of a Territory, like those of a State, shall decide for themselves whether slavery shall or shall not exist within their limits?" Why did he not perform this imperative duty by voting against Mr. Cobb, who made northern votes for Mr. Buchanan by advocating this same "absurd, monstrous and dangerous theory of 'non-action' and 'unfriendly legislation'" when he was appointed secretary of the treasury? And, in short, why did he not prove his fidelity to a high sense of duty by protesting against my selection as chairman of the Senate's Committee on Territories in the Democratic caucus by a unanimous vote, at every session that he has been a senator, from 1850 to 1858, with a full knowledge of my opinions? The inference is, that Mr. Gwin, from his remarks on the "Dred Scott decision," is prepared to offer it as an excuse for the disregard for so many years of that profound sense of duty which he owed to the people of California. It may be that before the decision his mind was not clear as to the sense of duty which now moves him. Of that decision he said:

"In March, 1857, the Supreme Court decided this question, in all its various relations, in the case of Dred Scott. That decision declares that neither Congress nor a Territorial legislature possesses the power either to establish or to exclude slavery from the Territory, and that it was a power which exclusively belonged to the States; that the people of a Territory can exercise this power for the first time when they form a constitution; that the right of the people of any State to carry their slaves into a common Territory of the United States, and hold them there during its existence as such, was guaranteed by the Constitution of the United States; that it was a right which could neither be subverted nor evaded, either by non-action, by direct or indirect Congressional legislation, or by any law passed by a Territorial legislature."

Surely Mr. Gwin had never read the opinion of the Court in the case of "Dred Scott," except as it had been perverted for partisan purposes by newspapers, when he undertook to expound it to the good people of California.

It so happens that the court did not decide any one of the propositions so boldly and emphatically stated in the "Grass Valley" speech!

The court did not declare that "neither Congress nor a Territorial legislature possessed the power either to establish or exclude slavery from a

Territory, and that it was a power which exclusively belonged to the States."

The court did not declare "that the people of a Territory can exercise this power for the first time when they come to form a constitution.

The court did not declare "that the right of the people in any State to carry their slaves into a common Territory of the United States, and hold them there during its existence as such, was guaranteed by the Constitution of the United States."

The court did not declare "that it was a right which could neither be subverted nor evaded, either by non-action, by direct or indirect Congressional legislation, or by any law passed by a Territorial legislature."

Neither the decision nor the opinion of the court affirms any one of those propositions, either in express terms or by fair legal intendment.

This version of the "Dred Scott Decision" had its origin in the unfortunate Lecompton controversy, and is one of the many political heresies to which it gave birth.

PROTECTION TO AMERICAN CITIZENS ABROAD.

On the 18th of February, 1859, President Buchanan had sent to Congress a special message, in which he urged the necessity of passing " a law conferring upon the President of the United States the authority to employ a sufficient military or naval force, whenever it might be necessary to do so, for the protection of American citizens when out of the immediate jurisdiction of the United States. Mr. Douglas spoke in favor of such a law, and said: "I think sir, that the President of the United States ought to have the power to redress sudden injuries upon our citizens, or outrages upon our flag, without waiting for the action of Congress. The Executive of every other powerful nation on earth has that authority. Our merchants are now being driven out of the trade in the Mexican and South American ports, for the want of authority in the Executive to demand and enforce instant redress the moment the outrage is perpetrated. I go further, sir; I would intrust the Executive with the authority, when an outrage is perpetrated upon our ships or commerce, to punish it instantly. I desire the President of the United States to have as much authority to protect American citizens, American property, and the American flag, abroad, as the Executive of every other civilized nation on earth possesses."

SLAVE PROPERTY IN THE TERRITORIES.

On the 23d of February, in a debate on the Legislative Appropriation Bill, Mr. Brown, of Mississippi, made a speech in the Senate, insisting on a code of laws protecting slavery in the Territories. Admitting that, if the people of the Territories did not want negroes, they could lawfully legislate so as to accomplish their purpose, he assumed that it was the right and duty of Congress to enact laws to sustain it against the popular will. Taking Mr. Douglas' position on the question (as he said) for granted, Mr. Brown declared that he wished to hear from other Democratic senators from the free States, and to know whether they would vote to protect the rights of slaveholders in the Territories. No one rising for several minutes after, Mr. Brown concluded his remarks, and the Senate being about to proceed to the consideration of other subjects, Mr. Douglas arose and observed that if no other northern Democratic senator desired to be heard on the points presented by the senator from Mississippi, he craved the attention of the Senate for a while. He thanked Mr. Brown for taking his position for granted on the question presented to the other northern Democrats. He had yet to know that there was one Democrat in the free States who would vote to protect slavery in the Territories by Congressional enactment against the popular decision. In this speech he shows that all property in the Territories, including slaves, is, and must be, subject to the local law of the Territorial legislature: that the Territorial legislature has the same power over slaves in the Territory, as it has over all other property ; and no more: he explains his Freeport speech; reminds the Senate that his past record shows that he would never vote for a Congressional slave code for the Territories; shows the absurdity of such a code; and demonstrates that if the people of a Territory want slavery there, they will enact laws for its protection: he shows that it was the intent of the Nebraska Bill to confer on the Territorial legislature all the power that Congress possessed on the subject of slavery, to let them wield it as the people of the Territory chose: he elucidates the truly equitable and just provisions of that bill, and shows that it expressly forbids the enactment of a Congressional slave code for the Territories.

In the course of his remarks he said:

The senator from Mississippi and myself agree that under the decision of the Supreme Court, slaves are property, standing on an equal footing with all other property; and that consequently, the owner of slaves has the same right to carry his slave with him to a Territory, as the owner of any other species of property has to carry *his* property there. The right of transit to and from the Territories is the same for one species of property as it is for all others. Thus far the senator from Mississippi and myself agree—that slave property in the Territories stands on an equal footing with every other species of property. Now, the question arises, to what extent is property, slaves included, subject to the local law of the Territory? Whatever power the Territorial legislature has over other species of property, extends, in my judgment, to the same extent, and in like manner, to slave property. The Territorial legislature has the same power to legislate in respect to slaves, that it has in regard to any other property, to the same extent, and no further. If the senator wishes to know what power it has over slaves in the Territories, I answer, let him tell me what power it has to legislate over every other species of property, either by encouragement or by taxation, or in any other mode, and he has my answer in regard to slave property.

But the senator says that there is something peculiar in slave property, requiring further protection than other species of property. If so, it is the misfortune of those who own that species of property. He tells us that, if the Territorial legislature fails to pass a slave code for the Territories, fails to pass police regulations to protect slave property, the absence of such legislation practically excludes slave property as effectually as a constitutional prohibition would exclude it. I agree to that proposition. He says, furthermore, that it is competent for the Territorial legislature, by the exercise of the taxing power, and other functions within the limits of the Constitution, to adopt unfriendly legislation which practically drives slavery out of the Territory. I agree to that proposition. That is just what I said, and all I said, and just what I meant by my Freeport speech in Illinois, upon which there has been so much comment throughout the country.

* * * * * * * *

The senator from Mississippi says they ought to pass such a code; but he admits that it is immaterial to inquire whether they ought or ought not to do it; for if they do not want it, they will not enact it; and if they do not do it, there is no mode by which you can compel them to do it. He admits there is no compulsory means by which you can coerce the Territorial legislature to pass such a law; and for that reason he insists that, in case of non-action by the Territorial legislature, it is the right and duty of southern senators and representatives to demand affirmative action by Congress in the enactment of a slave code for the Territories. He says that it is not necessary to put the question to me, whether I would vote for a Congressional slave code. He desire to know of all other northern Democrats what they will do; he does not wish an answer from me. I am much obliged to him for taking it for granted, from my past record, that I never would vote for a slave code in the Territories by Congress; and I have yet to learn that there is a man in a free State of this Union, of any party, who would.

The senator from Mississippi defined it very well in his speech. His position was, that while the Constitution gave him the right of protection in a Territory for his slave property, it did not, of itself, furnish adequate protection. He drew a distinction between the right and the fact, and said that the protection could only be furnished by legislation; that legislation could only come from one of two sources—the Territorial legislature or the Congress of the United States. He would look to the Territorial legislature in the first instance. If he got adequate legislation there, he was content; but if the Territorial legislature failed to act, and give him that adequate legislation, in the form of what is commonly called a slave code, such non-action was equivalent to a denial of his rights; and, losing his rights, it was no consolation to him that he had been deprived of them by the non-action of a Territorial legislature; and hence he would demand of Congress the passage of laws to protect his slaves, and to punish men for running them off; to furnish such remedies for the violation of his rights as he thought he was entitled to from the Territorial legislature. He said he would demand this from Congress. He further said that he would base his demand on Congress to pass this slave code on the ground that the Territorial legislature was the creature of Congress; and, if it did not do its duty, Congress should pass such laws as were necessary to protect slave property in the Territories.

All I have to say, on the point presented by the senator from Missouri, is this: while our Constitution does not provide remedies for stealing negroes, it does not provide remedies for stealing dry-goods, or horses, or any other species of property. You cannot protect any property in the Territories, without laws furnishing remedies for its violation, and penalties for its abuse. Nobody pretends that you are going to pass laws of Congress making a criminal code for the Territories, with reference to other species of property. The Congress of the United States never yet passed an act creating a criminal code for any organized Territory. It simply organizes the Territory, and leaves its legislature to make its own criminal code. Congress never passed a law to protect any species of property in the organized Territories; it leaves its protection to the Territorial Legislatures. The question is, whether we shall make an exception as to slavery? The Supreme Court makes no such distinction. It recognizes slaves as property. When they are taken to a Territory, they are on an equal footing with other property, and dependent upon the same system of legislation, for protection, as other property. While all other property is dependent on the Territorial legislation for protection, I hold that slave property must look to the same authority for its protection.

SLAVERY DEPENDENT ON THE LOCAL LAW.

I leave all kinds of property, slaves included, to the local law for protection; and I will not exert the power of Congress to interfere with that local law with reference to slave property, or any other kind of property. If the people think that particular laws on the subject of property are beneficial to their interests, they will enact them. If they do not think such laws are wise, they will refrain from enacting them. They will protect slaves there, provided they want slavery; and they will want slavery, if the climate be such that the white man cannot cultivate the soil, so as to render negro compulsory labor necessary. Hence, it becomes a question of climate, of production, of self-interest, and not a question of legislation, whether slavery shall, or shall not exist there.

But the senator from Mississippi says he has a right to protection. The owner of every other species of property may say he has a right to protection. The man dealing in liquors may think that, inasmuch as his stock of liquors is property, he has a right to protection. The man dealing in an inferior breed of cattle, may think he has a right to protection; but the people of the Territory may think it is their interest to improve the breed of stock by discrimination against inferior breeds; and hence they may fix a higher rate of taxation on the one than on the other.

I am willing to test this question by the illustration the senator presents of a Maine liquor law. I shall not stop to inquire whether the Maine liquor law is constitutional or not; first, because Congress is not the tribunal to decide it; and secondly, because, by the platform to which the senator from Mississippi and myself both stand pledged as the rule for our political action, it is provided that that question shall be sent to the court to test the constitutionality of the law, and we shall not come to Congress to repeal the law. When the Nebraska Bill was first pending in the Senate, it contained the old clause that the Territorial laws should be sent here, and, if disapproved by Congress, should be void. The discussion proceeded on the basis that we were conferring the whole power of legislation on the Territory, subject only to the Constitution of the United States, with the right in the Territorial legislature " to form and regulate their domestic institutions in their own way;" and that if any man was aggrieved by such legislation, he should have a right to appeal to the Supreme Court of the United States to test its validity, but should not come to Congress to repeal the obnoxious law. When that argument was made, a distinguished senator from Ohio, not now here (Mr. Chase), asked us why we kept that clause in the bill requiring the laws of the Territory to be sent here for approval or disapproval. We could not answer the inquiry, and hence we struck out the provision requiring the Territorial laws to be sent here for approval or disapproval, upon the avowed ground, at the time, that the Territorial legislature might pass just such laws as they wanted, with the right of appeal by any one aggrieved to the Supreme Court to test their constitutionality, but not to Congress to annul them. I undertake to say that this was the distinct understanding among the northern and southern Democrats at that time, and among all the friends of the Kansas Nebraska Bill. It was agreed, that while we might differ as to the extent of the power of the Territorial legislature on these questions, we would make a full grant of legislative authority to the legislature of the Territory, with the right to pass such laws as they chose, and the right of anybody to appeal to the court to decide upon the validity and constitutionality of such laws, but not to come to Congress for their annulment. Hence, if the Territorial legislature should pass the Maine liquor law, and anybody was dissatisfied with the provisions of that act, and thought it violated his constitutional right, he could not come to Congress for its annulment, but could appeal to the Supreme Court of the United States; and if that court decided the law to be constitutional, it must stand, no matter how obnoxious it might be to any portion of the American people. If it was unconstitutional, it became void without any interference by Congress, or any other legislative body. The Kansas Nebraska Bill was thus amended for the avowed purpose, at the time, of striking out the appeal to Congress, and substituting the appeal to the court.

SUPREME COURT TO SETTLE DIFFERENCES OF OPINION ON TERRITORIAL POWER.

After we had gone that far, a senator from New Hampshire

pointed out in the Nebraska Bill the fact, that no appeal could be taken to the Supreme Court of the United States unless the amount of property in controversy was $2,000 in value, and hence that a negro could not appeal for his freedom, nor could the owner of a single slave appeal to the Supreme Court to establish his title, if he thought that his rights were violated. In order to obviate that objection, we amended the bill by providing that where the title to property in slaves, or any question of personal freedom was the point in issue, the right of appeal to the Supreme Court should exist without reference to the amount in controversy.

Thus the Kansas Nebraska Bill stood, granting all rightful power of legislation on all subjects whatsoever to the Territorial legislature, subject only to the Constitution of the United States, provided they should not pass any law taxing the property of non-residents higher than that of residents, nor any law interfering with the primary disposition of the soil, nor impose any tax on the property of the United States; but there was no exception made as to slavery. The intent was to confer on the Territorial legislature all the power we had on the subject of slavery, to let them wield it for or against slavery as the people of the Territory chose; and the understanding was, that we would abide by whatever laws they might make, provided they did not violate the Constitution of the United States; and the Supreme Court was the only tribunal that could decide that question.

STANDS BY THE NEBRASKA BILL.

Now, sir, I stand on the Kansas-Nebraska Bill as it was expounded and understood at the time, with this full power in the Territorial legislature, with the right of appeal to the Supreme Court to test the validity of its laws, and no right whatever to appeal to Congress to repeal them in the event of our not liking them. I am ready to answer the inquiry of the senator from Mississippi, whether, if I believed the Maine liquor law to be unconstitutional and wrong, and if a Territorial legislature should pass it, I would vote here to annul it? I tell him no. If the people of Kansas want a Maine liquor law, let them have it. If they do not want it, let them refuse to pass it. If they do pass it, and any citizen thinks that law violates the Constitution, let him make a case and appeal to the Supreme Court. If the court sustains his objection, the law is void. If it overrules the objection, the decision must stand until the people, who alone are to be affected by it, who alone have an interest in it, may choose to repeal it. So I say with reference to slavery. Let the Territorial legislature pass just such laws in regard to slavery as they think they have a right to enact under the Constitution of the United States. If I do not like those laws, I will not vote to repeal them; if you do not like them, you must not vote to repeal them; but anybody aggrieved may appeal to the Supreme Court, and if they are constitutional, they must stand; if they are unconstitutional, they are void. That was the doctrine of non-intervention, as it was understood at the time the Kansas-Nebraska Bill was passed. That is the way it was explained and argued in the Senate, and in the House of Representatives, and before the country. It was distinctly understood that Congress was never to intervene for or against slavery, or for or against any other institution in the Territories; but leave the courts to decide all constitutional questions as they might arise, and the President to carry the decrees of the court into effect; and, in case of resistance to his authority in executing the judicial process, let him use, if necessary, the whole military force of the country, as provided by existing laws.

NON-INTERVENTION A DEMOCRATIC SHIBBOLETH.

I know that some gentlemen do not like the doctrine of non-intervention as well as they once did. It is now becoming fashionable to talk sneeringly of "your doctrine of non-intervention." Sir, that doctrine has been a fundamental article in the Democratic creed for years. It has been repeated over and over again in every national Democratic platform—non-intervention by Congress with slavery in the States and Territories. The Nebraska Bill was predicated on that idea—the Territorial legislature to have jurisdiction over all rightful subjects of legislation, not excepting slavery, with no appeal to Congress, but a right to appeal to the courts; and the legislation to be void, if the Supreme Court said it was unconstitutional; and valid, no matter how obnoxious, if the court said it was constitutional. Let me call attention to the language of the Kansas-Nebraska Bill. Its fourteenth section provides:

"That the Constitution and all laws of the United States, which are not locally inapplicable, shall have the same force and effect in the said Territory of Nebraska as elsewhere within the United States, except the eighth section of the act 'preparatory to the admission of Missouri into the Union,' approved March 6, 1820, *which, being* INCONSISTENT WITH THE PRINCIPLE OF NON-INTERVENTION BY CONGRESS WITH SLAVERY *in the States* AND TERRITORIES, *as recognized by the legislation of* 1850, *commonly called the Compromise measures,* IS HEREBY DECLARED INOPERATIVE *and* VOID; *it being the true intent and meaning of this act not to legislate slavery into any State or* TERRITORY, *nor to exclude it therefrom, but to leave the people* THEREOF *perfectly* FREE TO FORM AND REGULATE THEIR DOMESTIC INSTITUTIONS IN THEIR OWN WAY, SUBJECT ONLY TO THE CONSTITUTION OF THE UNITED STATES."

Thus, in the Nebraska Bill, it is declared that a Congressional enactment on the subject of slavery was inconsistent with the principle of non-intervention by Congress with slavery in the States and Territories. This same article of faith has gone into the various Democratic platforms, and especially into the Cincinnati platform. Every

Democrat, therefore, is pledged, by his platform and the organization of the party, against any legislation of Congress in the Territories for or against slavery, no matter how obnoxious the Territorial legislation may be. If it is unconstitutional, you have your remedy; go to the court and test the question. If it is constitutional, you agreed that the people of a Territory may have it. I hold you to the agreement.

The whole legislative power possessed by Congress over a Territory was, by that act, conferred on the Territorial legislature. There were exceptions on three points; but slavery was not one of the exceptions. I say, then, the intent was to give to the Territorial legislature all the power that we possessed; all that could be given under the Constitution; and the understanding was, that Congress would not interfere with whatever legislation they might enact.

Now, the senator from Alabama asks me whether the southern people, under the Constitution, have not the right to carry their slaves there? I answer, yes—the same right that you have to carry any other property. Then you ask, have they not a right to hold it there when they get it there? I answer, the same right that you have to hold any other property, subject to such local laws as the local legislature may constitutionally enact. Can you hold any other property without law to protect it? No. Then, can you hold slave property without law to protect it? No, is the answer. Then, will Congress pass laws to protect other property in the Territories? I answer, no. We have created Territorial legislatures *for that purpose.* We agreed that this government should not violate the principles of our Revolution, by making laws for a distant people, regulating their domestic concerns and affecting their rights of property, without giving them a representation. The doctrine that Congress is to regulate the rights of person and property, and the domestic concerns of a Territory, is the doctrine of the Tories of the Revolution. It is the doctrine of George III., and Lord North, his minister. Our fathers then said that they would not consent that the British parliament should pass laws touching the local and domestic concerns of the colonies, the rights of person and property, the family relations of the people of the colonies, without their consent. The parliament of Great Britain said they had the power. We said to them, "you may have the power, but you have not the moral right; it is violative of the great principles of civil liberty; violative of the rights of an Englishman, not to be affected in his property without his consent is given through his representatives." Because Great Britain insisted on exercising that identical power over these colonies, our fathers flew to arms, asserted the doctrine that every colony, every dependency, every Territory, had a right in its own domestic legislature to pass just such laws as its people chose touching their local and domestic concerns, recognizing the right of the imperial parliament to regulate imperial affairs, as I do the right of Congress to regulate the national and federal concerns of the people of a Territory.

Sir, I am asserting, on behalf the people of the Territories, just those rights which our fathers demanded for themselves against the claim of Great Britain. Because those rights were not granted to our fathers, they went through a bloody war of seven years. Am I now to be called upon to enforce that same odious doctrine on the people of a Territory, against their consent? I say, no. Organize a Territorial government for them; give them a legislature, to be elected by their own people; give them all the powers of legislation on all questions of a local and domestic character, subject only to the Constitution; and if they make good laws, let them enjoy their blessings; and if they make bad laws, let them suffer under them until they repeal them. If the laws are unconstitutional, let those aggrieved appeal to the court—the tribunal created by the Constitution to ascertain that fact. That is the principle on which we stood in 1854. It was on that principle and that understanding we fought the great political battle and gained the great victory of 1856. How many votes do you think Mr. Buchanan would have obtained in Pennsylvania if he had then said that the Constitution of the United States plants slavery in all the Territories, and makes it the duty of the Federal Government to keep it there and maintain it at the point of the bayonet and by federal laws, in opposition to the will of the people? How many votes would he have received in Ohio, or any other free State, on such a platform? Mr. Buchanan did not then understand the doctrines of popular sovereignty and self-government in that way.

I assert that in 1856, during the whole of that campaign, I took the same position I do now, and none other; and I will show that Mr. Buchanan pledged himself to the same doctrine when he accepted the nomination of the Cincinnati Convention. In his letter of acceptance, he says, referring to the Kansas-Nebraska Act:

"The recent legislation of Congress, respecting domestic slavery, derived, as it has been, from the original and pure fountain of legitimate political power, the will of the majority, promises ere long to allay the dangerous excitement. This legislation is founded upon principles as ancient as free government itself, and, in accordance with them, has simply declared that the people of a Territory, like those of a State, shall decide for themselves whether slavery shall or shall not exist within their limits."

This extract from Mr. Buchanan's letter, shows that he then understood that the people of a *Territory, like those of a State*, should decide for themselves whether slavery should or should not exist within their limits. I undertake to say, that wherever I went that year, his cause was advocated on that principle, as laid down in his letter of acceptance. The people of the North, at least, certainly understood him to hold the doctrine of self-government in Territories as well as in States, and as applicable to slave property as well as to all other species of property. I undertake to say, that he would not have carried one-half the Democratic vote in any free State, if he had not been thus understood; and I hope my friend from Mississippi had no allusion to this letter, when he said that in the next contest he did not desire "to cheat nor be cheated." I am glad that the senator from Mississippi means to have a clear, unequivocal, specific statement of our principles, so that there shall be no cheating on either side. I intend to use language which can be repeated in Chicago as well as in New Orleans, in Charleston the same as in Boston. We live under a common Constitution. No political creed is sound or safe which cannot be proclaimed in the same sense wherever the American flag waves over American soil. If the North and the South cannot come to a common ground on the slavery question, the sooner we know it the better. The Democracy of the North hold, at least, that the people of a Territory have the same right to legislate in respect to slavery, as to all other property; and that, practically, it results in this: if they want slavery, they will have it; and if they do not want it, it shall not be forced upon them by an act of Congress. The senator from Mississippi says that doctrine is right, unless we pass an act of Congress compelling the people of a Territory to have slavery whether they want it or not. The point he wishes to arrive at, is whether we are for or against Congressional intervention. If you repudiate the doctrine of non-intervention, and form a slave code by act of Congress, when the people of a Territory refuse it, you must step off the Democratic platform. We will let you depart in peace, as you no longer belong to us; you are no longer of us when you adopt the principle of Congressional intervention, in violation of the Democratic creed. I stand here defending the great principle of non-intervention by Congress, and self-government by the people of the Territories. That is the Democratic creed. The Democracy in the northern States have so understood it. No northern Democratic State ever would have voted for Mr. Buchanan, but for the fact that he was understood to occupy that position.

Gentlemen of the southern States, I tell you in all candor that I do not believe a Democratic candidate can ever carry any one northern Democratic State on the platform that it is the duty of the Federal Government to force the people of a Territory to have slavery when they do not want it. But if the true principles of State rights and popular sovereignty be maintained and carried out in good faith, as set forth in the Nebraska Bill, and as understood by the people in 1856, a glorious future awaits the Democracy.

CHAPTER XVI.

WAR OF THE PAMPHLETS.

Letters to Dorr and Peyton—Speeches in Ohio, and Cincinnati Platform—Charleston Convention—Presidental Aspirants—The Harper Article—Black's Reply—Appendix of Attorney General—Rejoinder of Senator Douglas—The Chase and Trumbull Amendments—Consistency of Senator Douglas.

DURING the spring and summer of 1859, Mr. Douglas received many letters from his personal friends, soliciting the use of his name as a candidate for the Presidency before the Charleston Convention, to one of which he replied as follows:

WASHINGTON, *Wednesday, June* 22, 1859.

MY DEAR SIR: I have received your letter inquiring whether my friends are at liberty to present my name in the Charleston Convention for the Presidential nomination.

Before the question can be finally determined, it will be necessary to understand distinctly upon what issue the canvass is to be conducted. If, as I have full faith they will, the Democratic party shall determine, in the Presidential election of 1860, to adhere to the principles embodied in the Compromise measures of 1850, and ratified by the people in the Presidential election of 1852, and re-affirmed in the Kansas-Nebraska Act of 1854, and incorporated into the Cincinnati platform in 1856, as expounded by Mr. Buchanan in his letter accepting the nomination, and approved by the people—in that event my friends will be at liberty to present my name to the Convention, if they see proper to do so. If, on the contrary, it shall become the policy of the Democratic party—which I cannot anticipate—to repudiate these, their time-honored principles, on which we have achieved so many patriotic triumphs, and if, in lieu of them, the Convention shall interpolate into the creed of the party such new issues

10

as the revival of the African slave-trade, or a Congressional slave code for the Territories, or the doctrine that the Constitution of the United States either establishes or prohibits slavery in the Territories, beyond the power of the people legally to control it as other property, it is due to candor to say that, in such an event, I could not accept the nomination if tendered to me. Trusting that this answer will be deemed sufficiently explicit,   I am, very respectfully, your friend,

                                        S. A. DOUGLAS.

To J. B. DORN, Esq., Dubuque, Iowa.

The publication of this letter produced immense enthusiasm among Mr. Douglas' friends all over the country, and particularly throughout the Northwest, and was followed by a pressing invitation from the Democratic State Central Committee of Ohio to visit that State and address the people in their pending canvass. In consequence of the ill-health of Mr. Douglas and his family, he was only able to make three speeches in Ohio—at Columbus, Cincinnati and Wooster, in each of which places the Democracy made immense gains at the fall election, averaging one thousand votes in each county. He was met in Cincinnati by large numbers of Democrats from Kentucky, Indiana, and other adjacent States, and wherever he went was greeted with the wildest enthusiasm.

We omit to insert extracts from these speeches, which are among the ablest and best of his political life, for the reason that they relate chiefly to the line of argument which has been so fully illustrated in the previous pages of this work. These speeches appeared in- the columns of the New York press the morning after their delivery, having been deemed of sufficient consequence to be telegraphed entire. A marked feature of these addresses was his solemn protest against the incorporation of any new tests of faith into the Democratic creed which would tend to divide and defeat the party, insisting upon "the re-adoption of the Cincinnati platform without the addition of a word or the subtraction of a letter."

We omitted to state, that on his way to Ohio, Mr. Douglas was induced, by the earnest entreaties of the Democrats of Pittsburg, to remain a day and address the people of that city in behalf of the regularly nominated State ticket, with a view to the pending election.

It was in this speech that Mr. Douglas, in kind but firm language, rebuked those Democrats who had permitted their passions to array them in opposition to the regular organization of their party, and thus contribute to the success of the common enemy.

Notwithstanding these speeches which had been so recently published throughout the country, the attorney-general of the United States did not hesitate, a few weeks afterward, in an anonymous pamphlet, the authorship of which he subsequently assumed, to call in question Mr. Douglas' fidelity to the party and the principles of the Cincinnati platform. In reply, after arraigning Judge Black and his confederates for their unnatural coalition with the Black Republicans in the memorable Illinois campaign, Mr. Douglas thus meets and crushes his assailant in his allegation that the former intended to insist on the Charleston Convention adopting his interpretation of the Cincinnati platform :

The administration claimed the right to " change and interpolate the Cincinnati platform, and prescribe new and different tests ;" while the gallant Democracy of that noble State denied " the right of any power on earth, except a like body," to change the Cincinnati platform or prescribe new tests ; and declared that " they will neither do it themselves, nor permit it to be done by others, but will recognize all men as Democrats who stand by and uphold Democratic principles."

We were assailed and proscribed because we did stand by the Cincinnati platform ; because we would not recognize the right of any power on earth except a regularly constituted convention of the party to change the platform and interpolate new articles into the creed ; because we would not sanction the new issues and submit to the new tests ; because we would not proscribe any Democrat, nor permit the proscription of Democrats in con sequence of difference of opinion upon questions which had arisen subsequently to the adoption of the platform; and because we recognized all men as Democrats who supported the nominees and upheld the principles of the party as defined by the last National Convention. It was upon this issue and for these reasons that the power and patronage of the Federal Government were wielded in concert with the Black Republicans for the election of their candidates in preference to the regular nominees of the Democratic party. This system of proscription still continues in Illinois, and is being extended throughout the Union, with the view of controlling the Charleston nomination. Fidelity to the Cincinnati platform and opposition to the new issues and tests prescribed by men in power, in direct conflict with the professions upon which they were elected, are deemed disqualifications for office and cause of removal.

THE CHARLESTON CONVENTION—PRESIDENTIAL ASPIRANTS.

The reasons for singling me out as the especial object for anathema will be found in the first page of the attorney-general's pamphlet, where he says:

"He (Douglas) has been for years a working, struggling candidate for the Presidency!"

Suppose it were true, that I am a Presidential aspirant; does that fact justify a combination by a host of other Presidential aspirants, each of whom may imagine that his success depends upon my destruction, and the preaching a crusade against me for boldly avowing now the same principles to which they and I were pledged at the last Presidential election? Is this a sufficient excuse for devising a new test of political orthodoxy; and, under pretext of fidelity to it, getting up a set of bolting delegates to the Charleston Convention in those States where they are unable to control the regular organization? The time is not far distant when the Democracy of the whole Union will be called upon to consider and pronounce judgment upon this question.

What authority has the attorney-general, aside from his fears and hopes, for saying that I am "a working, struggling candidate for the Presidency?" My best friends know that I have positively and peremptorily refused to have anything to do with the machinery of the conventions in the several States by which the delegates to the Charleston Convention are to be appointed. They know that personally I do not desire the Presidency at this time—that I prefer a seat in the Senate for the next six years, with the chance of a reëlection, to being President for four years, at my period of life. They know that I will take no steps to obtain the Charleston nomination, that I will make no sacrifice of principle, no concealment of opinions, no concession to power for the purpose of getting it. They know, also, that I only consented to the use of my name upon their earnest representations that the good of the Democratic party required it, and even then, upon the express condition that the Democratic party shall determine in the Presidential election of 1860, as I have full faith they will, to adhere to the principles embodied in the Compromise measures of 1850, and approved by the people in the Presidential election of 1852, and incorporated into the Kansas-Nebraska Act of 1854, and confirmed by the Cincinnati platform, and ratified by the people, in the Presidential election of 1856. Nor can the attorney-general pretend to be ignorant of the fact that the public were informed long since, that, "If, on the contrary, it shall become the policy of the Democratic party, which I cannot anticipate, to repudiate these their time-honored principles, on which we have achieved so many patriotic triumphs, and in lieu of them the convention shall interpolate into the creed of the party such new issues as the revival of the African slave trade, or a Congressional slave code for the Territories, or the doctrine that the Constitution of the United States either establishes or prohibits slavery in the Territories beyond the power of the people legally to control it, as other property, it is due to candor to say that in such an event I could not accept the nomination if tendered to me." Is this the language of a man who is working and struggling for the Presidency upon whatever terms, and by the use of whatever means it could be obtained? Or does this language justify that other charge, that I am making new issues and prescribing new tests in violation of the Cincinnati platform?

WOULD VOTE FOR DEMOCRATIC CANDIDATE, THOUGH NOT STANDING ON HIS PLATFORM

While I could have no hesitation in voting for the nominee of my own party, with whom I might differ on certain points, in preference to the candidate of the Black Republican party, whose whole creed is subversive of the Constitution and destructive of the Union, I am under no obligation to become a candidate upon a platform that I would not be willing to carry out in good faith, nor to accept the Presidency on the implied pledge to carry into effect certain principles, and then administer the government in direct conflict with them. In other words, I prefer the

position of senator, or even that of a private citizen, where I would be at
liberty to defend and maintain the well-defined principles of the Democratic party, to accepting a Presidential nomination upon a platform incompatible with the principle of self-government in the Territories, or the
reserved rights of the States, or the perpetuity of the Union under the
Constitution. In harmony with these views, I said in those very speeches
in Ohio, to which Judge Black refers in his appendix, that I was in favor
of conducting the great struggle of 1860 upon "the Cincinnati platform
without the addition of a word or the subtraction of a letter." Yet, in the
face of all these facts, the attorney-general does not hesitate to represent me as attempting to establish a new school of politics, to force new
issues upon the party, and prescribe new tests of Democratic faith.

In conclusion, I have only to suggest to Judge Black and his confederates in this crusade, whether it would not be wiser for them, and more
consistent with fidelity to the party which placed them in power, to exert
their energies and direct all their efforts to the redemption of Pennsylvania
from the thralldom of Black Republicanism, than to continue their alliance
with the Black Republicans in Illinois, with the vain hope of dividing and
defeating the Democratic party in the only western or northern State
which has never failed to cast her electoral vote for the regular nominee of
the Democratic party at any Presidential election.

WASHINGTON, *October,* 1859.

PROTECTION TO NATURALIZED CITIZENS—AFRICAN SLAVE TRADE.

Mr. Peyton, of Virginia, formerly of Chicago, having addressed a letter to Mr. Douglas, in which he informed him
that his views in respect to the rights of naturalized citizens
and the reopening of the African slave trade were the subject of misrepresentation in the Old Dominion, Mr Douglas
replied:

WASHINGTON, *Aug.* 2, 1859.

COLONEL JOHN L. PEYTON, Staunton, Va.:

MY DEAR SIR: You do me no more than justice in your kind letter, for which accept my thanks, in assuming that I do not concur with
the administration in their views respecting the rights of naturalized citizens, as defined in the "Le Clerc Letter," which, it is proper to observe,
have since been materially modified.

Under our Constitution there can be no just distinction between the rights of native-born and naturalized citizens to claim the protection of our government, at home and abroad. Unless naturalization releases the person naturalized from all obligations which he owed to his native country, by virtue of his allegiance, it leaves him in the sad predicament of owing allegiance to two countries, without receiving protection from either, a dilemma in which no American citizen should ever be placed.

Neither have you misapprehended my opinions in respect to the African slave trade. That question seriously disturbed the harmony of the convention which framed the federal Constitution. Upon it the delegates divided into two parties, under circumstances which, for a time, rendered harmonious action impossible. The one demanded the instant and unconditional prohibition of the African slave trade, on moral and religious grounds, while the other insisted that it was a legitimate commerce, involving no other consideration than a sound public policy, which each State ought to be permitted to determine for itself, so long as it was sanctioned by its own laws. Each party stood firmly and resolutely by its own position until both became convinced that this vexed question would break up the convention, destroy the federal Union, blot out the glories of the Revolution, and throw away all its blessings, unless some fair and just compromise could be formed on the common ground of such mutual concessions as were indispensable to the preservation of their liberties, Union, and independence.

Such a compromise was effected and incorporated into the Constitution, by which it was understood that the African slave trade might continue as a legitimate commerce in those States whose laws sanctioned it until the year 1808, from and after which time Congress might and would prohibit it forever, throughout the dominion and limits of the United States, and pass all laws which might become necessary to make such prohibition effectual. The harmony of the convention was restored, and the Union saved by this compromise, without which the Constitution could never have been made.

I stand firmly by this compromise, and by all the other compromises of the Constitution, and shall use my best efforts to carry each and all of them into faithful execution, and in the sense and with the understanding which they were originally adopted. I am irreconcilably opposed to the revival of the African slave trade, in any form and under any circumstances.   I am, with great respect, yours truly,

S. A. DOUGLAS.

THE HARPER ARTICLE.

In the September (1859) number of "Harper's Magazine," Mr. Douglas published over his own name, an article entitled "Popular Sovereignty in the Territories: The Dividing Line between Federal and Local Authority." This article was read with avidity by the public, and for some days after its appearance, nothing else was talked of in political circles. It is a clear elucidation of the line that divides the authority of the Federal Government from that of local authorities; and of the great principle that every distinct political community, loyal to the Constitution and the Union, is entitled to all the rights, privileges, and immunities of self-government in respect to their local concerns and internal polity, subject only to the Constitution of the United States. He exposes the erroneous views entertained by the "Republican" party on these points: shows that the courts in a Territory derive all their powers from the Territorial legislature: that all powers conferred on Congress by the Constitution, must be exercised by Congress in the manner prescribed in the Constitution; but that Congress may establish local governments, and invest them with powers which Congress itself cannot constitutionally exercise.

He shows by the records of the provincial legislature of Virginia, that in 1772, the Virginians were unwilling to have slavery forced upon them: that in 1776, the inhuman use of the royal negative, in refusing the colony of Virginia permission to exclude slavery from her limits by law, was one of the reasons for separating from Great Britain: and that in all the thirteen colonies, slavery was regarded as a domestic question, to be considered and determined by each colony to suit itself, without the intervention of the British parliament. He proves that the principle of popular sovereignty was at the very foundation of the causes that led to the Revolution: showing that the patriots of 1776 fought for the inalienable right of local self-government, with the clear understanding that when the despotism of the British parliament was thrown off, no Congressional despotism was to be substituted for it.

He proves by a citation of Jefferson's plan for the government of the first Territory ever owned by the United States, that by it, the right of Congress to bind the people of the Territories without their consent was emphatically ignored; and the people therein recognized as the source of all local power: that in forming the Constitution of the United States in 1787, the Convention took the British constitution for their model, conferring upon the Federal Government the same powers which, as colonies, they had been willing to concede to the British government, and reserving to the States and to the people, the rights for which the Revolution had been fought. He shows that the clause in the Constitution which gives to Congress " power to dispose of, and make all needful rules and regulations for the Territory "— refers exclusively to property, in contradistinction to persons and communities; but does not authorize Congress to interpose or interfere with the internal polity of the people who may reside upon lands which the United States once owned.

He alludes to the erroneous views that have been put forth in regard to the Dred Scott case; and shows that *the slavery question* was not included in the class of prohibited powers to which the Constitution alluded. He describes the steps by which the Compromise measures of 1850 were formed, and the principles on which they were based; and shows that they are the same principles upon which the Nebraska Bill of 1854 was formed.

We give a few extracts from the article, which possesses a permanent historical value, in the Appendix to this work.

10*

The appearance of the Harper article caused, as has been stated, the most profound sensation in political circles.

The exposition of the question produced consternation and dismay in the camp of the assailants of Judge Douglas. Their hope was to secure the confidence and favor of the South by conceding their right to plant slavery in the Territories in opposition to the wishes of the people, and in defiance of the Territorial authorities; and at the same time, satisfy the North by withholding all legislative protection and judicial remedies, without which the right becomes a naked, useless, worthless possession. The exposure of Mr. Douglas opened their eyes to the dangers of their perilous position, and made it obvious, even to their comprehension, that they could no longer successfully maintain the ground they then occupied. Afraid to advance and pursue their doctrines to their logical consequences, and ashamed to retreat and return to the impregnable position of popular sovereignty, which they had so recently abandoned, they began to look about for some new expedient to relieve themselves from the awkward dilemma into which they had been driven by one short article in " Harper's Magazine." Accordingly Judge Black was deputed to frame an answer to the masterly paper of Mr. Douglas.

The attorney-general's reply to the Harper article appeared in the " Washington Constitution," the central organ of the assailants of Judge Douglas, in October. A few days after, Mr. Douglas made a speech at Wooster, in which he replied to the pamphlet of the attorney-general. The latter functionary published an appendix to his former article, and on the 17th of November, Mr. Douglas published a rejoinder, from which we make the following extracts :

In my reply to Judge Black I produced and quoted the decisions of the Supreme Court of the United States, in which the following propositions were solemnly and authoritatively established as the law of the land:

1st. That the state of slavery is a mere municipal regulation, founded upon and limited to the range of Territorial laws.

2d. That the laws of one State or country can have no force or effect in another *without its consent*, express or implied.

3d. That, in the absence of any positive rule upon the subject, affirming or denying or restraining the operation of the foreign law or laws of one State or country in their application to another, the courts will presume the tacit adoption of them by the government of the place where they are sought to be enforced, unless they are repugnant to its policy, or prejudicial to its interests.

The attorney-general neither admits nor denies the correctness of these propositions, nor does he either admit or deny that the courts have so decided. To admit their correctness would necessarily involve an abandonment of his position and a confession that he had been wrong from the beginning. To deny them would bring him in direct conflict with the authority of the court and expose him to an inevitable conviction by the record.

*　　*　　*　　*　　*　　*　　*

Judge Black has not attempted to reconcile his opinion with the decision of the court. No man in his senses can fail to perceive that if the court is right, Judge Black is inevitably wrong. Although the whole legal controversy between Judge Black and myself turns on this one point, I did not choose, in my reply, to offset my individual opinion against his, or to bring the two into comparison. As the question at issue could only be determined by authority, I said:

"Of course I express no opinion of my own, since I make it a rule to acquiesce in the decisions of the courts upon all legal questions."

And again, in concluding what I had to say on the legal points at issue, I added:

"In all that I have said, I have been content to assume the law to be as decided by the Supreme Court of the United States, without presuming that my individual opinion would either strengthen or invalidate their decisions."

If Judge Black could reconcile it with his dignity and sense of duty to act on the same assumption, there could be no controversy between him and me in regard to the law of the case. According to the doctrine of the court, a white man, with a negro wife and mulatto children, under a marriage lawful in Massachusetts, on removal into a Territory, could not maintain that interesting "private relation," under the laws of Massachusetts, without the consent or tacit adoption of the Massachusetts law by the Territorial government. On the contrary, if Judge Black's view of the axiomatic principle of public law be correct, this disgusting and demoralizing system of amalgamation may be introduced and maintained in the Territories under the law of Massachusetts, in defiance of the wishes of the people and in contempt of all Territorial authority, until "they get a constitutional convention or the machinery of a State government in their hands." It is true that Judge Black limits this right to those places where there is no law "in direct conflict with it ;" but he also says in the same pamphlet that the Territories " have no attribute of sovereignty about them," and, therefore, are incapable of making any law in conflict with this "private relation" which is lawful in Massachusetts.

According to the doctrine of the court, a Turk, with thirteen wives, under a marriage lawful in his own country, could not move into the Territories of the United States with his family and maintain his marital rights under the laws of Turkey without the consent or tacit adoption of the Turkish law by the Territorial government.

In accordance with the Black doctrine (I use the term for convenience and with entire respect), polygamy may be introduced into all the territories, maintained under the laws of Turkey, " until the people of the Territory get a constitutional convention or the machinery of a State government into their hands," with competent authority to make laws in conflict with this " private relation."

According to the doctrine of the court, the peddler with his clocks, the liquor-dealer with his whiskies, the merchant with his goods, and the master with his slaves, on removal to a Territory, cannot hold, protect, or sell their property under the laws of the States whence they came, respectively, without the consent or tacit adoption of those laws by the Territorial government.

According to the Black doctrine, however, any one person, black or white, from any State of the Union, and from any country upon the globe, may remove into the Territories of the United States, and carry with him the law of the State or country whence he came, for the protection of any " right of property, private relation, condition, or status, lawfully existing in such State or country," without the consent and in defiance of the authority of the Territorial government, and maintain the same " until they get a constitutional convention or the machinery of a State government into their hands."

This is the distinct issue between Judge Black and the Supreme Court of the United States. It is not an issue between the attorney-general and myself, for in the beginning of the controversy I announced my purpose " to assume the law to be as decided by the court, without presuming that my individual opinion would either strengthen or invalidate their decisions."

*   *   *   *   *   *   *

But if it be true, as contended by Judge Black, that the Territories cannot legislate upon the subject or slavery, or any other right of property, private relation, condition, or *status*, lawfully existing in

another State or country, it necessarily results that the Territorial legislature cannot adopt the laws of other States or countries for the
protection of such rights and institutions, and consequently that the
courts cannot *presume* the tacit adoption of such laws by the Territorial government in the absence of any power to adopt them. Here,
again, we see that the doctrine of Judge Black, if it does not conclusively establish a right without the possibility of a remedy, is
certainly equivalent to the Wilmot Proviso in its practical results, so
far as the institution of slavery is concerned. I demonstrated this
proposition to him in my "reply" so conclusively that he did not
venture to deny it, much less attempt to answer the argument in his
"rejoinder."

I do not deem it necessary to notice in detail the many strange
and unaccountable misrepresentations in his "rejoinder" of the matters of fact and law set forth in my "reply," to which he was professing to respond. One or two instances will suffice as specimens
of the manner in which the attorney-general is in the habit of disposing of authorities which stand as insuperable obstacles in the path
of his argument. In my "reply" I quoted the following paragraph
from Judge Story's "Conflict of Laws," to show that he, at least,
thought the law was precisely the reverse of what Judge Black supposed it to be:

"There is a uniformity of opinion among foreign jurists and foreign tribunals
in giving no effect to the state of slavery of a party, whatever it may have been
in the country of his birth, or that in which he had been previously domiciled,
unless it is also recognized by the laws of the country of his actual domicil, and
where he is found, and it is sought to be enforced. [After citing various authorities, Judge Story proceeds:] In Scotland the like doctrine has been
solemly adjudged. The tribunals of France have adopted the same rule, even
in relation to slaves coming from and belonging to their own colonies. This is
also the undisputed law of England."

Now for Judge Black's reply to these passages from Judge Story:
"These passages (will the reader believe it?) merely show that a
slave becomes free when taken to a country *where slavery is* NOT
TOLERATED *by law !*" Substituting the words "not *tolerated* by law"
for the words "unless it is also *recognized* by law," Judge Black
reverses Judge Story's meaning, and makes that learned jurist declare
the law to be *precisely the reverse* of what Judge Story stated it to
be! "*Will the reader believe it?*" Not content with changing the
language and reversing the meaning, and citing it, in its altered form,
as evidence that I had misapplied the quotation, the attorney-general has the audacity to exclaim in parenthesis, for the purpose of
giving greater emphasis to his allegation, "will the reader believe
it?" Judge Black cannot avoid the responsibility which justly
attaches to such conduct by the pretence that slavery was prohibited
by law in Scotland, England and France, for the reason that the
reports of the cases show that the laws of those countries were *silent*
upon the subject, and that the decisions were made upon the distinct

ground that there was no law *recognizing* slavery, and *not* upon the ground that it was prohibited by law.

*   *   *   *   *   *   *

I will now devote a few words to a more pleasing and agreeable duty, by presenting to the public some of the beneficial results of this discussion. The attorney-general has been forced, by the exigencies of the controversy, step by step and with extreme reluctance, to make several important confessions, which necessarily involve an abandonment, on the part of his clients, of various pernicious heresies with which the country has been threatened for the last two years.

First, that slavery exists in the Territories by virtue of the Constitution of the United States. . . . Hence, we find on the second page of Judge Black's pamphlet these emphatic words: " *The Constitution certainly does not establish slavery in the Territories or anywhere else. Nobody in this country ever thought or said so.*"

This confession is ample reward for all the labor that the article in "Harper's Magazine" cost me, protesting, however, that I am acquainted with no rule of Christian morality which justifies gentlemen in saying "that nobody in this country ever thought or said so," in the face of Mr. Buchanan's Silliman letter and Lecompton message. This confession is presumed to have the sanction of the President and his cabinet, and therefore may be justly regarded as an official and authoritative abandonment of the pernicious heresy with which the country has been irritated for the last two years, *that slavery exists in the Territories by virtue of the Constitution of the United States.*

*   *   *   *   *   *   *

Another political heresy, which is in substance, although not in terms, abandoned in Judge Black's rejoinder, is "*that the Territories have no attribute of sovereignty about them.*"

It will be recollected that in my Harper article I drew a parallel between our Territories and the American Colonies, and showed that each possessed the exclusive power of legislation in respect to their internal polity; that, according to our American theory, in contradistinction to the European theory, this right of self-government was not derived from the monarch or government, but was inherent in the people.

*   *   *   *   *   *   *

In reply, Judge Black argued that this claim involved the possession of sovereignty by the people of the Territories; that "they have no attribute of sovereignty about them;" that "they are public corporations established by Congress to manage the local affairs of the inhabitants, like the government of a city established by a State legislature;" that "there is probably no city in the United States whose powers are not larger than those of a federal Territory;" and in fact, adopting the Tory doctrine of the Revolution, that all political power is derived from the crown or government, and not inherent in the people.

In my reply I showed that the people of the Territories do pass laws for the protection of life, liberty and property, and, in pursuance of those laws, do deprive the citizen of life, liberty and property, whenever the same become forfeited by crimes; that they exercise the sovereign power of taxation over all private property within their limits, and divest the title for non-payment of taxes; that they exercise the sovereign power of creating corporations, municipal, public and private; that they possess "*legislative power*" over "all rightful subjects of legislation consistent with the Constitution and the organic act;" and I quoted the language of Chief Justice Marshall, in delivering the unanimous opinion of the Supreme Court, that "*all legislative powers appertain to sovereignty.*"

Now let us see with what bad grace and worse manners, and yet how *completely the attorney-general backs down from his main position,* that the Territories "have no attribute of sovereignty about them :"

"Every half-grown boy in the country who has given the usual amount of study to the English tongue, or who has occasionally looked into a dictionary, knows that the sovereignty of a government consists in its uncontrollable right to exercise the highest power. But Mr. Douglas tries to clothe the Territories with the 'attributes of sovereignty,' not by proving the supremacy of their jurisdiction in any matter or thing whatsoever, but merely by showing that they may be, and some of them have been, authorized to legislate within certain limits, to exercise the right of *eminent domain,* to lay and collect *taxes* for territorial purposes, to deprive a citizen of *life, liberty or property,* as a punishment for crime, and to *create corporations. All this is true enough,* but it does by no means follow that the provisional government of a Territory is, therefore, a sovereign in any sense of the word."

ABSURDITIES OF BLACK'S ARGUMENTS.

So he surrenders at last. This discussion furnishes a single example of what perseverance can accomplish. It has taken a long time to drive the attorney-general into the admission that the people of a Territory are clothed with the LAW-MAKING POWER; with the right "to *legislate* within certain limits" (that is to say, upon "all rightful subjects of legislation consistent with the Constitution"); with "the right of eminent domain, to lay and collect taxes for Territorial purposes, to deprive a citizen of life, liberty, and property, as a punishment for crime, and to create corporations." I am not quite sure that "every half-grown boy in the country who has given the usual amount of study to the English tongue, or has occasionally looked into a dictionary," does know that these powers are all "attributes of sovereignty;" but I am very confident that no respectable court, jurist, or lawyer, "on this side of China" (Judge Black alone excepted), ever exposed their ignorance by questioning it, much less had the audacity to deny it. Since *the fact is admitted,* that the Territories do possess and may rightfully exercise those "legislative powers" which are recognized throughout the civilized world as the very highest attributes of sovereignty—the power over life, liberty and property—I shall not waste time in disputing with the attorney-general about the *name* by which he chooses to call them. It is sufficient for my purpose that I have at last forced him into the admission that the law-making power over all rightful subjects of legislation appertaining to life, liberty, and property, resides in, and may be rightfully exercised by the Territories, subject only to the limitations of the Constitution.

This brings to my notice another important confession in Judge Black's rejoinder, intimately connected with the preceding, which is: THAT IT IS AN INSULT TO THE AMERICAN PEOPLE TO SUPPOSE THAT THE PEOPLE OF ANY ORGANIZED TERRITORY WOULD ABUSE THE RIGHT OF SELF-GOVERNMENT IF IT WERE CONCEDED TO THEM.

This last confession, taken in connection with the previous admission of the power, removes the last vestige of any substantial objection to the doctrine of popular sovereignty in the Territories. Unable to make any plausible argument against it in theory and upon principle, as explained in "Harper's Magazine," Judge Black expended all the powers and energies of his intellect in his first pamphlet to render the doctrine odious and detestable upon the presumption of its probable practical results. He argued that it might result in "legislative robbery;" that "they may take every kind of property in mere caprice, or for any purpose of lucre or malice, without process of law, and without providing for compensation;" that "they may order the miners to give up every ounce of gold that has been dug at Pike's Peak;" that they may "license a band of marauders to despoil the emigrants crossing the Territory."

These were the arguments employed by the attorney-general, in the beginning of this controversy, to render the doctrine of popular sovereignty odious and detestable in the eyes of all honest men, and to prepare the minds of the people for the favorable reception of his new doctrine, that property in the Territories must be protected under the laws of the State whence the owner removed. Very soon, however, the lawyers began to amuse themselves and the public by exposing the folly and absurdity of the pretence that the Territorial courts could apply the judicial remedies prescribed by the legislature of Kentucky, or of any other State. Becoming ashamed of his position, Judge Black wrote an appendix to his pamphlet, in which he declared that while the "title which the owner acquired in the State" from whence he removed must be respected in the Territory, "THE ABSURD INFERENCE which some persons have drawn from it is *not true*, that the master also takes with him the JUDICIAL REMEDIES which were furnished him at the place where his title was acquired," and that "the respective rights and obligations of the parties must be protected and enforced *by the law prevailing at the place where they are supposed to be violated.*"

By this time it was my turn to reply, when I showed that his doctrine, if true, established a RIGHT WITHOUT A REMEDY, and if the people of the Territories could not be trusted in the management of their own affairs, and in the protection of life, liberty, and property, *they could not be relied upon to provide the remedies!* This reply was made in good faith, and believed to be pertinent to the issue and fatal to his position. Instead of receiving it in good temper, obviating the force of it by fair argument, if it were possible for him to do so, he flies into a rage and denies that he "said that an emigrant to a Territory had a right to his property *without a remedy*," and that "*it is an insult to the American people to suppose that any community can be organized within the limits of our Union who will tolerate such a state of things.*" Listen to his patriotic indignation at the bare suggestion that the people of the Territories cannot be trusted to guard and protect the rights of property and provide the remedies :

"I never said that an immigrant to a Territory had a right to his property *without a remedy ;* but I admit that he must look for his remedy to the law of his new domicil. It is true that he takes his life, his limbs, his reputation, and his property, and with them he takes nothing but his naked right to keep them and enjoy them. He leaves the judicial remedies of his previous domicil behind him. It is also true that in a Territory just beginning to be settled, he may need remedies for the vindication of his rights above all things else. In his new home there may be bands of base marauders, without conscience or the fear of God before their eyes, who are ready to rob and murder, and spare nothing that man or woman holds dear. In such a time it is quite possible to imagine an abolition legislature whose members owe their seats to Sharpe's rifles and the money of the Emigration Aid Society. Very possibly a legislature so chosen might employ itself in passing laws *unfriendly* to the rights of honest men and *friendly* to the business of the robber and the murderer. I concede this, and Mr. Douglas is entitled to all the comfort it affords him. But it is an insult to the American people to suppose, that any community can be organized within the limits of our Union, who will tolerate such a state of things."

Why did Judge Black insult the American people by supposing and assuming that they would do these things if left free to regulate their own internal polity and domestic affairs in their own way? It was deemed a necessary expedient in order to render popular sovereignty and its advocates odious and detestable. Why then did he, in the course of the same discussion, turn round and say it was an insult to the American people to suppose that the people of the Territories would do those things when allowed to regulate their own affairs in their own way? This, too, was in turn deemed a necessary expedient in order to avoid the horn of the dilemma into which he had been fairly driven, and escape the odium of an attempt to deceive the southern people, of which he had been fairly convicted of advocating a "*right without a remedy.*"

To what desperate shifts will men resort or be driven when they deliberately abandon *principle* FOR *expediency?* No more striking or humiliating illustration of this truth was ever given than this controversy presents. Each change of ground, every shifting of position has been done as an expedient to avoid what at the time was deemed a worse alternative. The ground on which Mr. Buchanan was elected, that "the people of a Territory, like those of a State, shall decide for themselves whether slavery shall or shall not exist within their limits," was changed, and in lieu of it the position assumed that "slavery exists in the Territories by virtue of the Constitution," as an expedient to obtain the support of certain southern ultras and fire-eaters who had always opposed popular sovereignty, on the supposition that without such support Mr. Buchanan's administration would be in a minority in the two houses of Congress. The confession that "the Constitution certainly does not establish slavery in the Territories, nor anywhere else," was made, and the position that slavery may be protected in the Territories under the laws of other States, assumed as an expedient to avoid the necessity of supporting a Congressional slave code. The confession that the people of the Territories may exercise legislative powers over all righful subjects of legislation, pertaining to life, liberty, and property, was made as an expedient to avoid the odium of advocating a right without a remedy, by showing that the Territorial legislatures might lawfully and rightfully pass all laws and prescribe all judicial remedies necessary for the protection of property of every description, slavery included. The declaration that it is an insult to the American people to suppose that the people of the Territories, when left free to manage their own affairs in their own way, would be guilty of "legislative robbery," would confiscate private property, seize it in mere spite, etc., was deemed a necessary expedient for the purpose of proving that the people might safely be trusted to furnish the protection and provide the remedies without which slaves could not be held and slave property protected in the Territories under the laws of other States.

*   *   *   *   *   *   *

Turning from Judge Black to Dr. Gwin, it is but respectful to say a few words upon his letter, which illuminated the columns of the central organ of my assailants the day previous to Judge Black's rejoinder. The identity of language, thought, and style, which pervades the two productions, while rejecting the idea that they could have been written with the same pen, furnishes conclusive evidence that great men will think alike when in the same vein. For example—

Dr. Gwin says:

"The *difference* BETWEEN MR. DOUGLAS AND THE DEMOCRATIC PARTY, sustained by this decision of the Supreme Court of the United States, *is this*," etc., etc.

Judge Black says:

"*The whole dispute* (as far as it is a doctrinal dispute) BETWEEN MR. DOUGLAS AND THE DEMOCRATIC PARTY *lies substantially in these two propositions*," etc., etc.

This coincidence, without wearying the reader with other examples, will suffice to show the unity of purpose and harmony of design with which my assailants pursue me. To separate "Mr. Douglas" from the "Democratic party" seems to be the patriotic end to which they all aim. They may as well make up their minds to believe, if they have not already been convinced of the fact by the bitter experience of the last two years, that *the thing cannot be done.* I gave them notice, at the initial point of this crusade, that no man or set of men on earth, save one, could separate me from the Democratic party; and as I was that one, and the only one who had the power, I did not intend to do it myself nor permit it to be done by others!

At this point (Nov. 7), Mr. Douglas was forced to stop writing by a seve reattack of inflammatory rheumatism, which soon prostrated him with a dangerous illness, from which he was not expected at one time to recover. In a moment of consciousness he directed the unfinished manuscript to be taken to the printer, with a note which concludes as follows:

"I am too feeble, however, to add more. Here let the controversy close for the present, and perhaps for ever."

THE CHASE AND TRUMBULL AMENDMENT.

We cannot close this chapter without referring to "the record" to which Mr. Douglas alludes in his brief "note" as wishing to comment on in reply to Mr. Gwin. It will be found in the "Congressional Globe" of the First Session of the thirty-third Congress, vol. xxviii. It completely exposes the attempted trickery of the Chase amendment. It shows what the Senate regarded as the true meaning of that clause in the Kansas Nebraska Bill which left the people of the Territories perfectly free " to *form* and *regulate* their *domestic institutions* in their own way," and that that meaning was, in the language of Senator Badger, " *an unrestricted* and *unreserved* reference to the *Territorial authorities* or the *people* themselves to determine *upon the question of slavery.*"

After the appearance of the Harper article, Mr. Gwin of California endeavored to produce the impression that neither

Mr. Douglas nor other senators understood, when the Kansas Nebraska Bill was before them, that the people of the Territories could legislate on the subject of slavery during the Territorial condition ; and that had senators so understood the bill, it would have destroyed the measure ; and further, that Mr. Douglas, if he took a different view of the bill from that, acted in bad faith to the Senate and the country in not saying so *" before the bill became a law."*

The records of Congress show the very reverse of this to be the fact. The record shows that both Mr. Douglas and the Democratic as well as other senators understood the Kansas Nebraska Bill to mean that the people of the Territories, while in the Territorial condition, could legislate on slavery as on any other domestic affair. It shows, also, that both Mr. Chase's amendment and Mr. Trumbull's amendment were legislative tricks, gotten up for political effect outside of Congress.

As the Kansas Nebraska Bill stood before Mr. Chase offered his amendment, it read :

It being the true intent and meaning of this act not to legislate slavery into any Territory or State, nor to exclude it therefrom, but to leave the people therein perfectly free to form and regulate their domestic institutions in their own way, subject only to the Constitution of the United States.

Mr. Chase's amendment proposed to add these words :

Under which the people of the Territory, through their appropriate representatives, may, if they see fit, *prohibit the existence of slavery therein.*

Mr. Chase made a brief speech in support of his amendment, in the course of which he said :

After I have obtained a vote upon this question, I shall want to know, and if no other senator shall do it, I will move amendments calculated to ascertain, whether it be intended to give the principle of non-intervention asserted by the bill full scope. If it is to be adopted, I want to see it adopted and fully carried out.

Mr. Pratt said : Mr. President, the principle which the senator from Ohio adopts as the principle of his amendment, is that the question shall be left entirely and exclusively to the people whether they will prohibit slavery or not. Now, for the purpose of testing the sincerity of the senator, and for the purpose of deducing the principle of his amendment correctly, I propose to amend it by inserting after the word " prohibit " the words " or introduce," so that if my amendment be adopted, and the amendment of the senator from Ohio as so amended be introduced as part of the bill, the principle which he says he desires to have tested will be inserted in the bill—that the people of the Territories shall have power to prohibit or introduce slavery as they may see proper. I suppose the question will be taken on the amendment which I offer to the amendment.

Mr. Seward.—Is an amendment to an amendment to an amendment in order ?

Mr. Chase.—The amendment which I offered is an amendment to an amendment.

The Presiding Officer.—The amendment of the senator from Maryland is not now in order.

Mr. Pratt.—Perhaps the senator from Ohio will accept it.

Mr. Chase, in the course of his reply, said : Now, sir, I desire to have the sense of the Senate on the question, whether the Territorial legislatures to which you propose to refer this great question—vital to the future destiny of the people who are to emigrate into these Territories—can, subject to the Constitution, protect themselves, if they see fit to do so, from slavery. The senator from Maryland, Mr. Pratt, has proposed an amendment to my amendment. I cannot accept it, but it will be entirely within the power of the Senate to agree to his if they see fit to do so.

Mr. Shields.—If the honorable senator will permit, I will suggest to him, if he wishes to test that proposition, to put the converse as suggested by the honorable senator from Maryland, and then it will be a fair proposition. Let the senator from Ohio accept the amendment of the senator from Maryland for the purpose of testing the question.

Mr. Chase.—I was about to state why I could not accept the amendment of the senator from Maryland. I have no objection that the vote shall be taken on it, and it is probable that it would receive the sanction of a majority here, but with my views of the Constitution, I cannot vote for it. I do not believe that a Territorial legislature, though it may have power to protect the people against slavery, is constitutionally competent to introduce it.

Senator Badger, of North Carolina, took Mr. Chase in hand, and exposed the insincerity of the Ohio senator, and also told what was *the true meaning of the bill.* He said :

Mr. President, I have understood, I find, correctly the purport of the amendment offered by the honorable senator from Ohio. The purposes of the amendment, and the effect of the amendment, if adopted by the Senate, and standing as it does, are clear and obvious. *The effect of the amendment, and the design of the amendment, are to overrule and subvert the very proposition introduced into the bill upon the motion of the chairman of the Committee on Territories,* (Mr. Douglas.) Is not that clear? The position, as it stands, *is an unrestricted and unreserved reference to the Territorial authorities, or the people themselves,* to determine upon the question of slavery; and, therefore, by the very terms, as well as by the obvious meaning and legal operations of that amendment (of Mr. Pratt), TO ENABLE THEM EITHER TO EXCLUDE OR TO INTRODUCE OR TO ALLOW SLAVERY. If, therefore, the amendment proposed by the senator from Ohio were appended to the bill in the connection in which he introduces it, the necessary and inevitable effect of it *would be to control and limit the language which the Senate had just put into the bill,* and to give it this construction, that though Congress leaves them to regulate their own domestic institutions as they please, yet in regard to the subject matter of slavery, *the power is confined to the exclusion or prohibition of it.* I say this is both the legal effect and the manifest design of the amendment. The legal effect is obvious upon the statement; the design is obvious upon the refusal of the gentleman to incorporate in his amendment what was suggested by my honorable friend from Maryland, the propriety and fairness of which were instantly seen by my friend from Illinois (Mr. Shields.)

    *   *   *   *   *   *   *   *   *

I have no hesitation, therefore, in saying that I shall vote against the amendment of the senator from Ohio. The clause as it stands is ample. It submits the whole authority to the Territory to determine for itself. That in my judgment is the place where it ought to be put. *If the people of these Territories choose to exclude slavery, so far from considering it a wrong done to me or to my constituents, I shall not complain of it. It is their own business."*

    *   *   *   *   *   *   *   *   *

The question being taken by yeas and nays on the amendment of Mr. Chase, it resulted yeas 10, nays 36.

YEAS—Messrs. Chase, Dodge of Wis., Fessenden, Fish, Foote, Hamlin, Seward, Smith, Sumner and Wade—10.

NAYS—Messrs. Adams, Atchison, Badger, Bell, Benjamin, Brodhead, Brown, Butler, Clay, Clayton, Dawson, Dixon, Dodge of Iowa, Douglas, Evans, Fitzpatrick, Gwin, Houston, Hunter, Johnson, Jones of Iowa, Jones of Tennessee, Mason, Morton, Norris, Pettit, Pratt, Rusk, Sebastian, Shields, Slidell, Stuart, Toucey, Walker, Weller and Williams—36.

And so the amendment was rejected. It will be observed

that Dr. Gwin, who quotes Mr. Douglas' vote against the Chase amendment as conclusive evidence that the Nebraska Bill was not intended to confer on the Territorial legislature the power of introducing or excluding slavery, was present participating in these proceedings, without uttering one word of dissent or disapprobation of the speeches of Messrs. Pratt, Shields and Badger, when the latter declared that the bill as it stood without the Chase amendment, " submits the whole authority to the Territorial legislature to determine for itself," " and that if the people of these Territories choose to exclude slavery, so far from my considering it a wrong done to me or my constituents, I shall not complain of it—it is their own business."

The reader will doubtless be curious to know why it happened that so many of the senators who participated in the removal of Mr. Douglas from the chairmanship of the Committee on Territories for construing the Nebraska Bill in the same manner as Mr. Badger construed it the day before it received their votes, could have remained silent in their places without one word of dissent or protest.

The Trumbull proposition referred to by Dr. Gwin, was offered as an amendment to the bill for the admission of Kansas into the Union as a State, two years after the passage of the Kansas-Nebraska Act, and was rejected solely upon the ground that it was irrelevant to the bill for the admission of a State, and not because it did not declare the true intent and meaning of the Kansas-Nebraska Act.

It was in the following words :

And be it further enacted :—
That the provision in the act "to organize the Territories of Kansas and Nebraska," which declares it to be "the true intent and meaning of said act not to legislate slavery into any Territory or State, or to exclude it therefrom, but to leave the people thereof perfectly free to form and regulate their domestic institutions in their own way, subject only to the Constitution of the United States," was intended to and does confer upon or leave

to the people of the Territory of Kansas full power at any time through its Territorial legislature to exclude slavery from said Territory, or to recognize or regulate it therein.

The official report of the proceedings on this amendment (see App. to "Cong. Globe," July 2d, 1856) shows that this amendment was discussed by Senators Benjamin, Trumbull, Fessenden, Cass, Douglas, Bigler, Toucey, Hale, Seward and Bayard, and that no one of them denied or intimated that the amendment did not declare the true intent and meaning of the original act, and that those who opposed it did so upon the ground that it was irrelevant to the bill under consideration.

MR. CASS said: Now, in respect to myself, I suppose the Senate knows clearly my views. I believe the original act gave the Territorial legislature of Kansas full power to exclude or allow slavery. . . . . This being my view, I shall vote against the amendment.

MR. DOUGLAS said: The reading of the amendment inclines my mind to the belief, that in its legal effect it is precisely the same with the original act, and almost in the words of that act. Hence, I should have no hesitancy in voting for it, except that it is putting on this bill a matter which does not belong to it.

MR. BIGLER said: Now, sir, I am not prepared to say what the intention of the Congress of 1854 was, because I was not a member of that Congress. I will not vote on this amendment, because I should not know that my vote was expressing the truth. I agree too, with the senator from Michigan (Mr. Cass), and the senator from Illinois (Mr. Douglas), that this is substantially the law as it now exists.

MR. TOUCEY said: Now, I object to this amendment as superfluous, nugatory, worse than that, as giving grounds for misrepresentation. It leaves the subject precisely where it is left in the Kansas-Nebraska Bill.

MR. BAYARD said: I have an objection to the amendment proposed by the honorable senator from Illinois (Mr. Trumbull), which to me would be perfectly sufficient, independent of any other: and that is, it is nothing more or less than an attempt to give a judicial exposition by the Congress of the United States to the Constitution; and I hold that they have no right to usurp judicial power.

The question being taken by yeas and nays on the amendment, resulted, ayes 11, nays 34, as follows:

YEAS—Messrs. Allen, Bell, of N. H., Collamer, Durkee, Fessenden, Foote, Foster, Hale, Seward, Trumbull and Wade—11.

NAYS—Messrs. Adams, Bayard, Benjamin, Biggs, Bigler, Bright, Brodhead, Brown, Cass, Clay, Crittenden, Dodge, Douglas, Evans, Fitzpatrick, Geyer, Hunter, Iverson, Johnson, Jones, of Iowa, Mallory, Mason, Pratt, Pugh, Reid, Sebastian, Slidell, Stuart, Thompson, of Kentucky, Toombs, Toucey, Weller, Wright and Yulee—34.

So the amendment was rejected.

Upon this transcript from the records we have three comments to make, which cannot fail to impress the reader.

First, That during this whole debate no senator pretended that Mr. Trumbull's amendment did not declare the true intent and meaning of the Nebraska Act, according to its legal effect and plain reading.

Second, That every senator who spoke against the amendment, assigned as the sole reason for his vote, either that it was irrelevant or an attempt by Congress to usurp judicial power.

Third, That those senators who now arraign and condemn Mr. Douglas as too unsound to be chairman of the Territorial Committee for no other reason than that he now construes the Kansas-Nebraska Act precisely as he then did, listened to this debate without one word of dissent, and by silence have acquiesced in the construction which the author of the bill distinctly affirmed in their presence. Indeed, it may be said that this construction of the act was unanimously affirmed by the Senate, on this occasion—the Republicans assenting to it by their votes in favor of the amendment, and all the others by their acquiescence in the reasons assigned by Messrs. Cass, Douglas, Bayard, Bigler and Toucey for voting against it. If, however, these senators shall attempt to escape the conclusion under cover of the reasons assigned by Mr. Bayard, that the amendment was " nothing more or less than an attempt to give a judicial exposition,. by the Congress of the United

11

States, to the Constitution," and " that they have no right
to usurp judicial power," with what consistency can these
gentlemen meet in secret caucus and propose resolutions, to
be offered in open Senate, as a platform for the Charleston
Convention; thus "giving a judicial exposition," by the
caucus and the Senate, to the Constitution, on the identical
point which Mr. Bayard denounced as "a usurpation of
judicial power," and in the justice of which denunciation
they all appeared at the time to acquiesce?   Would it not
be well, at the next meeting of the senatorial caucus, to give
a satisfactory answer to this inquiry ?

CHAPTER XVII.

PROTECTION OF STATES FROM INVASION—THE SENATORIAL CAUCUS.

Great Speech of Mr. Douglas on the Harper's Ferry Invasion—Anxiety to hear him—His Speeches in Reply to Senators Fessenden, Jeff. Davis, and Seward—The Caucus of Senators—Their Utopian Platform.

THE first session of the 36th Congress met on the first Monday in December, 1859. The great practical measure of the session was the proposition of Mr. Douglas, embraced in the resolution which he offered on the 16th of January, 1860, instructing the Judiciary Committee to report a bill to protect each State from invasion by people of other States.

A day or two before the introduction of this resolution, a sharp passage at arms took place in the Senate between Mr. Douglas and Messrs. Clay, Jeff. Davis, and Green, which is thus described by the correspondent of the "New York Herald :"

Mr. PUGH, of Ohio, a sharp, keen, and plucky debater, and the right-hand man of Mr. Douglas, brought the controversy to a focus. There was a good deal of cross-firing and sharp-shooting against the doctrines and speeches of the Little Giant, from Green, Iverson, Clay, Davis, Gwin, and other southsiders, till at length the Little Giant himself was brought to the floor.

He complained of ill-health; but he never looked better in his life —never appeared fresher in the ring, and never acquitted himself more to the admiration of his friends. He was like a stag at bay, and right and left he dashed among his pursuers. It is useless here to repeat this branch of the debate. It was the feature of the day and of the session.

Mr. Douglas announced to-day that he will abide by the decision of the convention, for the sake of the Democratic party, though he will not accept its nomination except upon the doctrine of popular sovereignty, as enunciated in the Cincinnati platform.

EXTRACTS FROM THE DEBATE.

This was Mr. Douglas's first appearance in the Senate after his severe and protracted illness, and it was thought rather ungenerous in these senators to make a combined and concerted attack upon him under the circumstances. It is conceded, however, by all who listened to the debate, that he never bore himself more gallantly or came out of a contest more successfully. The objects of the assaults upon him were to justify his removal from the Committee on Territories, upon the ground that he held opinions incompatible with the Democratic creed. We give several extracts from this important debate.

In reply to Mr. Davis of Mississippi, Mr. Douglas said:

I have never complained of my removal from the chairmanship of the Committee on Territories, and I never intended to allude to that subject in this body; but I do assert that the record proves that the Senate knew for eleven years that I held the identical opinions which I expressed in my Freeport speech, and which are now alleged as the cause of my removal; and during that period, with a full knowledge of those opinions, which were repeated over and over again in this body, within the hearing of every member of the Senate, I was, by the unanimous vote of the body, made chairman of that committee, being reëlected each year for eleven years. The cause now assigned for my removal is that I hold the identical opinions to-day that I held and repeatedly expressed during that whole period. If this be the true state of the facts, what does it prove? Simply, that those who removed me changed at the end of the eleven years, and I was not sound because I did not change as suddenly as they. My only offence consists in fidelity to the principles that I had avowed during that whole period. If at the end of that time my opinions were incompatible with those of a majority, it shows that the majority had changed their policy but that I had not changed my opinions.

Mr. Green answered by charging that Mr. Douglas, in 1856, had declared in the Senate that the question, in respect to the extent of the power of a Territorial legislature over the subject of slavery, was a judicial question, which could be alone authoritatively determined by the Supreme Court of the United States.

Mr. Douglas, in reply, said :

In 1856 I did say it was a judicial question, and I said it over and over again before 1856. I have said it since that time. I declared in my Illinois speeches that it was a judicial question, I have declared the same thing in every publication I have made during the last year. I assert, now, that it is a judicial question. The point is that for years it was no want of soundness in principle that I held one side of that judicial question while others held the opposite. I assert that the Senate did know which side of the judicial question I held. But I have always said that I would abide the decisions of the Supreme Court, not only as a matter of policy but from considerations of duty. I take the law as expounded by the Supreme Court, I receive the Dred Scott decision as an authoritative exposition ; but I deny that the point now under consideration has been decided in the Dred Scott case. There is no one fact in that case upon which it could have arisen. The lawyers engaged on each side never dreamt that it did arise in the case. It is offensive and injurious to the reputation of the court to say that they decided a great question which had been the subject of agitation to the extent of convulsing the whole country, when it did not arise in the case, and when it was not argued by counsel. Sir, it would prove the court unworthy to decide the great question in a civilized country if it would take cognizance of a case when there was no fact upon the record upon which it could arise, when the counsel on either side never dreamt that it was in issue, when there was no argument on it, and foreclose the right of self-government to thousands and hundreds of thousands of people without a hearing. But one word more : I assert, and the debates will prove, that the understanding of the Kansas-Nebraska

Bill was that this was a judicial question to be decided when it should arise on a Territorial enactment.

The speech of the senator from Va. (Mr. Hunter), shows clearly that it was to arise on a Territorial enactment, and all the speeches of all of us show that it was in that way and at that time that this judicial question was expected to arise and be decided. The understanding was that when a Territorial legislature passed an act on this subject, of which any man complained, he should be able to bring the matter before the Supreme Court; and to facilitate the court in getting jurisdiction, we amended the bill by putting in a clause providing that a case affecting the title to slaves might be taken up to the Supreme Court without reference to the amount involved. That clause was inserted in order to get this judicial question before the Supreme Court of the United States. How? On a Territorial enactment, and nobody ever dreamt that the court was going in a decision on a case which did not affect that question to decide this point without argument and without notice, and preclude the rights of the people without allowing them to be heard. Whenever a Territorial legislature shall pass an act divesting or attempting to divest or impair or prejudice the right to slave property, and a case under that act shall be brought before the Supreme Court, I will abide by the decision and help in good faith to carry it out.

Mr. Clay, of Alabama, was the next to assail Mr. Douglas and to impeach the soundness of his principles and the consistency of his course upon the slavery question. In reply to him, Mr. Douglas said:

I say to the gentleman from Alabama, that while I have sought no sympathy and desire no sympathy, I shrink from no vindication of myself. I leave the public to judge whether there has not been rather a doubling of teams on me every time I have engaged in debate for the last two years. After fighting an unholy alliance in my own State, between federal officeholders and abolitionists, and triumphing over them, did I come here at the last session and make any parade of that fact? No, sir, I remained silent. I made no vindication of myself; I made no complaint of my removal from the chair of the Territorial Committee; I never alluded to it, and the matter would never have passed my lips if it had not been thrust in

my face in debate in the Senate to-day. The discussion of last year
was brought on by others and not by me, and yet we have been told
by a senator (Mr. Gwin) while making a speech in the country, that
those who removed me from the head of that committee expected me
to defend myself, and complained that I waited until the end of the
session, after I had been tried, condemned and executed in my absence. Sir, I had no defence to make. I scorn to make any defence.
I stood conscious of the rectitude of my own motives and the correctness of my own actions. I claimed the right to hold and vindicate
my own opinions, and to impeach no other man's conduct or the
integrity of his purpose. I yield to every senator the right of differing from me, and I never make a test on him for doing so.

*　　*　　*　　*　　*　　*　　*　　*

I have but a word more to say now, and that is on another point.
The senator from Alabama tells me that if he had not supposed that
I had changed my opinions, he would never have extended to me the
right hand of fellowship as a Democrat. Well, sir, I do not know
that my Democracy would have suffered much if he never had. I
am willing to compare records with him as a Democrat. I never
make speeches, proclaiming to the world that if I cannot get my
man nominated I will bolt the convention and break up the Democratic party, and then talk about the right hand of Democratic
fellowship. Sir, that senator has placed himself beyond the pale of
Democratic fellowship, by the pronunciamento that he will not abide
the decision of the National Convention, if the speeches, which I see
attributed to him in the newspapers, are true. I do not understand
this thing of belonging to an organization, going into a convention
and abiding by the result if you win and bolting if you lose. I never
thought that it was deemed fair dealing in any profession. If you
take the winnings when you gain, I always thought you had to pay
your bets when you lost: a man who tells me and the world that he
only goes into a convention to abide the result in the event of its
deciding in his favor, has no right to talk about extending the hand
of Democratic fellowship. Now, sir, I have the kindest feelings
toward the gentleman personally. He has a right to differ from
me; he has a right to bolt the Charleston Convention; he has a right
to proclaim to the world beforehand that he means to do so; but he
has no right to go into the convention unless he intends to abide the

result. He has no right to claim that he belongs to the convention and say that he will bolt the nominee; and hence I say to that senator, with all kindness, that if he does not extend to me the right hand of Democratic fellowship I shall survive the stroke. If I should happen to be the nominee of the Charleston Convention, and he should vote against me, I am not certain that it would diminish my majority in his own State. I am not counting his support. Permit me to say to that senator that it will be time enough to threaten that he will not vote for me when I ask him to do it. Permit me to say further to him that I am doing quite as much honor to him if I consent to accept his vote, as he will do me by conferring it.

*   *   *   *   *   *   *   *

When threats are made of not extending the hand of Democratic fellowship, I should like to understand who it is that has the right to say who is in the party and who not. I believe that more than two-thirds of the Democracy of the United States are with me on this disputed point. James Buchanan received about eighteen hundred thousand votes at the last election, more than twelve hundred thousand of them in the free States, and something over six hundred thousand in the slaveholding States, and you have heard it said by the senator from Ohio to-day, and I believe it, that ninety-nine out of every one hundred Democrats in the northern States agreed with him and me on this question. Then one-third of the Democratic party are going to read out the remaining two-thirds. Your candidate will have a good chance of election if you shall have done it, will he not ?

The only importance attached to the question of the chairmanship of the Committee on Territories is this: heretofore no test has been made as to a man's opinions on this judicial question, and hence I could hold the position of chairman by a unanimous vote, without objection ; but now it is made a test. I do not make it—I only resist your test if you make it on me. While I do not want the chairmanship—while I have performed labor enough on that committee, for eleven and a half years, to be anxious to get rid of it—yet the country cannot fail to take notice that my removal at the end of eleven years, is significant in one of two points of view. It was either personal or political. I acquit every man of the suspicion that it was personal. Then it must have been political. What does it signify ? It is a proclamation to the Senate that a man holding the opinions I do is not sound enough to serve as chairman of a committee. Is he sound enough for a cabinet officer, for a district attorney, for a collector of the port, for a post-master, for a lighthouse-keeper? All these classes of officers are now being removed, except cabinet officers, for holding the same opinions as myself. If you were to nominate for the Presidency a man who intends to pursue this proscriptive policy that every man holding the opinions I do is marked as a victim for vengeance the moment your candidates are elected, what chance have you of electing them?"

After a colloquy between Mr. Davis and Mr. Douglas, the latter proceeded :

" I seek no war with any senator on either side of the chamber, and especially I seek none on political issues with Democratic senators. Every word I have said has been in defence of myself against the imputation that I had changed my line of policy, which I utterly deny. I did understand, and I understand now, that when applications are made to the present Administration for office, the question of a man's opinion on popular sovereignty is asked, and the applicant is proscribed if he agree with me in opinion. The country understands therefore that if a man representing this proscriptive policy is the next President, every man in the country who holds the opinions of the senator from Ohio and myself is to be proscribed from every office, high or low. Such is now the case. Is any gentleman prepared to take the Charleston nomination with the understanding that he is to proscribe two-thirds of the party, and then degrade himself so low as to seek the votes of the men whom he has marked as his victims? If no tests are to be made, there can be harmony ; if these tests are to be made, one-third will not subdue two-thirds. I do not intend to surrender an opinion or to try and force one upon any other senator or citizen. I arraign no man because of his opinions."

INCIDENTS OF THE GREAT SPEECH.

On Monday, the 23d of January, the resolution submitted on the 16th instant having been made the special order for that day, Mr. Douglas addressed the Senate in its support. It was known in Washington for some time previously that he would speak on that day, and this fact drew to the Capitol an immense concourse of people. It would seem that the mantles of Clay and Webster have fallen upon the shoulders of Douglas, for it is well known that for years past it is only necessary to say "Douglas speaks to-day," in order to have the Senate chamber thronged by all the wit and beauty in the capital. On this occasion, although it was known that Mr. Douglas would not begin to speak till nearly two in the afternoon, yet as early as ten in the morning, numerous groups of people were seen wending their way to the Capitol. At eleven, the galleries were full, and the tide of silk and satin, cambric and crinoline, continued to gather in the avenues and lobbies. Crowds of ladies and gentlemen continued to pour in, till at noon every seat in the immense chamber was occupied, and all the standing-place jammed. The members of the House of Representatives came in almost in a body, and occupied the floor. The foreign diplomatic corps too, were present in full force. Never before had there been such a scene in the new chamber.

Douglas was to speak—not for Illinois, not for the West, but for the pacification of the whole country, and the perpetuity of the Union.

The reader will comprehend the character of this speech from the subjoined extracts:

INVASION OF STATES.

The hour having arrived for the consideration of the special order, the Senate proceeded to consider the following resolution, submitted by Mr. Douglas on the 16th instant:

"*Resolved*, That the Committee on the Judiciary be instructed to report a bill for the protection of each State and Territory of the Union against invasion by the authorities or inhabitants of any other State or Territory; and for the suppression and punishment of conspiracies or combinations in any State or Territory with intent to invade, assail, or molest the gov ernment, inhabitants, property, or institutions of any other State or Territor y of the Union."

Mr. DOUGLAS.—Mr. President, on the 25th of November last, the governor of Virginia addressed an official communication to the President of the United States, in which he said:

" I have information from various quarters, upon which I rely, that a conspiracy of formidable extent, in means and numbers, is formed in Ohio, Pennsylvania, New York, and other States, to rescue John Brown and his associates, prisoners at Charlestown, Virginia. The information is specific enough to be reliable. . . . .
" Places in Maryland, Ohio, and Pennsylvania, have been occupied as depots and rendezvous by these desperadoes, unobstructed by guards or otherwise, to invade this State, and we are kept in continual apprehension of outrage from fire and rapine. I apprise you of these facts in order that you may take steps to preserve peace between the States."

To this communication the President of the United States, on the 28th of November, returned a reply, from which I read the following sentence:

" I am at a loss to discover any provision in the Constitution or laws of the United States which would authorize me to 'take steps' for this purpose."
[That is, to preserve the peace between the States.]

This announcement produced a profound impression upon the public mind, especially in the slaveholding States. It was generally received and regarded as an official and authoritative announcement that the Constitution of the United States confers no power upon the Federal Government to protect the several States of this Union against invasion from the other States. I shall not stop to inquire whether the President meant to declare that the existing laws confer no authority upon him, or that the Constitution empowers Congress to enact no laws which would authorize the federal interposition to protect the States from invasion; my object is to raise the inquiry, and to ask the judgment of the Senate and of the House of Representatives on the question, whether it is not within the power of Congress, and the duty of Congress, under the Constitution, to enact all laws which are necessary and proper for the protection of each and every State against invasion, either from foreign powers or from any portion of the United States.

*   *   *   *   *   *

Sir, what were the causes which produced the Harper's Ferry outrage? Without stopping to adduce evidence in detail, I have no hesitation in expressing my firm and deliberate conviction that the Harper's Ferry crime was the natural, logical, inevitable result of the doctrines and teachings of the Republican party, as explained and enforced in their platform, their partisan presses, their pamphlets and books, and especially in the speeches of their leaders in and out of Congress. (Applause in the galleries.)

Order being restored, Mr. Douglas proceeded:

I was remarking that I considered this outrage at Harper's Ferry as the logical, natural consequence of the teachings and doctrines of the Republican party. I am not making this statement for the purpose of crimination or partisan effect. I desire to call the attention of members of that party to a reconsideration of the doctrines that they are in the habit of enforcing, with a view to a fair judgment whether they do not lead directly to those consequences on the part of those deluded persons who think that all they say is meant in real earnest, and ought to be carried out. The great principle that underlies the organization of the Republican party is violent, irreconcilable, eternal warfare upon the institution of American slavery, with the view of its ultimate extinction throughout the land; sectional war is to be waged until the cotton fields of the South shall be cultivated by free labor, or the rye fields of New York and Massachusetts shall be cultivated by slave labor. In furtherance of this article of their creed, you find their political organization not only sectional in its location, but one whose vitality consists in appeals to northern passion, northern prejudice, northern ambition against southern States, southern institutions, and southern people.

*   *   *   *   *   *

Can any man say to us that although this outrage has been perpetrated at Harper's Ferry, there is no danger of its recurrence? Sir, is not the Republican party still embodied, organized, sanguine, confident of success, and defiant in its pretensions? Does it not now hold and proclaim the same creed that it did before this invasion? It is true that most of its representatives here disavow the acts of John Brown at Harper's Ferry. I am glad that they do so; I am rejoiced that they have gone thus far; but I must be permitted to say to them that it is not sufficient that they disavow the act, unless they also repudiate and denounce the doctrines and teachings which produced the act. Those doctrines remain the same; those teachings are being poured into the minds of men throughout the country, by means of speeches, and pamphlets, and books, and through partisan presses. The causes that produced the Harper's Ferry invasion are now in active operation. Is it true that the people of all the border States are required by the Constitution to have their hands tied, without the power of self-defence, and remain patient under a threatened invasion in the day or in the night? Can you expect people to be patient, when they dare not lie down to sleep at night without first stationing sentinels around their houses to see if a band of marauders and murderers are not approaching with torch and pistol? Sir, it requires more patience than freemen ever should cultivate, to submit to constant annoyance, irritation and apprehension. If we expect to preserve this Union, we must remedy, within the Union, and in obedience to the Constitution, every evil for which disunion would furnish a remedy.

Upon the conclusion of this speech Mr. Fessenden attempted to break its force by a violent partisan attack on Mr. Douglas and the Democratic party; to which Mr. Douglas instantly replied, repelling the assaults and vindicating the position of the Democratic party upon the slavery question. We invite attention to extracts:

MR. DOUGLAS' REPLY.

Sir, I desire a law that will make it a crime, punishable by imprisonment in the penitentiary, after conviction in the United States court, to make a conspiracy in one State, against the people, property, government, or institutions of another. Then we shall get at the root of the evil. I have no doubt that gentlemen on the other side will vote for a law which pretends to comply with the guarantees of the Constitution, without carrying any force or efficiency in its provisions. I have heard men abuse the Fugitive Slave Law, and express their willingness to vote for amendments; but when you came to the amendments which they desired to adopt, you found they were such as would never return a fugitive to his master. They would go for any fugitive slave law that had a hole in it big enough to let the negro drop through and escape; but none that would comply with the obligations of the Constitution. So we shall find that side of the House voting for a law that will, in terms, disapprove of unlawful expeditions against neighboring States, without being efficient in affording protection.

But the senator says it is a part of the policy of the northern Democracy to represent the Republicans as being hostile to southern institutions. Sir, it is a part of the policy of the northern Democracy, as well as their duty, to speak the truth on that subject. I did not suppose that any man would have the audacity to arraign a brother senator here for representing the Republican party as dealing in denunciation and insult of the institutions of the South. Look to your Philadelphia platform, where you assert the sovereign power of Congress over the Territories for their government, and demand that it shall be exerted against those twin relics of barbarism—polygamy and slavery.

*   *   *   *   *   *   *   *

I have said and repeat that this question of slavery is one of climate, of political economy, of self-interest, not a question of legislation. Wherever the climate, the soil, the health of the country are such that it cannot be cultivated by white labor, you will have African labor, and compulsory labor at that. Wherever white labor can be employed cheapest and most profitably, there African labor will retire and white labor will take its place.

You cannot force slavery by all the acts of Congress you may make on one inch of territory against the will of the people, and you cannot, by any law you can make, keep it out from one inch of American territory where the people want it. You tried it in Illinois. By the Ordinance of 1787, slavery was prohibited, and yet our people, believing that slavery would be profitable to them, established hereditary servitude in the Territory by Territorial legislation, in defiance of your federal ordinance. We maintained slavery there just so long as Congress said we should not have it, and we abolished it at just the moment you recognized us as a State, with the right to do as we pleased. When we established it, it was on the supposition that it was for our interest to do so.

*   *   *   *   *   *   *   *

My object is to establish firmly the doctrine that each State is to do its own voting, establish its own institutions, make its own laws without interference, directly or indirectly, from any outside power. The gentleman says that is squatter sovereignty. Call it squatter sovereignty, call it popular sovereignty, call it what you please, it is the great principle of self-government on which this Union was formed, and by the preservation of which alone can it be maintained. It is the right of the people of every State to govern themselves and make their own laws, and be protected from outside violence or interference, directly or indirectly. Sir, I confess the object of the legislation I contemplate is to put down this outside interference; it is to repress this "irrepressible conflict;" it is to bring the government back to the true principles of the Constitution, and let each people in this Union rest secure in the enjoyment of domestic tranquillity without apprehension from neighboring States. I will not occupy further time.

REPLY TO SENATOR DAVIS.

On the 26th of January, Mr. Douglas made the following remarks, in his reply to Gen. Jeff. Davis, senator from Mississippi.

Mr. Douglas.—I think if the senator from Mississippi had carefully read my speech, he would have found no necessity for vindicating the President of the United States from any criticism that I had made upon his letter, or from any issue that I had made with the President growing out of that letter. Certainly, in my speech, there is no criticism upon the President, none upon his letter, no issue made with him; on the contrary, an express disclaimer of any such issue. I quoted the paragraph from the President's letter in reply to Gov. Wise, and I will quote it again:

"I am at a loss to discover any provision in the Constitution or laws of the United States which would authorize me to take steps for this purpose." [That is, preserving the peace between the States.]

My impression, from reading the President's letter, was that he was inclined to the belief that the Constitution conferred no power upon the Federal Government to interfere. But still, it might be that such was not the President's meaning, and that he only wished to be understood as saying that existing laws conferred no authority upon him to interfere. Hence, in order to make no issue with the President upon that subject, I stated, I shall not stop to inquire whether he meant to be understood as denying the power of Congress to confer authority, or denying that the authority was yet conferred. My simple object was to obtain suitable legislation to redress similar evils in the future; that if the present laws were not sufficient—I believe there are none on the subject—Congress ought to enact suitable laws to the extent that the Constitution authorized, to prevent these invasions. I quoted it for the purpose of showing the necessity of legislation by Congress. My argument was founded upon that supposed necessity. I proceeded to demonstrate that the Constitution conferred the power on Congress to pass laws necessary and proper to protect the States, and I called upon Congress to exercise that power. I made no issue with the President.

But the senator intimates that the legislation of which I spoke would lead to an act of usurpation that would endanger the rights of the States, and yet goes on to prove that the President of the United States does not differ with me in regard to that constitutional power. If the President agrees with me on that point, I am glad of it. If he differs with me it would not change my opinions nor my action, but I respectfully submit, when I only propose such legislation as the Constitution authorizes and requires, it is hardly fair to say that that means an attack upon the sovereignty of the States.

The legislation that I propose on this point of combinations, was this: that it shall be lawful for the grand juries of the United States courts to indict all men who shall form conspiracies or combinations to invade a State or to disturb or molest citizens, property, or institutions; and that it shall be proper for the petit jury in the United States courts, under the judge, to try and convict the conspirators, and to punish them by confinement in the penitentiaries or prisons within the respective States where the conspiracies or combinations are formed. That was the power that I proposed should be conferred by law on the federal courts. I never proposed to intrust to the President an army to go and seek out conspiracies, to seek out combinations, and to punish them by military rule. My whole argument was that the federal courts should have jurisdiction over these conspiracies and combinations; that the conspirators should be indicted, and convicted according to law, and punished to the extent of their power. But in case of an organized body of men, or a military force in the act of invading, I would confer authority to use military force to the extent necessary to prevent that—not the conspiracy.

The senator says he has got that power now. The President of the United States, I apprehend, thought not, for this reason : He said the only power he had got was the authority conferred by the two acts to which he alluded, to wit: to protect the United States against invasion from foreign powers and Indian tribes; and he stated that the invasion of one State from another State did not come within the specifications of the statute for protecting the United States against foreign powers and Indian tribes. If the senator thinks that that power is there, when we get the legislation before us it will be proper to make amendments which will reach each objection he may raise. The two propositions I maintained in my argument, and those provided for in my resolution, were these : first to protect each State against invasion—the case of actual invasion being then in process of execution ; second, to make it criminal to form conspiracies and combinations in any State or Territory, or any place within the United States, against the institutions, property or government of any other State or Territory of this Union. Those were the propositions.

REPLY TO SENATOR SEWARD.

On the 29th of February, Mr. Seward made his great speech on the occasion of his presenting the Wyandott Constitution of Kansas. It was a speech of much ability, and no doubt, when he had concluded, Mr. Seward imagined that he had dealt a death-blow to the Democratic party. Mr. Douglas immediately replied to Mr. Seward, taking up *seriatim* the points of his speech, and scattering his sophistries to the winds. By general confession Mr. Douglas has rarely appeared to better advantage on the floor of the Senate than in this triumphant *extempore* reply to Mr. Seward. In the language of the correspondent of the " Cleveland Plaindealer," " He decapitated the mighty Philistine with his own sword.

The beautiful structure which had cost Mr. Seward so much time, labor, and travel, was in one brief hour scattered in fragments at the feet of the Little Giant."

The reader will find the reply of Mr. Douglas in a subsequent part of this work, from which we give brief extracts:

EXTRACTS FROM REPLY.

MR. PRESIDENT: I trust I shall be pardoned for a few remarks upon so much of the senator's speech as consists in an assault on the Democratic party, and especially with regard to the Kansas-Nebraska bill, of which I was the responsible author. It has become fashionable now-a-days for each gentleman making a speech against the Democratic party to refer to the Kansas-Nebraska act as a cause of all the disturbances that have since ensued. They talk about the repeal of a sacred compact that had been undisturbed for more than a quarter of a century, as if those who complained of violated faith had been faithful to the provisions of the Missouri Compromise. Sir, wherein consisted the necessity for the repeal or abrogation of that act, except it was that the majority in the northern States refused to carry out the Missouri Compromise in good faith ? I stood willing to extend it to the Pacific Ocean, and abide by it forever, and the entire South, without one exception in this body, was willing thus to abide by it; but the freesoil element of the northern States was so strong as to defeat that measure, and thus open the slavery question anew. The men who now complain of the abrogation of that act were the very men who denounced it, and denounced all of us who were willing to abide by it so long as it stood upon the statute-book. Sir, it was the defeat, in the House of Representatives, of the enactment of the bill to extend the Missouri Compromise to the Pacific Ocean, after it had passed the Senate on my own motion, that opened the controversy of 1850, which was terminated by the adoption of the measures of that year.

We carried those Compromise measures over the head of the senator of New York and his present associates. We, in those measures established a great principle, rebuking his doctrine of intervention by the Congress of the United States to prohibit slavery in the Territories. Both parties, in 1852, pledged themselves to abide by that principle and thus stood pledged not to prohibit slavery in the Territories by act of Congress. The Whig party affirmed that pledge, and so did the Democracy. In 1854 we only carried out, in the Kansas-Nebraska Act, the same principle that had been affirmed in the Compromise measures of 1850. I repeat that their resistance to carrying out in good faith the settlement of 1820, their defeat of the bill for extending it to the Pacific Ocean, was the sole cause of the agitation of 1850, and gave rise to the necessity of establishing the

principle of non-intervention by Congress with slavery in the Territories. . . . .

But, sir, the whole argument of that senator goes far beyond the
question of slavery, even in the Territories. His entire argument
rests on the assumption that the negro and the white man were equal
by Divine law, and hence that all laws and constitutions and governments in violation of the principle of negro equality are in violation
of the law of God. That is the basis upon which his speech rests.

He quotes the Declaration of Independence to show that the fathers
of the Revolution understood that the negro was placed on an equality
with the white man, by quoting the clause, " we hold these truths to
be self-evident that, all men are created equal, and are endowed
by their Creator with certain inalienable rights, among which are
life, liberty, and the pursuit of happiness." Sir, the doctrine of that
senator and of his party is—and I have had to meet it for eight
years—that the Declaration of Independence intended to recognize
the negro and the white man as equal under the Divine law, and
hence that all the provisions of the Constitution of the United States
which recognize slavery are in violation of the Divine law. In other
words, it is an argument against the Constitution of the United
States upon the ground that it is contrary to the law of God. The
senator from New York has long held that doctrine. The senator
from New York has often proclaimed to the world that the Constitution of the United States was in violation of the Divine law, and
that senator will not contradict the statement. I have an extract
from one of his speeches now before me, in which that proposition is
distinctly put forth. In a speech made in the State of Ohio, in 1848,
he said:

" Slavery is the sin of not some of the States only, but of them all; of not
one nationality, but of all nations. It perverted and corrupted the moral sense
of mankind deeply and universally, and this perversion became a universal
habit. Habits of thought become fixed principles. No American State has
yet delivered itself entirely from these habits. We, in New York, are guilty
of slavery still by withholding the right of suffrage from the race we have
emancipated. You, in Ohio, are guilty in the same way by a system of black
laws still more aristocratic and odious. It is written in the Constitution of the
United States that five slaves shall count equal to three freemen as a basis of
representation; and it is written, also, IN VIOLATION OF DIVINE LAW,
that we shall surrender the fugitive slave who takes refuge at our firesides from
his relentless pursuer."

LABOR STATES AND CAPITAL STATES.

The Senator from New York has coined a new definition of the
States of the Union—labor States and capital States. The capital
States, I believe, are the slaveholding States; the labor States are
the non-slaveholding States. It has taken that senator a good many
years to coin that phrase and bring it into use. I have heard him
discuss these favorite theories of his for the last ten years, I think,
and I never heard of capital States and labor States before. It
strikes me that something has recently occurred up in New England

that makes it politic to get up a question between capital and labor, and take the side of the numbers against the few. We have seen some accounts in the newspapers of combinations and strikes among the journeymen shoemakers in the towns there—labor against capital. The senator has a new word ready coined to suit their case, and make the laborers believe that he is on the side of the most numerous class of voters.

What produced that strike among the journeymen shoemakers? Why are the mechanics of New England, the laborers and the employees, now reduced to the starvation point? Simply because, by your treason, by your sectional agitation, you have created a strife between the North and the South, have driven away your southern customers, and thus deprive the laborers of the means of support. This is the fruit of your Republican dogmas. It is another step, following John Brown, of the "irrepressible conflict." Therefore we now get this new coinage of "labor States"—he is on the side of the shoemakers, (laughter), and "capital States"—he is against those that furnish the hides. (Laughter.) I think those shoemakers will understand this business. They know why it is that they do not get so many orders as they did a few months ago. It is not confined to the shoemakers; it reaches every mechanic's shop and every factory. All the large laboring establishments of the North feel the pressure produced by the doctrine of the "irrepressible conflict." This new coinage of words will not save them from the just responsibility that follows the doctrines they have been inculcating. If they had abandoned the doctrine of the "irrepressible conflict," and proclaimed the true doctrine of the Constitution, that each State is entirely free to do just as it pleases, have slavery as long as it chooses, and abolish it when it wishes, there would be no conflict; the northern and southern States would be brethren; there would be fraternity between us, and your shoemakers would not strike for higher prices.

* * * * * * * *

But, sir, if the senator from New York, in the event that he is made President, intends to carry out his principles to their logical conclusions, let us see where they will lead him. In the same speech that I read from a few minutes ago, I find the following. Addressing the people of Ohio, he said:

"You blush not at these things, because they have become as familiar as household words; and your pretended free-soil allies claim peculiar merit for maintaining these miscalled guarantees of slavery, which they find in the national compact. Does not all this prove that the Whig party have kept up with the spirit of the age; that it is as true and faithful to human freedom as the inert conscience of the American people will permit it to be? What then, you say, can nothing be done for freedom, because the public conscience remains inert? Yes, much can be done, everything can be done. Slavery can be limited to its present bounds."

That is the first thing that can be done—slavery can be limited to its present bounds. What else?

"It can be ameliorated. It can and must be abolished, and you and I can and must do it."

There you find are two propositions: first, slavery was to be limited to the States in which it was then situated. It did not then exist in any Territory. Slavery was confined to the States. The first proposition was that slavery must be restricted, and confined to those States. The second was, that he, as a New Yorker, and they, the people of Ohio, must and would abolish it; that is to say, abolish it in the States. They could abolish it nowhere else. Every appeal they make to Northern prejudice and passion, is against the institution of slavery everywhere, and they would not be able to retain their abolition allies, the rank and file, unless they held out the hope that it was the mission of the Republican party, if successful, to abolish slavery in the States as well as in the Territories of the Union.

And again in the same speech, the senator from New York advised the people to disregard constitutional obligations in these words:

"But we must begin deeper and lower than the composition and combination of factions or parties, wherein the strength and security of slavery lie. You answer that it lies in the Constitution of the United States and the constitutions and laws of slaveholding States. Not at all. It is in the erroneous sentiment of the American people. Constitutions and laws can no more rise above the virtue of the people than the limpid stream can climb above its native spring. Inculcate the love of freedom and the equal rights of man under the paternal roof; see to it that they are taught in the schools and in the churches; reform your own code; extend a cordial welcome to the fugitive who lays his weary limbs at your door, and defend him as you would your paternal gods; correct your own error, that slavery is a constitutional guaranty which may not be released, and ought not to be relinquished."

I know they tell us that all this is to be done according to the Constitution; they would not violate the Constitution except so far as the Constitution violates the law of God—that is all—and they are to be the judges of how far the Constitution does violate the law of God. They say that every clause of the Constitution that recognizes property in slaves, is in violation of the Divine law, and hence should not be obeyed; and with that interpretation of the Constitution, they turn to the South and say, "We will give you all your rights under the Constitution, as we explain it."

Then the senator devoted about a third of his speech to a very beautiful homily on the glories of our Union. All that he had said, all that any other man has ever said, all that the most eloquent tongue can ever utter, in behalf of the blessings and the advantages of this glorious Union, I fully indorse. But still, sir, I am prepared to say, that the Union is glorious only when the Constitution is preserved inviolate. He eulogized the Union. I, too, am for the Union; I indorse the eulogies; but still, what is the Union worth, unless the Constitution is preserved and maintained inviolate in all its provisions?

Sir, I have no faith in the Union-loving sentiments of those who will not carry out the Constitution in good faith, as our fathers made it. Professions of fidelity to the Union will be taken for naught, un-

.ess they are accompanied by obedience to the Constitution upon which the Union rests. I have a right to insist that the Constitution shall be maintained inviolate in all its parts, not only that which suits the temper of the North, but every clause of that Constitution, whether you like it or dislike it. Your oath to support the Constitution binds you to every line, word, and syllable of the instrument. You have no right to say that any given clause is in violation of the Divine law, and that, therefore, you will not observe it. The man who disobeys any one clause on the pretext that it violates the Divine law, or on any other pretext, violates his oath of office.

But, sir, what a commentary is this pretext that the Constitution is a violation of the Divine law, upon those revolutionary fathers whose eulogies we have heard here to-day. Did the framers of that instrument make a Constitution in violation of the law of God? If so, how do your consciences allow you to take the oath of office? If the senator from New York still holds to his declaration that the clause in the Constitution relative to fugitive slaves is a violation of the Divine law, how dare he, as an honest man, take an oath to support the instrument? Did he understand that he was defying the authority of Heaven when he took the oath to support that instrument?

THE SENATORIAL CAUCUS.

About the middle of February, 1860, the whole country was astounded by the report that some of the Democratic senators in Congress had been amusing themselves for want of something better to do, by constructing an entirely new platform for the Charleston Convention. It was at first laughed at as a good joke, but finally proved to be a fact. Well might the question be asked, "Who authorized *them* to make a platform for the party at the Charleston Convention? What business had they to meddle in the matter?" Certain gentlemen were named by them as a committee to arrange *something* to be presented to a wondering and admiring world as the new Democratic creed. Yet strange to say, this committee did not embody the talents or the wisdom of the Democratic party in the Senate. Was there no merit in Mr. Toombs, or Mr. Pearce, or Mr. Benjamin, or Mr. Polk, or Mr. Pugh, or Mr. Hammond, or Mr. Davis, or Mr. Nicholson, or Mr. Wigfall, that they were passed over in the formation of the committee?

The chairman of the Caucus, Mr. Bright, a bitter enemy of Mr. Douglas, appointed the following cast:

Mr. Green of Missouri, who had supplanted Mr. Douglas as chairman of the Committee on Territories; Mr. Fitch of Indiana, an ancient hater of Mr. Douglas; Mr. Bigler of Pennsylvania, the shadow of the President; Mr. Gwin of California, whose hostility to Mr. Douglas is implacable and proverbial; and Mr. Chestnut of South Carolina. Excepting Mr. Chestnut, who is really an amiable gentleman, and a man of great ability, of what singular material was this committee composed! and that, too, when there were such men as Mason, Hunter, Clingman, and Brown, in the Senate! This committee of five were to report their platform to the Democratic members of the Senate, in caucus; and after its approval there, it was to be introduced into the Senate for adoption.

Mr. Bright could not have selected a better committee for the purpose of heading off Mr. Douglas at Charleston. A manifesto was therefore expected from this committee of five, which would be pointedly directed to the overthrow of the distinguished senator from Illinois, and his doctrine of popular sovereignty. It was hoped by Messrs. Bright, Fitch, Gwin and Co., that by the action of this caucus, such new tests might be introduced at the Charleston Convention, as would make it impossible for Mr. Douglas to receive the nomination. The whole proceedings of the committee were what might have been anticipated.

PLATFORM OF THE CAUCUS.

The following are the material resolutions of the caucus platform:

4. *Resolved*, That neither Congress nor a Territorial legislature, whether by direct legislation or legislation of an indirect and unfriendly character, possesses the power to annul or impair the constitutional right of any citizen of the United States to take his slave property into the common Territories, and there hold and enjoy the same while the Territorial condition remains.

5. *Resolved,* That if experience should at any time prove that the judiciary and executive authority do not possess the means to insure adequate protection to constitutional rights in a Territory, and if the Territorial government should fail or refuse to provide the necessary remedies for that purpose, it will be the duty of Congress to supply such deficiency.

6. *Resolved,* That the inhabitants of a Territory of the United States, when they rightfully form a constitution to be admitted as a State into the Union, may then, for the first time—like the people of a State when forming a new constitution—decide for themselves whether slavery, as a domestic institution, shall be maintained or prohibited within their jurisdiction; and if Congress admit them as a State "they shall be received into the Union with or without slavery, as their constitution may prescribe at the time of their admission."

It remains to be seen what disposition the United States Senate will make of this Utopian piece of Senatorial-caucus patchwork; this modern bed of Procrustes. At all events, it is too short for the Little Giant.

The material and obnoxious features of the caucus platform will be found in those provisions in which the caucus, to use the language of Senator Bayard, on the Trumbull amendment, "attempted to give a judicial exposition of the Constitution, and to usurp judicial power" by deciding against the right of a Territorial legislature to control the slavery question in violation of the Cincinnati platform, and in advance of the decision of the Supreme Court of the United States.

These resolutions, when translated into plain English, in effect declare that if the people of a Territory desire slavery, and pass laws to introduce and protect it, Congress will not interfere with their decision; but if they do not want it, and so decide in their legislation, Congress ought to interfere, to force it on them, by the enactment of a code for its protection in the Territories.

Is this the boasted principle of non-intervention with slavery in States, Territories and the District of Columbia, to which the party was pledged by the Cincinnati platform?

Is this the principle, "ancient as free government itself," of which Mr. Buchanan spoke in his letter accepting the Cincinnati nomination, when he said that the Kansas-Nebraska Act "has simply declared that the people of a Territory, like those of a State, shall decide for themselves whether slavery shall or shall not exist within their limits?"

We should be doing injustice to the Democratic party—no less than to those gentlemen concerned—to omit to state the fact that the introduction of these resolutions was deemed unfortunate and improper by at least twelve southern senators, as was announced in caucus pending the discussion.

Nor is it unworthy of note to mention the further fact that Messrs. Pugh and Douglas are understood to have been the only senators from the free States who raised their voices in caucus against this gross departure from the usages, creed and established policy of the Democratic party. Nay, if well-accredited and uncontradicted rumors are to be believed, the main champions of these resolutions were Messrs. Bright, Fitch, Gwin and Lane—all representing free States.

Mr. Lane, who was so loud in his declarations, in 1856, in favor of the doctrines of popular sovereignty, and the right of the people to introduce or exclude slavery at their pleasure during their Territorial condition, is represented in the public press as having declared in the Senate caucus, that "he did not wish to live in a republic which would not protect slavery in the Territories by act of Congress—that he could not conceive how a southern man could consent to remain in the Union without such Congressional protection, and that he had no respect for any man who would not vote for an act of Congress, protecting slavery in the Territories."

CHAPTER XVIII.

THE STATE CONVENTIONS.

Conventions of Illinois, Indiana, Ohio, Minnesota, Iowa, Wisconsin and Michigan; also of Maine, New Hampshire, Vermont, Connecticut and New York—Claims of the North-west—Conclusion.

CONVENTIONS IN THE NORTHWEST.

THE northwestern States began to hold their State Conventions, and to elect delegates to the National Democratic Convention at Charleston, early in 1860.

Illinois was first in the field. She held her Convention at Springfield, on the 4th of January, 1860, and unanimously adopted, among others, the following resolutions:

Resolved, That the Democracy of Illinois do reassert and affirm the Cincinnati platform, in the words, spirit and meaning with which the same was adopted, understood and ratified by the people in 1856, and do reject and utterly repudiate all such new issues and tests as the revival of the African slave-trade, or a congressional slave code for the Territories, or the doctrine that slavery is a federal institution, deriving its validity in the several States and Territories in which it exists from the Constitution of the United States, instead of being a mere municipal institution, existing in such States and Territories "under the laws thereof."

Resolved, That the Democratic party of the Union is pledged in faith and honor, by the Cincinnati Platform and its indorsement of the Kansas-Nebraska Act, to the following propositions:

1. That all questions pertaining to African slavery in the Territories shall be forever banished from the halls of Congress.

2. That the people of the Territories respectively shall be left perfectly free to make such laws and regulations in respect to slavery and all other matters of local concern as they may determine for themselves, subject to no other limitations or restrictions than those imposed by the Constitution of the United States

3. That all questions affecting the validity or constitutionality of any Territorial enactments shall be referred for final decision to the Supreme Court of the United States, as the only tribunal provided by the Constitution which is competent to determine them.

Resolved, That we recognize the paramount judicial authority of the Supreme Court of the United States, as provided in the Constitution, and hold it to be the imperative duty of all good citizens to respect and obey the decisions of that tribunal, and to aid, by all lawful means, in carrying them into faithful execution.

Resolved, That the Democracy of Illinois repel with just indignation the injurious and unfounded imputation upon the integrity and impartiality of the Supreme Court, which is contained in the assumption on the part of the so-called Republicans, that, in the Dred Scott case, that august tribunal decided against the right of the people of the Territories to decide the slavery question for themselves, without giving them an opportunity of being heard by counsel in defence of their rights of self-government, and when there was no Territorial law, enactment or fact before the court upon which that question could possibly arise.

Resolved, That whenever Congress or the legislature of any State or Territory shall make any enactment, or do any act which attempts to divest, impair or prejudice any right which the owner of slaves, or any other species of property, may have or claim in any Territory or elsewhere, by virtue of the Constitution or otherwise, and the party aggrieved shall bring his case before the Supreme Court of the United States, the Democracy of Illinois, as in duty bound by their obligations of fidelity to the Constitution, will cheerfully and faithfully respect and abide by the decision, and use all lawful means to aid in giving it full effect according to its true intent and meaning.

Resolved, That the Democracy of Illinois view with inexpressible horror and indignation the murderous and treasonable conspiracy of John Brown and his confederates to incite a servile insurrection in the slaveholding States, and heartily rejoice that the attempt was promptly suppressed, and the majesty of the law vindicated, by inflicting upon the conspirators, after a fair and impartial trial, that just punishment which the enormity of their crimes so richly merited.

Resolved, That the Harper's Ferry outrage was the natural consequence and and logical result of the doctrines and teachings of the Republican party, as explained and enforced in their platforms, partisan presses, books and pamphlets, and in the speeches of their leaders, in and out of Congress, and for this reason an honest and law-abiding people should not be satisfied with the disavowal or disapproval by the Republican leaders of John Brown's *acts,* unless they also repudiate the doctrines and teachings which produced those monstrous crimes, and denounce all persons who profess to sympathize with murderers and traitors, lamenting their fate and venerating their memory as martyrs who lost their lives in a just and holy cause.

Resolved, That the delegates representing Illinois in the Charleston

Convention be instructed to vote for and use all honorable means to secure the readoption of the Cincinnati platform, without any additions or subtractions.

Resolved, That no honorable man can accept a seat as a delegate in the National Democratic Convention, or should be recognized as a member of the Democratic party, who will not abide the decisions of such convention and support its nominees.

Resolved, That we affirm and repeat the principles set forth in the resolutions of the last State Convention of the Illinois Democracy, held in this city on the 21st day of April, 1858, and will not hesitate to apply those principles wherever a proper case may arise.

Resolved, That the Democracy of the State of Illinois is unanimously in favor of Stephen A. Douglas for the next Presidency, and that the delegates from this State are instructed to vote for him, and make every honorable effort to procure his nomination.

THE NORTHWEST FOR DOUGLAS.

The convention then elected their 22 delegates; and they were all instructed to support Mr. Douglas for the nomination at Charleston.

Indiana held her convention at Indianapolis on the 11th of January, and passed resolutions nearly similar to the above and quite as strong in favor of Mr. Douglas. The 26 delegates to Charleston, from Indiana, were instructed by this convention to cast the vote of the State of Indiana as a unit for Mr. Douglas.

Ohio, had held her State Convention a few days before, and it had been equally unanimous in favor of Mr. Douglas. Ohio is entitled to 46 delegates to Charleston, all of whom were instructed by the State Convention to cast the vote of Ohio as a unit for Mr Douglas.

Minnesota, entitled to 8 delegates, instructed them to go as a unit for Mr. Douglas.

Iowa held her State Convention at Fort Des Moines, on the 22d of February. It was the largest convention ever held in the State. There were 518 delegates present, from all parts of the State. The resolutions were adopted unanimously among them were the following:

8. *Resolved*, That we recognize in the Hon. Stephen A. Douglas the man for the times, able in council, ripe in experience, honest and firm in purpose, and devotedly attached to the institutions of the country, whose nomination as the Democratic standard-bearer for the President would confer honor alike on the party and the country, and is a consummation devoutly to be wished; and that the delegates elected by this convention be and are hereby instructed to cast the vote of the State of Iowa in the Charleston Convention as a unit for Stephen A. Douglas so long as he is a candidate before that body, and to use every other honorable means to secure his nomination for the Presidency.

Another resolution cordially re-affirmed the principles of the platform of the National Democratic Convention at Cincinnati in 1856.

Wisconsin held her State Convention on the same day. The following resolutions were adopted by a vote of 165 ayes to 22 nays :

Resolved, That the Democratic party of Wisconsin will cordially support the nominee of the Charleston convention.

Resolved, That Stephen A. Douglas is the choice of the Democracy of Wisconsin for President of the United States—his eminent public services rendered the government and the country—his signal triumphs in the Senate and before the people—his admitted ability—his sound and just views of public policy—his devotion to the Constitution and the Union—render his name a tower of strength, and gives assurance to the conviction that, if nominated at Charleston, he will most certainly receive the electoral vote of Wisconsin. Therefore,

Resolved, That the entire delegation be instructed to vote for Stephen A. Douglas.

Michigan also held her State Convention on the same day. The convention was very full, every county in the State being represented.

The Committee on Resolutions reported a long series. They emphatically indorse the Cincinnati platform; recognize the paramount judical authority in the Supreme Court of the United States; express a fraternal regard for the citizens of every State, and denounce the invasion of Virginia as dangerous to the safety and prosperity of the country; appeal to their brethren in other States to bury local prejudices, and join Michigan in advocating the claims of the favorite of the North-west; present Douglas as their unanimous choice, and

instruct their delegates to use every honorable means to secure his nomination.

The resolutions were unanimously adopted amid great
enthusiasm. Patriotic Union speeches were made by the
State delegates, and all declared themselves uncompromising
Douglas men. The name of Douglas was always received
with the heartiest applause.

' Among the resolutions adopted, was the following :

> That admiring his broad, national statesmanship, his loyalty to
> true Democratic principles, his impartial defence of national rights
> against sectional claims, and that heroic courage which—in be-
> half of the right — quails at no difficulty or disaster, and confi-
> dent that under his matchless leadership the enthusiastic masses
> can and will sweep the Northwest from centre to circumference,
> the Democracy of Michigan present Stephen A. Douglas as their
> UNANIMOUS choice for the Presidency, and they hereby instruct
> their delegates to the Charleton Convention to spare no honor-
> able efforts to secure his nomination.

In the aggregate, these seven States have one hundred and
thirty-two delegates at Charleston, and give sixty-six votes
for President. They cast over 600,000 Democratic votes,
a number equal to all the Democrats in the fifteen Southern
States. They give one-third of the Democratic vote of the
Union, and contain more than one-quarter of the population
of the United States. By the census of the present year
they will be entitled to over ninety members of Congress.

THE CLAIMS OF THE NORTH-WEST.

While all the sections of the Union have each had their
Presidents—indeed while every leading State in the East and
South has had one or more of her sons honored with that
high office—the great North-west, with its millions of people,
has never had the Chief Magistrate taken from her limits.
The case of General Harrison can scarcely be quoted to dis-

prove this remark, as he held the office but one month, when it reverted, by his death, to Virginia.

For the first time in their history, the unfaltering Democracy of the seven north-western States, hitherto always divided in their choice, are a unit for Mr. Douglas, and, if nominated at Charleston, it is the belief of nearly all the intelligent men in that section he would carry every State west of the Ohio River. They present, as their favorite, confessedly the foremost statesman of the nation—one, the unvarnished record of whose achievements puts him on a towering pedestal and furnishes a crushing answer to all the calumnies of his enemies. They present a man whose private escutcheon slander has never befouled with its breath, and whose career has been characterized by a greater height of moral grandeur than has ever been reached by any statesman of his day.

CONCLUSION.

Combinations are thickening around him. Undoubtedly the favorite of the popular heart—beyond question the first choice of a large majority of the Democratic masses of the country—political conspirators are at work night and day to defeat his nomination at Charleston. No contrivance which artful malice can suggest is permitted to escape unavailed of. Political calumnies, for years sleeping in the grave where truth consigned them, are revived and revamped. Republicans and southern Disunionists, almost in open alliance, are conspiring to thwart this to them most hateful consummation, the former satisfied that Douglas' nomination is their mortifying, crushing defeat, the latter, assured that if nominated he will be elected, and all excuse for secession and revolution removed. But the conspiracy will not triumph. The people have taken up his cause, and will bring such a pressure of opinion on Charleston that the politicians will not disregard it.

The adjourned meeting of the Democratic Conven-tion to Baltimore, on the 18th day of June, is a matter of history. Mr. Douglas was nominated on the Second Ballot, he having received 180½ votes out of 194½ cast, when Mr. Church, of New York, offered the following :

Resolved, That Stephen A. Douglas having received two-thirds of all the votes cast in the National Democratic Convention, is, according to the rules of this Convention and the usages of the Democratic party, declared nominated for the office of President of the United States.

Messrs. Hoge, of Virginia, and Clark, of Missouri, then simultaneously seconded the resolution of Mr. Church declaring Judge Douglas nominated, according to the usages of the Democratic party and the rules of the Con-vention, by a two-thirds vote.

The resolution was adopted unanimously.

A scene of excitement then ensued that evinced the violence of the feeling so long pent up. The cheers were deafening, every person in the theatre rising, waving hats, handkerchiefs, and evincing the utmost enthu-siasm. The scene could not be exceeded in excitement. From the upper tier, banners long kept in reserve were unfurled and waved before the audience. On the stage appeared banners, one of which was borne by the delegation from Pennsylvania, bearing the motto, " Pennsylvania good for forty thousand majority for Douglas." Cheers for the " Little Giant," were responded to until all was in a perfect roar, inside the building and outside.

The Convention again rose *en masse*, and the scene of excitement was renewed, cheer after cheer being sent forth for the nominee.

Mr. Richardson, of Illinois, then made a speech, thanking the Conven-tion for the high honor conferred on his State in selecting for the candi-date for the Presidency her favorite son. Alluding to the seceders, he said that if the Democratic party should be defeated and perpetually ruined, they, the seceders, must bear the responsibility, not Douglas or his friends. In this connection he produced a letter from Mr. Douglas, dated Wash-ington, the 20th inst., authorizing and requesting his friends to withdraw his name if, in their judgment, harmony could be restored in the Demo-cratic ranks. Mr. Richardson then said that the course of the seceders had placed it out of the power of the friends of Mr. Douglas to make any use of the letter. He concluded by saying that when the Government fails to accomplish the object for which it was formed, let it go down.

The following is the letter of Mr. Douglas:

WASHINGTON, *June* 20—11, P.M.

MY DEAR SIR: I learn there is imminent danger that the Democratic party will be demoralized, if not destroyed, by the breaking up of the Convention. Such a result would inevitably expose the country to the perils of sectional strife between the Northern and Southern partisans of Congressional intervention upon the subject of slavery in the Territories. I firmly and conscientiously believe that there is no safety for the country, no hope for the preservation of the Union, except by a faithful and rigid adherence to the doctrine of non-intervention by Congress with slavery in the Territories. Intervention means disunion. There is no difference in principle between Northern and Southern intervention. The one intervenes for slavery, and the other against slavery; but each appeals to the passions and prejudices of his own section against the peace of the whole country and the right of self-government by the people of the Territories. Hence the docrine of non-intervention must be maintained at all hazards. But while I can never sacrifice the principle, even to obtain the Presidency, I will cheerfully and joyfully sacrifice myself to maintain the principle,

If, therefore, you and my other friends who have stood by me with such heroic firmness at Charleston and Baltimore shall be of the opinion that the principle can be preserved, and the unity and ascendency of the Democratic party maintained, and the country saved from the perils of Northern Abolitionism and Southern disunion by withdrawing my name and uniting with some other non-intervention Union-loving Democrat, I beseech you to pursue that course. Do not understand me as wishing to dictate to my friends; I have implicit confidence in your and their patriotism, judgment, and discretion. Whatever you may do in the premises will meet my hearty approval. But I conjure you to act with a single eye to the safety and welfare of the country, and without the slightest regard to my individual interest or aggrandizement. My interest will be best promoted, and my ambition gratified, and motives vindicated, by that course, on the part of my friends, which will be most effectual in saving the country from being ruled or ruined by a sectional party. The action of the Charleston Convention, by sustaining me by so large a majority on the platform, and designating me as the first choice of the party for the Presidency, is all the personal triumph I desire. This letter is prompted by the same motives which induced my dispatch four years ago, withdrawing my name from the Cincinnati Convention. With this knowledge of my opinions and wishes, you and your other friends must act upon your own convictions of duty.

Very truly, your friend,

S. A. DOUGLAS.

To HON. WM. A. RICHARDSON, Baltimore, Md.

THE PLATFORM ADOPTED.

In addition to and in explanation of the Cincinnati platform, the majority of our late National Convention, during its sessions at Charleston and Baltimore, adopted the following resolutions:

Resolved, That we, the Democracy of the Union, in Convention assembled, do hereby declare our affirmation of the resolutions unanimously adopted and declared as a platform of principles by the Democratic Convention at Cincinnati, in the year 1856, believing that Democratic principles are unchangeable in their nature when applied to the same subject-matters.

Resolved, That it is the duty of the United States to afford ample and complete protection to all its citizens, whether at home or abroad, and whether native or foreign born.

Resolved, That one of the necessities of the age in a military, commercial and postal point of view, is speedy communication between the Atlantic and Pacific States, and the Democratic party pledge such Constitutional power of the Government as will insure the construction of a Railroad to the Pacific coast, at the earliest practicable period.

Resolved, That the Democratic party are in favor of the acquisition of Cuba on such terms as shall be honorable to ourselves and just to Spain.

Resolved, That the enactments of State Legislatures to defeat the faithful execution of the Fugitive Slave law, are hostile in character and subversive to the Constitution, and revolutionary in their effects.

Resolved, That it is in accordance with the Cincinnati platform, that during the existence of Territorial Governments, the measure of restriction, whatever it may be, imposed by the Federal Constitution on the power of the Territorial Legislature over the subject of the domestic relations, as the same has been or shall hereafter be finally determined by the Supreme Court of the United States, should be respected by all good citizens, and enforced with promptness and fidelity by every branch of the General Government.

On this platform, word for word, as printed above, the majority of our late National Convention nominated the Hon. Stephen A. Douglas for President of the United States.

MR. DOUGLAS' LETTER OF ACCEPTANCE.

WASHINGTON, *Friday, June* 29, 1860.

GENTLEMEN: In accordance with the verbal assurance which I gave you when you placed in my hands the authentic evidence of my nomination for the Presidency by the National Convention of the Democratic party, I now send you my formal acceptance. Upon a careful examination of the platform of principles adopted at Charleston and reaffirmed at Baltimore, with an additional resolution which is in perfect harmony with the others, I find it to be a faithful embodiment of the time-honored principles of the Democratic party, as the same were proclaimed and understood by all parties in the Presidential contests of 1848, 1852, and 1856.

Upon looking into the proceedings of the Convention also, I find that the nomination was made with great unanimity, in the presence and with the concurrence of more than two-thirds of the whole number of delegates, and in accordance with the long-established usages of the party. My inflexible purpose not to be a candidate, nor accept the nomination under any contingency, except as the regular nominee of the National Democratic party, and in that case only upon the condition that the usages, as well as the principles of the party, should be strictly adhered to, had been proclaimed for a long time and become well known to the country. These conditions having all been complied with by the free and voluntary action of the Democratic masses and their faithful representatives, without any agency, interference, or procurement, on my part, I feel bound in honor and duty to accept the nomination. In taking this step, I am not unmindful of the responsibilities it imposes, but with firm reliance upon Divine Providence, I have the faith that the people will comprehend the true nature of the issues involved, and eventually maintain the right.

The peace of the country and the perpetuity of the Union have been put in jeopardy by attempts to interfere with and to control the domestic affairs of the people in the Territories, through the agency of the Federal Government. If the power and the duty of Federal interference is to be conceded, two hostile sectional parties must be the inevitable result—the one inflaming the passions and ambitions of the North, the other of the South, and each struggling to use the Federal power and authority for the aggrandizement of its own section, at the expense of the equal rights of the other, and in derogation of those fundamental principles of self-government which were firmly established in this country by the American Revolution, as the basis of our entire republican system.

During the memorable period of our political history, when the advocates of Federal intervention upon the subject of slavery in the Territories had well-nigh " precipitated the country into revolution," the northern interventionists demanding the Wilmot Proviso for the prohibition of slavery, and the southern interventionists, then few in number, and without a single Representative in either House of Congress, insisting upon Congressional legislation for the protection of slavery in opposition to the wishes of the people in either case, it will be remembered that it required all the wisdom, power and influence of a Clay and a Webster and a Cass, supported by the conservative and patriotic men of the Whig and Democratic parties of that day, to devise and carry out a line of policy which would restore peace to the country and stability to the Union. The essential living principle of that policy, as applied in the legislation of 1850, was, and now is, *non-intervention by Congress with slavery in the Territories.* The fair application of this just and equitable principle restored harmony and fraternity to a distracted country. If we now depart from that wise and just policy which produced these happy results, and permit the country to be again distracted; if precipitated into revolution by a sectional contest between Pro-Slavery and Anti-Slavery interventionists, where shall we look for another Clay, another Webster, or another Cass to pilot the ship of state over the breakers into a haven of peace and safety.

The Federal Union must be preserved. The Constitution must be maintained inviolate in all its parts. Every right guaranteed by the Constitution must be protected by law in all cases where legislation is necessary to its engagement. The judicial authority as provided in the Constitution must be sustained, and its decisions implicitly obeyed and faithfully executed. The laws must be administered and the constituted authorities upheld, and all unlawful resistance to these things must be put down with firmness, impartiality and fidelity if we expect to enjoy and transmit unimpaired to our posterity, that blessed inheritance which we have received in trust from the patriots and sages of the Revolution.

With sincere thanks for the kind and agreeable manner in which you have made known to me the action of the Convention,

I have the honor to be,

Your friend and fellow citizen,

S. A. DOUGLAS.

Hon. Wm. H. Ludlow, of New York; R. P. Dick, of North Carolina; P. C. Wickliff, of Louisiana, and others of Committee.

SPEECHES AND REPORTS.

—•••—

ON THE MEASURES OF ADJUSTMENT.

Delivered in the City Hall, Chicago, Illinois, Oct. 23, 1850.

THE agitation on the subject of slavery now raging through the breadth of the land presents a most extraordinary spectacle. Congress, after a protracted session of nearly ten months, succeeded in passing a system of measures, which are believed to be just to all parts of the Republic, and ought to be satisfactory to the people. The South has not triumphed over the North, nor has the North achieved a victory over the South. Neither party has made any humiliating concessions to the other. Each has preserved its honor, while neither has surrendered an important right, or sacrificed any substantial interest. The measures composing the scheme of adjustment are believed to be in harmony with the principles of justice and the Constitution.

And yet we find that the agitation is re-opened in the two extremes of the Union with renewed vigor and increased violence. In some of the southern States, special sessions of the legislatures are being called for the purpose of organizing systematic and efficient measures of resistance to the execution of the laws of the land, and for the adoption of disunion as the remedy. In the northern States, municipal corporations, and other organized bodies of men, are nullifying the acts of Congress, and raising the standard of rebellion against the authority of the Federal Government.

At the South, the measures of adjustment are denounced as a disgraceful surrender of southern rights to northern abolitionism.

At the North, the same measures are denounced with equal violence as a total abandonment of the rights of freemen to conciliate the slave power.

The southern disunionists repudiate the authority of the highest judicial tribunal on earth, upon the ground that it is a pliant and corrupt instrument in the hands of northern fanaticism.

The northern nullifiers refuse to submit the points at issue to the same exalted tribunal, upon the ground that the Supreme Court of the United States is a corrupt and supple instrument in the hands of the southern slavocracy.

For these contradictory reasons the people in both sections of the

Union are called upon to resist the laws of the land, and the authority of the Federal Government, by violence, even unto death and disunion. Strange and contradictory positions!

Both cannot be true, and I trust in God neither may prove to be. We have fallen on evil times, when passion, and prejudice, and ambition, can so blind the judgments and deaden the consciences of men, that the truth cannot be seen and felt. The people of the North, or the South, or both, are acting under a fatal delusion. Should we not pause, and reflect, and consider, whether we, as well as they, have not been egregiously deceived upon this subject? It is my purpose .this evening to give a candid and impartial exposition of these measures, to the end that the truth may be known. It does not become a free people to rush madly and blindly into violence, and bloodshed, and death, and disunion, without first satisfying our consciences upon whose souls the guilty consequences must rest.

The measures, known as the adjustment or compromise scheme, are six in number:

1. The admission of California, with her free constitution.
2. The creation of a Territorial government for Utah, leaving the people to regulate their own domestic institutions.
3. The creation of a Territorial government for New Mexico, with like provisions.
4. The adjustment of the disputed boundary with Texas.
5. The abolition of the slave trade in the District of Columbia.
6. The Fugitive Slave Bill.

The first three of these measures—California, Utah, and New Mexico—I prepared with my own hands, and reported from the Committee on Territories, as its chairman, in the precise shape in which they now stand on the statute-book, with one or two unimportant amendments, for which I also voted. I, therefore, hold myself responsible to you, as my constituents, for those measures as they passed. If there is anything wrong in them, hold me accountable; if there is anything of merit, give the credit to those who passed the bills. These measures are predicated on the great fundamental principle that every people ought to possess the right of forming and regulating their own internal concerns and domestic institutions in their own way. It was supposed that those of our fellow-citizens who emigrated to the shores of the Pacific and to our other territories, were as capable of self-government as their neighbors and kindred whom they left behind them; and there was no reason for believing that they have lost any of their intelligence or patriotism by the wayside, while crossing the Isthmus or the Plains. It was also believed, that after their arrival in the country, when they had become familiar with its topography, climate, productions, and resources, and had connected their destiny with it, they were fully as competent to judge for themselves what kind of laws and institutions were best adapted to their condition and interests, as we were who never saw the country, and knew very little about it. To question their competency to do this, was to deny their capacity for self-government. If they have the requisite intelligence and honesty to be intrusted with the enactment of laws for the government of white men, I know of no reason why they should not be deemed competent to legislate for the negro. If they are sufficiently enlightened to make laws for the protection of life, liberty, and property—of morals and education—to determine the relation of husband and wife—of parent and child—I am not aware that it requires any higher degree of civilization to regulate the affairs of master and servant. These things are all confided by the Constitution of each State to decide for itself, and I know of no reason why the same principle should not be extended to the Territories. My votes and acts have been in accordance with these views in all cases, except the instances in which I voted under your instructions. Those were your votes, and not mine. I entered my protest against them at the time—before and after they were recorded—and shall never hold myself responsible for them. I believed then, and believe now, that it was better for the cause of freedom, of humanity, and of republicanism, to leave the people interested to settle all these questions for themselves. They have intellect and consciences as well as we, and have more interest in doing that which is best for themselves and their posterity, than we have as their self-constituted and officious guardians. I deem it fortunate for the peace and harmony of the country that Congress, taking the same view of the subject, rejected the Proviso, and passed the bills in the shape in which I originally reported them. So far as slavery is concerned, I am sure that any man who will take the pains to examine the history of the question, will come to the conclusion that this is the true policy, as well as the sound republican doctrine. Mr. Douglas here went into a historical view of the subject, to show that slavery had never been excluded in fact from one inch of the American continent by act of Congress. When the federal Constitution was formed in '87, twelve of the thirteen States, then composing the Confederation, held slaves, and sustained the institution of slavery by their laws. Since that period slavery had been abolished in six of these twelve original slave States. How was this effected? Not by an act of Congress. Not by the interposition of the Federal Government. Congress had no power over the subject, and never attempted to interfere with it. Slavery was abolished in those States by the people of each, acting for themselves, and upon their own motion and responsibility. The people became convinced that it was for their own interests, and the interests of their posterity, pecuniarily and morally, and they did it of their own free will, and rigidly enforced their own laws.

So it was in the territory northwest of the Ohio River. By the act of Congress, known as the Ordinance of '87, slavery was prohibited by law, but not excluded *in fact*. Slavery existed in the Territories of Illinois and Indiana, in spite of the Ordinance, under the authority of the Territorial laws. Illinois was a slaveholding Territory in de-

fiance of the act of Congress, but became a free State by the action
of our own people, when they framed our State constitution, preparatory to their admission into the Union.   So it was with Indiana.
Oregon prohibited slavery by the action of her people under their
provisional government, several years before Congress established
a Territorial government.   In short, wherever slavery has been
excluded, and free institutions established, it has been done by the
voluntary action of the people interested.   Wherever Congress attempted to interfere in opposition to the wishes of the people of the
Territory, its enactments remained a dead letter upon the statute-
book, and the people took such legislative action as comported with
their inclinations and supposed interests.

Mr. Douglas then referred to the country acquired from Mexico,
and called the attention of the audience to the fact, that the abolitionists had all predicted that slavery would certainly be introduced
into those territories, unless Congress interfered and prohibited it by
law, and condemned him because he was opposed to such interference.   The problem is now solved.   What was then a matter of
opinion and disputation, has become a historical fact.   Time has
settled the controversy, and shown who was right and who was
wrong.   The Wilmot Proviso was not adopted.   Congress did not
prohibit slavery in those territories, and yet slavery does not exist in
them.   In California, it was prohibited by the people in the constitution with which that State was admitted into the Union.   It is
well known that the people of New Mexico, when they formed a
constitution with the view of asking admission, also prohibited slavery.   These facts show conclusively that all the predictions of the
abolitionists upon this subject have been falsified by history, and that
my own have been literally fulfilled.   I refer to these facts, not in the
spirit of self-gratulation, but to show that these men, who have
alarmed the friends of freedom, and for a time partially controlled
the popular sentiment, were themselves mistaken, and misled their
followers; at the same time that their doctrine was at war with the
whole spirit of our republican institutions.

But let us return to the measures immediately under discussion.
It must be conceded that the question of the admission of California
was not free from difficulty, independently of the subject of slavery.   There were many irregularities in the proceedings; in fact,
every step in her application for admission was irregular, when
viewed with reference to a literal compliance with the most approved
rules and usages in the admission of new States.   On the other hand,
it should be borne in mind that this resulted from the necessity of
the case.   Congress had failed to perform its duty—had established
no Territorial government, and made no provision for her admission
into the Union.   She was left without government, and was therefore compelled to provide one for herself.   She could not conform
to rules which had not been established, nor comply with laws which
Congress had failed to enact.   The same irregularities had occurred.

however, and been waived, in the admission of other States under peculiar circumstances. True, they had not all occurred in the case of any one State; but some had in one, others in another; so that, by looking into the circumstances attending the admission of each of the new States, we find that all of these irregularities, as they are called, had intervened and been waived in the course of our legislative history. Besides, the territory of California was too extensive for one State, (if we are to adopt the old States as a guide in carving out new ones,) being about three times the size of New York; and her boundaries were unnatural and unreasonable, disregarding the topography of the country, and embracing the whole mining region and her coast in the limits. Thus it will be seen that the slavery question was not the only real difficulty that the admission of California presented to the minds of calm and reflecting men; although it cannot be denied that it was the exciting cause, which stimulated a large portion of the people in one section to demand her instant admission, and in the other, to insist upon her unconditional rejection. Even in this point of view, I humbly conceive that the ultras in each extreme of the republic acted under a misconception of their true interests and real policy. The whole of California—from the very nature of the country, her rocks and sands, elevation above the sea, climate, soil, and productions—was bound to be free territory by the decision of her own people, no matter when admitted or how divided. Hence, if considered with reference to the preponderance of political power between the free and slaveholding States, it was manifestly the true policy of the South to include the whole country in one State; while the same reasons should have induced the North to subdivide it into as many States as the extent of the territory would justify. But, in my opinion. it was not proper for Congress to act upon any such principle. We should know no North, no South, in our legislation, but look to the interests of the whole country. By our action in this case, the rights and privileges of California and the Pacific coast were principally to be affected. By erecting the country into one State instead of three, the people are to be represented in the Senate by two in the place of six senators. If their interests suffer in consequence, they can blame no one but themselves, for Congress only confirmed what they had previously done. The problem in relation to slavery should have been much more easily solved. It was a question which concerned the people of California alone. The other States of the Union had no interest in it, and no right to interfere with it. South Carolina settled that question within her own limits to suit herself; Illinois has decided it in a manner satisfactory to her own people; and upon what principle are we to deprive the people of the State of California of a right which is common to every State in the Union?

The bills establishing Territorial governments for Utah and New Mexico are silent upon the subject of slavery, except the provision that, when they should be admitted into the Union as States, each should decide the question of slavery for itself. This latter provision was not incorporated in my original bills, for the reason that I conceived it to involve a principle so clearly deducible from the Constitution that it was unnecessary to embody it in the form of a legal enactment. But when it was offered as an amendment to the bills, I cheerfully voted for it, lest its rejection should be deemed a denial of the principle asserted in it. The abolitionists of the North profess to regard these bills as a total abandonment of the principles of freedom, because they do not contain an express prohibition of slavery; while the ultras of the South denounce the same measures as equivalent to the Wilmot Proviso.

Of the Texas boundary I have but little to say, for the reason that I have scarcely heard it alluded to since my return home, although many complaints are made against it in other portions of the free States. It was an unfortunate dispute, which could result in no practical benefit to either party, no matter how decided. The Territory in controversy was of no considerable value. If there was a spot on the face of the American continent more worthless than any other; if there was a barren waste more desolate—sands more arid, and rocks more naked than all others—it was the country in dispute between Texas and the United States. Distant from navigation, and almost inaccessible for want of means of communication; void of timber, fuel, water, or soil, with the exception of here and there a nook in the gorges of the mountains, it was entirely useless, save as it afforded hiding-places for the wild and roaming savages. And yet the controversy was none the less serious and fierce in consequence of the barrenness of the country. Texas believed it to be hers, and deemed it a point of honor to maintain her title at all hazards and against all odds. Many of the States entertained doubts of the validity of the Texan claim, while others considered it entirely without foundation. In this state of the case, each party having partial possession, was mustering troops to render its possession complete to the exclusion of the other. Many of the slaveholding States, from sympathy with the peculiar institutions of Texas, were preparing to array themselves on the one side, while most of the free States, from aversion to those institutions, were expected to array themselves on the other. Thus were we plunging headlong and madly into a civil war, involving results which no human wisdom could foresee, and consequences which could be contemplated only with horror.

Fortunately this unnatural struggle was averted by the timely and judicious interposition of Congress. The Committee on Territories, to whom the subject had been referred, found it impossible to ascertain and agree upon the true boundary line of Texas, and accordingly authorized me, as their chairman, to report a bill for adjusting the boundary upon an arbitrary but convenient line, drawn through the centre of the desert, and to pay Texas —— dollars for relinquishing her claim to the waste lands outside of that line. I, therefore, reported this provision, at the same time that I brought in the bills for California, Utah, and New Mexico, with the intention of moving to fill the blank with ten millions of dollars. When the Committee of Thirteen, which was subsequently appointed, united into one the several bills which had been reported by the Committee on Territories, and thus formed what has been known as the "Omnibus Bill," they made a slight change in the line which had been agreed upon by the Territorial Committee. Upon the defeat of the Omnibus, Mr. Pearce, of Maryland, brought in a separate bill for adjusting this boundary, predicated upon the principle, also, of an arbitrary but convenient line through the Desert, changing the courses, however, so as to obviate some objections which have been urged to the others, and paying Texas ten millions of dollars for relinquishing her claim. This bill, after having been joined in the House of Representatives to the bill establishing a Territorial government for New Mexico, passed both houses, and became the law of the land. The people of Texas have since ratified it at the polls by an overwhelming majority ; and thus this dangerous element of agitation has been withdrawn from the controversy by the mutual assent of the parties. And yet there are organized parties, in both extremes of the Union, who are striving to reopen the controversy by persuading the people that the rights and interests of their own particular section have been basely betrayed in the settlement of this question. At the South, it is boldly proclaimed, and every where repeated, that sixty thousand square miles of *slave territory* have been sold and converted into *free soil*. On the other hand, the northern nullifiers and abolitionists are industriously impressing it upon the people that more than fifty thousand square miles of *free soil* have been transferred to Texas, and converted into *slave territory* by the act of Congress adjusting the Texas boundary. Such are the extremities to which prejudice and ambition can lead desperate men! Neither party has gained or lost anything, so far as the question of slavery is concerned. Texas has gained ten millions of dollars, and the United States have saved, in blood and treasure, the expenses of a civil war.

The next in the series of measures was the bill for the abolition of the slave trade in the District of Columbia. This bill was prepared and reported by the Committee of Thirteen, and I gave it my cordial support. I has been represented at the South as a concession to the North, to induce us to perform our duties under the Constitution in the surrender of fugitives from labor, and much opposition has been raised against the whole scheme of adjustment on that account. I did not regard it in that light. My vote was given upon no such considerations. I believed each of the measures substantially right in itself, and, under the extraordinary circumstances by which we were surrounded, eminently wise and expedient. The bill does not abolish slavery in the District—does not emancipate the few slaves that are there, and interferes with no man's right of property. It simply provides that slaves shall not be brought from the surrounding

1*

States, or elsewhere, into the District for sale. In this respect, Congress only followed the example of the legislatures of Maryland, North Carolina, Kentucky, and, in fact, most of the slaveholding States. The country embraced within the limits of the District of Columbia, therefore, stands in precisely the same relation to the slave trade under this law, that it would have stood under the laws of Maryland, if it had never been separated from that State. What justification can there be then, for the assertion that this was a concession to the North? It does nothing more nor less than to apply the general principles of the legislation of a majority of the southern States to the District of Columbia. But, while it was no concession from one section to the other, I had a right to expect that those modern philanthropists who have declaimed so eloquently and violently against the disgrace of the National Capitol, by the slave trade within its precincts, would have rejoiced with exceeding joy at the passage of this act. I have listened in vain for one word of approval or commendation from the advocates of abolition or nullification. While the whole series of Compromise measures are denounced in coarse and unmeasured terms, not one word of congratulation to the friends of freedom—not a word of approval of the act or of the conduct of those who voted for it—is allowed to escape their lips. All the other measures of the scheme of adjustment are attempted to be kept in the background, and concealed from the public view, in order that more prominence and importance may be given to what they are pleased to call "The infamous Fugitive Slave Bill."

Before I proceed to the exposition of that bill, I will read the preamble and resolutions passed by the Common Council of this city, night before last.

Mr. Douglas then read as follows:

" *Whereas*, The Constitution of the United States provides that the privilege of the writ of habeas corpus shall not be suspended, unless when, in cases of rebellion or invasion, the public safety may require it; and,

" *Whereas*, The late act of Congress purporting to be for the recovery of fugitive slaves, virtually suspends the habeas corpus, and abolishes the right of trial by jury, and by its provisions, not only fugitive slaves, but white men, ' owing service' to another in another State, viz., the apprentice, the mechanic, the farmer, the laborer engaged on contract or otherwise, whose terms of service are unexpired, may be captured and carried off summarily, and without legal resource of any kind; and,

" *Whereas*, No law can be legally or morally binding on us which violates the provisions of the Constitution; and,

" *Whereas*, Above all, in the responsibilities of human life, and the practice and propagation of Christianity, the laws of God should be held paramount to all human compacts and statutes: Therefore,

" *Resolved*, That the Senators and Representatives in Congress from the free States, who aided and assisted in the passage of this infamous law, and those who basely sneaked away from their seats, and thereby evaded the question, richly merit the reproach of all lovers of freedom, and are fit only to be ranked with the traitors, Benedict Arnold and Judas Iscariot, who betrayed his Lord and Master for thirty pieces of silver.

" *And Resolved*, That the citizens, officers, and police of the city be, and they are hereby requested to abstain from all interference in the capture and delivering up of the fugitive from unrighteous oppression, of whatever nation, name, or color.

"*Resolved*, That the Fugitive Slave Law lately passed by Congress is a cruel and unjust law, and ought not to be respected by any intelligent community, and that this Council will not require the city police to render any assistance for the arrest of fugitive slaves.

"AYES—Ald. Milliken, Loyd, Sherwood, Foss, Throop, Sherman, Richards, Brady and Dodge.

"NAYS—Ald. Page and Williams."

But for the passage of these resolutions, said Mr. D., I should not have addressed you this evening, nor, indeed, at any time before my return to the Capitol. I have no desire to conceal or withhold my opinions, no wish to avoid the responsibility of a full and frank expression of them, upon this and all other subjects which were embraced in the action of the last session of Congress. My reasons for wishing to avoid public discussion at this time, were to be found in the state of my health and the short time allowed me to remain among you.

Now to the resolutions. I make no criticism upon the language in which they are expressed; that is a matter of taste, and in every thing of that kind I defer to the superior refinement of our city fathers. But it cannot be disguised that the polite epithets of "traitors, Benedict Arnold, and Judas Iscariot, who betrayed his Lord and Master for thirty pieces of silver," will be understood abroad as having direct personal application to my esteemed colleague, Gen. Shields, and myself. Whatever may have been the intention of those who voted for the resolutions, I will do the members of council the justice to say, that I do not believe they intended to make any such application. But their secret intentions are of little consequence, when they give their official sanction to a charge of infamy, clothed in such language that every man who reads it must give it a personal application. The whole affair, however, looks strange, and even ludicrous, when contrasted with the cordial reception and public demonstrations of kindness and confidence, and even gratitude for supposed services, extended to my colleague and myself upon our arrival in this city one week ago. Then we were welcomed home as public benefactors, and invited to partake of a public dinner, by an invitation numerously signed by men of all parties and shades of opinion. The invitation had no sooner been declined, for reasons which were supposed to be entirely satisfactory, and my colleague started for his home, than the Common Council, who are presumed to speak officially for the whole population of the city, attempted to brand their honored guests with infamy, and denounce them as Benedict Arnolds and Judas Iscariots! I have read somewhere that it was a polite custom, in other countries and a different age, to invite those whom they secretly wished to destroy to a feast, in order to secure a more convenient opportunity of administering the hemlock! I acquit the Common Council of any design of introducing that custom into our hospitable city. But I have done with this subject, so far as it has a personal bearing.

It is a far more important and serious matter, when viewed with reference to the principles involved, and the consequences which may result. The Common Council of the city of Chicago have assumed to themselves the right, and actually exercised the power, of determining the validity of an act of Congress, and have declared it void upon the ground that it violates the Constitution of the United States and the law of God! They have gone further; they declared, by a solemn, official act, that a law passed by Congress "ought not to be respected by any intelligent community," and have called upon "the citizens, officers, and police of the city" to abstain from rendering any aid or assistance in its execution! What is this but naked, unmitigated nullification? An act of the American Congress nullified by the Common Council of the city of Chicago! Whence did the council derive their authority? I have been able to find no such provision in the city charter, nor am I aware that the legislature of Illinois is vested with any rightful power to confer such authority. I have yet to learn that a subordinate municipal corporation is licensed to raise the standard of rebellion, and throw off the authority of the Federal Government at pleasure! This is a great improvement upon South Carolinian nullification. It dispenses with the trouble, delay, and expense of convening legislatures and assembling conventions of the people, for the purpose of resolving themselves back into their original elements, preparatory to the contemplated revolution. It has the high merit of marching directly to its object, and by a simple resolution, written and adopted on the same night, relieving the people from their oaths and allegiance, and of putting the nation and its laws at defiance! It has heretofore been supposed by men of antiquated notions, who have not kept up with the progress of the age, that the Supreme Court of the United States was invested with the power of determining the validity of an act of Congress passed in pursuance of the forms of the Constitution. This was the doctrine of the entire North, and of the nation, when it became necessary to exert the whole power of the government to put down nullification in another portion of the Union. But the spirit of the age is progressive, and is by no means confined to advancement in the arts and physical sciences. The science of politics and of government is also rapidly advancing to maturity and perfection. It is not long since that I heard an eminent lawyer propose an important reform in the admirable judicial system of our State, which he thought would render it perfect. It was so simple and eminently practicable, that it could not fail to excite the admiration of even the casual inquirer. His proposition was, that our judicial system should be so improved as to allow an appeal on all constitutional questions from the Supreme Court of this State to two justices of the peace! When that shall have been effected, but one other reform will be necessary to render our national system perfect, and that is, to change the federal Constitution, so as to authorize an appeal, upon all questions touching the validity of acts of Congress, from the Supreme Court of the United States to the Common Council of the city of Chicago!

So much for the general principles involved in the acts of the council. I will now examine briefly the specific ground of objection urged by the council against the Fugitive Slave Bill, as reasons why it should not be obeyed.

The objections are two in number: first, that it suspends the writ of habeas corpus in the time of peace, in violation of the Constitution; secondly, that it abolishes the right of trial by jury.

How the council obtained the information that these two odious provisions were contained in the law, I am unable to divine. One thing is certain, that the members of the council, who voted for these resolutions, had never read the law, or they would have discovered their mistake. There is not one word in it in respect to the writ of habeas corpus or the right of trial by jury. Neither of these subjects is mentioned or referred to. The law is entirely silent on those points. Is it to be said that an act of Congress which is silent on the subject, ought to be construed to repeal a great constitutional right by implication? Besides, this act is only an amendment—amendatory to the old law—the act of 1793—but does not repeal it. There is no difference between the original act and the amendment, in this respect. Both are silent in regard to the writ of habeas corpus and the right of trial by jury. If to be silent is to suspend the one and abolish the other, then the mischief was done by the old law fifty-seven years ago. If this construction be correct, the writ of habeas corpus has been suspended, and a trial by a jury abolished, more than half a century, without anybody ever discovering the fact, or, if knowing it, without uttering a murmur of complaint.

Mr. Douglas then read the whole of the act of 1793, and compared its provisions with the amendment of last session, for the purpose of showing that the writ of habeas corpus and the right of trial by jury were not alluded to or interfered with by either. But I maintain, said Mr. D., that the writ of habeas corpus is applicable to the case of the arrest of a fugitive under this law, in the same sense in which the Constitution intended to confer it, and to the fullest extent for which that writ is ever rightfully issued in any case. In this I am fully sustained by the opinion of Mr. Crittenden, the attorney-general of the United States. As soon as the bill passed the two houses of Congress, an abolition paper raised the alarm that the habeas corpus bill had been suspended. The cry was eagerly caught up, and transmitted by lightning upon the wires, to every part of the Union, by those whose avocation is agitation. The President of the United States, previous to signing the bill, referred it to the attorney-general, for his opinion upon the point whether any portion of it violated any provision of the Constitution of the

United States, and especially whether it could possibly be construed to suspend the writ of habeas corpus. I have the answer of the attorney-general before me, in which he gives it as his decided opinion that every part of the law is entirely consistent with the Constitution, and that it does not suspend the writ of habeas corpus. I would commend the argument of the attorney-general to the careful perusal of those who have doubts upon the subject. Upon the presentation of this opinion, and with entire confidence in its correctness, President Fillmore signed the bill.

[Here Mr. Douglas was interrupted by a person present, who called his attention to the last clause of the 6th section of the bill, which he read, and asked him what construction he put upon it, if it did not suspend the writ of habeas corpus.]

Mr. Douglas, in reply, expressed his thanks to the gentleman who propounded the inquiry. His object was to meet every point, and remove every doubt that could be possibly raised; and he expressed the hope that every gentleman present would exercise the privilege of asking him questions upon all points upon which he was not fully satisfied. He then proceeded to answer the question which had been propounded. That section of the bill provides for the arrest of the fugitive and the trial before the commissioner; and if the facts of servitude, ownership, and escape be established by competent evidence, the commissioner shall grant a certificate to that effect, which certificate shall be conclusive of the right of the person in whose favor it is issued to remove the fugitive to the State from which he fled. Then comes the clause which is supposed to suspend the habeas corpus: "*And shall prevent all molestation of said person or persons by any process issued by any court, judge, magistrate, or other person whomsoever.*"

The question is asked, whether the writ of habeas corpus is not a "PROCESS" within the meaning of this act? I answer, that it undoubtedly is such a "process," and that it may be issued by any court or judge having competent authority—not for the purpose of "molesting" a claimant, having a servant in his possession, with such a certificate from the commissioner or judge, but for the purpose of ascertaining the fact whether he has such a certificate or not; and if so, whether it be in due form of law; and if not, by what authority he holds the servant in custody. Upon the return of the writ of habeas corpus, the claimant will be required to exhibit to the court his authority for conveying that servant back; and if he produces a "certificate" from the commissioner or judge in due form of law, the court will decide that it has no power to "molest the claimant" in the exercise of his rights under the law and the Constitution. But if the claimant is not able to produce such certificate, or other lawful authority, or produces one which is not in conformity with law, the court will set the alleged servant at liberty, for the very reason that the law has not been complied with. The sole object of the writ of habeas corpus is to ascertain by what authority a person is held in custody; to release him if no such authority be shown; and to refrain from any molestation of the claimant, if legal authority be produced. The habeas corpus is necessary, therefore, to carry the fugitive law into effect, and, at the same time, to prevent a violation of the rights of freemen under it. It is essential to the security of the claimant, as well as the protection of the rights of those liable to be arrested under it. The reason that the writ of habeas corpus was not mentioned in the bill must be obvious. The object of the new law seems to have been, to amend the old one in those particulars wherein experience had proven amendments to be necessary, and in all other respects to leave it as it had stood from the days of Washington. The provisions of the old law have been subjected to the test of long experience—to the scrutiny of the bar and the judgment of the courts. The writ of habeas corpus had been adjudged to exist in all cases under it, and had always been resorted to when a proper case arose. In amending the law there was no necessity for any new provision upon this subject, because nobody desired to change it in this respect.

But why this extraordinary effort, on the part of the professed friends of the fugitive, to force such a construction upon the law, in the absence of any such obnoxious provision, as to deprive him of the benefit of the writ of habeas corpus? The law does not do so in terms; and if it is ever accomplished, it must be done by implication, contrary to the understanding of those who enacted it, and in opposition to the practice of the courts, acquiesced in by the people, from the foundation of the government. One would naturally suppose, that if there was room for doubt as to what is the true construction, those who claim to be the especial and exclusive friends of the negro would contend for that construction which is most favorable to liberty, justice, and humanity. But not so. Directly the reverse is the fact. They exhaust their learning, and exert all their ingenuity and skill, to deprive the negro of all rights under the law. What can be the motive? Certainly not to protect the rights of the free, or to extend liberty to the oppressed; for they strive to fasten upon the law such a construction as would defeat both of these ends. Can it be a political scheme, to render the law odious, and to excite prejudice against all who voted for it, or were unavoidably absent when it passed? No matter what the motive, the effects would be disastrous to those whose rights they profess to cherish, if their efforts should be successful.

Now, a word or two in regard to the right of trial by jury. The city council, in their resolutions, say that this law abolishes that right. I have already shown you that the council are mistaken—that the law is silent upon the subject, and stands now precisely as it has stood for half a century. If the law is defective on that point, the error was committed by our fathers in 1793, and the people have acquiesced in it ever since, without knowing of its existence or caring to remedy it. The new act neither takes away nor confers the right of trial by jury. It leaves it just were our fathers and the Constitution left it under the old law. That the right of trial by jury exists in this country for all men, black or white, bond or free, guilty or innocent, no man will be disposed to question who understands the subject. The right is of universal application, and exists alike in all the States of Union; it always has existed, and always will exist, so long as the Constitution of the United States shall be respected and maintained, in spite of the efforts of the abolitionists to take it away by the perversion of the fugitive law. The only question is, *where* shall this jury trial take place? Shall the jury trial be had in the State where the arrest is made, or the State from which the fugitive escaped? Upon this point the act of last session says nothing, and of course, leaves the matter as it stood under the law of '93. The old law was silent on this point, and therefore left the courts to decide it in accordance with the Constitution. The highest judicial tribunals in the land have always held that the jury trial must take place in the State under whose jurisdiction the question arose, and whose laws were alleged to have been violated. The same construction has always been given to the law for surrendering fugitives from justice. It provides also for sending back the fugitive, but says nothing about the jury trial, or where it shall take place. Who ever supposed that that act abolished the right of trial by jury? Every day's practice and observation teach us otherwise. The jury trial is always had in the State from which the fugitive fled. So it is with a fugitive from labor. When he returns, or is surrendered under the law, he is entitled to a trial by jury of his right of freedom, and always has it when he demands it. There is great uniformity in the mode of proceeding in the courts of the southern States in this respect. When the supposed slave sets up his claim, to the judge or other officer, that he is free, and claims his freedom, it becomes the duty of the court to issue its summons to the master to appear in court with the alleged slave, and there to direct an issue of freedom or servitude to be made and tried by a jury. The master is also required to enter into bonds for his own appearance and that of the alleged slave at the trial of the cause, and that he will not remove the slave from the county or jurisdiction of the court in the mean time. The court is also required to appoint counsel to conduct the cause for the slave, while the master employs his own counsel. All the officers of the court are required by law to render all facilities to the slave for the prosecution of his suit free of charge, such as issuing and serving subpœnas for witnesses, etc. If upon the trial the alleged slave is held to be a free man, the master is required to pay the costs on both sides. If, on the other hand, he is held to be a slave, the State pays the costs. This is the way in which the trial by jury stood under the old law; and the new one makes no change in this respect. If the act of last session be repealed, that will neither benefit nor injure the fugitive, so far as the right of trial by jury is concerned.

For these two reasons—the habeas corpus and the trial by jury—the Common Council have pronounced the law unconstitutional, and declared that it ought not to be respected by an enlightened community. I have shown that neither of the objections are well founded, and that if they had taken the trouble to read the law before they nullified it, they would have avoided the mistake into which they have fallen. I have spoken of the acts of the city council in general terms, and it may be inferred that the vote was unanimous. I take pleasure in stating that I learn from the published proceedings that there was barely a quorum present, and that Aldermen Page and Williams voted in the negative. Having disposed of the two reasons assigned by the Common Council for the nullification of the law, I shall be greatly indebted to any gentleman who will point out any other objection to the new law, which does not apply with equal force to the old one. My object in drawing the parallel between the new and old law is this: The law of '93 was passed by the patriots and sages who framed our glorious Constitution, and approved by the father of his country. I have always been taught to believe that they were men well versed in the science of government, devotedly attached to the cause of freedom and capable of construing the Constitution in the spirit in which they made it. That act has been enforced and acquiesced in for more than half a century, without a murmur or word of complaint from any quarter.

I repeat—will any gentleman be kind enough to point out a single objection to the new law, which might not be urged with equal propriety to the act of '93?

[Here a gentleman present arose, and called the attention of Mr. Douglas to the penalties in the seventh section of the new law, and desired to know if there were any such obnoxious provisions in the old one.]

Mr. Douglas then read the section referred to, and also the fourth section of the act of '93, and proceeded to draw the parallel between them. Each makes it a criminal offence to resist the due execution of the law; to knowingly and willfully obstruct or hinder the claimant in the arrest of the fugitive; to rescue such fugitive from the claimant when arrested; to harbor or conceal such person after notice that he or she was a fugitive from labor. In this respect the two laws were substantially the same in every important particular. Indeed the one was almost a literal copy of the other. I can conceive of no act which would be an offence under the one, that would not be punishable under the other. In the speeches last night, great importance was given to the clause which makes it an offence to harbor or conceal a fugitive. You were told that you could not clothe the naked, nor feed the hungry, nor exercise the ordinary charities toward suffering humanity, without incurring the penalty of the law. Is this a true construction of that provision? The act does not so read. The law says that you shall not "harbor or conceal such fugitive, *so as to prevent the discovery and arrest* of such person after notice or knowledge of the fact that such person was a fugitive from service or labor as aforesaid." This does not deprive you of the privilege of extending charities to the fugitive. You may feed him, clothe him, may lodge him, provided you do not harbor or conceal him, so as to prevent discovery and arrest, after notice or knowledge that he is a fugitive. The offence consists in preventing the discovery and arrest of the fugitive after knowledge of the fact, and not in the extending kindness and charities to him. This is the construction put upon a similar provision in the old law by the highest judicial tribunals in the land. The only difference between the old law and the new one, in respect to obstructing its execution, is to be found in the amount of the penalty, and not in the principle involved.

But it is further objected that the new law provides, in addition to the penalty, for a civil suit for damages, to be recovered by an action of debt by any court having jurisdiction of the cause. This is true; but it is also true that a similar provision is to be found in the old law. The concluding clause in the last section of the act of '93 is as follows:

" Which penalty may be recovered by and for the benefit of such claimant, by action of debt, in any proper court to try the same; *saving, moreover, to the person claiming such labor or service, his right of action for or on account of the said injuries, or either of them.*"

Thus it will be seen, that upon this point there is no difference between the new and the old law.

Is there any other provision of this law upon which explanation is desired?

[A gentleman present referred to the 10th section, and desired an explanation of the object and effect of the record from another State therein provided for.]

I am glad, said Mr. D., that my attention has been called to that provision; for I heard a construction given to it, in the speeches last night, entirely different to the plain reading and object of that section. It is said, that this provision authorizes the claimant to go before a court of record of the county and State where he lives, and there establish by ex-parte testimony, in the absence of the fugitive, the facts of servitude, of ownership, and escape; and when a record of these facts shall have been made, containing a minute description of the slave, it shall be conclusive evidence against a person corresponding to that description, arrested in another State, and shall consign the person so arrested to perpetual servitude. The law contemplates no such thing, and authorizes no such result. I have the charity to believe that those who have put this construction upon it have not carefully examined it. The record from another State predicated upon " satisfactory proof to such court or judge" before whom the testimony may be adduced, and the record made, is to be conclusive of two facts only:

1st. That the person named in this record does owe service to the person in whose behalf the record is made.

2d. That such person has escaped from service.

The language of the law is, that "the transcript of the record authenticated," etc., "shall be held and taken to be full and conclusive evidence of the fact of escape, and that the service or labor of such person escaping is due to the party in such record mentioned." The record is conclusive of these two facts, so far as to authorize the fugitive to be sent back for trial under the laws of the State whence he fled; *but it is no evidence that the person arrested here is the fugitive named in the record.* The question of *identity* is to be proven here to the satisfaction of the commissioner or judge, before whom the trial is had, by "*other and further evidence.*" This is the great point in the case. The whole question turns upon it. The man arrested may correspond to the description set forth in the record, and yet not be the same individual. We often meet persons resembling each other to such an extent that the one is frequently mistaken for the other. The identity of the person becomes a matter of proof—a fact to be established by the testimony of competent and disinterested witnesses, and to be decided by the tribunal before whom the trial is had, conscientiously and impartially, according to the evidence in the case. The description in the record, unsupported by other testimony, is not evidence of the identity. It is not inserted for the especial benefit of the claimant—much less to the prejudice of the alleged slave. It is required as a test of truth, a safeguard against fraud, which will often operate favorably to the fugitive, but never to his injury. If the description be accurate and true, no injustice can possibly result from it. But if it be erroneous or false, the claimant is concluded by it; and the fugitive, availing himself of the error, defeats the claim, in the same manner as a discrepancy between the allegations and the proof, in any other case, results to the advantage of the defendant. I repeat, that when an arrest is made under a record from another State, the identity of the person must be established by competent testimony. The trial in this instance, would be precisely the same as in the case of a white man arrested on a charge of being a fugitive from justice. The writ of the governor, predicated upon an indictment, or even an affidavit from another State, containing the charge of crime, would be conclusive evidence of the right to take the fugitive back; but the identity of the person in that case, as well as a fugitive from labor, must be proven in the State where the arrest is made, by competent witnesses, before the tribunal provided by law for that purpose. In this respect, therefore, the negro is placed upon a perfect equality with the white man who is so unfortunate as to be charged with an offence in another State, whether the charge by true or false. In some respects, the law guards the rights of the negro, charged with being a fugitive from labor, more rigidly than it does those of a white man who is alleged to be a fugitive from justice. The record from another State must be predicated upon "proof satisfactory to the court or judge" before whom it is made, and must set forth the "matter proved," before it can be evidence against a fugitive from labor, or for any purpose; whereas, an innocent white man, who is so unfortunate as to be falsely charged with a crime in another State, by the simple affidavit of an unknown person, without indictment or proof to the satisfaction of any court, is liable to be transported to the most distant portions of this Union for trial.

Here we find the act of last session is a great improvement upon the law of '93 in reference to fugitives, white or black, whether they fled from justice or labor. But it is objected that the testimony before the court making the record is *ex parte*, and therefore in violation of the principles of justice and the Constitution; because it deprives the accused of the privilege of meeting the witnesses face to face, and of cross-examination. Gentlemen forget that all proceedings for the arrest of fugitives are necessarily *ex parte*, from the nature of the case. They have fled beyond the jurisdiction of the court, and the object of the proceeding is, that they may be brought back, confront the witnesses, and receive a fair trial according to the Constitution and laws. If they would stay at home in order to attend the trial, and cross-examine the witnesses, the record would be unnecessary, and the fugitive law inoperative. It is no answer to this proposition to say that slavery is no crime, and therefore the parallel does not hold good. I am not speaking of the guilt or innocence of slavery. I am discussing our obligations under the Constitution of the United States. That sacred instrument says that a fugitive from labor "*shall be delivered up* on the claim of the owner." The same clause of the same instrument provides that fugitives from justice shall be delivered up. We are bound by our oaths to our God to see that claim as well as every other provision of the Constitution carried into effect. The moral, religious and constitutional obligations resting upon us, here and hereafter, are the same in the one case as in the other. As citizens, owing allegiance to the government and duties to society, we have no right to interpose our individual opinions and scruples as excuses for violating the supreme law of the land as our fathers made it, and as we are sworn to support it. The obligation is just as sacred, under the Constitution, to surrender fugitives from labor, as fugitives from justice. And the Congress of the United States, according to the decision of the Supreme Court, are as imperatively commanded to provide the necessary legislation for the one as for the other. The act of 1793, to which I have had occasion to refer so frequently, and which has been read to you, provided for these two cases in the same bill. The first half of that act, relating to fugitives from justice, applies, from the nature and necessity of the case, principally to white men; and the other half for the same reasons, applies exclusively to the negro race. I have shown you, by reading and comparing the two laws in your presence, that there is no constitutional guaranty—or common law right—or legal, or judicial privilege—for the protection of the white man against oppression and injustice, under the law, framed in 1793, and now in force, for the surrender of fugitives from justice, that does not apply in all its force in behalf of the negro, when arrested as a fugitive from labor, under the act of the last session. What more can the friends of the negro ask than, in all his civil and legal rights under the Constitution, he shall be placed on an equal footing with the white man? But it is said that the law is susceptible of being abused by perjury and false testimony. To what human enactment does not the same objection lie? You, or I, or any other man, who was never in California in his life, is liable, under the Constitution, to be sent there in chains for trial as a fugitive from justice, by means of perjury and fraud. But does this fact prove that the Constitution, and the laws for carrying it into effect, are wrong, and should be resisted, as we were told last night, even unto the dungeon, the gibbet and the grave? It only demonstrates to us the necessity of providing all the safeguards that the wit of man can devise, for the protection of the innocent and the free, at the same time that we religiously enforce, according to its letter and spirit, every provision of the Constitution. I will not say that the act recently passed for the surrender of fugitives from labor, accomplishes all this; but I will thank any gentleman to point out any one barrier against abuse in the old law, or in the law for the surrender of white men, as fugitives from justice, that is not secured to the negro under the new law. I pause, in order to give any gentleman an opportunity to point out the provision. I invite inquiry and examination. My object is to arrive at the truth—to repel error and dissipate prejudice—and to avoid violence and bloodshed. Will any gentleman point out the provision in the old law, for securing and vindicating the rights of the free man, that is not secured to him in the act of last session?

[A gentleman present rose and called the attention of Mr. Douglas to the provision for paying out of the treasury of the United States the expenses of carrying the fugitive back in case of anticipated resistance.]

Ah, said Mr. D., that is a question of dollars and cents, involving no other principle than the costs of the proceeding! I was discussing the question of human rights—the mode of protecting the rights of freemen from invasion, and the obligation to surrender fugitives under the Constitution. Is it possible that this momentous question, which only forty-eight hours ago was deemed of sufficient importance to authorize the city council to nullify an act of Congress, and raise the standard of rebellion against the Federal Government, has dwindled down into a mere petty dispute, who shall pay the costs of suit? This is too grave a question for me to discuss on this occasion. I confess my utter inability to do it justice. Yesterday the Constitution of the ocean-bound republic had been overthrown; the privileges of the writ of habeas corpus had been suspended; the right of trial by jury had been abolished; pains and penalties had been imposed upon every humane citizen who should feed the hungry and cover the naked; the law of God had been outraged by an infamous act of a traitorous Congress; and the standard of rebellion, raised by our city fathers, was floating in the breeze, calling on all good citizens to rally under its sacred folds, and resist with fire and sword—the payment of the costs of suit upon the arrest of a fugitive from labor!

I will pass over this point, and inquire whether there is any other provision of this law upon which an explanation is desired? I hope no one will be backward in propounding inquiries, for I have but a few days to remain with you, and desire to make a clean business of this matter on the present occasion. Is there any other objection?

[A gentleman rose, and desired to know why the bill provides for paying ten dollars to the commissioner for his fee in case he decided in favor of the claimant, and only five dollars if he decided against him.]

I presume, said Mr. Douglas, that the reason was that he would have more labor to perform. If, after hearing the testimony, the commissioner decided in favor of the claimant, the law made it his duty to prepare and authenticate the necessary papers to authorize him to carry the fugitive home; but if he decided against him, he had no such labor to perform. The law seems to be based upon the principle that the commissioner should be paid according to the service he should render—five dollars for presiding at the trial, and five dollars for making out the papers in case the testimony should require him to return the fugitive. This provision appears to be exciting considerable attention in the country, and I have been exceedingly gratified at the proceedings of a mass meeting held in a county not far distant, in which it was resolved unanimously that they could not be bribed, for the sum of five dollars, to consign a freeman to perpetual bondage! This shows an exalted state of moral feeling, highly creditable to those who participated in the meeting. I doubt not they will make their influence felt throughout the State, and will instruct their members of the legislature to reform our criminal code in this respect. Under our laws, as they have stood for many years, and probably from the organization of our State government, in all criminal cases, on the preliminary examination before the magistrates, and in all the higher courts, if the prisoner be convicted, the witnesses, jurors, and officers, are entitled to their fees and bills of costs; but if he be acquitted, none of them receive a cent. In order to diffuse the same high moral sense throughout the whole community, would it not be well, at their next meeting, to pass another resolution, that they would not be bribed by the fees and costs of suit in any case, either as witnesses, jurors, magistrates, or in any other capacity, to consign an innocent man to a dismal cell in the penitentiary, or expose him to an ignominious death upon the gallows? Such a resolution might do a great deal of good in elevating the character of our people abroad, at the same time that it might inspire increased confidence in the liberality and conscientiousness of those who adopted it.

Is there any other objection to this law ?

[A gentleman rose, and called the attention of Mr. Douglas to the provision vesting the appointment of the commissioners under it in the courts of law, instead of the President and Senate, and asked if that was not a violation of that provision of the Constitution which says that judges of the Supreme Courts, and of the inferior courts, should be appointed by the President and Senate.]

I thank the gentleman, said Mr. D., for calling my attention to this point. It was made in the speech of a distinguished lawyer last night, and evidently produced great effect upon the minds of the audience. The gentleman's high professional standing, taken in connection with his laborious preparation for the occasion, as was apparent to all, from his lengthy written brief before him, while speaking, inspired implicit confidence in the correctness of his position. My answer to the objection will be found in the Constitution itself, which I will read, so far as it bears upon this question :

" The President shall nominate, and by and with the consent of the Senate, shall appoint ambassadors, other public ministers, and consuls, judges of the Supreme Court, and all other officers of the United States, where appointments are not herein otherwise provided for, and which shall be established by law."

Now it will be seen that the words " inferior courts " are not mentioned in the Constitution. The gentleman in his zeal against the law, and his frenzy to resist it, interpolated these words, and then made a plausible argument upon them. I trust this was all unintentional, or was done with the view of fulfilling the "higher law." But there, is another sentence in this same clause of the Constitution which I have not yet read. It is as follows :

" But the Congress may by law vest the appointment of such *inferior officers* as they may think proper in the President alone, *in the Courts of Law,* or in the heads of Departments."

The practice under this clause has usually been to confer the power of appointing those inferior officers, whose duties were executive or ministerial, upon the President alone, or upon the head of the appropriate department ; and in like manner to give to the courts of law the privilege of appointing their subordinates, whose duties were in their nature judicial. What is meant by " inferior officers," whose appointment may be vested in the " courts of law," will be seen by reference to the 8th section of the Constitution, where the powers of Congress are enumerated, and among them is the following:

" To constitute tribunals *inferior to the Supreme Court.*"

Is the tribunal which is to carry the fugitive law into effect inferior to the Supreme Court of the United States? If it is, the Constitution expressly provides for vesting the appointment in the courts of law. I will remark, however, that these commissioners are not appointed under the new law, but in obedience to an act of Congress which has stood on the statute books for many years. If those who denounce and misrepresent the act of last session, had condescended to read it before they undertook to enlighten the people upon it, they would have saved themselves the mortification of exposure, as I will show by reading the first section.

Here Mr. Douglas read the law, and proceeded to remark: Thus it will be seen that these commissioners have been in office for years, with their duties prescribed by law, nearly all of which were of a judicial character, and that the new law only imposes additional duties, and authorizes the increase of the number. Why has not this grave constitutional objection been discovered before, and the people informed how their rights have been outraged in violation of the supreme law of the land? Truly, the passage of the fugitive bill has thrown a flood of light upon constitutional principles!

Is there any other objection to the new law which does not apply to the act of '93?

[A gentleman rose, and said that he would like to ask another question, which was this: if the new law was so similar to the old one, what was the necessity of passing any at all, since the old one was still in force?]

Mr. Douglas, in reply, said, that is the very question I was anxious some one should propound, because I was desirous of an opportunity of answering it. The old law answered all the purposes for which it was enacted tolerably well, until the decision by the Supreme Court of the United States, in the case of Priggs vs. the State of Pennsylvania, eight or nine years ago. That decision rendered the law comparatively inoperative, for the reason that there were scarcely any officers left to execute it. It will be recollected that the act of '93 imposed the duty of carrying it into effect upon the magistrates and other officers under the State governments. These officers performed their duties under that law, with fidelity, for about fifty years, until the Supreme Court, in the case alluded to, decided that they were under no legal obligation to do so, and that Congress had no constitutional power to impose the duty upon them. From that time, many of the officers refused to act, and soon afterward the legislature of Massachusetts, and many other States, passed laws making it criminal for their officers to perform these duties. Hence the old law, although efficient in its provisions, and similar in most respects, and especially in those now objected to, almost identical with the new law, became comparatively a dead letter for want of officers to carry it into effect. The judges of the United States courts were the only officers left who were authorized to execute it. In this State, for instance, Judge Drummond, whose residence was in the extreme northwest corner of the State, within six miles of Wisconsin and three of Iowa, and in the direction where fugitives were least likely to go, was the only person authorized to try the case.

If a fugitive was arrested at Shawneetown or Alton, three or four hundred miles from the residence of the judge, the master would attempt to take him across the river to his home in Kentucky or Missouri, without first establishing his right to do so. This was calculated to excite uneasiness and doubts in the minds of our citizens, as to the propriety of permitting the negro to be carried out of the State, without the fact of his owing service, and having escaped, being first proved, lest it might turn out that the negro was a free man and the claimant a kidnapper. And yet, according to the express term of the old law, the master was authorized to seize his slave wherever he found him, and to carry him back without process, or trial, or proof of any kind whatsoever. Hence, it was necessary to pass the act of last session, in order to carry into effect, in a peaceable and orderly manner, the provisions of the law and the Constitution on the one hand, and to protect the free colored man from being kidnapped and sold into slavery by unprincipled men on the other hand. The purpose of the new law is to accomplish these two objects—to appoint officers to carry the law into effect, in the place of the magistrates relieved from that duty by the decision of the Supreme Court, and to guard against harassing and kidnapping the free blacks, by preventing the claimant from carrying the negro out of the State, until he establishes his legal right to do so. The new law, therefore, is a great improvement in this respect upon the old one, and is more favorable to justice and freedom, and better guarded against abuse.

[A person present asked leave to propound another question to Mr. Douglas, which was this: "If the new law is more favorable to freedom than the old one, why did the southern slaveholders vote for it, and desire its passage?"]

Mr. Douglas said he would answer that question with a great deal of pleasure. The southern members voted for it for the reason that it was a better law than the old one—better for them, better for us, and better for the free blacks. It places the execution of the law in the hands of responsible officers of the government, instead of leaving every man to take the law into his own hands and to execute it for himself. It affords personal security to the claimant while arresting his servant and taking him back, by providing him with the opportunity of establishing his legal rights by competent testimony before a tribunal duly authorized to try the case, and thus allay all apprehensions and suspicions, on the part of our citizens, that he is a villain, attempting to steal a free man for the purpose of selling him into slavery. The slaveholder has as strong a desire to protect the rights of the free black man as we have, and much more interest to do so; for he well knows, that if outrages should be tolerated under the law, and free men are seized and carried into slavery; from that moment the indignant outcry against it would be so strong here and everywhere, that even a fugitive from labor could not be returned, lest he also might happen to be free. The interest of the slaveholder, therefore, requires a law which shall protect the rights of all free men, black or white, from any invasion or violation whatever. I ask the question, therefore, whether this law is not better than the old one—better for the North and the South—better for the peace and quiet of the whole country? Let it be remembered that this law is but an amendment to the act of '93, and that the old law still remains in force, except so far as it is modified by this. Every man who voted against this modification, thereby voted to leave the old law in force; for I am not aware that any member of either house of Congress ever had the hardihood to propose to repeal the law, and make no provisions to carry the Constitution into effect. But the cry of repeal, as to the new law, has already gone forth. Well, suppose it succeeds; what will those have gained who joined in the shout? Have I not shown that all the material objections they urge against the new law, apply with equal force to the old one? What do they gain, therefore, unless they propose to repeal the old law, also, and make no provision for performing our obligations under the Constitution? This must be the object of all men who take that position. To this it must come in the end. The real objection is not to the new law, nor to the old one, but to the Constitution itself. Those of you who hold these opinions, do not mean that the fugitive from labor shall be taken back. That is the real point of your objection. You would not care a farthing about the new law, or the old law, or any other law, or what provisions it contained, if there was a hole in it big enough for the fugitive to slip through and escape. Habeas corpuses—trials by jury—records from other States—pains and penalties—the whole catalogue of objections, would be all moonshine, if the negro was not required to go back to his master. Tell me, frankly, is not this the true character of your objection?

[Here several gentlemen gave an affirmative answer.]

Mr. Douglas said he would answer that objection by reading a portion of the Constitution of the United States. He then read as follows:

"No person held to service or labor in one State, under the laws thereof, escaping into another, shall, into consequence of any law or regulation therein, be discharged from such service or labor, *but shall be delivered up* on the claim of the party to whom such service or labor may be due."

This, said Mr. D., is the supreme law of the land, speaking to every citizen of the republic. The command is imperative. There is no avoiding—no escaping the obligation, so long as we live under, and claim the protection of, the Constitution. We must yield implicit obedience, or we must take the necessary steps to release ourselves from the obligation to obey. There is no other alternative. We must stand by the Constitution of the Union, with all its compromises, or we must abolish it, and resolve each State back into its original elements. It is, therefore, a question of union or disunion. We cannot expect our brethren of other States to remain faithful to the compact, and permit us to be faithless. Are we prepared, therefore, to execute faithfully and honestly the compact our fathers have made for us?

[Here a gentleman rose, and inquired of Mr. Douglas, whether the clause in the Constitution providing for the surrender of fugitive slaves was not in violation of the law of God?]

Mr. Douglas in reply: The divine law is appealed to as authority for disregarding our most sacred duties to society. The city council have appealed to it, as their excuse for nullifying an act of Congress; and a committee embodied the same principle in their resolutions to the meeting in this hall last night, as applicable both to the Constitution and laws. The general proposition that there is a law paramount to all human enactments—the law of the Supreme Ruler of Universe—I trust that no civilized and Christian people is prepared to question, much less deny. We should all recognize, respect, and revere the divine law. But we should bear in mind that the law of God, as revealed to us, is intended to operate on our consciences, and insure the performance of our duties as individuals and Christians. The divine law does not prescribe the form of government under which we shall live, and the character of our political and civil institutions. Revelation has not furnished us with a constitution—a code of international law—and a system of civil and municipal jurisprudence. It has not determined the right of persons and property—much less the peculiar privileges which shall be awarded to each class of persons under any particular form of government. God has created man in his own image, and endowed him with the right of self-government, so soon as he shall evince the requisite intelligence, virtue, and capacity to assert and enjoy the privilege. The history of world furnishes few examples where any considerable portion of the human race have shown themselves sufficiently enlightened and civilized to exercise the rights and enjoy the blessings of freedom. In Asia and Africa we find nothing but ignorance, superstition, and despotism. Large portions of Europe and America can scarcely lay claim to civilization and Christianity; and a still smaller portion have demonstrated their capacity for self-government. Is all this contrary to the laws of God? And if so, who is responsible? The civilized world have always held, that when any race of men have shown themselves so degraded, by ignorance, superstition, cruelty, and barbarism, as to be utterly incapable of governing themselves, they must, in the nature of things, be governed by others, by such laws as are deemed applicable to their condition. It is upon this principle alone that England justifies the form of government she has established in the Indies, and for some of her other colonies—that Russia justifies herself in holding her serfs as slaves, and selling them as a part of the land on which they live—that our Pilgrim Fathers justified themselves in reducing the negro and Indian to servitude, and selling them as property—that we in Illinois and most of the free States, justify ourselves in denying the negro and the Indian the privilege of voting, and all other political rights—and that many of the States of the Union justify themselves in depriving the white man of the right of the elective franchise, unless he is fortunate enough to own a certain amount of property.

These things certainly violate the principle of absolute equality among men, when considered as component parts of a political society or government, and so do many provisions of the Constitution of the United States, as well as the several States of the Union. In fact, no government ever existed on earth in which there was a perfect equality, in all things, among those composing it and governed by it. Neither sacred nor profane history furnishes an example. If inequality in the form and principles of government is therefore to be deemed a violation of the laws of God, and punishable as such, who is to escape? Under this principle all Christendom is doomed, and no Pagan can hope for mercy? Many of these things are, in my opinion, unwise and unjust, and, of course, subversive of republican principles; but I am not prepared to say that they are either sanctioned or condemned by the divine law. Who can assert that God has prescribed the form and principles of government, and the character of the political, municipal and domestic institutions of men on earth? This doctrine would annihilate the fundamental principle upon which our political system rests. Our forefathers held that the people had an inherent right to establish such Constitution and laws for the government of themselves and their posterity, as they should deem best calculated to insure the protection of life, liberty, and the pursuit of happiness; and that the same might be altered and changed as experience should satisfy them to be necessary and proper. Upon this principle the Constitution of the United States was formed, and our glorious Union established. All acts of Congress passed in pursuance of the Constitution are declared to be the supreme laws of the land, and the Supreme Court of the United States is charged with expounding the same. All officers and magistrates, under the Federal and State governments—executive, legislative, judicial, and ministerial—are required to take an oath to support the Constitution, before they can enter upon the performance of their respective duties. Any citizen, therefore, who in his conscience, believes that the Constitution of the United States is in violation of a " higher law," has no right, as an honest man, to take office under it, or exercise any other function of citizenship conferred by it. Every person born under the Constitution owes allegiance to it; and every naturalized citizen takes an oath support it. Fidelity to the Constitution is the only passport to the enjoyment of rights under it. When a senator elect presents his credentials, he is not allowed to take his seat until he places his hand upon the holy evangelist, and appeals to his God for the sincerity of his vows to support the Constitution. He, who does this, with a mental reservation or secret intention to disregard any provision of the Constitution, commits a double crime—is morally guilty of perfidy to his God and treason to his country!

If the Constitution of the United States is to be repudiated upon the ground that it is repugnant to the divine law, where are the friends of freedom and Christianity to look for another and a better? Who is to be the prophet to reveal the will of God and establish a Theocracy for us?

Is he to be found in the ranks of northern abolitionism, or of southern disunion; or is the Common Council of the city of Chicago to have the distinguished honor of furnishing the chosen one? I will not venture to inquire what are to be the form and principles of the new government, or to whom is to be intrusted the execution of its sacred functions; for, when we decide that the wisdom of our revolutionary fathers was foolishness, and their piety wickedness, and destroy the only system of self government that has ever realized the hopes of the friends of freedom, and commanded the respect of mankind, it becomes us to wait patiently until the purposes of the Latter Day Saints shall be revealed unto us.

For my part, I am prepared to maintain and preserve inviolate the Constitution as it is with all its compromises, to stand or fall by the American Union, clinging with the tenacity of life to all its glorious memories of the past and precious hopes for the future.

Mr. Douglas then explained the circumstances which rendered his absence unavoidable when the vote was taken on the fugitive bill in the Senate. He wished to avoid no responsibility on account of that absence, and therefore desired it to be distinctly understood that he should have voted for the bill if he could have been present. He referred to several of our most prominent and respected citizens by name, as personally cognizant of the fact that he was anxious at that time to give that vote. He believed the passage of that or some other efficient law a solemn duty, imperatively demanded by the Constitution. In conclusion, Mr. D. made an earnest appeal to our citizens to rally as one man to the defence of the Constitution and laws, and above all things, and under all circumstances, to put down violence and disorder, by maintaining the supremacy of the laws. He referred to our high character for law and order heretofore, and also to the favorable position of our city for commanding the trade between the North and South, through our canals and railroads, to show that our views and principles of action should be broad, liberal, and national, calculated to encourage union and harmony, instead of disunion and sectional bitterness. He concluded by remarking, that he considered this question of fidelity to the Constitution and supremacy of the laws, as so far paramount to all other considerations, that he had prepared some resolutions to cover these points only, which he would submit to the meeting, and take their judgment upon them. If he had consulted his own feelings and views only, he should have embraced in the resolutions a specific approval of all the measures of the compromise; but as the question of rebellion and resistance to the Federal Government has been distinctly presented, it has been thought advisable to meet that issue on this occasion, distinct and separate from all others.

Mr. Douglas then offered the following resolutions, which were adopted without a dissenting voice :

Resolved, That it is the sacred duty of every friend of the Union to maintain, and preserve inviolate, every provision of our federal Constitution.

Resolved, That any law enacted by Congress, in pursuance of the Constitution, should be respected as such by all good and law-abiding citizens, and should be faithfully carried into effect by the officers charged with its execution.

Resolved, That so long as the Constitution of the United States provides, that all persons held to service or labor in one State, escaping into another State, "SHALL BE DELIVERED UP on the claim of the party to whom the service or labor may be due," and so long as members of Congress are required to take an oath to support the Constitution, it is their solemn and religious duty to pass all laws necessary to carry that provision of the Constitution into effect.

Resolved, That if we desire to preserve the Union, and render our great Republic inseparable and perpetual, we must perform all our obligations under the Constitution, at the same time that we call upon our brethren in other States to yield implicit obedience to it.

Resolved, That as the lives, property and safety of ourselves and our families depend upon the observance and protection of the laws, every effort to excite any portion of our population to make resistance to the due execution of the laws of the land, should be promptly and emphatically condemned by every good citizen.

Resolved, That we will stand or fall by the American Union and its Constitution, with all its compromises, with its glorious memories of the past and precious hope of the future.

[The following was offered in addition by B. S. Morris, and also adopted :]

Resolved, That we, the people of Chicago, repudiate the resolutions passed by the Common Council of Chicago upon the subject of the Fugitive Slave Law passed by Congress at its last session.

On the succeeding night the common council of the city repealed their nullifying resolution by a vote of 12 to 1.

ON THE CLAYTON BULWER TREATY.

Delivered in the Senate of the United States, March 10 *and* 17, 1853.

On returning to the Senate of the United States at the special session, commencing on the 4th March, 1843, Senator Clayton, of Delaware, offered the following resolutions :

Resolved, That the President be respectfully requested, if compatible in his opinion with the public interest, to communicate to the Senate the propositions mentioned in the letter of the secretary of state accompanying the Executive message to the Senate of the 18th February last, as having been agreed upon by the Department of State, the British minister, and the state of Costa Rica, on the 30th of April, 1852, having for their object the settlement of the territorial controversies between the states and governments bordering on the river San Juan.

Resolved, That the secretary of state be directed to communicate to the Senate such information as it may be in the power of his department to furnish, in regard to the conflicting claims of Great Britain and the state of Honduras, to the island of Roatan, Bonacca, Utilla, Barbarat, Helene, and Morat, in or near the Bay of Honduras.

On the 8th and 9th of March, 1853, he addressed the Senate on the subject, and arraigned Senators Cass, Mason, and Douglas, for the part they had taken in the debate during the regular session. On the 10th of March, Mr. Douglas replied as follows:

MR. PRESIDENT: I have nothing to do with the controversy which has arisen between the senator from Delaware (Mr. Clayton) and my venerable friend from Michigan (Mr. Cass), who is now absent in consequence of the severe illness of one nearest and dearest to him. We all know enough of that senator to be assured that when he shall be in his place, he will be prompt to respond to any calls that may be made upon him. Neither have I anything to do with the dispute which has grown up among senators in respect to the boundary of Central America, and the position of the British settlement at the Balize. I leave that in the hands of those who have made themselves parties to the controversy. Nor shall I become a party to the discussion upon the issue between the senator from Delaware and the chairman of the Committee on Foreign Relations, in their report on that question. Not having been present when the committee made their report, and not yet having had the opportunity of reading it, I leave the chairman of the committee to vindicate his positions, as I doubt not he will prove himself abundantly able to do. I have, therefore, only to ask the attention of the Senate to such points as the senator from Delaware has chosen to make against a speech delivered by me a few weeks ago in this chamber.

The senator seems to complain that I should have questioned the propriety of withholding from the consideration of the Senate what is known as the Ilise treaty, and the substitution of the Clayton and Bulwer treaty in its place. Those two treaties presented a distinct issue of great public concern to the country; and it was a difference of opinion between him and me as to which system of policy should prevail. I advocated that system which would secure to the United States the sole and exclusive privilege of controlling the communication between the two oceans. He substituted that other policy which opened the privilege to a partnership between the United States and Great Britain. The senator has assigned various reasons for withholding the Ilise treaty from the consideration of the Senate. The first is, that it was concluded by Mr. Ilise without the authority of this government. That may be true, but it is the first time I have heard it argued as a valid reason for withholding from the consideration of the Senate a treaty the objects and provisions of which were desirable. The treaty with New Granada, which he so warmly commends in his speech, was made by Mr. Bidlack without authority. President Polk stated this fact in his message communicating the treaty to the Senate, and the senator from Delaware has read that message and incorporated it into his speech. He therefore knew that fact when he gave as a reason for withholding the Ilise treaty, that it was made without authority.

The treaty of peace with Mexico, to the provisions of which the senator has also referred on another point, was entered into by Mr. Trist, not only without authority, but in bold defiance of the instructions of our government to the contrary. The administration of President Polk did not feel at liberty to withhold these two treaties from the Senate, merely because they were made without authority or in defiance of instructions, for the reason that the objects intended to be accomplished by the treaty were desirable, and the provisions could be so modified by the Senate as to make the details conform to the objects in view. It may not be amiss for me to remind the senator from Delaware, that he was a member of the Senate at the time the Mexican treaty was submitted for ratification, and that he voted for it, notwithstanding it was concluded in opposition to the instructions of our government. If, therefore, the senator has any respect for the practice of the government heretofore, or for his own votes recorded upon the very point in controversy, he is not at liberty to object to the treaty upon the ground that it was concluded by our diplomatic agent without authority.

I understand the rule to be this: whenever the treaty is made in pursuance of instructions, the Executive is under an implied obligation to submit it to the Senate for ratification. But if it be entered into without authority, or in violation of instructions, the administration are at liberty to reject it unconditionally, or to send it to the Senate for advice, amendment, ratification, or rejection, according to their judgment of its merits. Whether the Hise treaty was perfect in all its provisions, or contained obnoxious features, is not the question. It furnished conclusive evidence that the government of Nicaragua was willing and anxious to confer upon the United States the exclusive and perpetual privilege of controlling the canal between the Atlantic and Pacific oceans, instead of a partnership between us and the European powers. The senator from Delaware (then secretary of state) had the opportunity of securing to his own country that inestimable privilege, either by submitting the Hise treaty to the Senate, with the recommendation that it be so modified as to obviate all the objections which he deemed to exist to some of its provisions, or by making a new treaty which should embrace the principle of an exclusive and perpetual privilege without any of the obnoxious provisions. He did not do either. He suppressed the treaty—refused to accept of an exclusive privilege to his own country—and caused a new treaty to be made, which should lay the foundation of a partnership between the United States and Great Britain and the other European powers.

The next reason assigned for withholding the Hise treaty from the Senate is that it had not been approved by Nicaragua. It is true that Nicaragua did not ratify that treaty; but why did she fail to do so? I showed conclusively in the speech to which the senator was replying that the non-approval was in consequence of his instructions, as secretary of state, to Mr. Squier, our chargé d'affaires to Nicaragua. It required the whole influence of the representative of our government in that country to prevent the ratification and approval of the Hise treaty by the state of Nicaragua. Sir, it is not a satisfactory reason for suppressing the treaty, therefore, that it had not been ratified by the other party, when the non-ratification was produced by the action of the agent of this government in pursuance of instructions.

Mr. CLAYTON.—I desire distinctly to understand the senator. If I understood him, he said that Mr. Hise's treaty was rejected in consequence of Mr. Squier's interference.

Mr. DOUGLAS.—Yes, sir.

Mr. CLAYTON.—And then I understand him to say that Mr. Squier did it by instruction.

Mr. DOUGLAS.—Yes, sir.

Mr. CLAYTON.—Now will the senator submit the truth to substantiate that assertion? I know of no such instruction.

Mr. DOUGLAS.—I will do that with a great deal of pleasure. Mr. Hise was sent to the Central American States by Mr. Polk. He negotiated a treaty with the state of Nicaragua—the treaty in question—on the 21st of June, 1849. Prior to that time he had been recalled, and Mr. Squier had been appointed by the administra tion which succeeded that of President Polk. Mr. Hise had received no knowledge of his removal; no instructions from the new administration at the time when he made the treaty. In the instructions which the secretary of state gave to Mr. Squier on the 2d of May, 1849, when he was about to proceed to Central America to supersede Mr. Hise, you will find that he was directed to "claim no peculiar privilege; no exclusive right; no monopoly of commercial intercourse" for the United States. I will read from the letter of instructions:

"We should naturally be proud of such an achievement as an American work; but if European aid be necessary to accomplish it, why should we repudiate it, seeing that our object is as honest as it is openly avowed, to claim no peculiar privilege; no exclusive right; no monopoly of commercial intercourse, but to see that the work is dedicated to the benefit of mankind, to be used by all on the same terms with us, and consecrated to the enjoyment and diffusion of the unnumbered and inestimable blessings which must flow from it to all the civilized world!"

Then, sir, after having instructed Mr. Squier as to the character of the treaty which he was to form—a treaty which was to open the canal to the world—a treaty which was to give us no peculiar privilege, and secure to us no exclusive right—after giving that instruction, the secretary, in the concluding paragraph, says:

"If a charter or grant of the right of way shall have been incautiously or inconsiderately made before your arrival in that country, seek to have it properly modified to answer the ends we have in view."

MR. CLAYTON.—Is that the passage?

MR. DOUGLAS.—That and the other together.

MR. CLAYTON.—I endeavored to correct the misapprehension of the honorable senator yesterday in reference to that. That is not an instruction to the minister to Central America in regard to the treaty made by Mr. Hise, or any other treaty. It is a direction to the minister to Central America to see that any contract which had been made by the local government should be so made as not to be assignable. If the gentleman will read the context, he will see at once that that does not allude to a treaty. It is merely, I say again, an instruction to the minister in that country to look to it, that the capitalists who were about to construct the canal should not speculate upon the work. There is nothing there touching a treaty; nothing whatever. The gentleman is entirely mistaken. The whole construction is in reference to the character of the contract o· charter.

MR. DOUGLAS.—I will read the preceding sentence, and we will see then who is mistaken:

"If they do not agree to grant us passage on reasonable and proper terms, refuse our protection and our countenance to procure the contract from Nicaragua"——

Mr. Clayton.—If the gentleman will look at the context which goes before, he will see that the word "they" refers to the capitalists.

Mr. Douglas.—I will read what goes before:

"See that it is not assignable to others; that no exclusive privileges are granted to any nation that will not agree to the same treaty stipulations with Nicaragua; that the tolls to be demanded by the owners are not unreasonable or oppressive; that no power be reserved to the proprietors of the canal or their successors to extort at any time hereafter, or unjustly to obstruct or embarrass the right of passage. This will require all your vigilance and skill. If they do not agree to grant us passage on reasonable and proper terms, refuse our protection and our countenance to procure the contract from Nicaragua. If a charter or grant of the right of way shall have been incautiously or inconsiderately made before your arrival in that country, seek to have it properly modified to answer the ends we have in view."

Mr. Clayton.—The honorable senator will observe that that does not refer to a treaty. The grant of the right of way was a different thing. It was a contract between the local government and the capitalists. Not a treaty at all.

Mr. Douglas.—The senator's explanation is doubtless satisfactory to himself. He may imagine that it will suit his present purposes to place upon his instructions the construction for which he now contends; but it is wholly unwarranted by the language he employed. His instructions speak of securing the right of way to "us." To whom did he allude in the word "us?" Did he refer to the capitalists, proprietors and speculators, who should become the owners of the charter? Was he one of the company, and therefore authorized to use the word "us," when speaking of the rights and privileges to be acquired of a foreign nation through his agency as secretary of state? I have supposed that Mr. Squier was sent to Central America to represent the United States, and to protect our rights and interests as a nation. I have always done the senator from Delaware the justice to believe that when he gave those instructions to Mr. Squier he was acting on behalf of his country to secure the right of way for a canal to the United States and not to a few capitalists and speculators under the title of "us." For the honor of our country I will still do him that justice, notwithstanding his disclaimer. His instructions also speak of the right of way to "nations," and caution Mr. Squier to see that "no exclusive privileges are granted to any nation," etc.

It is plain, therefore, that in the instructions relating to the securing the right of way for a canal to the nations of the earth, Mr. Squier was directed to see that no exclusive privilege was granted to any other nation, and not to claim any peculiar advantages for our own. Then follows the concluding paragraph, which has been read:

"If a charter or grant of the rights of way shall have been incautiously or inconsiderately made before your arrival in the country, seek to have it properly modified to answer the ends we have in view."

Modified how? If before the arrival of Mr. Squier in the country

Mr. Hise shall have acquired a charter or grant which sl ill secure peculiar privileges or exclusive rights for this country, he was to seek to have it so modified as to open the same rights and privileges to all other nations on equal terms. This is what I understand to be the meaning of those instructions, and it is clear that Mr. Squier understood them in the same way; for when he arrived in Nicaragua, and discovered, by a statement in a newspaper of the Isthmus, that Mr. Hise was about making a treaty for a canal, without knowing what its terms were, without waiting to ascertain its provisions, he sent at once a notice to the government of Nicaragua, that Mr. Hise was not authorized to treat—that he did not understand the policy and views of the new administration—that he had been recalled, and that any treaty he might make must be considered and treated as an unofficial act. He communicated this protest to the secretary of state on the same day, and then proceeded to his point of destination, where he made a treaty for the right of way for a canal to all nations on the partnership plan in pursuance of his instructions. These two treaties—the Hise treaty and the Squier treaty—were in the Department of State at the same time—the one having arrived about the middle of September, and the other about the first of October. It then became the duty of the senator from Delaware, as secretary of state, to decide between them: in other words, to determine whether he would accept of an exclusive privilege to his own country, or enter into partnership with the monarchies of Europe. He did determine that question, and his decision was in favor of the partnership, and against his own country having the exclusive control of the canal.

Then, sir, I think I was authorized to say what I did say, that the non-ratification of Hise treaty by the government of Nicaragua was procured by the agent of General Taylor's administration in that country, and that the agent acted under the authority of this government. He certainly acted in obedience to what he understood to be his instruction, and that is, the instruction, that if such a charter had been incautiously granted, to seek to have it modified to conform to the ends had in view, as stated in the instruction.

Mr. Clayton.—Will the senator allow me to interrupt him? It is not a very material point, still it is better to have it right than wrong. If the senator will only read the last paragraph, he will see that the charter or grant of the right of way which Mr. Squier was instructed to see was not incautiously made, was a very different thing, indeed, from the treaty; and he will see that that is the thing which I directed the minister to look to, as I stated, and endeavored to be understood yesterday, and as I was anxious to be understood by the gentleman on this point—what I instructed the minister to look to was that the contract of these capitalists should not be such as would enable them to extort from persons using the canal. The last sentence of the instruction applies, if he will look at it exclusively to the case of the contract, and not to that of the treaty.

One remark more: How is it possible for the gentleman to reconcile the fact, that the State Department could know or imagine that Mr. Hise had made a treaty on the 2d of May, 1850, when those instructions were given, when, in point of fact, Mr. Hise was not heard from until June afterward? How could I imagine any such thing? And again: how could I possibly suppose that Mr. Hise had made a treaty, or was going to make a treaty, when the records of the State Department showed me the instructions given to him by Mr. Buchanan, in which he tells Mr. Hise to make no treaty whatever with Nicaragua? If the gentleman can reconcile these things, I should be happy to hear him.

Mr. Douglas.—I will have less difficulty in reconciling these things with my views of his instructions than he will with his construction of them. I have already shown that the instructions related to the right of way to nations and not to individuals; that they were in favor of equal rights to all nations, and opposed to any peculiar privileges to our own country. Is it not as reasonable to suppose that the instructions meant what they said, as it is to conceive that our minister was directed to procure the modification of contracts previously entered into with individuals, and for the observance of which Nicaragua was supposed to have pledged her faith as a nation? Was our minister sent there to represent individuals in their schemes of procuring charters and contracts on private account, or to interfere with and prevent the faithful observance of such contracts as that government might previously have made with our own citizens or others? While this supposition might extricate the senator from his present difficulty on this point, it would not tend to elevate the character of our diplomacy during his administration of the State Department. I think I do the senator more justice by the construction I have put upon his conduct than he does by his own explanation.

But, sir, I wish to know whether I understand the senator now? Does he wish now to be understood as saying that he preferred an exclusive privilege to his own country to a partnership with England?

Mr. Clayton.—No, sir.

Mr. Douglas.—Ah! then as he did not prefer the exclusive privilege to a partnership with the European powers, does he wish the Senate to understand that he did not mean to convey his true idea in his instructions? If he preferred the partnership to the exclusive privilege, was it not his duty to make known that wish in his instructions? Why should he complain when I show that by his instructions he said precisely what he now avows to be his policy upon that subject? Why, sir, I am defending the consistency of his own opinions, according to his present views, by showing that his instructions embraced what he says now was his true policy—in favor of a partnership with other nations, instead of an exclusive privilege to our own country.

But, sir, whatever may have been his meaning in those instructions, it is undeniable that Mr. Squier understood them as I now do, and acted upon them accordingly. Hence, as I have already remarked, before he arrived upon the theatre of his operations, and upon the mere authority of a newspaper paragraph, that Mr. Hise was about making such a treaty, he sent ahead a messenger to inform the government of Nicaragua that Mr. Hise had no authority to treat upon the subject—that he had been recalled—that he was not informed of the views and purposes of the new administration—and that whatever treaty he made must be regarded and treated as an unofficial act—and requesting that "new negotiations may be entered upon at the seat of government."

The new negotiations were immediately opened accordingly, and on the 3d of September terminated in a treaty, which was a substitute for that which Mr. Hise had previously made. I do not understand that the Hise treaty was formally rejected or disavowed by the government of Nicaragua. It was treated as an unofficial act—a mere nullity—upon the authority of Mr. Squier's protest. I again submit the question to the Senate, therefore, whether I am not fully justified in the statement that the non-approval of the Hise treaty by the government of Nicaragua was in consequence of the action of the agent of this government in that country, under the instructions of the senator from Delaware as secretary of state? I am only surprised that he should attempt to avoid the responsibility of the act, since, when hard pressed in this discussion, he has been driven into the admission that he preferred a partnership with the monarchies of the Old World to an exclusive privilege for his own country. If such were his opinions and preferences, he was bound by every consideration of duty and patriotism to have given the instructions, and produced the result which I have attributed to him. Why not avow that which he now acknowledges to have been his purpose, in obedience to what he conceived to be his duty? I only ask him to assume the responsibility and consequences of his own conduct, and then to assign such reasons as he may be able in justification.

The next reason which he gives for suppressing the Hise treaty is totally inconsistent with the first. He alleges that the clause guaranteeing the independence of Nicaragua was wholly inadmissible, and could never receive his sanction. In a report which was communicated to the House of Representatives in 1850, he assigned the same reason, and stated that such a guaranty was a departure from our uniform policy, and had no precedent in our history except in the one case of the French colonies in America.

Of course courtesy requires me to acknowledge that the senator really believes that this was one of the reasons which induced him to withhold the Hise treaty from the Senate. I must be permitted, however, to inform him that he is entirely mistaken: that the clause in question did not constitute an objection in his mind at that time that it is an afterthought which he has since seized hold of to justify an act which he had previously performed upon totally different grounds. The evidence of these facts will be found recorded in a dispatch written by the senator from Delaware, as secretary of state, on the 20th of October, 1849, to Mr. Lawrence, our minister to England. The document containing this dispatch was printed and laid upon our tables a few days since, and is entitled Senate Ex. Doc. No. 27. It will be remembered that the Hise treaty was communicated to the Department of State on the 15th of September, and the Squier treaty about the first of October of the same year. On the 20th of October, Mr. Clayton (in the dispatch to which I refer), discussed our relations with the Central American states at great length—among other things communicated to Mr. Lawrence the substance of these two treaties—and directed him to make the same known to Lord Palmerston. I read from the dispatch:

"If, however, the British government shall reject these overtures on our part, and shall refuse to coöperate with us in the generous and philanthropic scheme of rendering the interoceanic communication by the way of the port and river San Juan free to all nations upon the same terms, we shall deem ourselves justified in protecting our interests independently of her aid, and despite her opposition or hostility. With a view to this alternative, we have a treaty with the state of Nicaragua, a copy of which has been sent to you, and the stipulations of which you should unreservedly impart to Lord Palmerston. You will inform him, however, that this treaty was concluded without a power or instruction from this government; that the President had no knowledge of its existence, of the intention to form it, until it was presented to him by Mr. Hise, our late chargé d'affaires to Guatemala, about the 1st of September last; and that, consequently, we are not bound to ratify it, and will take no step for that purpose, if we can, by arrangements with the British government, place our interests upon a just and satisfactory foundation. But, if our effort for this end should be abortive, the President will not hesitate to submit this or some other treaty which may be concluded by the present chargé d'affaires to Guatemala, to the Senate of the United States for their advice and consent, with a view to its ratification; and if that enlightened body should approve it, he also will give it his hearty sanction, and will exert all his constitutional power to execute its provisions in good faith—a determination in which he may confidently count upon the good will of the people of the United States."

Here we find the true reason assigned for withholding the Hise treaty from the Senate. It was to induce Great Britain to enter into partnership with us. Lord Palmerston is informed that if Great Britain refuses our offer of a partnership, that " we shall deem ourselves justified in protecting our interests independently of her aid, and in despite of her opposition or hostility," and that " with a view to this alternative," he held the Hise treaty in reserve, to be submitted to the Senate for ratification or not, dependent upon the decision of Great Britain in relation to the partnership. This is the only reason assigned for withholding the treaty from the Senate. The pretext that it was made without authority is expressly negatived by the threat to accept the exclusive privilege, in the event that England refuses to enter into the partnership. Not a word of objection that it guarantees the independence of Nicaragua! But the testimony does not stop here. This same dispatch furnishes affirmative evidence—conclusive and undeniable—that the "guaranty" constituted no portion of his objection to the Hise treaty—was not deemed objectionable by him at that time—but, on the contrary, was looked upon with favor, and actually proposed by Mr. Clayton himself as a desirable provision which might be incorporated into a treaty for the protection of the canal! I read from the same dispatch:

"You may suggest, for instance, that the United States and Great Britain should enter into a treaty guaranteeing the independence of Nicaragua, Honduras and Costa Rica, which treaty may also guarantee to British subjects the privileges acquired in those States by the treaties between Great Britain and Spain, provided that the limits of those States on the east be acknowledged to be the Carribean Sea."

Now, sir, let me ask the senator from Delaware what becomes of his pretext that he deemed the guaranty of the independence of Nicaragua an insuperable objection to the Hise treaty? Have I not proven by his own dispatches, written at the time, that such an idea could never have entered his brain when he determined to withhold the treaty from the Senate?—that it was an afterthought upon which he has since seized as an excuse for an act which had been previously done with a view to another object, and for different reasons?

I will now proceed to consider the fourth objection made by the senator to the Hise treaty. He goes on to criticise its various provisions, denounces them as ridiculous, as absurd, as unconstitutional, and he puts the question with an air of triumph whether there was a man in this body who would have voted for all the provisions of that treaty. Sir, I have no fancy for that species of special pleading which attempts to avoid the real issue by a criticism upon mere details which are subject to modification at pleasure. Does not the senator know that when a treaty is made, the objects of which are desirable, while the details are inadmissible, the practice has been to send it to the Senate, that the object may be secured and the details so modified as to conform to the ends in view? Whoever supposed before that a treaty, desirable in its leading features, was to be rejected by the department, merely because there was an obnoxious provision in it? I could turn upon the senator with an air of as much triumph, if I had practised it as well, and ask him if there was a man in this body who would have voted for the Mexican treaty of peace as it was sent to us by the Executive? Do we not all know that the treaty which was ratified by about four-fifths of the Senate came to us in a shape in which it could not receive one solitary vote upon either side of the chamber? Do we not know that Mr. Polk in his message communicating the treaty intimated that fact, and called the attention of the Senate to the obnoxious provisions? While it contained provisions which would exclude the President from the possibility of ever ratifying it, which would have prevented every senator from giving his sanction to it, yet inasmuch as the main objects of the treaty met the approval of the President, and it was only matters of detail that were obnoxious and inadmissible, he sent it to the Senate that its details might be made to harmonize with its objects. Sir, the vote to strike out the obnoxious features in the treaty was unanimous. Not one man in the body, not even the senator from Delaware, dared to affirm those clauses or vote to keep them in the treaty. Having perfected it so as to suit the views of about four-fifths of the Senate, it was ratified with the vote of the senator recorded in the affirmative, according to my recollection.

If, therefore, the senator from Delaware had followed the practice which he sanctioned by his own vote in the case of the Mexican treaty, he would have sent the Hise treaty to the Senate for amendment and ratification, even if the details had been obnoxious to all the objections he now urges to them. For this reason I do not deem it necessary to occupy the time of the Senate in reply to his objections relative to making a canal outside the limits of the United States, or the creation of a company either by Congress or the President for that purpose. I care not whether these provisions were admissible or inadmissible. It is not material to the argument. It can have no bearing upon the question. The Hise treaty was evidence of one great fact, which should never be forgotten, and that fact is, that Nicaragua was willing and anxious to grant the United States forever the exclusive right and control over a ship canal between the two oceans. The secretary of state (Mr. Clayton), knew that fact. If the details were not acceptable to him, he could have availed himself of the main provisions and made the details to suit himself; I confine myself therefore to the great point that you might have had the exclusive privilege if you had desired it. You refused it with your eyes open, and took a partnership in lieu of it. All about the details is a matter of moonshine. You could have modified them to suit yourself before sending the treaty to the Senate, or you could have followed the example of Mr. Polk, in the case of the Mexican treaty, and sent it to the Senate with the recommendation that the details be thus modified.

All this talk about obnoxious features and objectionable provisions —about guarantees of independence and want of authority to make the treaty—must be regarded as miserable attempts to avoid the main point at issue. Why this pitiful equivocation, if the senator was really in favor of the European partnership in preference to the exclusive privilege for the United States, as all his acts prove—the whole tenor of his correspondence clearly and conclusively prove— was the case? If he thinks his policy was right, why not frankly avow the truth, and justify upon the merits? I am not to be diverted from my purpose by his assaults upon the administration of President Polk, nor by his array of great names in opposition to the views I entertain. History will do justice to Mr. Polk and Mr. Buchanan

upon this as well as all other questions connected with their administration of the government. In the speech to which the senator
professed to reply, I did not make an allusion to party politics. I do
not think the term Whig or Democrat can be found in the whole
speech. I am sure that it does not contain a partisan reference to
the state of political parties in the country during the period to
which my remarks applied. I attempted to discuss the question
upon its merits, independent of the fact whether my views might come
in conflict with those professed by either of the great parties, or
entertained by the great men of our country at some former period.
I should have been better satisfied if the senator had pursued the
same course, instead of calling upon Jackson, Polk and Buchanan,
and sheltering himself behind their great names, while attempting to
detract from their fame by representing them as having sacrificed the
interests and honor of their country.

MR. CLAYTON.—I deny it. There was not one word in my speech
which went to arraign Mr. Polk or General Jackson, or anybody.
There was nothing like a party spirit in this speech. If the gentleman so understood me, he entirely misunderstood me. I stated the
fact that Mr. Polk and Mr. Buchanan had been applied to by the
local government of Nicaragua for the intervention of this government to protect it from the aggressions of the British. I stated, and
proved the fact, that the Monroe doctrine had never been carried
out—that Mr. Polk on that occasion had declined to interfere; but
I disclaim entirely assailing him, and endeavor to reconcile his whole
course of conduct as being consistent with what he stated in the
House of Representatives on the Panama mission.

MR. DOUGLAS.—I accept the explanation. It is perfectly satisfactory, but I am very unfortunate in apprehending the meaning of
language. He said that Mr. Polk had avowed himself in favor of
asserting the Monroe doctrine. He then said that Mr. Polk had
abandoned and refused to carry it out when this question arose. He
said the President of Nicaragua, to use his own language, "poked
that declaration into Mr. Polk's own teeth."

MR. CLAYTON.—I used no such word.

MR. DOUGLAS.—At least, that he thrust it into his teeth.

MR. CLAYTON.—I did not.

MR. DOUGLAS.—Well, never mind about the precise word. At all
events, he went on to show that Mr. Polk was pledged to the Monroe doctrine, that he failed to carry it out, that no administration
ever carried it out, that it had been abandoned whenever a question
arose which gave an opportunity for carrying it into effect. When
he chose to put Mr. Polk into the position of making declarations
and violating them, making protests and abandoning them, making
threats and never executing them, I very naturally supposed, according to the notion of a western man, that he was attacking him.
(Laughter.)

MR. CLAYTON.—I endeavor to show that Mr. Polk had made his

recommendation to the Congress of the United States that he was perfectly justifiable in not considering that as the established doctrine of the country, because the Congress of the United States had never adopted it. On that principle I endeavor to reconcile the course of Mr. Polk with itself. The gentleman has undertaken to represent me as assailing Mr. Polk, when if he had paid attention to what I said—unfortunately he was out during the greater portion of the time I was discussing the subject—he would have seen that I was endeavoring to prove that the course of that President of the United States, in this particular, was made liable to the exception which is taken to it; that he was not bound by the declaration of the Monroe doctrine unless Congress adopted it, because he was not the government.

MR. DOUGLAS.—Of course I accept the explanation of the senator with a great deal of pleasure, and I am gratified to know that I misapprehend him; but it really did appear to me that I was justified in putting that construction upon what he said, inasmuch as he went on to show that when he came into the State Department, he found Great Britain with her protectorate over the Mosquito coast, and spreading over more than half of Central America—that during Mr. Polk's administration, and while he was negotiating the treaty of peace with Mexico, Great Britain seized the town of San Juan, at the mouth of the proposed canal, and that Mr. Polk and Mr. Buchanan remained silent, without even a protest against this unjustifiable aggression; and when he denounced that seizure as an act originating in hostility to this country, to cut off communication with our Pacific possessions; and when he said that it would have been wiser to have closed the door and shut out the British lion, than to allow him to enter unresisted, and then attempt to expel him; and when he boasted of having expelled the British lion after Mr. Polk and Mr. Buchanan had permitted him to enter the house in contempt of their declaration of the Monroe doctrine, I really thought that he was attempting to censure Mr. Polk for letting the lion come in; but it seems I was mistaken. He did not mean that, and not meaning it, upon my word I do not know what he did mean. (Laughter.)

When I heard all this, and much more of the same tenor, it occurred to me that it amounted to a pretty good arraignment of Mr. Polk and his administration; and that his object was to glorify himself and General Taylor, at the expense of Mr. Buchanan and Mr. Polk, by accusing the latter of having tamely submitted to British aggressions of great enormity, which the former promptly rebuked by expelling the British from Central America. Let me ask him the question—did the Clayton and Bulwer treaty expel the British from Central America? Has England abandoned her protectorate? What power has she surrendered? What functionary has she recalled? What portion of the country—what inch of territory has she given up? Will the senator from Delaware inform me what England has abandoned in pursuance or by virtue of the Clayton and Bulwer treaty? I can show him where she has extended her possessions since the date of that treaty, and in contempt of its stipulations. I can point him to the seizure of the Bay Islands and the erection of them into a colony—to the extension of her jurisdiction in the vicinity of the Balize—to her invasion of the Territory of Honduras on the main land—and to the continuance of her protectorate over the Mosquito coast. I can point him to a series of acts designed by Great Britain to increase her power and extend her possessions in that quarter. Will he point me to any one act by which she has reduced her power or curtailed her possessions? He boasts of having expelled the British from Central America. Will he have the kindness to inform the Senate how, when, and where this has been effected? Where is the evidence to sustain this declaration? I called for information on this point in my speech the other day. The senator replied to all other parts of that speech in detail and at great length. Of course, want of time was the reason for his omission to respond to these pertinent inquiries. (Laughter.)

Mr. CLAYTON.—No, sir; I replied to it, but the senator was out of his seat.

Mr. DOUGLAS.—I was in my seat the most of the time the senator was speaking on that part of the subject, but unfortunately I heard no response to this interrogatory. Now, sir, in regard to this Bay Island colony, I may be permitted to say, although it is by the way of digression from the line of argument which I was marking out for myself, that it presents a clear case not only in derogation of the Monroe doctrine, but in direct violation and contempt of the Clayton and Bulwer treaty. I will do the senator the justice to say, that the Bay Island colony has not been erected in pursuance of the treaty, but in derogation of its provisions. The question arises, are we going to submit tamely to the establishment of this new colony? If we acquiesce in it we submit to a double wrong—a contravention of our avowed policy in regard to European colonization on this continent; and a palpable and open violation of the terms and stipulations of the Clayton and Bulwer treaty. If we tamely submit to this twofold wrong, the less we say henceforth in regard to European colonization on the American continent, the better for our own credit.

Here is a case where we must act promptly if we ever intend to act. I do not wish to make an issue with England about the Balize —she has been in possession there longer than our nation has existed as an independent republic. I do not wish to make an issue with her in regard to Jamaica, because she cannot surrender it upon our demand without dishonor, and she is bound to fight if driven to an extremity on that point. I do not want to make an issue with her in reference to any colony she has upon the continent or adjacent to it, where she may be said to have had a long and peaceful possession. Sir, if I was going to make the issue on any one of these points, I would pursue a more manly course by declaring war at once instead of resorting to such an expedient. I would make the issue solely and distinctly on the Bay Island colony, for the reason that there she is clearly in the wrong, the act having been done in violation of her plighted faith. It was done in contempt of our avowed policy. She cannot justify it before the civilized world, and therefore, dare not fight upon such an issue. England will fight us when her honor compels her to do it, and she will fight us for no other cause. We can require Great Britain to discontinue the Bay Island colony, and I call upon the friends of the Clayton-Bulwer treaty, whose provisions are outraged by that act, to join in the demand that that colony be discontinued. Upon that point we are in the right: England is in the wrong; and she cannot, she dare not fight upon it. And, sir, when England backs out of one colony upon our remonstrance, it will be a long time before she will establish another upon this continent without consulting us. And, sir, when England shall have refrained from interfering in the affairs of the American continent without consulting the wishes of this government, what other power on earth will be willing to stand forward and do that which England concedes it prudent not to attempt? I may be permitted to say, therefore, that the only issue that I desire to see at this time, upon our foreign relations, as they are now presented to me, is upon the Bay Island colony : and let us require that that be discontinued, and that the terms of our treaty stipulations be obeyed and fulfilled. When that issue shall have been made and decided in our favor, we will not have much need for general resolutions about the Monroe doctrine in future.

But, sir, this was a digression. The point that I was discussing was this: that while it has been a matter of boast for years that the Clayton and Bulwer treaty drove Great Britain out of Central America, she has not surrendered an inch ; and what is more, she is now proposing negotiations with us with a view to new arrangements, by which she shall hereafter give up her protectorate.. Yes, sir, your late secretary of state and President, Everett and Fillmore, have communicated to Congress the fact that the British minister was proposing new negotiations, new arrangements, by which Great Britain shall hereafter give up that which the senator makes it a matter of boast that he had secured by his treaty. That is a little curious. I do not understand this self-gratulation of having accomplished a great and wonderful object, by the expelling of the British lion from the place where Mr. Polk allowed him to come and abide, and still a new negotiation or a new arrangement is deemed necessary to secure that which the senator from Delaware boasts of having accomplished long since !

England professes to be desirous of surrendering her protectorate. Then, why does she not do it? The British minister proposes to open negotiations by which England shall withdraw her authority from Central America, and the late secretary of state (Mr. Everett) entertains the proposition favorably, while the senator from Delaware congratulates the country upon his having effected the desired end in his treaty three years ago.

If Messrs. Everett and Fillmore were correct in entertaining Mr. Crampton's proposition for a new arrangement, certainly the senator from Delaware is at fault in saying that his treaty expelled the British from Central America. My opinion as to whether it did expel them or not, is a matter of not much consequence. I have always thought the language of the treaty was so equivocal, that no man could say with certainty, whether it did abolish the protectorate or not. One clause seemed to abolish it; another seemed to recognize its existence, and to restrain its exercise; and you could make as good an argument on one side as the other. But I gave notice at the time the treaty was ratified, that I would take the American side, and stand by the senator from Delaware in claiming that England was bound to quit; but our late secretary of state and the President, Everett and Fillmore, think otherwise; and now it becomes a question whether new negotiations to accomplish that very desirable object are necessary or not?

Mr. President, I return to the point which I was discussing when the senator interrupted me, and led me off in this digression, to wit. That the simple question presented in this matter, when stripped of all extraneous circumstances, was this: Should we have accepted, when tendered, an exclusive right of way forever, from one ocean to the other? The senator from Delaware thought not, and the administration of General Taylor sustained him in his view of the question. I thought we ought to have embraced the offer which tendered us the exclusive control forever over this great interoceanic canal.

The senator attempts to sustain his position by quoting the authority of General Jackson and Mr. Polk. Sir, he is unfortunate in his quotation. I do not think that, fairly considered, he has any such authority. I am aware that in 1835 that senator offered a resolution in this body, which was adopted, recommending a negotiation to open the Isthmus to all nations, and that General Jackson sent out Colonel Biddle to collect and report information on the subject; but when the resolution was adopted, the question was then presented under circumstances very different from those which existed when the senator suppressed the Hise treaty. At that time the Central American States had granted to the Netherlands the privilege of making a canal. Others had already secured the privilege, and in that point of view it was reasonable to suppose that the most we could do was to get an equal privilege with European nations. That was not the case presented when the exclusive privilege was offered to us and the offer declined by the senator from Delaware without consulting the Senate.

But there is no evidence that General Jackson ever entertained the opinions attributed to him. Colonel Biddle, who was appointed by General Jackson to explore the routes and collect and report information, availed himself of his official position to obtain an exclusive privilege to himself and his associates on private account. When the existence of this private contract came to the knowledge of the secretary of state, Mr. Forsyth, he reprimanded our chargé at

New Granada, for having given any countenance to it. And why?
Not because it contained an exclusive privilege to the United States,
for it did not give us any privilege. Mr. Biddle had been sent out
there to get information to be laid before the administration. He
had no power to negotiate—no authority to open diplomatic relations. He had no power to take any one step in procuring the privilege. He made use of his official position, and, in the opinion of the
administration, abused it, by securing a private grant to himself,
without the authority, protection, or sanction of the government of
his own country.

Mr. Forsyth was indignant because his agent had disobeyed his
authority, and turned the public employment into a private specula-
tion. That is not the question presented here. That contract did
not give the United States the privilege at all. It gave it to
Colonel Biddle and his associates. But I find nothing in that transaction, and in all the public documents relating to it, to show that
General Jackson would have refused the exclusive privilege to his
own country if it had been tendered to him.

How is it, then, with Mr. Polk? According to my recollection
of the facts, New Granada had granted the privilege of making a
canal to a Frenchman by the name of Du Quesne—I will not be certain of his name—and it was desirable to get permission to carry the
mails across there. The grant had passed into the possession of a
citizen of a foreign power, and the most that our government could
ask, was to be put upon an equal footing with that other power. It
did not present the question of the privilege being tendered to us,
and we refusing to accept it.

But I shall take no time in going into a vindication of those administrations. In the remarks that I made the other day, I chose to
vindicate my own course without reference to past administrations
or present party associations, and I will pursue the same line of debate now. One word upon the point, made by the senator, that the
Hise treaty was unconstitutional. Was it not constitutional to
accept the exclusive privilege to the United States? If it was not,
and his constitutional objection is valid, it goes a little too far. If
you had no right to accept an exclusive privilege to us under the
Constitution, what right had you to take a partnership privilege in
company with Great Britain? If you had no right to take the
privilege for the benefit of American citizens alone, what right had
you to take one for the benefit of Englishmen and Americans jointly?
If you have no right to make a treaty by which you will protect an
American company in making that canal, what right had you to
make a treaty by which you pledged yourselves to protect a British
company in making the same work? I choose to put the senator
upon the defensive, and let him demonstrate his right to do this
thing jointly with England, and then I will draw from his argument
my right to do it for the benefit of America alone. I choose to put
him in the position of demonstrating the existence of the constitu

tional power. He, in his treaty, exercised the power. I have not. And he, having exercised it, having pledged the faith of the nation to do the act, I have a right to call upon him to show the authority, under the Constitution of the United States, to make a guaranty jointly with England for the benefit of English subjects as well as American citizens; and when he proves the existence of that power, he has proved the right of the government to do the same thing for the benefit of America and American citizens, omitting England and British subjects.

Sir, as I before said, I have no fondness for this special pleading about the peculiar provisions of a treaty, when the real point was the extent of the privilege which we should accept. Now, sir, I was in favor of an exclusive privilege, and I will tell you why. I desired to see a canal made; and when made, I desired to see it under the control of a power enabled to protect it. I desired to see it open to the commerce of the whole world, under our protection upon proper terms. How was that to be done, except by an exclusive privilege to ourselves? Then, let us open it to the commerce of the world on such terms and conditions as we should deem wise, just and politic. Could we not do this as well by our volition as England could in conjunction with us? Would it not be as creditable to us as a nation to have acquired it ourselves, and then opened it freely, as to have gone into a partnership by which we should have no control in prescribing the terms upon which it should be opened? And besides, if the grant had been made to us, and we had accepted it, and then thrown it open to the commerce of all nations on our own terms and conditions, we held in our hands a right which would have been ample security for every nation under heaven to keep the peace with the United States. The moment England abused the privilege by seizing any more islands, by establishing any more colonies, by invading any more rights, or by violating any more treaties, we would use our privileges, shut up the canal, and exclude her commerce from the Pacific. We would hold a power in our hands which might be exercised at any moment to preserve peace and prevent injustice. Peace and progress being our aim, we should still have continued to be the only government on earth whose public policy from the beginning has been justly and honestly to enforce the laws of nations with fidelity toward all the nations. Sir, when you surrendered that exclusive right, you surrendered a great element of power, which in our hands would have been wielded in the cause of justice for the benefit of mankind.

I was not for such a restrictive policy as would exclude British vessels from going through the canal, or the vessels of any other nation which should respect our rights. I would let them all pass, as long as they did not abuse the privilege; close it against them when they did. I insist that the American people occupy a position on this continent which rendered it natural and proper that we should exercise that power. I have no fear of a war with England. I have none now. War should be avoided as long as possible. But, sir, you need have no apprehension of a war with her, for the reason that if we keep in the right, she dare not fight us, and she will not, especially for anything relating to American affairs. She knows she has given a bond to keep the peace, with a mortgage on all her real estate in America as collateral security, and she knows she forfeits her title to the whole, without hope of redemption, if she commits a breach of the bond. She will not fight unless compelled. We could have fortified that canal at each end, and in time of war could have closed it against our enemies, and opened it at our own pleasure. We had the power of doing it; for the Hise treaty contained provisions for the construction of fortifications at each terminus and at such points along the line of the canal as we thought proper. We had the privilege of fortifying it, and we had the right to close it against any power which should abuse the privilege which we conferred.

Then, sir, what was the objection to the acceptance of that exclusive privilege? I do not see it, sir. I know what were the private arguments urged in times which have gone by, and which I trust never will return; that England and other European powers never would consent that the United States should have an exclusive control over the canal. Well, sir, I do not know that they would have consented, but of one thing I am certain, I would never have asked their consent. When Nicaragua desired to confer the privilege, and when we were willing to accept it, it was purely an American question with which England had no right to interfere. It was an American question about which Europe had no right to be consulted. Are we under any more obligation to consult European powers about an American question than the allied powers were, in their Congress, to consult us, when establishing the equilibrium of Europe by the agency of the Holy Alliance? America was not consulted then. Our name does not appear in all the proceedings. It was a European question, about which it was presumed America had nothing to say. This question of a canal in Nicaragua, when negotiations were pending to give it to us, was so much an American question, that the English government was not entitled to be consulted. England not consent! She will acquiesce in your doing what you may deem right so long as you consent to allow her to hold Canada, the Bermudas, Jamaica, and her other American possessions. I hope the time has arrived when we will not be told any more that Europe will not consent to this, and England will not consent to that. I heard that argument till I got tired of it when we were discussing the resolutions for the annexation of Texas. I heard it again on the Oregon question, and I heard it on the California question. It has been said on every occasion whenever we had an issue about acquiring territory, that England would not consent; yet she has acquiesced in whatever we had the courage and the justice to do. And why? Because we kept ourselves in the right. England was so situated with her possessions on this continent, that she dare not fight in an

3

unjust cause. We would have been in the right to have accepted the privilege of making this canal, and England would never have dared to provoke a controversy with us. I think the time has come when America should perform her duty according to our own judgment, and our own sense of justice, without regard to what European powers might say with respect to it. I think this nation is about of age. I think we have a right to judge for ourselves. Let us always do right, and put the consequences behind us.

But, sir, I do not wish to detain the Senate upon this point, or to prolong the discussion. I have a word or two to say in reply to the remarks of the senator from Delaware upon so much of my speech as related to the pledge in the Clayton and Bulwer treaty, never to annex any portion of that country. I objected to that clause in the treaty, upon the ground that I was unwilling to enter into a treaty stipulation with any European power in respect to this continent, that we would not do in the future, whatever our duty, interest, honor, and safety, might require in the course of events. The senator infers that I desire to annex Central America because I was unwilling to give a pledge that we never would do it. He reminded me that there was a clause in the treaty with Mexico containing the stipulation, that in certain contingencies we would never annex any portion of that country. Sir, it was unnecessary that he should remind me of that provision. He has not forgotten how hard I struggled to get that clause out of the treaty where it was retained in opposition to my vote. Had the senator given me his aid then to defeat that provision in the Mexican treaty, I would be better satisfied now with his excuse for having inserted a still stronger pledge in his treaty. But having advocated that pledge then, he should not attempt to avoid the responsibility of his own act by citing it as a precedent. I was unwilling to bind ourselves by treaty for all time to come never to annex any more territory. I am content for the present with the territory we have. I do not wish to annex any portion of Mexico now. I did not wish to annex any part of Central America then, nor do I at this time.

But I cannot close my eyes to the history of this country for the last half century. Fifty years ago the question was being debated in this Senate whether it was wise or not to acquire any territory on the west bank of the Mississippi, and it was then contended that we could never with safety extend beyond that river. It was at that time seriously considered whether the Alleghany Mountains should not be the barrier beyond which we should never pass. At a subsequent date, after we had acquired Louisiana and Florida, more liberal views began to prevail, and it was thought that perhaps we might venture to establish one tier of States west of the Mississippi; but in order to prevent the sad calamity of an undue expansion of our territory, the policy was adopted of establishing an Indian Territory, with titles in perpetuity, all along the western borders of those States, so that no more new States could possibly be created in that direction. That barrier could not arrest the onward progress of our people. They burst through it, and passed the Rocky Mountains, and were only arrested by the waters of the Pacific. Who then is prepared to say that in the progress of events, having met with the barrier of the ocean in our western course, we may not be compelled to turn to the north and to the south for an outlet. How long is it since the gentleman from Delaware himself thought that the time would never arrive when we would want California? I am aware that he was of that opinion at the time we ratified the treaty, and annexed it.

Mr. CLAYTON.—How?

Mr. DOUGLAS.—By his voting for Mr. Crittenden's resolutions declaring that we did not want any portion of Mexican territory. He will find his vote in this volume which I hold in my hand. I am aware that he belonged to that school of politicians who thought we had territory enough. I have not forgotten that a respectable portion of this body, but a few years ago, thought it would be preposterous to bring a country so far distant as California, and so little known, into the Union. But it has been done; and now since California has become a member of the confederacy, with her immense commerce and inexhaustible resources, we are told that the time will never come when the territory lying half way between our Atlantic and Pacific possessions will be desirable. Central America is too far off, because it is half way to California, and on the main, direct route—on the very route upon which you pay your senators and representatives in Congress their mileage in coming to the capitol of the nation! The usual route of travel, the public highway, the half-way house from one portion of the country to the other, is so far distant that the man who thinks the time will ever come when we will want it, is deemed a madman!

Mr. CLAYTON.—Does the senator apply those sentiments to me? I do not think so.

Mr. DOUGLAS.—I simply say that such an opinion was indicated by the vote of the gentleman on the resolution of Mr. Crittenden.

Mr. CLAYTON.—The senator is entirely mistaken on that point.

Mr. DOUGLAS.—In order to save time, I waive the point as to the senator's vote, although it is recorded in the volume before me, and he can read it at his leisure. But I am not mistaken in saying that the senator on yesterday did ridicule the idea that we were ever to want any portion of Central America. He was utterly amazed, and in his amazement inquired where were these boundaries ever to cease. He wanted to know how far we were going, and if we expected to spread over the entire continent. I do not think we will do it in our day, but I am not prepared to prescribe limits to the area over which Democratic principles may safely spread. I know not what our destiny may be. I try to keep up with the spirit of the age, to keep in view the history of the country, see what we have done, whither we are going, and with what velocity we are moving, in order to be prepared for those events which it is not in the power of man to thwart.

You may make as many treaties as you please to fetter the limits of this giant republic, and she will burst them all from her, and her course will be onward to a limit which I will not venture to describe. Why the necessity of pledging your faith that you will never annex any more of Mexico? Do you not know that you will be compelled to do it; that you cannot help it; that your treaty will not prevent it, and that the only effect it will have will be to enable European powers to accuse us of bad faith when the act is done, and associate American faith and Punic faith as synonymous terms? What is the use of your guaranty that you will never erect any fortifications in Central America; never annex, occupy, or colonize any portion of that country? How do you know that you can avoid doing it? If you make the canal, I ask you if American citizens will not settle along its line; whether they will not build up towns at each terminus; whether they will not spread over that country, and convert it into an American State; whether American principles and American institutions will not be firmly planted there? And I ask you how many years you think will pass away before you will find the same necessity to extend your laws over your own kindred that you found in the case of Texas? How long will it be before that day arrives? It may not occur in the senator's day nor mine. But so certain as this republic exists, so certain as we remain a united people, so certain as the laws of progress which have raised us from a mere handful to a mighty nation, shall continue to govern our action, just so certain are these events to be worked out, and you will be compelled to extend your protection in that direction.

Sir, I am not desirous of hastening the day. I am not impatient of the time when it shall be realized. I do not wish to give any additional impulse to our progress. We are going fast enough. But I wish our public policy, our laws, our institutions, should keep up with the advance in science, in the mechanic arts, in agriculture, and in everything that tends to make us a great and powerful nation. Let us look the future in the face, and let us prepare to meet that which cannot be avoided. Hence I was unwilling to adopt that clause in the treaty guaranteeing that neither party would ever annex, colonize, or occupy any portion of Central America. I was opposed to it for another reason. It was not reciprocal. Great Britain had possession of the island of Jamaica. Jamaica was the nearest armed and fortified point to the terminus of the canal. Jamaica at present commands the entrance of the canal; and all that Great Britain desired was, inasmuch as she had possession of the only place commanding the canal, to procure a stipulation that no other power would ever erect a fortification nearer its terminus. That stipulation is equivalent to an agreement that England may fortify, but that we never shall. Sir, when you look at the whole history of that question you will see that England, with her far-seeing, sagacious policy, has attempted to circumscribe and restrict and restrain the free action of this government. When was it that Great Britain seized the possession of the terminus of this canal? Just six days after the signing of the treaty which secured to us California! The moment England saw, that by the pending negotiations with Mexico, California was to be acquired, she collected her fleets and made preparations for the seizure of the port of San Juan, in order that she might be gatekeeper on the public highway to our new possessions on the Pacific. Within six days from the time we signed the treaty, England seized by force and violence the very point now in controversy. Is not this fact indicative of her motives? Is it not clear that her object was to obstruct our passage to our new possessions? Hence I do not sympathize with that feeling which the senator expressed yesterday, that it was a pity to have a difference with a nation so friendly to us as England. Sir, I do not see the evidence of her friendship. It is not in the nature of things that she can be our friend. It is impossible she can love us. I do not blame her for not loving us. Sir, we have wounded her vanity and humbled her pride. She can never forgive us. But for us, she would be the first power on the face of the earth. But for us, she would have the prospect of maintaining that proud position which she held for so long a period. We are in her way. She is jealous of us, and jealousy forbids the idea of friendship. England does not love us; she cannot love us, and we do not love her either. We have some things in the past to remember that are not agreeable. She has more in the present to humiliate her that she cannot forgive.

I do not wish to administer to the feeling of jealousy and rivalry that exists between us and England. I wish to soften and allay it as much as possible; but why close our eyes to the fact that friendship is impossible while jealousy exists. Hence England seizes every island in the sea and rock upon our coast where she can plant a gun to intimidate us or to annoy our commerce. Her policy has been to seize every military and naval station the world over. Why does she pay such enormous sums to keep her post at Gibraltar, except to hold it *"in terrorem"* over the commerce of the Mediterranean? Why her enormous expense to maintain a garrison at the Cape of Good Hope, except to command the great passage on the way to the Indies? Why is she at the expense to keep her position on the little barren islands, Bermuda and the miserable Bahamas, and all the other islands along our coast, except as sentinels upon our actions? Does England hold Bermuda because of any profit it is to her? Has she any other motive for retaining it except jealousy which stimulates hostility to us? Is it not the case with all her possessions along our coast? Why, then, talk about the friendly bearing of England toward us when she is extending that policy every day? New treaties of friendship, seizure of islands, and erection of new colonies in violation of her treaties, seem to be the order of the day. In view of this state of things, I am in favor of meeting England as we meet a rival; meet her boldly, treat her justly and fairly, but make no humiliating concession even for the sake of peace. She has as much reason to make concessions to us as we have to make them to her. I would not willingly disturb the peace of the world; but, sir, the Bay Island colony must be discontinued. *It violates the treaty.*

Now, Mr. President, it is not my purpose to say another word upon our foreign relations. I have only occupied so much time as was necessary to put myself right in respect to the speech made by the senator from Delaware. He advocates one line of policy in regard to our foreign relations, and I have deemed it my duty to advocate another. It has been my object to put the two systems by the side of each other that the public might judge between us.

Mr. Mason having continued the debate on Monday, March 14th, Mr. Clayton occupied a portion of that and the succeeding days in a reply to Mr. Douglas—to which, on Wednesday, the 17th of March, Mr. Douglas responded:

Mr. PRESIDENT: I had a right to expect that the senator from Delaware, in his reply, would have ventured upon an argument against the positions which I had assumed in my former speech, and which he had assailed. It will be observed, upon a close examination, that he has evaded nearly every point in controversy between us, under the cover of free indulgence in coarse personalities. I do not complain of this. He had a right to choose his own course of discussion. Perhaps it was prudent in him to pursue the course which he adopted. I shall not follow his example, however. I may not have the same inducements that may have prompted him. If I had been driven from nearly every position I had assumed in debate—if nearly every material fact I had asserted had been negatived and disproved by official documents bearing my own signatures—if I had been convicted of giving one explanation of my conduct at one time, and at other times different and contradictory reasons, I might be prompted to seek refuge under personalities from the exposure that might be made. Sir, I pass that all by.

The senator, as a last resort, attempted to get up unkind feelings between my political friends and myself in regard to this debate. He endeavored to show that my speech was an assault upon every senator who took a different course. He went further, and charged that I, as a Presidential candidate, was pursuing this course in order to destroy and break down rivals in my own party. Sir, these insidious and disreputable assaults do not disturb my equanimity. The object is to enlist, from prejudice and unworthy motives, a sympathy in the course of discussion which he has attempted to maintain. But I appeal to the Senate if I assailed any senator upon this floor, either in regard to the Hise treaty or the Clayton and Bulwer treaty. I appeal to the Senate if I mentioned the name of any senator, or stated how any one man had voted. I did not disclose even how the vote stood. No citizen in America would have known the vote of any senator on this floor from my speech, or from my participation in the recent discussion; and I have yet to learn that a vindication of my own course involves an assault upon those who chose to differ with me. I have not understood the speeches of the senator from Michigan (Mr. Cass) and of the senator from Virginia (Mr. Mason) and of other senators, who have spoken on this question, in opposition to some of my views, as an attack on myself. It was their duty to vindicate their own course with the reasons which prompted them; and it was my right and my duty to give the reasons which induced and compelled me to pursue the course that I did.

I do not choose to occupy the time of the Senate in a matter that partakes so much of a personal character. But the senator cannot avail himself of that argument in vindication of his course in suppressing the Hise treaty. He is not supported by that array of names which he has produced for that act. No one of the senators ever did sustain him, so far as I know, in suppressing the Hise treaty. That treaty was never submitted to the Senate for ratification. The Senate were never permitted to examine it. The treaty, to this day, has been withheld from the Senate. You will have to go elsewhere than to the files of this body to find that treaty. How can it be said that senators have sustained him in his rejection of the Hise treaty, when he had deprived the Senate of an opportunity of showing whether they were for or against it? Sir, he cannot have the benefit of those names which he has quoted to shelter him upon that point.

Again, sir, he has quoted all the eminent names from General Jackson down to the present time, to support him in his refusal to accept of the exclusive control of the canal for his own country. Sir, he has no authority thus to quote them; he has no authority for saying that any one of those eminent statesmen were opposed to such a privilege as the Hise treaty showed that we could have acquired. It is true that when Central America granted a privilege to a company in the Netherlands to make this canal, the administration of General Jackson, under that state of facts, were content with asserting our right to an equal participation. It is also true that when a Frenchman had procured a charter for a railroad across the isthmus of Panama, and thus it had gone into the hands of foreigners, the administration of President Polk were content to assert our claim to an equal right. But it is not true that either of them ever refused to accept an exclusive privilege for this country when voluntarily tendered.

I am not going to occupy the attention of the Senate with an array of names for or against this proposition. I quoted no names in my first argument. I addressed myself to the merits of the question, and chose to decide it by arguments upon its merits, and not by the authority of great names. I would rather see the senator sustain his position now by arguments upon the merits of his own official action, and not by an appeal to the action of great men who lived at a different period, and whose acts were dependent upon entirely different circumstances.

One word more, and I proceed to the main point at issue. The senator has accused me of having attempted to make this a party question. How did I attempt it? In my speech of February last, to which he replied, he cannot find the term Whig or Democrat, or a political allusion, or a partisan argument. I explained my own principles of action as evinced in my votes; and I expressly stated that they were not sanctioned by either Whig or Democratic adminis trations upon some of the points. I did not invoke the aid of sympa thy of party. I was willing to stand upon the truth and the soundness of my own record, and leave the future to determine whether I was right or wrong on the question. Sir, partisan politics have been introduced by the senator, and not by me. The senator, in his speech in reply to me, endeavored to show that Democratic administrations had done this, and Democratic administrations had done that, and appealed to partisan authority, to sustain himself. I admit his right to introduce party questions, and to appeal to party names as author- ity. I have not done it, and I deny his right to charge it upon me. Sir, I invoked the aid of no partisan feeling or party organization for the support of the position I maintained. But when the senator showed that a majority of my own party, on the ratification of the Clayton and Bulwer treaty, had recorded their names in opposition to mine, he ought to have been content, without charging that I was making it a party question. It was not a very agreeable thing to me to be compelled to differ with three-fourths of the Senate, including a majority of my own political friends, and nothing but a sense of duty would have compelled me to take the responsibility of such a course.

Now, let us go back to the real point. Why all these attempts to avoid the main issue? In the first place the senator denied that he was responsible for not sending the Hise treaty to the Senate, inas- much as it had been rejected by Central America. Then, when I showed that the rejection of that treaty was procured by his own agent in obedience to his instructions, he denied the existence of the instructions. When I produced the instructions, and showed that the agent acted in obedience to what he believed to be their true meaning, the senator acknowledged his opposition to the treaty, and justified it upon the ground that it guaranteed the independence of Nicaragua. When I showed that he could not have objected to it on that ground, for the reason that at that very time he proposed a guaranty, in connection with Great Britain, of the independence of Nicaragua, he abandons that position, and is driven to the extremity of seeking refuge under what he chooses to consider obnoxious details. When I showed that his objections to the details could not avail him, because it was no reason for withholding the treaty according to the usages of the Senate, he then comes to the point that it was better to have a partnership privilege than an exclusive one. That brings us to the real question. Why could we not have come to it at once? If he was right in his preference for a European partnership over an exclusive privilege to his own country, why did he not avow the fact at once and justify his conduct, instead of wasting the time of the Senate in requiring me to prove facts which ought to have been confessed, and which have been proven by his own written testimony, in opposition to his own denial?

In his last speech the senator chose to persevere in representing me as the advocate of a canal to be made through Central America, with funds from the Treasury of the United States. I need not remind the senator that he had no authority, from anything I have said, to attribute to me such a purpose. I certainly did not assume any such position, while my remarks were calculated to negative such an idea. My position was this: that while negotiating for the right of way for a canal from the Atlantic to the Pacific, we should have accepted the offer to our own government of the exclusive right to control it, instead of a partnership with England and the other powers of the earth. The Hise treaty granted the privilege either to the United States or to an American company under our protection, at our option. I insisted that we had the same right to take it to ourselves that we had to take it jointly with other powers. It requires no further exertion of constitutional power to execute and maintain and regulate an exclusive privilege to America than it did to execute and maintain a partnership privilege with European powers. Hence his objections upon that score must fall to the ground. The simple question was, whether it would have been wise to accept that privilege. Sir, I think it would have been. I am not going to repeat the argument I made the other day upon that point. If it had been given to us, we could have opened the canal to the world upon such terms as we deemed proper. We could have withdrawn the use of it whenever a nation failed to respect our rights. It would have been a bond of peace instead of being an apple of discord between us and other nations; because when you bring all the great Powers of the earth into partnership, constant disputes will arise as to the nature and extent of the rights of the respective parties. The history of these negotiations proves this fact.

But, sir, let me ask the senator what he has gained by his rejection of the Hise treaty? He has given the world to understand by his speeches that he has accomplished two great objects: the one to open a canal between the Atlantic and the Pacific oceans—the other to put a stop to British encroachments in Central America. Has he accomplished either of those objects? I ask what privilege he has gained to make a canal? He has not even secured the right of way for a canal, either jointly or separately. He is responsible for having defeated the project of a canal between the two oceans. He refused the grant of the right of way, because it gave the right to control the work exclusively to his own country. The treaty which he caused to be made, failed to receive the sanction of the Senate. Thus we are left without any right of way—without any charter, right, or privilege. Instead of accomplishing that object, he is responsible for its defeat. All that he has to boast of is, that he deprived his own country of an inestimable privilege, the necessity and importance of which are now conceded on all hands.

What, then, have we gained by his diplomacy? Why, sir, after having failed in getting the privilege of making the canal, either jointly or separately, he makes a treaty with Great Britain by which, if we hereafter secure it, the privilege is given to Great Britain as well as to ourselves. The Clayton and Bulwer treaty provides that any right of way or communication which may be secured at any future time, shall be open alike to England and the United States, and under the joint control and protection of the two powers. We have a treaty with England about a canal in Central America, but we have none with any of the Central American States. Let me ask, then, how much have we gained? Has he expelled the British from Central America by his treaty? What inch of country have they given up. What right have they abandoned? What functionary have they withdrawn? Where is the evidence that you have driven the British from Central America? Are they not still in the full enjoyment of their protectorate upon the Mosquito coast? Have you driven them from the Balize?

The senator from Michigan (Mr. Cass), and the chairman of the Committee on Foreign Relations (Mr. Mason), in their speeches, have maintained that the Clayton and Bulwer treaty would fairly include the Balize as a part of Central America. But the senator from Delaware, while acting as the secretary of state, gave a construction to that treaty which excludes the Balize. The senator, therefore, is estopped from saying that he has expelled the British from the Balize. The fact shows that he has not driven the British protectorate from the coast. We find that instead of leaving Central America, the British have not only established a colony at the Bay Islands, but, if the newspaper information received by the last steamers can be credited, they have bombarded the towns upon the main land, and taken forcible possession of a part of the state of Honduras. Then I repeat the question to the senator, what has he gained? I can tell him what has resulted from his negotiation. He has recognized the right of Great Britain and all European powers to interfere with the affairs of the American states. He has recognized that right by a treaty; and he has guaranteed to England that we will use our good offices to enable them to enter into arrangements with these Central American states. He has excluded the idea that the question of the Central American states is an American question, and by his negotiation has opened it as a European question. In other words, he has, by his treaty, abolished what is known as the Monroe doctrine, with reference to a large portion of the American continent.

This brings me to the examination of another question. The senator from Delaware chose to arraign me upon that portion of my speech, in which I stated that I was unwilling to give a pledge never to annex any more territory to the United States. He then went on to argue against annexation, said we were pledged, and that the pledge given was correct, and attempted to vindicate it. He arraigned me for having said that such a treaty could not be enforced through all time to come. I explained to him that my idea was that the growth of this country was so great and so rapid that the barriers of any treaty would be irresistibly broken through by natural causes, over which we had no control; and hence that the treaty ought not to have been made. He told me that the explanation made it worse, and that he would show that the doctrine involved moral turpitude: that he was amazed and grieved that any one here from this high place should proclaim such a sentiment.

Sir, I will proceed to show my authority on that point, which I think he will be compelled to respect. In taking that position, I only reiterated the opinions expressed by the late secretary of state, and now senator from Massachusetts (Mr. Everett), in his letter to the Comte de Sartiges, a few months ago, in respect to the island of Cuba; and when the senator from Delaware arraigns me for uttering sentiments involving a want of respect for treaty stipulations, I will turn him over to the senator from Massachusetts and to ex-President Fillmore, and allow them to settle that issue between themselves. I wish to call the attention of the senator to the letter of Mr. Everett to the Comte de Sartiges. In that letter you find the following passage in regard to a proposed convention stipulating that we would never annex Cuba;

"The convention would be of no value unless it were lasting; accordingly its terms express a perpetuity of purpose and obligation. Now, it may well be doubted whether the Constitution of the United States would allow the treaty-making power to impose a permanent disability on the American government for all coming time, and prevent it, under any future change of circumstances, from doing what has been so often done in times past. In 1803 the United States purchased Louisiana of France, and in 1819 they purchased Florida of Spain. It is not within the competence of the treaty-making power in 1852 effectually to bind the government in all its branches; and for all coming time not to make a similar purchase of Cuba."

The senator from Delaware will see that the late secretary of state, Mr. Everett, by the direction of President Fillmore, has pronounced such a guaranty to be a violation of the Constitution of the United States, and the exercise of an authority not conferred by that instrument. Sir, if the Constitution gave no authority to make a pledge by this government that we will never annex Cuba, I suppose it does not authorize a pledge never to annex Central America. The constitutional objection applies to the Clayton and Bulwer treaty, in relation to Central America, with the same force that it did to. the proposed convention in respect to Cuba. They take higher ground than I did. I was not willing to do that which would involve a breach of faith in the progress of events. But I did not go so far as to deny the constitutional power to make such a treaty. And, therefore, I ask the senator why he did not arraign President Fillmore—

why he did not arraign the late secretary of state, Mr. Everett, for uttering those monstrous sentiments, instead of hurling his anathemas upon my head, as if I had been the only man in America who ever ventured to proclaim such opinions? According to the opinions of President Fillmore, and his secretary of state, as promulgated in Mr. Everett's celebrated letter, and applauded by the almost unanimous voice of the American people, the Clayton and Bulwer treaty was a palpable violation of the Constitution of the United States. But Mr. Fillmore and Mr. Everett were not content with denying the power of this government, under the Constitution, to enter into this treaty stipulation. They deny its propriety, its justice, its wisdom, as well as the right to make it. I will read a passage upon this point:

" There is another strong objection to the proposed agreement. Among the oldest traditions of the Federal Government is an aversion to political alliances with European powers. In his memorable Farewell Address, President Washington says : ' The great rule of conduct for us in regard to foreign nations is, in extending our commercial relations to have with them as little political connection as possible. So far as we have already formed engagements, let them be fulfilled with perfect good faith. Here let us stop.' President Jefferson, in his inaugural address, in 1801, warned the country against entangling alliances. This expression, now become proverbial, was unquestionably used by Mr. Jefferson in reference to the alliance with France of 1778, an alliance at the time of incalculable benefit to the United States. but which in less than twenty years came near involving us in the wars of the French Revolution, and laid the foundation of heavy claims upon Congress not extinguished to the present day. It is a significant coincidence that the particular provision of the alliance which occasioned these evils was that under which France called upon us to aid her in defending her West Indian possessions against England. Nothing less than the unbounded influence of Washington rescued the Union from the perils of that crisis and preserved our neutrality."

As the senator from Delaware is fond of the authority of great names, I not only furnish him with the name of the late secretary of state, and that of the late President of the United States, upon the points to which I have referred, but I have the authority of these gentlemen for saying that his doctrine with regard to Central America is in violation of the solemn warnings of the Father of his Country, and in derogation of the protests of Mr. Jefferson, repeated over and over again during his eventful life. I find that the late secretary of state has again, in another passage, summed up the objections which I entertained to the Clayton and Bulwer treaty, and I will call the attention of the Senate to it. It is this:

" But the President has a graver objection to entering into the proposed convention. He has no wish to disguise the feeling, that the compact, although equal in its terms. would be very unequal in substance   France and England, by entering into it, would disable themselves from obtaining possession of an island remote from their seats of government, belonging to another European power, whose natural right to possess it must always be as good as their own —a distant island, in another hemisphere, and one which by no ordinary or peaceful course of things could ever belong to either of them. If the present balance of power in Europe should be broken up; if Spain should become un-able to maintain the island in her possession, and France and England should be engaged in a death-struggle with each other, Cuba might then be the prize of the victor. Till these events all take place, the President does not see how Cuba can belong to any European power but Spain. The United States, on the other hand, would, by the proposed convention, disable themselves from making an acquisition which might take place without any disturbance of ex-isting foreign relations, and in the natural order of things."

If the prosposed guaranty never to annex Cuba was not reciprocal as between the United States and England, how is it that it can be said that a similar guaranty respecting Central America was reci-procal? Every argument urged by the late secretary of state against reciprocity in one, applies with equal force to the other. It may be said that Cuba stands at the entrance of the Gulf of Mexico; but it can be said with equal truth that Central America is upon the public highway to our Pacific possessions. Both stand as gates to this pub-lic highway, and every argument urged in relation to the one is equally applicable to the other.

Now I have to quote the late secretary of state and President Fillmore against the senator from Delaware on another point. When I remarked that the history of this country showed that our growth and expansion could not be resisted, and would inevitably break through whatever barriers might be erected by the present genera-tion to restrain our future progress, the senator from Delaware as-sumed the right to rebuke me for uttering sentiments implying per-fidy and moral turpitude. He desired to know if sentiments of that kind were to be tolerated in the American Senate? Let him hear his friend from Massachusetts on that point, in the same docu-ment:

"That a convention such as is proposed would be a transitory arrangement, sure to be swept away by the irresistible tide of affairs in a new country, is, to the apprehension of the President, too obvious to require a labored argument. The project rests on principles applicable, if at all, to Europe, where interna-tional relations are in their basis of great antiquity, slowly modified for the most part in the progress of time and events; and not applicable to America, which, but lately a waste, is filling up with intense rapidity, and adjusting, on natural principles, those territorial relations which on the first discovery of the continent were in a good degree fortuitous." . . . .
"But whatever may be thought of these last suggestions, it would seem im-possible for any one who reflects upon the events glanced at in this note to mistake the law of American growth and progress, or think it can ultimately arrested by a convention like that proposed. In the judgment of the Presi-dent, it would be as easy to throw a dam from Cape Florida to Cuba, in the hope of stopping the flow of the Gulf Stream, as to attempt, by a compact like this, to fix the fortunes of Cuba, now and for hereafter, or, as expressed in the French text of the convention, 'pour le présent comme pour l'avenir,' that is for all coming time."

There the senator is told that such a stipulation might be applica-ble to European politics, but would be unsuited and unfitted to Ame-rican affairs; that he has mistaken entirely the system of policy,

which should be applied to our own country, that he has predicated
his action upon those old, antiquated notions which belong to the
stationary and retrograde movements of the Old World, and find no
sympathy in the youthful, uprising aspirations of the American heart.
I indorse fully the sentiment. I insist that there is a difference, a
wide difference, between the system of policy which should be pursued
in America and that which would be applicable to Europe. Europe
is antiquated, decrepit, tottering on the verge of dissolution. When
you visit her, the objects which enlist your highest admiration are
the relics of past greatness; the broken columns erected to departed
power. It is one vast graveyard, where you find here a tomb indicating the burial of the arts; there a monument marking the spot
where liberty expired; another to the memory of a great man,
whose place has never been filled. The choicest products of her
classic soil consists in relics, which remain as sad memorials of departed glory and fallen greatness! They bring up the memories of
the dead, but inspire no hope for the living! Here everything is
fresh, blooming, expanding, and advancing. We wish a wise, practical policy adapted to our condition and position. Sir, the statesman who would shape the policy of America by European models,
has failed to perceive the antagonism which exists in the relative
position, history, institutions—in everything pertaining to the Old
and the New World.

The senator from Delaware seems always to have had his back
turned upon his own country, and his eye intently fixed upon Europe
as the polar star of all his observations. If it would not be deemed
an indelicate interposition between the senator from Delaware and
his friend from Massachusetts (Mr. Everett), I should be inclined to
say that the criticism of the late secretary of state, although not intended for the senator from Delaware, is strictly applicable to his
diplomacy, and fully deserved. I shall not go into the discussion of
that question, however. I deny the right of the senator from Delaware to come back at me on that point. I shall certainly turn him
over to his friend from Massachusetts (Mr. Everett), because he will
not dare to accuse him of political prejudices and partisan feelings.
He has said severer things of the senator's diplomacy than I thought
the rules of the Senate would authorize me to indulge in. The ex-
President of the United States has sanctioned them, and now I think
I am at liberty to refer to them, for if it were not within the rules of
courtesy and diplomacy, they would not be sent here. But, sir, I
may be permitted to add that the nation has sanctioned them too;
for I am not aware that a State paper was ever issued in America
that received a heartier response in most of its principles, than the
letter of the late secretary of state to the Comte de Sartiges, to
which I have referred. Sir, if he had done nothing else to render
his administration of the State Department illustrious, his name
would live in all coming time in that diplomatic letter, as one who
could appreciate the spirit of the age, and perceive the destiny of the
nation. No document has ever received such a universal sanction

of the American people as the one to which I have referred, condemning and repudiating the diplomacy of the senator from Delaware in relation to the American continent.

Mr. President, I have not much more to add. The senator has arraigned me also for having attempted to arouse unkind feelings between the United States and England. I deny that the arraignment is just.

I have attempted no such thing. I have never attempted to foster jealousies or unkind feelings between our own country and any other. I have attempted to plant our relations on amicable terms, by speaking the truth plainly as we and they know it to exist. The remarks that I have made about friendly relations between the two countries, were drawn out by his statement that England was known to be so "friendly" to us. I said to him I did not think the friendly relations of England constituted any claim upon our gratitude. I have seen no evidence of that friendship. I said frankly I did not think that England loved us, and it was useless for us to pretend that we loved her. The history of the two countries proves it. The daily action of the two countries proves it. England is spending her millions to maintain her fortifications all along our coast; at the Bermudas, the Bahamas, and at Jamaica, and on every rock and barren waste along the American coast. What does she keep them up for? Does she make money out of them? Why, you all know that they are a source of unbounded expenditure to her. Does it extend her commerce? Does it employ her shipping? Not at all. Why does she keep them? In order to point her guns at America.

Well, if she is so friendly to us, and we are so friendly to her, what necessity is there for pointing her cannon all the time at us? And if these are evidences of friendship, why do we not reciprocate it by sending over a few cannon and planting them on every little island and rock near her coast? If we were to seize upon every military and naval position, and expend millions in keeping up fortifications all along her coast, would that be any evidence of friendly feeling on our part toward England? I do not see it.

Again: the moment it was discovered that we were to acquire California as a consequence of the Mexican war, England sent her armed ships and seized possession of the town of San Juan, and I have the authority of the senator from Delaware for saying there is reason to believe that the act was done out of hostility to the American government. Why did she want the town of San Juan? Simply for the reason that by the Mexican treaty our possessions had been enlarged upon the Pacific coast, and it evidently became necessary, in order to preserve this Union and maintain our commerce, that we should have the line of intercommunication between the two oceans so as to connect the Atlantic and Pacific States together; and therefore, in order to cut off our right of way, in order to establish a toll gate upon our public highway, she seized possession of that point as the one from which she could annoy us most.

The senator will not pretend that he believes that act originated in friendly feelings toward us on the part of England. I have his authority in his public documents for saying that he believes it originated in motives of jealousy and hostility. The object was, not to advance her own interest, not to increase her own commerce, not to extend her own power, but to restrain, fetter, and cripple our energies and our power. Are these acts evidence of friendship on her part toward us, and are we so constituted that we feel grateful for them? Sir, let us not play the hypocrite upon this subject. Let us speak out the naked truth, plainly and boldly. We feel that this seizure of every rock and island upon our coast, and converting them into garrisoned fortresses, with guns to bear on American commerce and American interests, are no evidence of friendship. We feel that these attempts to surround and fetter us, and hem us in, are evidences of hostility, which it is our duty plainly to see and boldly to resist. Sir, the way to establish friendly relations with England is, to let her know that we are not so stupid as not to understand her policy, nor so pusillanimous as to submit to her aggressions. The moment she understands that we mean what we say, and will carry out any principle we profess, she will be very careful not to create any point of difference between us. It is want of candor and frankness that keeps the two nations in conflict with each other. I say, that as long as this policy of hemming us in, and fettering us, and trying to restrain our growth and curtail our power continues, we cannot feel friendly and kindly toward her; and so long as she persists in that policy, we ought not to believe that she feels kindly toward us. If we tell her so, she will do one of two things; either abandon her aggressive course, or avow her hostility; and of all things let us know whether she is our friend or our enemy. Therefore, I will repeat very frankly, that it is useless to endeavor to conceal the fact that there are jealousies between us and England growing out of rival interests, and that her policy has for its aim to restrain our power rather than increasing her own. Our policy is, to enhance our own power and greatness, without attempting to restrain hers. Ours is generous, honorable, and justifiable; hers is illiberal, unkind, unjust, and we ought to tell her so.

I believe, Mr. President, I have said all I have to say upon this question. My object has been simply to reply to the points raised by the senator in his speech. I do not wish to travel over the ground again. There are many other points in the discussion into which I could have gone. There are many other positions that the documents which have been lately published would furnish me ample material for prolonging the discussion, but I do not wish to occupy the time of the Senate. I only wish to show that the real points at issue are: first, that the senator preferred a partnership with England to an exclusive privilege to his own country for the great interoceanic canal. Secondly, that he believes in the policy of pledging this country never to annex any more territory in all time to come. I repudiate that policy. These are the main points between us, and the last point, in the course of the discussion, seems to have become the material one. He is opposed to all further annexation, and wishes to make treaties now to restrain us in all time to come from extending our possessions.

I do not wish to annex any more territory now. But I avow freely that I foresee the day when you will be compelled to do it, and cannot help it, and when treaties cannot prevent the consummation of the act. Hence my policy would be to hold the control of our own action, give no pledges upon the subject, but bide our time, and be at liberty to do whatever our interest, our honor, and duty may require when the time for action may come. An old, decrepit nation, tottering and ready to fall to pieces, may well seek for pledges and guaranties from a youthful, vigorous, growing power, to protect her old age. But a young nation, with all her freshness, vigor, and youth, desires no limits fixed to her greatness, no boundaries to her future growth. She desires to be left free to exercise her own powers, exert her own energies, according to her own sense of duty in all coming time. This, sir, is the main issue between us, and I am ready to submit it to the Senate and to the country.

[Senator Butler, in continuation of the debate on the same day, having assailed some of the positions maintained by Senator Douglas, and pronounced a eulogy upon England and her literature, Senator Douglas replied:]

Mr. President: In reply to the senator from South Carolina, I wish to state to him, without going into the controversy as to which is the right policy for the President when a treaty contains objects desirable and details obnoxious, that he will find an example in point in the case of the Mexican treaty containing provisions which the President and Senate both regarded as unconstitutional, yet the President sent the treaty here, and pointed out the obnoxious parts. The senator and those acting with him modified it, perfected it, voted for it, and ratified it in opposition to my vote, and it became the law of the land. It is a case precisely in point, and I merely mention it, and leave that part of the question.

Mr. Butler.—I think the Mexican treaty was sent as an entirety. We amended it no doubt, but it was sent as an entirety by President Polk, saying that Mr. Trist had usurped power which he did not possess. It was exactly one of those instances in which the treaty had been made, and he asked the Senate to adopt it, but he sent it in as an entire thing.

Mr. Douglas.—The President sent it in, stating that there were certain provisions in it which must be striken out before it could be sanctioned by him. But now to another point: The gentleman commented upon a remark that I had made, and which also was contained in the letter of the late secretary of state (Mr. Everett), and seems to suppose that we were advocating the doctrine of not observing the faith of treaties. That did not put us before the country in the true position which we have assumed. My position is this.

that we should never make a treaty which we cannot carry into full execution; that good faith requires us not to make a treaty unless we intend to execute it, nor make one which we probably cannot be able to execute. My argument, therefore, was an argument against the making of treaties improperly upon points that were unnecessary, and which could not be carried into effect, and not in favor of violating any treaties that had been made. It was an argument in favor of the sanctity of treaties; and those who make treaties profusely and recklessly, binding us for all time to come without reference to the ability in future to execute them, are the ones who ought to be arraigned, if anybody should be, for not being faithful to treaty stipulations. I wish, therefore, to make this explanation, in order that no misapprehension as to the position which I have assumed may be entertained in any quarter.

The senator referred to a remark of mine in regard to the decay and decline of European powers, and made it the excuse for a eulogium upon England as the source from which we have derived everything that is valuable in science and art; in literature, law, and politics.

When I am reminded of the greatness of England, as connected with her statesmen and orators, and the illustrious names of Hampden and Sydney are pointed to as examples, I cannot fail to remember—I can never forget—that the same England which gave them birth, and should have felt a mother's pride and love in their virtues and services, persecuted her noble sons to the dungeon and the scaffold, and attempted to brand their names with infamy in all coming time, for the very causes which have endeared them to us and filled the republican world with their fame! Nor am I unmindful of the debt of gratitude which the present generation owes to the brilliant galaxy of great names whose fortune it was to have been born and to have suffered in England, and whose labors and researches in political, legal, and physical science—in literature, poetry, and art, have added so much lustre on their native land. Some pursued their labors under the protection and patronage of the English government—others in defiance of her tyranny and vengeance. I award all credit and praise to the authors of all the blessings and advantages we have inherited from that source.

I cannot go as far as the senator from South Carolina. I cannot recognize England as our mother. If so, she is and ever has been a cruel and unnatural mother. I do not find the evidence of her affection in her watchfulness over our infancy, nor in her joy and pride at our ever-blooming prosperity and swelling power, since we assumed an independent position.

The proposition is not historically true. Our ancestry were not all of English origin. They were of Scotch, Irish, German, French, and of Norman descent as well as English. In short, we inherit from every branch of the Caucasian race. It has been our aim and policy to profit by their example—to reject their errors and follies—and to retain, imitate, cultivate, perpetuate all that was valuable and desirable. So far as any portion of the credit may be due to England and Englishmen—and much of it is—let it be freely awarded and recorded in her ancient archives, which seem to have been long since forgotten by her, and the memory of which her present policy toward us is not well calculated to revive. But, that the senator from South Carolina, in view of our present position and of his location in this Confederacy, should indulge in glowing and eloquent eulogiums of England for the blessings and benefits she has conferred and is still lavishing upon us, and urge these considerations in palliation of the wrongs she is daily perpetrating, is to me amazing. He speaks in terms of delight and gratitude of the copious and refreshing streams which English literature and science are pouring into our country and diffusing throughout the land. Is he not aware that nearly every English book circulated and read in this country contains lurking and insidious slanders and libels upon the character of our people and the institutions and policy of our government? Does he not know that abolitionism, which has so seriously threatened the peace and safety of this republic, had its origin in England, and has been incorporated into the policy of that government for the purpose of operating upon the peculiar institutions of some of the States of this confederacy, and thus render the Union itself insecure? Does she not keep her missionaries perambulating this country, delivering lectures and scattering broadcast incendiary publications, designed to incite prejudices, hate, and strife between the different sections of this Union? I had supposed that South Carolina and the other slaveholding States of this confederacy had been sufficiently refreshed and enlightened by a certain species of English literature, designed to stir up treason and insurrection around his own fireside, to have excused the senator from offering up praises and hosannas to our English mother! (Applause in the galleries.) Is not the heart, intellect, and press of England this moment employed in flooding America with this species of "English literature?" Even the wives and daughters of the nobility and the high officers of government have had the presumption to address the women of America, and in the name of philanthropy appeal to them to engage in the treasonable plot against the institutions and government of their own choice in their native land, while millions are being expended to distribute "Uncle Tom's Cabin" throughout the world, with the view of combining the fanaticism, ignorance, and hatred of all the nations of the earth in a common crusade against the peculiar institutions of the State and section of this Union represented by the senator from South Carolina; and he unwittingly encourages it, by giving vent to his rapturous joy over these copious and refreshing streams with which England is irrigating the American intellect. (Renewed applause in the galleries.)

THE PRESIDING OFFICER (MR. RUSK in the chair).—There must be order in the galleries. If there is not, they will be ordered to be cleared.

Mr. Adams.—I desire to ask that the galleries may be cleared if such an outrage occurs again.

Mr. Douglas.—I hope it will be done. It is manifestly improper to have such proceedings in the galleries.

The Presiding Officer.—It certainly will be done, if the same thing occurs again.

Mr. Butler.—I have but one word to say in reply to the senator from Illinois. When I spoke of our gratitude to England, I did not allude to the sentimental kind of literature to which the senator refers. I thought I indicated the authors of the literature to which I referred; and I do not thank the senator for going out of his way, and indicating impure streams, as if they had a connection with my remark, for there are impure streams flowing from other sources besides Great Britain; and there are impure examples in other parts of the world besides Great Britain. When I spoke of it, I spoke in emphatic terms of those writers who have poured upon us what the senator himself will not deny to be refreshing streams; what I hope he will regard as refreshing to him, and to the intelligence of the age. I named authors. Will he dissent from Burke? Will he dissent from Chatham? Will he dissent from Shakspeare? Will he dissent from the literature, and the eloquence, and the example, and the tone of feeling of Hampden and Sidney? Sir, when I spoke in the spirit of a man judging the literature of England, I did not expect to be diverted by this miserable allusion to "Uncle Tom's Cabin." (Laughter.) That may do for an *ad captandum*, but it is not a manly mode of meeting what I said in relation to the literature of England.

Mr. Douglas.—I spoke in terms of reverence and respect of the monuments and tombstones which were found in England, to the great men, to their patriotism, to their legal learning and science and poetry, and all that was great and noble and admirable. I spoke of them with respect as a matter of the past; but, sir, I do not think it was a legitimate argument to go back two or three centuries past to justify English aggressions in the present upon this continent; and when I heard the laudations and eulogiums upon past English history in palliation of present English enormity, with commendations upon the refreshing streams which she is now pouring into this country to enlighten our people, I thought it was right and proper to remind the senator himself of some of the present conduct of England, which should be borne in mind when he pronounced eulogies upon her conduct. I am talking of the present and its bearing upon the future. It is that to which I am directing my remarks, and not to the past.

Mr. Butler.—I should like to know how England is to be responsible for "Uncle Tom's Cabin." Is England the indorser of it? I have alluded to the masterly intellects of England, and not to the spurious, miserable, sickly sentimentality of the day. If such literature as that to which he alludes is to be taken as a standard, England is not the only place in which it is found. She is no more responsible for that miserable cant in relation to this subject than others. But with regard to England, in all our commercial relations, in all our connection with her as a civilized nation, I presume the honorable senator would not be disposed to postpone her to any other any other nation.

Mr. Douglas.—I would neither postpone nor give her the preference. I have no eulogium to make upon her. I will treat her as our duty as a nation requires.

Mr. Butler.—I have pronounced no other eulogium than history yields to her literature, commerce and civilization, and we are bound to maintain our relations with England if we intend to be a civilized nation ourselves. I made no allusion to the kind of literature which the senator has brought in debate. We can find this miserable sentimentality anywhere, and there are many other things which the senator might as well have brought in, which would have been as pertinent to the debate. He had better get up a discussion of the Maine liquor law. (Laughter.) I do not see why he could not. It has about as much connection with the question as the other.

Mr. Douglas.—I have introduced into this discussion none of these extraneous topics. I have contented myself with replying when others have brought them forward and thrust them upon me. My object has been to confine the debate to the points at issue between the senator from Delaware and myself, and I have not departed from that line except when compelled to do so by the remarks of others.

The discussion having been continued on subsequent days by Mr. Clayton and Mr. Everett, Mr. Douglas closed the debate with the following remarks :

Mr. President : I do not intend to prolong the discussion ; but I think it due to myself and the occasion to make a word of comment upon one remark which fell from the eminent senator from Massachusetts. I understood him to concur in the opinion expressed by the senator from Delaware, that his letter in relation to Cuba, which proclaimed the principle that no pledge was to be made by this government in regard to the future condition of that island, was not applicable to the Central American states. I cannot consent, even for the sake of harmonizing the political relations of those two senators, to be placed in a false position. I am not willing, even by their concurrence, to be put in a position of having made a misapplication of that letter. The main point to which I referred in the letter of Mr. Everett to the Comte de Sartiges was the denial of any constitutional power in this government to make the pledge, that in all coming time we would not acquire any territory which, in the course of events, might become desirable and necessary. If it was not competent under the Constitution to make such a stipulation in reference to the island of Cuba, where does he find the constitutional authority to make it in the Clayton and Bulwer treaty in respect to Central America? If there be a want of constitutional power in the one case, does not the same absence of authority exist in the other, and should it not be equally binding upon the consciences of men in all cases? Therefore, until they remove that constitutional barrier, I cannot permit those two senators to place themselves upon a common platform, and accuse me of having made a misapplication of the letter to the French minister. The senator from Delaware has asserted the existence of the power, and exercised it in the Clayton and Bulwer treaty, while the senator from Massachusetts has denied its existence in the official dispatch to which I have referred. That is all I desired to say on that point.

So far as the senator's remarks relate to the preservation of peace, I fully and cordially agree with him. If there is any one line of policy more dear to my heart than all others, it is that which shall avoid any just cause of war, and preserve peace in all time to come. If there be a difference of opinion between us, it is upon the point as to which line of policy will best accomplish that object. I believe that the true policy is to make no pledges at present which are to bind our successors in all time to come with reference to a state of facts which now does not exist, but then may require action. I have not said that I wish to annex any portion of Central America to this country. I only protest against the pledge that our successors shall not do that which their interest, duty and honor may require when the time for action comes. With these remarks, I am willing to close the discussion.

ON THE NEBRASKA TERRITORY.

Delivered in the Senate, January 30, 1854.

The Senate, as in Committee of the Whole, proceeded to the consideration of the bill to organize the Territory of Nebraska.

MR. DOUGLAS.—Mr. President, when I proposed, on Tuesday last, that the Senate should proceed to the consideration of the bill to organize the Territories of Nebraska and Kansas, it was my purpose only to occupy ten or fifteen minutes in explanation of its provisions. I desired to refer to two points ; first to those provisions relating to the Indians, and second to those which might be supposed to bear upon the question of slavery.

The committee, in drafting the bill, had in view the great anxiety which had been expressed by some members of the Senate to protect the rights of the Indians, and to prevent infringements upon them. By the provisions of the bill, I think we had so clearly succeeded, in that respect, as to obviate all possible objection upon that score. The bill itself provides that it shall not operate upon any of the rights or lands of the Indians, nor shall they be included within the limits of those Territories, until they shall, by treaty with the United States, expressly consent to come under the operations of the act, and be incorporated within the limits of the Territories. This provision certainly is broad enough, clear enough, explicit enough, to protect all the rights of the Indians as to their persons and their property.

Upon the other point, that pertaining to the question of slavery in the Territories, it was the intention of the committee to be equally explicit. We took the principles established by the Compromise acts of 1850 as our guide, and intended to make each and every provision of the bill accord with those principles. Those measures established and rest upon the principles of self-government, that the people should be allowed to decide the question of their domestic institutions for themselves, subject only to such limitations and restrictions as are imposed by the Constitution of the United States, instead of having them determined by an arbitrary or geographical line.

The original bill, reported by the committee as a substitute for the bill introduced by the senator from Iowa (Mr. Dogde), was believed to have accomplished this object. The amendment which was subsequently reported by us was only designed to render that clear and specific, which seemed, in the minds of some, to admit of doubt and misconstruction. In some parts of the country the original substitute was deemed and construed to be an annulment or a repeal of what has been known as the Missouri Compromise, while in other parts it was otherwise construed. As the object of the committee was to conform to the principles established by the Compromise measures of 1850, and to carry those principles into effect in the

Territories, we thought it was better to recite in the bill precisely what we understood to have been accomplished by those measures, viz., that the Missouri Compromise, having been superseded by the legislation of 1850, has become and ought to be declared inoperative ; and hence we propose to leave the question to the people of the States and the Territories, subject only to the limitations and provisions of the Constitution.

Sir, this is all that I intended to say, if the question had been taken up for consideration on Tuesday last; but since that time occurrences have transpired which compel me to go more fully into the discussion. It will be borne in mind that the senator from Ohio (Mr. Chase) then objected to the consideration of the bill, and asked for its postponement until this day, on the ground that there had not been time to understand and consider its provisions ; and the senator from Massachusetts (Mr. Sumner) suggested that the postponement should be for one week for that purpose. These suggestions seeming to be reasonable, in the opinions of senators around me, I yielded to their request, and consented to the postponement of the bill until this day.

Sir, little did I suppose, at the time that I granted that act of courtesy to those two senators, that they had drafted and published to the world a document, over their own signatures, in which they arraigned me as having been guilty of a criminal betrayal of my trust, as having been guilty of an act of bad faith and been engaged in an atrocious plot against the cause of free government. Little did I suppose that these two senators had been guilty of such conduct when they called upon me to grant that courtesy, to give them an opportunity of investigating the substitute reported by the committee. I have since discovered that on that very morning the "National Era," the abolition organ in this city, contained an address, signed by certain abolition confederates, to the people, in which the bill is grossly misrepresented, in which the action of the committee is grossly perverted, in which our motives are arraigned and our characters calumniated. And, sir, what is more, I find that there was a postscript added to the address, published that very morning, in which the principal amendment reported by the committee was set out, and then coarse epithets applied to me by name. Sir, had I known those facts at the time that I granted that act of indulgence, I should have responded to the request of those senators in such terms as their conduct deserved, so far as the rules of the Senate and a respect for my own character would have permitted me to do. In order to show the character of this document, of which I shall have much to say in the course of my argument, I will read certain passages:

" We arraign this bill as a gross violation of a sacred pledge; as a criminal betrayal of precious rights ; as part and parcel of an atrocious plot to exclude from a vast unoccupied region emigrants from the Old World, and free laborers from our own States, and convert it into a dreary region of despotism, inhabited by masters and slaves."

A Senator.—By whom is the address signed?

Mr. Douglas.—It is signed " S. P. Chase, senator from Ohio; Charles Sumner, senator from Massschusetts; J. R. Giddings and Edward Wade, representatives from Ohio; Gerrit Smith, representative from New York; Alexander De Witt, representative from Massachusetts;" including, as I understand, all the abolition party in Congress.

Then, speaking of the Committee on Territories, these confederates use this language :

" The *pretences*, therefore, that the Territory, covered by the positive prohibition of 1820, sustains a similar relation to slavery with that acquired from Mexico, covered by no prohibition except that of disputed constitutional or Mexican law, and that the compromises of 1850 require the incorporation of the pro-slavery clauses of the Utah and New Mexico Bill in the Nebraska Act, are mere *inventions, designed to cover up from public reprehension meditated bad faith.*"

"Mere inventions to cover up bad faith." Again:

" Servile demagogues may tell you that the Union can be maintained only by submitting to the demands of slavery."

Then there is a postscript added, equally offensive to myself, in which I am mentioned by name. The address goes on to make an appeal to the legislatures of the different States, to public meetings, and to ministers of the Gospel in their pulpits, to interpose and arrest the vile proceeding which is about to be consummated by the senators who are thus denounced. That address, sir, bears date Sunday, January 22, 1854. Thus it appears that, on the holy Sabbath, while other senators were engaged in divine worship, these abolition confederates were assembled in secret conclave, plotting by what means they should deceive the people of the United States, and prostrate the character of brother senators. This was done on the Sabbath day, and by a set of politicians, to advance their own political and ambitious purposes, in the name of our holy religion.

But this is not all. It was understood from newspapers that resolutions were pending before the legislature of Ohio proposing to express their opinions upon this subject. It was necessary for these confederates to get up some exposition of the question by which they might facilitate the passage of the resolutions through that legislature. Hence you find that, on the same morning that this document appears over the names of these confederates in the abolition organ of this city, the same document appears in the New York papers— certainly in the " Tribune," " Times " and " Evening Post "—in which it is stated, by authority, that it is " signed by the senators and a majority of the representatives from the State of Ohio "—a statement which I have every reason to believe was utterly false, and known to be so at the time that these confederates appended it to the address. It was necessary, in order to carry out this work of deception, and to hasten the action of the Ohio legislature, under a misapprehension of the real facts, to state that it was signed, not only by the abolition confederates, but by the whole Whig representation, and a portion of the Democratic representation in the other house from the State of Ohio.

MR. CHASE.—Mr. President——

MR. DOUGLAS.—Mr. President, I do not yield the floor. A senator who has violated all the rules of courtesy and propriety, who showed a consciousness of the character of the act he was doing by concealing from me all knowledge of the fact—who came to me with a smiling face, and the appearance of friendship, even after that document had been uttered—who could get up in the Senate and appeal to my courtesy in order to get time to give the document a wider circulation before its infamy could be exposed; such a senator has no right to my courtesy upon this floor.

MR. CHASE.—Mr. President, the senator mistates the facts——

MR. DOUGLAS.—Mr. President, I decline to yield the floor.

MR. CHASE.—And I shall make my denial pertinent when the time comes.

THE PRESIDENT.—Order!

MR. DOUGLAS.—Sir, if the senator does interpose, in violation of the rules of the Senate, a denial of the fact, it may be that I shall be able to nail that denial, as I shall the statements in this address which are over his own signature, as a wicked fabrication, and prove it by the solemn legislation of this country.

MR. CHASE.—I call the senator to order.

THE PRESIDENT.—The senator from Illinois is certainly out of order.

MR. DOUGLAS.—Then I will only say that I shall confine myself to this document, and prove its statements to be false by the legislation of the country. Certainly that is in order.

MR. CHASE.—You cannot do it.

MR. DOUGLAS.—The argument of this manifesto is predicated upon the assumption that the policy of the fathers of the republic was to prohibit slavery in all the territory ceded by the old States to the Union, and made United States territory, for the purpose of being organized into new States. I take issue upon that statement. Such was not the practice in the early history of the government. It is true that in the territory northwest of the Ohio River slavery was prohibited by the Ordinance of 1787; but it is also true that in the territory south of the Ohio River, slavery was permitted and protected; and it is also true that in the organization of the Territory of Mississippi, in 1798, the provisions of the Ordinance of 1787 were applied to it, with the exception of the sixth article, which prohibited slavery. Then, sir, you find upon the statute-books under Washington and the early Presidents, provisions of law showing that in the southwestern territories the right to hold slaves was clearly implied or recognized, while in the northwest territories it was prohibited.

The only conclusion that can be fairly and honestly drawn from that legislation is, that it was the policy of the fathers of the republic to prescribe a line of demarkation between free Territories and slave-holding Territories by a natural or a geographical line, being sure to make that line correspond, as near as might be, to the laws of climate, of production, and all those other causes that would control the institutions and make it either desirable or undesirable to the people inhabiting the respective Territories.

Sir, I wish you to bear in mind, too, that this geographical line, established by the founders of the republic between free Territories and slave Territories, extended as far westward as our territory then reached; the object being to avoid all agitation upon the slavery question by settling that question forever, as far as our territory extended, which was then to the Mississippi River.

When, in 1803, we acquired from France the territory known as Louisiana, it became necessary to legislate for the protection of the inhabitants residing therein. It will be seen, by looking into the bill establishing the Territorial government in 1805 for the Territory of New Orleans, embracing the same country now known as the State of Louisiana, that the Ordinance of 1787 was expressly extended to that Territory, except the sixth section, which prohibited slavery. That act implied that the Territory of New Orleans was to be a slaveholding Territory by making that exception in the law. But, sir, when they came to form what was then called the Territory of Louisiana, subsequently known as the Territory of Missouri, north of the thirty-third parallel, they used different language. They did not extend to it any of the provisions of the Ordinance of 1787. They first provided that it should be governed by laws made by the governor and the judges, and, when in 1812 Congress gave to that Territory, under the name of the Territory of Missouri, a Territorial government, the people were allowed to do as they pleased upon the subject of slavery, subject only to the limitations of the Constitution of the United States. Now what is the inference from that legislation? That slavery was, by implication, recognized south of the thirty-third parallel; and north of that the people were left to exercise their own judgment and do as they pleased upon the subject, without any implication for or against the existence of the institution.

This continued to be the condition of the country in the Missouri Territory up to 1820, when the celebrated act which is now called the Missouri Compromise was passed. Slavery did not exist in, nor was it excluded from, the country now known as Nebraska. There was no code of laws upon the subject of slavery either way: First, for the reason that slavery had never been introduced into Louisiana, and established by positive enactment. It had grown up there by a sort of common law, and been supported and protected. When a common law grows up, when an institution becomes established under a usage, it carries it so far as that usage actually goes, and no further. If it had been established by direct enactment, it might have carried it so far as the political jurisdiction extended; but, be that as it may, by the act of 1812, creating the Territory of Missouri, that Territory was allowed to legislate upon the subject of slavery as it saw proper, subject only to the limitations which I have stated; and the country not inhabited or thrown open to settlement was set apart as Indian country, and rendered subject to Indian laws. Hence, the local legislation of the State of Missouri did not reach into that Indian country, but was excluded from it by the Indian code and Indian laws. The municipal regulations of Missouri could not go there until the Indian title had been extinguished, and the country thrown open to settlement. Such being the case, the only legislation in existence in Nebraska Territory at the time that the Missouri act passed, namely, the 6th of March, 1820, was a provision, in effect, that the people should be allowed to do as they pleased upon the subject of slavery.

The Territory of Missouri having been left in that legal condition, positive opposition was made to the bill to organize a State government, with a view to its admission into the Union; and a senator from my State, Mr. Jesse B. Thomas, introduced an amendment, known as the eighth section of the bill, in which it was provided that slavery should be prohibited north of 36° 30′ north latitude, in all the country which we had acquired from France. What was the object of the enactment of that eighth section? Was it not to go back to the original policy of prescribing boundaries to the limitation of free institutions, and of slave institutions, by a geographical line, in order to avoid all controversy in Congress upon the subject? Hence they extended that geographical line through all the territory purchased from France, which was as far as our possessions then reached. It was not simply to settle the question on that piece of country, but it was to carry out a great principle, by extending that dividing line as far west as our territory went, and running it onward on each new acquisition of territory. True, the express enactment of the eighth section of the Missouri act, now called the Missouri Compromise, only covered the territory acquired from France; but the principles of the act, the objects of its adoption, the reasons in its support, required that it should be extended indefinitely westward, so far as our territory might go, whenever new purchases should be made.

Thus stood the question up to 1845, when the joint resolution for the annexation of Texas passed. There was inserted in that joint resolution a provision, suggested in the first instance and brought before the House of Representatives by myself, extending the Missouri Compromise line indefinitely westward through the Territory of Texas. Why did I bring forward that proposition? Why did the Congress of the United States adopt it? Not because it was of the least practical importance, so far as the question of slavery within the limits of Texas was concerned; for no man ever dreamed that it had any practical effect there. Then why was it brought forward? It was for the purpose of preserving the principle, in order that it might be extended still further westward, even to the Pacific Ocean, whenever we should acquire the country that far. I will here read that clause. It is the third article, second section, and is in these words:

"New States, of convenient size, not exceeding four in number, in addition to said State of Texas having sufficient population, may hereafter, by the consent of said State, be formed out of the territory thereof, which shall be entitled to admission under the provisions of the federal Constitution. And such States as may be formed out of that portion of said Territory lying south of thirty-six degrees thirty minutes north latitude, commonly known as the Missouri Compromise line, shall be admitted into the Union, with or without slavery, as the people of each State asking admission may desire. And, in such State or States as shall be formed out of said Territory north of said Missouri Compromise line, slavery or involuntary servitude (except for crime) shall be prohibited."

It will be seen that it contains a very remarkable provision, which is, that when States lying north of 36° 30' apply for admission, slavery shall be prohibited in their constitutions. I presume no one pretends that Congress could have power thus to fetter a State applying for admission into this Union; but it was necessary to preserve the principle of the Missouri Compromise line, in order that it might afterward be extended; and it was supposed that while Congress had no power to impose any such limitation, yet, as that was a compact with the State of Texas, that State could consent for herself that, when any portion of her own Territory, subject to her own jurisdiction and control, applied for admission, her constitution should be in a particular form; but that provision would not be binding on the new State one day after it was admitted into the Union. The other provision was that such States as should lie south of 36° 30' should come into the Union with or without slavery, as each should decide in its constitution. Then, by that act, the Missouri Compromise was extended indefinitely westward, so far as the State of Texas went, that is, to the Rio del Norte; for our Government at that time recognized the Rio del Norte as its boundary. We recognized, in many ways, and among them by even paying Texas for it ten millions of dollars, in order that it might be included in and form a portion of the Territory of New Mexico.

Then, sir, in 1848, we acquired from Mexico the country between the Rio del Norte and the Pacific Ocean. Immediately after that acquisition, the Senate, on my own motion, voted into a bill a provision to extend the Missouri Compromise indefinitely westward to the Pacific Ocean, in the same sense and with the same understanding with which it was originally adopted. That provision passed this body by a decided majority, I think by ten at least, and went to the House of Representatives, and was defeated there by northern votes.

Now, sir, let us pause and consider for a moment. The first time that the principles of the Missouri Compromise were ever abandoned, the first time they were ever rejected by Congress, was by the defeat of that provision in the House of Representatives in 1848. By whom was that defeat effected? By northern votes with Freesoil proclivities. It was the defeat of that Missouri Compromise that reopened the slavery agitation with all its fury. It was the defeat of that Missouri Compromise that created the tremendous struggle of 1850. It was the defeat of that Missouri Compromise that created the necessity for making a new compromise in 1850. Had we been faithful to the principles of the Missouri Compromise in 1848, this question would not have arisen. Who was it that was faithless? I undertake to say it was the very men who now insist that the Missouri Compromise was a solemn compact, and should never be violated or departed from. Every man who is now assailing the principle of the bill under consideration, so far as I am advised, was opposed to the Missouri Compromise in 1848. The very men who now arraign me for a departure from the Missouri Compromise are the men who successfully violated it, repudiated it, and caused it to be superseded by the Compromise measures of 1850. Sir, it is with rather bad grace that the men who proved faithless themselves, should charge upon me and others, who were ever faithful, the responsibilities and consequences of their own treachery.

Then, sir, as I before remarked, the defeat of the Missouri Compromise in 1848 having created the necessity for the establishment of a new one in 1850, let us see what that compromise was.

The leading feature of the Compromise of 1850 was Congressional non-intervention as to slavery in the Territories; that the people of the Territories, and of all the States, were to be allowed to do as they pleased upon the subject of slavery, subject only to the provisions of the Constitution of the United States.

That, sir, was the leading feature of the Compromise measures of 1850. Those measures, therefore, abandoned the idea of a geographical line as the boundary between free States and slave States; abandoned it because compelled to do it from an inability to maintain it; and in lieu of that, substituted a great principle of self-government, which would allow the people to do as they thought proper. Now the question is, when that new compromise, resting upon that great fundamental principle of freedom, was established, was it not an abandonment of the old one—the geographical line? Was it not a supersedure of the old one within the very language of the substitute for the bill which is now under consideration? I say it did supersede it, because it applied its provisions as well to the north as to the south of 36° 30'. It established a principle which was equally applicable to the country north as well as south of the parallel of 36° 30'—a principle of universal application. The authors of this abolition manifesto attempted to refute this presumption, and maintain that the Compromise of 1850 did not supersede that of 1820, by quoting the proviso to the first section of the act to establish the Texan boundary, and create the Territory of New Mexico. That proviso was added, by way of amendment, on motion of Mr. Mason, of Virginia.

I repeat, that in order to rebut the presumption, as I before stated, that the Missouri Compromise was abandoned and superseded by the principles of the Compromise of 1850, these confederates cite the following amendment, offered to the bill to establish the boundary of Texas and create the Territory of New Mexico in 1850:

"*Provided*, That nothing herein contained shall be construed to impair or qualify anything contained in the third article of the second section of the joint resolution for annexing Texas to the United States, approved March 1, 1845, either as regards the number of States that may hereafter be formed out of the States of Texas or otherwise."

After quoting this proviso, they make the following statement, and attempt to gain credit for its truth by suppressing material facts which appear upon the face of the same statute, and which, if produced, would conclusively disprove the statement:

"It is solemnly declared in the very compromise acts, 'that *nothing herein contained shall be construed to impair or qualify* the prohibition of slavery north of thirty-six degrees thirty minutes;' and yet, in the face of this declaration, that sacred prohibition is said to be overthrown. Can presumption further go?"

I will now proceed to show that presumption could not go further than is exhibited in this declaration.

They suppress the following material facts, which, if produced, would have disproved their statement. They first suppress the fact that the same section of the act cuts off from Texas, and cedes to the United States all that part of Texas which lies north of 36° 30'. They then suppress the further fact that the same section of the law cuts off from Texas a large tract of country on the west, more than three degrees of longitude, and adds it to the territory of the United States. They then suppress the further fact that this territory thus cut off from Texas, and to which the Missouri Compromise line applied, was incorporated into the Territory of New Mexico. And then what was done? It was incorporated into that Territory with this clause:

"That, when admitted as a State, the said Territory, or any portion of the same, shall be received into the Union with or without slavery, as their constitution may prescribe at the time of its adoption."

Yes, sir, the very bill and section from which they quote, cuts off all that part of Texas which was to be free by the Missouri Compromise, together with some on the south side of the line, incorporates it into the Territory of New Mexico, and then says that the Territory, and every portion of the same, shall come into the Union with or without slavery, as it sees proper.

What else does it do? The sixth section of the same act provides that the legislative power and authority of this said Territory of New Mexico shall extend to all rightful subjects of legislation consistent with the Constitution of the United States and the provisions of the act, not excepting slavery. Thus the New Mexican Bill, from which they make that quotation, contains the provision that New Mexico, including that part of Texas which was cut off, should come into the Union with or without slavery, as it saw proper ; and in the meantime that the Territorial legislature should have all the authority over the subject of slavery that they had over any other subject, restricted only by the limitation of the Constitution of the United States and the provisions of the act. Now, I ask those senators, do not those provisions repeal the Missouri Compromise, so far as it applied to the country cut off from Texas? Do they not annul it? Do they not supersede it? If they do, then the address which has been put forth to the world by these confederates is an atrocious falsehood. If they do not, then what do they mean when they charge me with having, in the substitute first reported from the committee, repealed it, with having annulled it, with having violated it, when I only copied those precise words? I copied the precise words into my bill, as reported from the committee, which were contained in the New Mexico Bill. They say my bill annuls the Missouri Compromise. If it does, it had already been done before by the act of 1850; for these words were copied from the act of 1850.

MR. WADE.—Why did you do it over again?

MR. DOUGLAS.—I will come to that point presently. I am now dealing with the truth and veracity of a combination of men who have assembled in secret caucus upon the Sabbath day, to arraign my conduct and belie my motives. I say, therefore, that their manifesto is a slander either way ; for it says that the Missouri Compromise was not superseded by the measures of 1850, and then it says that the same words in my bill do repeal and annul it. They must be adjudged guilty of one falsehood in order to sustain the other assertion.

Now, sir, I propose to go a little further, and show what was the real meaning of the amendment of the senator from Virginia, out of which these gentlemen have manufactured so much capital in the newspaper press, and have succeeded by that misrepresentation in procuring an expression of opinion from the State of Rhode Island in opposition to this bill. I will state what its meaning is.

Did it mean that the States north of 36° 30' should have a clause in their constitutions prohibiting slavery? I have shown that it did not mean that, because the same act says that they might come in with slavery, if they saw proper. I say it could not mean that for another reason: The same section containing that proviso cut off all that part of Texas north of 36° 30', and hence there was nothing for it to operate upon. It did not, therefore, relate to the country cut off. What did it relate to? Why, it meant simply this: By the joint resolution of 1845, Texas was annexed, with the right to form four additional States out of her territory ; and such States as were south of 36° 30' were to come in with or without slavery, as they saw proper ; and in such State or States as were north of that line, slavery should be prohibited. When we had cut off all north of 36° 30', and thus circumscribed the boundary and diminished the territory of Texas, the question arose, how many States will Texas be entitled to under this circumscribed boundary. Certainly not four, it will be argued. Why? Because the original resolution of annexation provided that one of the States, if not more, should be north of 36° 30'. It would leave it, then, doubtful whether Texas was entitled to two or three additional States under the circumscribed boundary.

In order to put that matter to rest, in order to make a final settlement, in order to have it explicitly understood what was the meaning of Congress, the senator from Virginia offered the amendment that nothing therein contained should impair that provision, either as to the number of States or otherwise, that is, that Texas should be entitled to the same number of States with her reduced boundaries as she would have been entitled to under her larger boundaries; and those States shall come in with or without slavery, as they might prefer, being all south of 36° 30', and nothing to impair that right shall be inferred from the passage of the act. Such, sir, was the meaning of that proposition. Any other construction of it would stultify the very character and purpose of its mover, the senator from Virginia. Such, then, was not only the intent of the mover, but such is the legal effect of the law; and I say that no man, after reading the other sections of the bill, those to which I have referred, can doubt that such was both the intent and the legal effect of that law.

Then I submit to the Senate if I have not convicted this manifesto, issued by the abolition confederates, of being a gross falsification of the laws of the land, and by that falsification that an erroneous and injurious impression has been created upon the public mind. I am sorry to be compelled to indulge in language of severity ; but there is no other language that is adequate to express the indignation with which I see this attempt, not only to mislead the public, but to malign my character by deliberate falsification of the public statutes and the public records.

In order to give greater plausibility to the falsification of the terms of the Compromise measures of 1850, the confederates also declare in their manifesto that they (the Territorial bills for the organization of Utah and New Mexico) "applied to the territory acquired from Mexico, and to that only. They were intended as a settlement of the controversy growing out of that acquisition, and of that controversy only. They must stand or fall by their own merits."

I submit to the Senate if there is an intelligent man in America who does not know that that declaration is falsified by the statute from which they quoted. They say that the provisions of that bill was confined to the territory acquired from Mexico, when the very section of the law from which they quoted that proviso did purchase a part of that very territory from the State of Texas. And the next section of the law included that territory in the Territory of New Mexico. It took a small portion also of the old Louisiana purchase, and added that to the Territory of New Mexico, and made up the rest out of the Mexican acquisitions. Then, sir, your statutes show, when applied to the map of the country, that the Territory of New Mexico was composed of country acquired from Mexico, and also of territory acquired from Texas, and of territory acquired from France; and yet in defiance of that statute, and in falsification of its terms, we are told, in order to deceive the people, that the bills were confined to the purchase made from Mexico alone; and in order to give it greater solemnity, they repeat it twice, fearing that it would not be believed the first time. What is more, the Territory of Utah was not confined to the country acquired from Mexico. That Territory, as is well known to every man who understands the geography of the country, includes a large tract of rich and fertile country, acquired from France in 1803, and to which the eighth section of the Missouri Act applied in 1820. If these confederates do not know to what country I allude, I only reply that they should have known before they uttered the falsehood, and imputed a crime to me.

But I will tell you to what country I allude. By the treaty of 1819, by which we acquired Florida and a fixed boundary between the United States and Spain, the boundary was made of the Arkansas River to its source, and then the line ran due north of the source of the Arkansas to the 42d parallel, then along on the 42d parallel to the Pacific Ocean. That line, due north from the head of the Arkansas, leaves the whole middle part, described in such glowing terms by Colonel Fremont, to the east of the line, and hence a part of the Louisiana purchase. Yet, inasmuch as that middle part is drained by the waters flowing into the Colorado, when we formed the territorial limits of Utah, instead of running that air-line, we ran along the ridge of the mountains, and cut off that part from Nebraska, or from the Louisiana purchase, and included it within the limits of the Territory of Utah.

Why did we do it? Because we sought for a natural and convenient boundary, and it was deemed better to take the mountains as a boundary, than by an air-line to cut the valleys on one side of the mountains, and annex them to the country on the other side. And why did we take these natural boundaries, setting at defiance the old boundaries? The simple reason was that so long as we acted upon the principle of settling the slave question by a geographical line, so long we observed those boundaries strictly and rigidly; but when that was abandoned, in consequence of the action of free-soilers and abolitionists—when it was superseded by the Compromise measures of 1850, which rested upon a great universal principle—there was no necessity for keeping in view the old and unnatural boundary. For that reason, in making the new Territories, we formed natural boundaries, irrespective of the source whence our title was derived. In writing these bills I paid no attention to the fact whether the title was acquired from Louisiana, from France, or from Mexico; for what difference did it make? The principle which we had established in the bill would apply equally well to either.

In fixing those boundaries, I paid no attention to the fact whether they included old territory or new territory—whether the country was covered by the Missouri Compromise or not. Why? Because the principles established in the bills superseded the Missouri Compromise. For that reason we disregarded the old boundaries; disregarded the territory to which it applied, and disregarded the source from whence the title was derived. I say, therefore, that a close examination of those acts clearly establishes the fact that it was the intent, as well as the legal effect of the Compromise measures of 1850, to supersede the Missouri Compromise, and all geographical and territorial lines.

Sir, in order to avoid any misconstruction, I will state more distinctly what my precise idea is upon this point. So far as the Utah and New Mexico bills included the territory which had been subject to the Missouri Compromise provision, to that extent they absolutely annulled the Missouri Compromise. As to the unorganized territory not covered by those bills, it was superseded by the principles of the Compromise of 1850. We all know that the object of the Compromise measures of 1850 was to establish certain great principles, which would avoid the slavery agitation in all time to come. Was it our object simply to provide for a temporary evil? Was it our object to heal over an old sore, and leave it to break out again? Was it our object to adopt a mere miserable expedient to apply to that territory, and to that alone, and leave ourselves entirely at sea, without compass, when new territory was acquired, or new territorial organizations were to be made?

Was that the object for which the eminent and venerable senator from Kentucky (Mr. Clay) came here and sacrificed even his last energies upon the altar of his country? Was that the object for which Webster, Clay, Cass, and all the patriots of that day, struggled so long and so strenuously? Was it merely the application of a temporary expedient, in agreeing to stand by past and dead legislation, that the Baltimore platform pledged us to sustain the Compromise of 1850? Was it the understanding of the Whig party, when they adopted the Compromise measures of 1850 as an article of political faith, that they were only agreeing to that which was past, and had no reference to the future? If that was their meaning; if that was their object, they palmed off an atrocious fraud upon the American people. Was it the meaning of the Democratic party, when we pledged ourselves to stand by the Compromise of 1850, that we spoke only of the past, and had no reference to the future? If so, it was a gross deception. When we pledged our President to stand by the Compromise measures, did we not understand that we pledged him as to his future action? Was it as to his past conduct? If it had been in relation to past conduct only, the pledge would have been untrue as to a very large portion of the Democratic party. Men went into that convention who had been opposed to the Compromise measures—men who abhorred those measures when they were pending—men who never would have voted affirmatively on them. But, inasmuch as those measures had been passed and the country had acquiesced in them, and it was important to preserve the principle in order to avoid agitation in the future, these men said, we waive our past objections, and we will stand by you and with you in carrying out these principles in the future.

Such I understand to be the meaning of the two great parties at Baltimore. Such I understand to have been the effect of their pledges. If they did not mean this, they meant merely to adopt resolutions which were never to be carried out, and which were designed to mislead and deceive the people for the mere purpose of carrying an election.

I hold, then, that, as to the territory covered by the Utah and New Mexico bills, there was an express annulment of the Missouri Compromise; and as to all the other unorganized territories, it was superseded by the principles of that legislation, and we are bound to apply those principles to the organization of all new territories, to all which we now own, or which we may hereafter acquire. If this construction be given, it makes that compromise a final adjustment. No other construction can possibly impart finality to it. By any other construction, the question is to be reopened the moment you ratify a new treaty acquiring an inch of country from Mexico. By any other construction, you reopen the issue every time you make a new Territorial government. But, sir, if you treat the Compromise measures of 1850 in the light of great principles, sufficient to remedy temporary evils, at the same time that they prescribe rules of action applicable everywhere in all time to come, then you avoid the agitation forever, if you observe good faith to the provisions of these enactments, and the principles established by them.

Mr. President, I repeat that, so far as the question of slavery is concerned, there is nothing in the bill under consideration which does not carry out the principle of the Compromise measures of 1850, by leaving the people to do as they please, subject only to the provisions of the Constitution of the United States. If that principle is wrong, the bill is wrong. If that principle is right, the bill is right. It is unnecessary to quibble about phraseology or words; it is not the mere words, the mere phraseology, that our constituents wish to judge by. They wish to know the legal effect of our legislation.

The legal effect of this bill, if it be passed as reported by the Committee on Territories, is neither to legislate slavery into these Territories nor out of them, but to leave the people to do as they please, under the provisions and subject to the limitations of the Constitution of the United States. Why should not this principle prevail? Why should any man, North or South, object to it? I will especially address the argument to my own section of country, and ask why should any northern man object to this principle? If you will review the history of the slavery question in the United States, you will see that all the great results in behalf of free institutions which have been worked out, have been accomplished by the operation of this principle, and by it alone.

When these States were colonies of Great Britain, every one of them was a slaveholding province. When the Constitution of the United States was formed, twelve out of the thirteen were slaveholding States. Since that time six of those States have become free. How has this been effected? Was it by virtue of abolition agitation in Congress? Was it in obedience to the dictates of the Federal Government? Not at all; but they have become free States under the silent but sure and irresistible working of that great principle of self-government which teaches every people to do that which the interests of themselves and their posterity morally and pecuniarily may require.

Under the operation of this principle, New Hampshire became free, while South Carolina continued to hold slaves; Connecticut abolished slavery, while Georgia held on to it; Rhode Island abandoned the institution, while Maryland preserved it; New York, New Jersey and Pennsylvania abolished slavery, while Virginia, North Carolina, and Kentucky retained it. Did they do it at your bidding? Did they do it at the dictation of the Federal Government? Did they do it in obedience to any of your Wilmot Provisoes or Ordinances of '87? Not at all; they did it by virtue of their rights as freemen under the Constitution of the United States, to establish and abolish such institutions as they thought their own good required.

Let me ask you, where have you succeeded in excluding slavery by an act of Congress from one inch of the American soil? You may tell me that you did it in the Northwest Territory by the Ordinance of 1787. I will show you by the history of the country that you did not accomplish any such thing. You prohibited slavery there by law, but you did not exclude it in fact. Illinois was a part of the Northwest Territory. With the exception of a few French and white settlements, it was a vast wilderness, filled with hostile savages, when the Ordinance of 1787 was adopted. Yet, sir, when Illinois was organized into a Territorial government, it established and protected slavery, and maintained it in spite of your Ordinance and in defiance of its express prohibition. It is a curious fact, that, so long as Congress said the Territory of Illinois should not have slavery, she actually had it; and on the very day when you withdrew your Congressional prohibition the people of Illinois, of their own free will and accord, provided for a system of emancipation.

Thus you did not succeed in Illinois Territory with your Ordinance or your Wilmot Proviso, because the people there regarded it as an invasion of their rights. They regarded it as a usurpation on the part of the Federal Government. They regarded it as violative of the great principles of self-government, and they determined that they would never submit even to have freedom so long as you forced it upon them.

Nor must it be said that slavery was abolished in the constitution of Illinois in order to be admitted into the Union as a State, in compliance with the Ordinance of 1787; for they did no such thing. In the Constitution with which the people of Illinois were admitted into Union, they absolutely violated, disregarded, and repudiated your Ordinance. The Ordinance said that slavery should be forever prohibited in that country. The constitution with which you received them into the Union as a State provided that all slaves then in the State should remain slaves for life, and that all persons born of slave parents after a certain day should be free at a certain age, and that all persons born in the State after a certain other day, should be free from the time of their birth. Thus their State constitution, as well as their Territorial legislation, repudiated your Ordinance. Illinois, therefore, is a case in point to prove that whenever you have attempted to dictate institutions to any part of the United States, you have failed. The same is true, though not to the same extent, with reference to the Territory of Indiana, where there were many slaves during the time of its Territorial existence, and I believe also there were a few in the Territory of Ohio.

But, sir, these abolition confederates, in their manifesto, have also referred to the wonderful results of their policy in the States of Iowa and the Territory of Minnesota. Here, again, they happen to be in fault as to the laws of the land. The act to organize the Territory of Iowa did not prohibit slavery, but the people of Iowa were allowed to do as they pleased under the Territorial government; for the sixth section of that act provided that the legislative authority should extend to all rightful subjects of legislation except as to the disposition of the public lands, and taxes in certain cases, but not excepting slavery. It may, however, be said by some that slavery was prohibited in Iowa by virtue of that clause in the Iowa act which declared the laws of Wisconsin to be in force therein, inasmuch as the Ordinance of 1787 was one of the laws of Wisconsin. If, however, they say this, they defeat their object, because the very clause which transfers the laws of Wisconsin to Iowa, and makes them of force therein, also provides that those laws are subject to be altered, modified, or repealed by the Territorial legislature of Iowa.

Iowa, therefore, was left to do as she pleased. Iowa, when she came to form a constitution and State government, preparatory to admission into the Union, considered the subject of free and slave institutions calmly, dispassionately, without any restraint or dictation, and determined that it would be to the interest of her people in their climate, and with their productions, to prohibit slavery; and hence Iowa became a free State by virtue of this great principle of allowing the people to do as they please, and not in obedience to any federal command.

The abolitionists are also in the habit of referring to Oregon as another instance of the triumph of their abolition policy. There again they have overlooked or misrepresented the history of the country. Sir, it is well known, or if it is not, it ought to be, that for about twelve years you forgot to give Oregon any government or any protection; and during that period the inhabitants of that country established a government of their own, and by virtue of their own laws, passed by their own representatives before you extended your jurisdiction over them, prohibited slavery by a unanimous vote. Slavery was prohibited there by the action of the people themselves, and not by virtue of any legislation of Congress.

It is true that, in the midst of the tornado which swept over the country in 1848, 1849 and 1850, a provision was forced into the Oregon bill prohibiting slavery in that Territory; but that only goes to show that the object of those who pressed it was not so much to establish free institutions as to gain a political advantage by giving an ascendency to their peculiar doctrines in the laws of the land; for slavery having been already prohibited there, and no man proposing to establish it, what was the necessity for insulting the people of Oregon by saying in your law that they should not do that which they had unanimously said they did not wish to do? That was the only effect of your legislation so far as the Territory of Oregon was concerned.

How was it in regard to California? Every one of these abolition confederates, who have thus arraigned me and the Committee on Territories before the country, and have misrepresented our position, predicted that unless Congress interposed by law, and prohibited slavery in California, it would inevitably become a slaveholding State. Congress did not interfere; Congress did not prohibit slavery. There was no enactment upon the subject; but the people formed a State constitution, and therein prohibited slavery.

Mr. WELLER.—The vote was unanimous in the convention of California for prohibition.

Mr. DOUGLAS.—So it was in regard to Utah and New Mexico. In 1850, we who resisted any attempt to force institutions upon the people of those Territories inconsistent with their wishes and their right to decide for themselves, were denounced as slavery propagandists. Every one of us who was in favor of the Compromise measures of 1850 was arraigned for having advocated a principle proposing to introduce slavery into those Territories, and the people were told, and made to believe, that, unless we prohibited it by act of Congress, slavery would necessarily and inevitably be introduced into these Territories.

Well, sir, we did establish the Territorial governments of Utah and New Mexico without any prohibition. We gave to these abolitionists a full opportunity of proving whether their predictions would prove true or false. Years have rolled round, and the result is before us. The people there have not passed any law recognizing, or establishing, or introducing, or protecting slavery in the Territories.

I know of but one Territory of the United States where slavery does exist, and that one is where you have prohibited it by law; and it is this very Nebraska country. In defiance of the eighth section of the act of 1820, in defiance of Congressional dictation, there have been, not many, but a few slaves introduced. I heard a minister of the Gospel the other day conversing with a member of the Committee on Territories upon this subject. This preacher was from that country, and a member put this question to him: "Have you any negroes out there?" He said there were a few held by the Indians. I asked him if there were not some held by white men? He said there were a few under *peculiar circumstances*, and he gave an instance. An abolition missionary, a very good man, had gone there from Boston, and he took his wife with him. He got out into the country but could not get any help; hence he, being a kind-hearted man, went down to Missouri and gave $1,000 for a negro, and took him up there as "help." (Laughter.) So, under peculiar circumstances, when these freesoil and abolition preachers and missionaries go into the country, they can buy a negro for their own use, but they do not like to allow any one else to do the same thing. (Renewed laughter.) I suppose the fact of the matter is simply this: there the people can get no servants—no "help," as they are called in the section of country where I was born—and from the necessity of the case, they must do the best they can, and for this reason a few slaves have been taken there. I have no doubt that whether you organize the Territory of Nebraska or not, this will continue for some little time to come. It certainly does exist, and it will increase as long as the Missouri Compromise applies to the Territory; and I suppose it will continue for a little while during their Territorial condition, whether a prohibition is imposed or not. But when settlers rush in—when labor becomes plenty, and therefore cheap, in that climate, with its productions—it is worse than folly to think of its being a slaveholding country. I do not believe there is a man in Congress who thinks it could be permanently a slaveholding country. I have no idea that it could. All I have to say on that subject is, that, when you create them into a Territory, you thereby acknowledge that they ought to be considered a distinct political organization. And when you give them in addition a legis-

nature, you thereby confess that they are competent to exercise the powers of legislation. If they wish slavery, they have a right to it. If they do not want it, they will not have it, and you should not attempt to force it upon them.

I do not like, I never did like, the system of legislation on our part, by which a geographical line, in violation of the laws of nature, and climate and soil, and of the laws of God, should be run to establish institutions for a people contrary to their wishes; yet, out of a regard for the peace and quiet of the country, out of respect for past pledges, and out of a desire to adhere faithfully to all compromises, I sustained the Missouri compromise so long as it was in force, and advocated its extension to the Pacific ocean. Now, when that has been abandoned, when it has been superseded, when a great principle of self-government has been substituted for it, I choose to cling to that principle, and abide in good faith, not only by the letter, but by the spirit of the last compromise.

Sir, I do not recognize the right of the abolitionists of this country to arraign me for being false to sacred pledges, as they have done in their proclamations. Let them show when and where I have ever proposed to violate a compact. I have proved that I stood by the compact of 1820 and 1845, and proposed its continuance and observance in 1848. I have proved that the freesoilers and abolitionists were the guilty parties who violated that compromise then. I should like to compare notes with the abolition confederates about adherence to compromises. When did they stand by or approve of any one that was ever made?

Did not every abolitionist and freesoiler in America denounce the Missouri Compromise in 1820? Did they not for years hunt down ravenously, for his blood, every man who assisted in making that compromise? Did they not in 1845, when Texas was annexed, denounce all of us who went for the annexation of Texas, and for the continuation of the Missouri Compromise line through it? Did they not, in 1848, denounce me as a slavery propagandist for standing by the principles of the Missouri Compromise, and proposing to continue it to the Pacific Ocean? Did they not themselves violate and repudiate it then? Is not the charge of bad faith true as to every abolitionist in America, instead of being true as to me and the committee, and those who advocate this bill?

They talk about the bill being a violation of the Compromise measure of 1850. Who can show me a man in either house of Congress who was in favor of those Compromise measures in 1850, and who is not now in favor of leaving the people of Nebraska and Kansas to do as they please upon the subject of slavery, according to the principle of my bill? Is there one? If so, I have not heard of him. This tornado has been raised by abolitionist, and abolitionists alone. They have made an impression upon the public mind, in the way in which I have mentioned, by a falsification of the law and the facts; and this whole organization against the Compromise measures of 1850 is an abolition movement. I presume they had some hope of getting a few tender-footed Democrats into their plot; and, acting on what they supposed they might do, they sent forth publicly to the world the falsehood that their address was sighed by the senators and a majority of the representatives from the State of Ohio; but when we come to examine signatures, we find no one Whig there, no one Democrat there; none but pure, unmitigated, unadulterated abolitionists.

Much effect, I know, has been produced by this circular, coming as it does with the imposing title of a representation of a majority of the Ohio delegation. What was the reason for its effect? Because the manner in which it was sent forth implied that all the Whig members from that State had joined in it; that part of the Democrats had signed it; and then that the two abolitionists had signed it, and that made a majority of the delegation. By this means it frightened the Whig party and the Democracy in the State of Ohio, because they supposed their own representatives and friends had gone into this negro movement, when the fact turns out to be that it was not signed by a single Whig or Democratic member from Ohio.

Now, I ask the friends and the opponents of this measure to look at it as it is. Is not the question involved the simple one, whether the people of the Territories shall be allowed to do as they please upon the question of slavery, subject only to the limitations of the Constitution? That is all the bill provides; and it does so in clear, explicit and unequivocal terms. I know there are some men, Whigs and Democrats, who, not willing to repudiate the Baltimore platform of their own party, would be willing to vote for this principle, provided they could do so in such equivocal terms that they could deny that it means what it was intended to mean in certain localities. I do not wish to deal in any equivocal language. If the principle is right, let it be avowed and maintained. If it is wrong, let it be repudiated. Let all this quibbling about the Missouri Compromise, about the territory acquired from France, about the act of 1820, be cast behind you; for the simple question is, will you allow the people to legislate for themselves upon the subject of slavery? Why should you not?

When you propose to give them a Territorial government, do you not acknowledge that they ought to be erected into a political organization; and when you give them a legislature, do you not acknowledge that they are capable of self-government? Having made that acknowledgment, why should you not allow them to exercise the rights of legislation? Oh, these abolitionists say they are entirely willing to concede all this, with one exception. They say they are willing, to trust the Territorial legislature, under the limitations of the Constitution, to legislate upon the rights of inheritance, to legislate in regard to religion, education, and morals, to legislate in regard to the relations of husband and wife, of parent and child, of guardian and ward, upon everything pertaining to the dearest rights and interests of white men, but they are not willing to trust them to legislate in regard to a few miserable negroes. That is their single exception. They acknowledge that the people of the Territories are capable of deciding for themselves concerning white men, but not in relation to negroes. The real gist of the matter is this: Does it require any higher degree of civilization, and intelligence, and learning, and sagacity, to legislate for negroes than for white men? If it does, we ought to adopt the abolition doctrine, and go with them against this bill. If it does not—if we are willing to trust the people with the great, sacred, fundamental right of prescribing their own institutions, consistent with the Constitution of the country—we must vote for this bill. That is the only question involved in the bill. I hope I have been able to strip it of all the misrepresentation, to wipe away all of that mist and obscurity with which it has been surrounded by this abolition address.

I have now said all I have to say upon the present occasion. For all, except the first ten minutes of these remarks, the abolition confederates are responsible. My object, in the first place, was only to explain the provisions of the bill, so that they might be distinctly understood. I was willing to allow its assailants to attack it as much as they pleased, reserving to myself the right, when the time should approach for taking the vote, to answer in a concluding speech all the arguments which might be used against it. I still reserve—what I believe common courtesy and parliamentary usage awards to the chairman of a committee and the author of a bill—the right of summing up after all shall have been said which has to be said against this measure.

I hope the compact which was made on last Tuesday, at the suggestion of these abolitionists, when the bill was proposed to be taken up, will be observed. It was that the bill, when taken up to-day, should continue to be considered from day to day until finally disposed of. I hope they will not repudiate and violate that compact, as they have the Missouri Compromise and all others which have been entered into. I hope, therefore, that we may press the bill to a vote; but not by depriving persons of an opportunity of speaking.

I am in favor of giving every enemy of the bill the most ample time. Let us hear them all patiently, and then take the vote and pass the bill. We who are in favor of it know that the principle on which it is based is right. Why, then, should we gratify the abolition party in their effort to get up another political tornado of fanaticism, and put the country again in peril, merely for the purpose of electing a few agitators to the Congress of the United States? We intend to stand by the principle of the Compromise measures of 1850.

ON NEBRASKA AND KANSAS.

Delivered in the Senate, March 3, 1854.

MR. PRESIDENT: before I proceed to the general argument upon the most important branch of this question, I must say a few words in reply to the senator from Tennessee (Mr. Bell), who has spoken upon the bill to-day. He approves of the principles of the bill; he thinks they have great merit; but he does not see his way entirely clear to vote for the bill, because of the objections which he has stated, most of which relate to the Indians.

Upon that point, I desire to say that it has never been the custom in territorial bills to make regulations concerning the Indians within the limits of the proposed Territories. All matters relating to them it has been thought wise to leave to subsequent legislation, to be brought forward by the Committee on Indian Affairs. I did venture originally in this bill to put in one or two provisions upon that subject; but, at the suggestion of many senators on both sides of the chamber, they were stricken out, in order to allow the appropriate committee of the Senate to take charge of that subject. I think, therefore, since we have stricken from the bill all those provisions which pertain to the Indians, and reserved the whole subject for the consideration and action of the appropriate committee, we have obviated every possible objection which could reasonably be urged upon that score. We have every reason to hope and trust that the Committee on Indian Affairs will propose such measures as will do entire justice to the Indians, without contravening the objects of Congress in organizing those Territories.

But, sir, allusion has been made to certain Indian treaties, and it has been intimated, if not charged in direct terms, that we were violating the stipulations of those treaties in respect to the rights and lands of the Indians. The senator from Texas (Mr. Houston), made a very long and interesting speech on that subject; but it so happened that most of the treaties to which he referred were with Indians not included within the limits of this bill. We have been informed, in the course of the debate to-day, by the chairman of the Committee on Indian Affairs (Mr. Sebastian), that there is but one treaty in existence relating to lands or Indians within the limits of either of the proposed Territories, and that is the treaty with the Ottawa Indians, about two hundred persons in number, owning about thirty-four thousand acres of land. Thus it appears that the whole argument of injustice to the red man, which in the course of this debate has called forth so much sympathy and indignation, is confined to two hundred Indians, owning less than two townships of land. Now, sir, is it possible that a country, said to be five hundred thousand square miles in extent, and large enough to make twelve such States as Ohio, is to be consigned to perpetual barbarism merely on account of that small number of Indians, when the bill itself expressly provides that those Indians and their lands are not to be included within the limits of the proposed Territories, nor to be subject to their laws or jurisdiction? I would not allow this measure to invade the rights of even one Indian, and hence I inserted in the first section of the bill that none of the tribes with whom we have treaty stipulations should be embraced within either of the Territories, unless such Indians shall voluntarily consent to be included therein by treaties hereafter to be made. If any senator can furnish me with language more explicit, or which would prove more effectual in securing the rights of the Indians, I will cheerfully adopt it.

Well, sir, the senator from Tennessee, in a very kind spirit, here raises the objection for me to answer, that this bill includes Indians within the limits of these Territories with whom we have no treaties; and he desires to know what we are to do with them. I will say to him, that that is not a matter of inquiry which necessarily or properly arises upon the passage of this bill; that is not a proper inquiry to come before the Committee on Territories. You have in all your Territorial bills included Indians within the boundaries of the Territories. When you erected the Territory of Minnesota, you had not extinguished the Indian title to one foot of land in that Territory west of the Mississippi River, and to the major part of that Territory the Indian title remains unextinguished to this day. In addition to those wild tribes, you removed Indians from Wisconsin and located them within Minnesota since the Territory was organized. It will be a question for the consideration of the Committee on Indian Affairs, and for the action of Congress, when, in settlement and civilization, it shall become necessary to change the present policy in respect to the Indians. When you erected the Territorial government of Oregon, a few years ago, you embraced within it all the Indians living in the Territory without their consent, and without any such reservations in their behalf as are contained in this bill. You had not at that time made a treaty with those Indians, nor extinguished their title to an acre of land in that Territory, nor indeed have you done so to this day. So it is in the organization of Washington Territory. You ran the lines around the country which you thought ought to be within the limits of the Territory, and you embraced all the Indians within those lines; but you made no provision in respect to their rights or lands; you left that matter to the Committee on Indian Affairs, to the Indian laws, and to the proper department, to be arranged afterward as the public interests might require. The same is true in reference to Utah and New Mexico.

In fact, the policy provided for in this bill, in respect to the Indians, is that which is now in force in every one of the Territories. Therefore, any senator who objects to this bill on that score should have objected to and voted against every Territorial bill which you have now in existence. Yet my friend from Texas has taken occasion to remind the Senate several times that it was a matter of pride —and it ought to be a matter of patriotic pride with him—that he voted for every measure of the Compromise of 1850, including the Utah and New Mexico Territorial bills, embracing all the Indians within their limits. My friend from Tennessee, too, has been very liberal in voting for most of the Territorial bills; and I therefore trust that the same patriotic and worthy motives which induced him to vote for the Territorial acts of 1850 will enable him to give his support to the present bill, especially as he approves of the great principle of popular sovereignty upon which it rests.

The senator from Tennessee remarked further, that the proposed limits of these two Territories were too extensive; that they were large enough to be erected into eight different States; and why, he asked, the necessity of including such a vast amount of country within the limits of these two Territories? I must remind the senator that it has always been the practice to include a large extent of country within one Territory, and then to subdivide it from time to time as the public interest might require. Such was the case with the old Northwest Territory. It was all originally included within one Territorial government. Afterward Ohio was cut off; and then Indiana, Michigan, Illinois and Wisconsin, were successively erected into separate Territorial governments, and subsequently admitted into the Union as States.

At one period, it will be remembered, the Territory of Wisconsin included the country embraced within the limits of the States of Wisconsin and Iowa, and a part of the State of Michigan, and the Territory of Minnesota. There is country enough within the Territory of Minnesota to make two or three States of the size of New York. Washington Territory embraces about the same area. Oregon is large enough to make three or four States as extensive as Pennsylvania; Utah two or three, and New Mexico four or five of like dimensions. Indeed, the whole country embraced within the proposed Territories of Nebraska and Kansas, together with the States of Arkansas, Missouri and Iowa, and the larger part of Minnesota, and the whole of the Indian country west of Arkansas, once constituted a Territorial government, under the name of the Missouri Territory. In view of this course of legislation upon the subject of Territorial organization, commencing before the adoption of the Constitution of the United States and coming down to the last session of Congress, it surely cannot be said that there is anything unusual or extraordinary in the size of the proposed Territory which should compel a senator to vote against the bill, while he approves of the principles involved in the measure.

It has also been urged in debate that there is no necessity for these Territorial organizations; and I have been called upon to point out any public and national considerations which require action at this time. Senators seem to forget that our immense and valuable possessions on the Pacific are separated from the States and organized Territories on this side of the Rocky Mountains by a vast wilderness, filled by hostile savages; that nearly a hundred thousand emigrants pass through this barbarous wilderness every year, on their way to California and Oregon; that these emigrants are American citizens, our own constituents, who are entitled to the protection of law and government; and that they are left to make their way, as best they may, without the protection or aid of law or government.

The United States mails for New Mexico and Utah, and all official communications between this government and the authorities of those Territories, are required to be carried over these wild plains, and through the gorges of the mountains, where you have made no provision for roads, bridges, or ferries, to facilitate travel, or forts or other means of safety to protect life. As often as I have brought forward and urged the adoption of measures to remedy these evils, and afford security against the dangers to which our people are constantly exposed, they have been promptly voted down as not being of sufficient importance to command the favorable consideration of Congress. Now, when I propose to organize the Territories, and allow the people to do for themselves what you have so often refused to do for them, I am told that there are not white inhabitants enough permanently settled in the country to require and sustain a government. True, there is not a very large population there, for the very good reason that your Indian code and intercourse laws exclude the settlers, and forbid their remaining there to cultivate the soil. You refuse to throw the country open to settlers, and then object to the organization of the Territories upon the ground that there is not a sufficient number of inhabitants.

The senator from Connecticut (Mr. Smith) has made a long argument to prove that there are no inhabitants in the proposed Territories, because nearly all of those who have gone and settled there have done so in violation of certain old acts of Congress which forbid the people to take possession of and settle upon the public lands until after they should be surveyed and brought into market.

I do not propose to discuss the question whether these settlers are technically legal inhabitants or not. It is enough for me that they are a part of our own people; that they are settled on the public domain; that the public interests would be promoted by throwing that public domain open to settlement; and that there is no good reason why the protection of law and the blessings of government should not be extended to them. I must be permitted to remind the senator that the same objection existed in its full force to Minnesota, to Oregon and to Washington, when each of those Territories were organized; and that I have no recollection that he deemed it his duty to call the attention of Congress to the objection, or considered it of sufficient importance to justify him in recording his own vote against the organization of either of those Territories.

Mr. President, I do not feel called upon to make any reply to the argument which the senator from Connecticut has urged against the passage of this bill upon the score of expense in sustaining these Territorial governments, for the reason that, if the public interests require the enactment of the law, it follows as a natural consequence that all the expenses necessary to carry it into effect are wise and proper.

I will now proceed to the consideration of the great principle involved in the bill, without omitting, however, to notice some of those extraneous matters which have been brought into this discussion with the view of producing another anti-slavery agitation. We have been told by nearly every senator who has spoken in opposition to this bill, that at the time of its introduction the people were in a state of profound quiet and repose; that the anti-slavery agitation had entirely ceased; and that the whole country was acquiescing cheerfully and cordially in the Compromise measures of 1850, as a final adjustment of this vexed question.

Sir, it is truly refreshing to hear senators who contested every inch of ground in opposition to those measures when they were under discussion, who predicted all manner of evils and calamities from their adoption, and who raised the cry of repeal, and even resistance, to their execution, after they had become the laws of the land—I say it is really refreshing to hear these same senators now bear their united testimony to the wisdom of those measures, and to the patriotic motives which induced us to pass them in defiance of their threats and resistance, and to their beneficial effects in restoring peace, harmony and fraternity to a distracted country. These are precious confessions from the lips of those who stand pledged never to assent to the propriety of those measures, and to make war upon them so long as they shall remain upon the statute-book. I well understand that these confessions are now made, not with the view of yielding their assent to the propriety of carrying those enactments into faithful execution, but for the purpose of having a pretext for charging upon me, as the author of this bill, the responsibility of an agitation which they are striving to produce. They say that I, and not they, have revived the agitation. What have I done to render me obnoxious to this charge? They say I wrote and introduced this Nebraska Bill. That is true; but I was not a volunteer in the transaction. The Senate, by a unanimous vote, appointed me chairman of the Territorial Committee, and associated five intelligent and patriotic senators with me, and thus made it our duty to take charge of all Territorial business. In like manner, and with the concurrence of these complaining senators, the Senate referred to us a distinct proposition to organize this Nebraska Territory, and required us to report specifically upon the question. I repeat, then, we were not volunteers in this business. The duty was imposed upon us by the Senate. We were not unmindful of the delicacy and responsibility of the position. We were aware that from 1820 to

1850 the abolition doctrine of Congressional interference with slavery in the Territories and new States had so far prevailed as to keep up an incessant slavery agitation in Congress and throughout the country, whenever any new Territory was to be acquired or organized. We were also aware that, in 1850, the right of the people to decide this question for themselves, subject only to the Constitution, was substituted for the doctrine of Congressional intervention. The first question, therefore, which the committee were called upon to decide, and indeed the only question of any material importance, in framing this bill, was this: Shall we adhere to and carry out the principle recognized by the Compromise measures of 1850, or shall we go back to the old exploded doctrine of Congressional interference, as established in 1820 in a large portion of the country, and which it was the object of the Wilmot Proviso to give a universal application, not only to all the Territory which we then possessed, but all which we might hereafter acquire? There were no other alternatives. We were compelled to frame the bill upon the one or the other of these two principles. The doctrine of 1820 or the doctrine of 1850 must prevail. In the discharge of the duty imposed upon us by the Senate, the committee could not hesitate upon this point, whether we consulted our individual opinions and principles, or those which were known to be entertained and boldly avowed by a large majority of the Senate. The two great political parties of the country stood solemnly pledged before the world to adhere to the Compromise measures of 1850, "in principle and substance." A large majority of the Senate, indeed every member of the body, I believe, except the two avowed abolitionists (Mr. Chase and Mr. Sumner), profess to belong to the one or the other of these parties, and hence was supposed to be under a high moral obligation to carry out the "principle and substance" of those measures in all new Territorial organizations. The report of the committee was in accordance with this obligation. I am arraigned, therefore, for having endeavored to represent the opinions and principles of the Senate truly; for having performed my duty in conformity with the parliamentary law; for having been faithful to the trust reposed in me by the Senate. Let the vote this night determine whether I have thus faithfully represented your opinions. When a majority of the Senate shall have passed the bill; when a majority of the States shall have indorsed it through their representatives upon this floor; when a majority of the South and a majority of the North shall have sanctioned it; when a majority of the Whig party and a majority of the Democratic party shall have voted for it; when each of these propositions shall be demonstrated by the vote this night on the final passage of the bill, I shall be willing to submit the question to the country, whether, as the organ of the committee, I performed my duty in the report and bill which have called down upon my head so much denunciation and abuse.

Mr. President, the opponents of this measure have had much to

5

say about the mutations and modifications which this bill has under-gone since it was first introduced by myself, and about the alleged departure of the bill, in its present form, from the principle laid down in the original report of the committee as a rule of action in all future Territorial organizations. Fortunately there is no neces-sity, even if your patience would tolerate such a course of argument at this late hour of the night, for me to examine these speeches in detail, and to reply to each charge separately. Each speaker seems to have followed faithfully in the footsteps of his leader—in the path marked out by the abolition confederates in their manifesto, which I exposed on a former occasion. You have seen them on their wind-ing way, meandering the narrow and crooked path in Indian file, each treading close upon the heels of the other, and neither ventur-ing to take a step to the right or left, or to occupy one inch of ground which did not bear the foot-print of the abolition champion. To answer one, therefore, is to answer the whole. The statement to which they seem to attach the most importance, and which they have repeated oftener perhaps than any other, is, that, pending the Compromise measures of 1850, no man in or out of Congress ever dreamed of abrogating the Missouri Compromise; that from that period down to the present session, nobody supposed that its validity had been impaired, or anything done which rendered it obligatory upon us to make it inoperative hereafter; that at the time of sub-mitting the report and bill to the Senate, on the 4th of January last, neither I nor any member of the committee ever thought of such a thing; and that we could never be brought up to the point of abro-gating the eighth section of the Missouri act until after the senator from Kentucky introduced his amendment to my bill.

Mr. President, before I proceed to expose the many misrepresenta-tions contained in this complicated charge, I must call the attention of the Senate to the false issue which these gentlemen are endeavor-ing to impose upon the country, for the purpose of diverting public attention from the real issue contained in the bill. They wish to have the people believe that the abrogation of what they call the Missouri Compromise was the main object and aim of the bill, and that the only question involved is, whether the prohibition of slavery north of 36° 30' shall be repealed or not? That which is a mere incident, they choose to consider the principal. They make war on the means by which we propose to accomplish an object, instead of openly resisting the object itself. The principle which we propose to carry into effect by the bill is this: That Congress shall neither legislate slavery into any Territories or State, nor out of the same; but the people shall be left free to regulate their domestic concerns in their own way, subject only to the Constitution of the United States.

In order to carry this principle into practical operation, it becomes necessary to remove whatever legal obstacles might be found in the way of its free exercise. It is only for the purpose of carrying out this great fundamental principle of self-government that the bill renders the eighth section of the Missouri act inoperative and void.

Now, let me ask, will these senators who have arraigned me, or any one of them, have the assurance to rise in his place and declare that this great principle was never thought of or advocated as applicable to Territorial bills in 1850; that, from that session until the present, nobody ever thought of incorporating this principle in all new Territorial organizations; that the Committee on Territories did not recommend it in their report; and that it required the amendment of the senator from Kentucky to bring us up to that point? Will any one of my accusers dare to make this issue, and let it be tried by the record? I will begin with the compromises of 1850. Any senator who will take the trouble to examine our journals will find that on the 25th of March of that year I reported from the Committee on Territories two bills including the following measures: The admission of California, a Territorial government for Utah, a Territorial government for New Mexico, and the adjustment of the Texas boundary. These bills proposed to leave the people of Utah and New Mexico free to decide the slavery question for themselves, in the precise language of the Nebraska Bill now under discussion. A few weeks afterward, the Committee of Thirteen took those two bills and put a wafer between them, and reported them back to the Senate as one bill, with some slight amendments. One of those amendments was, that the Territorial legislatures should not legislate upon the subject of African slavery. I objected to that provision upon the ground that it subverted the great principle of self-government upon which the bill had been originally framed by the Territorial Committee. On the the first trial, the Senate refused to strike it out, but subsequently did so, after full debate, in order to establish that principle as the rule of action in Territorial organizations.

Upon this point I trust I will be excused for reading one or two sentences from some remarks I made in the Senate on the 3d of June, 1850:

"The position that I have ever taken has been that this, the slavery question, and all other questions relating to the domestic affairs and domestic policy of the Territories, ought to be left to the decision of the people themselves, and that we ought to be content with whatever way they would decide the question, because they have a much deeper interest in these matters than we have, and know much better what institutions will suit them, than we, who have never been there, can decide for them."

Again, in the same debate, I said:

"I do not see how those of us who have taken the position which we have taken, (that of non-interference,) and have argued in favor of the right of the people to legislate for themselves on this question, can support such a provision without abandoning all the arguments which we urged in the Presiden tial campaign in the year 1848, and the principles set forth by the honorable senator from Michigan in that letter which is known as the 'Nicholson letter.' We are required to abandon that platform; we are required to abandon those principles, and to stultify ourselves, and to adopt the opposite doctrine; and for what? In order to say that the people of the Territories shall not have such institutions as they shall deem adapted to their condition and their wants. I do not see, sir, how such a provision as that can be acceptable either to the people of the North or the South."

Mr. President, I could go on and multiply extract after extract from my speeches in 1850, and prior to that date, to show that this doctrine of leaving the people to decide these questions for themselves is not an "after-thought" with me, seized upon, this session, for the first time, as my calumniators have so frequently and boldly charged in their speeches during this debate, and in their manifesto to the public. I refused to support the celebrated Omnibus Bill in 1850 until the obnoxious provision was stricken out, and the principle of self-government restored, as it existed in my original bill. No sooner were the Compromise measures of 1850 passed, than the abolition confederates, who lead the opposition to this bill now, raised the cry of repeal in some sections of the country, and in others forcible resistance to the execution of the law. In order to arrest and suppress the treasonable purposes of these abolition confederates, and avert the horrors of civil war, it became my duty, on the 23d of October, 1850, to address an excited and frenzied multitude at Chicago, in defence of each and all of the Compromise measures of that year. I will read one or two sentences from that speech, to show how those measures were then understood and explained by their advocates:

" These measures are predicated on the great fundamental principle that every people ought to possess the right of forming and regulating their own internal concerns and domestic institutions in their own way."

Again:

" These things are all confided by the Constitution to each State to decide for itself, and I KNOW OF NO REASON WHY THE *same principle should not be confided to the Territories.*"

In this speech it will be seen that I lay down a general principle of universal application, and make no distinction between Territories north or south of 36° 30'.

I am aware that some of the abolition confederates have perpetrated a monstrous forgery on that speech, and are now circulating through the abolition newspapers the statement that I said that I would " cling with the tenacity of life to the compromise of 1820 " This statement, false as it is—a deliberate act of forgery, as it is known to be by all who have ever seen or read the speech referred to—constitutes the staple article out of which most of the abolition orators at the small anti-Nebraska meetings manufacture the greater part of their speeches. I now declare that there is not a sentence, a line, even a word in that speech, which imposes the slightest limitation on the application of the great principle embraced in this bill in all new Territorial organizations, without the least reference to the line of 36° 30'.

At the session of 1850–51, a few weeks after this speech was made at Chicago, and when it had been published in pamphlet form and circulated extensively over the States, the legislature of Illinois proceeded to revise its action upon the slavery question, and define its position on the compromise of 1850. After rescinding the resolutions adopted at a previous session, instructing my colleague and myself to vote for a proposition prohibiting slavery in the Territories, resolutions were adopted approving the Compromise measures of 1850. I will read one of the resolutions, which was adopted in the House of Representatives, by a vote of 61 yeas to 4 nays:

"*Resolved*, That our liberty and independence are based upon the right of the people to form for themselves such a government as they may choose; that this great privilege—the birthright of freemen, the gift of Heaven, secured to us by the blood of our ancestors—ought to be extended to future generations; and no limitation ought to be applied to this power, in the organization of any Territory of the United States, of either a Territorial government or a State Constitution: *Provided*, The government so established shall be republican, and in conformity with the Constitution."

Another series of resolutions having passed the Senate almost unanimously, embracing the same principle in different language, they were concurred in by the House. Thus was the position of Illinois, upon the slavery question defined at the first session of the legislature after the adoption of the Compromise of 1850.

Now, sir, what becomes of the declaration which has been made by nearly every opponent of this bill, that nobody in this whole Union ever dreamed that the principle of the Utah and New Mexican bill was to be incorporated into all future Territorial organizations? I have shown that my own State so understood and declared it at the time in the most implicit and solemn manner. Illinois declared that our "liberty and independence" rest upon this "principle;" that the principle "ought to be extended to future generations;" and that "NO LIMITATION OUGHT TO BE APPLIED TO THIS POWER IN THE ORGANIZATION OF ANY TERRITORY OF THE UNITED STATES." No exception is made in regard to Nebraska. No Missouri Compromise lines; no reservations of the country north of 36° 30'. The principle is declared to be be the "birthright of freemen:" the "gift of Heaven, to be applied without limitation," in Nebraska as well as Utah, north as well as south of 36° 30'.

It may not be out of place here to remark that the legislature of Illinois, at its recent session, has passed resolutions approving the Nebraska Bill; and among the resolutions is one in the precise language of the resolution of 1851, which I have just read to the Senate.

Thus I have shown, Mr. President, that the legislature and people of Illinois have always understood the Compromise measures of 1850 as establishing certain principles as rules of action in the organization of all new Territories, and that no limitation was to be made on either side of the geographical line of 36° 30'.

Neither my time nor your patience will allow me to take up the resolutions of the different States in detail, and show what has been the common understanding of the whole country upon this point. I am now vindicating myself and my own action against the assaults of my calumniators; and, for that purpose, it is sufficient to show that, in the report and bill which I have presented to the Senate, I have only carried out the known principles and solemnly declared will of the State whose representative I am. I will now invite the attention of the Senate to the report of the committee, in order that it may be known how much, or rather how little, truth there is for the allegation which has been so often made and repeated on this floor, that the idea of allowing the people in Nebraska to decide the slavery question for themselves was a "sheer after-thought," conceived since the report was made, and not until the senator from Kentucky proposed his amendment to the bill.

I read from that portion of the report in which the committee lay down the principle by which they propose to be governed:

"In the judgment of your committee, those measures (Compromise of 1850) were intended to have a far more comprehensive and enduring effect than the mere adjustment of the difficulties arising out of the recent acquisition of Mexican territory. They were designed to establish certain great principles, which would not only furnish adequate remedies for existing evils, but *in all time to come* avoid the perils of a similar agitation, *by withdrawing the question of slavery from the halls of Congress and the political arena, and committing it to the arbitrament of those who were immediately interested in and alone responsible for its consequences.*"

After making a brief argument in defence of this principle, the report proceeds, as follows:

"From these provisions, it is apparent that the Compromise measures of 1850 affirm and rest upon the following propositions:

"First, that all questions pertaining to slavery in the Territories, and in the new States to be formed therefrom, are to be left to the decision of the people residing therein, by their appropriate representatives, to be chosen by them for that purpose."

And in conclusion, the report proposes a substitute for the bill introduced by the senator from Iowa, and concludes as follows:

"The substitute for the bill which your committee have prepared, and which is commended to the favorable action of the Senate, proposes to carry these propositions and principles into practical operation, in the precise language of the Compromise measures of 1850."

Mr. President, as there has been so much misrepresentation upor this point, I must be permitted to repeat that the doctrine of the report of the committee, as has been conclusively proved by these extracts, is—

First, That the whole question of slavery should be withdrawn from the halls of Congress, and the political arena, and committed to the arbitrament of those who are immediately interested in and alone responsible for its existence.

Second, The applying this principle to the Territories and the new States to be formed therefrom, all questions pertaining to slavery were to be referred to the people residing therein.

Third, That the committee proposed to carry these propositions and principles into effect in the precise language of the compromise measures of 1850.

Are not these propositions identical with the principles and provisions of the bill on your table? If there is a hair's breadth of discrepancy between the two, I ask any senator to rise in his place and point it out. Both rest upon the great principle, which forms the basis of all our institutions, that the people are to decide the question for themselves, subject only to the Constitution.

But my accusers attempt to raise up a false issue, and thereby divert public attention from the real one, by the cry that the Missouri Compromise is to be repealed or violated by the passage of this bill. Well, if the eighth section of the Missouri Act, which attempted to fix the destinies of future generations in those Territories for all time to come, in utter disregard of the rights and wishes of the people when they should be received into the Union as States, be inconsistent with the great principle of self-government and the Constitution of the United States, it ought to be abrogated. The legislation of 1850 abrogated the Missouri Compromise, so far as the country embraced within the limits of Utah and New Mexico was covered by the slavery restriction. It is true, that those acts did not in terms and by name repeal the act of 1820, as originally adopted, or as extended by the resolutions annexing Texas in 1845, any more than the report of the Committee on Territories proposes to repeal the same acts this session. But the acts of 1850 did authorize the people of those Territories to exercise " all rightful powers of legislation consistent with the Constitution," not excepting the question of slavery; and did provide that, when those Territories should be admitted into the Union, they should be received with or without slavery as the people thereof might determine at the date of their admission. These provisions were in direct conflict with a clause in a former enactment, declaring that slavery should be forever prohibited in any portion of said Territories, and hence rendered such clause inoperative and void to the extent of such conflict. This was an inevitable consequence, resulting from the provisions in those acts which gave the people the right to decide the slavery question for themselves, in conformity with the Constitution. It was not necessary to go further and declare that certain previous enactments, which were incompatible with the exercise of the powers conferred in the bills, "are hereby repealed." The very act of granting those powers and rights have the legal effect of removing all obstructions to the exercise of them by the people, as prescribed in those Territorial bills. Following that example, the Committee on Territories did not consider it necessary to declare the eighth section of the Missouri act repealed. We were content to organize Nebraska in the precise language of the Utah and New Mexican bills. Our object was to leave the people entirely free to form and regulate their domestic institutions and internal concerns in their own way, under the constitution; and we deemed it wise to accomplish that object in the exact terms in which the same thing had been done in Utah and New Mexico by the acts of 1850. This was the principle upon which the committee reported; and our bill was supposed, and is now believed, to have been in accordance with it. When doubts were raised whether the bill did fully carry out the principle laid down in the report, amendments were made, from time to time, in order to avoid all misconstruction, and make the true intent of the act more explicit. The last of these amendments was adopted yesterday, on the motion of the distinguished senator from North Carolina (Mr. Badger), in regard to the revival of any laws or regulations which may have existed prior to 1820. That amendment was not intended to change the legal effect of the bill. Its object was to repel the slander which had been propagated by the enemies of the measures in the North, that the southern supporters of the bill desired to legislate slavery into these Territories. The south denies the right of Congress either to legislate slavery into any Territory or State, or out of any Territory or State. Non-intervention by Congress with slavery in the States or Territories is the doctrine of the bill, and all the amendments which have been agreed to have been made with the view of removing all doubts and cavil as to the true meaning and object of the measure.

Mr. President, I think I have succeeded in vindicating myself and the action of the committee from the assaults which have been made upon us in consequence of these amendments. It seems to be the tactics of our opponents to direct their arguments against the unimportant points and incidental questions which are to be affected by carrying out the principle, with the hope of relieving themselves from the necessity of controverting the principle itself. The senator from Ohio (Mr. Chase) led off gallantly in the charge that the committee, in the report and bill first submitted, did not contemplate the repeal of the Missouri Compromise, and could not be brought to that point until after the senator from Kentucky offered his amendment. The senator from Connecticut (Mr. Smith) followed his lead, and repeated the same statement. Then came the other senator from Ohio (Mr. Ward), and the senator from New York (Mr. Seward), and senator from Massachusetts (Mr. Sumner), all singing the same song, only varying the tune.

Let me ask those senators what they mean by this statement? Do they wish to be understood as saying that the report and first form of the bill did not provide for leaving the slavery question to the decision of the people in the terms of the Utah Bill? Surely they will not dare to say that, for I have already shown that the two measures were identical in principle and enactment. Do they mean to say that the adoption of our first bill would not have had the legal effect to have rendered the eighth section of the Missouri Act "inoperative and void," to use the language of the present bill? If this be not their meaning, will they rise in their places and inform the Senate what their meaning was? They must have had some object in giving so much prominence to this statement, and in repeating it so often. I address the question to the senators from Ohio and Massachusetts (Mr. Chase and Mr. Sumner). I despair in extorting a response from them, for, no matter in what way they may answer upon this point, I have in my hand the evidence over their own signatures, to disprove the truth of their answer. I allude to their appeal or manifesto to the people of the United States, in which they arraign the bill and report, in coarse and savage terms, as a proposition to repeal the Missouri Compromise, to violate plighted faith, to abrogate a solemn compact, etc. etc. This document was signed by those two senators in their official capacity, and published to the world before any amendments had been offered to the bill. It was directed against the committee's first bill and report, and against them alone. If the statements in this document be true, that the first bill did repeal the eighth section of the Missouri Act, what are we to think of the statements in their speeches since, that such was not the intention of the committee, was not the recommendation of the report, and was not the legal effect of the bill? On the contrary, if the statements in their subsequent speeches are true, what apology do those senators propose to make to the Senate and country for having falsified the action of the committee in a document over their own signatures, and thus spread a false alarm among the people, and misled the public mind in respect to our proceedings? These senators cannot avoid the one or the other of these alternatives. Let them seize upon either, and they stand condemned and self-convicted; in the one case by their manifesto, and in the other by their speeches.

In fact, it is clear that they have understood the bill to mean the same thing, and to have the same legal effect in whatever phase it has been presented. When first introduced, they denounced it as a proposition to abrogate the Missouri restriction. When amended, they repeated the same denunciation, and so on each successive amendment. They now object to the passage of the bill for the same reason, thus proving conclusively that they have not the least faith in the correctness of their own statements in respect to the mutations and changes in the bill.

They seem very unwilling to meet the real issue. They do not like to discuss the principle. There seems to be something which strikes them with terror when you invite their attention to this great fundamental principle of popular sovereignty. Hence you find that all the memorials they have presented are against repealing the Missouri Compromise, and in favor of the sanctity of compacts—in favor of preserving plighted faith. The senator from Ohio is cautious to dedicate his speech with some such heading as "Maintain Plighted Faith." The object is to keep the attention of the people as far as possible from this principle of self-government and constitutional rights.

Well, sir, what is this Missouri Compromise, of which we have heard so much of late? It has been read so often that it is not necessary to occupy the time of the Senate in reading it again. It was an act of Congress, passed on the 6th of March, 1820, to authorize the people of Missouri to form a constitution and a State government, preparatory to the admission of such State into the Union. The first section provided that Missouri should be received into the Union "on an equal footing with the original States in all respects whatsoever." The last and eighth section provided that slavery should be "for ever prohibited" in all the territory which had been acquired from France north of 36° 30', and not included within the limits of the State of Missouri. There is nothing in the terms of the law that purports to be a compact, or indicates that it was anything more than an ordinary act of legislation. To prove that it was more than it purports to be on its face, gentlemen must produce other evidence, and prove that there was such an understanding as to create a moral obligation in the nature of a compact. Have they shown it?

I have heard but one item of evidence produced during this whole debate, and that was a short paragraph from Niles's Register, published a few days after the passage of the act. But gentlemen aver that it was a solemn compact, which could not be violated or abrogated without dishonor. According to their understanding, the contract was that, in consideration of the admission of Missouri into the Union, on an equal footing with the original States in all respects whatsoever, slavery should be prohibited forever in the Territories north of 36° 30'. Now, who were the parties to this alleged compact? They tell us that it was a stipulation between the North and the South. Sir, I know of no such parties under the Constitution. I am unwilling that there shall be any such parties known in our legislation. If there is such a geographical line, it ought to be obliterated for ever, and there should be no other parties than those provided for in the Constitution, viz.: the States of this Union. These are the only parties capable of contracting under the Constitution of the United States.

Now, if this was a compact, let us see how it was entered into. The bill originated in the House of Representatives, and passed that body without a southern vote in its favor. It is proper to remark, however, that it did not at that time contain the eighth section, prohibiting slavery in the Territories; but in lieu of it, contained a provision prohibiting slavery in the proposed State of Missouri. In the Senate, the clause prohibiting slavery in the State was stricken out, and the eighth section added to the end of the bill, by the terms of which slavery was to be forever prohibited in the Territory not embraced in the State of Missouri north of 36° 30'. The vote on adding this section stood, in the Senate, 34 in the affirmative, and 10 in the negative. Of the northern senators, 20 voted for it and 2 against it. On the question of ordering the bill to a third reading as amended, which was the test vote on its passage, the vote stood 24 yeas and 20 nays. Of the northern senators, 4 only voted in the affirmative, and 18 in the negative. Thus it will be seen that, if it was intended to be a compact, the North never agreed to it. The northern senators voted to insert the prohibition of slavery in the Territories; and then, in the proportion of more than four to one voted against the passage of the bill. The North, therefore, never signed the compact, never consented to it, never agreed to be bound by it. This fact becomes very important in vindicating the character of the North for repudiating this alleged compromise a few months afterward. The act was approved and became a law on the 6th of March, 1820. In the summer of that year, the people of Missouri formed a constitution and State government, preparatory to admission into the Union, in conformity with the act. At the next session of Congress the Senate passed a joint resolution, declaring Missouri to be one of the States of the Union, on an equal footing with the original States. This resolution was sent to the House of Representatives, where it was rejected by northern votes, and thus Missouri was voted out of the Union, instead of being received into the Union under the act of the 6th of March, 1820, now known as the Missouri Compromise. Now, sir, what becomes of our plighted faith, if the act of the 6th of March, 1820, was a solemn compact, as we are now told? They have all rung the changes upon it, that it was a sacred and irrevocable compact, binding in honor, in conscience, and morals, which could not be violated or repudiated without perfidy and dishonor! The two senators from Ohio (Mr. Chase and Mr. Wade), the senator from Massachusetts (Mr. Sumner), the senator from Connecticut (Mr. Smith), the senator from New York (Mr. Seward), and perhaps others, have all assumed this position.

MR. SEWARD.—Whoever will refer to my antecedents will find that in the year 1850 I expressed opinions on the subject of legislative compromises between the North and South, which, at that day were rejected and repudiated.

MR. DOUGLAS.—If the object of the senator is to go back, and go through all his opinions, I cannot yield the floor to him; but if his object is now to show that the North did not violate the Missouri compromise, I will yield.

MR. SEWARD.—If the honorable senator will allow me just one

minute and a half, without dictating what I shall say within that minute and a half, I shall be satisfied.

MR. DOUGLAS.—Certainly, I will consent to that.

MR. SEWARD.—I find that the honorable senator from Illinois is standing upon the ground upon which I stood in 1850. I have nothing to say now in favor of that ground. On this occasion, I stand upon the ground, in regard to compromises, which has been adopted by the country. Then, when the senator tells me that the North did not altogether, willingly, and unanimously, consent to the compromise of 1820, I agree to it; but I have been overborne in the country, on the ground that if one northern man carried with him a majority of Congress he bound the whole North. And so I hold in regard to the compromise of 1820, that it was carried by a vote which has been held by the South and by the honorable senator from Illinois to bind the North. The South having received their consideration and equivalent, I only hold him, upon his own doctrine and the doctrine of the South, bound to stand to it. That is all I have to say upon that point.

A few words more will cover all that I have to say about what the honorable senator may say hereafter as to the North repudiating this contract. When I was absent, I understood the senator alluded to the fact that my name appeared upon a paper which was issued by the honorable senator from Ohio, and some other members of Congress, to the people, on the subject of this bill. Upon that point it has been my intention throughout to leave to the honorable senator from Illinois, and those who act with him, whatever there is of merit, and whatever there is of responsibility for the present measure, and for all the agitation and discussion upon it. Therefore, as soon as I found, when I returned to the Capitol, that my name was on that paper, I caused it to be made known and published, as fully and extensively as I could, that I had never been consulted in regard to it; that I know nothing about it; and that the merit of the measure, as well as the responsibility, belonged to the honorable senator from Ohio, and those who coöperated with him; and that I had never seen the paper on which he commented; nor have I in any way addressed the public upon the subject.

MR. DOUGLAS.—I wish to ask the senator from New York a question. If I understood his remarks when he spoke, and if I understand his speech as published, he averred that the Missouri Compromise was a compact between the North and the South; that the North performed it on its part; that it had done so faithfully for thirty years; that the South had received all its benefits, and the moment these benefits had been fully realized, the South disavowed the obligations under which it had received them. Is not that his position?

MR. SEWARD.—I am not accustomed to answer questions put to me, unless they are entirely categorical, and placed in such a shape that I may know exactly, and have time to consider, their whole extent. The honorable senator from Illinois has put a very broad question

What I mean to say, however, and that will answer his purpose, is, that his position, and that the position of the South is, that this was a compromise; and I say that the North has never repudiated that compromise. Indeed, it has never had the power to do so. Missouri came into the Union, and Arkansas came into the Union, under that compromise; and, whatever individuals may have said, whatever individuals, more or less humble than myself, may have contended, the practical effect is, that the South has had all that she could get by that compromise, and that the North is now in the predicament of being obliged to defend what was left to her. I believe that answers the question.

Mr. Douglas.—Now, Mr. President, I choose to bring men directly up to this point. The senator from New York has labored in his whole speech to make it appear that this was a compact; that the North had been faithful; and that the South acquiesced until she got all its advantages, and then disavowed and sought to annul it. This he pronounced to be bad faith; and he made appeals about disorder. The senator from Connecticut (Mr. Smith) did the same thing, and so did the senator from Massachusetts (Mr. Sumner), and the senator from Ohio (Mr. Chase). That is the point to which the whole abolition party are now directing all their artillery in this battle. Now, I propose to bring them to the point. If this was a compact, and if what they have said is fair, or just, or true, who was it that repudiated the compact?

Mr. Sumner.—Mr. President, the senator from Illinois, I know, does not intend to misstate my position. That position, as announced in the language of the speech which I addressed to the Senate, and which I now hold in my hand, is, "this is an infraction of solemn obligations, assumed beyond recall by the South, on the admission of Missouri into the Union as a slave State;" which was one year after the act of 1820.

Mr. Douglas.—Mr. President, I shall come to that; and I wish to see whether this was an obligation which was assumed "beyond recall." If it was a compact between the two parties, one party has been faithful, it is beyond recall by the other. If, however, one party has been faithless, what shall we think of them, if, while faithless, they ask a performance?

Mr. Seward.—Show it.

Mr. Douglas.—That is what I am coming to. I have already stated that, at the next session of Congress, Missouri presented a constitution in conformity with the act of 1820; that the Senate passed a joint resolution to admit her; and that the House refused to admit Missouri in conformity with the alleged compact, and, I think, on three distinct votes, rejected her.

Mr. Seward.—I beg my honorable friend, for I desire to call him so, to answer me frankly whether he would rather I should say what I have to say in this desultory way, or whether he would prefer that I should answer him afterward; because it is with me a rule in the Senate never to interrupt a gentleman, except to help him in his argument.

Mr. Douglas.—I would rather hear the senator now.

Mr. Seward.—What I have to say now, and I acknowledge the magnanimity of the senator from Illinois in allowing me to say it, is, that the North stood by that compact until Missouri came in with a constitution, one article of which denied to colored citizens of other States the equality of privileges which were allowed to all other citizens of the United Sates, and then the North insisted on the right of colored men to be regarded as citizens, and entitled to the privileges and immunities of citizens. Upon that a new compromise was necessary. I hope I am candid.

Mr. Douglas.—The senator is candid, I have no doubt, as he understands the facts; but I undertake to maintain that the North objected to Missouri because she allowed slavery, and not because of the free-negro clause alone.

Mr. Seward.—No sir.

Mr. Douglas.—Now I will proceed to prove that the North did not object, solely on account of the free-negro clause; but that in House of Representatives at that time, the North objected as well because of slavery as in regard to free negroes. Here is the evidence. In the House of Representatives, on the 12th of February, 1821, Mr. Mallory, of Vermont, moved to amend the Senate joint resolution for the admission of Missouri, as follows:

" To amend the said amendment, by striking out all thereof after the words *respects*, and inserting the following : ' Whenever people of the said State, by a convention, appointed according to the manner provided by the act to authorize the people of Missouri to form a constitution and State government, and for the admission of such State into the Union on an equal footing with the original States, and to prohibit slavery in certain Territories, approved March 6, 1820, adopt a constitution conformably to the provisions of said act, and shall, IN ADDITION *to said provisions, further provide, in and by said constitution, that neither slavery nor involuntary servitude shall ever be allowed in said State of Missouri*, unless inflicted as a punishment for crimes committed against the laws of said State, whereof the party accused shall be duly convicted : *Provided*, That the civil condition of those persons who now are held to service in Missouri shall not be affected by this last provision.' "

Here I show, then, that the proposition was made that Missouri should not come in unless, in addition to complying with the Missouri Compromise, so called, she would go further, and prohibit slavery within the limits of the State.

Mr. Seward.—Now, then, for the vote.

Mr. Douglas.—The vote was taken by yeas and nays. I hold it in my hand. Sixty-one northern men voted for that amendment, and thirty-three against it. Thus the North, by a vote of nearly two to one, expressly repudiated a solemn compact upon the very matter in controversy, to wit: that slavery should not be prohibited in the State of Missouri.

Mr. Weller.—Let the senator from New York answer that.

Mr. Douglas.—I should like to hear his answer.

Mr. Seward.—I desire, if I shall be obtrusive by speaking in this way, that senators will at once signify, or that any senator will signify, that I am obtrusive. But I make these explanations in this way, for the reason that I desire to give the honorable senator from Illinois the privilege of hearing my answer to him as he goes along. It is simply this: That this doctrine of compromises is, as it has been held, that if so many northern men shall go with so many southern men as to fix the law, then it binds the North and South alike. I therefore have but one answer to make: the vote for the restriction was less than the northern vote given against the compromise.

Mr. Douglas.—Well, now, we come to this point: We have been told, during this debate, that you must not judge of the North by the minority, but by the majority. You have been told, that the minority, who stood by the Constitution and the rights of the South, were dough-faces.

Mr. Seward.—I have not said so. I will not say so.

Mr. Douglas.—You have all said so in your speeches, and you have asked us to take the majority of the North.

Mr. Seward.—I spoke of the practical fact. I never said anything about dough-faces.

Mr. Douglas.—You have asked us to take the majority instead of the minority.

Mr. Seward.—The majority of the country.

Mr. Douglas.—I am talking of the majority of the northern vote.

Mr. Seward.—No, sir.

Mr. Douglas.—I hope the senator will hear me. I wish to recall him to the issue. I stated that the North in the House of Representatives voted against admitting Missouri into the Union under the act of 1820, and caused the defeat of that measure; and he said that they voted against it on the ground of the free-negro clause in her constitution, and not upon the ground of slavery. Now, I have shown by the evidence that it was upon the ground of slavery, as well as upon the other ground; and that a majority of the North required not only that Missouri should comply with the compact of 1820, so called, but that she should go further, and give up the whole consideration which the senator says the South received from the North for the Missouri Compromise. The compact, he says, was that, in consideration of slavery being permitted in Missouri, it should be prohibited in the Territories. After having procured the prohibition in the Territories, the North, by a majority of votes, refused to admit Missouri as a slaveholding State, and in violation of the alleged compact, required her to prohibit slavery as a further condition of her admission. This repudiation of the alleged compact by the North is recorded by yeas and nays, sixty-one to thirty-three, and entered upon the Journal, as an imperishable evidence of the fact. With this evidence before us, against whom should the charge of perfidy be preferred?

Sir, if this was a compact, what must be thought of those who violated it almost immediately after it was formed? I say it was a calumny upon the North to say that it was a compact: I should feel a flush of shame upon my cheek, as a northern man, if I were to say that it was a compact, and that the section of the country to which I belong received the consideration, and then repudiated the obligation in eleven months after it was entered into. I deny that it was a compact in any sense of the term. But if it was, the record proves that faith was not observed; that the contract was never carried into effect; that after the North had procured the passage of the act prohibiting slavery in the Territories, with a majority in the House large enough to prevent its repeal, Missouri was refused admission into the Union as a slaveholding State, in conformity with the act of March 6, 1820. If the proposition be correct, as contended for by the opponents of this bill, that there was a solemn compact between the North and the South, that, in consideration of the prohibition of slavery in the Territories, Missouri was to be admitted into the Union in conformity with the act of 1820, that compact was repudiated by the North and rescinded by the joint action of the two parties within twelve months from its date. Missouri was never admitted under the act of the 6th of March, 1820. She was refused admission under that act. She was voted out of the Union by northern votes, notwithstanding the stipulation that she should be received; and, in consequence of these facts, a new compromise was rendered necessary, by the terms of which Missouri was to be admitted into the Union conditionally—admitted on a condition not embraced in the act of 1820, and, in addition, to full compliance with all the provisions of said act. If, then, the act of 1820, by the eighth section of which slavery was prohibited in the Territories, was a compact, it is clear to the comprehension of every fair-minded man that the refusal of the North to admit Missouri, in compliance with its stipulations, and without further conditions, imposes upon us a high moral obligation to remove the prohibition of slavery in the Territories, since it has been shown to have been procured upon a condition never performed.

Mr. President, inasmuch as the senator from New York has taken great pains to impress upon the public mind of the North the conviction that the act of 1820 was a solemn compact, the violation or repudiation of which by either party involves perfidy and dishonor, I wish to call the attention of that senator (Mr. Seward) to the fact, that his own State was the first to repudiate the compact and to instruct her senators in Congress not to admit Missouri into the Union in compliance with it, nor unless slavery should be prohibited in the State of Missouri.

Mr. Seward.—That is so.

Mr. Douglas.—I have the resolutions before me, in the printed Journal of the Senate. The senator from New York is familiar with the fact, and frankly admits it:

"State of New York,
In Assembly, *November* 13, 1820.

" Whereas the legislature of this State, at the last session, did instruct their senators and request their representatives in Congress to oppose the admission, as a State, into the Union, of any territory not comprised within the original boundaries of the United States, without making the prohibition of slavery therein an indispensable condition of admission ; and whereas this legislature is impressed with the correctness of the sentiments so communicated to our senators and representatives : Therefore—

" *Resolved* (if the honorable the Senate concur herein), That this legislature does approve of the principles contained in the resolutions of the last session ; and further, if the provisions contained in any proposed constitution of a new State deny to any citizens of the existing States the privileges and immunities of citizens of such new State, that such proposed constitution should not be accepted or confirmed ; the same, in the opinion of this legislature, being void by the Constitution of the United States. And that our senators be instructed, and our representatives in Congress be requested, to use their utmost exertions to prevent the acceptance and confirmation of any such constitution."

It will be seen by these resolutions, that at the previous session the New York legislature had " instructed " the senators from that State " to oppose the admission, as a State, into the Union of any territory not comprised within the original boundaries of the United States, without making the prohibition of slavery therein an indispensable condition of admission."

These instructions are not confined to territory north of 36° 30'. They apply, and were intended to apply, to the whole territory west of the Mississippi, and to all territory which might hereafter be acquired. They deny the right of Arkansas to admission as a slave-holding State, as well as Missouri. They lay down a general principle to be applied and insisted upon everywhere, and in all cases, and under all circumstances. These resolutions were first adopted prior to the passage of the act of March 6, 1820, which the senator now chooses to call a compact. But they were renewed and repeated on the 13th of November, 1820, a little more than eight months after the Missouri Compromise, as instructions to the New York senators to resist the admission of Missouri as a slaveholding State, notwithstanding the stipulations in the alleged compact. Now, let me ask the senator from New York by what authority he declared and published in his speech that the act of 1820, was a compact which could not be violated or repudiated without a sacrifice of honor, justice and good faith. Perhaps he will shelter himself behind the resolutions of his State, which he presented this session, branding this bill as a violation of plighted faith.

Mr. Seward.—Will the senator allow me a word of explanation ?

Mr. Douglas.—Certainly, with a great deal of pleasure.

Mr. Seward.—I wish simply to say that the State of New York, for now thirty years, has refused to make any compact on any terms by which a concession should be made for the extension of slavery. But, by the practical action of the Congress of the United States, compromises have been made, which, it is held by the honorable senator from Illinois and by the South, bind her against her consent and approval. And, therefore, she stands throughout this whole matter upon the same ground—always refusing to enter into a compromise, always insisting upon the prohibition of slavery within the Territories of the United States. But, on this occasion, we stand here with a contract which has stood for 30 years, notwithstanding our protest and dissent, and in which there is nothing left to be fulfilled except that part which is to be beneficial to us. All the rest has been fulfilled, and we stand here with our old opinions on the whole subject of compromises, demanding fulfillment on the part of the South, which the honorable senator from Illinois on the present occasion represents.

MR. DOUGLAS.—Mr. President, the senator undoubtedly speaks for himself very frankly and very candidly.

MR. SEWARD.—Certainly I do.

MR. DOUGLAS.—But I deny that on this point he speaks for the State of New York.

MR. SEWARD.—We shall see.

MR. DOUGLAS.—I will state the reason why I say so. He has presented here resolutions of this State of New York which have been adopted this year, declaring the act of March 6, 1820, to be a "solemn compact."

I read from the second resolution :

" But at the same time duty to themselves and to the other States of the Union demands that when an effort is making to violate a solemn compact whereby the political power of the State and the privileges as well as the honest sentiments of its citizens will be jeoparded and invaded, they should raise their voice in protest against the threatened infraction of their rights, and declare that the negation or repeal by Congress of the Missouri Compromise will be regarded by them as a violation of right and of faith, and destructive of that confidence and regard which should attach to the enactment of the federal legislature."

Mr. President, I cannot let the senator off on the plea that I, for the sake of the argument, in reply to him and other opponents of this bill, have called it a compact ; or that the South have called it a compact ; or that other friends of Nebraska have called it a compact which has been violated and rendered invalid. He and his abolition confederates have arraigned me for a violation of a compact, which, they say, is binding in morals, in conscience and honor. I have shown that the legislature of New York, at its present session, has declared it to be " a solemn compact," and that its repudiation would " be regarded by them as a violation of right, and of faith, and destructive of confidence and regard." I have also shown, that if it be such a compact, the State of New York stands self-condemned and self-convicted as the first to repudiate and violate it.

But since the senator has chosen to make an issue with me in respect to the action of New York, with the view of condemning my conduct here, I will invite the attention of the senator to another portion of these resolutions. Referring to the fourteenth section of the Nebraska Bill, the legislature of New York says:

" That the adoption of this provision would be in derogation of the truth, a gross violation of plighted faith, and an outrage and indignity upon the free States of the Union, whose assent has been yielded to the admission into the Union of Missouri and of Arkansas, with slavery, in reliance upon the faithful observance of the provision (now sought to be abrogated) known as the Missouri Compromise, whereby slavery was declared to be " forever prohibited in all that territory ceded by France to the United States, under the name of Louisiana, which lies north of 36° 30′ north latitude, not included within the limits of the State of Missouri."

I have no comments to make upon the courtesy and propriety exhibited in this legislative declaration, that a provision in a bill, reported by a regular committee of the Senate of the United States, and known to be approved by three-fourths of the body, and which has since received the sanction of their votes, is "in derogation of truth, a gross violation of plighted faith, and an outrage and indignity," etc. The opponents of this measure claim a monopoly of all the courtesies and amenities, which should be observed among gentlemen, and especially in the performance of official duties; and I am free to say that this is one of the mildest and most respectful forms of expression in which they have indulged. But there is a declaration in this resolution to which I wish to invite the particular attention of the Senate and the country. It is the distinct allegation that "the free States of the Union," including New York, yield their "assent to the admission into the Union of Missouri and Arkansas, with slavery, in reliance upon the faithful observance of the provision known as the Missouri Compromise."

Now, sir, since the legislature of New York has gone out of its way to arraign the State on matters of truth, I will demonstrate that this paragraph contains two material statements in direct "derogation of truth." I have already shown, beyond controversy, by the records of the legislature and by the journals of the Senate, that New York never did give her assent to the admission of Missouri with slavery! Hence, I must be permitted to say, in the polite language of her own resolutions, that the statement that New York yielded her assent to the admission of Missouri with slavery is in "derogation of truth!" and, secondly, the statement that such assent was given "in reliance upon the faithful observance of the Missouri Compromise" is equally "in derogation of truth." New York never assented to the admission of Missouri as a slave State, never assented to what she now calls the Missouri Compromise, never observed its stipulations as a compact, never had been willing to carry it out; but, on the contrary, has always resisted it, as I have demonstrated by her own records.

Mr. President, I have before me other journals, records and instructions, which prove that New York was not the only free State that repudiated the Missouri Compromise of 1820 within twelve months from its date. I will not occupy the time of the Senate at this late hour of the night by referring to them, unless some opponent of the bill renders it necessary. In that event, I may be able to place other senators and their States in the same unenviable position in which the senator from New York has found himself and his State.

I think I have shown, that to call the act of the 6th of March, 1820, a compact, binding in honor, is to charge the northern States of this Union with an act of perfidy unparalleled in the history of legislation or of civilization. I have already adverted to the facts, that in the summer of 1820 Missouri framed her constitution, in conformity with the act of the 6th of March; that it was presented to Congress at the next session; that the Senate passed a joint resolution declaring her to be one of the States of the Union, on an equal footing with the original States; and that the House of Representatives rejected it, and refused to allow her to come into the Union, because her constitution did not prohibit slavery.

These facts created the necessity for a new compromise, the old one having failed of its object, which was, to bring Missouri into the Union. At this period in the order of events—in February, 1821, when the excitement was almost beyond restraint, and a great fundamental principle, involving the right of the people of the new States to regulate their own domestic institutions, was dividing the Union into two great hostile parties—Henry Clay, of Kentucky, came forward with a new compromise, which had the effect to change the issue, and make the result of the controversy turn upon a different point. He brought in a resolution for the admission of Missouri into the Union, not in pursuance of the act of 1820, not in obedience to the understanding when it was adopted, and not with her constitution as it had been formed in conformity with that act, but he proposed to admit Missouri into the Union upon a "fundamental condition," which condition was to be in the nature of a solemn compact between the United States on the one part and the State of Missouri on the other part, and to which "fundamental condition" the State of Missouri was required to declare her assent in the form of "a solemn public act." This joint resolution passed, and was approved March 2, 1821, and is known as Mr. Clay's Missouri Compromise, in contradistinction to that of 1820, which was introduced into the Senate by Mr. Thomas, of Illinois. In the month of June, 1821, the legislature of Missouri assembled and passed the "solemn public act," and furnished an authenticated copy thereof to the President of the United States, in compliance with Mr. Clay's compromise, or joint resolution. On August 10, 1821, James Monroe, President of the United States, issued his proclamation, in which, after reciting the fact that on the 2d of March, 1821, Congress had passed a joint resolution "providing for the admission of the State of Missouri into the Union, on a certain condition;" and that the general assembly of Missouri, on the 26th of June, having, "by a solemn public act, declared the assent of the said State of Missouri to the fundamental condition contained in said joint resolution," and having furnished him with an authentic copy thereof, he, "*in pursuance of the resolution of Congress aforesaid,*" declared the admission of Missouri to be complete.

I do not deem it necessary to discuss the question whether the conditions upon which Missouri was admitted were wise or unwise. It is sufficient for my present purpose to remark, that the "fundamental condition" of her admission related to certain clauses in the constitution of Missouri in respect to the migration of free negroes into that State; clauses similar to those now in force in the constitutions of Illinois and Indiana, and perhaps other States; clauses similar to the provisions of law in force at that time in many of the old States of the Union; and, I will add, clauses which, in my opinion, Missouri had a right to adopt under the Constitution of the United States. It is no answer to this position to say, that those clauses in the constitution of Missouri were in violation of the Constitution. If they did conflict with the Constitution of the United States, they were void; if they were not in conflict, Missouri had a right to put them there, and to pass all laws necessary to carry them into effect. Whether such conflict did exist is a question which, by the Constitution, can only be determined authoritatively by the Supreme Court of the United States. Congress is not the appropriate and competent tribunal to adjudicate and determine questions of conflict between the constitution of a State and that of the United States. Had Missouri been admitted without any condition or restriction, she would have had an opportunity of vindicating her constitution and rights in the Supreme Court—the tribunal created by the Constitution for that purpose.

By the condition imposed on Missouri, Congress not only deprived that State of a right which she believed she possessed under the constitution of the United States, but denied her the privilege of vindicating that right in the appropriate and constitutional tribunals, by compelling her, "by a solemn public act," to give an irrevocable pledge never to exercise or claim the right. Therefore Missouri came in under a humiliating condition—a condition not imposed by the Constitution of the United States, and which destroys the principle of equality which should exist, and by the Constitution does not exist, between all the States of this Union. This inequality resulted from Mr. Clay's compromise of 1821, and is the principle upon which that compromise was constructed. I own that the act is couched in general terms and vague phrases, and therefore may possibly be so construed as not to deprive the State of any right she might possess under the Constitution. Upon that point I wish only to say, that such a construction makes the "fundamental condition" void, while the opposite construction would demonstrate it to be unconstitutional. I have before me the "solemn public act" of Missouri to this fundamental condition. whoever will take the trouble to read it will find it the richest specimen of irony and sarcasm that has ever been incorporated into a public act.

Sir, in view of these facts I desire to call the attention of the sen.

ator from New York to a statement in his speech, upon which the greater part of his argument rested. His statement was, and it is now being published in every abolition paper, and repeated by the whole tribe of abolition orators and lecturers, that Missouri was admitted as a slaveholding State, under the act of 1820; while I have shown, by the President's proclamation of August 10, 1821, that she was admitted in pursuance of the resolution of March 2, 1821. Thus it is shown that the material point of his speech is contradicted by the highest evidence—the record in the case. The same statement I believe was made by the senator from Connecticut (Mr. Smith), and the senators from Ohio (Mr. Chase and Mr. Wade), and the senator from Massachusetts (Mr. Sumner). Each of these senators made and repeated this statement, and upon the strength of this erroneous assertion called upon us to carry into effect the eighth section of the same act. The material fact upon which their arguments rested being overthrown, of course their conclusions are erroneous and deceptive.

MR. SEWARD.—I hope the senator will yield for a moment, because I have never had so much respect for him as I have to night.

MR. DOUGLAS.—I see what course I have to pursue in order to command the senator's respect. I know now how to get it. (Laughter.)

MR. SEWARD.—Any man who meets me boldly commands my respect. I say that Missouri would not not have been admittted at all into the Union by the United States except upon the compromise of 1820. When that point was settled about the restriction of slavery it was settled in this way; that she should come in with slavery and that all the rest of the Louisiana purchase, which is now known as Nebraska, should be forever free from slavery. Missouri adopted a constitution, which was thought by the northern States to infringe upon the right of citizenship guaranteed by the Constitution of the United States, which was a new point altogether; and upon that point debate was held, and upon it a new compromise was made, and Missouri came into the Union upon the agreement, that, in regard to that question, she submitted to the Constitution of the United States, and so she was admitted into the Union.

MR. DOUGLAS.—Mr. President, I must remind the senator again that I have already proven that he was in error in stating that the North objected to the admission of Missouri merely on account of the free-negro clause in her constitution. I have proven by the vote that the North objected to her admission because she tolerated slavery; this objection was sustained by the North by a vote of nearly two to one. He cannot shelter himself, therefore, under the free-negro dodge, so long as there is a distinct vote of the North objecting to her admission; because, in addition to complying with the act of 1820, she did not also prohibit slavery, which was the only consideration that the South was to have for agreeing to the prohibition of slavery in the Territories. Then, having deprived the senator, by conclusive evidence from the records, of that pretext, what do I drive him to? I compel him to acknowledge that a new compromise was made.

MR. SEWARD.—Certainly there was.

MR. DOUGLAS.—Then, I ask, why was it made? Because the North would not carry out the first one. And the best evidence that the North did not carry out the first one is the senator's admission that the South was compelled to submit to a new one. Then, if there was a new compromise made, did Missouri come in under the new one or the old one?

MR. SEWARD.—Under both.

MR. DOUGLAS.—This is the first time, in this debate, it has been intimated that Missouri came in under two acts of Congress. The senator did not allude to the resolution of 1821 in his speech; none of the opponents of this bill have said it. But it is now admitted that she did not come into the Union under the act of 1820 alone. She had been voted out under the first compromise, and this vote compelled her to make a new one, and she came in under the new one; and yet the senator from New York, in his speech, declared to the world that she came in under the first one. This is not an immaterial question. His whole speech rests upon that misapprehension or misstatement of the record.

MR. SEWARD.—You had better say misapprehension.

MR. DOUGLAS.—Very well. We will call it by that name. His whole argument depends upon that misapprehension. After stating that the act of 1820 was a compact, and that the North performed its part of it in good faith, he arraigns the friends of this bill for proposing to annul the eighth section of the act of 1820 without first turning Missouri out of the Union, in order that slavery may be abolished therein by the act of Congress. He says to us, in substance: "Gentlemen, if you are going to rescind the compact, have respect for that great law of morals, of honesty, and of conscience which compels you first to surrender the consideration which you have received 'under the compact.'" I concur with him in regard to the obligation to restore the consideration when a contract is rescinded. And inasmuch as the prohibition in the Territories north of 36° 30' was obtained, according to his own statement, by an agreement to admit Missouri as a slaveholding State on an equal footing with the original States, "in all respects whatsoever," as specified in the first section of the act of 1820; and, inasmuch as Missouri was refused admission under said act, and was compelled to submit to a new compromise in 1821, and was then received into the Union on a fundamental condition of inequality, I call on him and his abolition confederates to restore the consideration which they have received, in the shape of a prohibition of slavery north of 36° 30', under a compromise which they repudiated, and refused to carry into effect. I call on them to correct the erroneous statement in respect to the admission of Missouri, and to make a restitution of the consideration by voting for this bill. I repeat, that this is not

an immaterial statement.   It is the point upon which the abolitionists
rest their whole argument.   They could not get up a show of pretext against the great principle of self-government involved in this
bill, if they could not repeat all the time, as the senator from New
York did in his speech, that Missouri came into the Union with
slavery, in conformity to the compact which was made by the act
of 1820, and that the South, having received the consideration, is
now trying to cheat the North out of her part of the benefits.   I
have proven that, after abolitionism had gained its points so far as
the eighth section of the act prohibited slavery in the Territory,
Missouri was denied admission by northern votes until she entered
into a compact by which she was understood to surrender an important right now exercised by several States of the Union.

Mr. President, I did not wish to refer to these things.   I did not
understand them fully in all their bearings at the time I made my
first speech on this subject; and, so far as I was familiar with them,
I made as little reference to them as was consistent with my duty;
because it was a mortifying reflection to me, as a northern man, that
we had not been able, in consequence of the abolition excitement
at the time, to avoid the appearance of bad faith in the observance
of legislation, which has been denominated a compromise.   There
were a few men then, as there are now, who had the moral courage
to perform their duty to the country and the Constitution, regardless
of consequences personal to themselves.   There were ten northern
men who dared to perform their duty by voting to admit Missouri
into the Union on an equal footing with the original States, and with
no other restriction than that imposed by the Constitution.   I am
aware that they were abused and denounced as we are now; that
they were branded as dough-faces, traitors to freedom, and to the
section of the country whence they come.

Mr. Geyer.—They honored Mr. Lanman, of Connecticut, by burning him in effigy.

Mr. Douglas.—Yes, sir; these abolitionists honored Mr. Lanman
in Connecticut just as they are honoring me in Boston, and other
places, by burning me in effigy.

Mr. Cass.—It will do you no harm.

Mr. Douglas.—Well, sir, I know it will not; but why this burning
in effigy?   It is the legitimate consequences of the address which
was sent forth to the world by certain senators, whom I denominated,
on a former occasion, as the abolition confederates.   The senator
from Ohio presented here the other day a resolution—he says unin-
tentionally, and I take it so—declaring that every senator who advocated this bill was a traitor to his country, to humanity, and to God;
and even he seemed to be shocked at the results of his own advice
when it was exposed.   Yet he did not seem to know that it was, in
substance, what he had advised in his address, over his own signature, when he called upon the people to assemble in public meetings
and thunder forth their indignation at the criminal betrayal of pre-

cious rights; when he appealed to ministers of the Gospel to desecrate their holy calling, and attempted to inflame passions, and fanaticism, and prejudice against senators who would not consider themselves very highly complimented by being called his equals? And yet, when the natural consequences of his own action and advice came back upon him, and he presents them here, and is called to an account for the indecency of the act, he professes his profound regret and surprise that anything should have occurred which could possibly be deemed unkind or disrespectful to any member of this body!

*　　*　　*　　*　　*　　*　　*　　*　　*

The senator's explanation does not help him at all. He says he did not state under what act Missouri came in; but he did say, as I understood him, that the act of 1820 was a compact, and that, according to that compact, Missouri was to come in with slavery, provided slavery should be prohibited in certain Territories, and did come in in pursuance of the compact. He now uses the word " compact." To what compact does he allude? Is it not to the act of 1820? If he did not, what becomes of his conclusion that the eighth section of that act is irrepealable? He will not venture to deny that his reference was to the act of 1820. Did he refer to the joint resolution of 1821, under which Missouri was admitted? If so, we do not propose to repeal it. We admit that it was a compact, and that its obligations are irrevocably fixed. But that joint resolution does not prohibit slavery in the Territories. The Nebraska Bill does not propose to repeal it, or impair its obligation in any way. Then, sir, why not take back your correction, and admit that you did mean the act of 1820, when you spoke of irrevocable obligations and compacts? Assuming then, that the senator meant what he is now unwilling either to admit or deny, even while professing to correct me, that Missouri came in under the act of 1820, I aver that I have proven that she did not come into the Union under that act. I have proven that she was refused admission under that alleged compact. I have, therefore, proven incontestably that the material statement upon which his argument rests is wholly without foundation, and unequivocally contradicted by the record.

Sir, I believe I may say the same of every speech which has been made against the bill, upon the ground that it impared the obligation of compacts. There has not been an argument against the measure, every word of which in regard to the faith of compacts is not contradicted by the public records. What I complain of is this: The people may think that a senator, having the laws and journals before him, to which he could refer, would not make a statement in contradiction of those records. They make the people believe these things, and cause them to do great injustice to others, under the delusion that they have been wronged, and their feelings outraged. Sir, this address did for a time mislead the whole country. It made the legislature of New York believe that the act of 1820 was a compact which it would be disgraceful to violate; and, acting under that delusion, they framed a series of resolutions, which, if true and just, convict that State of an act of perfidy and treachery unparalleled in the history of free governments. You see, therefore, the consequence of these misstatements. You degrade your own State, and induce the people, under the impression that they have been injured, to get up a violent crusade against those whose fidelity and truthfulness will in the end command their respect and admiration. In consequence of arousing passions and prejudices, I am now to be found in effigy, hanging by the neck, in all the towns where you have the influence to produce such a result. In all these excesses, the people are yield‑ing to an honest impulse, under the impression that a grievous wrong has been perpetrated. You have had your day of triumph. You have succeeded in directing upon the heads of others a torrent of insult and calumny from which even you shrink with horror, when the fact is exposed that you have become the conduits for conveying it into this hall. In your State, sir (addressing himself to Mr. Chase) I find I am burnt in effigy in your abolition towns. All this is done because I have proposed, as it is said, to violate a compact! Now, what will those people think of you when they find out that you have stimulated them to these acts, which are disgraceful to your State, disgraceful to your party, and disgraceful to your cause, under a misrepresentation of the facts, which misrepresentation you ought to have been aware of, and should never have been made.

MR. CHASE.—Will the senator permit me to say a few words?

MR. DOUGLAS.—Certainly.

MR. CHASE.—Mr. President, I certainly regret that anything has occurred in my State which should be otherwise than in accordance with the disposition which I trust I have ever manifested to treat the senator from Illinois with entire courtesy. I do not wish, how‑ever, to be understood, here or elsewhere, as retracting any state‑ment which I have made, or being unwilling to reassert that state‑ment when it is directly impeached. I regard the admission of Mis‑souri, and the facts of the transaction connected with it, as constitut‑ing a compact between the two sections of the country; a part of which was fulfilled in the admission of Missouri, another part in the admission of Arkansas, and other parts of which have been fulfilled in the admission of Iowa, and the organization of Minnesota, but which yet remains to be fulfilled in respect to the Territory of Nebraska, and which, in my judgment, will be violated by the repeal of the Missouri prohibition. That is my judgment. I have no quarrel with senators who differ with me; but upon the whole facts of the trans‑action, however, I have not changed my opinion at all, in conse‑quence of what has been said by the honorable senator from Illinois. I say that the facts of the transaction, taken together, and as under‑stood by the country for more than thirty years, constitute a com‑pact binding in moral force; though, as I have always said, being embodied in a legislative act, it may be repealed by Congress, if Con‑gress see fit.

Mr. Douglas.—Mr. President, I am sorry that the senator from Ohio has repeated the statement that Missouri came in under the compact which he says was made by the act of 1820. How many times have I to disprove the statement? Does not the vote to which I have referred show that such was not the case? Does not the fact that there was a necessity for a new compromise show it? Have I not proved it three times over? and is it possible that the senator from Ohio will repeat it in the face of the record, with the vote staring him in the face, and with the evidence which I have produced? Does he suppose that he can make his own people believe that his statement ought to be credited in opposition to the solemn record? I am amazed that the senator should repeat the statement again unsustained by the fact, by the record, and by the evidence, and overwhelmed by the whole current and weight of the testimony which I have produced.

The senator says, also, that he never intended to do me injustice, and he is sorry that the people of his State have acted in the manner to which I have referred. Sir, did he not say, in the same document to which I have already alluded, that I was engaged, with others, in "a criminal betrayal of precious rights," in an "atrocious plot?" Did he not say that I and others were guilty of "meditated bad faith?" Are not these his exact words? Did he not say that "servile demagogues" might make the people believe certain things, or attempt to do so? Did he not say everything calculated to produce and bring upon my head all the insults to which I have been subjected publicly and privately—not even excepting the insulting letters which I have received from his constituents, rejoicing at my domestic bereavements, and praying that other and similar calamities may befall me? All these have resulted from that address. I expected such consequences when I first saw it. In it he called upon the preachers of the Gospel to prostitute the sacred desk in stimulating excesses; and then, for fear that the people would not know who it was that was to be insulted and calumniated, he told them, in a postscript, that Mr. Douglas was the author of all this iniquity, and that they ought not to allow their rights to be made the hazard of a Presidential game! After having used such language, he says meant no disrespect—he meant nothing unkind! He was amazed that I said in my opening speech that there was anything offensive in this address; and he could not suffer himself to use harsh epithets, or to impugn a gentleman's motives! No! not he! After having deliberately written all these insults, impugning motive and character, and calling upon our holy religion to sanctify the calumny, he could not think of losing his dignity by bandying epithets, or using harsh and disrespectful terms!

Mr. President, I expected all that has occurred, and more than has come, as the legitimate result of that address. The things to which I referred are the natural consequences of it. The only revenge I seek is to expose the authors, and leave them to bear, as best they may, the just indignation of an honest community, when the people discover how their sympathies and feelings have been outraged, by making them the instruments in performing such desperate acts.

Sir, even in Boston I have been hung in effigy. I may say that I expected it to occur even there, for the senator from Massachusetts lives there. He signed his name to that address; and for fear the Boston abolitionists would not know that it was he, he signed it " Charles Sumner, senator from Massachusetts." The first outrage was in Ohio, where the address was circulated under the signature of " Salmon P. Chase, senator from Ohio." The next came from Boston—the same Boston, sir, which, under the direction of the same leaders, closed Faneuil Hall to the immortal Webster in 1850, because of his support of the Compromise measures of that year, which all now confess have restored peace and harmony to a distracted country. Yes, sir, even Boston, so glorious in her early history—Boston, around whose name so many historical associations cling, to gratify the heart and exalt the pride of every American—could be led astray by abolition misrepresentations so far as to deny a hearing to her own great man, who had shed so much glory upon Massachusetts and her metropolis! I know that Boston now feels humiliated and degraded by the act. And, sir (addressing himself to Mr. Sumner), you will remember that when you came into the Senate, and sought an opportunity to put forth your abolition incendiarism, you appealed to our sense of justice by the sentiment, "Strike, but hear me first." But when Webster went back in 1850 to speak to his constituents in his own self-defence, to tell the truth, and to expose his slanderers, you would not hear him, but *you struck first!*

Again, sir, even Boston, with her Faneuil Hall consecrated to liberty, was so far led astray by abolitionism, that when one of her gallant sons—gallant by his own glorious deeds, inheriting a heroic Revolutionary name, had given his life to his country upon the bloody field of Buena Vista; and when his remains were brought home, even that Boston, under abolition guidance and abolition preaching, denied him a decent burial, because he lost his life in vindicating his country's honor upon the southern frontier! Even the name of Lincoln, and the deeds of Lincoln, could not secure for him a decent interment, because abolitionism follows a patriot beyond the grave. (Applause in the galleries.)

THE PRESIDING OFFICER (MR. MASON in the chair).—Order must be preserved.

MR. DOUGLAS.—Mr. President, with these facts before me, how could I hope to escape the fate which had followed these great and good men? While I had no right to hope that I might be honored as they had been, under abolition auspices, have I not a right to be proud of the distinction and the association? Mr. President, I regret these digressions. I have not been able to follow the line of argument which I had marked out for myself, because of the many interruptions. I do not complain of them. It is fair that gentlemen should make them, inasmuch as they have not the opportunity or replying; hence I have yielded the floor, and propose to do so cheerfully whenever any senator intimates that justice to him or his position requires him to say anything in reply.

Returning to the point from which I was diverted:

I think I have shown that, if the act of 1820, called the Missouri Compromise, was a compact, it was violated and repudiated by a solemn vote of the House of Representatives in 1821, within eleven months after it was adopted. It was repudiated by the North by a majority vote, and that repudiation was so complete and successful as to compel Missouri to make a new compromise, and she was brought into the Union under the new compromise of 1821, and not under the act of 1820. This reminds me of another point made in nearly all the speeches against this bill, and, if I recollect right, was alluded to in the abolition manifesto; to which, I regret to say, I had occasion to refer so often. I refer to the significant hint that Mr. Clay was dead before any one dared to bring forward a proposition to undo the greatest work of his hands. The senator from New York (Mr. Seward) has seized upon this insinuation, and elaborated it, perhaps, more fully than his compeers; and now the abolition press suddenly, and as if by miraculous conversion, teems with eulogies upon Mr Clay and his Missouri Compromise of 1820.

Now, Mr. President, does not each of these senators know that Mr. Clay was not the author of the act of 1820? Do they not know that he disclaimed it in 1850 in this body? Do they not know that the Missouri restriction did not originate in the house of which he was a member? Do they not know that Mr. Clay never came into the Missouri controversy as a compromiser until after the compromise of 1820 was repudiated, and it became necessary to make another? I dislike to be compelled to repeat what I have conclusively proven, that the compromise which Mr Clay effected was the act of 1821, under which Missouri came into the Union, and not the act of 1820. Mr. Clay made that compromise after you had repudiated the first one. How, then, dare you call upon the spirit of that great and gallant statesman to sanction your charge of bad faith against the South on this question?

MR. SEWARD.—Will the senator allow me a moment?

MR. DOUGLAS.—Certainly.

MR. SEWARD.—In the year 1851 or 1852, I think 1851, a medal was struck in honor of Henry Clay, of gold, which cost a large sum of money, which contained eleven acts of the life of Henry Clay. It was presented to him by a committee of citizens of New York, by whom it had been made. One of the eleven acts of his life which was celebrated on that medal, which he accepted, was the Missouri Compromise of 1820. This is my answer.

MR. DOUGLAS.—Are the words " of 1820 " upon it?

MR. SEWARD.—It commemorates the Missouri Compromise.

MR. DOUGLAS.—Exactly. I have seen that medal; and my recollection is that it does not contain the words "of 1820." One of the great acts of Mr. Clay was the Missouri Compromise, but what Missouri Compromise? Of course, the one which Henry Clay made, the one which he negotiated, the one which brought Missouri into the Union, and which settled the controversy. That was the act of 1821, and not the act of 1820. It tends to confirm the statement which I have made. History is misread and misquoted, and these statements have been circulated and disseminated broadcast through the country, concealing the truth. Does not the senator know that Henry Clay, when occupying that seat in 1850 (pointing to Mr. Clay's chair), in his speech of the 6th of February of that year, said that nothing had struck him with so much surprise as the fact that historical circumstances soon passed out of recollection; and he instanced, as a case in point, the error of attributing to him the act of 1820. (Mr. Seward nodded assent.) The senator from New York says that he does remember that Mr. Clay did say so. If so, how is it, then, that he presumes now to rise and quote that medal as evidence that Henry Clay was the author of the act of 1820?

MR. SEWARD.—I answer the senator in this way: that Henry Clay, while he said he did not disavow or disapprove of that compromise, transferred the merit of it to others who were more active in procuring it than he, while he had enjoyed the praise and the glory which were due from it.

MR. DOUGLAS.—To that I have only to say, that it cannot be the reason; for Henry Clay, in that same speech, did take to himself the merit of the compromise of 1821, and hence it could not have been modesty which made him disavow the other. He said that he did not know whether he had voted for the act of 1820 or not; but he supposed that he had done so. He furthermore said that it did not originate in the house of which he was a member, and that he never did approve of its principles; but that he may have voted, and probably did vote for it, under the pressure of the circumstances.

Now, Mr. President, as I have been doing justice to Mr. Clay on this question, perhaps I may as well do justice to another great man, who was associated with him in carrying through the great measures of 1850, which mortified the senator from New York so much, because they defeated his purpose of carrying on the agitation. I allude to Mr. Webster. The authority of his great name has been quoted for the purpose of proving that he regarded the Missouri Act as a compact—an irrepealable compact. Evidently the distinguished senator from Massachusetts (Mr. Everett) supposed that he was doing Mr. Webster entire justice when he quoted the passage which he read from Mr. Webster's speech of the 7th of March, 1850, when he said that he stood upon the position that every part of the American continent was fixed for freedom or for slavery by irrepealable law.

The senator says that, by the expression "irrepealable law," Mr. Webster meant to include the compromise of 1820. Now, I will!

show that that was not Mr. Webster's meaning—that he was never
guilty of the mistake of saying that the Missouri Act of 1820 was an
irrepealable law. Mr. Webster said in that speech, that every foot
of territory in the United States was fixed as to its character for freedom or slavery by an irrepealable law. He then inquired if it was
not so in regard to Texas? He went on to prove that it was; because, he said, there was a compact in express terms between Texas
and the United States. He said the parties were capable of contracting, and that there was a valuable consideration; and hence, he contended, that in that case there was a contract binding in honor, and
morals, and law; and that it was irrepealable without a breach of
faith.

He went on to say:

"Now, as to California and New Mexico, I hold slavery to be excluded from
those Territories by a law even superior to that which admits and sanctions it
in Texas—I mean the law of nature, of physical geography, the law of the
formation of the earth."

That was the irrepealable law which he said prohibited slavery in
the Territories of Utah and New Mexico. He next went on to speak
of the prohibition of slavery in Oregon, and he said it was an "entirely useless, and, in that connection, senseless proviso."

He went further, and said:

"That the whole territory of the States in the United States, or in the
newly-acquired territory of the United States, has a fixed and settled character,
now fixed and settled by law, which cannot be repealed in the case of Texas
without a violation of public faith, and cannot be repealed by any human
power in regard to California or New Mexico; that, *under one or other of these
laws*, every foot of territory in the States, or in the Territories, has now
received a fixed and decided character."

What irrepealable laws? "One or the other" of those which he
had stated. One was the Texas compact, the other the law of nature
and physical geography; and he contended that one or the other
fixed the character of the whole American continent for freedom or
for slavery. He never alluded to the Missouri Compromise, unless it
was by the allusion to the Wilmot Proviso in the Oregon Bill, and
there he said it was a useless, and, in that connection, senseless
thing. Why was it a useless and a senseless thing? Because it was
re-enacting the law of God; because slavery had already been prohibited by physical geography. Sir, that was the meaning of Mr.
Webster's speech. My distinguished friend from Massachusetts (Mr.
Everett), when he reads the speech again, will be utterly amazed to
see how he fell into such an egregious error as to suppose that Mr.
Webster had so far fallen from his high position as to say that the
Missouri Act of 1820 was an irrepealable law.

Mr. Everett.—Will the gentleman give way for a moment?
Mr. Douglas.—With great pleasure.
Mr. Everett.—What I said on that subject was, that Mr. Webster,

in my opinion, considered the Missouri Compromise as of the nature of a compact. It is true, as the senator from Illinois has just stated, that Mr. Webster made no allusion, in express terms, to the subject of the Missouri restriction. But I thought then, and I think now, that he referred in general terms to that as a final settlement of the question, in the region to which it applied. It was not drawn in question then on either side of the House. Nobody suggested that it was at stake. Nobody intimated that there was a question before the Senate whether that restriction should be repealed or should remain in force. It was not distinctly, and in terms, alluded to, as the gentleman correctly says, by Mr. Webster or anybody else. What he said in reference to Texas, applied to Texas alone. What he said in reference to Utah and New Mexico, applied to them alone ; and what he said with regard to Oregon, to that Territory alone. But he stated in general terms, and four or five times, in the speech of the 7th of March, 1850, that there was not a foot of land in the United States or its Territories, the character of which, for freedom of slavery, was not fixed by some irrepealable law; and I did think then, and I think now, that by the "irrepealable law," as far as concerned the territory north of 36° 30′ and included in the Louisiana purchase, Mr. Webster had reference to the Missouri restriction, as regarded as of the nature of a compact. That restriction was copied from one of the provisions of the Ordinance of 1787, which are declared in that instrument itself to be articles of compact. The Missouri restriction is the article of the Ordinance of 1787 applied to the Louisiana purchase. That this is the correct interpretation of Mr. Webster's language, is confirmed by the fact that he said more than once, and over again, that all the North lost by the arrangement of 1859, was the non-imposition of the Wilmot Proviso upon Utah and New Mexico. If, in addition to that, the North had lost the Missouri restriction over the whole of the Louisiana purchase, could he have used language of that kind, and would he not have attempted, in some way or other, to reconcile such a momentous fact with his repeated statements that the measures of 1850 applied only to the territories newly acquired from Mexico?

MR. DOUGLAS.—Mr. President, I will explain that matter very quickly. Mr. Webster's speech was made on the 7th of March, 1850, and the Territorial bills and the Texas boundary bill were first reported to the Senate by myself on the 25th of the same month. Mr. Webster's speech was made upon Mr. Clay's resolution, when there was no bill pending. Then the Omnibus Bill was formed about the 1st of May subsequently ; and hence this explains the reason why Mr. Webster did not refer to the principle involved in these acts, and to the necessary effect of carrying out the principle.

MR. EVERETT.—The expression of Mr. Webster, which I quoted in my remarks on the 8th of February, was from a speech of Mr. Soulé's amendment, offered, I think, in June. In addition to this, I have before me an extract from a still later speech of Mr. Webster, made quite late in the session, on the 17th of July, 1850, in which he reiterated that statement. In it he said:

"And now, sir, what do Massachusetts and the North, the anti-slavery States, lose by this adjustment? What is it they lose? I put that question to every gentleman here, and to every gentleman in the country. They lose the application of what is called the 'Wilmot Proviso' to these Territories, and that is all. There is nothing else, I suppose, that the whole North are not ready to do. They wish to get California into the Union; they wish to quiet New Mexico; they desire to terminate the dispute about the Texan boundary in any reasonable manner, cost what it reasonably may. They make no sacrifice in all that. What they do sacrifice is exactly this: The application of the 'Wilmot Proviso' to the Territory of New Mexico and the Territory of Utah, and that is all."

Could Mr. Webster have used language like this if he had understood that, at the same time, the non-slaveholding States were losing the Missouri restriction, as applied to the whole vast territory included in the bills now before the Senate?

Mr. DOUGLAS.—Of course that was all, and if he regarded the Missouri prohibition in the same light that he did the Oregon prohibition, it was a useless, and, in that connection, a senseless proviso; and hence the North lost nothing by not having that same senseless, useless proviso applied to Utah and New Mexico. Now, to show the senator that he must be mistaken as to Mr. Webster's authority, let me call his attention back to this passage in his 7th of March speech:

"Under one or other of these laws, every foot of territory in the States or Territories has now received a fixed and decided character."

What laws did he refer to when he spoke of "one or other of these laws?" He had named but two, the Texas compact and the law of nature, of climate, and physical geography, which excluded slavery. He had mentioned none other; and yet he says "one or other" prohibited slavery in all the States or Territories—thus including Nebraska, as well as Utah and New Mexico.

Mr. EVERETT.—That was not drawn in question at all.

Mr. DOUGLAS.—Then if it was not drawn in question, the speech should not have been quoted in support of the Missouri Compromise. It is just what I complain of, that, if it was not thus drawn in question, that use ought not to have been made of it. Now, Mr. President, it is well known that Mr. Webster supported the Compromise measures of 1850, and the principle involved in them, of leaving the people to do as they pleased upon this subject. I think, therefore, that I have shown that these gentlemen are not authorized to quote the name either of Mr. Webster or Mr. Clay in support of the position which they take, that this bill violates the faith of compacts. Sir, it was because Mr. Webster went for giving the people in the Territories the right to do as they pleased upon the subject of slavery, and because he was in favor of carrying out the Constitution in regard to fugitive slaves, that he was not allowed to speak in Faneuil Hall.

6*

Mr. Everett.—That was not my fault.

Mr. Douglas.—I know it was not; but I say it was because he took that position; it was because he did not go for a prohibitory policy; it was because he advocated the same principles which I now advocate, because he went for the same provisions in the Utah Bill which I now sustain in this bill, that Boston abolitionists turned their backs upon him, just as they burnt me in effigy. Sir, if identity of principle, if identity of support as friends, if identity of enemies fix Mr. Webster's position, his authority is certainly with us, and not with the abolitionists. I have a right, therefore, to have the sympathies of his Boston friends with me, as I sympathized with him when the same principle was involved.

Mr. President, I am sorry that I have taken up so much time; but I must notice one or two points more. So much has been said about the Missouri Compromise Act, and about a faithful compliance with it by the North, that I must follow that matter a little further. The senator from Ohio (Mr. Wade) has referred, to-night, to the fact that I went for carrying out the Missouri Compromise in the Texas resolutions of 1845, and in 1848, on several occasions; and he actually proved that I never abandoned it until 1850. He need not have taken the pains to prove that fact; for he got all his information on the subject from my opening speech upon this bill. I told you then that I was willing, as a northern man, in 1845, when the Texas question arose, to carry the Missouri Compromise line through that State, and in 1848 I offered it as an amendment to the Oregon Bill. Although I did not like the principle involved in that act, yet I was willing, for the sake of harmony, to extend to the Pacific, and abide by it in good faith, in order to avoid the slavery agitation. The Missouri Compromise was defeated then by the same class of politicians who are now combined in opposition to the Nebraska Bill. It was because we were unable to carry out that compromise, that a necessity existed for making a new one in 1850. And then we established this great principle of self-government which lies at the foundation of all our institutions. What does his charge amount to? He charges it, as a matter of offence, that I struggled in 1845 and in 1848 to observe good faith; and he and his associates defeated my purpose, and deprived me of the ability to carry out what he now says is the plighted faith of the nation.

Sir, as I have said, the South were willing to agree to the Missouri Compromise in 1848. When it was proposed by me to the Oregon Bill, as an amendment, to extend that line to the Pacific, the South agreed to it. The Senate adopted that proposition, and the House voted it down. In 1850, after the Omnibus Bill had broken down, and we proceeded to pass the Compromise measures separately, I proposed, when the Utah Bill was under discussion, to make a slight variation of the boundary of that Territory, so as to include the Mormon settlements, and not with reference to any other question; and it was suggested that we should take the line of 36° 30'. That would have accomplished the local objects of the amendment very well. But when I proposed it, what did those freesoilers say? What did the senator from New Hampshire (Mr. Hale), who was then their leader in this body, say? Here are his words:

"MR. HALE.—I wish to say a word as a reason why I shall vote against the amendment. I shall vote against 36° 30', because I think there is an implication in it. (Laughter.) I will vote for 37° or 36° either, just as it is convenient; but it is idle to shut our eyes to the fact that here is an attempt in this bill—I will not say it is the intention of the mover—to pledge this Senate and Congress to the imaginary line of 36° 30', because there are some historical recollections connected with it in regard to this controversy about slavery. I will content myself with saying that I never will, by vote or speech, admit or submit to anything that may bind the action of our legislation here to make the parallel of 36° 30' the boundary line between slave and free territory. And when I say that, I explain the reason why I go against the amendment."

These remarks of Mr. Hale were not made on a proposition to extend the Missouri Compromise line to the Pacific, but on a proposition to fix 36° 30' as the southern boundary line of Utah, for local reasons. He was against it because there might be, as he said, an implication growing out of historical recollections in favor of the imaginary line between slavery and freedom. Does that look as if his object was to get an implication in favor of preserving sacred this line, in regard to which gentlemen now say there was a solemn compact? That proposition may illustrate what I wish to say in this connection upon a point which has been made by the opponents of this bill, as to the effect of an amendment inserted on the motion of the senator from Virginia (Mr. Mason), into the Texas Boundary Bill. The opponents of this measure rely upon that amendment to show that the Texas compact was preserved by the acts of 1850. I have already shown, in my former speech, that the object of the amendment was to guaranty to the State of Texas, with her circumscribed boundaries, the same number of States which she would have had under her larger boundaries, and with the same right to come in with or without slavery, as they please.

We have been told over and over again that there was no such thing intimated in debate as that the country cut off from Texas was to be relieved from the stipulation of that compromise. This has been asserted boldly and unconditionally, as if there could be no doubt about it. The senator from Georgia (Mr. Toombs), in his speech, showed that, in his address to his constituents of that State, he had proclaimed to the world that the object was to establish a principle which would allow the people to decide the question of slavery for themselves, north as well as south of 36° 30'. The line of 36° 30' was voted down as the boundary of Utah, so that there should not be even an implication in favor of an imaginary line to divide freedom and slavery. Subsequently, when the Texas Boundary Bill was under consideration, on the next day after the amendment of the senator from Virginia had been adopted, the record says:

"Mr. Sebastian moved to add to the second article the following:

"'On the condition that the territory hereby ceded may be, at the proper time, formed into a State, and admitted into the Union, with a constitution with or without the prohibition of slavery therein, as the people of the said Territory may at the time determine.'"

Then the senator from Arkansas did propose that the territory cut off should be relieved from that restriction in express terms, and allowed to come in according to the principles of this bill. What was done? The debate continued:

"Mr. Foote.—Will my friend allow me to appeal to him to move this amendment when the Territorial Bill for New Mexico shall be up for consideration? It will certainly be a part of that bill, and I shall then vote for it with pleasure. Now it will only embarrass our action."

Let it be remarked, that no one denied the propriety of the provision. All seemed to acquiesce in the principle; but it was thought better to insert it in the Territorial bills, as we are now doing, instead of adding it to the Texas Boundary Bill. The debate proceeded:

"Mr. Sebastian.—My only object in offering the amendment is to secure the assertion of this principle beyond a doubt. The principle was acquiesced in without difficulty in regard to the Territorial government established for Utah, a part of this acquired territory, and it is proper, in my opinion, that it should be incorporated in this bill.

"Messrs. Cass, Foote, and others.—Oh, withdraw it.

"Mr. Sebastian.—I think this is the proper place for it. It is uncertain whether it will be incorporated in the other bill referred to, and the bill itself may not pass."

It will be seen that the debate goes upon the supposition that the effect was to release the country north of 36° 30' from the obligation of the prohibition; and the only question, was whether the declaration that it should be received into the Union "with or without slavery," should be inserted in the Texas Bill or the Territorial Bill.

The debate was continued, and I will read one or two other passages:

"Mr. Foote.—I wish to state to the senator a fact of which, I think, he is not observant at this moment; and that is, that the senator from Virginia has introduced an amendment, which is now a part of the bill, which recognizes the Texas compact of annexation in every respect.

"Mr. Sebastian.—I was aware of the effect of the amendment of the senator from Virginia. It is in regard to the number of States to be formed out of Texas, and is referred to only in general terms."

Thus it will be seen that the senator from Arkansas then explained the amendment of the senator from Virginia, which had been adopted, in precisely the same way in which I explained it in my opening speech. The senator from Arkansas continued:

"If this amendment be the same as that offered by the senator from Virginia, there can certainly be no harm in reaffirming it in this bill. to which I think it properly belongs."

Thus it will be seen that nobody disputed that the restriction was to be removed; and the only question was, as to the bill in which that declaration would be put. It seems, from the record, that I took part in the debate, and said:

"MR. DOUGLAS.—This boundary as now fixed, would leave New Mexico bounded on the east by the 103° of longitude up to 36° 30', and then east to 100°; and it leaves a narrow neck of land between 36° 30' and the old boundary of Texas, that would not naturally and properly go to New Mexico when it should become a State. This amendment would compel us to include it in New Mexico, or to form it into another State. When the principle shall come up in the bill for the organization of a Territorial government for New Mexico, no doubt the same vote which inserted it in the Omnibus Bill, and the Utah Bill, will insert it there.
"Several senators.—No doubt of it."

Upon that debate the amendment of the senator from Arkansas was voted down, because it was avowed and distinctly understood that the amendment of the senator from Virginia, taken in connection with the remainder of the bill, did release the country ceded by Texas north of 36° 30' from the restriction; and it was agreed that if we did not put it into the Texas Boundary Bill it should go into the Territorial Bill. I stated, as a reason why it should not go into the Texas Boundary Bill, that if it did it would be a compact, and would compel us to put the whole ceded country into one State, when it might be more convenient and natural to make a different boundary. I pledged myself then that it should be put into the Territorial Bill; and when we considered the Territorial bill for New Mexico, we put in the same clause, so far as the country ceded by Texas was embraced within that Territory, and it passed in that shape. When it went into the house, they united the two bills together, and thus this clause passed in the same bill, as the senator from Arkansas desired.

Now, sir, have I not shown conclusively that it was the understanding in that debate that the effect was to release the country north of 36° 30', which formerly belonged to Texas, from the operation of that restriction, and to provide that it should come into the Union with or without slavery, as its people should see proper?

That being the case; I ask the senator from Ohio (Mr. Chase) if he ought not to have been cautious when he charged over and over again that there was not a word or a syllable uttered in debate to that effect? Should he not have been cautious when he said that it was a mere after-thought on my part? Should he not have been cautious when he said that I never even dreamed of it up to the 4th of January of this year? Whereas the record shows that I made a speech to that effect during the pendency of the bills of 1850. The same statement was repeated by nearly every senator who followed him in debate in opposition to this bill; and it is now being circulated over the country, published in every abolition paper, and read on every stump by every abolition orator, in order to get up a prejudice

against me and the measure I have introduced. Those gentlemen
should not have dared to utter the statement without knowing
whether it was correct or not.   These records are troublesome things
sometimes. It is not proper for a man to charge another with a
mere after-thought because he did not know that he had advocated
the same principles before.   Because he did not know it he should
not take it for granted that nobody else did. Let me tell the senators
that it is a very unsafe rule for them to rely upon.   They ought to
have had sufficient respect for a brother senator to have believed,
when he came forward with an important proposition, that he had
investigated it.   They ought to have had sufficient respect for a
committee of this body to have assumed that they meant what they
said.

When I see such a system of misinterpretation and misrepresentation of views, of laws, of records, of debates, all tending to mislead
the public, to excite prejudice, and to propagate error, have I not a
right to expose it in very plain terms, without being arraigned for
violating the courtesies of the Senate ?

Mr. President, frequent reference has been made in debate to the
admission of Arkansas as a slaveholding State, as furnishing evidence
that the abolitionists and freesoilers, who have recently become so
much enamored with the Missouri Compromise, have always been
faithful to its stipulations and implications. I will show that the
reference is unfortunate for them.   When Arkansas applied for
admission in 1836, objection was made in consequence of the provisions of her constitution in respect to slavery.   When the abolitionists and freesoilers of that day were arraigned for making that
objection, upon the ground that Arkansas was south of 36° 30′, they
replied that the act of 1820 was never a compromise, much less a
compact, imposing any obligation upon the successors of those who
passed the act to pay any more respect to its provisions than to any
other enactment of ordinary legislation.   I have the debates before
me, but will occupy the attention of the Senate only to read one or
two paragraphs.   Mr. Hand of New York, in opposition to the
admission of Arkansas as a slaveholding State, said :

"I am aware, it will be, as it has already been contended, that by the
Missouri Compromise, as it has been preposterously termed, Congress has
parted with its right to prohibit the introduction of slavery into the territory
south of 36° 30′ north latitude."

He acknowledged that by the Missouri Compromise, as he said it
was preposterously termed, the North was estopped from denying
the right to hold slaves south of that line; but, he added :

"There are, to my mind, insuperable objections to the soundness of that
proposition."

Here they are :

"In the first place, there was no compromise or compact whereby Congress
surrendered any power, or yielded any jurisdiction ; and, in the second place,

If it had done so, it was a mere legislative act, that could not bind their successors; it would be subject to a repeal at the will of any succeeding Congress."

I give these passages as specimens of the various speeches made in opposition to the admission of Arkansas by the same class of politicians who now oppose the Nebraska Bill upon the ground that it violates a solemn compact. So much for the speeches. Now for the vote. The journal which I hold in my hand, shows that forty-nine northern votes were recorded against the admission of Arkansas.

Yet, sirs, in utter disregard—and charity leads me to hope, in profound ignorance—of all these facts, gentlemen are boasting that the North always observed the contract, never denied its validity, never wished to violate it; and they have even referred to the cases of the admission of Missouri and Arkansas as instances of their good faith.

Now, is it possible that gentlemen could suppose these things could be said and distributed in their speeches without exposure? Did they presume that, inasmuch as their lives were devoted to slavery agitation, whatever they did not know about the history of that question did not exist? I am willing to believe, I hope it may be the fact, that they were profoundly ignorant of all these records, all these debates, all these facts, which overthrow every position they have assumed. I wish the senator from Maine (Mr. Fessenden), who delivered his maiden speech here to-night, and who made many sly stabs at me, had informed himself upon the subject before he repeated all these groundless assertions. I can excuse him for the reason that he has been here but a few days, and having enlisted under the banner of the abolition confederates, was unwise and simple enough to believe that what they had published could be relied upon as stubborn facts. He may be an innocent victim. I hope he can have the excuse of not having investigated the subject. I am willing to excuse him on the ground that he did not know what he was talking about, and it is the only excuse which I can make for him. I will say, however, that I do not think he was required by his loyalty to the abolitionists to repeat every disreputable insinuation which they made. Why did he throw into his speech that foul innuendo about "a northern man with southern principles," and then quote the senator from Massachusetts (Mr. Sumner) as his authority? Ay, sir, I say that foul insinuation. Did not the senator from Massachusetts, who first dragged it into this debate, wish to have the public understand that I was known as a northern man with southern principles? Was not that the allusion? If it was, he availed himself of a cant phrase in the public mind, in violation of the truth of history. I know of but one man in this country who ever made it a boast that he was "a northern man with southern principles," and *he* (turning to Mr. Sumner) was *your* candidate for the Presidency in 1848. (Applause in the galleries.).

THE PRESIDING OFFICER (MR. MASON).—Order, order.

MR. DOUGLAS.—If his sarcasm was intended for Martin Van Buren, it involves a family quarrel, with which I have no disposition to interfere. I will only add that I have been able to discover nothing in the present position or recent history of that distinguished states- man, which would lead me to covet the *sobriquet* by which he is known—"a northern man with southern principles."

Mr. President, the senators from Ohio and Massachusetts (Mr. Chase and Mr. Sumner), have taken the liberty to impeach my motives in bringing forward this measure. I desire to know by what right they arraign me, or by what authority they impute to me other and dif- ferent motives than those which I have assigned. I have shown from the record that I advocated and voted for the same principles and provisions in the compromise acts of 1850, which are embraced in this bill. I have proven that I put the same construction upon those measures immediately after their adoption that is given in the report which I submitted this session from the Committee on Territories. I have shown the legislature of Illinois at its first session, after those measures were enacted, passed resolutions approving them, and de- claring that the same great principles of self-government should be incorporated into all Territorial organizations. Yet, sir, in the face of these facts, these senators have the hardihood to declare that this was all an "afterthought" on my part, conceived for the first time dur- ing the present session ; and that the measure is offered as a bid for Presidential votes! Are they incapable of conceiving that an honest man can do a right thing from worthy motives? I must be permitted to tell those senators that their experience in seeking political prefer- ment does not furnish a safe rule by which to judge the character and principles of other senators!

I must be permitted to tell the senator from Ohio that I did not obtain my seat in this body, either by a corrupt bargain or a dis- honorable coalition! I must be permitted to remind the senator from Massachusetts that I did not enter into any combinations or arrangements by which my character, my principles, and my honor, were set up at public auction or private sale in order to procure a seat in the Senate of the United States! I did not come into the Senate by any such means.

MR. WELLER.—But there are some men whom I know that did.

MR. CHASE (to Mr. Weller.) Do you say that I came here by a bargain? Whoever says that I came here by a corrupt bargain states what is false.

MR. DOUGLAS.—It will not do for the senator from Ohio to return offensive expressions after what I have said and proven. Nor can I permit him to change the issue, and thereby divert public attention from the enormity of his offence, in charging me with unworthy motives; while performing a high public duty, in obedience to the expressed wish and known principles of my State. I choose to maintain my own position, and leave the public to ascertain, if they do not understand how and by what means he was elected to the Senate.

Mr. Chase.—If the senator will allow me, I will say, in reply to the remarks which the senator has just made, that I did not understand him as calling upon me for any explanation of the statement which he said was made in regard to a Presidential bid. The exact statement in the address was this—it was a question addressed to the people: "Would they allow their dearest rights to be made the hazards of a Presidential game?" That was the exact expression. Now, sir, it is well known that all these great measures in the country are influenced, more or less, by reference to the great public canvasses which are going on from time to time. I certainly did not intend to impute to the senator from Illinois—and I desire always to do justice—in that any improper motive. I do not think it is an unworthy ambition to desire to be a President of the United States. I do not think that the bringing forward of a measure with reference to that object would be an improper thing, if the measure be proper in itself. I differ from the senator in my judgment of the measure. I do not think the measure is a right one. In that I express the judgment which I honestly entertain. I do not condemn his judgment, I do not make, and I do not desire to make, any personal imputations upon him in reference to a great public question.

Mr. Douglas.—I wish to examine the explanation of the senator from Ohio, and see whether I ought to accept it as satisfactory. He has quoted the language of the address. It is undeniable that that language clearly imputed to me the design of bringing forward this bill with a view of securing my own election to the Presidency. Then, by way of excusing himself for imputing to me such a purpose, the senator says that he does not consider it "an unworthy ambition;" and hence he says that, in making the charge, he does not impugn my motives. I must remind him that, in addition to that insinuation, he only said, in the same address, that my bill was a "criminal betrayal of precious rights;" he only said it was "an atrocious plot against freedom and humanity;" he only said that it was "meditated bad faith;" he only spoke significantly of "servile demagogues;" he only called upon the preachers of the Gospel and the people at their public meetings to denounce and resist such a monstrous iniquity. In saying all this, and much of the same sort, he now assures me in the presence of the Senate, that he did not mean the charge to imply an "unworthy ambition;" that it was not intended as a "personal imputation" upon my motives or character; and that he meant "no personal disrepect" to me as the author of the measure. In reply, I will content myself with the remark, that there is a very wide difference of opinion between the senator from Ohio and myself in respect to the meaning of words, and especially in regard to the line of conduct which, in a public man, does not constitute an unworthy ambition.

Mr. Sumner.—Will the senator from Illinois yield the floor to me for a moment?

Mr. Douglas.—As I presume it is on the same point, I will hear the testimony.

Mr. Sumner.—Mr. President, I shrink always instinctively from any effort to repel a personal assault. I do not recognize the jurisdiction of this body to try my election to the Senate; but I do state, in reply to the senator from Illinois, that if he means to suggest that I came into the body by any waiver of principles; by any abandonment of my principles of any kind; by any effort or activity of my own, in any degree, he states that which cannot be sustained by the facts. I never sought, in any way, the office which I now hold; nor was I a party, in any way, directly or indirectly, to those efforts which placed me here.

Mr. Douglas.—Sir, the senator from Massachusetts comes up with a very bold front, and denies the right of any man to put him on defence for the manner of his election. He says it is contrary to his principles to engage in personal assaults. If he expects to avail himself of the benefit of such a plea, he should act in accordance with his professed principles, and refrain from assaulting the character and impugning the motives of better men than himself. Everybody knows that he came here by a coalition or combination between political parties holding opposite and hostile opinions. But it is not my purpose to go into the morality of the matters involved in his election. The public know the history of that notorious coalition, and have formed its judgment upon it. It will not do for the senator to say that he was not a party to it, for he thereby betrays a consciousness of the immorality of the transaction, without acquitting himself of the responsibilities which justly attach to him. As well might the receiver of stolen goods deny any responsibility for the larceny, while luxuriating in the proceeds of the crime, as the senator to avoid the consequences resulting from the mode of his election, while he clings to the office. I must be permitted to remind him of what he certainly can never forget, that when he arrived here to take his seat for the first time, so firmly were senators impressed with the conviction that he had been elected by dishonorable and corrupt means, there were very few who, for a long time, could deem it consistent with personal honor to hold private intercourse with him. So general was that impression, that for a long time he was avoided and shunned as a person unworthy of the association of gentlemen. Gradually, however, these injurious impressions were worn away by his bland manners and amiable deportment; and I regret that the senator should now, by a violation of all the rules of courtesy and propriety, compel me to refresh his mind upon these unwelcome reminiscences.

Mr. Chase.—If the senator refers to me, he is stating a fact of which I have no knowledge at all. I came here ——

Mr. Douglas.—I was not speaking of the senator from Ohio, but of his confederate in slander, the senator from Massachusetts (Mr. Sumner). I have a word now to say to the other senator from Ohio (Mr. Wade). On the day when I exposed this abolition address, so full of slanders and calumnies, he arose and stated that, although his name was signed to it, he had never read it; and so willing was he to indorse an abolition document, that he signed it in blank, without knowing what it contained.

The senator from New York (Mr. Seward), when I was about to call him to account for this slanderous production, promptly denied that he ever signed the document. Now, I say, it has been circulated with his name attached to it; then I want to know of the senators who sent out the document, who forged the name of the senator from New York?

MR. CHASE.—I am glad that the senator has asked that question. I have only to say in reference to that matter, that I have not the slightest knowledge in regard to the manner in which various names were appended to that document. It was prepared to be signed, and was signed, by the gentlemen here who are known as Independent Democrats, and how any other names came to be added to it is more than I can tell.

MR. DOUGLAS.—It is not a satisfactory answer, for those who confess to the preparation and publication of a document filled with insult and calumny, with forged names attached to it for the purpose of imparting to it respectability, to interpose a technical denial that they committed the crime. Somebody did forge other people's names to that document. The senators from Ohio and Massachusetts (Mr. Chase and Mr. Sumner), plead guilty to the authorship and publication; upon them rests the responsibility of showing who committed the forgery.

Mr. President, I have done with these personal matters. I regret the necessity which compelled me to devote so much time to them. All I have done and said has been in the way of self-defence, as the Senate can bear me witness.

Mr. President, I have also occupied a good deal of time in exposing the cant of these gentlemen about the sanctity of the Missouri Compromise, and the dishonor attached to the violation of plighted faith. I have exposed these matters in order to show that the object of these men is to withdraw from public attention the real principle involved in the bill. They well know that the abrogation of the Missouri Compromise is the incident and not the principal of the bill. They well understand that the report of the committee and the bill propose to establish the principle in all Territorial organizations, that the question of slavery shall be referred to the people to regulate for themselves, and that such legislation should be had as was necessary to remove all legal obstructions to the free exercise of this right by the people.

The eighth section of the Missouri Act standing in the way of this great principle must be rendered inoperative and void whether expressly repealed or not, in order to give the people the power of regulating their own domestic institutions in their own way, subject only to the Constitution.

Now, sir, if these gentlemen have entire confidence in the correctness of their own position, why do they not meet the issue boldly and fairly, and controvert the soundness of this great principle of popular sovereignty in obedience to the Constitution? They know full well that this was the principle upon which the colonies separated from the crown of Great Britain, the principle upon which the battles of the Revolution were fought, and the principle upon which our republican system was founded. They cannot be ignorant of the fact that the Revolution grew out of the assertion of the right on the part of the imperial government to interfere with the internal affairs and domestic concerns of the colonies. In this connection I will invite attention to a few extracts from the instructions of the different colonies to their delegates in the Continental Congress, with a view of forming such a union as would enable them to make successful resistance to the efforts of the crown to destroy the fundamental principle of all free government by interfering with the domestic affairs of the colonies.

I will begin with Pennsylvania, whose devotion to the principles of human liberty, and the obligations of the Constitution, has acquired for her the proud title of the Key-stone in the arch of republican States. In her instructions is contained the following reservation:

"Reserving to the people of this colony the sole and exclusive right of regulating the internal government and police of the same."

And, in a subsequent instruction, in reference to suppressing the British authority in the colonies, Pennsylvania uses the following emphatic language:

"Unanimously declare our willingness to concur in a vote of the Congress declaring the United Colonies free and independent States, provided the forming the government and the regulation of the internal police of this colony be always reserved to the people of the said colony."

Connecticut, in authorizing her delegates to vote for the Declaration of Independence, attached to it the following condition:

"Saving that the administration of government, and the power of forming governments for, and the regulation of the internal concerns and police of each colony, ought to be left and remain to the respective colonial legislatures."

New Hampshire annexed this proviso to her instructions to her delegates to vote for independence:

"Provided the regulation of our internal police be under the direction of our own assembly."

New Jersey imposed the following condition:

"Always observing that, whatever plan of confederacy you enter into, the regulating the internal police of this province is to be reserved to the colonial legislature."

Maryland gave her consent to the Declaration of Independence upon the condition contained in this proviso :

"And that said colony will hold itself bound by the resolutions of a majority of the United Colonies in the premises, provided the sole and exclusive right of regulating the internal government and police of that colony be reserved to the people thereof."

Virginia annexed the following condition to her instructions to vote for the Declaration of Independence :

"Provided that the power of forming government for, and the regulations of the internal concerns of the colony, be left to respective colonial legislatures."

I will not weary the Senate in multiplying evidence upon this point. It is apparent that the Declaration of Independence had its origin in the violation of that great fundamental principle which secured to the people of the colonies the right to regulate their own domestic affairs in their own way : and that the Revolution resulted in the triumph of that principle, and the recognition of the right asserted by it. Abolitionism proposes to destroy the right, and extinguish the principle for which our forefathers waged a seven years' bloody war, and upon which our whole system of free government is founded. They not only deny the application of this principle to the Territories, but insist upon fastening the prohibition upon all the States to be formed out of those Territories. Therefore, the doctrine of the abolitionists—the doctrine of the opponents of the Nebraska and Kansas Bill, and of the advocates of the Missouri restriction— demand Congressional interference with slavery, not only in the Territories, but in all the new States to be formed therefrom. It is the same doctrine when applied to the Territories and new States of this Union, which the British government attempted to enforce by the sword upon the American colonies. It is this fundamental principle of self-government which constitutes the distinguishing feature of the Nebraska Bill. The opponents of the principle are consistent in opposing the bill. I do not blame them for their opposition. I only ask them to meet the issue fairly and openly, by acknowledging that they are opposed to the principle which it is the object of the bill to carry into operation. It seems that there is no power on earth, no intellectual power, no mechanical power that can bring them to a fair discussion of the true issue. If they hope to delude the people, and escape detection for any considerable length of time under the catch-word "Missouri Compromise," and "faith of compacts," they will find that the people of this country have more penetration and intelligence than they have given them credit for.

Mr. President, there is an important fact connected with this slavery resolution, which should never be lost sight of. It has always arisen from one and the same cause. Whenever that cause has been removed, the agitation has ceased; and whenever the cause has been renewed, the agitation has sprung into existence. That cause is, and ever has been, the attempt on the part of Congress to interfere with the question of slavery in the Territories and new States formed therefrom. Is it not wise, then, to confine our action within the sphere of our legitimate duties, and leave this vexed question so take care of itself in each State and Territory, according to the wishes of the people thereof, in conformity to the forms and in subjection to the provisions of the Constitution?

The opponents of the bill tell us that agitation is no part of their policy, that their great desire is peace and harmony; and they complain bitterly that I should have disturbed the repose of the country by the introduction of this measure. Let me ask these professed friends of peace and avowed enemies of agitation, how the issue could have been avoided? They tell me that I should have let the question alone—that is, that I should have left Nebraska unorganized, the people unprotected, and the Indian barrier in existence, until the swelling tide of emigration should burst through, and accomplish by violence what it is the part of wisdom and statesmanship to direct and regulate by law. How long could you have postponed action with safety? How long could you maintain that Indian barrier, and restrain the onward march of civilization. Christianity, and free government by a barbarian wall? Do you suppose that you could keep that vast country a howling wilderness in all time to come, roamed over by hostile savages, cutting off all safe communication between our Atlantic and Pacific possessions? I tell you that the time for action has come, and cannot be postponed. It is a case in which the "let-alone" policy would precipitate a crisis which must inevitably result in violence, anarchy, and strife.

You cannot fix bounds to the onward march of this great and growing country. You cannot fetter the limbs of the young giant. He will burst all your chains. He will expand, and grow, and increase, and extend civilization, Christianity, and liberal principles. Then, sir, if you cannot check the growth of the country in that direction, is it not the part of wisdom to look the danger in the face, and provide for an event which you cannot avoid? I tell you, sir, you must provide for continuous lines of settlement from the Mississippi Valley to the Pacific Ocean. And in making this provision, you must decide upon what principles the Territories shall be organized; in other words, whether the people shall be allowed to regulate their domestic institutions in their own way, according to the provisions of this bill, or whether the opposite doctrine of Congressional interference is to prevail. Postpone it, if you will; but whenever you do act, this question must be met and decided.

The Missouri Compromise was interference; the Compromise of 1850 was non-interference, leaving the people to exercise their rights under the Constitution. The Committee on Territories were compelled to act on this subject. I, as their chairman, was bound to meet tne question. I chose to take the responsibility, regardless of consequence personal to myself. I should have done the same thing last year, if there had been time : but we know, considering the late period at which the bill then reached us from the House, that there was not sufficient time to consider the question fully, and to prepare a report upon the subject. I was therefore persuaded by friends to allow the bill to be reported to the Senate, in order that such action might be taken as should be deemed wise and proper.

The bill was never taken up for action, the last night of the session having been exhausted in debate on the motion to take up the bill. This session, the measure was introduced by my friend from Iowa (Mr. Dodge) and referred to the Territorial Committee during the first week of the session. We have abundance of time to consider the subject; it was a matter of pressing necessity, and there was no excuse for not meeting it directly and fairly. We were compelled to take our position upon the doctrine either of intervention or non-intervention. We chose the latter, for two reasons ; first, because we believed that the principle was right; and, second, because it was the principle adopted in 1850, to which the two great political parties of the country were solemnly pledged.

There is another reason why I desire to see this principle recognized as a rule of action in all time to come. It will have the effect to destroy all sectional parties and sectional agitations. If, in the language of the report of the committee, you withdraw the slavery question from the halls of Congress and the political arena, and commit it to the arbitrament of those who are immediately interested in and alone responsible for its consequences, there is nothing left out of which sectional parties can be organized. It never was done, and never can be done on the bank, tariff, distribution, or any other party issue which has existed, or may exist, after this slavery question is withdrawn from politics. On every other political question these have always supporters and opponents in every portion of the Union —in each State, county, village, and neighborhood—residing together in harmony and good-fellowship, and combating each other's opinions and correcting each other's errors in a spirit of kindness and friendship. These differences of opinion between neighbors and friends, and the discussions that grow out of them, and the sympathy which each feels with the advocates of his own opinions in every other portion of this wide-spread republic, adds an overwhelming and irresistible moral weight to the strength of the confederacy.

Affection for the Union can never be alienated or diminished by any other party issues than those which are joined upon sectional or geographical lines. When the people of the North shall all be rallied under one banner, and the whole South marshalled under another banner, and each section excited to frenzy and madness by hostility to the institutions of the other, then the patriot may well tremble for the perpetuity of the Union. Withdraw the slavery question from the political arena, and remove it to the States and

Territories, each to decide for itself, such a catastrophe can never happen. Then you will never be able to tell, by any senator's vote for or against any measure, from what State or section of the Union he comes.

Why, then, can we not withdraw this vexed question from politics? Why can we not adopt the principle of this bill as a rule of action in all new Territorial organizations? Why can we not deprive these agitators of their vocation, and render it impossible for senators to come here upon bargains on the slavery question? I believe that the peace, the harmony, and perpetuity of the Union require us to go back to the doctrines of the Revolution, to the principles of the Constitution—the Compromise of 1850, and leave the people, under the Constitution, to do as they may see proper in respect to their own internal affairs.

Mr. President, I have not brought this question forward as a northern man or as a southern man. I am unwilling to recognize such divisions and distinctions. I have brought it forward as an American senator, representing a State which is true to this principle, and which has approved of my action in respect to the Nebraska Bill. I have brought it forward not as an act of justice to the South more than to the North. I have presented it especially as an act of justice to the people of those Territories, and of the States to be formed therefrom, now and in all time to come.

I have nothing to say about northern rights or southern rights. I know of no such divisions or distinctions under the Constitution. The bill does equal and exact justice to the whole Union, and every part of it; it violates the rights of no State or Territory, but places each on a perfect equality, and leaves the people thereof to the free enjoyment of all their rights under the Constitution.

Now, sir, I wish to say to our southern friends, that if they desire to see this great principle carried out, now is their time to rally around it, to cherish it, preserve it, make it the rule of action in all future time. If they fail to do it now, and thereby allow the doctrine of interference to prevail, upon their heads the consequence of that interference must rest. To our northern friends, on the other hand, I desire to say, that from this day henceforward, they must rebuke the slander which has been uttered against the South, that they desire to legislate slavery into the Territories. The South has vindicated her sincerity, her honor on that point, by bringing forward a provision, negativing, in express terms, any such effect as the result of this bill. I am rejoiced to know that, while the proposition to abrogate the eighth section of the Missouri Act comes from a free State, the proposition to negative the conclusion that slavery is thereby introduced comes from a slaveholding State. Thus, both sides furnish conclusive evidence that they go for the principle, and the principle only, and desire to take no advantage of any possible misconstruction.

Mr. President, I feel that I owe an apology to the Senate for having occupied their attention so long, and a still greater apology for having discussed the question in such an incoherent and desultory manner. But I could not forbear to claim the right of closing this debate. I thought gentlemen would recognize its propriety when they saw the manner in which I was assailed and misrepresented in the course of this discussion, and especially by assaults still more disreputable, in some portions of the country. These assaults have had no other effect upon me than to give me courage and energy for a still more resolute discharge of duty. I say frankly that, in my opinion, this measure will be as popular at the North as at the South, when its provisions and principles shall have been fully developed and become well understood. The people at the North are attached to the principles of self-government; and you cannot convince them that that is self-government which deprives a people of the right of legislating for themselves, and compels them to receive laws which are forced upon them by a legislature in which they are not represented. We are willing to stand upon this great principle of self-government everywhere; and it is to us a proud reflection that, in this whole discussion, no friend of the bill has urged an argument in its favor which could not be used with the same propriety in a free State as in a slave State, and *vice versa.* But no enemy of the bill has used an argument which would bear repetition one mile across Mason and Dixon's line. Our opponents have dealt entirely in sectional appeals. The friends of the bill have discussed a great principle of universal application, which can be sustained by the same reasons, and the same arguments, in every time and in every corner of the Union.

ON BRITISH AGGRESSION.

On the 7th of June, 1858, the subject of British Aggression being under consideration, Mr. Douglas said:

I agree, Mr. President, with most that has been said by my friend from Georgia (Mr. Toombs), and especially that we ought to determine what we are to do in reference to the outrages upon our flag in the Gulf of Mexico and the West Indies before we decide the amount of money we shall vote for war purposes. If we are going to content ourselves with simple resolutions that we will not submit to that which we have resolved for half a century should never be repeated, I see no use in additional appropriations for navy or for army; if we are going to be contented with loud-sounding speeches, with defiance to the British lion, with resolutions of the Senate alone, not concurred in by the other house, conferring no power on the Executive, merely capital for the country, giving no power to the Executive to avenge insults or prevent their repetition, what is the use of voting money? I find that patriotic gentlemen are ready to talk loud, resolve strong; but are they willing to appropriate the money—are they willing to confer on the Executive power to repel these insults, and to avenge them whenever they may be perpetrated? Let us know whether we are to submit and protest, or whether we are to authorize the President to resist and to prevent the repetition of these offences. If senators are prepared to vote for a law reviving the act of 1839, putting the army, the navy, volunteers, and money at the disposal of the President to prevent the repetition of these acts, and to punish them if repeated, then I am ready to give the ships and the money; but I desire to know whether we are to submit to these insults with a simple protest, or whether we are to repel them.

Gentlemen ask us to vote ships and money, and they talk to us about the necessity of a ship in China, and about outrages in Tampico, and disturbances in South America, and Indian difficulties in Puget Sound. Every enemy that can be found on the face of the earth is defied, except the one that defies us. Bring in a proposition here to invest the President with power to repel British aggression on American ships, and what is the response? High-sounding resolutions, declaring in effect, if not in terms, that whereas Great Britain has perpetrated outrages on our flag and our shipping, which are intolerable and insufferable, and must not be repeated; therefore, if she does so again, we will whip Mexico, or we will pounce down upon Nicaragua, or we will get up a fight with Costa Rica, or we will chastise New Granada, or we will punish the Chinese, or we will repel the Indians from Puget Sound (laughter); but not a word about Great Britain! What I desire to know, is whether we are to meet this issue with Great Britain? I am told we shall do it when we are prepared. Sir, when will you be prepared to repel an insult, unless when it is given?

England has her ships of war, of various sizes, searching our vessels, firing across their bows, firing into their rigging, subjecting them to search, not only in the Gulf of Mexico, but in the Caribbean sea and upon the Atlantic. It is not confined to one captain, or one vessel, or one locality, but the outrages are committed by various ships, by the Styx, on the coast of Cuba; by the Forward, five hundred miles east of there; by the Buzzard, a thousand miles from Cuba. Every arrival at our ports brings us information of the repetition of these offences, clearly demonstrating the fact that they are not accidental. They are not confined to one locality. They are not the acts of one ship or of one officer. They are the result of orders from Great Britain to execute this system of outrages on the American flag and American commerce. Are we to submit to it? If so, let us not say another word about it, pass no resolutions, make no speeches, vote no extra appropriations that we would not vote if these things had not occurred. If, on the contrary, we are not going to submit to them, why not act as we did on the northeastern boundary question in 1839? When the news arrived here on the 2d of March, 1839, that an American citizen had been taken prisoner on the disputed boundary of Maine, showing a disposition on the part of Great Britain to insist on her claim to the exclusive possession of that country, instantly the Senate, by a unanimous vote, passed a bill authorizing the President to repel any attempt on the part of Great Britain to enforce that claim, and, for that purpose, putting at his disposal the army, the navy, the militia, fifty thousand volunteers, and ten millions of money, to enable him to execute the will of the nation in that respect.

Now, sir, why not revive that act, striking out the disputed boundary and inserting "her claims to the right of visitation and search," and then every provision of that bill would be applicable to the present case. My friend from Missouri (Mr. Green) calls my attention to the vote of the House of Representatives on that occasion. It stood 197 in the affirmative, and 6 in the negative. The vote in the Senate was forty-one in the affirmative, none in the negative. Your Clays, your Calhouns, your Websters, the great men of former times, were here then; men differing in politics in times of high party strife, at a period when Mr. Van Buren was President, and Clay, Webster, and Calhoun led the opposition. Still, the moment this outrage was perpetrated by Great Britain upon our rights, all party dissensions were hushed; the opposition and the administration stood as one man when the honor of the nation was assaulted. They did not hesitate to confer upon Mr. Van Buren the power to resist the outrages committed by Great Britain, in case they should be persevered in.

Why not now revive the same law which was then passed by a unanimous vote in the Senate, and with only six dissenting voices in the other house, and confer upon President Buchanan the same power and authority which was then conferred upon President Van Buren on the motion of Mr. Senator Buchanan? Do that, and then I am prepared to vote the ships, the money, the men, anything, everything, necessary to indicate our firm resolve. Yes, sir, I will go further, I will vote the ships and the money even now, trusting that Congress, before it adjourns, will arm the President with the necessary power and authority to prevent a repetition of these aggressions. I am, however, extremely unwilling to bury up the outrages of Great Britain under all the talk and noise that is made about the injuries perpetrated by the South American republics. I know that in South America outrages have been perpetrated on our commerce, on our citizens and their property, which ought to have been punished on the spot. I know they are continuing, and will continue, from day to day, and year to year, until you clothe the Executive with the authority to punish them as promptly as the British government punish similar outrages on their commerce and their rights; but these things have been going on in South America for years. They are weak, feeble, unstable powers, entitled to our sympathy and our contempt mingled together. While I would clothe the Executive with power to punish them, I would only do it after I had avenged the insults perpetrated by Great Britain, or I would in the same act authorize the President to avenge them.

Sir, I tremble for the fame of America, for her honor, and for her character, when we shall be silent in regard to British outrages; and avenge ourselves by punishing the weaker powers instead of grappling with the stronger. I never did fancy that policy, nor admire that chivalry which induced a man, when insulted by a strong man of his own size, to say that he would whip the first boy he found in the street, in order to vindicate his honor; or, as is suggested by a gentleman behind me, that he would go home and whip his wife (laughter), in order to show his courage, inasmuch as he was afraid to tackle the full grown man who had committed the aggression.

Sir, these outrages cannot be concealed, they cannot have the go-by; we must meet them face to face. Now is the time when England must give up her claim to search American vessels, or we must be silent in our protests and resolutions and valorous speeches against that claim. It will not do to raise a navy for the Chinese seas, nor for Puget Sound, nor for Mexico, nor for the South American republics. It may be used for those purposes, but England must first be dealt with. Sir, we shall be looked upon as showing the white feather, if we strike a blow at any feeble power, until these English aggressions and insults are first punished, and security is obtained that they are not to be repeated.

I shall vote for the amendment offered by my friend from Florida, under the authority of Committee on Naval Affairs, providing for ten sloops-of-war. I shall also vote for the proposition of my friend from North Carolina for the ten gun-boats. I wish he had increased the number to fifty, because I understand they can be constructed for about $100,000 apiece, and $5,000,000 would give you fifty gun-boats, vessels of a character more serviceable for coast defence than any other vessels you could have. They could enter every harbor, every creek, every bay, every nook where it is necessary to afford protection, and each one of them singly would be strong enough in time of war to capture an enemy's merchant vessel, and bring it into port or sink it, as easily as a seventy-four, or the largest class of ships of war. I would increase the number of gun-boats to fifty—I would give the sloops asked for by the committee, but I would never permit this Congress to adjourn, after all the resolutions we have had reported and all the brave speeches we have made, until we give the President power, and thereby make it his duty, to repel in future every repetition of these British outrages on our flag; and to use the army, the navy, the militia, and the treasury, to any extent which may be necessary for that purpose.

I concur entirely with the senator from Virginia in the reasons he has given for the necessity of applying the provisions of the bill which he has reported from the Committee on Foreign Relations, as a substitute for one I introduced, to Mexico, Nicaragua, Costa Rica and New Granada; but I do not perceive the necessity of limiting the application to those countries, and not extending it beyond them. If his objection be true that my proposition was to confer a war-making power upon the President, then, by applying the whole power of these provisions to Mexico, and the other three countries, he confers a war-making power to that extent. I suppose, if it is no violation of principle to give the President a war-making power as applied to one country, it is no more so to give it to him generally. The objection I had to his provision was this: I had introduced a bill to authorize the President, in cases of flagrant violations of the law of nations, under circumstances admitting of no delay, to repel and punish the aggression. The senator from Virginia takes the provisions of that bill and indorses them as to four feeble, crippled powers, and omits the very country that is now committing outrages upon our flag and our shipping. I had introduced a bill, general in its provisions, applicable to England, France, Spain, Mexico, Central America, South America—everywhere where there were flagrant violation upon our flag, under circumstances admitting of no delay.

It does not follow that for every belligerent act we shall declare war. The senator from Virginia, in his report, as chairman of the Committee on Foreign Relations, quoted Chief Justice Marshall to show that the practice of the right of search was a belligerent act. All belligerent acts do not necessarily produce war. You may repel them, you may grant letters of marque and reprisal—there are various remedies short of war for repelling and redressing belligerent acts. It does not follow, by any means, when one nation perpetrates a violation of right against another, which, of itself, is a belligerent act, that war is the inevitable consequence, any more than it follows, when one gentleman says something offensive to another, that a peremptory challenge is a necessary result. A demand for explanation may be necessary. There are preludes to a declaration. So it is between nations. There may be a belligerent act performed. It leads to negotiation, to remonstrance. When these means fail, then the question comes, whether our rights or our honor are involved to such an extent as to make it imperative to go to war as a final resort?

If this violation of the freedom of the seas were a new thing; if the assertion of the right to search American vessels were now made for the first, or even the second time, we might not, although treating it as a belligerent act, deem it necessary to go to war. But when the question has gone through half a century of dispute; when it has reached such a point that we refuse to discuss the question of right any further; when we have asserted that the argument is exhausted, and that the only thing left is to resort to resistance if it be persevered in any further; it will not do for us, in the face of these outrages repeated each day, to be silent with regard to them, and proceed to legislate for the punishment of Mexico, Nicaragua, and other weak and feeble powers at a distance. The bill reported by the senator from Virginia would be right if it were brought forward at a time when the aggravation came from those countries, and not from England. I will vote for it. But to pass that by itself, and remain silent with regard to these British outrages, is to confess to the world that we are afraid of Great Britain, but we will maintain our courage by punishing some smaller, feebler, weaker power. I do not bring forward the proposition to revive the act of the 3d of March, 1839, as a substitute for the bill reported by the senator from Virginia, as he imagines. On the contrary, the two bills ought to go together. The one which I bring forward is applicable to England, and to her alone. It covers the present quarrels between us and England; not as a war measure, but as a peace measure. The only change that I make between that act, as I bring it forward now, and as it was in the shape in which it originally passed, is to strike out the words "territory in dispute," and insert "the claim of the right of search." Then the two cases are parallel, and the provision is as applicable to one as it is to the other.

Sir, there was one member of this body, who, when the measure was brought in, in 1839, was disposed to treat it as an act of war, until the great minds of the Senate, the patriots of that day, came forward, and said: no, Great Britain is performing a belligerent act; we must resist it at all hazards; if she perseveres in the wrong, then the consequences be on her head, for having persevered in the wrong. Hence, you find that Clay, Calhoun, Webster, Buchanan, and the leaders of the Senate of all parties of that day, united with entire unanimity in conferring upon President Van Buren the power to resist it. One man only hesitated. A distinguished and respected senator from New Jersey made the very point that is now being made, as to its being an act of war; but a distinguished senator from Mississippi appealed to him, after a preliminary vote had been taken, and it was ascertained that the Senate were unanimous with one exception, not to persevere in his opposition, but allow the Senate to stand unanimous in the assertion of a principle upon which all agreed; and Mr. Southard, in deference to the opinion of the remainder of the Senate, waived his objections, and allowed the bill to pass by a unanimous vote.

Sir, did it turn out to be a measure of war then? On the contrary, it resulted in peace, and you were saved from a war with Great Britain on the northeastern boundary question, by the unanimity of Congress, at that time, in preparing to repel the assault. The vote in the Senate was unanimous, and in the House of Representatives it was 197 against 6. This unanimity among the American people, as manifested by their representatives, saved the two countries from war, and preserved peace between England and the United States upon that question. If the Senate had been nearly equally divided in 1839; if there had been but half a dozen majority for the passage of that measure; if the vote had been nearly divided in the House of Representatives, England would have taken courage from the divisions in our own councils; she would have pressed her claim to a point that would have been utterly inadmissible, and incompatible with our honor, and war would have been the inevitable consequence.

The true peace measure is that which resents the insult and redresses the wrong promptly upon the spot with a unanimity that shows the nation cannot be divided. Unanimity now, prompt action, and determined resistance to this claim of the right of search is the best peace measure, and the only peace measure to which you can resort. You have said that this nation will not submit to the right of search; every department of this government has repeated it, all political parties unite in the sentiment; there is one point on which the American people are united, and on which they have stood for half a century. It is violated now. The question is, whether we shall present the same unanimity in resistance that we do in denying the right to commit the outrage. Unanimity on our part, unanimity in our councils, firm resolve, but kind and respectful words will preserve peace. Sir, I desire peace. I would lament a war with England, or with any other power, as much as any other man in the Senate. Nor do I think that my constituents desire war, but I believe that the true way to prevent it is to be prepared to resist aggression the moment it is made. What is the argument we hear used to-day? The senator from South Carolina (Mr. Hammond), who knows that I have for him the highest respect, portrays to us our weak, feeble, and defenceless condition; our thousands of miles of coast; our small navy; our limited resources; to show that we are not ready for a war now. Sir, let Great Britain believe that picture, and she will be ready now for a war with us.

Our vacillation, our hesitation, our nervousness about the defence-less condition of our coasts and of our cities, are the sources of en-couragement to England.

Sir, I repel the idea that the American coast is so defenceless as represented. I have passed round a great portion of the British coast, and I undertake to assert that the American coast is in a bet-ter condition of defence than that of Great Britain. New York is better defended than Liverpool or London to-day. It is easier for a fleet to enter the harbor of Liverpool or London than New York. There are not as many obstacles in the way in the British cities as in the American. It is possible that a steam fleet might run by the fortifications into either. It is not probable it would ever escape from there if it did; but it is possible that it might effect its escape. But, sir, I do not believe that our coast is more exposed than hers, and I do not believe our commerce is more exposed than hers. I do not believe England is any better prepared for war with us than we are with her. If she has a larger navy, she has a more exposed interest to protect by that navy. She has her troubles in India; she has them at the Cape; she has them all over the world; and her navy is divided, and her army divided to protect them in those detached places on every continent, and every island of the globe. Sir, the extent of her power spreading all around the globe is one of the greatest sources of her weakness; and the other fact that she is a commercial nation, and we are an agricultural people shows that she may be ruined, and her citizens starved, while we, although at war abroad, are happy and prosperous at home. Her statesmen have more respect for us in this particular than we have for ourselves. They will never push this question to the point of war. They will look you in the eye, march to you steadily, as long as they find it is prudent. If you cast the eye down, she will rush upon you. If you look her in the eye steadily, she will shake hands with you as friends, and have respect for you.

Suppose she should not, my friend from South Carolina asks me. If she does not, then we will appeal to the God of battles; we will arouse the patriotism of the American nation; we will blot out all distinction of party; and the voice of faction will be hushed; the American people will be a unit; none but the voice of patriotism will be heard; and from the North and the South, from the East and the West, we will come up as a band of brothers, animated by a common spirit and a common patriotism, as were our fathers of the Revolution, to repel the foreign enemy, and afterward differ as we please, and discuss at our leisure, matters of domestic dispute.

As to my proposition for fifty gun-boats instead of twenty, I have only to say that I prefer the larger number; and with all the respect I have for the senator from Mississippi and his superior knowledge on all matters of military defence, I must be permitted to entertain doubts whether he is correct in this particular. As to the usefulness of those vessels called gun-boats, the experience of the last few years shows that a gun-boat can wander from the Carolina coast, and can venture to sea. England constructed immense numbers of them expressly for the Black Sea and the Baltic during the Russian war; and she used them with great effect. She used them in the Gulf of Finland and at Sweaborg. They were built expressly for that service, and had to go three thousand miles to get to the Black Sea, and nearly two thousand to get into the Gulf of Finland. England has sent them to the West Indies; and the very outrages of which we now complain are being perpetrated by gun-boats. The Forward, that seized our vessels five hundred miles east of the Island of Cuba, on the high seas, is a gun-boat. The Buzzard, that seized our vessels one thousand miles from Cuba, off in the Atlantic ocean, is a gun-boat. All the vessels England is using now, for the annoyance of our commerce, are gun-boats—that very despised little craft which the senator from Mississippi thinks will never venture out from shore. I think that if a gun-boat is powerful enough to stop our merchantmen on the high seas, search them, and take them into port, or do what she pleases with them, such vessels will be efficient enough in time of war for us to annoy the enemy's commerce with. I think daily experience proves that these gun-boats are efficient not only in the defence of harbors, in running into the mouths of rivers and shallow bays, but in annoying the enemy's commerce, as they are being used by England for that very purpose at this time.

It so happens that only one of the vessels of Great Britain that have been perpetrating these outrages on our commerce, which has hovered around the coast of Cuba, is not a gun-boat, but small side-wheel steamer—the Styx.

ON THE INVASION OF STATES,

AND REPLY TO MR. FESSENDEN.

Delivered in the Senate of the United States, January 23, 1860.

The hour having arrived for the consideration of the special order, the Senate proceeded to consider the following resolution, submitted by Mr. Douglas on the 16th instant:

"*Resolved*, That the Committee on the Judiciary be instructed to report a bill for the protection of each State and Territory of the Union against invasion by the authorities or inhabitants of any other State or Territory; and for the suppression and punishment of conspiracies or combinations in any State or Territory with intent to invade, assail, or molest the government, inhabitants, property, or institutions of any other State or Territory of the Union."

MR. DOUGLAS.—Mr. President, on the 25th of November last, the Governor of Virginia addressed an official communication to the President of the United States, in which he said:

"I have information from various quarters, upon which I rely, that a conspiracy of formidable extent, in means and numbers, is formed in Ohio, Pennsylvania, New York, and other States, to rescue John Brown and his associates, prisoners at Charlestown, Virginia. The information is specific enough to be reliable. . . . . .
"Places in Maryland, Ohio, and Pennsylvania, have been occupied as depots and rendezvous by these desperadoes, and unobstructed by guards or otherwise, to invade this State, and we are kept in continual apprehension of outrage from fire and rapine. I apprise you of these facts in order that you may take steps to preserve peace between the States."

To this communication, the President of the United States, on the 28th of November, returned a reply from which I read the following sentence:

"I am at a loss to discover any provision in the Constitution or laws of the United States which would authorize me to 'take steps' for this purpose." [That is, to preserve the peace between the States.]

This announcement produced a profound impression upon the public mind and especially in the slaveholding States. It was generally received and regarded as an authoritative announcement that the Constitution of the United States confers no power upon the Federal Government to protect each of the States of this Union against invasion from the other States. I shall not stop to inquire whether the President meant to declare that the existing laws confer no authority upon him, or that the Constitution empowers Congress to enact laws which would authorize the federal interposition to protect the States from invasion; my object is to raise the inquiry, and to ask the judgment of the Senate and of the House of Representatives on the question, whether it is not within the power of Congress, and the duty of Congress, under the Constitution, to enact all laws which may be necessary and proper for the protection of each and every State against invasion, either from foreign powers or from any portion of the United States.

The denial of the existence of such a power in the Federal Government has induced an inquiry among conservative men—men loyal to the Constitution and devoted to the Union—as to what means they have of protection, if the Federal Government is not authorized to protect them against external violence. It must be conceded that no community is safe, no State can enjoy peace or prosperity, or domestic tranquillity, without security against external violence. Every State and nation of the world, outside of this Republic, is supposed to maintain armies and navies for this precise purpose. It is the only legitimate purpose for which armies and navies are maintained in time of peace. They may be kept up for ambitious purposes, for the purposes of aggression and foreign war; but the legitimate purpose of a military force in time of peace is to insure domestic tranquillity against violence or aggression from without. The States of this Union would possess that power, were it not for the restraints imposed upon them by the federal Constitution. When that Constitution was made, the States surrendered to the Federal Government the power to raise and support armies, and the power to provide and maintain navies, and not only thus surrendered the means of protection from invasion, but consented to a prohibition upon themselves which declares that no State shall keep troops or vessels of war in time of peace.

The question now recurs, whether the States of this Union are in that helpless condition, with their hands tied by the Constitution, stripped of all means of repelling assaults and maintaining their existence, without a guaranty from the Federal Government, to protect them against violence. If the people of this country shall settle down into the conviction that there is no power in the Federal Government under the Constitution to protect each and every State from violence, from aggression, from invasion, they will demand that the cord be severed, and that the weapons be restored to their hands with which they may defend themselves. This inquiry involves the question of the perpetuity of the Union. The means of defence, the means of repelling assaults, the means of providing against invasion, must exist as a condition of the safety of the States and the existence of the Union.

Now, sir, I hope to be able to demonstrate that there is no wrong in this Union for which the Constitution of the United States has not provided a remedy. I believe, and I hope I shall be able to maintain, that a remedy is furnished for every wrong which can be perpetrated within the Union, if the Federal Government performs its whole duty. I think it is clear, on a careful examination of the Constitution, that the power is conferred upon Congress, first, to provide for repelling invasion from foreign countries ; and, secondly, to protect each State of this Union against invasion from any other State, Territory, or place, within the jurisdiction of the United States. I will first turn your attention, sir, to the power conferred upon Congress to protect the United States—including States, Territories, and the District of Columbia ; including every inch of ground within our limits and jurisdiction—against foreign invasion. In the eighth section of the first article of the Constitution, you find that Congress has power—

" To raise and support armies ; to provide and maintain a navy ; to make rules for the government and regulation of the land and naval forces ; to provide for calling forth the militia to execute the laws of the Union, suppress insurrections, and repel invasions."

These various clauses confer upon Congress power to use the whole military force of the country for the purpose specified in the Constitution. They shall provide for the execution of the laws of the Union ; and, secondly, suppress insurrections. The insurrections there referred to are insurrections against the authority of the United States—insurrections against a State authority being provided for in a subsequent section, in which the United States cannot interfere, except upon the application of the State authorities. The invasion which is to be repelled by this clause of the Constitution is an invasion of the United States. The language is, Congress shall have power to " repel invasions." That gives the authority to repel the invasion, no matter whether the enemy shall land within the limits of Virginia, within the District of Columbia, within the Territory of New Mexico, or anywhere else within the jurisdiction of the United States. The power to protect every portion of the country against invasion from foreign nations having thus been specifically conferred, the framers of the Constitution then proceeded to make guaranties for the protection of *each of the States* by federal authority. I will read the fourth section of the fourth article of the Constitution :

" The United States shall guarantee to every State in this Union a republican form of government, and shall protect each of them against invasion ; and, on application of the legislature, or of the Executive, (when the legislature cannot be convened,) against domestic violence."

This clause contains three distinct guaranties : first, the United States shall guarantee to every State in this Union a republican form of government ; second, the United States shall protect each of them against invasion ; third, the United States shall, on application of the legislature, or of the Executive, when the legislature cannot be convened, protect them against domestic violence. Now, sir, I submit to you whether it is not clear, from the very language of the Constitution, that this clause was inserted for the purpose of making it the duty of the Federal Government to protect each of the States against invasion from any other State, Territory, or place within the jurisdiction of the United States? For what other purpose was the clause inserted? The power and duty of protection as against foreign nations had already been provided for. This clause occurs among the guaranties from the United States to each State, for the benefit of each State, for the protection of each State, and necessarily from other States, inasmuch as the guaranty had been given previously as against foreign nations.

If any further authority is necessary to show that such is the true construction of the Constitution, it may be found in the forty-third number of the "Federalist," written by James Madison. Mr. Madison quotes the clause of the Constitution which I have read, giving these three guaranties; and, after discussing the one guaranteeing to each State a republican form of government, proceeds to consider the second, which makes it the duty of the United States to protect each of the States against invasion. Here is what Mr. Madison says upon that subject:

" A protection against invasion is due *from every society to the parts composing it.* The latitude of the expression here used seems to secure each State, not only against foreign hostility, but against ambitious or vindictive enterprises of its more powerful neighbors. The history both of ancient and modern confederacies proves that the weaker members of the Union ought not to be insensible to the policy of this article."

The number of the "Federalist," like all the others of that celebrated work, was written after the Constitution was made, and before it was ratified by the States, and with a view to securing its ratification; hence the people of the several States, when they ratified this instrument, knew that this clause was intended to bear the construction which I now place upon it. It was intended to make it the duty of every society to protect each of its parts; the duty of the Federal Government to protect each of the States; and, he says, the smaller States ought not to be insensible to the policy of this article of the Constitution.

Then, sir, if it be made the imperative duty of the Federal Government, by the express provision of the Constitution, to protect each of the States against invasion or violence from the other States, or from combinations of desperadoes within their limits, it necessarily follows that it is the duty of Congress to pass all laws necessary and proper to render that guaranty effectual. While Congress, in the early history of the government, did provide legislation, which is supposed to be ample to protect the United States against invasion from foreign countries and the Indian tribes, they have failed, up to this time, to make any law for the protection of each of the States against invasion from within the limits of the Union. I am unable to account for this omission; but I presume the reason is to be found in the fact that no Congress ever dreamed that such legislation would ever become necessary for the protection of one State of this Union against invasion and violence from her sister States. Who, until the Harper's Ferry outrage, ever conceived that American citizens could be so forgetful of their duties to themselves, to their country, to the Constitution, as to plan an invasion of another State, with a view of inciting servile insurrection, murder, treason, and every other crime that disgraces humanity? While, therefore, no blame can justly be attached to our predecessors in failing to provide the legislation necessary to render this guaranty of the Constitution effectual; still, since the experience of last year, we cannot stand justified in omitting longer to perform this imperative duty.

The question then remaining is, what legislation is necessary and proper to render this guaranty of the Constitution effectual? I presume there will be very little difference of opinion that it will be necessary to place the whole military power of the government at the disposal of the President, under proper guards and restrictions against abuse, to repel and suppress invasion when the hostile force shall be actually in the field. But, sir, that is not sufficient. Such legislation would not be a full compliance with this guaranty of the Constitution. The framers of that instrument meant more when they gave the guaranty. Mark the difference in language between the provision for protecting the United States against invasion and that for protecting the States. When it provided for protecting the United States, it said Congress shall have power to "*repel* invasion." When it came to make this guaranty to the States it changed the language and said the United States shall "*protect*" each of the States against invasion. In one instance, the duty of the government is to repel; in the other, the guaranty is that they will protect. In other words, the United States are not permitted to wait until the enemy shall be upon your borders; until the invading army shall have been organized and drilled and placed in march with a view to the invasion; but they must pass all laws necessary and proper to insure protection and domestic tranquillity to each State and Territory of this Union against invasion or hostilities from other States and Territories.

Then, sir, I hold that it is not only necessary to use the military power when the actual case of invasion shall occur, but to authorize the judicial department of the government to suppress all conspiracies and combinations in the several States with the intent to invade a State, or molest or disturb its government, its peace, its citizens, its property, or its institutions. You must punish the conspiracy, the combination with intent to do the act, and then you will suppress it in advance. There is no principle more familiar to the legal profession than that wherever it is proper to declare an act to be a crime, it is proper to punish a conspiracy or combination with intent to perpetrate the act. Look upon your statute books, and I presume you will find an enactment to punish the counterfeiting of the coin of the United States; and then another section to punish a man for having countefeit coin in his possession *with intent* to pass it; and another section to punish him for having the molds, or dies, or instruments for counterfeiting, *with intent* to use them. This is a familiar principle in legislative and judicial proceedings. If the act of invasion is criminal, the conspiracy to invade should also be made criminal. If it be unlawful and illegal to invade a State, and run off fugitive slaves, why not make it unlawful to form conspiracies and combinations in the several States with intent to do the act? We have been told that a notorious man who has recently suffered death for his crimes upon the gallows, boasted in Cleaveland, Ohio, in a public lecture, a year ago, that he had then a body of men employed in running away horses from the slaveholders of Missouri, and pointed to a livery stable in Cleaveland which was full of the stolen horses at that time.

I think it is within our competency, and consequently our duty, to pass a law making every conspiracy or combination in any State or Territory of this Union to invade another with intent to steal or run away property of any kind, whether it be negroes, or horses, or property of any other description, into another State, a crime, and punish the conspirators by indictment in the United States courts, and confinement in the prisons or penitentiaries of the State or Territory where the conspiracy may be formed and quelled. Sir, I would carry these provisions of law as far as our constitutional power will reach. I would make it a crime to form conspiracies with a view of invading States or Territories to control elections, whether they be under the garb of Emigrant Aid Societies of New England, or Blue Lodges of Missouri. (Applause in the galleries.) In other words, this provision of the Constitution means more than the mere repelling of an invasion when the invading army shall reach the border of a State. The language is, it shall protect the State against invasion; the meaning of which is, to use the language of the preamble to the Constitution, to insure to each State domestic tranquillity against external violence. There can be no peace, there can be no prosperity, there can be no safety in any community, unless it is secured against violence from abroad. Why, sir, it has been a question seriously mooted in Europe, whether it was not the duty of England, a power foreign to France, to pass laws to punish conspiracies in England against the lives of the princes of France. I shall not argue the question of comity between foreign States. I predicate my argument upon the Constitution by which we are governed, and which we have sworn to obey, and demand that the Constitution be executed in good faith so as to punish and suppress every combination, every conspiracy, either to invade a State or to molest its inhabitants, or to disturb its property, or to subvert its institutions and its government. I believe this can be effectually done by authorizing the United States courts in the several States to take jurisdiction of the offence, and punish the violation of the law with appropriate punishments.

It cannot be said that the time has not yet arrived for such legis-lation. It cannot be said with truth that the Harper's Ferry case will not be repeated, or is not in danger of repetition. It is only necessary to inquire into the causes which produced the Harper's Ferry outrage, and ascertain whether those causes are yet in active operation, and then you can determine whether there is any ground for apprehension that that invasion will be repeated. Sir, what were the causes which produced the Harper's Ferry outrage? Without stopping to adduce evidence in detail, I have no hesitation in expressing my firm and deliberate conviction that the Harper's Ferry crime was the natural, logical, inevitable result of the doc-trines and teachings of the Republican party, as explained and enforced in their platform, their partisan presses, their pamphlets and books, and especially in the speeches of their leaders in and out of Congress. (Applause in the galleries.)

I was remarking that I considered this outrage at Harper's Ferry as the logical, natural consequence of the teachings and doctrines of the Republican party. I am not making this statement for the purpose of crimination or partisan effect. I desire to call the atten-tion of members of that party to a reconsideration of the doctrines that they are in the habit of enforcing, with a view to a fair judg-ment whether they do not lead directly to those consequences, on the part of those deluded persons who think that all they say is meant, in real earnest, and ought to be carried out. The great principle that underlies the Republican party is violent, irreconcila-ble, eternal warfare upon the institution of American slavery, with the view of its ultimate extinction throughout the land ; sectional war is to be waged until the cotton field of the South shall be culti-vated by free labor, or the rye fields of New York, and Massachu-setts shall be cultivated by slave labor. In furtherance of this article of their creed, you find their political organization not only sectional in its location, but one whose vitality consists in appeals to northern passion, northern prejudice, northern ambition against southern States, southern institutions, and southern people. I have had some experience in fighting this element within the last few years, and I find that the source of their power consists in exciting the prejudices and the passions of the northern section against those of the southern section. They not only attempt to excite the North against the South, but they invite the South to assail and abuse and traduce the North. Southern abuse, by violent men, of northern statesmen and northern people, is essential to the triumph of the Republican cause. Hence the course of argument which we have to meet is not only repelling the appeals to northern passion and preju-dice, but we have to encounter their appeals to southern men to assail us, in order that they may justify their assaults upon the plea of self-defence.

Sir, when I returned home in 1858, for the purpose of canvassing Illinois, with a view to reëlection, I had to meet this issue of the "irrepressible conflict." It is true that the senator from New York had not then made his Rochester speech, and did not for four months afterward. It is true that he had not given the doctrine that precise name and form; but the principle was in existence, and had been proclaimed by the ablest and the most clear-headed men of the party. I will call your attention, sir, to a single passage from a speech, to show the language in which this doctrine was stated in Illinois before it received the name of the "irrepressible conflict." The Republican party assembled in State convention in June, 1858, in Illinois, and unanimously adopted Abraham Lincoln as their candidate for United States senator. Mr. Lincoln appeared before the convention, accepted the nomination, and made a speech—which had been previously written and agreed to in caucus by most of the leaders of the party. I will read a single extract from that speech:

"In my opinion, it [the slavery agitation] will not cease until a crisis shall have been reached and passed. 'A house divided against itself cannot stand.' I believe this government cannot endure permanently, half slave and half free. I do not expect the house to fall, but I do expect it will cease to be divided. It will become all one thing or all the other. Either the opponents of slavery will arrest the further spread of it, and place it where the public mind shall rest in the belief that it is in the course of ultimate extinction; or its advocates will push forward till it shall become alike lawful in all the States—old as well as new, North as well as South."

Sir, the moment I landed upon the soil of Illinois, at a vast gathering of many thousands of my constituents to welcome me home, I read that passage, and took direct issue with the doctrine contained in it as being revolutionary and treasonable, and inconsistent with the perpetuity of this Republic. That is not merely the individual opinion of Mr. Lincoln; nor is it the individual opinion merely of the senator from New York, who four months afterward asserted the same doctrine in different language; but, so far as I know, it is the general opinion of the members of the Abolition or Republican party. They tell the people of the North that unless they rally as one man, under a sectional banner, and make war upon the South with a view to the ultimate extinction of slavery, slavery will overrun the whole North, and fasten itself upon all the free States. They then tell the South, unless you rally as one man, binding the whole southern people into a sectional party, and establish slavery all over the free States, the inevitable consequence will be that we shall abolish it in the slaveholding States. The same doctrine is held by the senator from New York in his Rochester speech. He tells us that the States must all become free, or all become slave; that the South, in other words, must conquer and subdue the North, or the North must triumph over the South, and drive slavery from within its limits.

Mr. President, in order to show that I have not misinterpreted the position of the senator from New York, in notifying the South that, if they wish to maintain slavery within their limits, they must also fasten it upon the northern States, I will read an extract from his Rochester speech :

" It is an irrepressible conflict between opposing and enduring forces : and it means that the United States must and will, sooner or later, become either entirely a slaveholding nation, or entirely a free-labor nation. Either the cotton and rice fields of South Carolina, and the sugar plantations of Louisiana, will ultimately be tilled by free labor, and Charleston and New Orleans become marts for legitimate merchandise alone, or else the rye fields and wheat fields of Massachusetts and New York must again be surrendered by their farmers to slave culture and to the production of slaves, and Boston and New York become once more markets for trade in the bodies and souls of men."

Thus, sir, you perceive that the theory of the Republican party is, that there is a conflict between two different systems of institutions in the respective classes of States—not a conflict in the same States, but an irrepressible conflict between the free States and the slave States ; and they argue that these two systems of State cannot permanently exist in the same Union ; that the sectional warfare must continue to rage and increase with increasing fury until the free States shall surrender, or the slave States shall be subdued. Hence, while they appeal to the passions of our own section, their object is to alarm the people of the other section, and drive them to madness, with the hope that they will invade our rights as an excuse for some of our people to carry on aggressions upon their rights. I appeal to the candor of senators, whether this is not a fair exposition of the tendency of the doctrines proclaimed by the Republican party. The creed of that party is founded upon the theory that, because slavery is not desirable in our States, it is not desirable anywhere ; because free labor is a good thing with us, it must be the best thing everywhere. In other words, the creed of their party rests upon the theory that there must be *uniformity* in the domestic institutions and internal polity of the several States of this Union. There, in my opinion, is the fundamental error upon which their whole system rests. In the Illinois canvass, I asserted, and now repeat, that uniformity in the domestic institutions of the different States is neither possible nor desirable. That is the very issue upon which I conducted the canvass at home, and it is the question which I desire to present to the Senate. I repeat, that uniformity in domestic institutions of the different States, is neither possible nor desirable.

Was such the doctrine of the framers of the Constitution ? I wish the country to bear in mind that when the Constitution was adopted, the Union consisted of thirteen States, twelve of which were slaveholding States, and one a free State. Suppose this doctrine of uniformity on the slavery question had prevailed in the Federal Convention, do the gentlemen on that side of the House think that freedom would have triumphed over slavery ? Do they imagine that the one free State would have outvoted the twelve slaveholding States.

and thus have abolished slavery throughout the land by a Constitutional provision? On the contrary, if the test had then been made, if this doctrine of uniformity on the slavery question had then been proclaimed and believed in, with the twelve slaveholding States against one free State, would it not have resulted in a constitutional provision fastening slavery irrevocably upon every inch of American soil, North as well as South? Was it quite fair in those days for the friends of free institutions to claim that the Federal Government must not touch the question, but must leave the people of each State to do as they pleased, until under the operation of that principle they secured the majority, and then wield that majority to abolish slavery in the other States of the Union?

Sir, if uniformity in respect to domestic institutions had been deemed desirable when the Constitution was adopted, there was another mode by which it could have been obtained. The natural mode of obtaining uniformity was to have blotted out the State governments, to have abolished the State Legislatures, to have conferred upon Congress legislative power over the municipal and domestic concerns of the people of all the States, as well as upon Federal questions affecting the whole Union; and if this doctrine of uniformity had been entertained and favored by the framers of the Constitution, such would have been the result. But, sir, the framers of that instrument knew at that day, as well as we now know, that in a country as broad as this, with so great a variety of climate, of soil, and of production, there must necessarily be a corresponding diversity of institutions and domestic regulations, adapted to the wants and necessities of each locality. The framers of the Constitution knew that the laws and institutions which were well adapted to the mountains and valleys of New England, were ill-suited to the rice plantations and the cotton-fields of the Carolinas. They knew that our liberties depended upon reserving the right to the people of each State to make their own laws and establish their own institutions, and control them at pleasure, without interference from the Federal Government, or from any other State or Territory, or any foreign country. The Constitution, therefore, was based, and the Union was founded, on the principle of dissimilarity in the domestic institutions and internal polity of the several States. The Union was founded on the theory that each State had peculiar interests, requiring peculiar legislation, and peculiar institutions, different and distinct from every other State. The Union rests on the theory that no two States would be precisely alike in their domestic policy and institutions.

Hence, I assert that this doctrine of uniformity in the domestic institutions of the different States is repugnant to the Constitution, subversive of the principles upon which the Union was based, revolutionary in its character, and leading directly to despotism if it is ever established. Uniformity in local and domestic affairs in a country of great extent is despotism always. Show me centralism prescribing uniformity from the capital to all of its provinces in their local and domestic concerns, and I will show you a despotism as odious and as insufferable as that of Austria or of Naples. Dissimilarity is the principle upon which the Union rests. It is founded upon the idea that each State must necessarily require different regulations; that no two States have precisely the same interests, and hence do not need precisely the same laws; and you cannot account for this confederation of States upon any other principle.

Then, sir, what becomes of this doctrine that slavery must be established in all the States or prohibited in all the States? If we only conform to the principles upon which the Federal Union was formed, there can be no conflict. It is only necessary to recognize the right of the people of every State to have just such institutions as they please, without consulting your wishes, your views, or your prejudices, and there can be no conflict.

And, sir, inasmuch as the Constitution of the United States confers upon Congress the power coupled with the duty of protecting each State against external aggression, and inasmuch as that includes the power of suppressing and punishing conspiracies in one State against the institutions, property, people, or government of every other State, I desire to carry out that power vigorously. Sir, give us such a law as the Constitution contemplates and authorizes, and I will show the senator from New York that there is a constitutional mode of repressing the "irrepressible conflict." I will open the prison door to allow conspirators against the peace of the Republic and the domestic tranquility of our States to select their cells wherein to drag out a miserable life, as a punishment for their crimes against the peace of society.

Can any man say to us that although this outrage has been perpetrated at Harper's Ferry, there is no danger of its recurrence? Sir, is not the Republican party still embodied, organized, confident of success, and defiant in its pretensions? Does it not now hold and proclaim the same creed that it did before this invasion? It is true that most of its representatives here disavow the *acts* of John Brown at Harper's Ferry. I am glad that they do so; I am rejoiced that they have gone thus far; but I must be permitted to say to them that it is not sufficient that they disavow the act, unless they also repudiate and denounce the doctrines and teachings which produced the act. Those doctrines remain the same; those teachings are being poured into the minds of men throughout the country by means of speeches and pamphlets and books and through partisan presses. The causes that produced the Harper's Ferry invasion are now in active operation. It is true that the people of all the border States are required by the Constitution to have their hands tied, without the power of self-defence, and remain patient under a threatened invasion in the day or in the night? Can you expect people to be patient, when they dare not lie down to sleep at night without first stationing sentinels around their houses to see if a band of marauders and murderers are not approaching with torch and pistol? Sir, it requires more patience than freemen ever should cultivate, to submit to constant annoyance, irritation and apprehension. If we expect to preserve this Union, we must remedy, within the Union and in obedience to the Constitution, every evil for which disunion would furnish a remedy. If the Federal Government fails to act, either from choice or from an apprehension of the want of power, it cannot be expected that the States will be content to remain unprotected.

Then, sir, I see no hope of peace, of fraternity, of good feeling, between the different portions of the United States, except by bringing to bear the power of the Federal Government to the extent authorized by the Constitution—to protect the people of all the States against any external violence or aggression. I repeat, that if the theory of the Constitution shall be carried out by conceding the right of the people of every State to have just such institutions as they choose, there cannot be a conflict, much less an "irrepressible conflict," between the free and the slaveholding States.

Mr. President, the mode of preserving peace is plain. This system of sectional warfare must cease. The Constitution has given the power, and all we ask of Congress is to give the means, and we, by indictments and convictions in the federal courts of our several States, will make such examples of the leaders of these conspiracies as will strike terror into the hearts of the others, and there will be an end of this crusade. Sir, you must check it by crushing out the conspiracy, the combination, and then there can be safety. Then we shall be able to restore that spirit of fraternity which inspired our revolutionary fathers upon every battle-field; which presided over the deliberations of the convention that framed the Constitution, and filled the hearts of the people who ratified it. Then we shall be able to demonstrate to you that there is no evil unredressed in the Union for which disunion would furnish a remedy. Then, sir, let us execute the Constitution in the spirit in which it was made. Let Congress pass all the laws necessary and proper to give full and complete effect to every guaranty of the Constitution. Let them authorize the punishment of conspiracies and combinations in any State or Territory against the property, institutions, people or government of any other State or Territory, and there will be no excuse, no desire, for disunion. Then, sir, let us leave the people of every State perfectly free to form and regulate their domestic institutions in their own way. Let each of them retain slavery just as long as it pleases, and abolish it when it chooses. Let us act upon that good old golden principle which teaches all men to mind their own business and let their neighbors alone. Let this be done, and this Union can endure forever as our fathers made it, composed of free and slave States, just as the people of each State may determine for themselves.

Mr. Fessenden having replied at some length to Mr. Douglas, he made the following rejoinder:

Mr. Douglas.—Mr. President, I shall not follow the senator from Maine through his entire speech, but simply notice such points as demand of me some reply. He does not know why I introduced my resolution; he cannot conceive any good motive for it; he thinks there must be some other motive besides the one that has been avowed. There are some men, I know, who cannot conceive that a man can be governed by a patriotic or proper motive; but it is not among that class of men that I look for those who are governed by motives of propriety. I have no impeachment to make of his motives. I brought in this resolution because I thought the time had arrived when we should have a measure of practical legislation. I had seen expressions of opinion against the power from authorities so high that I felt it my duty to bring it to the attention of the Senate. I had heard that the senator from Virginia had intimated some doubt on the question of power, as well as of policy. Other senators discussed the question here for weeks when I was confined to my sick bed. Was there anything unreasonable in my coming before the Senate at this time, expressing my own opinion, and confining myself to the practical legislation indicated in the resolution? Nor, sir, have I in my remarks gone outside of the legitimate argument pertaining to the necessity for this legislation. I first showed that there had been a great outrage; I showed what I believed to be the causes that had produced the outrage, and that the causes which produced it were still in operation; and argued that, so long as the party to which the gentlemen belong remains embodied in full force, those causes will still threaten the country. That was all.

The senator from Maine thinks he will vote for the bill that will be proposed to carry out the objects referred to in my resolution. Sir, whenever that senator and his associates on the other side of the chamber will record their votes for a bill of the character described in my resolution and speech, I shall congratulate the country upon the progress they are making toward sound principles. Whenever he and his associates will make it a felony for two or more men to conspire to run off fugitive slaves, and punish the conspirators by confinement in the penitentiary, I shall consider that wonderful changes have taken place in this country. I tell the senator that it is the general tone of sentiment in all those sections of the country where the Republican party predominate, so far as I know, not only not to deem it a crime to rescue a fugitive slave, but to raise mobs to aid in the rescue. He talks about slandering the Republican party when we intimate that they are making a warfare upon the rights guaranteed by the Constitution. Sir, where, in the towns and cities with Republican majorities, can you execute the Fugitive Slave Law? Is it in the town where the senator from New York resides? Do you not remember the Jerry rescuers? Is it at Oberlin, where the mob was raised that made the rescue last year and produced the riot?

Why not make it a crime to form conspiracies and combinations to run off fugitive slaves, as well as to run off horses, or any other property ? I am talking about conspiracies which are so common in all our northern States, to invade and enter, through their agents, the slave States, and seduce away slaves and run them off by the underground railroad, in order to send them to Canada. It is these conspiracies to perpetrate crime with impunity, that keep up the irritation. John Brown could boast, in a public lecture in Cleveland, that he and his band had been engaged all the winter in stealing horses and running them off from the slaveholders in Missouri, and that the livery stables were then filled with stolen horses, and yet the conspiracy to do it could not be punished.

Sir, I desire a law that will make it a crime, punishable by imprisonment in the penitentiary, after conviction in the United States court, to make a conspiracy in one State, against the people, property, government, or institutions, of another. Then we shall get at the root of the evil. I have no doubt that gentlemen on the other side will vote for a law which pretends to comply with the guaranties of the Constitution, without carrying any force or efficiency in its provisions. I have heard men abuse the Fugitive Slave Law, and express their willingness to vote for amendments; but when you came to the amendments which they desired to adopt, you found they were such as would never return a fugitive to his master. They would go for any fugitive slave law that had a hole in it big enough to let the negro drop through and escape; but none that would comply with the obligations of the Constitution. So we shall find that side of the chamber voting for a law that will, in terms, disapprove of unlawful expeditions against neighboring States, without being efficient in affording protection.

But the senator says it is a part of the policy of the northern Democracy to represent the Republicans as being hostile to southern institutions. Sir, it is a part of the policy of the northern Democracy, as well as their duty, to speak the truth on that subject. I did not suppose that any man would have the audacity to arraign a brother senator here for representing the Republican party as dealing in denunciation and insult of the institutions of the South. Look to your Philadelphia platform, where you assert the sovereign power of Congress over the Territories for their government, and demand that it shall be exerted against those twin relics of barbarism—polygamy and slavery.

Mr. President, for what purpose does the Republican party appeal to northern passions and northern prejudices against southern institutions and the southern people, unless it is to operate upon those institutions ? They represent southern institutions as no better than polygamy; the slaveholder as no better than the polygamist; and complain that we should intimate that they did not like to associate with the slaveholder any better than with the polygamist.

I have always noticed that those men who were so far off from the slave States that they did not know anything about them, are most anxious for the fate of the poor slave. Those men who are so far off that they do not know what a negro is, are distressed to death about the condition of the poor negro. (Laughter.) But, sir, go into the border States, where we associate across the line, where the civilities of society are constantly interchanged; where we trade with each other, and have social and commercial intercourse, and there you will find them standing by each other like a band of brothers. Take southern Illinois, southern Indiana, southern Ohio, and that part of Pennsylvania bordering on Maryland, and there you will find social intercourse; commercial intercourse; good feeling; because those people know the condition of the slave on the opposite side of the line; but just in proportion as you recede from the slave States, just in proportion as the people are ignorant of the facts, just in that proportion party leaders can impose on their sympathies and honest prejudices.

Sir, I know it is the habit of the Republican party, as a party, wherever I have met them, to make the warfare in such a way as to try to rally the whole North on sectional grounds against the South. I know that it is to be the issue, and it is proven by the speech of the senator from New York, which I quoted before, and that of Mr. Lincoln, so far as they are authority. I happen to have those speeches before me. The senator from Maine has said that neither of these speeches justified the conclusion that they asserted, that the free States and the slave States cannot coëxist permanently in the same republic. Let us see whether they do or not. Mr. Lincoln says:

"A house divided against itself cannot stand. I believe this government cannot endure permanently, half slave and half free."

Then he goes on to say they must all be one thing or all the other, or else the Union cannot endure. What is the meaning of that language, unless it is that the Union cannot permanently exist, half slave and half free—that it must all become one thing or all become the other? That is the declaration. The declaration is that the North must combine as a sectional party, and carry on the agitation so fiercely, up to the very borders of the slaveholding States, that the master dare not sleep at night for fear that the robbers, the John Browns, will come and set his house on fire, and murder the women and children, before morning, It is to surround the slaveholding States by a cordon of free States, to use the language of the senator; to hem them in, in order that you may smother them out. The senator avowed, in his speech to-day, their object to be to hem in the slave States, in order that slavery may die out. How die out? Confine it to its present limits; let the ratio of increase go on by the laws of nature; and just in proportion as the lands in the slaveholding States wear out, the negroes increase, and you will soon reach that point where the soil will not produce enough to feed the slaves; then hem them in, and let them starve out—let them die out by starvation.

That is the policy—hem them in, and starve them out. Do as the French did in Algeria, when the Arabs took to the caverns—smoke them out, by making fires at the mouths of the caverns, and keep them burning until they die. The policy is, to keep up this agitation along the line; make slave property insecure in the border States; keep the master constantly in apprehension of assault, till he will consent to abandon his native country, leaving his slaves behind him, or to remove them further south. If you can force Kentucky thus to abolish slavery, you make Tennessee the border State, and begin the same operation upon her.

But sir, let us see whether the senator from New York did not proclaim the doctrine that free States and slave States cannot permanently exist in the same republic. He said:

"It is an irrepressible conflict between opposing and enduring forces; and it means that the United States must, and will, sooner or later, become either entirely a slaveholding nation or entirely a free-labor nation."

The opposing conflict is between the States; the Union cannot remain as it now is, part free and part slave. The conflict between free States and slave States must go on until there is not a slave State left, or until they are all slave States. That is the declaration of the senator from New York. The senator from Maine tried to make the Senate believe that I had misrepresented the senator from New York and Mr. Lincoln, of Illinois, in stating that they referred to a conflict between States. He said that all they meant was that it was a conflict between free labor and slave labor in the same State.

Now, sir, let me submit to that man's candor whether he will insist on that position. They both say the contest will go on until the States become all free or all slave. Then, when is the contest going to end? When they become all slave? Will there not be the same conflict between free labor and slave labor, after every State has become a slave State, that there is now? If that was the meaning, would the conflict between slave labor and free labor cease even when every State had become slaveholding? Have not all the slaveholding States a large number of free laborers within their limits; and if there is an irrepressible conflict between free labor and slave labor, will you remove that conflict by making the States all slave? Yet, the senator from New York says they must become all slave or all free before the conflict ceases. Sir, that shows that the senator from New York meant what I represented him as meaning. It shows that a man who knows the meaning of words, and has the heart to express them as they read, cannot fail to know that that was the meaning of those senators. The boldness with which a charge of misrepresentation may be made in this body will not give character to it when it is contradicted by the facts. I dislike to have to repel these charges of unfairness and misrepresentation; yet the senator began with a series of innuendoes, with a series of complaints of misrepresentation, showing that he was afraid to meet the real issues of his party, and would make up for that by personal assaults and innuendoes against the opposite party.

He goes back to a speech of mine in opposition to the Lecompton constitution, in which I said that if you would send that constitution back and let the people of Kansas vote for or against it, if they voted for a free State or a slave State I would go for it without caring whether they voted slavery up or down. He thinks it is a great charge against me that I do not care whether the people vote it up or vote it down.

The idea is taken from a speech in the Senate—the first speech I made against the Lecompton constitution. It was quoted all over Illinois by Mr. Lincoln in the canvass, and I repeated the sentiment each time it was quoted against me, and repeated it in the South as well as the North. I say this: if the people of Kansas want a slave State, it is their business, not mine; if they want a free State, they have a right to have it; and hence, I do not care, so far as regards my action, whether they make it a free State or not; it is none of my business. But the senator says he does care, he has a preference between freedom and slavery. How long would this preference last if he was a sugar planter in Louisiana, residing on his estate, instead of living in Maine? Sir, I hold the doctrine that a wise statesman will adapt his laws to the wants, conditions and interests of the people to be governed by them. Slavery may be very essential in one climate and totally useless in another. If I were a citizen of Louisiana I would vote for retaining and maintaining slavery, because I believe the good of that people would require it. As a citizen of Illinois I am utterly opposed to it, because our interests would not be promoted by it. I should like to see the Abolitionist who would go and live in a southern country that would not get over his scruples very soon and have a plantation as quickly as he could get the money to buy it.

I have said and repeat that this question of slavery is one of climate, of political economy, of self-interest, not a question of legislation. Wherever the climate, the soil, the health of the country are such that it cannot be cultivated by white labor, you will have African labor, and compulsory labor at that. Wherever white labor can be employed cheapest and most profitably, there African labor will retire and white labor will take its place.

You cannot force slavery by all the acts of Congress you may take on one inch of territory against the will of the people, and you cannot by any law you can make keep it out from one inch of American territory where the people want it. You tried it in Illinois. By the Ordinance of 1787, slavery was prohibited, and yet our people, believing that slavery would be profitable to them, established hereditary servitude in the Territory by territorial legislation, in defiance of your federal ordinance. We maintained slavery there just so long as Congress said we should not have it, and we abolished it at just the moment you recognized us as a State, with the right to do as we pleased. When we established it, it was on the supposition that it was our interest to do so. When we abolished it, we did so because experience proved that it was not our interest to have it. I hold that slavery is a question of political economy, to be determined by climate, by soil, by production, by self-interest, and hence the people to be affected by it are the most impartial jury to try the fact, whether their interest requires them to have it or not.

But the senator thinks it is a great crime for me to say that I do not care whether they have it or not. I care just this far: I want every people to have that kind of government, that system of laws, that class of institutions, which will best promote their welfare, and I want them to decide for themselves; and so that they decide it to suit themselves, I am satisfied, without stopping to inquire or caring which way they decide it. That is what I meant by that declaration, and I am ready to stand by it.

The senator has made the discovery—I suppose it is very new, for he would not repeat anything that was old, after calling me to account for expressing an idea that had been heard of before—that I re-opened the agitation by bringing in the Nebraska Bill in 1854; and he tries to put the responsibility of the crimes perpetrated by his political friends, and in violation of the law, upon the provisions of the law itself. We passed a bill to allow the people of Kansas to form and regulate their own institutions to suit themselves. No sooner had we placed that law on the statute-book, than his political friends formed conspiracies and combinations in the different New England States to import a set of desperadoes into Kansas to control the elections and the institutions of that country in fraud of the law of Congress.

Sir, I desire to make the legislation broad enough to reach conspiracies and combinations of that kind; and I would also include combinations and conspiracies on the other side. My object is to establish firmly the doctrine that each State is to do its own voting, establish its own institutions, make its own laws without interference, directly or indirectly, from any outside power. The gentleman says that is squatter sovereignty. Call it squatter sovereignty, call it popular sovereignty, call it what you please, it is the great principle of self-government on which this Union was formed, and by the preservation of which alone it can be maintained. It is the right of the people of every State to govern themselves and make their own laws, and be protected from outside violence or interference, directly or indirectly. Sir, I confess the object of the legislation I contemplate is to put down this outside interference; it is to repress this "irrepressible conflict;" it is to bring the government back to the true principles of the Constitution, and let each people in this Union rest secure in the enjoyment of domestic tranquillity without apprehension from neighboring States.

·ON THE ADMISSION OF KANSAS UNDER THE WYAN-DOTT CONSTITUTION.

IN REPLY TO MR. SEWARD AND MR. TRUMBULL.

Delivered in the Senate of the United States, February 29, 1860.

MR. PRESIDENT : I trust I shall be pardoned for a few remarks upon so much of the senator's speech as consists in an assault on the Democratic party, and especially with regard to the Kansas-Nebraska bill, of which I was the responsible author.   It has become fashionable now-a-days for each gentleman making a speech against the Democratic party to refer to the Kansas-Nebraska Act as the cause of all the disturbances that have since ensued.   They talk about the repeal of a sacred compact that had been undisturbed for more than a quarter of a century, as if those who complained of violated faith had been faithful to the provisions of the Missouri Compromise.   Sir, wherein consisted the necessity for the repeal or abrogation of that act, except it was that the majority in the northern States refused to carry out the Missouri Compromise in good faith ?   I stood willing to extend it to the Pacific Ocean, and abide by it forever, and the entire South, without one exception in this body, was willing thus to abide by it; but the freesoil element of the northern States was so strong as to defeat that measure, and thus open the slavery question anew.   The men who now complain of the abrogation of that act were the very men who denounced it, and denounced all of us who were willing to abide by it so long as it stood upon the statute-book.   Sir, it was the defeat, in the House of Representatives, of the enactment of the bill to extend the Missouri Compromise to the Pacific Ocean, after it had passed the Senate on my own motion, that opened the controversy of 1850, which was terminated by the adoption of the measures of that year.

We carried those Compromise measures over the head of the senator from New York and his present associates.   We, in those measures, established a great principle, rebuking his doctrine of intervention by the Congress of the United States to prohibit slavery in the Territories.   Both parties, in 1852, pledged themselves to abide by that principle, and thus stood pledged not to prohibit slavery in the Territories by act of Congress.   The Whig party affirmed that pledge, and so did the Democracy.   In 1854 we only carried out, in the Kansas-Nebraska Act, the same principle that had been affirmed in the Compromise measures of 1850. . I repeat that their resistance to carrying out in good faith the settlement of 1820, their defeat of the bill for extending it to the Pacific Ocean, was the sole cause of the agitation of 1850, and gave rise to the necessity of establishing the principle of non-intervention by Congress with slavery in the Territories.

Hence I am not willing to sit here and allow the senator from New York, with all the weight of authority he has with the powerful party of which he is the head, to arraign me and the party to which I belong with the responsibility for that agitation which rests solely upon him and his associates. Sir, the Democratic party was willing to carry out the Compromise in good faith. Having been defeated in that for the want of numbers, and having established the principle of non-intervention in the Compromise measures of 1850, in lieu of it, the Democratic party from that day to this has been faithful to the new principle of adjustment. Whatever agitation has grown out of the question since, has been occasioned by the resistance of the party of which that senator is the head, to this great principle which has been ratified by the American people at two Presidential elections. If he was willing to acquiesce in the solemn and repeated judgment of that American people to which he appeals, there would be no agitation in this country now.

But, sir, the whole argument of that senator goes far beyond the question of slavery, even in the Territories. His entire argument rests on the assumption that the negro and the white man were equal by Divine law, and hence that all laws and constitutions and governments in violation of the principle of negro equality are in violation of the law of God. That is the basis upon which his speech rests.

He quotes the Declaration of Independence to show that the fathers of the Revolution understood that the negro was placed on an equality with the white man, by quoting the clause, " we hold these truths to be self-evident, that all men are created equal, and are endowed by their Creator with certain inalienable rights, among which are life, liberty, and the pursuit of happiness." Sir, the doctrine of that senator and of his party is—and I have had to meet it for eight years—that the Declaration of Independence intended to recognize the negro and the white man as equal under the Divine law, and hence that all the provisions of the Constitution of the United States which recognize slavery are in violation of the Divine law. In other words, it is an argument against the Constitution of the United States upon the ground that it is contrary to the law of God. The senator from New York has long held that doctrine. The senator from New York has often proclaimed to the world that the Constitution of the United States was in violation of the Divine law, and that senator will not contradict the statement. I have an extract from one of his speeches now before me, in which that proposition is distinctly put forth. In a speech made in the State of Ohio, in 1848, he said:

" Slavery is the sin of not some of the States only, but of them all; of not one nationality, but of all nations. It perverted and corrupted the moral sense of mankind deeply and universally, and this perversion became a universal habit. Habits of thought become fixed principles. No American State has yet delivered itself entirely from these habits. We, in New York, are guilty of slavery still by withholding the right of suffrage from the race we have emancipated. You, in Ohio, are guilty in the same way by a system of black laws still more aristocratic and odious. It is written in the Constitution of the United States that five slaves shall count equal to three freemen as a basis of representation; and it is written, also, IN VIOLATION OF DIVINE LAW, that we shall surrender the fugitive slave who takes refuge at our firesides from his relentless pursuer."

There you find his doctrine clearly laid down, that the Constitution of the United States is "in violation of the Divine law," and therefore, is not to be obeyed. You are told that the clause relating to fugitive slaves, being in violation of the Divine law, is not binding on mankind. This has been the doctrine of the senator from New York for years. I have not heard it in the Senate to-day for the first time. I have met in my own State, for the last ten years, this same doctrine, that the Declaration of Independence recognized the negro and the white man as equal; that the negro and white man are equals by Divine law, and that every provision of our Constitution and laws which establishes inequality between the negro and the white man, is void, because contrary to the law of God.

The senator from New York says, in the very speech from which I have quoted, that New York is yet a slave State. Why? Not that she has a slave within her limits, but because the Constitution of New York does not allow a negro to vote on an equality with a white man. For that reason he says New York is still a slave State; for that reason every other State that discriminates between the negro and the white man is a slave State, leaving but a very few States in the Union that are free from his objection. Yet, notwithstanding the senator is committed to these doctrines, notwithstanding the leading men of his party are committed to them, he argues that they have been accused of being in favor of negro equality, and says the tendency of their doctrine is the equality of the white man. He introduces the objection, and fails to answer it. He states the proposition and dodges it, to leave the inference that he does not indorse it. Sir, I desire to see these gentlemen carry out their principles to their logical conclusion. If they will persist in the declaration that the negro is made the equal of the white man, and that any inequality is in violation of the Divine law, then let them carry it out in their legislation by conferring on the negroes all the rights of citizenship the same as on white men. For one, I never held to any such doctrine. I hold that the Declaration of Independence was only referring to the white man—to the governing race of this country, who were in conflict with Great Britain, and had no reference to the negro race at all, when it declared that all men were created equal.

Sir, if the signers of that declaration had understood the instrument then as the senator from New York now construes it, were they not bound on that day, at that very hour, to emancipate all their slaves? If Mr. Jefferson had meant that his negro slaves were created by the Almighty his equals, was he not bound to emancipate the slaves on the very day that he signed his name to the Declaration of Independence? Yet no one of the signers of that declaration emancipated his slaves. No one of the States on whose behalf the declaration was signed, emancipated its slaves until after the Revolution was over. Every one of the original colonies, every one of the thirteen original States, sanctioned and legalized slavery until after the Revolution was closed. These facts show conclusively that the Declaration of Independence was never intended to bear the construction placed upon it by the senator from New York, and by that enormous tribe of lecturers that go through the country delivering lectures in country school-houses and basements of churches to abolitionists, in order to teach the children that the Almighty had put his seal of condemnation upon any inequality between the white man and the negro.

Mr. President, I am free to say here—what I have said over and over again at home—that, in my opinion, this government was made by white men for the benefit of white men and their posterity for ever, and should be administered by white men, and by none other whatsoever.

Mr. DOOLITTLE.—I will ask the honorable senator, then, why not give the Territories to white men?

Mr. DOUGLAS.—Mr. President, I am in favor of throwing the Territories open to all the white men, and all the negroes, too, that choose to go, and then allow the white men to govern the Territory. I would not let one of the negroes, free or slave, either vote or hold office anywhere, where I had the right, under the Constitution, to prevent it. I am in favor of each State and each Territory of this Union taking care of its own negroes, free or slave. If they want slavery, let them have it; if they desire to prohibit slavery, let them do it; it is their business, not mine. We in Illinois tried slavery while we were a Territory, and found it was not profitable; and hence we turned philanthropists and abolished it, just as our British friends across the ocean did. They established slavery in all their colonies, and when they found they could not make any more money out of it, abolished it. I hold that the question of slavery is one of political economy, governed by the laws of climate, soil, productions, and self-interest, and not by mere statutory provision. I repudiate the doctrine, that because free institutions may be best in one climate they are, necessarily, the best everywhere; or that because slavery may be indispensable in one locality, therefore it is desirable everywhere. I hold that a wise statesman will always adapt his legislation to the wants, interests, condition, and necessities of the people to be governed by it. One people will bear different institutions from another. One climate demands different institutions from another.

I repeat, then, what I have often had occasion to say, that I do not think uniformity is either possible or desirable. I wish to see no two States precisely alike in their domestic institutions in this Union. Our system rests on the supposition that each State has something in her condition or climate, or her circumstances, requiring laws and institutions different from every other State of the Union. Hence I answer the question of the senator from Wisconsin, that I am willing that a Territory settled by white men shall have negroes, free or slave, just as the white men shall determine, but not as the negroes shall prescribe.

The senator from New York has coined a new definition of the States of the Union—labor States and capital States. The capital States, I believe, are the slaveholding States; the labor States are the non-slaveholding States. It has taken that senator a good many years to coin that phrase and bring it into use. I have heard him discuss these favorite theories of his for the last ten years, I think, and I never heard of capital States and labor States before. It strikes me that something has recently occurred up in New England that makes it politic to get up a question between capital and labor, and take the side of the numbers against the few. We have seen some accounts in the newspapers of combinations and strikes among the journeymen shoemakers in the towns there—labor against capital. The senator has a new word ready coined to suit their case, and make the laborers believe that he is on the side of the most numerous class of voters.

What produced that strike among the journeymen shoemakers? Why are the mechanics of New England, the laborers and the employees, now reduced to the starvation point? Simply because, by your treason, by your sectional agitation, you have created a strife between the North and the South, have driven away your southern customers, and thus deprive the laborers of the means of support. This is the fruit of your Republican dogmas. It is another step, following John Brown, of the "irrepressible conflict." Therefore we now get this new coinage of "labor States"—he is on the side of the shoemakers (laughter), and "capital States"—he is against those that furnish the hides. (Laughter.) I think those shoemakers will understand this business. They know why it is that they do not get so many orders as they did a few months ago. It is not confined to the shoemakers; it reaches every mechanic's shop and every factory. All the large laboring establishments of the North feel the pressure produced by the doctrine of the "irrepressible conflict." This new coinage of words will not save them from the just responsibility that follows the doctrines they have been inculcating. If they had abandoned the doctrine of the "irrepressible conflict," and proclaimed the true doctrine of the Constitution, that each State is entirely free to do just as it pleases, have slavery as long as it chooses, and abolish it when it wishes, there would be no conflict:

the northern and southern States would be brethren; there would be fraternity between us, and your shoemakers would not strike for higher prices.

*   *   *   *   *   *   *   *

Sir, the feeling among the masses of the South we find typified in the dress of the senator from Virginia (Mr. Mason); they are determined to wear the homespun of their own productions rather than trade with the North. That is the feeling which has produced this state of distress in our manufacturing towns.

The senator from New York has also referred to the recent action of the people of New Mexico, in establishing a code for the protection of property in slaves, and he congratulates the country upon the final success of the advocates of free institutions in Kansas. He could not fail, however, to say, in order to preserve what he thought was a striking antithesis, that popular sovereignty in Kansas meant State sovereignty in Missouri. No, sir, popular sovereignty in Kansas was stricken down by unholy combination in New England to ship men to Kansas—rowdies and vagabonds—with the Bible in one hand and Sharpe's rifle in the other, to shoot down the friends of self-government. Popular sovereignty in Kansas was stricken down by the combinations in the northern States to carry elections under pretence of emigrant aid societies. In retaliation, Missouri formed aid societies too; and she, following your example, sent men into Kansas, and then occurred the conflict. Now, you throw the blame upon Missouri merely because she followed your example, and attempted to resist its consequences. I condemn both; but I condemn a thousand-fold more those that set the example and struck the first blow, than those who thought they would act upon the principle of fighting the devil with his own weapons, and resorted to the same means that you had employed.

But, sir, notwithstanding the efforts of emigrant aid societies, the people of Kansas have had their own way, and the people of New Mexico have had their own way. Kansas has adopted a free State; New Mexico has established a slave Territory. I am content with both. If the people of New Mexico want slavery, let them have it, and I never will vote to repeal their slave code. If Kansas does not want slavery, I will not help anybody to force it on her. Let each do as it pleases. When Kansas comes to the conclusion that slavery will not suit her, and promote her interest better than the prohibition, let her pass her own slave code; I will not pass it for her. Whenever New Mexico gets tired of her code, she must repeal it for herself; I will not repeal it for her. Non-intervention by Congress with slavery in the Territories is the platform on which I stand.

But I want to know why will not the senator from New York carry out his principles to their logical conclusions? Why is there not a man in that whole party, in this body or the House of Representatives, bold enough to redeem the pledges which that party has

made to the country ? I believe you said, in your Philadelphia
platform, that Congress had sovereign power over the Territories
for their government, and that it was the duty of Congress, to prohibit, in all the Territories, those twin relics of barbarism, slavery
and polygamy. Why do you not carry out your pledges? Why do
you not introduce your bill? The senator from New York says they
have no new measures to originate ; no new movement to make; no
new bill to bring forward. Then what confidence shall the American people repose in your faith and sincerity, when, having the
power in one House, you do not bring forward a bill to carry out
your principles? The fact is, these principles are avowed to get
votes in the North, but not to be carried into effect by acts of Congress. You are afraid of hurting your party if you bring in your
bill to repeal the slave code of New Mexico ; afraid of driving off the
conservative men ; you think it is wise to wait until after the election.
I should be glad to have confidence enough in the sincerity of the
other side of the chamber to suppose that they had sufficient
courage to bring forward a law to carry out their principles to their
logical conclusions. I find nothing of that. They wish to agitate,
to excite the people of the North against the South to get votes for
the Presidential election ; but they shrink from carrying out their
measures lest they might throw off some conservative voters who do
not like the Democratic party.

But, sir, if the senator from New York, in the event that he is
made President, intends to carry out his principles to their logical
conclusions, let us see where they will lead him. In the same speech
that I read from a few minutes ago, I find the following. Addressing the people of Ohio, he said :

" You blush not at these things, because they have become as familiar as
household words ; and your pretended free-soil allies claim peculiar merit for
maintaining these miscalled guaranties of slavery, which they find in the national compact. Does not all this prove that the Whig party have kept up
with the spirit of the age ; that it is as true and faithful to human freedom as
the inert conscience of the American people will permit it to be? What then,
you say, can nothing be done for freedom, because the public conscience remains inert ? Yes, much can be done, everything can be done. Slavery can
be limited to its present bounds."

That is the first thing that can be done—slavery can be limited to
its present bounds. What else ?

" It can be ameliorated. It can and must be abolished, and you and I can and
must do it."

There you find are two propositions : first, slavery was to be limited
to the States in which it was then situated. It did not then exist in
any Territory. Slavery was confined to the States. The first proposition was that slavery must be restricted, and confined to those
States. The second was, that he, as a New Yorker, and they, the
people of Ohio, must and would abolish it; that is to say, abolish it

in the States. They could abolish it nowhere else. Every appeal they make to Northern prejudice and passion, is against the institution of slavery everywhere, and they would not be able to retain their abolition allies, the rank and file, unless they held out the hope that it was the mission of the Republican party, if successful, to abolish slavery in the States as well as in the Territories of the Union.

And again in the same speech, the senator from New York advised the people to disregard constitutional obligations in these words:

" But we must begin deeper and lower than the composition and combination of factions or parties, wherein the strength and security of slavery lie. You answer that it lies in the Constitution of the United States and the constitutions and laws of slaveholding States. Not at all. It is in the erroneous sentiment of the American people. Constitutions and laws can no more rise above the virtue of the people than the limpid stream can climb above its native spring. Inculcate the love of freedom and the equal rights of man under the paternal roof; see to it that they are taught in the schools and in the churches; reform your own code ; extend a cordial welcome to the fugitive who lays his weary limbs at your door, and defend him as you would your paternal gods ; correct your own error, that slavery is a constitutional guaranty which may not be released, and ought not to be relinquished."

I know they tell us that all this is to be done according to the Constitution; they would not violate the Constitution except so far as the Constitution violates the law of God—that is all—and they are to be the judges of how far the Constitution does violate the law of God. They say that every clause of the Constitution that recognizes property in slaves, is in violation of the Divine law, and hence should not be obeyed; and with that interpretation of the Constitution, they turn to the South and say, " We will give you all your rights under the Constitution, as we explain it."

Then the senator devoted about a third of his speech to a very beautiful homily on the glories of our Union. All that he has said, all that any other man has ever said, all that the most eloquent tongue can ever utter, in behalf of the blessings and the advantages of this glorious Union, I fully indorse. But still, sir, I am prepared to say, that the Union is glorious only when the Constitution is preserved inviolate. He eulogized the Union. I, too, am for the Union ; I indorse the eulogies; but still, what is the Union worth, unless the Constitution is preserved and maintained inviolate in all its provisions?

Sir, I have no faith in the Union-loving sentiments of those who will not carry out the Constitution in good faith, as our fathers made it. Professions of fidelity to the Union will be taken for naught, unless they are accompanied by obedience to the Constitution upon which the Union rests. I have a right to insist that the Constitution shall be maintained inviolate in all its parts, not only that which suits the temper of the North, but every clause of that Constitution, whether you like it or dislike it. Your oath to support the Constitution binds you to every line, word, and syllable of the instrument. You have no right to say that any given clause is in violation of the Divine

law, and that, therefore, you will not observe it. The man who disobeys any one clause on the pretext that it violates the Divine law,
or on any other pretext, violates his oath of office.

But, sir, what a commentary is this pretext that the Constitution is
a violation of the Divine law, upon those revolutionary fathers whose
eulogies we have heard here to-day. Did the framers of that instrument make a Constitution in violation of the law of God? If so, how
do your consciences allow you to take the oath of office? If the senator. from New York still holds to his declaration that the clause in the
Constitution relative to fugitive slaves is a violation of the Divine
law, how dare he, as an honest man, take an oath to support the instrument? Did he understand that he was defying the authority of
Heaven when he took the oath to support that instrument?

Thus, we see, the radical difference between the Republican party
and the Democratic party is this: we stand by the Constitution as
our fathers made it, and by the decisions of the constituted authorities as they are pronounced in obedience to the Constitution. They
repudiate the instrument, substitute their own will for that of the
constituted authorities, annul such provisions as their fanaticism, or
prejudice, or policy, may declare to be in violation of God's law, and
then say: "We will protect all your rights under the Constitution as
expounded by ourselves; but not as expounded by the tribunal created for that purpose."

Mr. President, I shall not occupy further time in the discussion of
this question to-night. I did not intend to utter a word; and I
should not have uttered a word upon the subject, if the senator from
New York had not made a broad arraignment of the Democratic
party, and especially of that portion of the action of the party for
which I was most immediately responsible. Everybody knows that I
brought forward and helped to carry through the Kansas-Nebraska
act, and that I was active in support of the compromise measures of
1850. I have heard bad faith attached to the Democratic party for
that act too long to be willing to remain silent and seem to sanction
it even by tacit acquiescence.

Mr. TRUMBULL having replied,

Mr. DOUGLAS responded as follows: I have but a few words to
say, in reply to my colleague; and first on the question, whether
Illinois was a slave Territory or not, and whether we ever had
slavery in the State. I dislike technical denials, conveying an idea
contrary to the fact. My colleague well knows, and so do I, that,
practically, we had slaves there while a Territory, and after we became a State. I have seen him dance to the music of a negro slave
in Illinois many a time, and I have danced to the same music myself.
[Laughter.] We have both had the same negro servants to black our
boots and wait upon us, and they were held as slaves. We know,
therefore, that slavery did exist in the State in fact, and slavery did
exist in the Territory in fact; and his denial relates exclusively to
the question whether slavery was legal. Whether legal or not, it

existed in fact. The master exercised his dominion over the slave, and those negroes were held as slaves until 1847, when we established the new Constitution. There are gentlemen around me here, who know the fact—gentlemen who were nursed by slaves in Illinois. No man familiar with the history of Illinois will deny the fact. The quibble is, that the Territorial laws authorizing the introduction of slaves were void because the ordinance of 1787 said slavery was prohibited.

Notwithstanding that ordinance, the old French inhabitants, who had slaves before the ordinance, paid no attention to it, and held slaves still. Slaves were held there all the time that Illinois was a Territory; and after it became a State they were held till they all died out, and their children became emancipated under the constitution. It is a fact; we all know it. That gentlemen have seen many of those old French slaves, who were held in defiance of the ordinance. Whether they were lawfully held or not, the Territorial authorities sustained the rights of the master. Not only were slaves held by the French before the ordinance, but the Territorial legislature passed a law in substance to this effect: any citizen might go to Kentucky, or any other State or Territory, where slaves were held, and bring slaves into the Territory of Illinois, take them to a county court, and in open court enter into an indenture by which the slave and his posterity were to serve him for ninety-nine years; and in the event that the slave refused to enter into the indenture, the master should have a certain time to take him out of the Territory and sell him. The senator now says that law was not valid. Valid or not, it was executed; slaves were introduced, and they were held; they were used; they were worked; and they died slaves. That is the fact. I have had handed to me a book showing the number of slaves in Illinois at the taking of the various censuses, by which it appears that, when the census of 1810 was taken, there were in Illinois 168 slaves; in 1820, 917; in 1830, 747; and in 1840, 331. In 1850 there were none, for the reason that, in 1847, we adopted a new constitution that prohibited slavery entirely, and by that time they had nearly all died. The census shows that at one time there were as many as nine hundred slaves, and at all times the dominion of the master was maintained.

The fact is, that the people of the Territory of Illinois, when it was a Territory, were almost all from the southern States, particularly from Kentucky and Tennessee. The southern end of the State was the only part at first settled—that part called Egypt—because it is the land of letters and of plenty. Civilization and learning all originated in Egypt. The northern part of the State, where the political friends of my colleague now preponderate, was then in the possession of the Indians, and so were northern Indiana and northern Ohio; and a Yankee could not get to Illinois at all, unless he passed down through Virginia and over into Tennessee and through Kentucky. The consequence was, that ninety-nine out of a hundred of the settlers were from the slave States. They carried the old family servants with them, and kept them. They were told, "Here is an ordinance of Congress passed against your holding them." They said, "What has Congress to do with our domestic institutions? Congress had better mind its own business, and let us alone; we know what we want better than Congress;" and hence they passed this law to bring them in and make them indentured. Under that, they established slavery and held slaves as long as they wanted them. When they assembled to make the constitution of Illinois, in 1818, for admission into the Union, nearly every delegate to the convention brought his negro along with him to black his boots, play the fiddle, wait upon him, and take care of his room. They had a jolly time there; they were dancing people, frolicksome people, people who enjoyed life; they had the old French habits. Slaves were just as thick there as blackberries.

But they said "Experience proves that it is not going to be profitable in this climate." There were no scruples about it. Every one of them was nursed by it. His mother and his father held slaves. They had no scruples about its being right, but they said, "We cannot make any money by it, and as our State runs way off north up to those eternal snows, perhaps we shall gain population faster if we stop slavery and invite in the northern population;" and, as a matter of political policy, state policy, they prohibited slavery themselves. How did they prohibit it? Not by emancipating, setting at liberty, the slaves then in the State, for I believe that has never been done by any legislative body in America, and I doubt whether any one will ever arrogate to itself the right to divest property already there; but they provided that all slaves then in the State should remain slaves for life; that all indentured persons should fulfill the terms of their indentures. Ninety-nine years was about long enough, I reckon, for grown persons at least.

All persons of slave parents, after a certain time, were to be free at a certain age, and all born after a certain other period, were to be free at their birth. It was a gradual system of emancipation. Hence, I now repeat, that so long as the ordinance of 1787, passed by Congress, said Illinois should not have slavery, she did have it; and the very first day that our people arrived at that condition that they could do as they pleased, to wit, when they became a State, they adopted a system of gradual emancipation; but still slavery continued in the State, as the census of 1820, the census of 1830, and the census of 1840, show, until the new constitution of 1847, when nearly all those old slaves had died out, and probably there were not a half-dozen alive. That was the way slavery was introduced and expired in Illinois. Whatever quibbles there may be about legal construction, legal right, these are the facts.

Look into the Territorial legislation, and you will find as rigorous a code for the protection of slave property as in any State; a code prescribing the control of the master, providing that if a negro slave should leave his master's farm without leave, or in the night time, he should be punished by so many stripes, and if he committed such an offence he should receive so many stripes, and so on; as rigorous a code as ever existed in any southern State of this Union. Not only that, but after the State came into the Union, the State of Illinois reenacted that code, and continued it up to the time that slavery died out under the operation of the State constitution.

I dislike, sir, to have a controversy with my colleague about historical facts. I suppose the Senate of the United States has no particular interest in the early history of Illinois, but it has become obligatory on me to vindicate my statement to that extent.

Now, sir, a word about the repeal of the Missouri Compromise. I have had occasion to refer to that before in the Senate, and I am sorry to have to refer to it again.

My colleague arraigns me as chairman of the Committee on Territories against myself as a member of the Senate in 1854, upon the Nebraska Bill. He says that, as chairman of the committee, I reported that we did not see proper to depart from the example of 1850; that as the Mexican laws were not then repealed in terms, we did not propose in terms to repeal the Missouri restriction, but— there the senator stops, and there the essense of the report begins— but, the report added, this committee proposes to carry out the principles embodied in the Compromise measures of 1850 in precise language, and then we go on to state what those principles were; and one was, that the people of a Territory should settle the question of slavery for themselves, and we reported a bill giving them that· power.

But inasmuch as the power to introduce slavery, notwithstanding the Mexican laws, was conferred on the Territorial legislatures under the compromise measures of 1850, the right to introduce it into Kansas, notwithstanding the Missouri restriction, was also proposed to be conferred without expressly repealing the restriction. The legal effect was precisely the same. Afterward some gentlemen said they would rather have the legal effect expressed in plain language.

I said, "If you want a repealing act, have it: it does not alter the legal effect." I said so at the time, as the debates show; and hence I put in the express provision that the Missouri act was thereby repealed. It did not change the legal effect of the bill; but that variation of language has been the staple of a great many stump speeches, a great many miserable quibbles of county court lawyers, a great many attempts to prove inconsistency by small politicians in the country. Be it so. The people understand that thing. The object I had in view was to allow the people to do as they pleased. The first bill accomplished that; the amendment accomplished it. Whether that was the object of others or not, is another question. That was my object. The two bills, in my opinion, had the same legal effect; but I said if any one doubts it, I will make it plain.

Some said, " we doubt whether that gives the right." Then I made it plain, and brought it in in express terms, and he calls a change of language, without varying the legal effect, a change of policy. My colleague is welcome to make the most out of that. I have had that arraignment over and over again.

The senator has some doubt as to whether I am in good standing in my own party ; whether I am a good representative of northwestern Democracy. I have nothing to say about that. I will allow the people to speak in their conventions on that subject. Whether I represent the Democracy of Illinois or not, I shall not say. The people understand all that. I can only say that I have been in the Democratic party all my life, and I know what our Democrats mean. My colleague indorsed and approved the compromise measures of 1850. He was a Democrat a few years ago. Even in 1856, he declared, I believe, that he could not vote for me, if nominated, but he would vote for Mr. Buchanan ; but, after the nomination, he did not like the platform, and he went over. I have no objection to that ; it is all right enough. I never intended to taunt him with inconsistency ; but I do not think he is as safe and as authoritative an expounder of the Republican party as the senator from New York. The senator from New York says that a State that does not allow a negro to vote on an equality with a white man is a slave State. I read his speech here to-day. I suppose the senator from New York is a pretty good Republican. I thought he spoke with some authority for his party. I did not suppose those neophytes who had just come into the party were going to unsettle and unhorse the leader and embodiment of the party so quickly, and prescribe a platform that would rule out the senator from New York. I must be permitted, therefore, to take the authority of the leaders of the party in preference to those who are kept in the rank and file until they have served an apprenticeship. (Laughter.)

The senator from New York says it is slavery not to allow the negro to vote. Well, sir, I hold that that is political slavery. If you disfranchise a man, you make him a political slave. Deprive a white man of a voice in his government, and, politically, he is a slave. Hence the inequality you create is slavery to that extent. My colleague will not allow a negro to vote. He lives too far south in Illinois for that, decidedly. He has to expound the creed down in Egypt. They have other expositions up north. The creed is pretty black in the north end of the State ; about the centre it is a pretty good mulatto, and it is almost white when you get down into Egypt. It assumes paler shades as you go south. The Democrats of Illinois have one creed, and we can proclaim it everywhere alike.

The senator, my colleague, complains that I represent his party to be in favor of negro equality. No such thing, says he : " I tell my colleague to his teeth it is not so." There is something very fearful in the manner in which he said it ! Senators know that he is a dangerous man who says things to a man's teeth, and I shall be very cautious how I reply. But he says he does hold that by the law of God the negro and the white man are created equal; that is, he says, in a state of nature; and, therefore, he says he indorses that clause of the Declaration of Independence as including the negro as well as the white man. I do not think I misstate my colleague. He thinks that clause of the Declaration of Independence includes the negro as well as the white man. He declares, therefore, that the negro and the white man were created equal. What does that Declaration also say: "We hold these truths to be self-evident; that they are endowed by their Creator with certain *inalienable 'ights,* among which are life, liberty, and the pursuit of happiness." .f the negro and the white man are *created equal,* and that equality s an *inalienable* right, by what authority is my colleague and his party going to deprive the negro of that inalienable right which he got directly from God? He says the Republican party is not in favor of according to the negro an inalienable right which he received directly from his Maker. Oh, no; he tells me to my teeth that they are not in favor of that; they will not obey the laws of God at all. Their creed is to to take away inalienable rights. Well, I have found that out before, and that is just the reason I complain of them, that they are for taking away inalienable rights.

If they will cling to the doctrine that the Declaration of Independence conferred certain inalienable rights, among which, we are told, is equality between the white man and the negro, they are bound to make the human laws they establish conform to those God-given rights which are inalienable. If they believe the first proposition, as honest men, they are bound to carry the principle to its logical conclusion, and give the negro his equality and voice in the government; let him vote at elections, hold office, serve on juries, make him judge, governor, ("senator.") No, they cannot make him a senator, because the Supreme Court has decided that he is not a citizen. The Dred Scott decision is in the way. Perhaps that is the reason of the objection to the Dred Scott decision, that a negro cannot be a senator. I say, if you hold that the Almighty created the negro the equal of the white man, and that equality be an inalienable right, you are bound to confer the elective franchise and every other privilege of political equality on the negro. The senator from New York stands up to it like a man. His logic drove him there, and he had the honesty to avow the consequence of his own doctrine. That is to say, he did it before the Harper's Ferry raid. He did not say it quite as plainly to-day; for I will do the senator from New York the justice to say, that, in his speech to-day, I think he made the most successful effort, considered as an attempt to conceal what he meant. (Laughter.) He dealt in vague generalities; he dealt in disclaimers and general denials; and he covered it all up with a verbiage that would allow anybody to infer just what he pleased, but not to commit the senator to anything; and to let the country know that there was no danger from the success of the Republican party; that they did not mean any harm; that if men, believing in the truth of their doctrines, did go and commit invasions, murders, robberies, and treason, all they had to do was to disavow the men who were fools enough to believe them, and they are not responsible for the consequences of their own action!

Now, Mr. President, I wish my colleague were equally as frank as the senator from New York. That senator is in favor of the equality of the negro with the white man, or else he would not say that the Almighty guaranteed to them an inalienable right of equality. My colleague dare not deny the inalienable rights of the negro, for if he did, the Abolitionists would quit him. He dare not avow it, lest the old line Whigs should quit him; hence he is riding double on this question. I have no desire to conceal my opinions; and I repeat that I do not believe the negro race is any part of the governing element in this country, except as an element of representation in the manner expressly provided in the Constitution. This is a white man's government, made by white men for the benefit of white men, to be administered by white men and nobody else; and I should regret the day that we ever allowed the negroes to have a hand in its administration. Not that the negro is not entitled to any privileges at all; on the contrary, I hold that humanity requires us to allow the unfortunate negro to enjoy all the rights and privileges that he may safely exercise consistent with the good of society. We may, with safety, give them some privileges in Illinois that would not be safe in Mississippi; because we have but few, while that State has many. We will take care of our negroes, if Mississippi will take care of hers. Each has a right to decide for itself what shall be the relation of the negro to the white man within its own limits, and no other State has a right to interfere with its determination.

On that principle there is no "irrepressible conflict;" there is no conflict at all. If we will just take care of our own negroes, and mind our own business, we shall get along very well; and we ask our southern friends to do the same, and they seem pretty well disposed to do it. Therefore, I am in favor of just firing a broadside into our Republican friends over there, who will keep interfering with other people's business. That is the complaint I have of them. They keep holding up the negro for us to worship, and when they get the power, they will not give him the rights they claim for him; they will not give him his inalienable rights. New York has not given the negro those inalienable rights of suffrage yet. The senator from New York represents a slave State, according to his own speech; because New York does not allow the negro to vote on an equality with a white man. It is true, in New York they do allow a negro to vote, if he owns $250 worth of property, but not without. They suppose $250 just compensates for the difference between a rich negro and a poor white man. (Laughter.) They allow the rich negro to vote, and do not allow the poor one; and the senator from New York thinks that is a system of slavery. It may be; let New York decide that; it is her business. I do not want to interfere with it. Just let us alone. We do not want negro suffrage. We say "non-interference;" hands off. If you like the association of the negroes at the polls, that is your business; if you want them to hold office, so that they do not come here, give offices to them, if you choose; if you want them for magistrates, that is your business; but you must not send them here; because we do not allow anybody but citizens to hold seats on this floor; and, thank God, the Dred Scott case has decided that a negro is not a citizen.